MW00462944

BISON
BOOKS

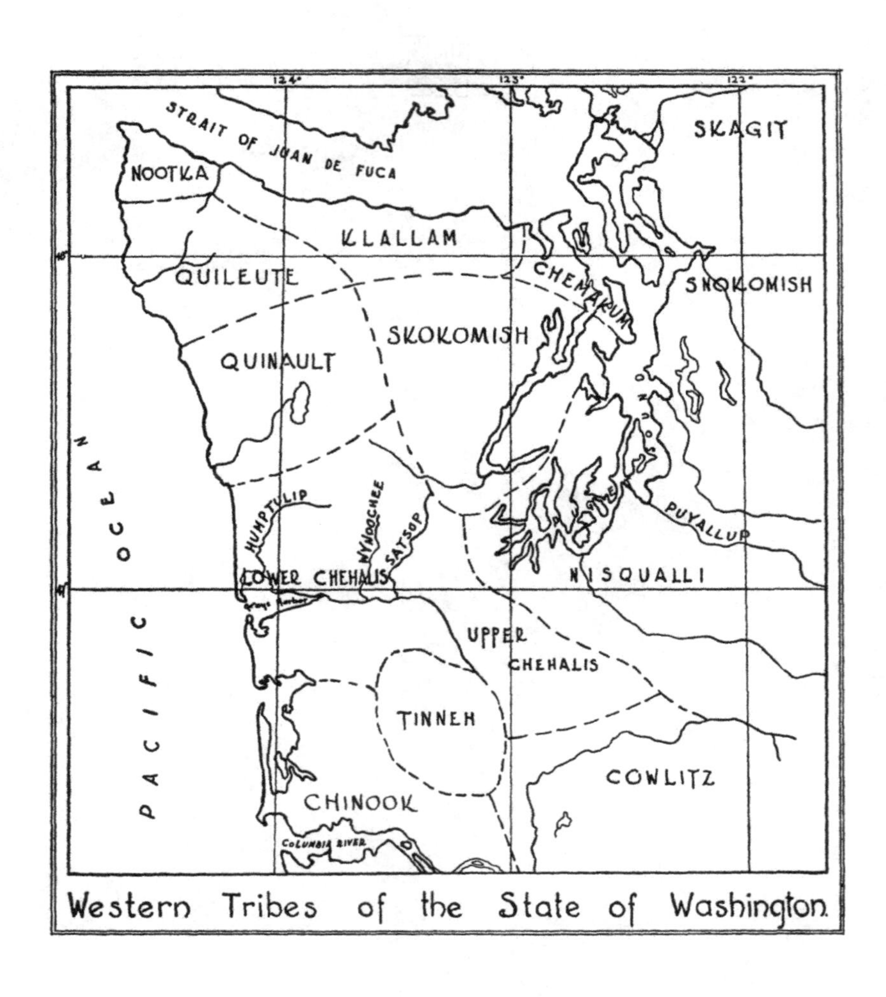

Western Tribes of the State of Washington.

FOLK-TALES
OF THE
COAST SALISH

COLLECTED AND EDITED BY
THELMA ADAMSON

INTRODUCTION TO THE BISON BOOKS EDITION BY
WILLIAM R. SEABURG AND LAUREL SERCOMBE

UNIVERSITY OF NEBRASKA PRESS
LINCOLN AND LONDON

Folk-Tales of the Coast Salish was originally published by the American Folklore Society in 1934. Reprinted by permission of the American Folklore Society (www.afsnet.org).

Manufactured in the United States of America
∞
First Nebraska paperback printing: 2009

Library of Congress Cataloging-in-Publication Data
Folk-tales of the Coast Salish / collected and edited by Thelma Adamson; introduction to the Bison Books edition by William R. Seaburg and Laurel Sercombe.
p. cm.
Originally published: New York: American Folklore Society, 1934.
Includes bibliographical references.
ISBN 978-0-8032-2668-5 (paper: alk. paper)
1. Coast Salish Indians—Folklore. 2. Tales—Washington (State) I. Adamson, Thelma.
E99.S21F65 2009
398.209797—dc22
2009031101

INTRODUCTION TO THE BISON BOOKS EDITION

WILLIAM R. SEABURG AND LAUREL SERCOMBE

THELMA ADAMSON

Thelma Adamson's monograph, *Folk-Tales of the Coast Salish*, first published seventy-five years ago by the American Folklore Society as Memoir 27, was—and remains—a major contribution to our knowledge of western Washington State Salish oral traditions. It contains 190 texts from nineteen consultants, almost all collected in English or in English translation. The bulk of the stories (155) represents Upper Chehalis and Cowlitz Salish narrative traditions, primarily myths and tales, and constitutes the largest published collection of oral literature for either of these groups. The monograph also presents Humptulip tales (14), Wynoochee tales (3), Satsop tales (3), Puyallup tales (4), White River tales (2), and Skokomish tales (9).

This collection has several notable features. It includes, for example, as many as four variants of the same tale-type and has a very useful forty-three-page section of abstracts with comparative notes from eight regional text collections prepared by Adele Froehlich, a former Barnard College student (Benedict 1935, 188). Although Adamson altered her consultants' language to conform to standard written English (explained below), she does not appear to have bowdlerized the texts.

Another valuable feature of this monograph is the numerous and informative footnotes. These annotations include: *ethnographic explications of untranslatable Native terms* ("A kind of magic power, accompanied by secret words. This magic is not to be confused with tamanoas. Except that it works wonders, it is entirely different. It is mainly a prerogative of women, and is especially efficacious in affairs of the heart" [91]); *storytellers' asides* ("The narrator said that she herself, when young, had a little dog just like the one that the young woman in this story owned. Since the little dog was with her continually, her family always told her this story as a lesson" [97]); *storytelling etiquette* ("This story is unfinished, so the narrator said. He explained, 'That's as far as I ever got with it. My uncle was telling me this story. The folks were talking about eating, and so I asked for something to eat. My uncle said, "Well, go eat now." He never told me the rest of it. It was against the law to ask for something to eat while hearing a story'" [120]); *characters' vocal qualities* ("Said in a big, deep voice" [140]); *consultants' gestures* ("Illustrated by straightening up the fingers" [189]); *consultants' acting* ("The narrator stood up and imitated Skunk's actions" [201]); *consultants' self-editing* ("This passage has been toned down. He is supposed to catch the craw-fish with his organ" [251]); and *the collector's elicitation techniques* ("I told Mrs. Northover the Moon and Sun story, hoping that she would recall it" [274]). These kinds of extra-textual details suggest that Adamson—although a newly minted field-worker—was a careful, observant, and perceptive researcher.

Futhermore, this collection provides a rich data source for those interested in the content and comparative analyses of Native texts told in English. Researchers seldom secured interpretive commentary regarding the stories they transcribed. But stories told directly in English often provide important clues about how the narrators felt about the stories, the characters, and the characters' actions—oral literary criticism in Alan Dundes's apt phrasing (2007 [1966]).

A preliminary investigation of two of Sophie Smith's Cowlitz Sahaptin texts, "Cougar and His Younger Brothers" (202–9) and "Spear Boy" (227–30), reveals several categories of interpretative commentary, for example: *descriptive details and explanations not required by the plot action* ("The little boy looked on, his eyes wide with amazement. The horns of the elk had merely scratched the dangerous being's throat as they went down" [203] and "The old man landed, smiling to himself" [208]); *characters' thoughts and feelings* ("She kept watching. The boy held the fish up and swallowed it whole. She sat down and began to wonder, 'Has he been doing this all the time?' The thought of it nearly killed her" [227] and "She ate well and was pleased with everything except the fact that the man's mother was Fire. This seemed very strange to her" [228]); *cultural background* ("They always cut the bark around the tree to make it fall" [207]); and *similes* ("'Br---,' it went, like a wind storm, breaking the trees along the way" [203]). These four categories of oral literary criticism are only a subset of the variety of types or categories one would find if the entire collection were carefully examined. Similar examples can be found in Elizabeth D. Jacobs's Nehalem Tillamook stories from Clara Pearson (1990 [1959]) and her Upper Coquille Athabaskan texts from Coquelle Thompson (Seaburg 2007), both collections recorded directly in English. We suggest that they may well constitute areal stylistic features of Northwest Indian stories told in English.

The original field notebooks in which Adamson transcribed this collection of stories in 1926 and 1927 have been lost. But a handful of typed transcripts of stories remain. Comparison of the typed-up notes with the published texts reveals Adamson's (and perhaps others') editing practices. To illustrate, the first paragraph of the typescript of Marion Davis's "Bluejay Goes to the Land of the Dead" is reproduced below. Material enclosed in square brackets has been added by us for clarification.

One time B.J. liv[ing] with Naw.[1] Were living in one house; finally B.J. got

> awful sick. Four or five days he had be[en] lying in bed—getting worse and worse. Finally he commenced to sing a little Ta[manowas] song, as lying on his back. He called Naw to come, and told her that his Ta[manowas] told him that Naw must come to his face and step over his eyes. "No, I wud—— I wouldn't show myself to you." "Oh, I'll die······· . My Ta[manowas] says you must do it." B.J. almost dead now, because now [Naw] hadn't done what his Ta[manowas] said. In tiny voice, "Ain't you going to do it? I'm going to die." (He was pretending (Page 31) to die.) Naw was disturbed now. "Oh, my b[rother] is going to die." "Oh, you aren't going to do it? The last breath I shall ever draw." So now [Naw] said, "Yes, I guess I can do it." So she kinda jumped over B.J.'s face. (Now that is where B.J. nearly died.) "You've got to go slow. That is too fast!" Naw said, "Oh, I don't want to show myself to you. What's the use?" Then B.J. nearly died again. "You've got to go a little slower—five times over my face." So Naw kinda jumped liked [like]—didn't want to show herself. B.J. kinda nearly died—long time before drew his breath again. Now the third time, Naw thought, "I guess he'll die. Better do what 2 [he] tells me." Told Naw to go slow now. So she did go more slowly. B.J. said, "Yes, that's kinda of all right, but a little too fast yet, for me." That's four times. Now fifth time, B.J. said, (Page 32) "Now you've got to stand in front of my face for a long time, and I'll get well. That's what my Ta[manowas] said." So Naw went and stood quite a while in front of B.J.'s eyes. "A little longer······ ," in tiny voice. "That's all right····." He got well then; he examined his sister pretty well. He was thinking what to do now, after that. What to do with her?

Comparison of this transcript excerpt with its published version (24–25) shows that Adamson made considerable changes to the consultant's English. What is gained by such editing is a reader-friendly Standard English text, one that silently glosses Davis's rural Indian English. But some things are lost by this "translation" as well. Although the plot structure remains the same, Davis's voice is smoothed over. With the loss of the performer's voice, nuances and shades of meaning are elided, and one consultant begins to sound like any other consultant. A few examples will suffice.

Some changes seem gratuitous: "finally B.J. got awful sick" changed to "Finally Bluejay took very sick," and "That's all right····" changed to "That's fine!" Other alterations shift meanings: "Naw was disturbed now" changed to "Naw was really frightened this time." Loss of hedges, such as "kinda," detracts from the ambivalence of the character and the humor of the scene: "So she kinda jumped over B.J.'s face" changed to "and jumped over Bluejay's face," and "So Naw kinda jumped liked [like]—didn't want to show herself" altered to "Instead Naw jumped over him again for she did not want to show herself." Marion's phrase "kinda jumped like" nicely captures the character's halfhearted—conflicted—attitude in a way the published version does not. Naw is torn between not wanting to expose herself and not wanting her brother to die, and the storyteller's hedges, originally in the typescript, effectively highlight this tension.

Adamson, we hasten to note, was not the only researcher to severely edit their consultants' English. Livingston Farrand's Quinault texts

(1902), Elizabeth D. Jacobs's Tillamook collection (1990 [1959]), and Ella E. Clark's anthology (1953) all show similar kinds of editing practices.

By 1932 Adamson had a six-hundred-page manuscript of Coast Salish folktales ready to vet for publication. This is according to a letter from Thelma to Melville Jacobs sent from Everson, Washington, her Nooksack fieldwork site, asking if the University of Washington "was in a position to publish some of my Coast Salish material" in their Publications in Anthropology series. The possibility of collaborating with the American Folklore Society (AFS) in a joint publication was also broached. We have no record of Jacobs's reply. According to Adamson, Erna Gunther had already told her that she "did not care for [more] folk-tales, as there were quite a number of volumes of folk-tales in the series already."[2] Gunther was looking for ethnographies instead.

Eventually a grant of $500 from the National Academy of Sciences, together with receipts from sales of AFS memoirs, allowed the Society to finance the volume out of Society funds, "the first time that a memoir" had "been published without private donation designated for the publication of a specific manuscript." This represented "a landmark in the history of the American Folklore Society" (Benedict 1934, 261).

Adamson apparently saw the manuscript of *Folk-Tales of the Coast Salish* into proof stage, although Jacobs (1959, 123) indicated that it "required lengthy editing" by Boas. The onset of a debilitating mental illness in 1933 prevented Adamson from finishing preparation of the book, leaving the task to then editor of the *Journal of American Folklore* Ruth Benedict. In a letter to Melville Jacobs, Benedict reported: "I suppose you know how ill Thelma is. I have had to have her husband gather together the proofs of her Salish Tales and I shall have to put them through the press as best I can without her proof reading."[3] Adamson's illness necessitated the hiring of Adele Froehlich, whose "careful work . . . both in the preparation of abstracts . . . and in proofreading and preparation of [the] manuscript has been invaluable" (Benedict 1935, 188). Sadly, *Folk-Tales of the Coast Salish* turned out to be the first and last of Thelma Adamson's publications.

Not only did Adamson collect myths and tales from her consultants, she also recorded a considerable amount of ethnographic data, primarily during her 1927 field trip to the Northwest. What remains of this material is a carbon copy of a 402-page typescript based on her field notebooks, now archived in the Melville Jacobs Collection at the University of Washington. Like her notebooks, the original typescript has been lost. The complete ethnographic material has never been published. Included in this typescript are a few stories of French provenience that were omitted from her *Folk-Tales of the Coast Salish*. Jay Miller, who has worked closely with these loosely organized typed notes, noted that "Adamson's material represents an impressive early ethnography and is particularly useful for religious and theological topics" (1999, 3).

Thelma Ramona Adamson, the daughter of William Ernest (1875–1941) and Lela Mae McKenzie Adamson (1874–1963), was born on

March 27, 1901, in Piru City, California.[4] Her father was an oil driller who was working in the California oil fields at the time of her birth. Her siblings included an older brother, Carl (1899–1981), and a younger sister, Aline (1909–57). Sometime during 1904 the family moved from California back to New Matamoras, Ohio, where Adamson spent her childhood years. Later, the family moved from New Matamoras to Marietta, Ohio, where Adamson graduated from Marietta High School and enrolled in Marietta College in 1919. According to a Marietta College Religious Census card, she was not a member of any church but was nominally a Baptist.[5]

Adamson majored in geology at Marietta College, graduating cum laude and Phi Beta Kappa in 1923. As an undergraduate she was apparently quite active in campus social life. She was a member of the women's basketball team, of the Alpha Nu Sigma sorority, and of the YWCA. For the academic year 1922–23 she was one of two students representing Alpha Nu Sigma on the student council, and she appeared on the masthead of the college newspaper, *The Olio*, as one of its two society editors. In addition, she was organization editor for the 1923 edition of the college yearbook, *Mariettana*. Adamson's profile in the 1923 *Mariettana* reads, in part: "'Pep' should have been 'Ted's' name for she is never still a minute. She plays basketball like a whizz, debates like an oldtimer, and dances—well, she just exists till a good orchestra comes to town. Next to all these things, her passion is for hats, any kind, any shape, any color. And anthropology is her favorite subject."

In her senior year Adamson was "one of three students in the United States to receive fellowships to the American School in France for the study of Anthropology."[6] She was the first Marietta College student to receive this award. According to the October 1923 issue of the *Marietta College Alumni Quarterly*, the American School in France for Prehistoric Studies was begun in 1921

> under the direction of Dr. Henri-Martin. The purpose of the school is to give American students an opportunity to obtain a first-hand acquaintance with paleolithic sites and with methods of prehistoric research. . . .
>
> Each year the school has been under the leadership of a director . . . during 1923 Dr. Arles [*sic*] Hrdlicka of the Smithsonian Institution, Washington.
>
> The plan to be followed under Dr. Hrdlicka's direction . . . this year is visiting many if not all the principal localities in Europe where either the actual skeletal remains of prehistoric man or his marvelous handiworks have been found. At the same time the important Museums and collections of prehistory will be seen and studied; and the newest opinions of the European anthropologists heard.

Adamson departed New York in late June aboard the ship *George Washington*, landing in Plymouth, England, on July 1, 1923. The *Alumni Quarterly* printed a letter (dated August 7, 1923) that Adamson had sent to her former Marietta professor Ralph W. Whipple, describing the first two months of her trip. It is not clear if she participated in any archaeological digs. She expected "to be assigned museum work mostly" during her fall and winter stay in Paris. "I have been told several times that I would not have to stay a whole year. The school at most can only last until Easter, as it did last year, because the courses in Paris are over with at that time. Miss Galrin [one of the other award recipients] has only a six months leave of absence and plans to come home the first of January; and Dr. Hrdlicka said I might come home then, since the summer has been so expensive." According to family tradition, it was in Paris that Adamson met her future husband, the physicist Edward O. Salant (1900-1978). She returned to the United States, departing from La Havre, France, and arriving on May 26, 1924, aboard the *Rochambeau*. Salant arrived in New York on the same voyage.

Adamson was admitted to Columbia University to pursue a graduate degree in anthropology in September 1924. She took course work in the academic year 1924–25, the summer of 1925, and the academic year of 1925–26. During her first year she took: Introduction to Comparative Anthropology (2 semesters) (Boas and Reichard), Anthropological Methods (Boas), Seminar in Anthropology (2 semesters) (Boas), Introduction to the Science of Language (Remy and Boas), Ethnology of North American Indians (Benedict), and Race Relations (Boas). During the summer session of 1925 she took Introduction to Anthropology and Fundamental Problems in the Study of Human Culture, both taught by Edward Sapir. Adamson's second year of course work at Columbia included: Seminar in Anthropology (Boas), The Negro in Africa and in America (2 semesters) (Herskovits), The Mythology of Primitive Peoples (Benedict), General Ethnography: Technology and Primitive Art (Goddard), Anthropometry: Biometrical Methods (2 semesters) (Boas), Languages of North America (Boas), Ethnology of North American Indians (Benedict), and Phonetics and Pronunciation (Tilly).

Little is known about Adamson's life as a graduate student. She became good friends with fellow anthropology graduate students Melville Jacobs and George Herzog. She may have already been engaged to her husband-to-be Edward O. Salant, who "received his BA from Columbia College in 1922 and his PhD in physical chemistry from the University of London in 1924" and was a Johnston scholar at Johns Hopkins University from 1925–27.[7]

During the summer of 1926, Thelma Adamson, Melville Jacobs, and Otto Klineberg drove across the country together in order to undertake field research with Native Americans in Washington State. Jacobs studied Klikitat Sahaptin language, folklore, and music; Klineberg conducted psychological testing with Yakima children; and Adamson studied Chehalis and Cowlitz Salish folklore.

In a letter from Klineberg to Seaburg (October 2, 1985), sixty years after the 1926 field trip, he said:

> I came to Columbia in the summer of 1925 to start work on my doctorate in psychology, but I was quickly fascinated by cultural anthropology and *identified* with both departments. Mel and I became good friends, and he

> (and Thelma) planned to spend the following summer to collect more material on mythological texts and language among Washington Indians, he suggested I join them and do something "psychological." Which I did, and it changed my life! I had seen little of Thelma until that summer, but we got along well, all three, and had a very pleasant trip—also very proper—together.

The first summer of Adamson's fieldwork "was devoted entirely to the recording of tales, especially from the Upper Chehalis and Cowlitz tribes" (xxxi). These texts, together with those recorded in 1927, comprise this volume. We have located three letters from Adamson's 1926 trip—one to Boas and two to Herzog.[8] Not too surprisingly, the picture of fieldwork drawn for her mentor Franz Boas differed somewhat from that sketched for fellow graduate student and friend George Herzog. From the letters to both correspondents it is clear that Adamson's first field research was not an unqualified success. Among the Chehalis, she wrote Boas, it was difficult to establish good working relationships: "I had some difficulty in assuring the Chehalis people, and I am not sure that they believe me even now, that I wasn't going to sell their stories and make a fortune from them. Some people were very nasty about it. Last year an Oakville girl in collaboration with an Indian, wrote a book called 'Honne, the Spirit of the Chehalis.' This led the people to believe that I was collecting the stories in order to sell them in book form later."[9]

After about three weeks at Chehalis she went to the Cowlitz river valley. She told Boas: "There are a few scattered families living there. I was very disappointed in this trip. It seemed that as soon as I would locate a family, they would decide to make a visit they had already planned. It is very difficult to find them home as they shift from one place to another." Her "chief complaint," she related to Boas, was the lack of good transportation: "I lose so much time in making distances. Often these people live in fairly inaccessible places, and I have to wait for stages to take me there. At Oakville, I often walked ten miles a day, as there was no other way to get around."

Adamson's trip to Toppenish and the Yakima Reservation in early August in search of Cowlitz families living there was also an exercise in frustration. She wrote Herzog: "Life isn't treating me nicely these days. I want to come home and I can't, and all because of one & *the only* Cowlitz family I care about. They just *won't* come home from the mountains, where they have been picking berries ever since I came here. I have been waiting for over two weeks now & they haven't put in their appearance yet. I've got to the point where I'll almost be disappointed if they do come. I am ready to come home."[10]

Adamson's letters to Herzog were written near the end of a three-month-long field trip—one that had been physically and probably emotionally tiring and lonely for her. The attitudes she evinced toward the people she was working with and towns she was living in should be seen in this context. "I began work about July 4th on the Chehalis reservation near Oakville Washington, a terrible dump of a town. I was marooned there for three weeks getting some fairly good stories on the whole. Since that time I haven't had such good luck. I spent nearly a week in the Cowlitz river valley without much success" as the "few scattered families there . . . all took a notion to go visiting shortly after I came around."[11] Her later letter to Herzog from Toppenish lamented: "To be alone in Toppenish is an experience one would not care to have more than once in a lifetime. There is absolutely nothing to do except to go to the movies every other night (the same movie is shown two nights in succession)."[12]

Her course work finished, Adamson probably spent the 1926–27 academic year working up her summer's field notes and perhaps thinking about a dissertation topic.

Adamson returned to southwest Washington during the summer of 1927 to continue her fieldwork. She noted in the introduction to the present volume, "The second summer's work was devoted to a study of the general culture of the Upper Chehalis and to a comparative study of the Cowlitz dialect; the tales obtained were merely incidental to that work" (xxxi).

In a letter to George Herzog, Adamson reported on her summer's fieldwork. As in her 1926 letters, she complained about being bored and about the provinciality of Oakville: "I really enjoyed seeing him [Melville Jacobs] very much, as he was the first person I have really had a chance to jabber and gossip with. He drove me down the high-way after dark and I smoked a Phillip Morris, the second cigarette I have had since I have been in Oakville. I think that I certainly would loose [*sic*] my boarding-place if I ever smoked a cigarette in public or near-public."[13] But her assessment of her fieldwork that summer was quite positive:

> I have been getting some very nice material. I have been digging out Ethnography all summer and have some quite nice things, particularly Guardian Spirit material. To be brief, I am getting as much of the old Chehalis culture as possible and hope to piece it together until it fills fairly decently a very large void hereto-fore in this part of the country, anthropologically speaking. I am really get[ting] material I never thought existed last year. I think that it is probably due to the fact that I know more what to look for and this year the Injuns are more used to me.

Boas also spent time in Oakville in the summer of 1927, perhaps six weeks or so, studying Chehalis grammar and recording texts in the language.[14] Adamson reported that she had "dabbled more or less in linguistics" and had found that "Salish phonetics are terrific but very interesting, and I feel that I manage them pretty well." In fact, Adamson's transcriptions are of fairly poor quality (Kinkade 1991, v–xii). Boas and Adamson also recorded a variety of song types on nineteen Edison wax cylinders while in the field together; Adamson collected an additional eighteen cylinders of music (Seeger and Spear 1987, 59–60). Transcriptions by George Herzog of seventeen of the songs appear as an appendix to this volume (422–30).[15]

In 1928 both Jacobs and Adamson were hired as instructors at the University of Washington. Jacobs described these appointments as follows: "In the spring of 1927 Dr. Leslie Spier resigned to go to the University of Oklahoma. Negotiations to secure Dr. Paul Radin failed in August. About September 1 Professor Franz Boas recommended that Miss Thelma Adamson and Mr. Melville Jacobs be appointed Associates in Anthropology at the University of Washington."[16] Jacobs began his appointment in January 1928 and Adamson in April 1928. Adamson taught one course during spring term, Indians of the Northwest Coast. Her salary was set "at the rate of $1600 a year for twelve months' service."[17]

It is not known how Adamson funded her 1926 research. According to Jacobs, her 1927 fieldwork was supported by a grant of $800 from Columbia University.[18] Her 1928 research, however, was funded by the newly established Committee on Research in Native American Languages, administered through the American Council of Learned Societies. Adamson was awarded $500 for her Nooksack research (Leeds-Hurwitz 1985, 135). In a letter from Boas to Edward Sapir and Leonard Bloomfield recommending Adamson's appropriation, Boas stated: "Miss Adamson has been working under my direction last summer among the Cowlitz. She is familiar in a general way with the structure of the Coast Salish languages. Her ear has been quite well trained in the exceedingly variable consonantic pronunciation which characterizes the Chehalis. The Nootsak are, according to what we know, the most divergent of the Puget Sound tribes and very few speakers of the language are left."[19]

Adamson had planned to spend a few days in fieldwork at Oakville in 1928 but apparently didn't make it.[20] In a June 17th letter to Franz Boas, written at Everson, Washington, she described the field situation with the Nooksack. The Nooksack language "has been entirely replaced by" Halkomelem—"and has been for some time." A number of individuals, though, still remembered some Nooksack, and she worked with one of them, George Swanaset. "He is, I believe, as informants go, rather good and seems to know a good deal of Nooksak. I have yet tried to get texts from him but shall very shortly." She asked Boas whether she should stick with Nooksack and "run the risk of getting an incomplete grammar" or work on Halkomelem or some other dialect. Unfortunately, it is not known whether or how he replied.

Adamson resigned her position at the University of Washington and left in September 1928, according to Jacobs, because of her marriage to Edward O. Salant.[21] She was probably married before she accepted the position and had kept it a secret from Boas, perhaps fearing that he would have been reluctant to recommend a married woman for such a job. Adamson's resignation from UW was apparently an embarrassment to Boas.[22]

At the end of 1928, Boas wrote a letter of support for Adamson's Social Science Research Council grant to study the Indian Shaker religion. His letter described her as "an exceedingly industrious worker" who "has much tact in handling the natives." He went on to say: "The problem suggested by her is one which has been discussed off and on as of considerable importance. Miss Adamson happened to become very intimate with the leader of the Shaker religion [Peter Heck—WRS] and she has unusual facility, therefore, of obtaining intimate information. The problem itself is of unusual interest for the understanding of the assimilation of primitive religions and Christianity." Adamson's proposal was not funded. None of Adamson's Nooksack field notes from 1928 have been located.

Adamson's dissertation, "Trickster and Transformer Myths of the Coast Salish," was approved May 6, 1929, but was never deposited with the Columbia University Library.[23] The Boas papers at the American Philosophical Society Library contain a copy of what appears to be Boas's reading report on the dissertation, reproduced here:

> Miss Thelma Adamson has made a comparative study of the Trickster and Transformer Cycle of Puget Sound. The essential point of her thesis is the discussion of the reason for separating these two figures of Indian mythology, which in other regions appear as a unit. For this purpose she has undertaken a detailed comparison of the Puget Sound material and of that of the Northwestern plateaus on the northern coast.
>
> The arrangement of the material does not bring out her point clearly because the discussion is interspersed with long abstracts of tales. It is understood that Miss Adamson will re-arrange the material so as to separate the discussion from the tales and so that the essential point will be brought out more clearly than it is at present presented. In this form the thesis will be a valuable contribution to our knowledge of American mythology.

For unknown reasons, perhaps the onset of tuberculosis and later mental illness, Adamson never submitted a revised dissertation, nor was the dissertation ever published, a requirement for the PhD at Columbia at that time. No copy of the dissertation draft has been located.

Adamson apparently came down with tuberculosis sometime during 1929 and spent time recuperating at a TB sanitarium at Saranac Lake, New York. In a letter to Boas from Saranac Lake, Adamson thanked him for sending her a copy of Oliver La Farge's recently published *Laughing Boy*. She continued: "I feel happier lately as I am rather certain of leaving here in April. I am to have an X-ray in two weeks. There's no reason why it shouldn't turn out well. I walk an hour and a half a day now and do about an hour's work in addition. In another week or so I shall be walking over two hours a day. I am very anxious to get back and can scarcely wait. The routine grows so monotonous."[24] It is not known when she left the sanitarium. Little is known of her activities during the rest of 1930 and 1931. She may have been preparing the manuscript of her *Folk-Tales of the Coast Salish*.

As part of an acculturation study under the direction of Ruth Benedict, Adamson conducted fieldwork on Nooksack during the summer of 1932 in Everson, Washington. This was the last known fieldwork undertaken by Adamson. As with her 1928 Nooksack notes, none of Adamson's 1932 field research has been located. Two wax cylinders of Nooksack songs recorded by Adamson constitute a separate collection in the Archives of Traditional Music at Indiana University (Seeger and Spear 1987, 26). It is not clear whether the recordings date from 1928 or 1932—probably 1928.

Little is known about Adamson's life from 1932 to 1941. Bits and pieces from Jacobs's and Herzog's correspondence files suggest that by 1933 she may have been experiencing the onset of the mental illness that eventually resulted in her institutionalization in about 1941 or 1942. In a letter to his wife, Elizabeth, Melville Jacobs wrote on December 13, 1934: "Learned from the anthropologists that Thelma never had a T.B. relapse at all; the theory is that she went melancholia for two years now, or had a nervous breakdown, or something, though she was reported as recently seen at a theatre, with Eddie, who reported her to somebody as 'much improved.' I'll get in touch with him soon."

During 1937 there was an exchange of letters between Jacobs and Herzog about Adamson's condition and the possibility of her visiting Melville and Elizabeth Jacobs in Seattle. Ruth Benedict also broached the possibility of Thelma's visiting the Jacobses: "Does the invitation to Thelma still hold? For the time is propitious, if it's still possible . . . it seems as though it might save Thelma. She has been having the new insulin treatment and is much better. Bloomingdale has raised the question of whether they should keep her there indefinitely, and it has been decided that she should try leaving."[25] But such a visit and stay with the Jacobses never transpired.

Thelma spent part of the summer of 1941 at Duneden Rest and Convalescent Home in Rockville Center, New York.[26] She left Duneden and became a resident of Brattleboro Retreat, a private psychiatric hospital in Brattleboro, Vermont, from around 1941–42 until the 1970s, apparently with a diagnosis of schizophrenia.[27] Edward Salant was granted a divorce from his wife in 1946 after making provisions for her maintenance and support for the rest of her life and for the payment of reasonable funeral expenses.[28] After leaving Brattleboro Retreat, Adamson lived in several group homes in Vermont. She died at the Springfield Convalescent Center, Springfield, Vermont, on April 12, 1983, at the age of eighty-two. Her cremated remains were interred in Grandview Cemetery at New Matamoras, Ohio.

GEORGE HERZOG

"Appendix: Songs" appears at the end of Adamson's collection of folktales (422–30). This appendix contains nineteen song transcriptions, including music notation by George Herzog and song texts provided mainly by Franz Boas.

Herzog's role in Adamson's work came out of both personal and professional connections between the two going back to their student days at Columbia University. In 1924 Boas had contacted Erich von Hornbostel, director of the Phonogramm-Archiv at Kaiser Friedrich-Wilhelms

Universität (Berlin University), seeking a student trained in comparative musicology and experienced with sound archiving to study with him at Columbia. Boas hoped to produce a scholar capable of conducting anthropological research in North American Indian music. Hornbostel recommended Herzog, who was then working as his unpaid research assistant in the Phonogramm-Archiv (Inman 1986, [1]).

The trajectory that brought George Herzog from Berlin to New York started in his native Budapest, where he received early training in music. His studies included piano instruction from Béla Bartók and composition classes with Zoltán Kodály, and it seems likely that he also became acquainted with their work collecting and studying folk songs (Nettl 1991, 270). Facing anti-Semitic university admission practices, he left Hungary in 1920 to study at the Academy of Music in Vienna. From there he moved to the Hochschule für Musik in Berlin, where he came under the influence of the emerging discipline of *vergleichende Musikwissenschaft*, or comparative musicology (Inman 1986, [1]). The "Berlin School" had been pioneered by psychologist Carl Stumpf and physician Otto Abraham, and the founding of the Phonogramm-Archiv was the direct result of their research activities. These scholars, along with Hornbostel, formalized the study of folk and so-called primitive music by combining empirical observation and analysis with a humanistic approach concerned with the motivation behind music expression in culture. Herzog's training in comparative musicology, together with his work at the Phonogramm-Archiv from 1922 through 1924, made him, seemingly, the perfect representative of Hornbostel and the "Berlin School" in the United States. He arrived in New York in 1925 to study with Boas at Columbia University (Inman 1986, [1]). Among his classmates that first year were Melville Jacobs, Otto Klineberg, and Thelma Adamson.

Herzog and Adamson appear to have become good friends, despite their different backgrounds (he a Hungarian Jew, she having grown up Baptist in Ohio). During the summer of 1926, when Adamson, Jacobs, and Klineberg made their overland trek to Washington State for field research, Adamson was feeling stranded in Chehalis when she wrote a long letter to Herzog back in New York: "I don't know where to begin, so much water has flowed under the bridge since I saw you last. As sum total I might say, 'I have been bored, I am bored, I shall be bored.' . . . Nothing ever happens here. At least in New York there are things to hear and see. Which reminds me, you *must* find me a Hungarian restaurant next fall."[29] Herzog and Adamson exchanged letters again the next summer, when he was conducting his first field trip in the Southwest, and she was back in western Washington continuing her research. Boas visited during part of this second field trip, bringing along an Edison cylinder recorder with which they recorded the songs that would be included in *Folk-Tales of the Coast Salish*.

It is clear that Boas expected Herzog not only to conduct his own research on Native American music but to be available to transcribe the songs other Boas students recorded during the course of their ethnographic and linguistic research (recordings Boas expected his students to make). Jacobs mentioned his hope that Herzog would eventually transcribe his own western Oregon recordings as well as Adamson's, Erna Gunther's, Arthur Ballard's, and Viola Garfield's.[30] Herzog confirmed his intention to do so and suggested, "All together one could do a pretty good survey with all this material."[31] Herzog was interested in the delineation of musical style and hoped to assemble enough recorded material to enable him to characterize the music of the Northwest Coast, with the ultimate aim of producing comparative studies of musical style in Native North America.

By the spring of 1933 Herzog had apparently been engaged to provide transcriptions of songs to be published as part of *Folk-Tales of the Coast Salish*. He had feared for a time that the nineteen Chehalis cylinder recordings made by Boas and Adamson in 1927 were lost, but in April, having located them in storage at the American Museum of Natural History, Herzog requested that nine of the cylinders be sent to him for transcription.[32] He was in the process of obtaining the song texts, some from Adamson and some from Boas. Herzog wrote to Adamson that, in addition to the Chehalis recordings, the Museum had two Dictaphone records (cylinders) numbered "20" and "21" with slips of paper containing song texts "in her writing" and the word "Nutsaq" in his writing.[33] These two recordings are something of a mystery. Adamson worked on Nooksack material in Everson, Washington, during the summers of 1928 and 1932, but her field notes from these trips have disappeared. The two cylinder recordings were apparently made during one of these trips, but no contextual information accompanies them. It seems likely they were made in 1928, as Herzog refers to them in 1933 as if they had been in the museum for several years and were just being rediscovered. We know that Adamson worked with consultant George Swanaset while in Everson in 1928, and it's likely that, if she recorded the two cylinders that year, the singer is Swanaset. Though the two songs on these recordings have no connection to Adamson's folktale collection—other than being additional examples of Coast Salish songs—it was decided to include them among the transcriptions in the appendix to *Folk-Tales of the Coast Salish*.

In June 1933 Herzog had finished fourteen song transcriptions and sent them to Adamson. By November she was too ill to deal with the details of publication, and the song transcriptions still hadn't been incorporated into the manuscript. In December Herzog sent copies of the transcriptions to Ruth Benedict, who was overseeing publication as editor of the *Journal of American Folklore* and the Memoirs of the American Folklore Society series.[34] There was still some confusion about what was to be included, and in early 1934 Herzog and Boas continued to correspond about the songs. Herzog completed several additional transcriptions of songs that Thelma had not planned to include but that went with texts Boas had collected.[35] In September, as the book was due at the printer, Herzog sent Benedict the final few transcriptions, along with the explanation of the symbols that were to precede the transcriptions.[36] Boas had wanted the songs to be inserted into the stories they accompanied, but by the time the transcriptions were finally compiled, the most practical approach was to keep them together in an appendix at the end of the volume.[37]

THE SONG TRANSCRIPTIONS

The nineteen songs transcribed in the appendix come from three recorded collections: 1) nineteen cylinders recorded in Oakville, Washington, by Boas and Adamson, summer 1927; 2) eighteen cylinders recorded in Oakville, Washington, by Adamson alone (following Boas's departure), summer 1927; and 3) two cylinders recorded in (probably) Everson, Washington, by Adamson in (probably) summer 1928. The original cylinders were deposited in the American Museum of Natural History. There they were given "P.R." (phonograph record) numbers, in the case of the 1927 recordings, and "D.R." (Dictaphone record) numbers, in the case of the 1928 recordings.

When Herzog moved from Columbia University to Indiana University in 1948, the Adamson and Adamson/Boas recordings were among the many collections of original cylinders he took with him. George List, director of the Archives of Traditional Music at Indiana University from 1954 to 1977, recalled the situation: "It seems that Herzog had received many of the collections with a promise to study them and publish the results. . . . The greatest problem was with the American Museum of Natural History in New York City. Herzog had received all their cylinders with the promise that he would catalog them. This he never did and never returned them" (List 1999, 4).

Negotiations between Indiana University and the American Museum of Natural History enabled the Archives of Traditional Music to produce copies of the recordings for the Museum while keeping the originals for its own collection. The Adamson and Adamson/Boas collections were eventually given the following accession numbers: 1) 54-131-F (Boas/Adamson 1927); 2) 54-130-F (Adamson 1927); and 3) 54-043-F (Adamson 1928). The American Museum of Natural History continues to hold the rights to the Adamson and Adamson/Boas recordings.

Of the nineteen transcriptions, eleven include page references to the folktale they accompany. Six of the remaining eight were recorded to accompany folktales collected by Boas (not included in Adamson's collection), and the last two are the Nooksack songs for which no documentation survives.

Herzog's song transcriptions employ standard European music notation enhanced with symbols or "diacritics" to depict a more precise description of the song as performed. His "Explanation of the Signs Used in the Transcriptions" (422) is nearly identical to that which accompanies the song transcriptions in his 1928 article "The Yuman Musical Style." In this work, his first major study of musical style, Herzog acknowledged the system outlined by Abraham and Hornbostel in their

1909 "Vorschläge für die Transkription exotischer Melodien" ("Proposals for the Transcription of Exotic Melodies") (Herzog 1928, 200). This system was intended to provide an objective means for the transcription and comparative study of music, also allowing for the transcriber's own observations, a synthesis of approaches intended "to treat transcription as a tool for discovery of musical intent" (Ellingson 1992, 125). The model developed by Abraham and Hornbostel avoids "overt Eurocentric bias while capturing aspects of expression and musicality" (Levine 2002, xxv), and it has been widely used by scholars. (Other approaches to transcription focus on different aspects of music and reflect a variety of orientations toward the role and meaning of music culturally.)

Herzog transcribed the nineteen songs by listening repeatedly to the recordings and notating what he heard. He then fit the song texts (along with English translations for eight of the nineteen) provided by Adamson and Boas to the music so as to indicate the pitch, articulation, and duration of each sung syllable. The number of beats per minute is indicated above the staff, and where a drum beat is present but not congruent with the vocal pulse, a second metric indication is made (such complex rhythmic relationships are a common feature of Coast Salish songs generally). In some cases Herzog added a separate line of notation for the drum beat below the music staff, and where he felt it necessary, he added an explanatory footnote (i.e., "almost syncopating with the beats of the singing" [424]). Adamson did not provide song texts for the first of the two Nooksack songs (D.R. 1) (430) or the White River song "Spitsxu Chant to Bring Rain" (P.R. 14b) (429). Herzog, required to do those transcriptions himself, commented, "The texts of . . . [these songs] are uncertain; they have been written down from the phonograph records" (422).

Finally, one error in the original appendix should be noted: "Lion's Gambling Song" (P.R. 24b) (424) should be "Rabbit's Gambling Song." Adamson and Boas both collected versions of the story of Mountain Lion and Rabbit's competition, and Adamson included two versions in her collection (52–55). According to a letter from Adamson to Herzog, both P.R. 24a (correctly titled "Lion's Gambling Song") and P.R. 24b were recorded to go with texts collected by Boas.[38] However the misidentification occurred, a comparison of the text of P.R. 24b with that of P.R. 15b (correctly titled "Rabbit's Gambling Song") shows clearly that it is Rabbit's song. He calls on his tamanoas for a cold, clear night to enable him to win the contest by leading Lion across the frozen lake, which cannot support his weight. Rabbit wins because of the power of his song.

With the challenge of Adamson's illness, the publication of *Folk-Tales of the Coast Salish* in 1934 could not have been completed without the determination of a number of individuals, particularly her teacher and mentor Franz Boas and her teacher and editor Ruth Benedict. Interestingly, 1934 was also the year of publication of Benedict's *Patterns of Culture*, a seminal work in the discipline of cultural anthropology and one that established Benedict as one of the preeminent scholars of her generation. George Herzog, whose appendix to *Folk-Tales* provides us with a rare window into the use of songs in Coast Salish stories, made a tremendous contribution to the budding field of comparative musicology (eventually to be called ethnomusicology) through his fieldwork, writings, and archival activities during the 1930s and 1940s. Sadly, the careers of both Adamson and Herzog ended early due to mental illness. Both died in 1983 at the age of eighty-two after many years of institutionalization.

ACKNOWLEDGMENTS

We wish to thank the many people who helped us in our search for this introduction. Thelma Adamson's niece, Mazie Stitt of Sudbury, Massachusetts, provided much valuable biographical and family information and permitted us access to Adamson's Columbia University record of transcript. The Registrar's Office, the Dawes Library, and the Office of Alumni Relations of Marietta College provided invaluable assistance in tracking down and photocopying items relating to Adamson's undergraduate career. The Libraries and the Office of Student Information Services of Columbia University were quite helpful in providing information about Adamson's graduate studies. The Vassar College Archives and Special Collections expedited access to Ruth Benedict's correspondence, and the Archives of Barnard College provided information regarding former student Adele Froehlich. Thanks also to Susanne J. Young, Jay Miller, and the late Maclyn P. Burg for patiently listening to many stories of discoveries and disappointments in the search for Thelma Adamson.

NOTES

An early draft of this introduction was presented by Seaburg at the Forty-eighth Annual Northwest Anthropological Conference, March 23–25, 1995, Portland State University, Portland, and later expanded and published (Seaburg 1999).

1. B.J. = Bluejay; Naw = Bluebird (Kinkade 1991).

2. Thelma Adamson to Melville Jacobs, 1932, Melville Jacobs Collection, University of Washington Libraries, Seattle, Washington (hereafter cited as MJC).

3. Ruth Benedict to Melville Jacobs, November 25, 1933, MJC.

4. An obituary in the *Marietta Times* (April 14, 1983) lists Torey Hills, California, as Adamson's place of birth. Her Columbia University transcript of record lists Peru City, California, while correspondence from Brattleboro Retreat indicates her place of birth as Piru City, California. According to Adamson's niece, Mazie Stitt, the oil field where Adamson's father worked was at Torey Mt., California (personal communication, 1996). The Adamson family went to California around July 1900 and returned to New Matamoras in 1904, then went on to Marietta around 1915–16. Mrs. Stitt's mother, Aline, attended early grade school in Marietta. Mrs. Stitt also remembered that Thelma's middle name, Ramona, was inspired by the novel *Ramona* by Helen Hunt Jackson and that Thelma and Lela were cared for by an Indian woman while in California.

5. Adamson's niece, Mazie Stitt, indicated that the family's religious affiliation was mostly Baptist (personal communication, October 22, 1986). Jay Miller believes that the family was probably American Baptist (personal communication, March 2009).

6. *Marietta Times*, April 29, 1923.

7. *Physics Today*, February 1979, 70.

8. Thelma Adamson to Franz Boas, August 9, 1926, American Philosophical Society Library, Philadelphia, Pennsylvania (hereafter cited as APS); Thelma Adamson to George Herzog, August 7 and 30, 1926, Archives of Traditional Music, Indiana University, Bloomington, Indiana (hereafter cited as ATM).

9. Adamson is referring to Palmer (1925).

10. Thelma Adamson to George Herzog, August 30, 1926, ATM.

11. Thelma Adamson to George Herzog, August 7, 1926, ATM.

12. Thelma Adamson to George Herzog, August 30, 1926, ATM.

13. Thelma Adamson to George Herzog, August 2, 1927, ATM.

14. According to Freeman (1965, 96–97), Boas collected fourteen notebooks of the Upper Chehalis dialect, containing "vocabulary, paradigms, and texts with interlinear translation." For a brief but valuable history of linguistic and ethnographic research on the Upper Chehalis, see Kinkade (1991, v–viii).

15. The Society for Ethnomusicology, Northwest Chapter, awards its Thelma Adamson Prize for the best student paper delivered at the annual chapter meeting.

16. Handwritten notes re. Jacobs's research, administration, and teaching, 1926–1928, MJC.

17. David Thomson to Thelma Adamson, October 11, 1927, APS.

18. Handwritten notes re. Jacobs's research, administration, and teaching, 1926–1928, MJC.

19. Franz Boas to Edward Sapir and Leonard Bloomfield, April 18, 1928, APS.

20. Thelma Adamson to Franz Boas, May 27 and June 17, 1928, APS.

21. Adamson was probably married in 1927 (U.S. Federal Census for 1930).

22. "I sometimes wonder what will happen when I say that I am married. I may tell it at any time if I think that it will give me more freedom—more freedom from such questions as where I live in the winter time and how much I pay for my room rent. Of course this is entirely entre-nous; I don't need to say that to you, of course." Thelma Adamson to George Herzog, August 2, 1927, ATM.

23. Eileen McIlvaine, personal communication, August 11, 1986.

24. Thelma Adamson to Franz Boas, March 4, 1930, APS.

25. Ruth Benedict to Melville Jacobs, June 11, 1937, MJC.

26. Thelma Adamson to Melville Jacobs, various dates, MJC. In one letter (July 16, 1941), Adamson said, "I have been writing a bit on some material of Waterman's and Ballard[']s that Ruth Benedict gave me before she left. There is a good deal of it and so I hope that I get it done eventually. I shall most likely abstract it also. There is a good deal of Puget Sound material now, or at least a fair amount. There used to be such little material from different places on the Northwest Coast."

27. Otto Klineberg, personal communication, October 2, 1985; State of Vermont Certificate of Death for Thelma Salant, #01339.

28. From a certified "Copy of the Final Decree for Divorce," no. 11981, in Circuit Court for Montgomery County, Maryland.

29. Thelma Adamson to George Herzog, August 7, 1926, ATM.

30. Melville Jacobs to George Herzog, May 17, 1932, and August 10, 1932, MJC.

31. George Herzog to Melville Jacobs, August 16, 1932, MJC.

32. George Herzog to Bella Waitzner, April 19, 1933, ATM.

33. George Herzog to Thelma Adamson, April 19, 1933, ATM; George Herzog to Thelma Adamson, undated, ATM.

34. George Herzog to Ruth Benedict, December 12, 1933, ATM.

35. George Herzog to Franz Boas, March 16, 1934, ATM.

36. George Herzog to Ruth Benedict, September 29, 1934, ATM.

37. For more on Herzog's life and career, see Inman (1986) and Nettl (1991).
38. Thelma Adamson to George Herzog, June 2, [1933], ATM.

REFERENCES

Benedict, Ruth F. 1934. Editor's report. *Journal of American Folklore* 47 (184/185): 260–61.

———. 1935. Editor's report. *Journal of American Folklore* 48 (188): 188.

Boas, Franz. 1927. Chehalis field notes. Manuscript in American Philosophical Society Library, Philadelphia.

Clark, Ella E. 1953. *Indian legends of the Pacific Northwest*. Berkeley: University of California Press.

Dundes, Alan. 2007 [1966]. Metafolklore and oral literary criticism. In *The meaning of folklore: The analytical essays of Alan Dundes*, ed. Simon J. Bronner, 77–87. Logan: Utah State University Press.

Ellingson, Ter. 1992. Transcription. In *Ethnomusicology: An introduction*, ed. Helen Myers, 110–52. New York: Norton.

Farrand, Livingston, and W. S. Kahnweiler. 1902. *Traditions of the Quinault Indians*. Vol. 4 of *Publications of the Jesup North Pacific Expedition*. New York: Memoirs of the American Museum of Natural History.

Freeman, John F. 1965. *A guide to manuscripts relating to the American Indian in the Library of the American Philosophical Society*. Philadelphia: American Philosophical Society.

Herzog, George. 1928. The Yuman musical style. *Journal of American Folklore* 41:183–231.

Inman, Carol F. 1986. George Herzog: Struggles of a sound archivist. *Resound: A Quarterly of the Archives of Traditional Music* 5 (1): [1–5].

Jacobs, Elizabeth D. 1990 [1959]. *Nehalem Tillamook tales*. Corvallis: Oregon State University Press.

Jacobs, Melville. 1959. Folklore. In *The anthropology of Franz Boas*, ed. Walter Goldschmidt, 119–38. American Anthropological Association, Memoir 89. Menasha WI: American Anthropological Association.

Kinkade, M. Dale. 1991. *Upper Chehalis dictionary*. University of Montana Occasional Papers in Linguistics 7. Missoula: University of Montana.

Leeds-Hurwitz, Wendy. 1985. The Committee on Research in Native American Languages. *Proceedings of the American Philosophical Society* 129 (2): 129–60.

Levine, Victoria Lindsay. 2002. *Writing American Indian music: Historic transcriptions, notations, and arrangements*. Recent Researches in American Music 44; Music of the United States of America 11. Middleton WI: A-R Editions.

List, George. 1999. The early days of the Archives. *Resound: A Quarterly of the Archives of Traditional Music* 18 (1): 4–5.

Miller, Jay. 1999. Chehalis area traditions. *Northwest Anthropological Research Notes* 33 (1): 1–72.

Nettl, Bruno. 1991. The dual nature of ethnomusicology in North America: The contributions of Charles Seeger and George Herzog. In *Comparative musicology and anthropology of music: Essays on the history of ethnomusicology*, ed. Bruno Nettl and Philip V. Bohlman, 266–76. Chicago: University of Chicago Press.

Palmer, Katherine V. W. 1925. *Honne, the Spirit of the Chehalis: The Indian interpretation of the origin of the people and animals—as narrated by George Saunders, collected and arranged by Katherine Van Winkle Palmer*. Geneva NY: Press of W. F. Humphrey.

Seaburg, William R. 1999. Whatever happened to Thelma Adamson?: A footnote in the history of Northwest anthropological research. *Northwest Anthropological Research Notes* 33 (1): 73–83.

———. 2007. *Pitch Woman and other stories: The oral traditions of Coquelle Thompson, Upper Coquille Athabaskan Indian*. Lincoln: University of Nebraska Press.

Seeger, Anthony, and Louise S. Spear, eds. 1987. *Early field recordings: A catalogue of cylinder collections at the Indiana University Archives of Traditional Music*. Bloomington: Indiana University Press.

Thelma Adamson, anthropology office, Columbia University, spring 1926. Courtesy of William R. Seaburg.

Thelma Adamson, making Edward O. Salant's initials with pebbles in the snow on a mountain pass on the trip west, June 1926. Courtesy of William R. Seaburg.

Thelma Adamson at Yellowstone Falls, June 1926. Courtesy of William R. Seaburg.

George Herzog in front of Journalism Building, Columbia University, spring 1926. Courtesy of William R. Seaburg.

CONTENTS.

INTRODUCTION.

The following collection of tales was obtained during the summers of 1926 and 1927 from a number of Coast Salish groups of western Washington. The first summer's work was devoted entirely to the recording of tales, especially from the Upper Chehalis and Cowlitz tribes. The second summer's work was devoted to a study of the general culture of the Upper Chehalis and to a comparative study of the Cowlitz dialect; the tales obtained were merely incidental to that work.

UPPER CHEHALIS.

The largest group of tales is from the Upper Chehalis, who now live on the Chehalis Reservation at Oakville, Washington. My principal informants, in the order named, were Peter Heck, Marion Davis, Jonas Secena and Pike Ben. Peter Heck's mother, Mary Heck,[1] who was past ninety years of age and the oldest member of the tribe, gave me a few tales. She told them in the Upper Chehalis dialect, Peter acting as interpreter. Joe Pete and his wife, Maggie, also told a few tales, and Dan Secena, Jonas' father, only one. All of the informants were born in Upper Chehalis territory and with the exception of Mr. Pete, were brought up there. Mr. Pete spent his youth among the Nisqually. Peter Heck was about sixty years old, Marion Davis and Pike Ben were considerably older, and Jonas Secena was forty.

There is only one group of tales, I should say, that does not belong in the Upper Chehalis group, — the Mink tales told by Pike Ben. I could not learn from Mr. Ben where he learned them, nor does his genealogy throw any light on the subject. His wife is a Puyallup and he may have learned them from her. Several individuals impressed upon me strongly that if I had any Mink tales, I should not consider them Upper Chehalis tales. As one person put it, "Mink belongs to the Sound." Mr. Ben got a lot of pleasure out of telling any tale and those about Mink appealed to him particularly. Since I am at a loss to say what Sound tribe they came from, I have included them in the Upper Chehalis group.

The Upper Chehalis call themselves Q'waya'ɩɬ. Approximately,

[1] Indian name Kwili'not.

their territory formerly extended along the Chehalis River from Chehalis to a little west of Oakville. This territory embraced Oakville and Rochester Prairies, large parts of Mima and Grand Mound Prairies, besides various smaller prairies.

COWLITZ.

The Cowlitz informants were Mary Iley, her sister Sophie Smith, James Cheholts (tciho'ł), Lucy Youckton, Mrs. Northover, and Minnie Case. The Cowlitz have no reservation and, because of this, were rather difficult to locate. Mrs. Youckton, who has lived on the Oakville Reservation for many years, put me in touch with Mrs. Iley. Mrs. Iley lives at Nesika, on the upper Cowlitz River, but I finally located her in 1926 near Wapeto, Yakima Reservation, where she was visiting Mrs. Smith. Mrs. Case (or Mrs. Bill) and Mrs. Northover were also living on Yakima Reservation in 1926. Another Cowlitz woman, Mrs. Johnnie Johnson, a sister of James Cheholts, was living on Yakima Reservation but she refused to tell any tales. Because they were so difficult to reach, and because so little time was left to me, I spent very little time with Mrs. Case and Mrs. Northover. The latter was ill at the time and could recall very few tales. In 1927 I located James Cheholts at Rochester, Washington, — not far from Oakville Reservation, and Mrs. Iley at Morton, Washington, where she was visiting her son. Unlike his sister, Mrs. Johnson, Mr. Cheholts was a willing informant, and told all the tales that he could remember, or that we had time for. He has had very little contact with his own people for years, so his stories are rather brief. All the informants were well past middle-age, — Mrs. Iley about seventy.

The Cowlitz call themselves L'αpu·'l'əmυx̂. Since there is a good deal of confusion as to the proper location of the tribe, I shall go into some detail regarding it.

The term Cowlitz is often applied to two distinct linguistic groups, the Taitnepam of Sahaptian stock, and the Cowlitz of Coast Salish stock. The Taitnepam are called Upper Cowlitz, the Coast Salish Cowlitz, Lower Cowlitz. The Taitnepam formerly lived and still live along the upper Cowlitz River in the vicinities of Mossy Rock, Nesika and Silver and Tilton Creeks. The Coast Salish Cowlitz — the L'αpu·'l'əmυx̂ — comprised three different geographical groups. One group, evidently the largest, lived along the Cowlitz River and its tributaries from above Toledo south to Castle Rock, roaming territory extending as far south as Kelso. In this group are the Toutle River Cowlitz, — a sub-group which calls itself sɩ·''q'w. A second group lived along the Newaukum (na'waqυm) River, a tributary of the Chehalis. The upper reaches of the Newaukum extend very close to Taitnepam territory. A third group lived on the Chehalis River in the vicinities of Pe Ell and Boisfort. The people of this group speak of themselves as Cowlitz, although some of the Upper Chehalis consider them a sub-group of their own tribe. Geographically, and linguistically so it would seem, the latter group is intermediate between Cowlitz and Upper Chehalis. The Upper Chehalis and Cowlitz dialects are closely related, and the two peoples, with some difficulty, can understand one another. The Newaukum Cowlitz intermarried with the Taitnepam and this resulted in a bi-lingual group. Mrs. Iley, Mrs. Smith and Mrs. Youckton belong to this group. Mrs. Iley's and Mrs. Smith's father was L'αpu·'l'əmʊx̣̑, their mother, Taitnepam and Yakima. Mrs. Iley speaks both Cowlitz and Taitnepam. Her husband is Taitnepam. Mrs. Smith once knew Cowlitz but through long contact with Sahaptians remembers only a few words. Mr. Cheholts and Mrs. Northover belong to the first group. Mr. Cheholts was born on Toutle River, as were his father and mother. According to him, the L'αpu·'l'əmʊx̣̑ who lived along the Cowlitz River had little contact with the Taitnepam. Mrs. Northover was born near Toledo and speaks Cowlitz. Mrs. Case belongs to the third group, the Boisfort group, and originally spoke Cowlitz. The members of the tribe are so scattered and have so little contact with one another that they rarely speak their own dialect; in most cases, they have replaced it with another. Although both Mrs. Smith and Mrs. Iley have been in very close contact with the Taitnepam, many of the tales they gave are quite similar to those of the Upper Chehalis. Practically all the terms used were Coast Salish. In the case of the trickster — transformer, the Taitnepam term Spilya'i (Coyote) and the Coast Salish term X̣wα'ni, for which there is no translation, were sometimes interchanged in the same tale. They maintained that the two characters were the same and that the interchange of terms did not matter.

HUMPTULIP.

The Humptulip tales were obtained in 1926 from Mrs. Lucy Heck, a Humptulip-Grays Harbor woman living on the Upper Chehalis Reservation at Oakville. She was about seventy years old and was brought up on Chinoose (Chenois) Creek, in Humptulip country. She learned the tales from her step-father, known to the Whites as Pete Simmons, or old man Simmons. Neither her father, father's brothers, mother nor mother's sisters knew how to tell tales. Pete Simmons was about a hundred years old when he died. He told the tales to Mrs. Heck when she was quite young, but told her no more after her marriage. He used to say to her, "If you never forget these stories, it is a sign that you will live to an old age."

Mrs. Heck told me all the tales that she could remember at the time, relating them in the Harbor dialect, while her husband, Silas Heck, an Upper Chehalis, acted as interpreter. I had hoped to get more information from her at some later time. Unfortunately, she died the next winter.

Since I have never visited the Grays Harbor country or had much contact with people speaking the Harbor dialect, I am somewhat at a disadvantage in checking the spelling of the place names that appear in Mrs. Heck's tales.

WYNOOCHEE AND SATSOP.

This small collection of tales was obtained during a short visit to Montesano, Washington, in 1927. The Wynoochee (wanu'ɨtci) informant was Jack Williams, a very old man and somewhat childish. The Satsop informant was Mrs. Simon Charley, also well up in years. According to the information I received, the Wynoochee lived along the Wynoochee River, the Satsop, along the Satsop River.

PUGET SOUND.

The Puyallup and Skokomish tales were obtained on Skokomish Reservation in 1926. The Puyallup informant was Jerry Meeker, who was visiting on the Reservation at the time. The Skokomish informant was Mrs. Mary Adams, who lived among the Puyallup during her youth. Both informants were past fifty. The White River tales were obtained from Marion Davis, Upper Chehalis informant. Mr. Davis learned the tales from his mother, a White River woman who was brought to Upper Chehalis territory when about five years old.

REMARKS.

With one or two exceptions,[1] the tales of this collection refer to the time "when all the animals were people". The Upper Chehalis term for this type of tale is sielɔ'ʾpt, the Cowlitz, sɔ'ʾpt. According to the Upper Chehalis, after the appearance of the transformer Moon, the birds and animals could no longer speak the human language. Moon was "master" of the animals and told them how the people in time to come should use them. Most of the characters in the tales are animals or birds, but in a few cases, the characters seem entirely human.

In olden times, the Upper Chehalis never told stories in the summer for fear snakes would crawl through the door. They waited until the drizzling fall rains had set in, or until after the first flurry of snow. As soon as spring came, they stopped in order to make the spring last a long time. There were no stories that belonged to a particular family or class. The narrator of a story and the listeners

[1] Two Cowlitz tales, The Horse Race and White Bear Takes Revenge, seem to me to belong to a different class of stories although not designated as such by the narrators.

had to lie flat on their backs when the story was being told, to avoid getting humps in their backs. The fire-man was the only one who was allowed to stir about and then only to keep the fire going. All that the listeners were permitted to say was hamu'qi. This was to show their appreciation and to urge the narrator on, especially when the story was getting good. The Secena family said that they had always heard oso'sos used instead of hamu'qi. The latter phrase is the one usually given; I have heard it used when a very old person was telling a story. Mary Heck said that two stories were always told in succession. I suppose this does not apply to exceptionally long stories, for one informant said that in the old days it took three nights to tell the Moon story; another said that it took one whole night. It was considered very bad manners for a child to fall asleep or ask for something to eat while an old person was telling him a story. An old person could demand that the child first swim in the river as pay for the story. This was merely in keeping with the arduous tasks required of young people to fit them for the harder life of maturity. The Cowlitz made a practice of sending a child to swim before or after a story was told, as pay for the story. The Heck family often used the phrase, "K'walale·'··i", at the end of their stories; a comment about the story is sometimes added to this. Various other people, although they do not use the phrase now, said that they had often heard it. The exact meaning is difficult to give. Like some songs that appear in tales, it seems to imply much more than it says. Some say that it means, "Soon his salmon will be all gone!" On the other hand, one informant said that he thought it meant something like, "Keep the hoodoo away from the salmon!" One person suggested that it was derived from k'walɛ', meaning black-salmon, which seems possible. The Secena family, who use oso'sos while listening to a story, also use oso'sos as an ending. There is no translation for this.

Taken as a whole, this collection of tales offers few surprises in the way of plots or incidents, many striking parallels being found in the mythologies of other Northwest Coast tribes. A considerable number of the tales and incidents are also found in the mythologies of the Interior Salish. The cross-references given refer to whole tales or episodes rather than to incidents.

A few Upper Chehalis and Cowlitz tales were given in text. Since I have no English versions of these, I have retold them in order to make the collection complete. In a number of the second year's tales, the conversations were given in text.

Comments in parentheses were added by the narrators, those in square brackets by me.

KEY TO THE PHONETIC SYSTEM USED.

I. CONSONANTS.

b, d, g	as in English except in Puget Sound dialects; in the latter dialects b and d are pronounced with semi-closure of the nose
p, t, k	as in English
q	velar k, like Arabic q
gw, kw, qw	labialized
p', t', k', q'	explosives
g'w, k'w, q'w	labialized explosives
pᵘ, tᵘ, kᵘ, qᵘ	p, t, k, q followed by whispered u
k·	as in English kin
k·'	explosive
c	like sh in English ship
s	like English s
tc	like ch in English church
ts	like ts in English
tc', ts'	explosives
x̭	like ch in German Bach
x̣	velar spirant
x·	like ch in German ich
x̭w, x̣w	labialized
x̭ᵘ, x̣ᵘ	x̭ and x̣ followed by whispered u
d̂j	like dg in English judge
l, m, n, w, y, h	as in English
ł	voiceless palatal lateral
L'	explosive ł but with slight initial t quality

II. VOWELS.

a	as in English father
ä	as in English hat
e	as in English fate
i	as in English pique
o	as in English note
ɑ	as in English but
ε	as in English met
ɩ	as in English pin

ɔ	approximately as in English law
ʋ	as in English put
ə	obscure vowel
ai	as in English island
au	as in English now
oi	true diphthong, o + i
ɔi	true diphthong, ɔ + i
a^a, e^i, $ɔ^ɔ$, $ɛ^ɛ$	a, e, ɔ, ɛ followed by echo vowel

III. DIACRITICAL MARKS.

ʾ	glottal stop; following consonants denotes explosive consonants.
ʿ	aspirant; denotes strongly aspirated consonant or marked release of glottal stop following vowel.
´ `	denote main and secondary stress accent.
·	placed after a letter denotes preceding long sound; repetition of denotes corresponding length of sound.
⌢	indicates short consonant or vowel.

I. UPPER CHEHALIS TALES.

THE FLOOD.

(First Version).[1]

Once upon a time the birds were people. Thrush (spi′tsx̣^{u}) wished to marry, but the parents of the girl whom he had decided upon did not approve of him. The young woman, however, wished to marry him. Finally her parents gave their consent and she and Thrush were married.

Thrush always had a dirty face; he never washed before he ate. "Why don't you wash your face?" his mother-in-law asked one day. Thrush did not answer. Next morning she asked again, "Why don't you wash your face?" Thrush did not reply. She asked him the same question five days in succession. "Why don't you wash your face? It's getting very dirty." The fifth day the young man said, "If I wash my face, something will happen." His wife's parents insisted nevertheless. "If you don't wash, we'll take our daughter away from you!" they said. "All right then, I'll wash my face," Thrush said.

He went to the river and sang,

> Father-in-law, mother-in-law,
> Keep moving back from the river.

He washed his face. The dirt rolled off, leaving his face streaked all over. It began to rain and rained all day. "Move back from the river. I washed my face as you asked," Thrush said to his father-in-law. The river continued to rise. It rained for many days and nights (perhaps forty days and nights). The water rose and covered everything. There was no place for the people to stand but in the water and no place for them to go. Many drifted away and were never found.[2]

Thrush's parents-in-law and his wife landed on this side (i. e., Upper Chehalis territory). Muskrat dived into the water and came out with some dirt. He dived five times. From the dirt he made a little mountain. He told the people to land there, where they would be safe. "This is the mountain that I have made for you

[1] Told by Peter Heck, 1926. See p. 413.

[2] When the French first made their appearance, they were called "drift-people", for it was believed that they may have been one of those groups of peoples who drifted away during the flood.

so that you can be safe," he said. This mountain is called Tiger Lily[1] (mαsi'łk'·'ι); when the next flood comes it will not be flooded.

After the water fell and the earth dried off, the ground was found to be covered with dried [fossil] whales. The earth was just like new, and the people could begin all over again.

When Thrush washed his face, the white showed through. That's why he has scratches on his face.

*

* *

This story is important, because so many people lost everything they owned. The next time the flood comes, we shall know where to go.

(Second Version).[2]

The people, many years ago before this world was changed, were not as people are now; in some ways, they were smarter than we are.

Thrush was a disgrace to the tribe: the people had noticed, for many years, that she would not wash her face or bathe; she would not go near the water. They had asked her time and again to wash her face or bathe. "My friends," Thrush would say, "if I should wash my face, something might happen to this earth. I give all my friends warning." One day at last she consented to wash her face, and as she washed drops of water fell from her face. Clouds started to form immediately. The world was going to end. It rained and rained (for fifty or sixty days. The Whites believe that it rained forty days). The whole world was flooded. All the people then took to boats or open canoes. (It must have been in the summer time, for grass and plants were growing.) They floated away in all directions. There was nothing to eat, and they were almost dying there in their canoes. The whole earth had become an ocean. Then all the great divers began to argue. "Which of us is the best swimmer?" they asked. Everyone then had a suggestion for finding land. There was no mountain there then, nothing but prairie land beneath the water. Everybody dived but could bring up nothing from the earth. Then the smallest boy, Muskrat, was to dive for some grass; he was to receive a robe as pay. "I'll pay you for your trouble. You shall bring us the earth," the chief said to him. At this time, everyone had tamanoas[3] (sα'x̣t'kwυlc). Then Muskrat got ready to dive; he had a little power himself. He told the people what he would do with his tamanoas, as he had never used it before. He dived in and got some

---

[1] Near the town of Gate; the mountain is called Black Mountain by the Whites.

[2] Told by Jonas Secena, 1926.

[3] The Chinook jargon term for guardian spirit, now in common usage. The one term is used to express either the singular or the plural.

earth. Then he threw the earth to the surface with his power. The people could see a little dot on the ocean. Five times, Muskrat threw a bit of dirt to the surface. The dirt began to swell and turned into a mountain. All the canoes then landed there. They waited there a long time for the water to fall. At last the water fell. Everything was lovely. Muskrat had made the mountain through the power of his tamanoas. He was the only one who had been able to reach the bottom. He received a fur coat as pay. The mountain is now known as Black Mountain. At Gate, — not far from Mima Prairie, — the earth still remains in the shape of waves. It extends like this for four or five miles. After the water had subsided, it was said, "There shall never again be a person who shall cause a flood when he washes his face." Thrush was condemned; she became a bird.

(Third Version).[1]

Thrush was very lazy. He would not clean himself; he always had a dirty face. He finally consented to wash himself, but said, "Watch out for a flood!" It rained and rained for a long time. Then Moon[2] said that it would not do for a flood to come when people washed their faces. And so he turned Thrush into a bird.

THE FLOOD.[3]

The flood began and all the people were drowned. They tried to go to the highest hills but could not save themselves; they tried to swim but drowned. Pheasant (skwi'nəm) flew up to the highest hill and sat on the tallest tree there. Even there he thought that he would soon die for the water began to rise over his tail. At last the water fell and only Pheasant was saved. When the water fell it left a mark on Pheasant's tail.

BUNGLING HOST.

(First Version).[4]

Bluejay had a home of his own. One day he asked his cousin,[5] Skwikwi'kʷ, to go with him to visit a certain family. They went up the river to visit Skwit (a bird). They went into the house. In a little while, Skwit told his children to take their baskets and get some salmon-berries. The children kept saying, "Kwit, kwit," and

---

[1] Told by Joe Pete, 1926.
[2] The Transformer; see pp. 158, 269, 276, 356, 374.
[3] Told by Marion Davis, 1927. Mr. Davis said that he had never heard of a flood story in which Muskrat dives for earth.
[4] Told by Peter Heck, 1926. See p. 393.
[5] Or brother.

soon had a great many berries. They came home with their baskets full. Bluejay ate as many berries as he could hold. Then he went to his canoe and got in. He called back, "Come to visit me." He reached home.

Next day, Bluejay watched for his visitor. After a while, he saw him coming. Then he told his cousin to clean the seat. Skwit and his children landed. Soon Bluejay told his own children to go out and look for some berries. The five children said, "Kwit, kwit," but they could not find any berries. Then Skwit said to Bluejay, "You are making your children suffer." His children then went out. They said, "Kwit, kwit," and returned with five baskets of berries. They gave them to Bluejay. Then they left.

Bluejay said to his cousin, "Let us visit Tsia'kwawa (a bird)." They set out in their canoe. Tsia'kwawa was glad to see them. He told his children to get some salmon-berries. The children said, "Tsia'kwawa, kele'tewa'," and got the berries. They offered some to Bluejay. Bluejay ate as many as he could hold. Then he got into his canoe, and called back, "Come and visit me." "Y-e-e-e-s, old man," Tsia'kwawa called back.

Next day, Bluejay watched for his visitors — whose hospitality he wished to return in the same way. Tsia'kwawa and his children arrived. Before long, Bluejay sent his own children out to get some salmon-berries. "Tsia'kwawa, kele'tewa'," they said, but could find no berries. "You are making your children suffer," Tsia'kwawa said to Bluejay. Then he sent his own children out and they came back with lots of berries. They gave the berries to Bluejay and then left.

Next morning, Bluejay said to his cousin, "Let us visit Beaver (łα'q'ʟ'tc)." Old Beaver was glad to see old Bluejay. He said to his children, "Get some red-berries." Bluejay thought, "I'm going to get something good now." Beaver's children brought back some willow branches about a foot long, and a basket full of blue mud. Beaver gave some of the branches and a dish of mud to Bluejay. Bluejay was very much surprised; he did not know how to eat these things. He started for home hungry. At his canoe he called back, "Come and visit me." "Y-e-e-e-s, old man," Beaver called back.

Bluejay watched for his visitors and cleaned a place for them. Before long, Beaver and his five children came. Bluejay then sent his own children to get some mud and willow branches. The children cut some willows and looked for some mud. They gave some to Beaver and he ate it without any hesitancy; he ate every bit of it. Bluejay did well this time. Beaver left.

Next morning, Bluejay said, "Let us visit Bear." They set out. They arrived at Bear's place and went up to the door. "Hwu··," Bear said. Bluejay was frightened. Bear did the same thing five times. The last time they went in. "Come in, old man," Bear said to Bluejay. Bear was sitting down. Bluejay was so frightened he was ready to jump out at any minute. Bear picked up a knife and sharpened it. Bluejay was afraid that Bear would cut him. But Bear looked at his own hand and cut it in five different places. Then he held it over the fire and the grease dripped out. He gave the grease to Bluejay to drink. Bluejay drank it. He finished, and went away in his canoe. "Come and visit me," he called back. "Y-e-e-e-s, old man," Bear answered.

Bluejay rolled himself in his blanket and lay down by the fireplace. Bear opened the door. Bluejay said, "Hwu··," thinking to frighten Bear as the latter had frightened him. But Bear paid no attention; he came right in and sat down. Bluejay sharpened his knife. He cut his hand, and cried out in pain, "U··." He had hurt himself. Bear said to him, "Poor old man, you don't have to do that." He asked for a knife, cut his own hand and roasted it over the fire. Then he gave the grease to Bluejay and went home.

Next morning, Bluejay said to his cousin, "Let us visit Sea Lion." They set out and arrived at the place. Just as they opened the door, Sea Lion said, "Hwu··." He frightened Bluejay five times; then he let them in. Bluejay was still very frightened. Sea Lion got up; he got a big knife and whetted it on his leg. Then he cut a piece of flesh off his side for Bluejay. Bluejay thought, "Oh, this is terrible — eating this flesh!" He finished the meat, and started home. He called back his usual invitation.

Bluejay was watching for his visitor. After a while, he saw him coming. "Clean a place," he said to his cousin. Bluejay then lay down in bed. Sea Lion opened the door. Bluejay said, "Hwu··." Sea-Lion was not the least bit frightened. Bluejay got out of bed. He whetted his carving knife on his lap. Then he began to feel his side, and cut it. "U··," he said and nearly fainted. A little black blood oozed out. Sea Lion said, "Oh, you are hurting yourself." He asked for a knife, cut a piece of his own flesh and gave it to Bluejay. Bluejay was that much to the good. Then Sea Lion left.

Next morning, Bluejay said, "Let us visit Fish Duck." They arrived at Fish Duck's place. Bluejay went in. After he had been there a while, Fish Duck told his children to get some fish. The children dived and brought up a great many. Fish Duck cooked the fish. Bluejay ate a great many. As he started home, he called back, "Come and visit me." "Y-e-e-e-s, old man," Fish Duck answered.

Bluejay was watching for his visitors. "He's coming! Get ready!" he called to his cousin. Fish Duck came with all his children. They sat down. In a little while Bluejay told his own children to go and get some fish. The children went to the river. They dived in, but when they came up they had no fish. They dived in again; the fish were too quick for them. "Your children are getting tired now," Fish Duck said. He told his own children to dive for some fish. The children dived in and came out with a great many fish for Bluejay.

Next day Bluejay said to his cousin, "Let us visit Shadow

(q'aq'a'yəx̣an)." They arrived at Shadow's place. Bluejay opened the door and looked in. There was no one there. He closed the door behind him. Just then someone laughed. He could not locate the sound. He walked around; he saw some beads lying on the bed. He grabbed them and pulled them. "Oh, you are hurting me," someone said. The beads were hanging from the people's noses. But the people were Shadows and invisible to Bluejay. He was puzzled; he sat down. Dried salmon fell down from the ceiling. Wood came through the door. He threw it out. He could not see anyone. Fire started on the fireplace. He poured water on it. "We were just going to cook for you, old man," someone said. Then Bluejay remained quiet, and waited to see what would happen. Pots began to move toward the fire. He waited quietly; after a while the food was done. The pots began to move from the fire. The food was dished out. A dish moved toward him. He still remained quiet. The dish was put right in front of him. So far, he had not seen a single person. He ate what was put before him. When he got down to the river, he called back, "Come and visit me." "Y-e-e-e-s, old man," someone answered.

Bluejay was watching for Shadow. Finally, he saw an empty canoe drifting down. "Someone has lost his canoe," he said. The canoe landed. Then Bluejay went to bed and hung some beads from his nose. He waited and waited. At last someone said, "Where's Bluejay? I can't see him." Bluejay looked; there was something cloudy there, but he could not make the thing out. So that was the last from Bluejay; Shadow went away.

(Second Version).[1]

A young widower with four children was living with his grandmother. That made six people in the one house. The man was Bluejay.

Old Bluejay said, "Grandmother, let's get up early. We'll go to see the old gent, old Bear." So old Bluejay, his grandmother, and his children went to visit Bear. Bear had a big plank house, and was sitting outside. "X̣u··, x̣u··," he said when he saw Bluejay. "You frighten me, old man," Bluejay said to him. "Well, come in, you and your wife," Bear said. "She's not my wife, she's my grandmother. I'm a widower. My children have come for breakfast," Bluejay said. "All right, old man, sit down. Take the best seat,"[2] Bear said. Then he went out to get a cedar basket, a large one. When he came back, the basket held a half-dozen large rocks to use in cooking. "Will you have some meat, my friend?" he asked. "All right," Bluejay said, thinking Bear had killed a deer or something. Old Bear took his butcher knife and sharpened it.[3] Bluejay could not see any meat.

[1] Told by Pike Ben, 1926.
[2] The rocking chair.
[3] On his whetstone.

Bear cut his thigh clear to the bone, took off a piece of meat, and then slapped the flesh back down. He boiled the meat for an hour. There was lots of fat on the soup that he was making. Bluejay, his grandmother, and the children ate the soup with a soup spoon.[1] Well, Bluejay finally finished his breakfast. He and Bear talked of various things.[2] About ten o'clock Bluejay said, "Bear, I'm going home, now." "Come again," Bear replied. Bluejay went down to the canoe. "Old gentleman, come to my place tomorrow morning," he called back.

Next morning, old Bear, his wife and two children went to see old Bluejay. Bluejay was outside waiting on top of the house. "Xu··, x̣u··," he said when he saw Bear, to frighten Bear, just as the latter had frightened him. But old Bear and his wife came right in; they were not frightened at all. Bluejay had only a miserable little seat to offer them.[3] Soon old Bluejay jumped up and put some water in his big basket, and heated some rocks. "Well, grandmother, where's my butcher knife?" he asked. The old lady had hidden it. "Hurry up! Find my butcher knife. The water is getting cold!" he said. At last, the old lady brought the knife and Bluejay sharpened it.[4] Then he whet it on his thigh and cut himself. "U··, wau, wau," he cried. His fingers were chilled and he had left the knife sticking in him. He was about dead. He fell down. "Too bad," Bear said to the woman, "I didn't want him to die." "Take the knife out," he said to one of the boys. Then he fixed Bluejay up. "Don't do it again," he said. Then he cut his own thigh as before. "Have some of my flesh," he said and went home. And so Bear did not get his breakfast.

Bluejay did not put a stop to his visits. "We've got to visit Fish Duck," he said to his family. He went down to Duck's place. Duck had a wife and six children. "I've just come to talk,"[5] Bluejay said. Soon Duck said to his children, "Boys! Girls! better get some trout, suckers, salmon!" All the fish he had mentioned were nice little deep-water fish. "I don't want to go myself, it's too cold," he added to his wife. The boys dived in, caught two or three trout, some carp, lots of good fish. Old Bluejay ate a nice breakfast of trout. Then he said to his grandmother, "Let's go back home now." At the canoe he called back, "Old gentleman, come to my place tomorrow morning." "All right. I'll be there tomorrow morning," Fish Duck called back.

Next morning Fish Duck came to Bluejay's. Bluejay told his children to do the same as Fish Duck's children had done. The old

---

[1] Bear also served Bluejay fresh bread, fresh coffee, new potatoes, fresh cake and fresh pie.

[2] They talked about the price of land, gold mines, the mining of gold, and the stores.

[3] A little old box.

[4] On his grindstone.

[5] About the law.

lady went out with her grandchildren to help get the fish. Bluejay himself dived in and came out with one gravel. Little Bluejay got nothing; he was too frightened. The old lady got one little bull-head. She was nearly out of breath and soaked through. So Fish Duck and his family got no breakfast at all. Then Fish Duck sent his family out and they came back with ten fish for Bluejay.

"We'll visit Seal," Bluejay said to his family. When they got there they found six little Seals in front of the fire, along with their father and mother. Soon Seal built a fire of sticks outside. Then he came back inside, got a stick and a hand-axe. He hit his son, the smallest of his six children, over the head. The boy died. He cut the boy's throat, seared his hide, scraped it with a knife, and scalded him as one would a hog. Then he put him in a basket with some hot rocks and boiled him. Bluejay and his family had a grand time, it was such a nice breakfast; the meat was very good. "Look, look," Bluejay's grandmother suddenly whispered. The little Seal had come to life, although they had already eaten him. There were six little Seals again. The meat was good; it was a good meal. Then Bluejay said, "It's time to go home now." At the canoe he called back, "Come to my place tomorrow." "All right," Seal answered.

Seal came to Bluejay's house. He and his wife sat down. Soon Bluejay went out, built a large fire and put some hot rocks in a basket. Then he came back in, hit his smallest son on the head, killed him, cut his throat, cut his head off, and dragged him outside. He seared him, then scraped him and boiled him. Seal ate the smallest of Bluejay's boys. Bluejay looked: his little boy had not come to life at all. He had lost him. He had thought that his son would come to life as Seal's son had.

Bluejay said to his grandmother, "Get up early tomorrow. We'll visit Beaver; we'll see if he has a good house." Next morning they went to Beaver's. Bluejay sat down, and talked of various things.[1] After a while Beaver said to his children, "Better take the canoe and go to the slough. Get some nice willow branches (about twenty inches long) and some black mud." The children brought back a bucket full of willow sticks; the mud was meant to be eaten.[2] Beaver piled all of this up;[3] this was the food that he himself always ate. Bluejay prayed and prayed to God to tell him how to eat it. God told him not to eat it. "You're not Beaver!" he said. "Take some home with you," Beaver said to Bluejay. "No, my teeth are no good," Bluejay answered. When he got to the canoe, Bluejay called back, "Old gentleman, come to my place tomorrow."

Beaver went to Bluejay's house and stayed a while. "Take a bucket and get some mud and cut off some brush," Bluejay said

---

[1] Of buying and selling land, and of flying-machines.
[2] In place of bread or cakes.
[3] On a little table.

to the old lady. When she returned, they piled the food high. Beaver smacked his mouth over it. It was good food.[1]

Bluejay said to his family, "Get up early tomorrow morning. We'll go to just one more house." They went down to the house. There was no one home. There were lots of beads hanging around. "Steal one," the old lady whispered. Bluejay grabbed a bead. "Kai, kai," some one cried. "What are you doing? You're grabbing me. Sit down. Don't steal a bead." It was Shadow. Soon a bucket began to move, move, move. The door opened and the bucket went outside; it went clear to the river and came back. (The Shadows only think they cook.) The basket was full of water — one salmon egg was floating on top. Soon there was a fire but not a man or woman was visible. The egg became two eggs, ten eggs. Then a large mat and a spoon[2] appeared. Bluejay ate. He took one egg home with him, thinking he could make lots of eggs with it. He invited Shadow to visit him, but I don't know if Shadow ever went.

(Third Version).[3]

Bluejay once went to visit the Shadows, although he did not know whom he could make friends with there. He could barely see them. His sister, who had married one of them, could interpret for him.[4] He saw some fine beads hanging on the wall and pulled at them. The beads were hanging from the Shadows' noses. "Don't do that; you might hurt them," his sister said. After a while they served him food. Then he went back home. Since he always liked to return a favor, he asked the Shadows to visit him to see what kind of home he had. Finally a Shadow returned the visit, but Bluejay could not make him understand him, for they were quite different from one another. After a while Shadow went home, his visit a complete failure. Every time Shadow failed to understand him, Bluejay would say, "What a queer person!"

Bluejay remained at home five days and then went to visit Bear. Bear had a fine winter-house; everything was nice and neat and there was plenty of meat. Bear (who must have been a bachelor for he lived alone) started a big fire. He was a large husky fellow. He held his hands over the fire, and the finest oil imaginable soon began to drip from them. He caught the drippings in a wooden dish shaped like a trough. As soon as there was enough, he handed the dish to Bluejay. "There's nothing like it!" Bluejay said, as he drank it. He visited several hours with Bear. When he was ready to leave, he thought of what he was going to say; he would like to do as Bear had done. "You must visit me," he said. "All right," Bear answered.

---

[1] Butter. [2] A silver spoon.

[3] Told by Jonas Secena, 1926.

[4] According to other informants, Bluejay's sister marries a ghost (ma'k'wt) instead of a shadow (q'aqa'yəx̣ɑn).

Bluejay had everything ready — everything was fixed up fine. Bear came and Bluejay began to talk and joke with him. When they had finished, Bluejay said, "Stay a while, brother, I'll start a fire and give you some lunch." Bluejay was under the impression that he had flesh like Bear's and could do the same thing with it. He built a fire and held his hands over the flame. His fingers only shrivelled from the heat; no oil or broth came out. Bear picked him up and soaked his fingers in water. Bluejay had failed. "I'll get a meal for you," Bear said. He held his hands over the fire and caught the drippings. Then they ate. As soon as they had finished, Bear left. Bluejay now had plenty of grease.

Bluejay remained home five days. He had now made up his mind to visit the ghosts, (who are not the same as the shadows). He visited the Land of the Dead; one of his relatives had married a ghost. He made mistakes continually while there. He saw an ear-bone and pulled at it, whereupon a woman let out a yell. He saw someone's feet and pulled at them. Out came a man's skeleton. Finally, they served him food, but he complained all the while he ate. Before he left he invited the ghosts to visit him. The ghosts came, but would not eat what he served them. They went back home, their visit a failure.

Another time, his living sister said, "When the people visit the bay, you must hang under the saddle.[1] She did not mean him to take her literally — she only meant that he should ask to be allowed to sit on the saddle. But he took her at her word, and got under the saddle. Every time someone moved, he was nearly crushed to death. The youngest boy in the crowd decided to see what was squirming beneath the saddle. He picked Bluejay up and bound up his bruises. At last they arrived at their destination. Their hosts fed them seal and whale oil. Bluejay's people told him to mix some kind of food with the oil, so that it would not make him sick. But he paid no attention and took sick on the way back.

Five days after his return, Bluejay decided to pay another visit. He would visit Beaver. Beaver had many children. The children went to the woods and returned with some pieces of wood. They served the wood with some mud and Bluejay ate it. After that, they had a few songs. Before he left, Bluejay invited Beaver to visit him, to see what kind of home he had. Bluejay felt happy about his visit. He and Beaver got along well, for unlike the ghosts and Shadows, Beaver was a human being.

After returning home, Bluejay decided to go down river. He found some muck in a swamp. He also found some wood that Beaver was used to eating. He took plenty of both home. Beaver, his children, and friends came. Bluejay prepared a large meal of wood and mud. This time he made a success, for his guests were

[1] Some brush in the bottom of the canoe. This entire passage does not belong here, see pp. 15, 287.

willing to eat what he served them. The food was better than they had at home, for the soil in which it was found was richer. They thanked Bluejay for the food, and after a little dancing they went home.

BLUEJAY AND CRANE.[1]

Crane (sq'was) had a fish-trap (ts'i'tpən). Bluejay went to him to ask for a bit of salmon. "Wasq'wa·'·s·," was all Crane would say. Bluejay pushed him in the chest and hurt him. Crane became angry and said, "We'll have a little fight. I'll come to your house. Get your crowd ready."

Bluejay went to Nettle. "Brother," he said, "you must help me. Here's a chance for you to use your dirty tricks." "All right," Nettle answered, "no one can touch me!" Bluejay then went to Bull-Thistle. "Brother," he said, "you must help me. I'm going to have a fight, and you can use your tricks." "Nettle and I are brothers," Thistle answered, "I'm ready to help you anytime. I'm always ready to help Nettle." Bluejay then went to Slipperiest Mud and said, "Brother, I need you; I'm going to have a fight." He slapped Mud all around his door so that his enemies would slip on it. He next went to Rotten Meat. "I need you fellows to help gas my enemies," he said. "All right," the Rotten Meats said. He went to Skunk (sma·'yın) and said, "Guard my door to help keep my enemies out." Skunk readily fell in with his plan. Bluejay also put other nasty things[2] around his house.

Crane was coming. He gave his warning (as Indians do on the war path), shouting from a distance.

Nettles and Thistles now grew thick around Bluejay's house and fairly covered the place. Bluejay had also enlisted Honeysuckle's aid and had tied the Honeysuckle up so that it would hook his enemies.

"Now our enemies are coming!" Bluejay shouted. Skunk was Bluejay's leader. Crane was coming on the run. Bluejay struck at him first. Crane got the best of him, whereupon Bluejay withdrew, as he knew he had plenty of help to fall back on. "Ka'tcatcatca,"[3] he kept saying, as he ran back and forth, outside. His enemies slipped and fell time and time again on the obstruction he had placed around his door, but did not injure themselves seriously. At last, Bluejay's aides were trampled down. But his best aide, Skunk, was still at the door, and Crane could not stand his odor. Bluejay saw that Crane could not overcome Skunk. Crane tried to get at Skunk, but the latter turned his hind quarters toward him and let

---

[1] Told by Jonas Secena, 1927. See p. 398.

[2] Probably excrements.

[3] He always says this when he is angry or excited.

his musk fly. He hit Crane right in the eyes. Crane then announced that he was ready to give up.

Next day Bluejay and Crane made up. Had it not been for Skunk, Bluejay would have been whipped badly, as all his other aides had been trampled to death.

THE CONTESTS.

(First Version).[1]

X̭wa'ips, Bluejay, and the latter's half-brother, Skwikwi'k^{w}, were living together. X̭wa'ips always stayed on top of the house, which was close to the bay, watching for something. Bluejay did not know what X̭wa'ips was watching for. Once more, X̭wa'ips went up on the roof and stayed there, looking over the bay. At last, he saw something coming out of the water in the path of the sunshine. It was Sea Otter. X̭wa'ips told Bluejay to get the canoe ready. Bluejay took a spear and went down to the water. X̭wa'ips had seen all he wanted to, — Sea Otter was quite close now. He was going to try to kill him. Just as they were ready to spear him, Sea Otter dived. They chased him; he was heading for the direction from which he had come. They had no chance to spear him. They kept on chasing him. They paddled away until they were a good distance from home; they could no longer see their home. Before long, some trees came into sight again. They were approaching shore. Sea Otter dived again and they chased him. He went in, close to shore. He dived again and came out on shore. He stood up. Now they saw that he was a man and had long hair. He shook off the water from one side of his head and then from the other. The water began to freeze. Bluejay sat still. He and X̭wa'ips would have an easy time of it, he was thinking. But he was cold and would have to warm himself somewhere. He stepped on the ice, slipped and fell down. X̭wa'ips picked him up and told him to stay where he was. Bluejay was getting colder all the time. X̭wa'ips said that since the ice was so slippery, Bluejay and Skwikwi'k^{w} should follow in his steps; wherever he stepped the ice would melt. When they got to the house, X̭wa'ips stood close to the door. Bluejay was anxious to go in; he was cold and hungry. He opened the door, but on one side there was a big dog ready to bite him. He went to the other side, but another dog was there. There was no way to get in. They waited a long time. Then X̭wa'ips said, "I think we can go in now." The dogs no longer bothered them.

Sea Otter was lying on a bed, his head covered with a blanket. They waited and waited. After a while Bluejay wanted to go out, but the dogs were still guarding the door. At last Sea Otter paid some attention to them. He told one of the two dogs to split some

[1] Told by Peter Heck, 1926. See p. 394.

wood; there was one little piece of wood lying on the altar.[1] The dog struck the wood with his long nose. Every time he struck it, a piece flew off. He soon had a large pile of wood, but the original piece still remained the same size. Then he made a fire. The fire smoked badly. Bluejay could not stand the smoke; he buried his nose in the ground. He wanted badly to go out but he saw no way to leave. He was tired out from sitting so long. The other dog was short and had a big stomach. Sea Otter ordered him to draw in all the smoke. The dog opened his mouth and drew all of it in. The room was soon cleared. Then Sea Otter told the first dog to cut the blubber. The dog cut it into long strips with his nose. "Let's go out," Bluejay said to X̂wa'ips. They went out. X̂wa'ips cut a piece of elderberry stalk and removed the pith to form a hollow tube. Then they went in again. The long-nosed dog dished out the food that he had cooked and served it on a little mat. They began to eat. There was so much food, they did not know how they were going to eat it all. Bluejay was glad enough to eat, as he was very hungry by this time. As soon as Bluejay had eaten all he could hold, X̂wa'ips got out his elderberry tubes. "Come close," he said to Bluejay. He shoved the tube down Bluejay's throat and out his anus. He did the same to Skwikwi'k^w. Then he had them dig a hole where they were sitting. Bluejay swallowed his food and it went right through him. "Oh," he said, "everything I eat, goes right through me!" He picked the food up and ate it over again. "Keep still. Just do as I say," X̂wa'ips said. But Bluejay would not remain quiet. They ate all the food and covered it up where it had fallen.

Sea Otter began to talk to X̂wa'ips. "What game shall we play?" he asked. "Anything you like," X̂wa'ips answered. "A foot race?" Sea Otter asked. "All right," X̂wa'ips said. Sea Otter said that Coyote (snik·'ʊ'l)[2] would represent his side. X̂wa'ips said that Bluejay would represent his, whereupon Bluejay jumped up and said, "Running is my trade! In my country, we have games of all kinds." Sea Otter bet a paddle and X̂wa'ips bet a blanket. "Take this along and hit Coyote with it," X̂wa'ips said aside to Bluejay, handing him a wooden club. Bluejay and Coyote began to race, Bluejay hopping along. "We'll pass[3] one another," Bluejay said to Coyote. As soon as he got a chance, Bluejay gave Coyote a whack with his club. Coyote dropped down; Bluejay had won.

"The next event will be a tree-climbing contest," Sea Otter's side announced. Bluejay was to climb against Squirrel. This contest was to be like the first one: they were to pass one another going up the tree. The tree had been made as slick as ice. Sea Otter bet a paddle and X̂wa'ips bet a blanket. X̂wa'ips had already won one

---

[1] Perhaps a part of the floor built above the ground?

[2] The same term is used for either Coyote or Fox.

[3] As I understand it, Bluejay starts at one end, Coyote at the other. On the way, they pass one another.

paddle. They went to the tree. On one side of the tree, Bluejay noticed a little lump. He chose this side for his. Squirrel passed him. He flew to another lump. Squirrel passed him again. When far up on the tree, he hit Squirrel on the head with his club. Squirrel fell down. X̯wa'ips had won another paddle.

"What shall we play next?" Sea Otter asked. "Whatever you like," X̯wa'ips said. "Seal will dive," Sea Otter then said. "Who will dive against him?" he asked. "Bluejay," X̯wa'ips said. Then they put up bets; Sea Otter bet a paddle again. "We shall pass one another, forward and back," Bluejay said to Seal. X̯wa'ips took some brush from their canoe and put it close to shore. He took Bluejay aside, and said, "Come here to this brush when you get out of breath and stick your mouth out." Bluejay and Seal dived. Bluejay passed Seal; then he came in close to shore and stuck his nose up through the brush. He went out again, passed Seal, and came back to the brush and stuck his nose out. The last time he passed Seal, he struck him on the head with a little hatchet. Seal floated up dead. "Seal has won!" the people said. "Bluejay can't stand diving; he's dead!" But they soon discovered it was Seal who was dead. Bluejay stayed out in the water a little while, and then came in.

"What shall we play now?" Sea Otter asked. "We'll have a sweating match," he finally said. They made a sweat-house and heated rocks. Bluejay was to try again; he was to try against little Mud Hen. The sweat-house was ready. Bluejay and Mud Hen went in. X̯wa'ips had slipped Bluejay a piece of ice. They covered themselves. Bluejay put the ice on his side to keep him cool. Mud Hen was sweating. They were to stay there until one of them burst. After a while, Bluejay hit Mud Hen. There was the sound of an explosion. "Bluejay has died!" the people shouted. They removed the blankets, Bluejay was quite all right, but Mud Hen was dead. Altogether Bluejay had won five[1] paddles.

The fifth match was the last; they were ready to go home now. But Sea Otter was trying to keep them longer, they found after they had started; he had made a lever[2] of ice that moved quickly up and down on the water. There were five of these levers. Perhaps Bluejay would be killed after all for having won the matches. They had not gone far when they came to the first lever. X̯wa'ips was sitting in the middle of the canoe and Bluejay was acting as captain. Just as the lever went up they paddled under, but Bluejay paddled so hard he broke his paddle. The lever came down and caught the end of the canoe, clipping off Bluejay's tail. They got through safely. They came to another lever. This one was going up and down faster than the first. X̯wa'ips waited a while before attempting it. "We're ready now! Paddle when I do!" he finally said. Just as the lever

[1] There was a fifth contest, but the narrator had forgotten it.

[2] See footnote 1, p. 161.

went up, they pulled. Bluejay lost another tail and broke another paddle. They got through safely. They came to another lever. This one was moving a little faster than the second. X̂wa'ips waited and waited. "Ready, now!" he said, and they pulled. Bluejay broke another paddle and lost another tail. They got through safely and went on. They came to another lever. This one was going a little too fast for them. How were they to make it? X̂wa'ips went close and waited and waited. The lever never once slowed down. At last X̂wa'ips said, "We must go now; do your best!" They pulled as fast as they could. The lever caught Bluejay on the tail again. They went on. They came to another lever. It was going so fast it did not seem to move at all. X̂wa'ips went close. He called upon his tamanoas[1] to see if it would do any good. He wept; it seemed that they would not be able to go through at all. Then the lever seemed to slow down a bit. "Get ready!" he said. They pulled. Bluejay lost more of his tail and broke his last paddle. This was the last lever. They were safe now. There was a house near-by. X̂wa'ips went to the house. A woman, Spider, lived there. "Can you take us home? We've lost our paddles,"[2] he said. "Oh, yes," Spider said, "go to my canoe. You'll find my rope there. Pull on it and it will take you up the river." X̂wa'ips went to the canoe and found the rope. "Whe̜n you get there, jerk the rope so that I can pull it back," Spider said. X̂wa'ips pulled and pulled at the rope and they got home. Then he jerked at the rope, and Spider learned that they had got there safely.

K'walale·'··i.

(Second Version).[3]

An old chief was living in a certain place. One day he told his people that they must make a trip to another place, beyond the ocean somewhere. The people knew then that the chief wanted them to go to this place to get some provisions, a certain kind of bead (tamo'x̣ᵘq̣s).

On a certain day they got ready. Nau told her brother Bluejay to go along with the others. She gave him some beads (tamo'x̣ᵘq̣s) and told him that when he got there, he should "put the beads around someone's head" — in exchange for food. She told him also to break off some bushes, and to put them in the bottom of the canoe so that he would not get wet. Old Bluejay understood her to say that he should go underneath the brush at the bottom of the canoe. And so carrying his beads in his little bag, he sneaked to the canoe before anyone else got there, and lay down flat between the brush and the bottom. All the people got ready and went down the

[1] Guardian spirit.
[2] Perhaps all of them break their paddles?
[3] Told by Marion Davis, 1927.

river in the canoe. They usually sat on their knees while they paddled, but this time they were sitting flat. They were paddling fast and had gone some distance, when they heard someone making a noise. Still paddling hard, they heard someone grunting again, "'Un, 'un." They kept on paddling. One man was sure that there was something there — he did not know what. But they started paddling again. At last the man was sure that there was something there and was determined to find out what it was. After the fifth grunt he looked underneath him. There was Bluejay with a dying look on his face. They told the chief about it. "What are you doing here?" the chief said to Bluejay. "Oh Nau told me to get between the brush and the canoe," Bluejay said. "You didn't do the right thing. You were under the brush. Your sister only meant you to get into the canoe and go along," the chief said.

After five days, they arrived at the trail that led down to the shore. The man they were to visit had a house up on the hill and this was his trail. The trail was very frosty and covered with ice. It was exceedingly slippery and they would certainly fall down if they stepped on it. The chief told them that they should not attempt to walk on the ice for the present. "Oh, I'm not afraid to walk on it!" Bluejay said. He jumped out, and right away took a tumble. He hurt his head badly and was quite stunned. He was out of his head for a while and very nearly died. His chief pleaded with him to behave himself. Bluejay listened, but looked very sick. Then the chief addressed his people. "I'll get out and try to walk on the trail that the other chief uses," he said. He told them that they should follow in his footsteps, as the ice would melt where he walked, and they would thus be saved a fall. All got out and followed right behind him. At last they arrived at the door. Two large dogs were tied there, one on each side of the door, to bite and kill any strangers who tried to get in. "I'm not afraid of dogs like that!" Bluejay said and tried to get ahead. But he jumped back as quickly as he could. "I told you that you should follow me," the chief said. Bluejay paid attention this time, for he had got a good scare. The chief led the way and walked right past the dogs. The dogs wagged their tails. His people came right behind him and the dogs never once threatened them. The chief opened the door, and the people followed him inside. The house was very large. There was no one there but the chief they had come to visit; he was lying on the bed. There was no wood. Bluejay was rather cold by this time and began to shiver. The chief arose from his bed. "How in the world are we ever going to get warm?" Bluejay was whispering to the others, "there's no wood! What a strange chief! He has no provisions, but here we are, coming just for provisions!" He was quite annoyed. After the chief had arisen, he called his servant to build a fire. There was only a tiny stick, which, Bluejay had complained, was too small to warm one sufficiently. A male servant came in and split the stick. Bluejay said, "What in the world is he doing, splitting such a small stick!" The slave cut it up into two or three cords of wood. Nau was there, too, trying to make Bluejay stop talking. But Bluejay kept right on. Finally, the servant built a very large fire. At first the fire would not burn and smoked a great deal. The smoke brought tears to Bluejay's eyes. He was angry and kept complaining, "What kind of chief is this anyway? His fire is smoky and won't burn. We have good fires that warm us properly." Nau tried to make him stop talking but he would not. Finally, the chief [their host] called a second servant. "Suck it in," he said, and the servant drew all the smoke into his stomach. Bluejay soon became quite warm — a little uncomfortably so. But he was happy at last. Finally he got too warm and complained. The chief then called another servant in. There was a tiny piece of whale meat there and Bluejay had noticed it. He was very hungry and complained that he would not get enough to eat. The servant cut up the whale meat and fat. He kept cutting it up until he had a large pile of it. Then he put it in a very large kettle and boiled it. Bluejay had one surprise after another — first the tiny piece of wood, the servant who drew in the smoke, and then the tiny piece of meat. They began to eat. (It is a custom in the stories that guests must eat every bit of food at a feast that is prepared for them by their hosts. If they leave anything, they are called common people, but if they eat it all, they are called highest class people from "such and such a place"). Bluejay's chief had planned that all of his people should take a hollow elder-wood stick, about three-quarters of a yard long, and push it down their throats and right out through their back-sides, so that everything they ate would pass right through them. He knew that there would be a great deal of food and had prepared them for this before they left. Bluejay was complaining to his chief all the time because they had put one of these tubes in him. "I'm pretty hungry," he would say, as the food passed right through him. "Just keep still, don't move about. We'll eat when all but a little of this food is gone," his chief would say. Finally, his chief thought it was time to remove the tubes. They took them out and Bluejay soon became satiated. "This is the way to eat!" he said, happy at last. His chief warned him to keep quiet. They had got rid of all the food but just the amount they could eat comfortably. They were now anxious to know what would follow. Finally word came to the visiting chief that there would be a diving-contest.

They went to the beach and sat down near the canoes. Their host, the chief, then announced, "Seal will dive on our side." The visiting chief was worried; no one could stay under as long as Seal, (who was a person at this time). He was sure that they would lose. "What shall we do? We'll certainly be beaten," he said to his people. Bluejay was walking about, stretching. "What's so difficult about diving? I can stay in all day without breathing," he said. His chief was surprised to hear this. After Bluejay had made this statement five times, his chief said, "Well, well! Let him do it; we'll see what he can do." And so they announced that Bluejay would dive against Seal. All made ready to see the sport at the ocean's edge; they lined their canoes up side by side. Bluejay then whispered to his chief, "Throw the brush out of the canoes and pile it thick along the shore-line, but close to the canoes." Bluejay was pretty smart! They had chosen a place in deep water for diving. "After we're out but a short time, I'll ask Seal if he is still there, and if he says 'yes', I'll rush back as fast as I can to the brush to get my breath. Then I'll rush back again and ask Seal if he is still there. If he is, I'll come right back to the brush. I'll do this five times," Bluejay said aside to his chief. He was going to cheat. Everyone was there to see the diving-contest; they were lined up all along the shore to see who would win. The loser would float up dead. The two contestants dived in. Bluejay swam back under water as quickly as he could to the brush and stayed there a long time. "Now I must rush back to ask Seal how he is," he said to his chief. "All right," the chief said. "Are you there?" Bluejay asked Seal. "Yes," Seal answered in a deep voice. Bluejay rushed back to the brush and stayed there a long time. "Now I must go back to Seal," he said. The third time he got back to his place, he was very nearly out of breath. "I'm so cold," he said, shaking all over. "Don't shake so much; the others will see the water stirring!" the chief said. When he came back the fourth time, it was already late afternoon and the sun was down. "Ox̭-o-o-o-o-o," he said, "I'm so cold!" The fifth time, the chief said, "Keep quiet! They'll hear you and discover that you are cheating." "Seal is out of breath now and doesn't speak distinctly," Bluejay said. "I'll beat him yet. He'll be floating before long." He was shaking all over. Finally someone was seen floating on the water. "Three cheers! Bluejay is dead. Seal can stay under all day," the opposing side cried. "Now I'll come out," Bluejay said. He rushed over to the other side of the canoe, kicked, and came out up to his chest. "No one can beat me!" he called. Everyone was very much surprised to learn that Bluejay had beaten Seal. Bluejay's side had won!

Next day, they were going to shoot at human targets; they would have to choose someone for this purpose who was quite nimble. The opposition chose Beaver for their target. "I'll be the target for our side," Bluejay said. His own people tried to stop him, but he said, "I'm very quick and can jump out of the way of an arrow." Everyone went to the place where the match was going to be held. Beaver was ready and Bluejay was ready. Beaver, except for his stomach, was rather flat, and so when they shot at him, he turned so that the arrows missed him on either side. Bluejay ducked arrows time and again. They kept this up for some time. The fifth time, Beaver got hit. Bluejay escaped because he was so very quick. His side had won again.

Next day the chief of the opposition wanted to get even. But in the end he failed for Bluejay was too smart for him. This chief asked, "Who is the fastest person here?" "K^u," Squirrel, one of his own people, said. And so the opposition chose Squirrel. Of course Bluejay wanted to compete again. "It's nothing to me. Of course I can race against Squirrel," he said. Then he suggested that they climb a tall smooth tree with no limbs. Bluejay was a smart one — he had already made a good heavy club; the one who lost would die. He suggested also that they circle around and around the tree, passing one another on the way up; they should not start this until some distance up. Squirrel should say, "K^u," when he was ready. The people agreed to this. Both started up. Finally Squirrel said, "K^u," and then Bluejay said, "K^u." They were both so far up, the people could not see them, but they could hear them give the first "k^u". Squirrel from then on went faster and faster. Bluejay found that he was falling a little behind. He was already dizzy and on the verge of falling off. He feared that he would be the one to die. But he was ready with his club; he would use it as soon as he got a chance. The people could now hear them saying, "K^u k^u k^u," faster and faster. Just as he and Squirrel met, Bluejay gave him a whack with his club. Everyone thought that Bluejay was falling. "Ah, we've been beaten; Bluejay is falling!" his own people said. But after a long time, old Bluejay came down. He had won again.

The beach people had no chance now to get even. Bluejay's people had won from them every time. Old Bluejay had cheated twice to win. By this time, his people were getting ready to go back. Everyone was buying provisions from the beach people. Finally old Bluejay went out and relieved himself. Instead of putting the beads around someone's head, as his sister had said, he put them around his excrements; the rest of his excrements he put in his basket.

They started home, everyone packing his basket. Everyone had some food but Bluejay; he had something quite different. (I always think that Bluejay was a queer one when he was a person. He was sometimes so smart, but at other times so crazy.) While paddling one man smelt something unpleasant. It became worse and worse. Then the people began to whisper to one another, "What smells so badly?" Nau[1] saw them coming and was glad that they were back; her brother would have some dried whale meat or salmon. Bluejay came into the house, and threw the smelly basket down in front of Nau. "What's in here — rotten salmon?" she asked. She looked into the basket, and finding nothing but excrements, nearly fainted. The

---

[1] Notice that while Nau is supposed to remain at home, she is mentioned as having been in the chief's house while Bluejay was complaining so much. In most of the stories in which Bluejay appears, she is always along to make him keep quiet. In keeping with the action of these stories, but contradictory to the plot of this one, she is suddenly made to appear. The narrator, of his own accord, pointed out this discrepancy.

people came in to see what was the matter. "But she told me to do this; she told me to bring her some excrements," Bluejay said. Thereupon, the chief gave Bluejay a scolding, "You aren't a child any longer. You must understand what your sister says to you. She said, 'bɛ'bədɩtc', which is some kind of food. You understood her to say, "bɑ'dtc'[1] (excrements)."

BLUEJAY AND THE YOUNG WOMAN.[2]

There was a good looking young woman. Bluejay wished to marry her, but he was not fit to be her husband.

The young woman died and her parents put her body up in a tree. Bluejay went to the tree and took the body down. The young woman had been dead five days. He stole the body. Then he started up the river, crying that his wife had died. He was on his way to a doctor.[3] The doctor told him to take his wife to the next doctor, who lived farther up the river. The second doctor could do nothing. Bluejay then took her to the third doctor. The doctor said, "I can't do anything for her; take her to the next." The fourth doctor said, "I can't do anything for her — she's been dead five days already; take her to the next doctor." The fifth doctor heard Bluejay crying. "Oh, the old fellow is crying for his wife," he said. He took the dead woman from the canoe and began to doctor her. He sang; his song said that the woman's little finger should begin to move first. The woman's little finger indeed began to move. Soon she got up, well.

Now Bluejay had a wife. The woman did not know how it happened that she was married to Bluejay. As soon as she came to, Bluejay started back down the river with her in their canoe. They went to his house and stayed there. Before long the woman's parents came to Bluejay's house and saw his wife. Later they spoke about her to one another. "She resembles our dead daughter," they said. After a second visit to Bluejay, they were convinced that the woman was their daughter. Finally they went to her burial place to make sure. There was nothing there. "Yes, Bluejay's wife is our daughter." And so they went after the woman and took her home.

Bluejay said, "If they take this woman from me, it is the last time that a dead person can be brought back to life. But if they leave her with me, the dead may be brought to life again."

Just as soon as her family took her home, the woman died again.

---

[1] For some reason the terms were given in the Sound dialect.
[2] Told by Mary Heck, 1927; interpreted by Peter Heck. See p. 398.
[3] That is, a shaman.

BLUEJAY GOES TO THE LAND OF THE DEAD.

(First Version).[1]

Bluejay's sister made her home with him. Each evening, as soon as it became dark, she would go away. Bluejay always wondered why she stayed away at night, but she would never say. One day she finally told him that she was going to marry a dead man (ma'k'wt).[2] Bluejay said, "All right; it's all right with me if you marry a dead man." Then she left him and he stayed all alone.

Bluejay wondered where to find his sister. At last he thought, "I'll see if I can't find some way of visiting her." But he did not know where the dead lived. Eventually he came to a river.[3] He did not see anyone on his side of the river. (The dead lived on the other side.) He shouted across for someone to come in a canoe and get him. He shouted and shouted and shouted. No one answered. The sun was going down as in mid-afternoon. Hungry and tired, he began to yawn.[4] "I'm getting tired," he said. Then he heard someone talking on the other side; his sister was scolding. "Why are you here? I thought you were going to stay over there on the other side of the river forever!" she was saying. "I'm only coming to visit you," Bluejay said. His sister said that she would send her husband over in a canoe to get him.

Bluejay could see the canoe coming. It landed. He went down to get in. At one end of the canoe there were some human bones. "What are these doing here!" he said, and threw the bones overboard. There was a large hole in the canoe.[5] "This is a dead man's canoe," he thought. He yawned. Then he could hear his sister saying, "Why did you throw the man out of the canoe? You almost drowned him." "I don't want a dead man in my canoe!" Bluejay called back. "That man is your brother-in-law," his sister said. She told him to close his eyes and not to look. He closed his eyes and saw a man coming in a good canoe. The man was about to land. Bluejay peeped a little: the canoe had a hole in it, and there was the dead man, the same as before. "Don't peep again," his sister called over, "keep your eyes closed or you'll drown my husband yet!" Bluejay closed his eyes again: a man was coming in a good canoe; the man landed. Bluejay kept his eyes closed and they started across and finally landed on the other side.

"Keep your eyes closed all the time — don't peep once!" his sister said to him. Bluejay now saw a great many people, children and houses. "A dead whale has washed ashore over there. I wish

---

[1] Told by Peter Heck, 1926. See p. 396.

[2] A ghost.

[3] He is now in the Land of the Dead; this river belongs to the dead.

[4] The ghosts cannot hear a shout, but can hear a yawn.

[5] A hole is bored in burial canoes to let the water run out.

you would go and get some meat," his sister said. He started off and reached the place where the whale was. Bones of the dead were lying around a tree. "This isn't a whale, it's a tree!" he said. He peeled some bark off and took it home. "I couldn't find a whale; I saw only a fir-tree," he said to his sister. "I kicked the bones away I saw there." "Yes, and you hurt those people when you were getting the meat!" his sister said. He put the bark on the fire. The pitch melted and dripped. Then he closed his eyes: some little boys were sitting by the fire, eating the pitch. He opened his eyes: there was nothing there but some little bones. He threw the bones outside. His sister said, "Why do you hurt those boys?" "There's nothing here but a piece of bark that I'm burning," he said.

"Go up the river with your brother-in-law to fish," his sister said to him. He closed his eyes and got into the canoe. His brother-in-law fished. Bluejay lay down in the canoe and kept his eyes closed. His brother-in-law caught a great many fish — the canoe was half-full. "I guess we're ready to go now," his brother-in-law said. Bluejay opened his eyes: there was only trash and chips. He threw both the trash and the bones out. When he got home, his sister said, "What do you mean by throwing the fish away and trying to drown my husband?" "Why, I only found some trash and a dead man's bones, so I threw them away," he said.

Well, they eventually grew tired of Bluejay. His sister said to him, "You'd better go home, you'd better go there and stay. I'll give you something to take with you." She got him ready and gave him a basket full of something. Bluejay did not know what was in the basket. His sister told him not to open it until he reached home. By the time he was half-way home, he was anxious to know what was in the basket. He thought he would untie it and take a peep. He untied the string at one end. Something flew out and went "tam···". Then more insects flew out, each with a "tam···". The basket was now only half-full. When he neared home, Bluejay opened the basket again. All the bees flew out. When the last bee was gone, he found a baby at the bottom of the basket. Some of the insects would have become fir-cones and things like that, the rest would have become berries. All these things, Bluejay lost to us. Furthermore, first-born babies now fly away, as the berries did.

Bluejay could not endure living alone. He decided to visit his sister again. He started for the Land of the Dead. He reached the river and shouted and shouted. He had forgotten all about yawning. As soon as he was tired of shouting, he began to yawn. Then they heard him. His sister was angry. "You've done a great deal of damage already," she said. Bluejay promised to behave himself. He went across the river in the canoe that was brought for him. He had closed his eyes and he kept them closed until he reached the other side. Then he shoved the bones overboard. "Why are you trying to drown my husband who was good enough to bring you over?" his sister asked. "I don't want a dead man's bones in my canoe!" he said.

Bluejay visited a number of houses, and at each one he found many bones. Sometimes he threw them out and got himself in trouble. No one wanted him there. "Go home and stay there; don't come again!" his sister said to him. "All right, you people don't want me here," he said. They gave him five buckets, graduated in size. "Take these buckets; where you come from, there are five prairies, all burning. You won't be able to go through, unless you sprinkle them with water," they said to him. "Use the smallest bucket of water for the first prairie, and so on." "All right," he said. He started off, packing his buckets. He came to a prairie, a small one. He saw that it was burning and realized that he could not get through without using water. He began to sing,

> "Yo'i[1], this is the burning prairie she
> told me about."

He took the largest bucket he had, and sprinkled the water from it on the prairie. He got through safely. He came to another prairie, which was also burning. He began to sing,

> "Yo'i, this is the burning prairie she
> told me about."

He used the water from the next largest bucket and got through safely. He came to another prairie. It was blazing almost to the sky. He began to sing,

> "Yo'i, this is the burning prairie she
> told me about."

He used the water from the third largest bucket. This time, he barely made it, for he had scarcely enough water. He came out on a larger prairie. It was blazing still higher. He sang,

> "Yo'i, this is the burning prairie she
> told me about."

Then he sprinkled water from the fourth largest bucket. He just made it, but he was half-burned now. He went on and came to the last prairie; this one was larger than any of the others. He started across, singing,

> "Yo'i, this is the burning prairie she
> told me about."

He used the water from his last bucket, the smallest one. When he was just half-way across, the water gave out. He spit on the fire, but it did not do any good. He burned to death. These burning prairies were to the dead, merely prairies ablaze with flowers.

[1] This is his sister's name.

Bluejay found himself once more in the Land of the Dead.[1] The canoe, full of holes, came for him, but to Bluejay it now appeared the finest canoe he had ever seen. In the canoe was a man wearing fine clothes. Bluejay reached the other side. "So you've come again! I told you never to come back!" his sister said. "But I want to stay here all the time now; after I left you got some very fine canoes," he said. "No, they're the same canoes," his sister said. "The people are now dressed wonderfully," he said.

Some people came in and said that there was a big time at the other end of the village. Bluejay went to the place where the people were dancing. He peeped in: they were dancing on their heads. He walked in and began to dance. But soon he too stood on his head and began to dance; he was dancing like the others now. Those who die by fire go to this place.[2] Those who die from sickness go to the other end of the village — where Bluejay's sister lived. If Bluejay had done as he should have, we could visit the dead and return. But Bluejay did not behave properly and now we cannot visit the dead. He always saw the bones and threw them away.

BLUEJAY GOES TO THE LAND OF THE DEAD.

(Second Version).[3]

Once upon a time, Bluejay and Nau were living in the same house. Finally Bluejay took very sick. He had been in bed for four or five days. He grew steadily worse. At last, he began to sing a little tamanoas song. While he lay on his back, he called Nau and told her that his tamanoas had said that she should come to his face and step over his eyes. "I won't do it," Nau said, "I won't show myself to you." "Oh, I shall die; my tamanoas says that you must do it," Bluejay said. Now Bluejay was on the point of death, for Nau had not done as his tamanoas had asked. In a tiny voice he asked, "Aren't you going to do it? I'm going to die." He was just pretending to die. Nau was really frightened this time. "Oh, my brother is going to die," she wept. "Oh, aren't you going to do it? It's the last breath I shall ever draw," Bluejay said. So Nau said, "Yes, I guess I can do it," and jumped over his face. Thereupon Bluejay very nearly died. "You've got to go slowly. That's too fast!" "Oh, I don't want to show myself to you. What's the use?" Nau said. Again Bluejay very nearly died. "You've got to go a

[1] He belongs there now because he is dead.

[2] The Second-Death, another part of the village. Those who go there can never return to life, but there is always the possibility that those who go to the first part can be returned to life, that is, if they have not been there too long. A certain kind of shaman can go there and bring back a person's soul (skwa'x̯ᵘkᵘx̯tən).

[3] Told by Marion Davis, 1927. Song, Appendix, p. 422.

little slower; you've got to go five times over my face," he said. Instead Nau jumped over him again for she did not want to show herself. Bluejay nearly died again; it was a long time before he drew his breath. Now the third time Nau thought, "I guess he'll die; I'd better do as he asks." "Go slowly now," Bluejay said. And she did go more slowly. "Yes, that's better, but you're still a little too fast for me," Bluejay said. This was the fourth time. The fifth time Bluejay said, "Now you've got to stand over my face for a long time and I'll get well; that's what my tamanoas said." So Nau stood quite a while over Bluejay's eyes. "Just a little longer, just a little longer," he said, in a tiny voice. "That's fine!" He recovered after that; he had examined his sister pretty well. He was thinking now what he should do with her.

He decided to sell her to a dead person; there was a large city of dead people and one of them had come over and asked to marry Nau. Bluejay planned a high-wedding for them. (At such a wedding, there are tamanoas dances; an outside tribe may be invited. All the men sit or stand on one side, and all the women on the other; they sing tamanoas songs.)

Bluejay began to sing. He had wanted to see Nau's privates and so he had asked her to step over his face. He sang,

> What was that you showed me, Nau?
> I'ᵓ ya e·'

While one side was dancing, Nau was taken to the dead people's village. Bluejay had made her marry. She lived with the dead for a long time. (Perhaps her husband became alive at night.)

Bluejay stayed in this world for some time. Then he thought he should visit his sister. He set out. On his way he passed five prairies. (The prairies are not burning on the way over.) He came to a large river. On the other side was the city where Nau was living. "I had better shout for someone to come and get me," Bluejay thought. He shouted but nobody came. "I·'hu," he shouted, as living people shout. No one answered. "I·'hu," he shouted again. No one answered. The sun was setting and he was getting tired. He shouted the third time. No one answered. The sun was quite low now; it was late in the day. He shouted again. No one came for him. He was sleepy and tired. He shouted the fifth time. No one came. He was very tired, and the sun was very low. He sat down and began to yawn, whereupon everyone on the other side came out. He saw a canoe coming across. There was no one in it. Some human bones were lying at one end. The canoe came right up to him. There was nothing in it but the bones; these bones were his brother-in-law. (At night, flesh would come to the bones, and the bones would come to life.) Bluejay got in; there was a hole right in the middle of the canoe. He was getting angry because of the bones. He gave them a kick. "What is this lying here!" He started across. The boat filled up so much with water, that it nearly sank. But Bluejay got across safely. When he reached the other side, he could see nothing but bones lying all about the village. Since it was still day, the dead were all asleep. (At night, they awake.) No one was there except Nau. "Why did you kick your brother-in-law?" she asked. "There was nothing but bones there," Bluejay answered. "Everyone is asleep now," she said.

Bluejay stayed there some time. During the day he kicked every bone he could find. "What's this?" he said. He had noticed some small bones and had kicked them; these bones were the daughter of the most important chief. That night Bluejay wondered what the noise was that he could hear. The parents of the child and every inhabitant of the village were weeping for her.

He stayed on. Finally a tree floated down the river, a whole tree. It was night (but daytime to these people). "There is a dead whale here," they said, "we're going to have lots of property now." "It's nothing but a log, a pitchy one," Bluejay said. But the pitch was whale-fat to the dead people. His sister tried to make him behave. He made a fire from the pitch and put it in the fire to melt. The children put a stick into the pitch, pulled some out, and ate it. Bluejay was very much surprised. "You'll get stuck," he said. His sister tried to stop him, but without success. He stayed a while longer; he had become a little accustomed to the place by this time.

At last he said, "I've got to go home tomorrow." "All right," his brother-in-law said, and prepared five buckets for him. "There are five prairies," his brother-in-law said, "if you have no water, you'll get burnt. When you come to the first prairie, sprinkle a little water from the bucket, with your hand. Every time you sprinkle some, say, 'łαtcʿ, łαtcʿ,' and the fire will go out. Be as sparing with the water as you can; otherwise you'll get burnt and won't be able to reach home."

Bluejay set out. He came to the first prairie and found it burning. "Oh, it's all right; I have some water," he said. He pulled out a basket, said, "łαtcʿ," and the fire cleared. When near the end of the prairie, he began to spill the water. He emptied two buckets, near the end. At the second prairie, he spilled some more water. He began to complain; three buckets were now empty. At the third prairie, he spilled water all over the place. He got burnt there; he died. Everything seemed so nice to him now.

He reached the river and shouted in the proper way. Everyone heard him. "Oh, what a nice new canoe!" he said when his brother-in-law came for him. His brother-in-law was very good-looking. "What was the matter before? Everything seems so different now, so nice!" he said. He was dead, all right! "What was the matter?" he said to his sister, "when I was here before, there was nothing but bones." "You got burnt on the way back. Now you are dead. Before, you were like me,"[1] she explained.

Bluejay stayed there only a little while, and then crossed over to another river, to the Second-Death[2] where people go who burn to death. Beyond the Second-Death is the Children's-City, beyond the Children's-City is the Return-to-Life. Those who go to the Second-Death do not sit up like us, but sit head down; this is why children are born head down. So the bluejay here on earth is not the real Bluejay, but only the sparks that flew up when Bluejay burned to death.

BLUEJAY GOES TO THE LAND OF THE DEAD.

(Third Version).[3]

Bluejay had a sister. A young man came to court her. He made love to her, just like any other young man, and she returned his affections. She decided to marry him. They set out for his home.

After they had walked some distance, the young woman noticed that her husband did not appear plainly to her, but looked something like a shadow. They went on and on. Finally her husband appeared more plainly to her. They had now arrived in the Land of the Dead, where ghosts become visible.[4] After crossing one prairie, and then passing some large trees, and then crossing still other prairies, they came to a large river. Here on the banks of the river, the young woman saw only old broken canoes, or canoes with holes in them. She told her husband that they could not cross in such an old canoe. He told her to get in. As she stepped forward, the canoe went "pop, pop, pop"[5] from the water that was seeping through. Her husband then told her to close her eyes very tightly. As soon as she closed her eyes, she said, "Oh, what a beautiful canoe!" She had discovered that she was sitting in a very nice canoe. In the distance, on the opposite bank of the beautiful river, was a fine village. Many beautiful young girls were living there. Everyone was having a good time dancing, and singing nice songs. The young woman stayed in this village with her husband.

---

[1] Nau is alive, but has learned to live with the dead. Of course, this is quite unorthodox; the living are not supposed to stay with the dead.

[2] There is some doubt as to just where the Second-Death is located. The first version of this story has it located at the end of the village; this version has it located in a village beyond the first village. These differences are really quite minor. The Land of the Dead is in the west, but the Children's-City is pretty far around to the east, according to some informants. Only very young children go to the Children's-City. Older children go to the same place as grown-ups. I hope to discuss all these points more fully in a future publication.

[3] Told by Maggie Pete, 1926.

[4] A belief that is not expressed in the other versions.

[5] As in English.

One day Bluejay decided to visit his sister. He looked everywhere, but could not find a way to get to her. At last he wandered to the banks of the river — where his sister lived — and shouted across to the other side. "Hwu··," he said. His sister answered him. She told him to yawn, as that was the only message the ghosts could understand. She told him that her husband would come across in a boat to get him, and warned him to keep his eyes closed.

Bluejay closed his eyes, but soon opened them again to see what was going on. An old canoe was coming toward him. In one corner lay a piece of bone. "Where is my brother-in-law?" he called over to his sister, "I see only a piece of bone in the canoe." She told him to keep his eyes closed — for she was the only one who could see him. Bluejay got into the canoe, but kept peeping out of the corner of one eye. He saw that the piece of bone was now a kind of shadow, his brother-in-law. They landed. His sister greeted him but warned him again to keep his eyes closed. But Bluejay was too inquisitive to obey her. He made a dive for a beautiful blue bead — this long,[1] and put it into either his mouth or his pocket. Immediately, he heard an "Oh!" from many people. "Bluejay, you've been up to something!" his sister said, "you've torn the bead from the nose of an orphan." (The child's parents had not yet died, so it was alone in ghost-land. For this reason, the ghosts were especially nice to the child; an orphan is always treated very nicely.)

Bluejay remained for some time in ghost-land, without being able to see anyone. Finally he decided to return home. His sister said that she would help him to return. She explained that he must first cross the river. Then he would come to five burning prairies. Although the first prairie — to his right — was very small, it was on fire. She gave him a small vessel of water, saying, "There is not much water here, but it is sufficient for crossing the burning prairies if you use it sparingly. You must sprinkle just enough water to make a path through the first one; save as much as you can for the last and largest."

Bluejay started out. Sure enough he came to a burning prairie. He wastefully sprinkled water for a path. When he came to the largest prairie, he found that he had been too careless with the water; he did not have enough to go through. That was the end of Bluejay; he was a person no longer.

Bluejay having burned to death, his soul started back to the Land of the Dead. His sister had already learned of his death from the ghosts (ghosts always know when a person dies). Bluejay came to the river. He said, "What a beautiful river! What a beautiful village." He found, too, that he could now see many people; his brother-in-law was just like any other man. He stared in amazement, while his sister said, "I told you not to do it! You're dead now!"

---

[1] Illustrating — the length of the first finger joint.

BLUEJAY GOES TO THE LAND OF THE DEAD.

(Fourth Version).[1]

Bluejay once had a daughter whom he loved very dearly. There was no one like her, so he thought. She died quite suddenly. He wept and wondered what he should do. For a while he even thought of suicide.

At last he went to the burial-grounds, dug a hole, and went under ground. Not long afterwards he found the trail that led to the Land of the Dead — a world of existence after death. He found himself in a great world. He saw an ocean and many wonderful sights but did not stop on the way. Eventually he found his daughter living with the ghosts. He could not understand the ghosts, and made many blunders. His daughter became tired of him; he did not belong there for he was not dead. Everything that bursts in the living world — the life[2] of anything that bursts here on earth — goes to this other world where the ghosts live. A large tree came to the beach of the dead while Bluejay was there. "Just look at that whale!" a ghost said. "Ha, ha, ha," Bluejay said, "that's not a whale, that's a fir-tree!"

While there, Bluejay gambled with the ghosts. "What will you bet?" the ghosts asked. "I'll bet my blue uniform for the berries and fruits you have," Bluejay said. They played the wheel-game. And so Bluejay gambled with the ghosts in the Land of the Dead; he bet his blue uniform for their berries and he won. "You shall deliver the fruits and berries to my country," he said. Because Bluejay won, we have lots of berries; if he had not won we would not have any berries.

Eventually Bluejay made up his mind to go home. His daughter had already married there; she now had a child, who belonged to the Land of the Dead. "I'll make you a present," his daughter said, "take it home, and don't come here again. You will have to pass through five prairies on the way back."

Bluejay took his daughter's gift — her baby. He came to the first burning prairie. His daughter had given him five buckets of water; she had told him to use the smallest bucket of water to put the fire out on the first prairie. But instead, he used the largest bucket of water first. "This is not a fire, it is only a prairie of flowers," he said. At the fourth prairie, he found himself short of water; he had been wasting water on the other prairies. Half-way through, he began to weep. He had disobeyed; this caused the baby to return. After this, he said, "Babies shall die and go to the World of the Dead,[3] and no one shall go to get them." He burned to death, and had to go back to the dead.

---

[1] Told by Jonas Secena, 1926.

[2] Life and soul are the same term.

[3] See footnote 1, p. 119. Dead babies can be recovered from their land, but only certain shamans can do this; it is a very difficult job to get them back and very few succeed.

ROBIN.[1]

Robin (s.wɩ′sk’q‘) went to camp so that his wife could dig lacamas with the other women. One morning she went out and stayed all day. As soon as she would dig a few lacamas, she would begin to peel them. She would peel and peel until she had a whole pile of peelings. "I don't see what they find to eat in this," she would say, until she came to the seeds. She did this every day. On the fourth day, she still had no lacamas. Then Robin thought, "I wonder what my wife does; she never has any lacamas." He followed her. There they lay — piles and piles of peelings. "I'll fix you when you come home!" he said to himself. He gathered some rocks, piled them up and put some wood on top to heat them. By the time his wife came home with her empty basket, the rocks were just right. "You haven't any lacamas?" he asked. "No," she answered. "Come here to me!" he said. He put her on the fire and burnt her face. She got so hot, she nearly died. She began to roll herself to the water. Rocks began to stick to her, for her body was very hot; she picked up rocks as she rolled. She rolled right into the water.

Then Robin began to regret what he had done. He looked under the water for her and began to weep. His wife stays under water to this day. She is the periwinkle (sk·’ɩk·ɩa′liłtsiˇ)[2]; the little rocks that stuck to her as she rolled are her house. When she walks and sticks her head out, the little house walks with her. She lives in shallow water or on the riffle.

At present, early in the morning and early in the evening, Robin sings as he sits upon a tree, sings for his wife, as old people do when they weep for their children:

K’o′iya k·u′wx·[3], k’o′ya[4] k·u′wx·
My dear wife, my dear wife,

k’o′ya k·u′wx·,
My dear wife,

k’o′ya k·u′wx·
My dear wife

he′ he′ he′.

---

[1] Told by Peter Heck, 1927. See p. 410.

[2] A little insect with a shell of minute gravel. It is used for bait.

[3] The narrator pointed out that this is an obsolete term for wife. The present term is tco′wł.

[4] The term k’o′iya or k’o′ya is very difficult to translate, the narrator said: it "touches on" wife or child. He preferred to translate it as given above. Evidently it is a term of endearment.

WREN KILLS OTTER.[1]

Wren (skwimɔ'ᵓmx·) was Nau's[2] grandson. Every day he went far up the river to fish. He fished with a net. When his canoe was about half full of fish from one end to the other, he would lie down and sleep until morning; then he would go home. One morning early, he happened to look at his fish. They were all gone! Nothing remained but a single head lying alongside him. He went home. He told his grandmother that someone had made away with all his fish.

That evening he went fishing again. When he had caught a desirable number, he lay down to sleep. Next morning all his fish were gone; there was just one head lying by his foot. He could not imagine what had happened; something must have come and taken his fish away. The same thing happened four times. The fifth time, he determined to keep watch. When his canoe was about half full of fish, he lay down and pretended to sleep, but he was keeping close watch. Someone boarded the canoe at the other end and began to eat. He ate and ate his way up the canoe until he was quite close. Wren got ready. He picked up his club. The thief was now eating right at his foot. He struck him with the club. It was Otter. And so Wren learned who was stealing his fish. "That's the fellow, all right!" he said. When he got home, he skinned Otter, cooked the meat, and dried the skin.

Next morning he went fishing again. He lay down to sleep. When he awoke, all his fish were there. He now had plenty of fish and still had some Otter-meat left.

Otter's family missed him; he had not returned. "What has happened? Has someone killed him?" they said. They decided to look for him. They sent Ts'a'maxwʋl[3] up the river to see if he could find him. "I had better visit Wren on the way," Ts'a'maxwʋl thought to himself. He arrived at Wren's house. He went in. Wren cooked some meat for him and he ate it. He was well fed, felt satiated, so he lay down. As he lay there, he looked up and saw some dry hides. He knew that one hide was that of the missing man. "That was Otter's meat I ate," he said to himself. He went out, without saying anything to Wren about what he had seen. He went home and reported what he had found. "On the way I stopped for a visit with Wren," he said; "he fed me meat and fish. After I had eaten I lay down. Then I happened to look up and saw a dry hide there. It is Otter's."

---

[1] Told by Peter Heck, 1926. See p. 406.

[2] Both Mr. Heck and Mr. Davis call Wren's grandmother Nau. Mr. Davis also calls Bluejay's sister by the same term, while Mr. Heck calls her Yu'i. Mr. Davis said that the two terms apply to the same bird. Both agreed that either Yu'i or Nau are bluebirds, a bit smaller than the bluejay.

[3] A little black bird, about the size of a lark, that lives near the river.

The people then learned what had happened to Otter. But how should they kill Wren? They must find some way to kill him. Otter's parents finally hit upon a plan. "We'll call a tamanoas gathering and have a dance, and invite him to come," they said. "All right," the others said. They began to fix the house. They called all the different birds. "Come down and have a good time," they sent word to Wren. They stuffed all the cracks of the house good and tight with moss so that no one could get out. Everyone came, each person painted in a certain manner. Wren came also. When they saw him coming, Otter's parents asked, "Who will kill him?" They had planned to kill him with a big scoop spoon, used for bailing a canoe. "Hawk (s.x̂wa'yat') is the man who can do it. When Wren goes around the room, Hawk can cover him with the spoon," someone suggested. "Hawk can't kill him; he's a coward," Bluejay said. Then someone suggested Fish Hawk. Bluejay did not approve of him, either. Then someone suggested White-headed Eagle (spaq'a'lən). But Bluejay would have none of them; all those birds who are able to kill other birds, Bluejay turned down. "I'm the only one who can do it. That's my trade," he said. Otter's parents overheard him. "Well then, you'd better help us," they said.

Wren, by this time, had reached the door of the house. He, too, had his own crowd. They were ready to come in and dance around the room. Wren began his tamanoas song, as he started in backwards[1]. He sang,

tsəlɛ' tsəlɛ' ɩt hi'yiya'
tsəlɛ' tsəlɛ' ɩt hi'yiya'
ɩt hi'eya'

Bluejay was ready. Snail was beating a tom-tom pole against the roof. Wren was hoping to open a crack in the corner of the house with his song. Bluejay made a dive at him with the scoop. Wren danced around the room five times. The fifth time, Bluejay pounced upon him with the scoop; he covered him and held him down. Just then, unnoticed by the others, Wren said, "Sʊp, sʊp." That was the last that was heard of him, for in the corner of the house he had made with his tamanoas a hole through which he had escaped.

Bluejay thought Wren was under his scoop. "Take the scoop off, we'll help you kill him!" the others said. Bluejay had been made a fool of by Wren. Under the scoop was Snail, wet with slime. Bluejay had caught the drummer! He sat down very much ashamed. All the Hawks and Eagles punched him in the nose.

Wren got home safely. They never caught him. Snail did not die, but he was covered with slime.

---

[1] The leader of a dancing group comes in backwards.

WREN KILLS ELK.

(First Version).[1]

Little Wren (ts'ats'ɛ''αp)[2] came home. His grandmother[3] told him that he ought to go out and hunt game. He thought, "It would be very good if I should go out and see what I can do." He went out and found a vine-maple. "This is a good place for me to sit. Now I shall call Elk (qe′letən) to come." He sang,

Come, come,
El- el- elk,
Let us play and run back
    and forth,
This side of the prairie,
That side of the prairie.

Soon he heard something coming,

L'pa·′·· L'pɛ·′··

"Oh, that's Elk!" he said. Tiny Mouse (ts'mɛ·′k·'eyυqs) came out. "Oh, I don't want you, you with tiny eyes and a sharp nose!" Wren said. "Oh, I thought you were calling me," Tiny Mouse said, and went back weeping, "Hi·′ hi·′."

Then Wren sang again,

Come, come,
El- el- elk,
Let us play and run back
    and forth,
This side of the prairie,
That side of the prairie.

Soon he heard someone coming,

L'pa·′·· L'pɛ·′··

He saw who it was and said, "It's not you I'm calling!" It was Mouse (sk'wata′ᵃn). "You're not Elk! You have a long tail sticking out and you steal all the time!" Mouse wept when Wren refused him and went back.

Wren called again,

Come, come,
El- el- elk,
Let us play and run back
    and forth,
This side of the prairie,
That side of the prairie.

---

[1] Told by Peter Heck, 1927. See p. 406.
[2] Wren goes either by this name or by the name of skwimɔ′ᵓmx·; the narrator sometimes interchanges the two terms in the same myth.
[3] Nau, evidently; see Wren Kills Otter, p. 31.

Someone was coming,

L'pa·'·· L'pɛ·'··

It was Deer. "You, big eyes, big ears, I don't want you!" Wren said. Deer turned around and wept. "I thought you were calling me!" he said and went back.

Wren sang again,

Come, come,
El- el- elk,
Let us play and run back
and forth,
This side of the prairie,
That side of the prairie.

Someone was coming,

L'pa·'·· L'pɛ·'··

It was Bear. "It's not you, with the small eyes, that I'm calling!" Wren said. Bear went back weeping. "I thought you were calling me!" he said.

Wren sang again,

Come, come,
El- el- elk,
Let us play and run back
and forth,
This side of the prairie,
That side of the prairie.

"Someone is coming." (He heard,)

L'.pa·'·· L'.pɛ·'··

"There's Elk-with-large-horns. Now I have him!" Wren said. Elk came and looked about. "Where's that man who was calling me?" he asked. Then he noticed Wren and said, "Where are you going through? Through my nose? You're so small, you'll die when I snort. Are you coming through my eye? I'll twitch my eyelid and you will die. Are you coming through my ear? If you do, I'll wiggle my ear and you will die. If you come through my armpit, I'll flap my arm and you will die. If you come through my anus, I'll evacuate you and you will die." Then — "tsʊp, tsʊp" — was all Elk heard. Wren had jumped right in through his backside. Wren cut Elk's heart and Elk fell down dead. He came out through Elk's mouth. He was dirty all over, but proud of himself. "Hoi'," he cried, "I'm skinning my elk now."

He cut Elk up and laid each piece out nicely, each in a separate place, — the legs, the ribs, the neck, the backbone, the fore-arms, the stomach fat, the kidney fat. He had everything ready; he put the head and bones in a tree and went home.[1] "Grandmother," he said, "make me five maple-bark pack straps." The old lady went to the woods and came back with the pack straps. Then they went to get the meat. They sat down. "What shall I give you to carry, grandmother, the breast?" Wren asked. "No," his grandmother said, "Raven[2] might call my privates 'breast'." Then Wren offered her all the different parts, but each of these his grandmother refused. At last he offered her the head and horns. To everything he suggested she said, "Raven might call my privates 'so and so'." Wren was getting tired. At last he said, "Well, shall I give you his genitals?" Then his grandmother began to sing,

> Hano'ɔɔ, my little grandson,
> Kills game for me —
> My little grandson.

Wren had five pack straps. He made five bundles of the meat and started to pack it home. His pack strap broke, for in the meantime, his grandmother was copulating with Elk's genitals. He went a short distance and his pack strap broke again; his grandmother was still copulating, near a log. He passed his grandmother five times and each time, his pack strap broke and he had to re-pack his load. As soon as he got the meat home, he cut it up for drying; he had plenty of it. Then he went back for the hide. He took the stomach fat from a vine-maple pole, where he had previously hung it so that it would be dry by the time he got the meat home. At last he got everything home. In olden times when they killed an elk, they removed all the meat from the legs and bones and laid the bones aside. Wren had done that. Afterwards he broke the bones and removed the marrow from the hip bone and all the others. After cleaning the marrow, he put it in the bladder of the same elk and hung it up in the house to dry.

After a while the meat was very nearly gone. Wren would go out every morning and not return until evening. The fourth time his marrow was just about gone. The fifth time there was none at all. "What's happened to the marrow?" he asked his grandmother. "Oh, it fell down and the little dog ate it," his grandmother answered. Wren got his dog and hit him on the throat; a little piece of marrow came out. "My dog didn't eat it all," he said. Then he seized his grandmother by the hair, hit her on the throat, and out came the marrow. She went out to the stream near the gravel pit, and wept,

> "My grandson hit me in the throat."

Raven heard her as she went down stream. He told the people and they went after her. They talked things over. "How can we play

[1] In 1927, I tried very hard to get from various informants, including the narrator of this story, some idea of how large game was butchered. I could get no definite answer. Then the whole thing came out in this story.
[2] Raven was her lover.

a joke on Wren? We'll take his grandmother back to him and give her to him as a wife," someone said. They dressed her well and sent word to Wren, "We're going to bring you a wife." They had a gathering as if for a formal wedding; they would take the old woman to him. But there would be no purchase-money; they were only going to play a joke on Wren. When they arrived with the old woman, they removed the coverings from her head and had her sit down by Wren. He did not recognize his grandmother.

Wren went out. When he came in, he wanted to joke with his wife, but she laughed with her mouth closed. When Wren teased her for the fifth time, she laughed with her mouth open. She had no teeth. Then he recognized her. "Oh, it's you!" he said.

K'walale·'·· i
"Someone has lots of dried salmon."

WREN KILLS ELK.

(Second Version).[1]

Wren (skwimɔ'ᵊmx·) and his grandmother, Nau, were living in the same house. Wren did not know what to do. "I guess I'll go out into the woods. Perhaps Elk will hear me, if I give him a song," he said. He went to the woods, but did not tell his grandmother that he was going to try to kill Elk. (Elk was very big.) He looked around for a suitable place to sing a song that would bring Elk to him. At last he found a place and sat down. "This is a good place for me." He began his song,

Come, come,
El- el- elk,
Let us run back and forth;
Come.

As he was singing, someone came along. It was Bear. He said to Bear, "No, sir! You're not the one for whom I'm singing. You black old thing! You've got to go back. I don't want you!" Old Bear began to weep because Wren did not like him. He went back into the woods.

Wren began his song again. Someone came along, but it was not Elk. It was Cougar. He said to Cougar, "You're not the one. I want Elk. You big-eyed one! You've got to go back." Cougar wept for a little while and then went back.

He sang his song. Wolf came along. He said to Wolf, "Oh, you short-faced one, you've got to go back! I want Elk. He's the one for whom I'm singing." Wolf went back, weeping.

He sang again. Deer came along. He said to Deer, "You big-eyed, long-eared one, I don't want you! I want Elk. He's the one for

---

[1] Told by Marion Davis, 1927. Song, Appendix, p. 423.

whom I'm singing." Deer wept a while and then went right back into the woods from which he had come.

He sang. Wildcat came along. He drove Wildcat back again. "You short-faced, striped one, you've got to go back! I'm singing for Elk."

He sang again. Skunk came along, running. "Oh, I'm singing for Elk. I don't want you, old black-striped back!" he said. Skunk wept and went back into the woods from which he had come.

He sang. Fisher came along. He said to him, "You've got to go back, you black, slim-nosed one! You're not the one I want. I want Elk to come." Fisher wept and went back into the woods from which he had come.

He sang. Coyote came along. Wren knew that this could not be Elk; this one was coming quietly, while Elk would come noisily, cracking sticks on the way. "Oh, you slim-faced one, you cunning thing! Go back, I don't want you."

All the little animals came along, but he sent them right back.

He sang. Finally he heard the sticks cracking. The bushes were waving. A pair of big horns were showing. The big-horned Elk was coming. "That's the one I want!" Wren said.[1] Elk came along and stood right in front of him. Wren said, "How would you like me to enter your body? Through your nose or through your eyes? Through your ears or through your arm-pit?" He mentioned every part of Elk's body. Elk said, "No, no, no!" to everything until Wren mentioned his anus. Then before he could say a word, Wren had jumped right into his back-side. Wren disappeared for a while. Elk just stood there. Wren cut Elk's liver and slashed his entrails. Elk's insides hurt so badly he did not know what to do. He was being badly hurt. Wren was still busy at work inside. Finally Elk fell down. Wren knew that Elk had fallen. After a while Wren came out, the color he is today, somewhat yellow, from Elk's bowels. He had killed Elk, all right! He stayed there some time, to see if Elk were really dead. What should he do? He would go home and tell his grandmother, Nau.

He told his grandmother that he had killed the Elk. Nau was very much surprised that he had killed the big animal. He told her to get a pack strap which women always have ready. "Are you sure you killed it?" Nau asked. "Yes, get your knife. We'll butcher it." Nau did not believe him but got a pack strap. They went over to get Elk. Nau wondered how Wren had killed Elk, but did not ask her grandson how he had done it. They began to butcher Elk. They laid everything separately, the legs, the forepart, the neck, the head, one fore-leg, the ribs, the backbone, the hind-quarters, the liver, the reproductive organs, everything was laid separately. They worked at it for a long time. The legs and so on, they cut up.

[1] The narrator said here: "I was surprised when they first told me this story — Wren is such a little thing to kill a big Elk!"

Finally they were ready to pack it home. Then Wren asked Nau, "What do you want to pack, grandmother? The ribs?" "No," she answered, "Raven might call my privates 'rib'." Raven was her lover. "A leg?" "No, Raven might call my privates 'leg'." "The head?" "No, Raven might call my privates 'head'." "Well, what do you want to carry? The liver?" "No, Raven might call my privates 'liver'." Wren named everything he could think of — one thing after another. "Well, what do you want? The ears?" he finally asked. "No, Raven might call my privates 'ears'." "Then what do you want, grandmother? The genitals? Do you want the entire hips?" Nau then burst into song,

> That's right, my grandchild,
> My grandchild can kill game.

She was dancing about while sitting down, so pleased to have been given the hind-quarters to carry. Then she fixed her load, tied it up and adjusted it on her forehead. She was packing the load rather low, it was so heavy for her. Wren noticed what she was doing and did not like it. He overtook her, arrived home before her and threw his load down. He went back for another and met his grandmother, who was not half-way home yet. He got a second load, took it home and came back. He then made a third trip and found his grandmother still there. He fixed his load and started back. His grandmother had still not reached home. Her pack was way down and wobbling about. He passed her and threw his meat down for the fourth time. His grandmother was still on her way. He went back, met his grandmother, and picked up his last load. He had packed all the meat, but Nau was still coming. Then Nau went into a big cedar tree where Wren could not see what she was doing. It was night when she came out, looking rather different.

Next day, they fixed a place over the fireplace to dry the meat. They dried the meat in the house and had lots of it — both dried meat and cooked meat.

Before long, Wren began to cry. He was squealing, "Yʊ'mɩ·····, yu'miyumi." "What do you want? Some cooked camas?" Nau asked. "No, no, no," he said, and began to squeal again. "Yu'miyumi," he was crying. "What do you want? Some carrots?" Nau asked. "No, no, no," Wren said, and began to squeal again. "Well, then, what do you want? Some berries?" She asked him everything she could think of. Finally she caught on to what he wanted: he was saying, "Yʊ'm˘yʊm˘." He was saying it a little more clearly by this time. "Is it elder berries you want?" she asked. She knew by this time pretty much what it was that he wanted, but she was going to make sure. "Is it yɔ·'myɔ·'m (intercourse) you want?" she asked. "Yes," Wren said. "Well, then, you must dig a place for my hump-back," Nau said. Wren looked at her back. He tried three times to dig a proper place. "It's all right now," he finally said. Nau tried to lie down but the place would not do at all. He dug at it again. "It's all right now," he said. Nau lay down. "No, it doesn't fit my back," she said. It still hurt her back. He dug again. Finally he called, "It's just right now." "No, dig again," she said. He dug again and called her. "Yes, it's all right now," she said. They lay down together and put the hide over them.

Ts'a'maxwʊl[1] and Sɔ·'ts'i[2] had heard that Wren and Nau had killed an elk near home. They talked about it to one another. "Now, we should go and see if it is true, and if it is, we'll eat some good elk meat," they said. They started up the river in a canoe. After a while, they were nearing Wren's and Nau's place. They were now close to the trail that led to the river, but still did not hear anyone. It was so quiet there did not seem to be anyone home. They stopped and talked for a while, but still there was not a sound from the house. There was probably no one there, they decided, but they would make sure. Ts'a'maxwʊl went slowly up to the house and peeped in. There was no one there; just the dry elk hide was lying in the middle of the room. It seemed to be moving. "Why, yes, it is moving!" he said to himself. He looked around again. No, there was no one there. He looked on for a while. The hide was moving up and down. "They're doing something under there, all right!" he said. He went back and told his companion about it. They did not know what to do. They had come to eat meat. "We had better go back down, and come back up, striking the canoe; one of them will hear us," they finally said. So they went down the river some distance, and came back up, striking the canoe as if they had just arrived, talking and making a lot of noise. Wren came down to the river when he heard the noise. "What's the news down below?" he asked. "Oh, there's little news except that Wren and Nau were having intercourse in their house; they had a hide over them, —" Ts'a'maxwʊl answered. "Call one of them," Nau said, "call Ts'a'maxwʊl and we'll fight him." Wren called Ts'a'maxwʊl to come in and fight. "If you throw him down," Nau said to Wren, "I'll throw the bark over him and burn him." "All right, we'll kill him," Wren said. Ts'a'maxwʊl came into the house, ready to fight. They had a rather wide piece of bark, already burning, to kill him with. They began to fight. Finally one was thrown and Nau threw the burning bark over him. In the meantime, old Ts'a'maxwʊl had run out. "A·····, ä' o'," he cried, happily, "Nau threw her grandchild into the fire to burn him." Nau heard him. "Oh, it is my grandchild!" she said. She took the bark away as quickly as she could, but her grandson was already dead. Nothing remained but his ashes. Thinking it was Ts'a'maxwʊl, she had been too slow in removing the bark. She stayed there for a while not knowing what to do. Finally she gathered up the ashes and charred bones. Then she went out to look for some pitch. She

[1] See footnote 3, p. 31.
[2] A kind of mountain owl.

came back again and tried to stick the little bones together as they had been formerly. She shaped them and stuck them together with pitch. Then she blew upon the object she had shaped. She blew and blew. At last little Wren came to life, chatted with her and told her how he felt. Next day Wren went out into the hot sun and stayed there a while. "I'm melting, grandmother, I'm melting, grandmother, I'm melting, grandmother," he began to shout. Nau went out to see her little grandchild. Yes, he was melting. She fixed him up again, and told him not to go out in the sun, for since he was put together only with pitch, he would quickly melt. Next day, Wren went out and sat in the same place — in the hot sun. "I'm melting, grandmother, I'm melting, grandmother, I'm melting, grandmother," he soon began to cry. Nau went out to him and talked to him as before. "Don't sit in the sunshine, you'll melt if you do," she said. Next day Wren went out and sat in the sunshine again. "I'm melting, grandmother," he shouted. He shouted five times. He was not the real Wren; he had been stuck together from ashes and bones. If he had not got burnt, he would be a big wren — and perhaps hunters would kill game in the same way that he killed Elk. His ashes turned into a wren, — a little one.

DOVE.[1]

There was once a story about Dove (x·o'ʼmalax̣ᵘ). I think it was something like this: Dove was once a person. He lost all his children and wept and wept. He wept so naturally that people could feel his human qualities. He wept so much that he turned into a bird. He still makes a noise as though he were weeping.[2]

CROW AND THE WOMEN.[3]

Crow was staying on the bay with five other women. "Let's go across the bay to look for some roots," one of them said. "How shall we go?" the others asked. "In a canoe," the one said. They got five paddles and all set out. They paddled and paddled but the canoe barely moved. "Paddle hard!" they said to one another. Then they sang, in time to their strokes. The canoe barely moved. Half way out in the bay, they sang again in time to their strokes. They were pushing their paddles edgewise through the water, and thus made no headway. Then the captain hit upon the right way to do it; she held her paddle broadside. The canoe suddenly shot ahead, and the rest of the women fell back, their legs up in the air. "I've got it now the way it should be! This is the right way to paddle," the captain said. On their way back, they made good time by paddling in the new way. We paddle that way today.

[1] Told by Peter Heck, 1927.
[2] This is a fragment only. The narrator did not remember the details.
[3] Told by Peter Heck, 1926. See p. 420.

CRANE.[1]

Crane had a faithless wife. Whenever he went out to fish she would meet her lover. No sooner would he return home than she would say, "Crane, I'm hungry. Go to the river and get me a fish." As soon as he was gone again she would look around to see if anyone was watching, and if not, she would summon her lover.

Crane always did as he was told; thus he was always fishing. In order to walk so lightly that the fish would not hear him, he would take his knife and cut away the flesh on either side of his legs. His wife sent him to the river so often for fish, that he cut away the flesh from his legs many times. That is why Crane has such thin legs at present.[2]

SYUYU'WəN.[3]

Syuyu'wən (a great-hunter) went out hunting. He came to an elk and shot it. The elk went on; Syuyu'wən did not follow it, but went in the opposite direction. Raven[4] went out into the woods. He saw the elk's tracks and followed them. There was blood on the tracks. He kept following them. There was more and more blood. At last the tracks led to the elk. He was very happy. He sat around, trying to decide what to do; perhaps the elk belonged to someone. He looked back again, and saw someone standing there. He was now somewhat embarrassed. "Did you kill this, Raven?" the man asked. "Who could it have been but me?" Raven said. "All right, you killed it," the man said. "Well, go ahead and skin it then," he added, and walked away. Raven set to work, and butchered the elk; he would have a lot of meat. When he had finished, he cut off the fat from the stomach and kidneys. He also cut a piece from the soft-spot under the ribs; he would take it home to cook. (This piece is cut from the stomach, beneath the ribs. They claim it is the sweetest piece of meat. When they butcher an elk, they always cut that piece off and cook it on the spot.) When he was ready to go home, Raven put the fat under his shirt just over his heart, and put the piece of meat on the other side. He had lots of children to feed.

He reached home feeling very important. He stood there ready to pull the fat out. But when he pulled it out, it was nothing but white moss that hangs from the trees. He looked at it, not knowing what to say. Then he reached under his shirt to pull out the piece of meat from the other side. It was a slice of rotten log. He did not know

---

[1] Told by Maggie Pete, 1926. See p. 410.

[2] This story is often told as a lesson to young wives who are inclined to be unfaithful, so the narrator said. In the version from Puget Sound, p. 369, the moral is more obvious: Crane, when he learns of his wife's infidelity, takes revenge by disfiguring her.

[3] Told by Peter Heck, 1927. See p. 401.

[4] The narrator said he was not sure whether the Raven incident should come first, or the Pheasant incident; either way, it works out the same.

what to do. He had already told his family that he had killed an elk. He went back to see about the elk. His children went with him to help pack the meat. When he got there where the meat should be lying, there was nothing but rotten wood. He felt very badly about it and did not know what was the matter; there was just nothing but rotten wood. He went home feeling bad.

Syuyu'wən went hunting again. He saw an elk and shot it. Then he went off in the opposite direction. Pheasant went into the woods. Soon he came to some fresh tracks left by an elk. He followed them. Then he saw the blood on the tracks. "Someone must have wanted this elk," he said. He tracked it down. The elk was lying on the ground, dead. Pondering, he sat down and waited. He looked up. A man was standing in front of him. "Ah, this is the one who killed the elk," Pheasant thought to himself. "Did you kill this?" the man asked him. "I'm a good-for-nothing, I couldn't kill it," Pheasant said. "Oh, all right, skin it, then," the man said, and left. Pheasant began to skin the elk. He took the hide off, cut the meat up and got the fat from the stomach and kidneys. Now he had it all ready. He did the same as Raven: he cut the piece off from underneath the ribs. Then, in the same way, he put the fat on one side underneath his jacket, and the piece of meat on the other. He started home. He was happy that the man had given him the elk. When he got home, he pulled the fat out from under his jacket, then the piece of meat. He cooked the meat. He had five children. When the meat was done, the little children ate with him. The youngest swallowed a little piece of meat and choked on it. Raven heard him choking. He cried, "A··, I hear Pheasant's child choking." He went right over to Pheasant's house and helped remove the piece of meat from the child's throat. He ate the piece of meat himself. Then he shouted to the others, so that they would know, "A··, Pheasant's boy choked on a piece of elk-meat!" There was general excitement about it. Then Raven asked Pheasant, "Did you kill the elk?" "No," Pheasant answered, "a man just gave me the elk-meat." "I killed an elk but it turned into a rotten log," Raven said. "The man asked me if I killed the elk and I said, 'I'm a good-for-nothing, I couldn't kill it'; then he told me to skin it and take it home," Pheasant explained. Then Raven said, "Well, yes, that man asked me, too, if I had killed the elk and I said I had." "You lied to the man; that's where you had bad luck. If anyone asks you a question you should tell the truth. The man asked me and I said 'no'," Pheasant said. Raven asked to go along with Pheasant, to get the meat. They went the next day. The meat was there and they took it home. Then Raven asked for a piece of the hide and Pheasant gave him half. They would have enough meat to last them for some time. Night came; it was going to be a very cold night; the stars were shining clearly. They went to bed. Raven put his children to sleep in one place; he had five children. From the piece of elk skin that Pheasant had given him, he pulled out a single hair. He pulled out five hairs altogether, and laid one on each of his boys; that was all they had for blankets. "This is enough to keep you warm," he said. The children went to sleep.

Next morning, Raven arose early. "What's the matter with the boys? They're just lying there. What's the matter with them?" He touched one of them; the boy was frozen stiff. Then Raven wept, "He got too hot and died!" Then Raven's wife wept, "He got too cold and died!" Raven did not like his wife to talk so: he had given the boys enough covers.[1]

K'walale·'··i

*

*   *

As soon as anyone finishes telling this story he says to the listening children, "Never lie, or claim anything that does not belong to you, for you can see what happened to Raven."

BEAR LOSES HIS TAIL.[2]

Old Bear used to be a man; he still has feet like a man. He once got lost and a fellow found him in the brush. Old Bear had gone down to a big lake; this was in Alaska somewhere. He had a long tail then. He sat down on the ice. It was on a bright day, about two o'clock in the afternoon. The ice began to melt a little. By four o'clock it had started to get cold again. "Jump!" the man said. Bear jumped two or three times like a horse and lost his tail.

COON AND HIS GRANDMOTHER.[3]

Coon was a little boy. He went down the trail in September, to find some grasshoppers. He ate and ate. He told his blind old grandmother that he would give her some of the grasshoppers, but instead he put twigs in her mouth. "I'll fix you!" the old lady said. She took a piece of charcoal from her fire and struck him on the nose with it. It left a black streak on his nose. "You shall make good meat[4] for you have deceived me," she said.

LION AND BEAR.[5]

Woodpecker (qaqα'm)[6] had two wives, Lion (x̣oqwa'lp) and Bear (k·ɩ'tʷʋn). Each woman had five children and Woodpecker

---

[1] The narrator said that there may be more to this story, but if so, he has forgotten it.
[2] Told by Pike Ben, 1926. See p. 412.
[3] Told by Pike Ben, 1926. See p. 407.
[4] Perhaps the old woman transforms him?
[5] Told by Peter Heck, 1926. See p. 407.
[6] Says, "Qa, qa, qa," when he flies.

was the father of the children. In August when the blackberries were ripe, Lion asked Bear to pick berries with her. They set out to get some. Bear picked only the ripe ones, while Lion picked only red ones. Before long, Lion said, "Come here, co-wife (nʊk·awa′s)." Bear went over and sat down alongside her. Then Lion began to look for lice on Bear's head. She could not find any, but sucked at her head, nevertheless. Then Bear looked for lice on Lion's head and found lizards and things like that. Everything that Bear found there, Lion ate. When they had finished, they went home.

Lion brought her husband only red berries. He ate some and said, "They're a little too sour." The berries that Bear had brought were nice and black, so he ate these instead. Lion had eaten all the ripe ones that she found herself. "Where did you find these nice berries?" Woodpecker asked Bear.

The women went out several times, and each time, as soon as their baskets were filled, Lion would say to Bear, "Come over here and find my louse for me." Then Lion would also look for lice in Bear's head. The fourth time, Lion bit Bear on the head and sucked the blood out. "Oh, you're hurting me!" Bear said. Then they went home. Next morning they were planning to go again. "I don't want to go; Lion is going to kill me," Bear said.

They went out for the fifth time. As soon as their baskets were filled, Lion called, "Come here, Bear, I see a louse crawling right onto your head." Then she chewed Bear's head off.

Both women had nursing babies. Lion cut both Bear's breasts off and put them under the berries in her basket. When she got home, she said to Bear's children, "Oh, children, your mother got lost; I'll go to look for her tomorrow morning." Then Woodpecker said to himself, "I guess she's killed that woman. Yes, that's what she's done!" Lion said to the youngest Bear, "Come, sleep with me tonight." Lion then took the breasts from her basket and laid them alongside the fire to roast. The baby peeped through the side of the bed, saw what she was doing and said, "Those are my mother's breasts!" Lion immediately hid the breasts. "No," she said, "your mother was lost; I'll go to look for her tomorrow." Later she cooked the breasts and ate them.

Early next morning, Lion was gone; she had gone back to eat the body. Woodpecker then made five bows for each of his ten children. "You boys sit on either side of the room and shoot at one another," he said. He had made arrows for the Lion children from weeds, but for the Bear children, he had made a stronger kind. The little Bears then lined up on one side, and the little Lions on the other. The Bears killed all five of the Lions. Then Woodpecker said to the Bears, "Go to your grandmother. The road forks; there is paint on the one that you must take. The other one is covered with bones and leads to Wolf's house."

The little Bears set out. On the way, they met little Black Bug. "If Lion should come along, swear at her and keep fighting with her," they said. Later they met Snail. "Lion killed our mother. If she should come along here, swear at her and fight with her a long time, so that she can't catch us," they said.

In the meantime, Woodpecker took the smallest of the dead boys, and so fixed his arms and legs with sticks, that he appeared to be running to meet his mother. Then Woodpecker made himself some wings so that he could fly away. Lion returned and saw her little son. "My dear boy," she said, "are you coming to meet mother?" The boy seemed to be running, but still he did not move. Lion soon discovered that he was dead. She threw her pack down and started to look for the little Bears. Every last one of them was gone. Then she began to growl and said, "Where's Woodpecker?" Woodpecker was sitting on a tree, ready to leave at any minute. "Did you find her?" he asked. She was furious and tried to bite him. He then jumped to another tree. She dug at the roots and tore them out. The tree fell. He then jumped to another tree. She felled this tree also, but she could not catch him; Woodpecker could fly now, and so he went away.

Woodpecker had told the little Bears to run around the house five times before they left. Lion finally found their tracks and followed them around. She hit upon their trail and followed them.

In the meantime, the little Bears had come to the road, but they had forgotten which trail to take; they took the road that was strewn with bones. They came to a house and did not quite know what to do. At last, they went in. "Sit down here, boys," old man Wolf said and locked the door. He had five sons, all hunters. Before long the eldest one returned carrying a deer. Then the second and third came in, each also carrying a deer. The fourth came in with a man's dead body, the fifth with a deer and an elk. The old man said, "Oh, my dear sons, you must have tamanoas pretty strong; I never thought you would get it so strong." Then he motioned toward the little Bears and said, "Here is your food that came in for breakfast." Poor little Bears, the door was locked! "Get that dry hide and give it to them for a blanket, so that we can hear them if they try to escape," the old man said to his sons.

The eldest of the little Bears had stuck some little sticks in the ground to raise the hide a bit. He dug a tunnel under the ground, so that they could escape. Finally, he was able to make a passage clear through to the outside. He put his smallest brother into the tunnel, thinking it was large enough for him. The little fellow could not squeeze through, however. The eldest boy dug some more. He had to dig five times before the youngest could squeeze through. Then all of them managed to do likewise. They ran as fast as they could go. It was just daylight when they got to the forks of the road. They could hear the Wolves talking excitedly; they had just taken the hide away, ready to eat them. They ran to their grandmother After-birth. "Father told us that we would be welcome here. Lion killed our mother." "Of course, sit down here," After-birth said.

In the meantime, Lion had set out after them. She met little Black Bug on the way, who swore at her. She kept tearing the ground up, but Bug always rolled away. She could not catch him and finally gave up. Then she came to Snail on a rotten log, who swore at her. He kept her there for a long time, but finally, she went on. The children by this time were safe in their grandmother's house.

Lion at last arrived at After-birth's house and knocked on the door. "Are the boys here?" she asked. "Yes, they're here," After-birth said. "Oh, I found your mother, boys. I said I'd come to get you," Lion said. Inside, the little boys were screaming and crying, they were so frightened. Lion opened the door a bit, but it came back with a bang. "My door is just like this one," she said. She was a bit frightened by this time. "Come on, boys, we have a great many berries now; your mother found them at the place where she was lost," she called in. Then the grandmother said, "Come on in." The door swung back a bit just then, and Lion could see the boys. "Come in backwards; that's the way I come in," After-birth called out. Aside, After-birth said to the door, "Don't move until she is half-way in." Lion came in backwards. The door cut her in two. Half of her body remained outside, struggling. The hind-part was inside. She could not do anything, for her head was dead. Then the grandmother said, "Well, go outside now, boys, and make a fire." The boys burned Lion's body. When Lion was nothing but ashes, the old woman said to her, "This is the last time anything like this shall happen. If a man has two or three wives, they shall be good to one another."

K'walale·'··i: someone has lots of food. Of three baskets full, one is already finished, one is half-way finished, and one just begun. As for little babies, they are in similar stages of formation. After-birth is always angry when babies die.

SKUNK.[1]

A chief had two daughters. "If you go out to pick berries," he said to them, "don't take the trail to the left that is sprinkled with bird feathers. Take the other trail, the one sprinkled with red paint."

The girls went out to pick berries. When they came to the forks of the trail they stopped. "What trail shall we take?" they said, "the one with feathers or the one with red paint?" They stayed

[1] Told by Marion Davis, 1927. See p. 404.

there quite a while, talking it over. The younger said, "You know what father said. He told us that we should not take the one with feathers, but the one with red paint." "Oh, no," the elder said, "we must take the one to the left with feathers." They talked it over, back and forth, five times. "Well, you may go if you like, but I won't," the younger finally said, and went back home.

The elder took the trail that she had decided upon. She walked and walked. It seemed to her that she was coming to an open place. In a little while, she did come out on an open spot of ground. There was a large house there. She went up to a little house standing close to the large one and peeped in. She saw a man, a good-looking fellow and rather youngish. He invited her in immediately. "Oh, my wife, come in, come in," he said. She went right in, for the man was handsome. He had a bit of meat on a rack, a bit of deer or bear fat — something like that.

Late evening found the young man having a good time in his little house, playing with the girl. Then someone called, "Where are you, Skunk? Come over here and carry my load into the house." The man who was calling had a large load of deer meat and wanted Skunk to carry it into the house for him. Skunk then said to his young wife, "My servants are calling me; they must want me for something." He went out for a while and then came back again to his wife.

Next day the owner of the house went out to hunt again. Late in the afternoon he called to Skunk, "Oh, Skunk, come here; take my load into the house." Skunk jumped up and said to his wife, "Oh, my servants are calling me. They usually do that when they want my advice for something." In a very short time he was back again. Then Skunk's master thought, "What's the matter with my servant? He seems in such a hurry to get back to his house lately."

The third day, rather late, Skunk's master called again, "Oh, Skunk, come over here and carry my load in." Skunk jumped up and said, "My servants are calling me; they must want my advice for something." By this time, the young woman was thinking, "What's the matter? Perhaps he's the slave instead of the master. If he were master, he wouldn't be living in this small house; he'd be living in the large house. He must be a low-class fellow." Skunk was back again in a very short time.

Skunk's master was thinking, "Skunk has queer habits lately. He merely throws my load in and then goes away. He used to stay a while and brag about my game, and then I'd give him a bit of fat. Now, he doesn't seem to care." He went over to Skunk's little house and peeped in. A good-looking young woman was laughing and playing with Skunk.

The fifth day, he called again, "Where are you Skunk? Come over here and take my load into the house." Skunk ran over as quickly as he could and then went right back. "Yes, that's just what I thought! He has a young woman there. Wonder where he got her," the master said to himself. He went over to the little house and peeped in again. "Yes, it's a young girl!" But the young woman was now rather thin and yellow and unhealthy looking from staying with Skunk so long.

For the sixth time, he called, "Oh, Skunk, come over here and get my load." By this time, he was scheming to get the young woman away from Skunk. "My load is not so far away — just over there; I got tired and left it there," he said to Skunk. Skunk ran as fast as he could to the load. His master, in the meantime, went immediately to the young woman and told her that she would die if she did not get away from Skunk's odor. "Skunk is a slave," he said. He wanted her to run away with him to a place beyond the sky, where they would stay. There was another world beyond the sky, he explained. "Oh, I guess what he says is true. I am getting thin and Skunk smells badly. I had better go away with this man," the young woman thought.

The two of them ran away from Skunk. The man was afraid of him, for Skunk might shoot his musk at them and kill them. They ran away, far up to the other world, and from there watched what Skunk was doing. The woman had already given birth to many little Skunks.

Skunk had to go a long way before he found the load. He started back with it, in a great hurry to get to his wife. He ran as fast as he could, and threw the load into his master's house. Then he ran to his own little house. His wife was gone. The little Skunks were running about the house. He looked everywhere for his wife and his master. He was very tired and sweaty from all this exertion. Finally, he gave up searching close by, and went far away from the house. He was very tired by this time. He came to a little spring that was nice and clear, like a well. "Why, there's my wife and that man, far down in the water!" he said. Instead of drinking, he turned around and sent his musk into the water. He looked in. There they were; he had not killed them, and this made him very angry. He turned around and sent his musk into the water again. His wife was now resting her head on the man's arm. He sent his musk into the water again. They were still there, laughing and having a good time together. He was so angry by this time, he did not know what to do. He rested, then sent his musk into the water again. There they were, laughing and having a good time. He lay down on the ground, face up and looked here and there. Then he saw them; they were far up in the next world, beyond the sky. It was only their reflections he had seen in the water. It was too far up to send his musk, he decided. Then he shouted, "How did you manage to get so far away from your customary abode?" Again he shouted, "How did you manage to get so far from your customary abode?" There was no answer. He was tired out from shouting. "Let him shout until he gets tired," the couple said. He shouted five times. They knew that he was very tired by this time. As soon as Skunk had begun to shout, the man had put five large rocks into the fire. The rocks were now quite hot. They could barely hear Skunk when he had called the last time. "You can't get up here, unless you come backside up," they called down, "you'll get here that way." Skunk started up. "I'm coming," he called. Then, with his head down and backside up, he called, "How far am I?" "A l-o-o-o-ng way," they answered. But as a matter of fact, Skunk was already half-way up. Still coming, he called again, "How far am I?" "You're still not half-way up," they called back faintly, in order to mislead him, for he was already quite near. His backside was a little open, as he was very much fatigued. They were afraid of him now. The rocks were red hot by this time, and they knew what they could do to drive him back. Still tired, Skunk asked, weakly, "How far am I?" "A long way yet," they answered faintly, dragging their words out. But Skunk was very close, his backside becoming more and more open as he became more fatigued. They rolled the rocks right into him. His anus shot right through him and out his mouth, red as fire and like a hoop. Since he could not do anything without his anus, Skunk had to go back.

His anus fell right into the middle of the river. Skunk knew that it had then floated down the river. When he came to the river, he rested a bit, and then followed the river down. He came to a house where someone was living. "Oh, chiefs," he called, "have you seen my property?" "Oh, chief, your property went floating down," the people answered. He followed the river down and down. He came to another house and called, "Oh, chiefs, have you seen my property?" "Oh, Skunk, your anus went floating down," the people answered. Skunk was furious. He thought, "If ever I find my property, you'll pay for this!" He came to another house and called, "Oh, chiefs, have you seen my property?" "Oh, chief, your property went floating down," the people answered. He came to another house and called, "Oh, chiefs, have you seen my property?" "Oh, Skunk, your anus went floating down," the people answered. He went farther down. He came to another house and called, "Oh, chiefs, have you seen my property?" "Oh, chief, your property went floating down," they answered.

He went on and on. There were no houses now. Finally, he heard some boys shouting and having a good time. "Wä'e', wä'e'," they were shouting. "What is going on ahead of me?" Skunk thought. The people of this place had found a pretty hoop floating down the river. Whenever they rolled it, it shone fiery-red. They had sent word to any number of people to come to see what they had found. The gathering was a very large one.

When he went closer, Skunk discovered what the gathering was about. "It is my property that they are having fun with!" he said. They were rolling the hoop back and forth between two sides. The hoop was coming in Skunk's direction. He sat down. "What shall I turn myself into, a boy or an old man?" he asked himself. "Oh, I shall turn myself into an old man and walk with a cane. Perhaps they'll say, 'Oh, this old man is coming to see our fine hoop-game.' Then I can walk right to the center of the field," he finally said. And so he turned himself into an old man and found a stick for a cane. He walked slowly, then rested, went on slowly and rested again, as if he were so old he could scarcely walk, but anxious, nevertheless, to see the precious hoop that was so nice, so valuable. The people did think of him as he had hoped they would. "Now, there's an old man coming to our celebration. He wants to see this hoop of ours," they said. Someone called, "So you have come to see this fine celebration of ours? You've never seen a hoop like this before!" "Yes, I've come over to see this hoop you young people have," Skunk answered. "Now, old man," they said, "you must come right to the center of the playground and sit down!" Skunk tottered over to the playground, where they made him sit down. Whenever they rolled the hoop, it shone beautifully and very red. "Hure·′·,"[1] one side shouted, as they rolled the hoop over to the other side. "Hure·′·," the other side shouted, as they rolled it back. The third time, Skunk was holding his cane just so, and was fixing his backside. When they were ready to roll the hoop again, Skunk said, "Come this way, anus." They rolled the hoop back to the other side. "Come this way, anus," Skunk said again. They rolled the hoop back in the other direction. "Come this way, anus," Skunk said again. He was getting ready to turn his backside toward the rolling hoop. "Come this way, anus," he said again. The hoop rolled close to him this time. When they sent the hoop back again, it rolled right into its proper place. Then Skunk immediately changed into his natural self. "Ah, you dogs! You were having fun with my property!" he said. He turned his backside toward the people at one end of the playground and sent his musk to them. Not a one survived. Then he turned his backside toward those at the other end of the playground and sent his musk to them. Every last one of them died.

Skunk started back up the river, thinking of his wife. He came to one of the houses where the people had told him that his anus had gone floating down the river. He went into the house and told the people there to plug every crack with moss, so that his good news would not escape, as he wanted them to remember it for always. As soon as they had done so, he shot his musk at them. Everyone died.

He kept on going up the river. He came to a house where the people had told him that they had seen his property floating down

[1] The same as in English.

the river. He did not do anything to these people. "What is the news?" they asked. "I have nothing to tell you; there is no news for you people," he said and went on.

He came to the third house, where the people had told him that they had seen his anus floating down the river. He went in and told them to stuff all the cracks with moss, for he had some news for them and did not want it to leak out. Then he turned his backside toward them, let his musk fly, and killed them all. Altogether he visited five different houses. He killed all those people who had said that his anus went floating down. But to all those who had said that his property went floating down, he was kind.

He went on. As he travelled, he thought, "Oh, you man who took my wife! You'll pay for it if I ever reach you! But perhaps both of you are dead by this time." He had travelled a long way and was already tired. Then he came upon a precious blanket (sL'a'L'ł).

In the meantime, Skwikwi'kʷ[1] had heard that a man, who was on his way up the river, was killing everyone. He had been thinking of some way to escape Skunk. "Shall I turn myself into a boy, an old man, a hide?" he had asked himself. "Yes, I shall turn myself into a hide, a shiny one," he had finally said.

Skunk noticed that he had come upon something nice. He kicked the blanket. "Oh, it's covered with maggots!" he said, "I'll just leave it." He went on a little farther, thinking all the while of the blanket. "I'll go back and get it," he said. He kicked it. "Oh, there are too many maggots!" he said, and went on. A little farther on, he thought, "Perhaps that wife of mine would like that blanket. Perhaps I should give it to her." And so he went back, got the blanket and tried to shake the maggots off. "Oh, there are too many; I'll just let it go," he said and went on. A little farther on, he thought, "If I don't take my wife something, she won't come back to me. I had better go back. No matter how many maggots there are, I'll brush them off." He went back again, shook the blanket hard and brushed it off nicely. The blanket was rather shiny now. "Oh, my nice wife will come back to me if I give this to her," he thought. He tied it up with a packstrap and started off carrying it. He kept on going, now feeling very happy. After he had gone a long way he began happily to plan how he could get his wife back. "Oh, I shall kill that man when I get there!" he thought. He went on and on and on. Finally, he heard someone whistling, "Hw····, hw····.[2]" He kept on going, as if he had not heard anyone whistling. Nevertheless, he was thinking about it. "Who can that be?" he thought. "Hw····, hw····." He listened, but kept on going. However, in his heart he was afraid. "What am I going to find here?" he thought. He now walked a little faster, but heard again, "Hw····, hw····." Then, "Hw····, hw····," he heard

[1] Sometimes called Whistle, or the Whistling-bird. See pp. 3, 12.

[2] Actual whistle each time.

again, this time a little louder. Then he straightened up and said, "I'm not afraid of anyone but Skwikwi'kʷ." He heard someone whistling again. This time he said, a little louder, "It's Skwikwi'kʷ!" He started to run with his pack. He heard someone whistling again and ran as fast as he could. Now someone was whistling continuously. He shot his musk again and again. He kept sending it out in a constant stream, until he ran out of it, and died right on the spot. Then Skwikwi'kʷ said, "There shall never again be a Skunk like this, a Skunk who kills people." Although skunk was once a large person who killed people, he is now only a small animal and would not kill anyone; he sends his musk, but it merely annoys with its disagreeable odor.

MOUNTAIN LION AND RABBIT GAMBLE

(First Version).[1]

Once upon a time, Rabbit and Mountain Lion (stca'tqɬəm) gambled. While Rabbit was on his way to a certain place, he met a very large fellow near the river. This fellow was Mountain Lion. "We shall slahal," Lion said, "the two of us against each other." (Usually, there are a lot of people on each side. The Upper Chehalis did not play slahal formerly. They played only the "wheel" game. Slahal is a Yakima game, that the Squally brought from there.) "I don't gamble in an ordinary way as most people do," Rabbit said, "I shall slahal you with my tamanoas. Help yourself the best way you can!"

They built a large fire and began to play. Before long Lion had lost nearly all his sticks. He jumped at Rabbit and very nearly caught him, but Rabbit had managed to get out of his way. Lion sang,

I'm going to swallow you,
I'm going to swallow you alive.

Rabbit was only a small fellow, but he had a great tamanoas to whom he now began to call; he called upon the sky, the stars, the sun, the moon; he sent his message to the other world. He sang,[2]

Slice it up,[3] blue sky,
Slice it up, blue sky,
Change color to blue,
Change color to blue.

On the fifth night Lion began to quarrel with him. "You've been cheating!" he said. It was freezing cold. Rabbit now had his ta-

[1] Told by Jonas Secena, 1926. See p. 412. Song, Appendix, p. 423.

[2] The song was sung in the Puyallup or Squally language, so the narrator said.

[3] He wants it to warm up just enough to melt the ice a little.

manoas ready. "The last stick is gone! I'm going to swallow you alive!" Lion said, pointing a (gambling) stick at him. Then he jumped at him. Rabbit fled across the frozen ice. "Come on, my friend," he called to Lion, "let's go out to the mountains." He had seen that the ice was not thick enough to bear Lion's weight. He took some kind of dirt[1] and rolled it into a compact little ball, like a marble, and sent it ringing across the ice. "See, Lion, the ice is thick," he said. Finally, he convinced Lion. He had a long pole ready. Lion started across on the ice. The ice began to break with him. Rabbit kept pushing him under with the pole, until Lion finally died and floated downstream.

MOUNTAIN LION AND RABBIT GAMBLE

(Second Version).[2]

Once upon a time Mountain Lion (sk·a′tq̣ʿɬəm)[3] offered to play slahal against any comer. Rabbit said, "I'll take you up. We won't stay just in one place; we'll travel toward the east as we gamble." Rabbit was very much afraid that Lion would catch him and eat him up, and so he had made this suggestion. It had just occurred to him that to the east of them was a large lake. If they did not stay in one place as they gambled, but kept on the go, they would at last reach the lake. Perhaps it would be a cold and frosty night when they got there. They would keep at it five nights.

They started their first night of play. Lion missed little Rabbit time and again. This made him very angry. At last Rabbit got hit and gave his slahal to Lion. Old Lion began his song,

tcʿo tcʿo tcʿo
tcʿo tcʿo tcʿo

His song meant that it should cloud up and then rain. He must have known that if he sang like this, it would cloud up and he would not have to cross the lake. Rabbit hit him right away again. Then Rabbit began his tamanoas song,

sax̣ sax̣e′lyə
sax̣ sax̣e′lyə
q’wɛx̣ q’wɛx̣ x̣ele′yə.

Rabbit's song asked for a clear night. He sang and wriggled his ears very nicely. Old Lion wanted the clouds to bring rain. But Rabbit wanted the sky blue and striped, as on a clear frosty night.

---

[1] His own excrements, evidently; see following version.
[2] Told by Marion Davis, 1927. Songs, Appendix, p. 424.
[3] There is some doubt as to the proper English equivalent. Some say Grizzly and others say Mountain Lion.

sax̣ sax̣e′lyə
sax̣ sax̣e′lyə
q’wɛx̣ q’wɛx̣ x̣ele′yə.

Rabbit was ahead. Lion sang as before,

tc‘o tc‘o tc‘o
tc‘o tc‘o tc‘o.

Next night they began again and sang as before. Lion missed Rabbit many times, then hit him. Then Lion started his song,

tc‘o tc‘o tc‘o
tc‘o tc‘o tc‘o.

He missed Rabbit a few times, then hit him again.

The third night they gambled again. Rabbit began his song. When Lion missed him he jumped at him. But Rabbit was already on the other side of the room, shaking away at his slahal. Lion knew why Rabbit wanted a cold and frosty night. Missed him again! He jumped at Rabbit, but the latter was already on the other side of the room, shaking away.

The fourth night they gambled again. Lion began his song,

tc‘o tc‘o tc‘o
tc‘o tc‘o tc‘o.

But there were no clouds at all; the sky was turning blue and the ground was frozen. This was just what Rabbit had wished for — so that he could kill Lion. Lion jumped at Rabbit again and again, but each time Rabbit would be on the other side of the room, shaking away, his ears up. Lion began his song again, but soon got hit.

The fifth night was cold and clear. Everything was frozen. The lake was covered with frost, and was frozen hard enough to hold a person. They began to slahal. Lion missed Rabbit time and time again. Old Lion jumped at Rabbit. Little Rabbit was already on the other side, shaking his slahal and tossing them up every which way, singing all the time. Lion could not catch him.

They set out again in the morning, Rabbit leading the way. Lion did not know where Rabbit was taking him. Rabbit was leading him to the lake. "How are we going to get across?" Lion asked when they got there. "This is where I'm going to kill you," Rabbit thought. "We can walk across," he said to Lion. "Oh, little brother, I can't do it," Lion said. Little Rabbit then sat down and evacuated; his feces froze as hard as a rock in no time at all. "Let's go over. What's the matter with you? We'll slahal across the lake," he said. "If I go across, I'll die; the lake will break through with me," Lion said. "Don't talk of dying!" Rabbit said, as he picked up one of his feces, hard as a rock, and sent it skimming across the ice, tinkling like a bell. "But I can't cross over as fast as that!" Lion said. Rabbit then threw a second feces across, this one skimming across, like the first. "Come, come," he said, "just look at me. You needn't be afraid. I'll go down on the ice, and jump around. You needn't be afraid." He then showed Lion how easily it could be done. "See, I didn't break through!" He threw another feces, and still another and another, until he had thrown all five of them across the ice. "Will you hold me if the ice starts to break?" Lion asked. "Oh, yes! Of course I'll help you. Here's a long pole; if you fall in, I'll pull you out," Rabbit said. (He was a smart little fellow!) Lion stepped slowly onto the ice. Little Rabbit jumped about. "Look at me! Just see how hard the ice is. You won't break through!" he said. Lion stepped softly. Little by little, he made his way across. When he was just half-way over, the ice began to crack. "Oh, brother, the ice is going to break!" he cried. "Oh, no," Rabbit said, "it always does that when one crosses slowly." At last, the ice gave way. "Take hold of me, brother! I'm going to drown!" Lion cried. "All right, I'll find you a stick to hold on to while I pull you out," Rabbit said. He cut a long forked stick with which to hold Lion's head under, so that he could not get out. He pushed the prongs into Lion and held him down for a long, long time. "He's probably dead now," he thought. But he held him down longer to make sure. "He's surely dead by this time," he finally thought. He took the stick out, but kept his eye on Lion for some time longer. "Yes, he's dead now," he finally said.

And so the little fellow got the best of Lion, and by his own cleverness saved himself from being eaten.

WOLF AND DEER GAMBLE.[1]

Wolf challenged Deer. "What do you say to a game of lal?"[2] "All right, let us gamble. Where shall we play?" Deer said. "Right here," Wolf said. "All right," Deer answered.

Now each side was ready to gamble; they put their mats down. "Which side shall start first?" someone asked. "Let the Wolves start it." Wolf started to sing,

> Shank of a deer,
> Shank of a deer,
> My pounding stick,
> My pounding stick.[3]

[1] Told by Peter Heck, 1927; recorded in text. See p. 412. Song, Appendix, p. 425.

[2] Swʊ′q'x̣ats', or lal; it is the "wheel" or disk game.

[3] Wolf means to say, "When I kill Deer, I shall use his shank for beating time to my tamanoas song." In a game like this, each player begins his song himself. Then a "song-catcher" catches the words and repeats them. Then all join in. This is the usual procedure in all ceremonials where tamanoas songs are sung.

Shank of a deer,
Shank of a deer,
My pounding stick,
My pounding stick.

"e····!"[1]

The first Deer sang his tamanoas song,

ma'L'ena, ma'L'ena,[2]
I shall jump to the tip of the hill.[3]

ma'L'ena, ma'L'ena,
I shall jump to the tip of the hill.

"wɛ····!"[4]

The Wolves moved a little closer to Deer's side.

ma'L'ena, ma'L'ena,
I shall jump to the tip of the hill.

ma'L'ena, ma'L'ena, ma'L'ena,
I shall jump to the tip of the hill.

"e····!"

Another Wolf started his tamanoas song,

ma'L'ena, ma'L'ena,
I shall head him off,
I shall head him off.[5]

ma'L'ena, ma'L'ena,
I shall head him off,
I shall head him off.

"he····!"

Another Deer started his tamanoas song,

ma'L'ena, ma'L'ena,
I shall float down the river.[6]

---

[1] A "hit", that is, Deer's side has guessed right, so it is Deer's turn to play. Sometimes "he····!" is used instead of "e····!" to indicate a "hit".

[2] An opening phrase.

[3] Deer means to say, "I shall jump to the tip of the hill and Wolf will never catch me."

[4] A "miss", that is, Wolf's side has failed to guess correctly, so Deer is entitled to start over again. Because Wolf's side has "missed", they lose one counter to Deer's side; every time a side "misses" they must give up a counter.

[5] Wolf means to say, "When Deer jumps to the tip of the hill, I shall head him off."

[6] Deer means to say, "I shall float down the river with just my eyes and nose sticking out, so Wolf can't catch me."

ma'ʟ'ena, ma'ʟ'ena,
I shall float down the river.

"wɛ····!"[1]

ma'ʟ'ena, ma'ʟ'ena,
I shall float down the river.

ma'ʟ'ena, ma'ʟ'ena,
I shall float down the river.

"he····!"[2]

"Sit down, old man," the Wolves said to one of their number, "perhaps you will have better luck than the rest of us." A third Wolf sang,

ma'ʟ'ena, ma'ʟ'ena,
I shall cut across the point.[3]

ma'ʟ'ena, ma'ʟ'ena,
I shall cut across the point.

"wɛ····!"[4]

ma'ʟ'ena, ma'ʟ'ena,
I shall cut across the point.

ma'ʟ'ena, ma'ʟ'ena,
I shall cut across the point.

"e····!"

"Sit down, old man," the Deer said to Red Salmon (sa'wanx̣ᵘ),[5] who was on their side. Red Salmon started his song,

ma'ʟ'ena, ma'ʟ'ena,
I shall crawl under — — —
I shall crawl under — — —[6]

ma'ʟ'ena, ma'ʟ'ena,
I shall crawl under — — —
I shall crawl under — — —

---

[1] Wolf's side has "missed" again, so they must give Deer's side still another counter. Deer's side, of course, is entitled to keep on playing until hit. The same Deer continues the play.

[2] Deer is hit at last, so it is now Wolf's turn. Deer's side has won two counters from the Wolves, but as yet the latter have not won any from the Deer.

[3] This Wolf means to say, "At the place where the river bends parallel to itself, I shall cut across and catch Deer as he floats down the river."

[4] Now the Wolves have won one counter.

[5] Sometimes translated silver-side.

[6] Red Salmon means to say, "I shall crawl under something in the river and hide there so Wolf can't catch me."

ma'ʟ'ena, ma'ʟ'ena,
I shall crawl under,
I shall crawl under.

"he····!"[1] "wɛ····!" Every time the Wolves missed, they moved closer to Deer's side.

ma'ʟ'ena, ma'ʟ'ena,
I shall crawl under — — —
I shall crawl under — — —

ma'ʟ'ena, ma'ʟ'ena,
I shall crawl under — — —
I shall crawl under — — —

"he····!"

"Come into the game," the Wolves said to Bear, who was on their side. Bear sang,

ma'ʟ'ena, ma'ʟ'ena,
I shall chew his head off,
— — — male-salmon head — — —[2]

ma'ʟ'ena, ma'ʟ'ena,
I shall chew his head off,
— — — male-salmon head — — —

"he····!"

Now Rabbit (s.x̂wa'i'ks), who claimed to be the younger brother of the Deer, was sitting right in the middle, and he had heard the Wolves plotting against them. "Get into the game, old man," the Deer said to him. Now Rabbit sang what he had heard.

Whispering against us,
— — my brothers[3] — — — —

Whispering against us,
— — my brothers — — — —

"he····!"[4] "wɛ····!" The Wolves moved a little closer to Deer's side.

Whispering against us,
— — my brothers — — — —

[1] I do not understand this "he...." immediately preceding the "wɛ....", unless it is, that the Wolves are cheating. They are probably claiming to have hit, but have actually missed.

[2] Bear means to say, "I shall catch Red Salmon when he hides in little creeks and chew his head off." Notice how each song progresses.

[3] That is, the Wolves are whispering against him and his brothers.

[4] See footnote 1.

Whispering against us,
— — my brothers — — — —

"he····!"

Now four on each side had played. "Sit down, old man," Wolf's side said to Old Wolf (ts'α'meps). Old Wolf sang,

qαyε'na qαyε'na,[1]
I shall scatter Deer's stomach,
Get ready, get ready.[2]

"he····!"

Now those on Wolf's side jumped at the Deer. The Deer ran away, the Wolves right after. But Deer forgot little Fawn (tε·'lqa), who was sleeping. Poor little thing! They left him.[3]

Rabbit and Wildcat fought. "Scratch me," Wildcat said, "let us see who is the stronger." Then Wildcat ripped a piece of flesh from Rabbit's side — clear from his stomach to his side. Rabbit was wounded.[4]

The Wolves finally returned to the scene of the game, and there they found little Fawn sleeping. "Throw him up on the roof of the house, my children," Old Wolf said. Then they threw him up on the roof of the house.

Morning came and all the Wolves went out hunting. Only the old man was left at home. He got little Fawn and brought him down. "Go look for a roasting-stick, as straight as can be," he said. Little Fawn went out. He started his song,

poi' poi' poi'
poi' poi' poi'
poi' poi' poi'.[5]

"I couldn't find any straight ones," he said when he returned. Then Old Wolf got him and threw him on top of the roof again. Fawn stayed there for another whole morning. When all the Wolves came back, they asked the old man, "Is he cooked yet ?" "No," the old man said. Old Wolf sent Fawn out four times for a roasting-stick and four times Fawn returned without one. Each time, Old Wolf threw him on top of the roof again. The fifth time that the old man sent him out, Fawn thought, "Here's my chance to skip!" He ran and ran and never came back. When the hunters returned, they asked, "Where is Fawn ?" "He isn't here. He ran away, that bad one," the old man said. That's why Wolf never catches Fawn.

[1] An opening phrase, like ma'L'ena; cannot be translated.
[2] Old Wolf means, "I'm too old any more to catch game, but Deer's guts will be my share." When he says, "Get ready," he is calling upon his side to jump at Deer's side.
[3] Said in broken speech.
[4] The narrator pointed out that the story does not say whether or not Rabbit escaped in the end.
[5] He is singing to make the sticks crooked, so that he can save his life.

COUGAR AND WILDCAT.

(Type One).[1]

Cougar (s.wa'wa) and his little brother Wildcat (x̣eˡwʋ's) made a home close to the river. "Take care of yourself," Cougar said to Wildcat, "I'm going out to hunt tomorrow morning." The following morning Cougar went out. In the afternoon he came back carrying a whole elk. He butchered and skinned it and then cooked some of the meat. When he had finished he said to Wildcat, "Be careful of the fire. Don't let it go out; if you do you won't be able to get any more." He went out again early next morning. Wildcat began to cook. He threw an entire piece of meat on the fire. His brother came home that night with another elk. The same thing happened four times. The fifth time he warned Wildcat as usual, "Be careful of the fire. If it should go out, don't borrow fire from anyone; just wait for me." Wildcat got up in the morning and cooked his meat in the same manner. The juice from the meat saturated the fire and it grew smaller and smaller. At last it went out entirely. Then Wildcat felt uneasy. Where could he get some fire? His brother had taken the fire-sticks with him. He saw some smoke from a house across the river. He swam across and peeped in the house. An old man said, "I smell Wildcat, I smell Wildcat." There was a bundle of burning wood on the fireplace. It was tied together with a string. "How shall I get a piece off?" Wildcat thought to himself. After a number of attempts, he found the old man asleep. He took the smallest piece from the bundle and ran out. The old man awoke too late. When he discovered his loss, he beat around wildly for a bit with his whip.

Wildcat tied the fire to the end of his tail. The fire began to hurt him. He grabbed it and put it on his forehead. His scalp began to burn and draw up in a bunch. Just when it was time for his brother to return, he had a big fire started. Cougar had already smelled Wildcat. "You went across the river to get some fire, didn't you?" he asked. He was angry enough to whip Wildcat. "I told you never to let the fire go out!" he scolded. Wildcat explained that meat was best when cooked directly on the flame. "Why didn't you get some roasting-sticks?" Cougar asked. "Now run down to the river to see if anyone is coming," he said. "No one is coming," Wildcat reported. Cougar sent him again. This time Wildcat saw a log coming across toward them. Cougar sent him again. The log was still coming toward them. Cougar sent him again. "Oh, he's on this side now! He's landing!" Wildcat reported.

The old man, łała'mak'wʋs[2], had turned himself into a log. "Now you'll have to save my flesh. Don't make a mistake!" Cougar said to Wildcat. When łała'mak'wʋs came, he said to Cougar, "I'm

[1] Told by Peter Heck, 1926. See p. 401.

[2] See p. 92.

going to play 'kʊslo'qᵘ'[1] with you; we're going to play up in a tree." "Watch for my flesh!" Cougar said to Wildcat once more. łała'mak'wʊs jumped up on the tree. Cougar jumped higher. "Grab me first," łała'mak'wʊs said. Cougar grabbed him. A chunk of flesh dropped down. Wildcat threw it on the fire. Then a piece of Cougar's flesh fell down. Wildcat laid it aside. The two men tore so much flesh from each other's bodies, that only the bones, heart and liver remained. Then łała'mak'wʊs tore out Cougar's liver. Wildcat threw it on the fire; he made a mistake. When łała'mak'wʊs's liver fell down, he laid it aside. When the latter's bones and heart fell down, he threw them on the fire. Cougar's bones and heart he saved. When Cougar had just about reassembled himself, he said, "This liver isn't mine!" "Yes it is!" Wildcat answered. There was nothing for Cougar to do but use łała'mak'wʊs's liver. The battle was over and he had won. łała'mak'wʊs was nothing but ashes. Cougar said, "This shall never happen in the next generation. If anyone should let his fire go out, he will be able to go to another's house and borrow some."

When Cougar was whole once more he said, "Get ready; we're going to move to some other place." They made a new home. "Take care of yourself. I'm going out hunting," Cougar said, "don't walk about everywhere. Stay here." He returned early with a large elk. "Look for some roasting sticks," he said to Wildcat. Wildcat went to look for the sticks. He began to sing,

> Who will eat with us?
> We have a large elk.

He ran home somewhat frightened. "Didn't I tell you not to say anything?" Cougar demanded. "Haven't you already a scarred face and a short tail?" Soon Q'ama'psəm (Slender-neck) came. They had to cook for him. They served the meat on a mat. Q'ama'psəm grabbed the mat at both ends and swallowed it whole. Cougar then cooked another quarter of meat. Q'ama'psəm ate it in the same manner. He ate about five different times. At last nothing was left to eat except the head and horns. "Where can I lie down to sleep?" he asked. "I'm pretty nearly satiated." "Here's my pillow," Cougar said, pointing to a root. Q'ama'psəm lay down, his head on the root. "Run, get a rock and sharpen it!" Cougar said to Wildcat. The latter brought the rock. The old man was asleep; he was snoring. "Go now!" Cougar said to Wildcat. Then Cougar struck the old man across the neck and cut it in two. Q'ama'psəm began to chase Cougar; he caught sight of Wildcat sauntering along. The two brothers started to run. Q'ama'psəm ran like the wind. He swept everything before him; trees began to fall. He chased one Cougar after another and killed them, but the fifth and youngest

[1] The name of the tree fight that follows.

one he could not catch.[1] Wildcat made a large mountain. Q'ama'psəm climbed up it. Then far on the other side of the mountain, a cyclone came and felled the trees. When Q'ama'psəm reached the other side, Wildcat made another mountain. This happened five times. The last time, Q'ama'psəm turned into the same kind of wind that he had made,[2] a cyclone. It was then ordained: nothing like this shall ever happen again; in future generations, should anyone desire to eat with a man who has killed an elk, he will do so without molesting the man.

Cougar and Wildcat met once more. "We must move again," Cougar said to Wildcat. After they had made their new home Cougar said, "I'm going out hunting. Stay right here. You've got me into enough trouble already." "All right, I'll behave myself," Wildcat promised. But Wildcat went out to the prairie and looked around. He wore a cape of dried elk skin. Two women, Cranes, were digging button lacamas. They were singing,

ɛwo', ɛwa',
ɛwo', ɛwa'.

"Who is digging lacamas where my brother burned the prairie?" Wildcat asked. The women then sang,

ɛnə'm, ɛnəm, it is we.

"What a nice blanket you have!" they said and tried to eat it. "We'll give you our button lacamas for it," they offered. Wildcat agreed to trade. He took the lacamas home and cooked them. Cougar came home somewhat tired. Wildcat got the lacamas and served them to him. Cougar was pleased. "Where did you get these? Did you dig this 'money'[3] yourself?" he asked. "Yes," Wildcat answered. He was not going to confess that he had traded his cape for them. "That's good. You could do this every day. You've done well so far, — you haven't called anyone to eat with us," Cougar said.

Wildcat saw the women again. They were singing and he sang, too. They offered again to trade their button lacamas for his blanket and he agreed. He hurried home to cook the lacamas. His brother was pleased with him.

Wildcat went to the prairie again. The women came right up to him. "Who is your brother?" they asked. "Cougar," he said. "May we go home with you?" they asked. "Well, I don't know if Cougar would like it," he answered. The women went along with him nevertheless. They cooked their lacamas. Wildcat now had two women with him. When Cougar came home, he was surprised to

---

[1] Notice that one Cougar now suddenly becomes five.
[2] The narrator said here, "A long time ago we used to have this kind of wind, but we don't have it now."
[3] Because of their shape, button lacamas are sometimes called "money".

find them there. They gave him some lacamas and asked to marry him. "Oh, I don't know, you might stay here if you like," he said.

Early next morning Cougar went hunting. The women went out on the prairie to dig. He caught sight of an elk, but the sound of the women singing on the prairie frightened it away. He now became a little angry with Wildcat. "Where did you get those women?" he asked. "They asked what kind of fellow you were and wanted to marry you," Wildcat explained. "All right, but we'll starve if they don't stop singing!" Cougar said.

Cougar went out again the following morning, but the women singing on the prairie frightened his elk away. "You see, you've got me into trouble again! We have no meat. Tell those women to go away or we'll starve to death!" he said to Wildcat.

The following morning, Cougar went hunting again. Wildcat told the women to leave. Cougar did not have to go far this time, for the women had gone to another place to dig. "We're going to move again and leave those women," he said to Wildcat.

They moved far off so that the two women could not find them. They made a new home. Cougar went hunting. Wildcat stayed home and cooked for himself.

Next morning, Cougar said, "Well, Wildcat, we'd better part. You've given me too much trouble. You go your way and I'll go mine. You can hunt the same as I." Wildcat began to weep. He was afraid to live by himself. "Nothing will bother you; I'll give you my old bow," Cougar said. Wildcat did not like this arrangement but he had to go. He set out, carrying a bow and arrow.

He had not gone far when he saw a field-mouse. "Oh, here's something nice!" he said to himself. He thought the little thing was game. He shot and killed it. He went a little farther and saw another. He shot and killed it. It was a long-tailed mouse. He went a little farther and saw another. It was a mole. He shot and killed it. He now had three different kinds of game. He saw another. It was a gopher. He now had four different kinds. He saw another and shot and killed it. It was a rabbit. He now had five different kinds of game. He made a fire and built a rack about a yard high; the fire was burning beneath the rack. He dressed his game and got ready to dry it. He tied his hair back and busied himself with the meat.

"Wonder what brother is doing?" Cougar thought to himself. He began to look for him. He saw some smoke in the distance and went there. He saw that Wildcat was busy. He stood back and watched, laughing to himself; it amused him. "What are you doing?" he asked at last. Wildcat was ashamed; he began to weep. "Have you killed an elk?" Cougar asked. "Yes, I'm drying it," Wildcat answered. Cougar could see the tiny game. "Oh, poor brother," he said, "this isn't game you have here. You must look for deer or elk. This isn't fit to eat. Go fetch the elk I brought for you." Wildcat fetched the elk. Then Cougar said, "Well, brother, from now on, you'd better follow me. Follow behind me wherever I go. I'll always kill some game for you and cover it with brush and trash. From now on, that's how you'll live." And so it is to-day: cougar always covers up some game and leaves it for wildcat, who follows after him.

K'walale·'··i.

COUGAR AND WILDCAT.

(Type Two).[1]

or, THUNDER.

Cougar (s.wa'wa) and Wildcat (x̣e¹wʋ's) were brothers. Cougar was a hunter. Early one morning, he went hunting. In the evening he returned with two elk on his back. They cooked the meat and ate some of it. Next morning, Cougar went hunting again. In the evening he returned with two deer on his back. The two of them now had quite a lot of meat. Next morning, Cougar said to his little brother, "Look for some poles so that we can cook some more meat." He told Wildcat not to say anything. "Just do as I say and bring the poles," he said. Not far from the house, Wildcat began to sing,

> Who will eat with us?
> We have lots of food, my brother and I.

Before long, he heard someone say, "I am the one who is going to eat with you." As soon as he got back to his brother, Wildcat said, "Someone is coming to eat with us." Cougar felt like whipping him. "I told you not to say anything!" he said. Then Cougar went out to look for a piece of rock. He found one, split it in two, and sharpened it. He came back to camp. Soon an old man came. "Old man, sit down here," Cougar said to him. Then he began to cook some meat for his visitor. When it was done, he gave it to him. The old man ate it quickly. He cooked some more and gave it to him. The old man ate it just as quickly as before. Cougar then cooked more meat and put a larger helping on the mat. The old man grabbed the mat at both ends and ate mat and all. Cougar was frightened now. He boiled the head and horns and put them on the mat. The old man grabbed it and put the whole thing in his mouth. He swallowed the head and horns whole. Cougar was watching closely to see if he would choke. But there was only a slight movement in the old man's throat. He had eaten the last of their meat. Then he said, "I'm getting sleepy. Where may I lie down?" "Right here, grandfather," Cougar said, pointing to a large root, "this is my

[1] Told by Peter Heck, 1926. While this story in some respects is very much like the preceding one, it is not considered merely a different version, but an entirely different story.

pillow." The old fellow lay down, his neck against the root. Then Cougar whispered to Wildcat, "Run as fast as you can! This fellow is going to eat us!" The old fellow was snoring. (He may have been a giant.) Cougar got the rock that he had sharpened and stood waiting. He struck the fellow across the neck with it. He had this in mind when he had told the old fellow to lie with his head against the root. He cut the fellow's head right off. Then he ran as fast as he could. He kept shouting to Wildcat, "Run as fast as you can! He's coming!" The old man caught Cougar. Then he caught the second Cougar.[1] It was just his head that was chasing them; he had left his body lying back at the camp. He caught four Cougars but he could not catch the fifth one. The fifth one got away from the old fellow, Q'ama'psəm.[2]

Q'ama'psəm then got on Wildcat's trail and began to chase him. Just as he was about to get him, Wildcat turned himself into a little hill. As soon as Q'ama'psəm caught up with him and began to chase him again, Wildcat turned himself into a hill again. When Q'ama'psəm was left some distance behind, Wildcat ran on again as fast as he could go. He had to change himself into a hill five different times. At last he came to a river. There was a house on the other side. He called over and asked the man there to come for him in his canoe. "What will you give me?" the man asked. Wildcat told him what he would pay. The man then came for him. "Go to the house. My daughter is there," he said. Wildcat went to the house. He found the girl there and stayed with her. He was frightened half to death; Q'ama'psəm was coming nearer every minute. "Don't worry, he'll never catch you!" the girl said. Thunder (sto'q^{u}) was the owner of the house.

Then Q'ama'psəm came. "I've got to go on!" Wildcat cried to the girl in fear. "No, stay here. Do as my father said," the girl said. Q'ama'psəm asked Thunder to take him across. "All right, but what will you pay me?" Thunder said. Q'ama'psəm offered almost everything, but Thunder was still not satisfied. Finally, Q'ama'psəm said, "Well, I'll give you my net." "All right," Thunder said. At this, Wildcat was so frightened, he nearly burst into tears. Thunder stretched his legs across the river. Q'ama'psəm was too frightened to cross. "You'll be safe! Come on!" Thunder said. Q'ama'psəm started across. Then Thunder moved his legs a little. "Don't do that, my good friend!" Q'ama'psəm cried in alarm. When he had got just about half-way across, Thunder shook his legs, and Q'ama'psəm fell off and drowned. The head rolled down to the Grays Harbor country. It stays there, near the Point. When there is going to be good weather, the head goes over to the Ts'x̣e'lɪs (Westport) side and makes a terrible noise. When there is going to be bad weather it goes over to the Demons Point side and does the same.

[1] As in the preceding story, one Cougar now becomes five.
[2] The old man's name is not revealed until this stage of the story.

Thunder told Wildcat to marry his daughter. One day Thunder said to him, "I have a log here that I can't split in two. It's a cedar log and I can only manage to split it a little. Crawl into the crack and pry it open for me." As soon as Wildcat crawled in, Thunder removed the wedges, and left him there, with the sides of the log pressing into him. Thunder started home weeping, "Oh, my son-in-law has met with an accident. He crawled into the log and the wedges came out; he's dead." In the meantime, Wildcat bent over and the log split in two. He picked up one half and packed it home. "I've brought home the log that you asked for," he said to Thunder. Thunder was very angry, for he thought that he had killed Wildcat.

Next day, Thunder said, "Oh, son-in-law, help me take the bark off this tree." Wildcat went over to the tree. It was a dead fir. "Sit down right here in a safe place," Thunder said. Then Thunder stripped off a piece of bark and it fell right on Wildcat. Thunder went home weeping, "Oh, my son-in-law has met with an accident. I was stripping off a piece of bark, when he walked right under the tree. The bark fell on him and killed him; he is buried there under the bark." But Wildcat had gone under the ground immediately the bark had fallen on him, and was safe. He crawled out, gathered up the bark, and packed it home. "Here's the bark that you wanted me to help you with," he said. Thunder was very angry.

Next day, Thunder said, "Well, we'll go fishing now." They went out, Thunder carrying some wedges in a basket. Wildcat obeyed Thunder and got into the basket. Thunder tied the basket up tightly and put it at one end of the canoe. Then he sunk the canoe and the basket toppled into the water. He went home weeping, "My son-in-law has met with an accident. I told him not to sit on the edge of the canoe but he would do it; he fell in and drowned." But his daughter said, "You were the cause of it, yourself; I don't believe that he accidentally fell off and drowned." In the meantime, Wildcat untied the basket under water, and ran out on shore. He came home, carrying the basket. "Here's something you lost; I found it," he said. Thunder could think of no way to kill him; he scarcely knew what to do next.

Next day, he said, "Get me some snow to eat. I'm very thirsty." Wildcat went to the mountains and got some snow from five different mountains. He rolled the snow into a little ball and started home with it. Thunder was surprised when he saw Wildcat coming; he had hoped that Wildcat would be killed by the mountain lions. "Here's the snow," Wildcat said, handing Thunder the tiny ball. "It's too small. There's not enough here for a bite," Thunder said. He ate and ate the snowball but could only eat a third of it. He had already eaten enough to chill him. He told Wildcat to throw the remainder outside. The snow then increased in size and completely covered the house so that Thunder could not get out. "Oh, son-in-law, take the snow back where you got it," he said. "All right,"

Wildcat said. He rolled all the snow into a tiny ball and took it back. Then he came back home.

Next day, Thunder said, "Son-in-law, go to the mountains and get my two pets; I want to play with them." Wildcat went to the mountains and found two lions. Thunder saw him coming; he had expected Wildcat to be killed. Wildcat brought the lions in, holding one in each arm. "Here are your pets," he said, throwing them into the room. The lions began to snarl and howl. Thunder was frightened; the lions did not act like pets. "Oh, son-in-law, take them back," he said. Wildcat took the lions back. After that, Thunder never bothered him. Wildcat got the best of those giants in every way.

K'walale·'··i

COUGAR AND WILDCAT.

(Types One and Two).[1]

Cougar (s.wa'wa) and Wildcat (patc'α'm) were brothers. Wildcat was five or seven years old, just old enough to talk and get around. Cougar was a grown man. Their father and mother were dead. Cougar was a good hunter; he made his living at hunting. At that time he was a person. Many dangerous beings more powerful than the people then lived on earth.

The two brothers often moved from place to place. One winter they caught a great many fish and killed many deer. They made tallow cakes from the deer fat. Cougar once said to Wildcat, "Be quiet when you go into the bushes for roasting sticks." But Wildcat began to sing, boasting of the quantity of their food supply,

> There is no one like my brother,
> There is no one like us,
> We have plenty to eat,
> Plenty of everything at home;
> How can we ever eat it all?

Then someone from the bushes said, "I am hungry." It was Q'ama'psəm, the dangerous being (pα'sa). He had a large head and a long neck; he was slender but tall. Cougar feared him for he was something more than human. "I will help you eat, my son," the dangerous being said to Wildcat. They went home. "Now you've done it!" Cougar said to Wildcat, "we're up against it!" He gave Q'ama'psəm everything he had to eat. The dangerous being swallowed it, but without once showing any movement in his throat. Finally, they decided to kill him. After a hard fight, Cougar did kill him. Then he and his naughty little brother ran away.

---

[1] Told by Jonas Secena, 1926.

When Cougar, who was unmarried, went out to hunt, he discovered a patch of strawberries on the prairie.[1] Wildcat went out every day to pick them for lunch. One day he heard someone singing. It was two young Geese-women, who were also people at that time. They questioned the boy. Finally they said, "Your brother should be married. We are going back with you and work for him. We'll ask him to marry us." They went back with Wildcat. But they soon made so much noise that they frightened the game away and Cougar could not supply any food. At last he and his little brother deserted the Geese.

They set out for the third time. They made camp on a river and stayed there for a long time. "Keep the fire going while I'm gone. Don't let it go out," Cougar said to Wildcat. But Wildcat ate his lunch of tallow and forgot about the fire. It went out completely. His brother would punish him severely. He made up his mind to go across the river to get some fire. His brother had forbidden him to go there where some smoke could be seen. "Keep away from there!" he had said, for a powerful dangerous being was said to live there.

Wildcat found the dangerous being lying down, asleep. He stuck his tail into the fire and swam back across the river. He had a fire going before Cougar returned. Cougar returned a short time before the dangerous being came to give them trouble. He noticed that their fire looked different. "I told my brother to stay away from that place!" he said to himself. The dangerous being had smelled Wildcat's hair burning and had already crossed over to their side of the river. "There are six or seven hollow stumps half way between here and that tree. Make a fire in one of them and I'll climb the tree," Cougar said to Wildcat, "I'll fight the dangerous being there. Now there's just one way that we can kill him: you must stand underneath the tree and throw into the fire every piece of him that falls." Wildcat did as Cougar said. Every time a piece of the dangerous being fell, he threw it into the fire. All of Cougar's flesh and parts, he saved. After the fight, he put Cougar together again. But he had made one mistake: he had saved the dangerous being's liver[2] and had thrown Cougar's into the fire. Cougar had a great tamanoas, that came to help put him in shape. "You've made a mistake. You've saved the dangerous being's liver instead of mine!" Cougar said to Wildcat. Cougar now has the liver of a dangerous being; that is why the people won't eat it.

After this trouble, Cougar made a camp for his little brother. "I'll always leave some venison for you," he said. Since that time, Cougar always leaves something buried for Wildcat.

No sooner had Cougar finished with the second dangerous being, than the head of the first, Q'ama'psəm, began to pursue him. Just

[1] The two brothers are now in a new home.
[2] The narrator interchanges liver and lungs.

the head came rolling along. Cougar began to run. He knew that the head was getting pretty close. He came to a bay. He could now hear something rolling and grumbling; it was the power of Q'ama'p-səm. He came to another place where he found a man fishing. It was Thunder, a middle-aged man. Every time he moved, he roared and flashed lightning. "I'm in a tight place," Cougar said to him, "I'm fleeing for my life; my enemy is close." "I'll help you, my boy. Don't lose your balance when you cross over," Thunder answered. Thunder then lay down across the bay and Cougar crossed over. This was at Grays Harbor or some place like that.[1] He reached Thunder's camp in safety. Thunder trusted Cougar. "Listen," he said to him, "you'll hear me condemn Q'ama'psəm's head." Cougar had just crossed the bay, when Q'ama'psəm came. "Cross over, but don't touch me with your cane,"[2] Thunder said to him, knowing that this was just what Q'ama'psəm would do. Q'ama'psəm did touch him with his cane.[3] Now something can be heard roaring in the ocean. It goes "rər··", like a cannon ball; it is Q'ama'psəm's head. Thunder then declared, "Nothing like this shall happen in the next generation."

Cougar stayed at Thunder's camp. He had to pay Thunder by carrying poles for him. He had his tamanoas with him, a power of his own. He went to some huge trees that were lying on the ground. He could not lift them by his own strength. But there was tamanoas in the air, all over the world. He slapped the log five times and it turned into a small pole. He lifted it to his shoulder and threw it into Thunder's camp. As soon as it struck the ground, it turned into normal size. He did the same thing five times and then had all the trees that Thunder wanted. "You have finished your work. You are free now," Thunder said.

Ever since he parted from his little brother, cougar buries some venison for him so that wildcat can help himself.

COUGAR AND WILDCAT.

(Type Two).[4]

Cougar (s.wa'wa) and Wildcat (x̣e¹wʋ's) were brothers. Cougar was a great hunter; he always killed elk and deer. Wildcat would not do anything. He was even too lazy to gather wood to cook the game that his brother had killed. He always wished that someone would come to help them eat the meat so that he would not have to look for wood. One day when he was in the forest gathering wood, he began to sing,

[1] The narrator explains here, "Since this story is found everywhere, it can apply to any bay."
[2] Evidently the "leg-bridge" motif is implied here.
[3] Thunder moves and rolls the head off into the water.
[4] Told by Joe Pete, 1926.

Who will come to eat with us ?
Who will come to eat with us ?

An old man came out and said, "I will eat with you." The old man ate up everything they had. Both Cougar and Wildcat were afraid that he would eat them, too.

They planned to get rid of him. They made a pillow of a big rock and the old man lay down with his head on it. As soon as he fell asleep, they would roll a big log from the fireplace onto his head and kill him. At last the old man fell asleep. They rolled the log down and cut his head off. The head chased them to Westport. There they found an old man living on the south side. They told him that an old man was chasing them. He stretched his legs across to the north side and they crossed over. When the head got there, he asked the old man if he had seen the boys. The old man said that he had and offered to take him across. When the head was half-way across, he drew his foot up and the head fell off and drowned. It drifted down to the ocean and is now a sign of good or bad weather; when the roar of the ocean is heard from the south, there will be a storm; when heard from the north, the weather will be good.[1]

FOX AND STEHE'N.[2]

Fox (snik·'υ'l) had five children. Stehe'n[3] had one grandchild, a young boy with a lame hip. Fox sent his boys out to look for tamanoas, and Stehe'n sent his grandchild out to do the same. In the evening, Fox's children returned. Stehe'n's grandchild also returned. The lame boy said to his grandfather, "The Foxes stay out on the prairie and catch grass-hoppers instead of looking for tamanoas." Next day Stehe'n sent his grandson out again, and Fox also sent his children out. They were preparing the young people, so that they could send them to a large gathering. But the young Foxes spent their time looking for grass-hoppers. Stehe'n's grandchild spent his time looking for tamanoas and did not deceive his grandfather. The young Foxes went out five times. Then their father said, "Well, my children, you may now go to the celebration. Some people who live far from here are playing the hoop-game." Fox wanted his children to steal the hoop, which was a very wonderful one; whenever it was rolled, it shone clear to heaven. "All right, we'll go," the young Foxes said. Their father thought that by this time, they must have very good tamanoas. Stehe'n said, "My boy wants to go along." "Certainly not," Fox answered, "your grandson is lame and won't be able to keep up

[1] The narrator said that this was a true weather omen.
[2] Told by Peter Heck, 1926. See p. 390.
[3] English equivalent unknown; an animal with stripes across shoulders, said to live in the mountains or along the river.

with my boys. They're very swift." They argued back and forth. Finally Fox said, "All right. He may go, but don't feel bad if he gets left behind or killed."

The young Foxes set out, and young Stehe'n went along with them. He managed to keep up with them. They arrived at the place, and saw the people playing with the hoop; the hoop belonged to some young princes. They went right to the center of the playground, where the players were rolling the hoop back and forth. One of the young Foxes made a motion as if to grab the hoop. Bluejay (payʊ'k'w) said to his sister, "He's trying to grab it!" Bluejay was the only one who had noticed this. The players rolled the hoop five times, and then the young Foxes grabbed it and ran. Young Stehe'n ran behind, limping. The people ran after them. They caught the eldest of the young Foxes. Just before his pursuers killed him, young Fox threw the hoop to his next brother. They then ran after the second one. They caught him and he threw the hoop to his third brother. The little lame boy was coming right behind him. They caught the third one and he threw the hoop to his next brother. They caught the fourth one and he threw the hoop to his next brother. Then they killed the fourth one. A little farther on, they caught the smallest of the young Foxes. He threw the hoop to young Stehe'n. Young Stehe'n caught it. "You'll get caught!" the youngest of the Foxes cried. Young Stehe'n ran. They chased him. Just as they were about to catch him, young Stehe'n slapped his hip. He ceased to limp. Then he called upon his tamanoas. "They've just about got me!" he cried. He slapped his hip and called again upon his tamanoas. Thereupon a fog came. The people chased him and chased him. The fog became thicker. Young Stehe'n had called upon his tamanoas to bring fog. His pursuers could no longer see, and so they lost sight of him. They lost their way and never returned home.[1] By this time, young Stehe'n had already left the fog behind.

Young Stehe'n shouted to his grandfather and Fox, "Ah, Fox, all your children were killed." Fox and Stehe'n heard someone shouting. They listened. "Ah, Fox," Stehe'n said, "your children have been killed." "No, it sounds as though your grandchild has been killed," Fox said. They could hear very plainly now. "Your children never got tamanoas at all," Stehe'n said. "See here, Stehe'n," Fox said, "if you don't believe me when I tell you that your grandchild was killed, we'll settle it one way or another: we'll urinate on one another. If your grandchild was killed, you'll turn yellow. If my children were killed, I'll turn yellow." Stehe'n agreed to this. They urinated on one another. Fox turned yellow. "There! Your sons were killed," Stehe'n said. Fox did not say anything, but he felt very bad.

---

[1] I learned a year later that these people became the Tamanoas.

The former lame boy returned, his hoop on his shoulder. He was lame no longer. "You'd better give me half of that," Fox said, "cut it in two. That hoop was the cause of my children's death. You've got to give me half." Young Stehe'n had obtained Swan as a tamanoas. "No," he said, "your boys spent their time eating grass-hoppers and never got a power. I can't give you half." Fox wept for his sons. Young Stehe'n divided the hoop equally with his grandfather. Fox is yellow to this day.

K'walale·'··i

STEELHEAD AND SPRING SALMON.

(First Version).[1]

Spring Salmon (ts'a'wł) had a young brother, Silver Eel (a'qws). Steelhead (sqe'oẋ) had a brother, Trout (pak'wa'wc).

Steelhead and his brother always came here in the winter. They always stayed in the Chehalis River as they belonged here, naturally. They travelled everywhere together. In the summer they would go down the river to the ocean and in the winter they would come back and make their living. Once upon a time, in the early spring, the two brothers were going down the river on their way to the ocean. Steelhead had a powerful tamanoas. Even if he should be killed and cut into many pieces, his tamanoas would bring him back to life. This was his power. While they were on their way, Steelhead said to his brother, "Let us rest now and have some lunch. Then we shall start off again." After they had finished eating, they heard someone coming up the river. They stopped and listened. At last a man and a boy came in sight. This man, whose head was very large, was Spring Salmon and the boy was his brother, Silver Eel. Although Spring Salmon's head was very large, his body was quite thin. Silver Eel was not especially fat either. Spring Salmon stopped, intending to make friends with Steelhead and Trout. "Can you tell me the way to the Falls at the head of the river?" he asked. Steelhead did not answer as Spring Salmon was a stranger. Furthermore, he did not like the man's looks nor those of his companion. Steelhead was a natural born fighter and here was a chance for a fight. Spring Salmon asked the same question, but this time in a rough voice, "Ä···, where is the way to the Falls?" As soon as he had finished, Steelhead said, "I don't know what you're talking about. I never listen to a person like you or take any interest in his business. Your head is large, your body is small and you look terrible." Thereupon Spring Salmon answered, "I'm asking you for the last time. If you don't answer, I'll break you to pieces." But Steelhead merely replied, "There's no one in this world who can do that!" "I'll break you to pieces!" Steelhead cried, and jumped at him. They fought

[1] Told by Jonas Secena, 1927. See p. 408.

all day. As the two chased one another back and forth on the riffle, Steelhead's younger brother, Trout, cried as loud as he could. Since that time, trout's mouth has been of normal size. At last Steelhead was beaten.

After his brother's death, Trout gathered up the bones and took them ashore; he knew that his dead brother, by the aid of his tamanoas could be revived.

Spring Salmon and Silver Eel had taken Steelhead's flesh, fat and oil to use for themselves; then they had gone on up the river to the Falls. Ever since that time, spring salmon has been nice and fat and so has silver eel, who used only the oil.

After he had taken Steelhead's bones ashore, Trout arranged them in their proper order. A few muscles remained and he arranged them in their proper order, also. Some of the bones were too badly crushed to be of any use. As soon as his tamanoas came to him, Steelhead came to his senses and directed his brother as his tamanoas had bidden him. "Find a short vine-maple and get some leaves," he said. It was springtime and the vine-maple was in blossom. Trout brought some blossoms, some tiny limbs, and leaves. Steelhead then began to pour the leaves and the blossoms into his body to take the place of his missing entrails. He whittled the limbs and used them in place of his broken bones. He recovered and stayed about the river for a few days. As soon as he was well enough to travel, he said to his young brother, "Let us go down the river and finish our trip to the ocean. I shall recover there, regain my flesh, but I shall forever have the vine-maple in my entrails. Part of my body, my fat and oil, is gone, but I shall live without it." He stayed in the ocean all that summer and returned the following winter, perfectly well.

Since that time, the spring salmon has come here every year, where formerly he did not belong. But Steelhead was always a native of the Chehalis River, even before X̣wɑnä'x̣wɑne created here. At present, he has some of the purity of the vine-maple in his body — its pure leaves and blossoms. Its limbs are his bones. Some of its oil is in his flesh. It would seem that vine-maple was his relative.

Steelhead and his brother fought no more with Spring Salmon. Both Salmon lived in the river from that time on.

STEELHEAD AND SPRING SALMON.

(Second Version).[1]

Steelhead had come up the Chehalis to spawn and now it was time for him to go back down home. He was nice and fat. He met Spring Salmon and Eel (a'q̣ws) on their way up. They attacked him and finally got the best of him, taking away all his fat. Spring

[1] Told by Peter Heck, 1927.

Salmon took some of the fat for himself and gave the rest to Eel. Then they let him go.

In some way Steelhead managed to obtain some iron-wood to make himself a new backbone but he could not think of anything that would serve as his skin. At last he found a skin that a snake had shed. "This shall be my skin," he said. He made his backbone from iron-wood; that's why he has a tough backbone.[1]

Now spring salmon and eel have steelhead's fat. That's why steelhead becomes very thin when it is time for him to go downstream. If it had not been for spring salmon and eel, steelhead would still be nice and fat.

MALƐ'ʾ.[2]

Malɛ'ʾ had a grandson. The old man owned two dogs. The young man would go out every day, and, when he returned in the evening, would make arrows. He did this for five evenings, but said nothing.

The young man had an enemy, Lion (waq̓'e'sx̣enasx̣ena).[3] After the fifth day, he was ready to fight his enemy and set out to find him. Lion always walked with his head between his legs, in order to see if anyone were coming behind him. The young man put some of his arrows in every little canyon along the Chehalis River, near the present town of Chehalis. He found his enemy quite some distance beyond, walking with his head down between his legs, and digging as he walked. He sneaked up in front of Lion, who was looking in the opposite direction, grabbed him by the back of the head, and cut his throat. He killed him right there on the spot. And so he did not have to use his arrows. That's why they call these canyons X̣a'lsənʾ[4] — because he did not have to use his arrows. Then he skinned Lion and packed the skin to all the different prairies. He took it to Squally, he took it everywhere, but none of the prairies were large enough to allow him to stretch the skin out to dry. He took it to one prairie after another. Finally he found one that was large enough. And there he spread the skin out over practically the whole of the prairie. That's why we call this prairie nɪx·q'wa'nx̣tən[5] (where a hide is spread out to dry).

Malɛ'ʾ has been left alone ever since his grandchild killed Lion, for the young man never returned. For some reason or other, Malɛ'ʾ[6] and his two dogs turned into a rock.[7]

---

[1] The old people used to cook salmon backbones and chew them for the juice, but they could never chew steelhead's.

[2] Told by Peter Heck, 1927. See p. 418.

[3] The Kathlamet have the same term; see BBAE: 26, p. 9, Boas.

[4] I cannot give the meaning of this term.

[5] Now known as Mima prairie.

[6] Mr. Heck told this story for a particular reason. Some people call Moon's mother Male'ʾ (or Mali'); others call Moon's grandmother this instead. These people maintain that Male'ʾ is a native term. On the other hand,

NORTHEAST WIND AND SOUTHWEST WIND.[1]

For a very long time, the animals were people. Year after year, the people had trouble with Northeast Wind (to'lotsən). Many died off; no one lived very long. (In this period, Elk[2] (qe'letən) was also taking the lives of those on earth.) The Northeast Wind continually raided the Southwest Wind (to'tc'αlc). Northeast Wind, along with his brothers, was commander of the tribes back east; he and his brothers nearly froze the people to death. They brought both snow and ice. The southwest people organized against them. Southwest Wind lived in the (Pacific) ocean. He declared war on Northeast Wind, who lived in the sky. Southwest Wind said, "We must make preparations. My grandmother will make the baskets in which to carry water." Everyone made ready for war. It was going to be difficult to reach the sky. All the young men — Bluejay, Crow, Wolf, Cougar, Bear, Snake, every last one of them — were going along. Snake (o'q'wa) was a great fellow, a warrior; he was cross-eyed. They made a trail up to the sky. Snow-bird had pulled the sky down by the aid of his tamanoas.[3] It was cold up there in the sky. They fought. No one from Southwest Wind's side was killed, but two were missing; Snake was one of them. He did not return, and later, they took it for granted that he had been killed.

Snake had a young sister, Toad. She wailed,

> Oh, my brother, he is cross-eyed,
> That's why he's missing.

But Snake eventually found his way home. He heard his sister wailing. He crept up to her, murdered her, and ate her. Thus, whenever a snake sees a toad, he murders her, for Toad once made fun of his cross-eyes.

The people again fought the Northeast Winds. The seven brothers came and caused the people to die of cold. Finally, Southwest Wind came from the ocean with boiling hot water, — which he brought through the air. He poured the water on the ice but it did no good. He went back to the ocean. His grandmother's help was his last hope: she was making a basket with tiny holes to use as a water-sprinkler. At last, Southwest Wind and his grandmother alone wiped out the Northeast Wind nation. Five of the seven brothers were killed. Only two still remain in the sky. (Southwest Wind also prevented Elk

---

Mr. Heck maintains that they had never called Moon's mother or grandmother this until after they had heard about the Virgin Mary from the Catholics. He said, however, that there was a native term similar to Male'', but that it was the name of a male character in a story. To prove his point, he told this story.

[7] At Lequito.

[1] Told by Jonas Secena, 1926. See p. 414.

[2] Here identified with a star, said to be probably Jupiter.

[3] The narrator added this incident a year later.

from killing any more earth people.) Snow and Frost still remain alive but no longer have the power to freeze people to death. Southwest Wind said, "Nothing like this shall happen to the new generation of peoples. There shall be snow and freezing weather, but they shall not kill people." That's why we still have a little snow and frost. But southwest wind always comes and melts them.

THE BATTLE WITH SNOW.[1]

The people were living in a certain village. Winter came and it began to snow. There were hard times. Before long the snow was so deep that it covered the houses. In order to visit one another, the people had to tunnel a passage-way under the snow from house to house. Every house was buried under. The people began to grow uneasy. They did not know what to do about it. "We must do something about it, or we'll starve and die right here," they said. Then the head man, the chief, said, "We can't do anything about the snow here; we'll have to fight Snow on his own ground." All agreed. "We'll fight," they said. As soon as the snow melted the chief said, "We'll go north. That's where Snow has his home." Early that fall they began their preparations. "We don't want the snow again this winter," they said. They gathered together all the frogs, snakes and animals to accompany them and set out.

They stopped over night. Next day they continued their journey. The next night they stopped again. The third night, the chief said, "From now on, we'll travel through the air, up through the sky." Every last one of them went up. (I don't know how they got there.) When evening came, they stopped again for the night. The next morning they were in heaven, in another world. They reached the place where Snow lived. "We'll attack him as early as we can," the chief said.

Mouse (sk'wata'^{a}n) went to Snow's house. She sneaked in and cut the strings of his bow to shreds. She went to the bow of the second Snow and cut it to shreds. She did the same to two others. By this time, it was daybreak and she had to leave. She had no time for the remaining bow. She fled back to her people. "Well, I've done something very useful to you. You'll surely whip them," she said. "That's good," the people answered.

Early the same morning, they marched upon Snow's house. There were five Snows, all brothers. They jumped for their bows and found four of them in shreds. Only the bow of the youngest Snow remained intact. The Earth-people fought with bows and arrows. The youngest Snow, alone, could do very little. He fled to the north. The Earth-people ransacked the house. They ran away with all the property and food they could find. Snake (o'q'wa) had no chance to get anything but a few yellow, white and red

[1] Told by Peter Heck, 1926. See p. 414.

basket straws, and a piece of buckskin, already smoked. The people left him and Rattlesnake to gather up the leavings. Rattlesnake eventually lost his bearings and never found his way home again.

The people returned. They had won from Snow; he had fled to the north. At last Snake found his way home. He heard his cousin, Frog, crying for him. But Frog's words were not very complimentary, in fact, they were slightly slanderous:

Snake was looking up like this,[1]
That's why he was left behind.

Snake was furious. But another of Frog's kind, Water-dog, was crying properly for his cousin Snake. Now, Snake was satisfied. He gave Water-dog his buckskin. That's why water-dog has a tough hide. To another of Water-dog's kind, Lizard, he gave some of the basket straws. That's why lizard has stripes. To these two cousins who had cried properly for him, he gave presents. But Frog received nothing. "I'll never be friends again with you, Frog!" Snake said. Whenever snake sees frog he bites him and swallows him. This is how their enmity began.

Rattlesnake, left behind, finally found his way down from heaven, but he landed east-of-the-mountains, in Yakima country. The Chehalis country was his original home. That's why we have no rattlesnakes here today.

Snake put the remaining basket straws on his back. That's why some snakes have nice yellow or white stripes on their backs.

Thus the Snows were beaten. Only the youngest one remains. That's why we don't have much snow now. If Mouse had not cut the bows, we would still have deep snows. The youngest brother, who alone survived, brings the snow. At that time snow was a human being.

K'walale·'··i

THE SEAL HUNTER.[2]

The people were living in a village. A certain man had five sons, all of whom had tamanoas. Each one, however, had a different kind. The third had sea-hunter's tamanoas; he could kill seal, whale, or anything that lived in the sea. That was his trade. The eldest son was a canoe builder; he made Chinook canoes. He had no other occupation.

The younger of these two brothers went seal hunting. He came home with one seal. Next day, he dressed and cooked it. Then he invited the people to eat with him. His elder brother, the canoe maker, did not go to the feast but his wife did. The seal-hunter then

[1] That is, somewhat cross-eyed.
[2] Told by Peter Heck, 1926. See p. 416.

gave his sister-in-law some meat for his brother. When the canoe maker came home in the evening, his wife told him about the feast. "Your brother did not send you any meat," she said. She had hidden the meat for herself.

Next day the younger brother went seal hunting again. He caught one seal. The following day he dressed the seal and cooked it. Then he invited the people to eat with him. His elder brother did not come, so he gave his sister-in-law some meat to take to him. When her husband came home that evening, the woman told him the same story. "Your brother did not send you anything to eat," she said. Then her husband became angry with his brother who was so greedy.

Next day the younger brother went hunting again and caught one seal. Then he cooked the seal and invited the people as before. He gave his sister-in-law some meat to take to his brother. The woman did not give her husband the meat but hid it for herself. By this time the canoe maker was very angry with his younger brother. "I must do something to him for this. He doesn't like me. I must make a seal," he said to himself. He cut a piece of cedar and set to work to carve it like a seal. He fixed it and towed it to the bay. The cedar seal merely floated down the bay. He caught it and towed it in. It merely floated as before. He fixed it over, but still it merely floated. But then it suddenly did a little more than float — it seemed to move a bit, also. "I've just about got it now," he said. He took it out. Then he threw it in. The seal dived and came out again. He did not quite know what it was, but something still seemed to be wrong with the seal. He fixed it again and threw it in. The seal dived and came out.[1] He ordered it to dive again, and it obeyed. He then put it on the fire and it cracked all over in spots. After that, he ordered it to go to the place where the seals were accustomed to stay. "Stay there in the middle," he said. "When my brother comes, the seals always become frightened, but you must stay there." The seal then went to the place and landed. The other seals soon began to flock around him; he was the largest of them all.

The three brothers[2] came to the place where the seals stayed. They tried to catch the largest ones. The largest one of all did not move fast enough and they speared him. He reared off through the water and pulled so hard on their line that they could not kill him. He pulled them westward. The linesman tried to pull and hold but his hand stuck to the line. His two brothers told him to let go. They were now far out of sight of the timberline. The two brothers then tried to help but their hands also stuck to the line. They were being pulled out into the ocean. They began to think that the seal never

[1] Illustrating.

[2] It would seem that the seal-hunter is now accompanied by two of his brothers. More than one person is now necessary for the action of the story.

would come out. They went night and day for five whole days. At last they saw some trash drifting on the water. Then before long they saw some timber. They were now headed for shore. When the seal struck shore, it just lay there. It was nothing but a piece of cedar — it was no longer a seal. The brothers then realized what had happened. "Our brother did this to us! It was he, all right!" they said to one another. They landed and stepped out of their canoe. Their hands no longer stuck to the line.

They found themselves in a strange country. "We don't know where we are, but somebody must live here," they said. They pulled their canoe far up on the beach. Then the two elder brothers tipped the canoe over their little brother, so that he would be safe while they went off to investigate. They came to a river that showed signs of habitation. Before long they found a very large house and looked in. An old man was lying on the bed, warming his back by the fire. He knew them and said, "Come in, grandchildren." They were pleased that he had said 'grandchildren'. They went in. "Are you the young men who went away to buy a seal — a seal your brother made?" he asked. They nudged one another as if to say, "How does he know all this?" They admitted that they were the young men in question. "Are there only the two of you?" he then asked. "No, we left our little brother on the shore," they answered. "Run right back and get him! I have some very large mosquitoes there," he said. They went back to the canoe immediately and found a large hole in it. Nothing but blood stains remained where their little brother had lain. "The mosquitoes must have eaten him up," they decided. "Where's your brother?" the old man asked as soon as they got back. "The mosquitoes evidently ate him up," they answered. The old man's name was Ne′pius; he was a giant but his visitors were of normal size. "Well, boys," he said, "you're pretty far from home and I don't know how you're ever going to get back."

Ne′pius owned a fish-trap. "Grandchildren," he said to the young men, "I'm going fishing now." He left them. He had a net sunk for fish. "Don't look, grandchildren, when you hear anything," he had said before he left. Before long, they heard him say, "ʔchi·′ iyəhı′·." They peeped through the cracks: he was pulling up something very heavy. He had just got it up, when it fell back again. He came back to the house. He was very angry and kicked the fire-logs so that the sparks flew in their direction. One of them got burnt.

Next day, Ne′pius again announced to the young men that he was going fishing and told them not to look when they heard a noise. But as soon as they heard him grunt, they could not restrain themselves; they just had to see what he was doing. Ne′pius lost his catch again. He came into the house angry and kicked the fire toward them.

Next day Ne′pius did not go fishing. He told his visitors to be on the lookout for something to happen. Before long they heard someone chopping trees farther up the river. Another old man, L'αmx̣αma·'ɩp[1], had a fish-trap there. He was angry because Ne'pius had a trap below him. He was throwing trees, limbs and all, into the river so that they would float down and spoil Ne'pius's trap. Ne'pius went down the river to investigate the damage. He picked up five trees that had lodged against his trap and threw them right over it. He then came back to the house and gave each of the young men some sort of a wooden hammer with a handle. "Use this on that fellow when he comes to fight me," he said. But the hammer was so heavy they could not lift it. They took the burning logs from the fireplace instead and pushed them against L'αmx̣αma·'ɩp as he was fighting with Ne'pius. When the fight was over, the old fellow asked Ne'pius, "Where did you get these rascals?"

This was his fifth attempt to get the best of Ne'pius.

Ne'pius went fishing four times. The fifth and last time, he told the young men, as before, that they must not look when they heard a noise. They heard the noise but did not look. He returned to the house with some fish, as they had obeyed orders for once. "Well, grandchildren," he said, "we have some fish now, something good to eat." The fish proved to be a whale. He cut off the tail and gave them a roasting stick for it. "Here, grandchildren, use this for a roasting stick," he said. But the stick was so heavy they could not lift it. And the whale's tail was so heavy they could not lift it, either. "What's the matter, boys?" he asked. He then cooked the tail for them. Later he asked, "Would you like to go home?" "Yes," they answered, "but we don't know how to get there." Then he told them to go to their "grandfather" and ask him to take them home. "He lives near here and always goes up your way," he explained. When they got to their "grandfather" they found that he was Whale. "Are you the young men with whom the seal ran away?" he asked. "Yes, we are," they answered, "Ne'pius told us to ask you to take us home. He said you always go that way." "When I am ready to go, I'll take you," he promised.

When Whale was ready, he came to the young men and said, "Well, I'm ready now, but I don't know how you two will manage as I always travel under water." However, he took a knife and cut a hole in himself large enough for them to crawl into. They were afraid but they crawled in and closed the door. They came to a village and Whale made his first stop. He came out of the water and they opened the door. "Is this the place?" he asked. They came out and looked around. "No," they said and closed the door. They went on. After they had travelled a long way, Whale came out at another village. "Is this the place?" he called. They came out and looked. "No," they said. Whale dived back in again. They came to another village and Whale stopped. They opened the door.

[1] Also a giant. See p. 124.

"Is this the place?" he asked. "No," they said and he dived back in again. He went on and on. Finally he came out at another village. They opened the door. "Is this the place?" he asked. "No," they said and he dived in again. He came out at another village. "Is this the place?" he asked. "Yes, grandfather," they said, "will you help us land on that side?" "All right," Whale said. Then they explained, "All on the bay side are against us, but all on the shore side are in sympathy with us." Whale landed and they got out.

The two young men went immediately to their father and mother. "There's a whale that brought us here out in the bay," they said. The news of a dead whale out in the bay soon spread throughout the village. Everybody went out to get some blubber. All those who were angry with the young men worked on the water side[1] [or bayside]. They cut the blubber lengthwise and laid it back. But just as they had about finished and were standing close to the body, the whale rolled over and killed them all. The brother who had made the seal was among those killed. After that it was ordained that anyone who did not get enough to eat at a feast should not become angry or make an imitation seal with which to trick someone.

THE QWEQWASTA'IMUX̂.

(First Version).[2]

In the beginning, there was a northwest warrior who was travelling all over the world. He once came to a tribe from whom he borrowed a canoe. It was an ocean-going canoe and would hold about twenty people. He went hunting and spying in this, for he was a warrior; he had warriors' tamanoas. After he had been out on the ocean for a few hours, a storm blew up. The storm soon became very wild. He did not know much about the canoe and a wave carried him down to a place where no human had ever lived. He clung to his paddle. Finally, his canoe went to pieces. He found himself in an ocean channel. Then along came a large tree, roots and all. He clung to the tree and pulled himself up. There he lived for many days. All that time, he was calling upon his tamanoas to help him. At last he landed among the Qweqwasta'imvx̂ tribe (imaginary people). These people were very small, like boys of three or four years. None of them were of natural size. They took him home so that he could warm himself and kept him there until he was able to eat. They gave him salmon and other things. He lived there for several years, during which time he saw many wonderful things.

The Qweqwasta'imux̂ were having trouble with another tribe. Their visitor went to see what was going on, as he was a warrior and liked to see anything pertaining to fighting. He arrived at that

[1] The side farthest from shore.

[2] Told by Jonas Secena, 1926. See p. 419.

section of the tribe that was being raided by the enemy. He saw that the Geese came along and dropped their feathers. The feathers, flying in all directions, stuck the Qweqwasta'imux̂ and killed them. He was surprised to find that it was nothing but feathers that was killing them. This aroused his curiosity. He went over to one of the dead people and pulled a feather out of him. Before long, the person came to. He then pulled the feathers out of all the dead people. Then he made a weapon for killing the Geese. He made an arrow from red fir and a bow from yew wood. The whole tribe learned to make and to use this weapon. Thus, after many years, the Qweqwasta'imux̂ were at last freed from their enemies. Their visitor told them that the Geese would make good food and so, before long, they were making part of their living from the Geese. After that, they treated their visitor like a good fellow.

The Qweqwasta'imux̂ lived on sea food, a slender little shell[1] (like a piece of macaroni). They would break the shell on the end and suck out the contents. This was their chief nourishment.

After the warrior had been with them for about three years, they helped him to return home. While on the way back—he had already reached this world — he came to a place where a great war was going on. He stopped with the tribe that was being defeated. He went out to the place where they were fighting and found that they had no weapons with which to fight the enemy. The enemy were fighting with a slinger, a sharp stick like an arrow, attached to a cord of elk-tendon. The slinger could travel a long way. One day, when the fight was taking place on water, he made a bow and gave it to his friends, who had never used a bow before. They whipped the enemy in one battle and pursued them to their homes. They killed all those of a certain age and made slaves of the children. The warrior stayed with these people for some time and then they sent him back this way. It took him six or seven years before he got home.

He could never prove to his own people that the Qweqwasta'imux̂ were real people.

THE QWESTA'IMUX̂

(Second Version).[2]

Two men once stole some salmon from the Qwesta'imux̂.[3] They saw a little man diving; he came out with a salmon on each finger. They stole his salmon when he was not looking. The little man came out of the water, and from the end of his canoe looked about. He saw that two men had stolen his salmon. Although he was very

[1] The dentalia.
[2] Told by Peter Heck, 1927.
[3] Tiny people, who are believed to have lived in the north.

tiny, he was very strong; without any difficulty, he picked up the two men and carried them home.

The Qwesta'imux̯ told the men that someone was coming to fight them. "Here they come!" the Qwesta'imux̯ said at last. Their enemies proved to be the Ducks.[1] Hell Diver (sənx·ɔ'l') was the only woman with the Ducks. The Ducks flew above the Qwesta'imux̯ and shot their feathers at them; their feathers were their arrows. Whenever the Ducks got down too low, Hell Diver, who was flying beneath them, would shout, "Down too low!" The two men beat the Ducks with sticks. They removed the feathers from the wounded and the latter recovered. Then they showed them how to fight the Ducks. The two men cooked the dead Ducks. The Qwesta'imux̯ gave them their freedom for helping them.

They gave the men a canoe but refused to give them any dentalia (x̣aʟ'e''ɩk·). The Qwesta'imux̯ had great heaps of little shells piled up. They had sucked the insides out and had thrown the shells away. (These shells were the dentalia.) The two men, however, wanted very much to have some of the dentalia, so they put pitch on the bottoms of their canoes to pick the shells up. There were various kinds — the short variety and the long variety; they stuck to the bottom of the canoe. That's how dentalia first got here.

THE YOUNG MAN WHO WAS STOLEN BY LION.[2]

The people were living together in a village. They were having a big time, a dance. They had invited some outsiders to come. They intended to dance all night. Near morning, they would feed their guests.

One woman, while there, had given birth to a child. She was outside in a shed. She longed to go in and look on. But the people were afraid of her. (They fear a woman who has just given birth to a child.) The woman finally left her baby, went up to the house, and peeped through a crack. She was so absorbed, that she forgot all about her baby. Suddenly, she remembered him, and went back. In the meantime, someone had stolen her child. She wept. Before long, the others heard her and learned what had happened. They suspected that Lion (X̣oqwa'lp) had stolen the child.

Lion had indeed stolen the child. Crane (sq'was) had also been a party to the theft. The two of them intended to rear the child as their own. In the meantime, the big time kept on. Lion went out to look for (what was to her) roots and berries. She carried a basket with a small mouth. When she got back home, she emptied her basket; it was filled with lizards and other such disagreeable things. She squeezed some juice from a lizard over the baby's mouth. The

[1] X̣a'tx̣at (singular form) or q'ɛ·'letsti'la (singular form); the two terms are interchangeable.
[2] Told by Peter Heck. See p. 418.

baby did not like this; he shook his head and cried and cried. Next day, Lion went out again. Crane went out also. He got a newly hatched salmon[1] and took it home. He rolled the tiny fish in some leaves and buried it in the ashes. As soon as it was done, he fed it to the baby. The baby liked it.

Everyone was afraid to attempt the child's rescue. Lion would kill them if they went near her. In five days' time the child had grown considerably. Crane made him a bow and arrow and told him what had happened. The boy was already a big fellow (for, in all the stories, children grow up in five days). "If you want to kill Lion, you can," Crane said, "when you start after her, don't creep upon her from behind, for she will see you; she always digs roots with her head down between her legs. Approach her from the front."

The youth went out and found a place where there were reptiles and rotten logs. There was Lion, digging just as Crane had said. He approached her from the front, and, when close to her, shot her. Crane had said, "As soon as you hit her, run to my mountain over there; I have a tree there. Climb the tree and she won't be able to get you. Then splice the tree to the end of your bow and climb up to heaven." Lion did not know who had shot her. The youth ran away immediately and was soon some distance away. He climbed the mountain and found Crane's tree. Lion came to the tree, but she did not know how to climb and had to turn back. She would go home and eat Crane.

In the meantime, Crane made wings so that he could fly. He had some arrows, and as soon as he saw Lion coming he shot her. She jumped at him. Then he flew away from her and shot again. He shot her five times, and the fifth time, he killed her. Then he made a fire and burned her. "This shall never happen again. Whenever a woman gives birth to a child outside, no one shall steal her child," he said to her burning body. When Crane flies, he says, "Sq'as, sq'as, sq'as."

The youth spliced his bow to the tree and climbed up to heaven. He came out on a large prairie covered with grass. He did not know where to go. It was very early in the morning. He took the trail through the open prairie. Before long, he saw a grey dog coming. Then he saw that there were five grey dogs. Behind them was a grey man. "Where did you come from?" the man asked. "I am the one who was stolen by Lion; Crane told me to come here to escape her," the youth answered. "Very well, young man, I have five daughters. Go to my house and stay with them," the man said. The youth felt better after this encounter.

He travelled all day. At last he saw five black dogs and a dark man. "Where are you from?" the man asked. "I was stolen by Lion; Crane told me to climb a tree and come up here," the youth answered. "Oh, yes, we have already heard that," the man said.

[1] Called "eyes-tied-together."

"Go to my house. I have five daughters; stay with them. I'm on my way down."

The youth went to the five girls. From the nose of each girl, hung an elongation shaped like an organ. He did not want to stay with these girls, but felt compelled to. Late in the evening, the dark man returned. He was packing a dead deer and a dead man, both of whom he had killed. The youth did not wish to eat human flesh and shoved the meat off his plate.

In the meantime, the grey man had returned home. "Did a youth come here?" he asked his daughters. "No, we haven't seen him," they said. "Well, then, go and get him," he said. The dark man was Evening, the grey man, Dawn. The girls set out for Evening's home.

The black girls fought the grey girls for the possession of the young man. The latter saw that the grey girls were pretty and decided to run away with them. Thus the grey girls won, for the young man preferred them. Dawn was satisfied when he saw the young man with them. Dawn always brought home good meat; he never returned with human bodies. The young man stayed there, for he could find no complaint with his new home. "You may have my youngest daughter," Dawn said to him. "Very well," he answered.

Dawn hunted continually. He would start out early every morning. The young man had noticed a nice little basket hanging on the wall. One day he and his wife went out to swim. When they returned, he went into the house to look for a comb. He could not find one and thought, "Perhaps there's one in the basket hanging there." Instead of a comb, he found a pretty young woman, who was smiling. She was the prettiest girl he had ever seen. He immediately jumped into bed and covered up. When the old man returned, he asked, "What's the matter with the youth?" "Oh, we went swimming, and after we returned, he wanted a comb. He looked in the basket for one, and then immediately threw himself on the bed and covered up," his youngest daughter explained. "Take the basket down for him," the old man said. The girl came out of the basket. The old man told her to sleep with the young man. The young man then took the girl for his wife and had no more to do with his former wife.

The young woman bore him twins; the children were born stuck together. When one walked forward, the other walked backward, and vice-versa. One day the young couple were sitting down outside. The young man began to scratch his head. "You must have a louse; lie down here and I will look for it," his wife said. As he lay on the ground, the young man idly pulled up some grass and made a hole in the ground. Through the hole, he saw far down to earth. He could see many buildings, only one of which was smoking. He jerked his head away from his wife and went to bed. When his father-in-law came home that night, he asked, "What's the matter with the youth?" "Oh, I was lousing his head; he pulled up some grass and made a hole. He looked down to earth and saw some old buildings there. It made him feel badly, so he went to bed," the young man's wife said. "You two may leave now; that's his home down there. Go over to your grandmother and ask her if she can take you down there," the old man said. The old woman, to whom he referred, was Spider. In the meantime, the old man prepared a great deal of meat and other things. The young couple went to Spider. "My father told us to ask you to take us down; my husband here pulled up some grass and made a hole through which he could see down to earth. He saw some buildings there — his former home from which he was stolen," the young woman said. "Very well, I'll let you down," the old grandmother said. The couple put all their belongings into Spider's basket, and then got in themselves. "Jerk the rope as soon as you get down, so that I can pull my basket back up," Spider said. They went down. As soon as they reached the earth, they jerked the rope and the basket started back up.

The young man went to the well and sat there to see who would come for water. Before long, a blind boy came crawling down for a drink. He went over to the boy and said, "Hello, brother." "Don't say that to me, Bluejay," the boy said. The boy thought that this was Bluejay making fun of him. "I am the one who was stolen; now I have returned," the young man said to him. Then he took hold of his young brother and blew upon his eyes. The blind boy then recovered his sight. The young man then slapped him on the head, for the boy was somewhat bald. The boy's hair then became thick. "Run back to your mother and tell her that your elder brother, who was stolen, has returned," the young man said. The little fellow ran back to his mother, who tried to strike him when he gave her the news. "You're Bluejay and are just making fun of me," she said, "my son was stolen." The boy explained that he could see now and that he had a thick growth of hair. "My brother said to bring you to the well," he said. At last he persuaded his mother to go with him. "Oh, my poor mother, you are blind, too," her elder son said when he saw her. He blew on her eyes, restoring her sight. Then he slapped her on the head, restoring her hair. "Go back to the house; sweep it and clean it well," he said.

The woman and the boy went back to the house, swept it and removed the refuse. Then the young man and his wife came to the house. There were some mats in one corner of the house, tied to the wall. (In the old houses, there was a beam through the middle of the house, just high enough to walk under.) Bluejay began to call to the blind boy from the beam, where he had gone to defecate, "Come, clean my back side." "Get a piece of burning wood and stick it on him," the young man said to his brother. The boy got the piece of burning wood and burned Bluejay's backside. "U··," Bluejay cried, "why did you do that?" He did the same thing five times to see what was up. Finally, he peeped through the walling of mats. "Why, there's the young man who was stolen!" he said. He began to weep. Now he knew why he had got his back side burnt.[1]

That evening, the young father planned a game for his twins. He made them some little bows and arrows; they would have a shooting-match. Some hanging fungi would serve as targets. One child would shoot at the fungi at one end of the house, the other, at the fungi at the other end. Bluejay began to think about the children. "They're the strangest boys I've ever seen. Imagine, walking like that!" he said and picked up a stick. "Let them alone!" his sister said. The children walked past him five times. The last time, he struck at them — right where they were joined together — and separated them. One child fell this way, one fell that. Both were dead. Then Bluejay said to them, "This shall never happen again. When twins are born hereafter, they will not be stuck together." If it had not been for Bluejay, twins would still be born stuck together.

K'walale·'··i

SPEAR.[2]

Spear[3] (ts'a'x̣k·ən)[4] had a sister, Pαsi'nos, who always went out to get fern roots. Spear had put up a fish trap. As soon as his sister finished cooking the fern roots, he would come in and eat. He always put the base of his palm over his mouth as he ate, and his sister would wonder what was the matter with him.

Spear was always going to his trap, and his sister was always gathering fern roots. Spear could not eat anything but fern roots; that was why his sister had to go out for them so often.

But Spear was catching fish right along in his trap and was eating them all, himself. He did not tell his sister anything about it. He would save the salmon eggs and tie them to his wrist. When he ate, he would put his hand up to his mouth, so that his sister could not see what he was doing.

Pαsi'nos wondered continually why her brother always ate from his wrist. She could not figure out why he did this. It never occurred to her that if he should make a catch, he would eat it all himself and not give her any. She would think about it all day long. At last, deciding that he was deceiving her in some way, she said, "It would be best if I should leave that bad one and marry the chief, silver-side (sa'wanx̂u). I shall go far off and leave him."

---

[1] The narrator realized that this passage and the preceding one are also found in the Moon myth; see p. 172.

[2] Told by Mary Heck, 1927; interpreted by Peter Heck. See p. 417.

[3] That is, a salmon-spear.

[4] Throughout the story, the boy is called by the native term, but for the sake of convenience, I have used the English equivalent.

Next morning, she got ready and set out to find her intended husband. Then Spear discovered that his sister had gone. "What is the matter with my sister? Why hasn't she returned?" he said. He worried about it; he knew where she had gone, but still he wanted to find her. He went home and looked around to see which way she had gone. Her tracks led down to the river and then into the water. He followed until he was up to his neck, and then went back. "Oh, I know where she went. She must have gone to get married." He worried a great deal about his sister and how to find her. He went here and there, and cried and cried. He knew where she was, but still he wanted to go to her. "Oh, I think I'll go to see her," he said at last. He travelled, and travelled, and travelled (I don't know how many thousand miles) before he came to the large winter-house, where the earth and sky join. He went into the house. His sister was sitting down; she now had a little baby silver-side.

Spear, looking around, saw the sky, which reaches to the earth; there was nothing but sky. (They say that the sky is a blue rock; that is what we see when we look up.) Soon an old man arose and went outside. Then he began to call,

Come, come,
El- el- elk.

He called five times. Spear wondered why the old man was calling. Soon he heard something coming. An elk was standing close to the old man. Then he heard something fall to the ground. The old man had killed the elk and it had fallen with a thump. The old man then began to butcher it. When he came to the hind leg joints, he cut them across, but did not remove the feet from the hide. He cut all four legs at the joints and also cut the carcass off at the neck, but left the head intact in the skin. He did not cut the hide open at the legs, but just pulled the [whole] hide off, inside out. He had left the forelegs on, also. He rolled the carcass out, and stood the hide up on its feet. Then he told the elk [that is, the hide, with head and legs intact] to get up and go.

He cooked the entire carcass and served it whole in a trough-dish, wide at the top. He placed it before Spear. While Spear was eating, a woman, his brother-in-law's sister, came in. She had been picking huckleberries and had five little baskets, graduating in size until the last was very small. "What small baskets they use for picking berries!" Spear thought. The woman emptied the smallest basket into another trough-dish and served it to him. "It's so small I shan't get enough to eat," he thought, and was very dissatisfied. He ate every bit of the elk meat, the whole thing, and began on the huckleberries. He ate and ate. But still there were just as many berries on his plate as there were to start with. He could not finish them, because he had said, "What small baskets they use! I shan't get enough to satisfy me." That was why the berries had not decreased any in quantity. At last he gave up; he could not eat them all and pushed his plate aside. His sister came in and put the dish away.

The people were on the alert; they were waiting for someone, but Spear had not noticed this. He thought that his sister, her husband, and the old man, were the only people living in the house. The sun had gone down and it was growing dark. Then Spear heard someone howling at the river. The noise came closer and closer. "What can this be?" he thought. It was right at the door, now. He did not know that this was a customary thing with the people[1] of this place; it was their tamanoas howling. The newcomers opened the door. Spear watched closely. They came in dancing. There were many of them. Each one was holding something in his hand, — straight roasting-sticks, forked roasting-sticks, spears, broken spear-strings and so on. Everything that is used here on earth by the people to catch them with, they held in their hands. These were the black-salmon (k'walɛ'ʾ).[2]

Soon Spear heard the same noise again — the sound of howling. It came closer to the house. Then he heard a sound like the pounding of a tom-tom pole against the roof. All came in dancing, as the black-salmon had done; they held the same things in their hands. They danced around five times and then sat down. They were the silver-side (sa'wanx̂ᵘ).

Soon Spear heard the same sound as before. Now, they were at the door, pounding. All came in dancing, as the others had done. They had everything that the people here on earth use to catch them with, — broken spears and so on. In turn, they showed the people how proud they were of the property they had brought back. They were the dog-salmon (sno'nx̂ᵘ). They had gone from their world to the earth, in order to earn property.

Soon Spear heard the same noise. In a little while, they were at the door. They came in dancing, but they did not have much property with them; each one had very little. They danced five times around and then sat down. They were the spring-salmon (ts'a'wł). They did not have much property, for they would always hide so that the people could not catch them easily, while the others would always come up here [to earth] to have a good time and were given all the tools that are broken in catching them. They say that these things are presents to them from the people; but the spring-salmon would always hide from the people and that is why they got no presents.

---

[1] These are not real people, but (as I understand it from remarks the interpreter made) real fishes. They are not like other characters, who, although bearing fish names, are really considered human beings until transformed.

[2] This and the following terms for the various classes of salmon are given in the singular form.

Soon Spear heard the same noise again. They came to the door and did the same as the others — came in dancing. They had scarcely anything with them. They danced around five times and then sat down. They were the steelhead-salmon (sqe'ox̣) and did not have much property, for they would never play as the others would. They considered themselves too high-class to play. They stayed away, so that the people could not catch them and so they got no present.

These were the five nations of salmon, but all of them lived in the one house and were the children of the old man, who always stayed at home. His name was Sqwe'lius. His children, however, always came to this world — in all its rivers. His daughter's name was World's End[1] (nama'itαmx·).

After all the people had finished dancing, they went to bed. This was the first night of sleep for Spear; he had not slept since he had been there.

Toward morning, the people began to get up, and made preparations for leaving. They were gone before daylight. Only the four of them were left. Spear began to worry about what he was going to eat. But soon World's End took hold of her nephew, little silver-side, killed him, and cooked him for Spear to eat. Then Spear thought, "This is strange, feeding me my nephew!" When World's End served him the salmon, she said, "Eat the meat but save the bones. Put them in just one place, and don't break any." "All right," Spear said. He put every bone aside. Soon nothing was left but bones. Then Sqwe'lius came for the bones, covered them with a mat or something, and soon the bones became a little silver-side. The boy had come to life. He got up and walked around the same as before, although his uncle had eaten his body.

Spear stayed there five days, and each day they fed him his nephew, who always came to life afterwards. The fifth day, they fed him the boy again and he ate all of the meat but just one little piece, a little piece of bone with meat on it, the cheek-bone. When they tried to put the boy together, they found that a piece of bone was missing; Spear had not sucked the meat off it. They could not put little silver-side back together again, and he did not come to life. He died.

Then Spear's sister said, "You'll have to go back home for you've killed my son. If you had not killed him, you could have remained here with me, for I'm never going to return." After his sister had told him to go home, Spear thought, "I suppose it's just as well if I do, but I'm not going back the way I came. I'm not going back by way of the earth, but through the air." He set out.

He travelled a long way, and at last arrived at a large winter-house. He knew nothing about it, but went in anyway. A young woman was sitting down. He just "hit her heart".[2] "Oh, that's a

[1] The woman who gave Spear the berries.

[2] That is, he fell in love with her at first sight.

fine looking young woman; I should like her to be my wife, she's so pretty," he thought. He stayed there. Before long he heard the rumble of thunder. "Don't be afraid," the girl said, "it is my father coming back." Thunder's noise was terrific, and came closer and closer. Spear was frightened. Thunder (sto'qᵘ) was at the door now. He had no sooner arrived than he noticed Spear. Immediately he said, "If you want my daughter, you may have her for your wife." Spear was happy; this was just what he wanted. So the woman became his.

Spear slept with the woman that night. In the morning, all arose. Then Thunder said to his son-in-law, "You'll stay here with me. I'll let you alone for five days, but after the fifth day, I'll make you a person like myself; I'll teach you how to become Thunder." Spear remained there. At last the five days were up. On the fifth day, Thunder said, "Now I am going to teach you." They fixed Spear up and told him to try. He tried but could not do what he was supposed to do. They told him to clap his hands (or wings) but he could not make the noise. The following day, Thunder took him out again; he fixed him up at another place. But still Spear could not succeed. He was puzzled how to become like Thunder. After the fourth unsuccessful trial, he was frightened. "If I can't learn on my last trial, perhaps he'll kill me. I'd better leave. This place is dangerous (pɑ'sa). If I don't do what they tell me, they'll kill me." So he went on.

He travelled quite a way before he came to another winter-house. It was a large house, from which the smoke was coming. There was a smaller house to the side. He went up to the large house and peeped in. There was another good looking woman there. He went in. Soon a man returned. The latter no sooner entered, than he said to Spear, "If you want my daughter, you may marry her." Spear was happy. Now he had another wife. The two went to bed. In the morning, Spear's wife arose. Long afterward, Spear tried to get up, but found something heavy sticking to his back; it was a board. "Oh, I am in a dangerous place. I don't know how to take this off. I must get out of here," he thought. When he arose, he brought the whole board up with him, sticking to his back. He passed the little house. An old woman peeped out and said, "You had better wait." Then she took some dog-fish oil and began to work. She named the oil secretly with k·'ɪts'sta'ni[1] and oiled his back and sides. Pretty soon the board came off. Then she said to him, "Those people in whose house you stopped, are the Pitch People (itq̧wa'wł). No one stops there, they're afraid to. Any one visiting there gets stuck." As soon as the board was removed Spear went on.

---

[1] A kind of magic power, accompanied by secret words. This magic is not to be confused with tamanoas. Except that it works wonders, it is entirely different. It is mainly a prerogative of women, and is especially efficacious in affairs of the heart. See pp. 171, 378.

He travelled and travelled. At last he came to another house, from which the smoke was coming. He could not pass by without taking one look. There was an old man inside, and so he went in. "Where are you from?" the old man asked. "Oh I am he whose sister is married to silver-side, the chief. I went by way of the earth to see her, but I'm returning through the air," Spear answered. "Oh my grandson, while you're on your way back, you'll meet the owner of this trail — he loves the trees and roads where you are travelling. He's an old man like me, and carries a cane. If he meets you, he'll kill you and eat you. I say, grandson, I have a tree of my own there. When you see the old man coming, look about. You'll see a dead white-fir. It is mine. If this fellow chases you, climb it. The bark will fall on him. If he gets a chance, he'll eat you up. His name is łała'mak'wʊs[1]." After this advice, Spear started on his way again. Before long he saw the old fellow. "There he is, the man I was told about." The old fellow had already seen him. Spear looked about and found the tree. He climbed up. łała'mak'wʊs came up. "Where is the man I am to meet? Oh, I guess he has gone to his tree," he said. He began to climb after Spear. The first old man had said to Spear, "Whisper to the tree to let its bark fall." Spear whispered. Soon the bark fell down and the dangerous being fell with it. "There he is dead," Spear said. Then he made a fire of this bark, just as the first old man had told him, and threw the fellow in, and burned him up. "From now on, should people chance to meet, they shall just pass one another by; no one shall claim the road or trees or anything of the sort. This is how it will be in the next generation. They shall exchange greetings and go on their way," he said. After the body had burned and a few bones were left, he took a rock and smashed them to pieces.

Spear set out again. He travelled and travelled. Finally he came to a river. There was a fish-trap (ts'i'tpən) there and he crossed over on it. A house was on the other side. He entered. A young woman was sitting down; an old man was sitting down, too. "Oh grandson," the old man said, "sit by my daughter. You may be her husband, if you like." Spear sat down close to the young woman. The old man was named Ne'pius[2]. "There is another trap above here. The man who owns it and I are enemies," Ne'pius said. Then Spear's father-in-law told what trouble he had always had with the owner. "You shall help me. He will be down here this evening. He always breaks my trap. If you kill him, I shall be glad." Spear thought, "All right. I shall kill both of you." The other fellow soon came, made a noise at the trap and went away. "Come, help me," Ne'pius said to Spear. Farther up, his enemy had put some trees in the river, so that they would float down and take the trap with them. But the trap did not break and Ne'pius and Spear threw the

[1] See p. 60.
[2] A giant; there are several characters who bear this name; see pp. 79, 240.

logs over the trap. Then the other old fellow thought, "The trap has always broken before; there must be something wrong this time," and went to fight. He and Ne'pius fought. He threw Ne'pius down. Spear saw that Ne'pius was down. Thereupon he killed the other old fellow and then killed Ne'pius. He made a fire, threw the first one in, and did the same with his father-in-law. He burned them both. As they were burning, he said, "This will never happen in the next generation. No one shall put a trap above another's. There shall be just one trap for many people." As soon as he had finished, he said, "I can't stay here. I shall have to go on, and leave my wife."

Then Spear set out, deserting his wife. He travelled and travelled. At last, he came to a house by the side of the road. He looked in. A middle aged woman was lying on her bed. He entered. "Oh grandmother, are you lying down because you are ill?" "Oh grandson," she answered, "I'm not ill, I'm blind. Where are you from?" Spear answered, "Oh I am he whose sister is married to chief silver-side. When I visited her, I travelled by way of the world's-end, but now I'm going home through the sky. Grandmother, aren't you able to sit up?" The old lady arose from her bed and took a seat. Spear held her head and blew upon her eyes.[1] "Can you see me?" he asked. "Yes," she answered, "I can see you." "Very well, I shall blow once more," he said. The woman looked about. Her eyesight was now normal. "I'm going back to the place from which I started. I don't know yet what I shall be when I reach home. Perhaps I shall be a toy for the next generation. This much I have done for you, grandmother, I have restored your sight," Spear said.

When Spear was ready to start out, the old lady, whose name was Tax̂wa'ʼasti, said to him, "Be very careful when you're travelling. Before long you'll meet an old man coming on the road. He has a long tail. He will switch you to death with it, if he gets the chance. Try to see him first, then hide and shoot him." Spear went on. Before long he saw the man. "Well, this is the one whom I was told to beware of." He hid. The old man came right up to the spot where Spear was standing, stopped and said, "Wonder where that man is I was told I would meet." Before he could turn toward Spear, the latter shot him three times and killed him. This man was Cougar (s.wa'wa). Then Spear built a fire and burned him. He said to the burning Cougar, "In the next generation, if people should chance to meet, they will just pass by without trying to kill one another." And then when nothing remained but the ashes, he said to them, as they flew away, "You shall be just animals [cougars]. You shall be wild and people will eat your flesh."

Spear went on, and came to another house from which smoke was rising. He stopped, as he wished to see what was there. He peeped

[1] See pp. 86, 172.

through the door. An old woman was lying on the bed. Her name was To'tαmx·[1]. Just as he peeped in, she asked, "Where are you from?" "Oh I am he whose sister is married to silver-side, the chief. When I visited her, I travelled to the end of this world, but now I'm going back through the sky," he said. "You are the one who has been killing the dangerous beings as you travelled. Everyone has heard of you and of what you are doing," the old woman said. "Perhaps it is I," Spear answered. "My grandson, when you reach a prairie, you'll hear someone shouting. They are getting ready for you; that's why they're shouting. They're going to kill you," she said. Spear answered, "Oh grandmother, that is good." Then he went on. He came to the prairie and heard the shouting. The people were lined up, and were going through the motion of fighting. He started toward them. When they saw him, they shouted in full force. He went up to them. "Oh, my cousins, what are you doing that makes you so happy? Is there something going on here?" he asked. "Oh yes," they answered, "we're waiting for Spear; he's killing all the dangerous beings and we don't want it. We're going to kill him." "So that is what you are doing! You people stand right where you are forever! If the people of the next generation care to eat you, they may, although you shan't be real food. They may find use for you," he said to them. They never learned who he was. They became the wild-rhubarb (t'α'mts) and remained there in a bunch where Spear left them.[2]

Spear went on. After he had travelled a long way, he noticed a place that seemed rather familiar. He did not know at what place he had come down to earth again. It looked like his old home place. Before long, he noticed smoke coming from a house and went toward it. He saw a woman there and asked her, "Whose house is this?" "Oh," she said, "this is Spear's house. When you left there, I came back, too. You had better stay here." The woman was his own sister. "No, I left this house once, and I shall never return to it. I shall be a toy for the children; little children will gather me, and make a toy of me. You must become something, also. We can't stay in this house any longer," Spear said. Then he went away and changed himself into a flower. His sister changed herself into something also.[3] Spear-flower (or sheep's-nose) comes every May and is the flower that the children gather to use for toys.

---

[1] A kind of root, that sticks up out of the ground alone, as if separated from the rest of the tree.

[2] See p. 164. As far as I know, Spear is not considered a Transformer, although he acts very much like one. I have never heard anyone but Mary Heck tell this story.

[3] It is not known what she changed herself into; of course, she still bears the name pαsi'nos.

THE ORIGIN OF MENSTRUATION.[1]

An old man[2] was the first person to menstruate. The flow came through his eyes. A number of young girls, observing the blood on his eyes, laughed about it and made fun of him. The old man took something or other and wiped the blood from his eyes. He then threw it at the girls. "You girls have made fun of me and now you shall get it yourselves," he said. If the girls had not made fun of the old man, men would menstruate instead of women and would have to sleep outside alone for a certain length of time.

STAR HUSBAND.

(First Version).[3]

Two girls were once sleeping out. One said to the other, "See that great big star up there in the sky? I wish I could have that star." The other said, "See that tiny star way off there? You can scarcely see it. I wish I could have that one."

That night, the girls found men sleeping with them — men lying alongside of them. The girl who had wished for the big star, had an ugly old man sleeping with her. He was so old that his eyes were red and the skin beneath them drawn down. The girl who had wished for the tiny star, found a nice young man sleeping with her.

(Second Version).[4]

Two girls lay down one night to sleep. They wished for the stars. The elder one wished for a small, dim star. The younger said, "I want that large, bright one." When they awoke next morning, they found themselves with two old men; the stars had taken them up to the sky. The elder of the two men, who was really a very old man, shone more brightly than the other. The girls had to live with these two men; the stars had heard what they had said.[5]

They lived there for sometime as they did not know how to get back home. Then one day Spider (t'u'pa) came up there. They told Spider what had happened; they had been abducted but did not know what to do about it. "You are indeed far from home — you are in another world," Spider said. "I can go to high places and get back down again easily. I have a string that stretches so far it never

[1] Told by Peter Heck, 1927. See p. 420.

[2] The old man's name is not known.

[3] Told by Peter Heck, 1926. Mr. Heck gave this story only at my request. See p. 418.

[4] Told by Jonas Secena, 1927.

[5] The Upper Chehalis believe that the stars are people like themselves but live in a different world.

comes to an end. If you want to go back home, I can let you down."[1] Spider put the girls, one at a time, into a basket and let it down on a string. That is how the girls got down. Spider came down also. The girls lived thereafter on this earth.

*

* *

At the end of this myth, so the narrator said, the chief always gave the following "law" (ox̂wa'nt'wa'ni˘), the truth of which has often been proved:

> Girls should not wish for anything like this — anything far away. It is uncalled for; bad luck may come to them. They should be careful what they say and what they do; they will have a long life if they do not wish for anything far off.

DOG HUSBAND.

(First Version).[2]

There was once a beautiful young woman whom many young men wished to marry. But she said "no" to all of them and turned them away. She was a very active person. She was always out digging material for baskets that she could sell, or picking berries.

She had a pet, a small house dog just so high,[3] that was continually at her heels. The little dog slept at the foot of her bed. One night a man came to her bed and slept with her. "Who can this be?" she asked herself. It was the little dog who had changed himself into a man. But she was never able to find out who the man was and never once suspected her dog. This went on for sometime. At last her parents noticed that she was pregnant. They were very angry for she had disgraced them. One day, when she was out digging, the whole village decided to go away and leave her. They abandoned their houses and poured water on all the fireplaces so that she would have no fire. They took all the food and utensils that they owned and left. But the girl's grandmother felt sorry for her. She secretly dug a little hole in the ashes of her fireplace and buried there quite deep a bit of lighted bark enclosed in a large clam shell.

When the young woman returned, she found the village deserted. At first she felt very badly, but since she was so used to doing things for herself, she decided that she could manage well enough alone. She ran from one fireplace to another but found only sopping wet

---

[1] The stars were enormous eaters; no matter how much they ate, they never became satiated.

[2] Told by Maggie Pete, 1926. See p. 399.

[3] Illustrating.

ashes. Then she thought, "Grandmother! She must have left something for me." Sure enough, she found the bit of burning bark. Before long the people, who had moved across to an island, saw smoke coming from one of their houses on the mainland.

The young woman took sick. She gave birth to four male pups and one girl. The girl grew very quickly. The mother took care of her puppies. They were real puppies for she would pick them up and sling them the length of the floor. The little girl slept with her mother.

Each day the mother would leave her offspring and go to the beach to dig clams. As soon as she turned her back, she would hear a terrible racket, the sound of people romping around. One night after she and her daughter had gone to bed, she coaxed the little girl to tell her what all the racket was about that she heard each day. The little girl refused to tell her. But one morning she had a change of heart and whispered, "Mother, my little brothers are not puppies at all! Just as soon as you leave, they take off their coats, throw them in the corner by the door, and play. They always tell me to watch the door, and as soon as I see you coming, they put their coats back on." "You must help me," her mother said, "I am going to fool them. Stand by the door and as soon as they pile their clothes in the corner, let me know." She fooled her puppy-children. She threw a shawl around her digging stick and, as soon as her little daughter gave her a sign, rushed into the house and threw her son's clothes into the fire. A grown dog, that had remained in the village, also became a man as soon as he removed his shaggy coat.[1] The naked little boys sat there, ashamed. She diapered them immediately.

The little boys grew very quickly. They were soon bringing in a lot of meat to their mother — elk and deer that they had shot with their bows and arrows. The family became very prosperous. They stored up a great deal of food. By this time, the people on the island had noticed that smoke was always rising from the site of their former home. Bluejay was becoming suspicious. "I suspect grandmother," he had already said. Then one day he said, "I smell the fat of elk or deer. Grandmother, you have it!" Now the people learned that the old woman had been going at night to visit her granddaughter and had brought home many good things to eat. Grandmother had paddled over to the mainland in her little old canoe. They decided to move back. They started out in their canoes, but a storm came up and all were drowned but the old lady in her little canoe.[2]

---

[1] The narrator does not say so, but this grown dog must be the young woman's dog-husband.

[2] The narrator said that she herself, when young, had a little dog just like the one that the young woman in this story owned.Since the little dog was with her continually, her family always told her this story as a lesson.

DOG HUSBAND.

(Second Version).[1]

An old lady had five daughters. They lived close to the bay. One of the young women had a dog. The dog always seemed to be watching for someone. Before long, the young woman was found to be pregnant. The dog had changed himself into a man and had slept with her. Her mother, father, two uncles and other members of the family went off and left her. They were ashamed of her condition.

The young woman found herself deserted. But she soon discovered a fire-cord that some member of her family had left for her near the house post. With this, she was able to make a fire. She gave birth to four male pups and one daughter. About a month afterwards, those who had left her and moved across the bay, saw smoke near their former home. They thought that one of their number must have gone back to the place.

Whenever the tide was out, the young woman would go down to the beach to dig clams. She had a torch of pitch. The pups were growing fast and were already big fellows. One night, while at the beach, she heard from the house sounds like little children playing. She left her torch on the beach and went back to the house. "Oh, my sons! tʻ tʻ tʻ tʻ tʻ. They're not pups at all, but young men!" she cried. The boys were fair and had no wool at all. As soon as they had begun to dance that night, they had removed their dog-coats and laid them down. They had set their little sister, who had a bit of hair right on her eye, on top of this pile of coats. This thing had been going on for perhaps ten days. As soon as their mother was out of sight, they would build up a large fire. It was the little girl's duty to watch their mother on the beach — to see if her torch was still burning. "Is mother still there?" the boys would ask. "Yes, she's still digging clams," their sister would answer.

When their mother came home and surprised them, the boys went half crazy. She picked up a stick and cried, "Don't touch those coats!" Then she threw the coats into the fire and burned them up.

Next day, the boys walked upright like real men; they had human feet and hands. They made arrows and wore clothes for the first time. They were red haired, nice looking boys. They killed many ducks, geese, seals, — all kinds of game. From the beach, one could smell all kinds of food. Their grandmother came over from across the bay and saw that the former dog-children were now real people. They had lots of food and salmon of all kinds. This is the end of the story about the little dogs.

---

[1] Told by Pike Ben, 1926.

DOG HUSBAND.

(Third Version).[1]

Woodpecker (qaqα'm) had a home close to the river. He had one little girl. He was always making canoes. He went out one morning to work on a canoe; he could make all different kinds, which he sold for money. Next day, he went out again to work on his canoe. While working, he heard something making a noise. When he got home, the noise that he had heard was still on his mind and he was anxious to get back to work in order to hear it again. Early next morning, he went out again. While he was working — pounding and chopping — he could hear the noise, but as soon as he would stop, he could not hear it. He could not figure out a way to hear it more plainly. He went home, disturbed because he could not locate it. Next morning he went out again just for the purpose of hearing the noise. While working, he heard it once more; it sounded like a baby crying. At last he thought, "I'm going to tell my tools to do the work for me." He told them to strike against one another. He heard the noise again. He went some distance away and stopped to listen. It sounded like a baby crying. He started toward the noise and came to a hollow tree. He could hear a baby crying inside. He found a baby in a cradle; the baby had a flattener on its head. He looked the baby over and then left. He went home. "I've found a baby in a hollow tree. What shall I do with him? He will die if he's left there," he said to his wife. "Go get him," his wife said, and added, "But what shall we tell our daughter?" "We'll put her to sleep. I'll fix a place for you as if you were in child-birth," he said. He got the baby and gave him to his wife. They fixed a little shelter outside and the woman went there. When the little girl awoke, she asked, "Where's mother?" "Oh, your mother has just had a baby," her father said. "What is it, a girl or a boy?" she asked. "A boy," her father answered. "Oh, I have a little brother now!" she said.

The little girl thought about her brother a good deal. When he was five days old, he could already walk; he was a sturdy boy. Woodpecker made him a bow and arrow to practice shooting so that he would grow up to be a hunter and kill big game. The boy was very much pleased with his bow and used it for shooting around. His sister said, "Oh, brother, are you learning to shoot?" The two played together at shooting. Once the girl said, "Brother, shoot my hand. I'll bet you can't hit it!" The boy did not want to do it. At last he got tired of her coaxing and hit her right in the center of her hand. Then she cried out, "Nən, nən, nən, you shot my hand! My father found you in a hollow tree!" No one had told her this — she just knew it. The boy ran into the house and went to bed; he was angry because she had said that he was found in a hollow tree. He

[1] Told by Peter Heck, 1926.

was quite a big fellow by this time; he grew very rapidly. When Woodpecker got home, he asked his wife, "What's the matter with the boy?" "Oh," she explained, "his sister coaxed him to shoot her hand, and when he hit her, she said, 'My father found you in a hollow tree.' Then he felt bad and went to bed." "I guess he'll have to go, now. He won't be able to get along with her after this," Woodpecker said.

Woodpecker fixed his son up and gave him a lot of things to take with him. "When you come to a prairie, you will see a lot of women there digging lacamas. The trail is on this side; the women dig there. The trail leads through this and the following prairies; the women may notice you," he said to him.

The young man came to the first prairie and saw the women busy digging there. When he was about in the middle of the prairie, one of the women remarked, "Who is that handsome fellow?" All the others turned to look at him. There was just one who did not pay any attention to him. She said, "Ha, ha, he′, that's the fellow my father found in a hollow tree!" He got angry and killed her and burned her. But her hat[1] had fallen some distance away; it was her soul[2] (skwa′x̣̯^{u}k^{u}x̣̯tən).

He came to the second prairie, where there were more women digging lacamas. When he was just about in the middle of the prairie, one of the women said, "Who's that handsome fellow?" Then the others looked up and stared at him. There was one who did not so much as give him a glance, but she said, still without looking at him, "Ha, ha, he′, he's the fellow my father found in a hollow tree!" The young man turned around and said, "I thought that I had killed you!" He killed her and burned her. Her hat fell some distance away but he left it where it was and went on.

He came to the third prairie, where women were digging lacamas. When he was about in the middle of the prairie, one of the women said, "Who's that handsome fellow?" All of them except one stopped to look at him. She did not look, but said, "Ha, ha, he′, he's the fellow my father found in a hollow tree!" "I thought I had killed you!" he said. He turned back, killed her and burned her. Her hat fell off and lay some distance away, but he paid no attention to it.

He came to the fourth prairie, where women were digging lacamas. When he was just about in the middle of the prairie, one of the women said, "Who's that handsome fellow?" All but one stopped to look at him. She did not look at him, but said, "Ha, ha, he′, he's the fellow my father found in a hollow tree!" He turned back. "Here you are again! I thought I had killed you!" He killed her and burned her. He grabbed her hat and burned it too. "Nothing like this shall ever happen again. If a person is found and given a

[1] A soft, woven hat.

[2] This is only a folkloristic motif.

home, he shall be treated just like a brother." Ashes blew up and to these he said, "You shall be the lark (sqʋtsx̣a′), who always says something bad to people." Then he went on.

He came to the fifth and last prairie, where he saw some women digging lacamas. The girl that he had always seen was not there. But he did notice a very pretty young woman. "What can I do to get near her and talk to her ?" he thought. He kept hidden. "Women are afraid of snakes, so I can't be a snake," he thought. At last he said, "I'll be a little pup." And so he changed himself into a little dog, all covered with beads that his father had given him; he looked very pretty.

The little pup started out across the prairie and went up to the women. "Here comes a nice little dog!" someone said. They called him all kinds of nice names but he would not go any nearer. Then the pretty girl called and he went right up to her. He stayed there with her and refused to go to any of the others. After a while, the women started home. The little dog followed right after the pretty girl. They came to a village, and, upon arrival, started to cook. The little dog never once left the girl. "You're a strange dog!" Bluejay said. "Keep quiet, don't say anything that concerns the princess (a·′lsɩł)," his sister said. Bluejay kept watching the little dog. When bedtime came, the dog jumped up where the young woman slept and stayed there. "I've never seen a dog like that!" Bluejay said. Next morning, all got up and the dog jumped down from the bed. That morning, the women went out again to dig lacamas. The little dog went right along with his mistress and stayed there. In the evening, Bluejay called him but he refused to go to him. He gave him some bones, but the dog would touch only the meat on them, and even this, he cleaned before eating. Bluejay was suspicious and said so. "Don't annoy the princess about that dog!" his sister said. That night, the dog again lay down by the princess' side. During the night, he would change himself into a man. It never once occurred to the young woman that the man was her dog and so she returned his love.

Next day, all the women went out again to dig lacamas. They cooked as soon as they got home in the evening and fed the dog, who refused to eat bones. Bluejay said, "Come on, mister dog, give me some of that food!" The little dog gave him the bones. "You see," Bluejay said to his sister, "he understands me!"

The women went out again for the fourth time to dig lacamas and then it was noticed that the princess was getting big. "She's going to have a baby!" Bluejay said. "I'll bet that dog is a man; he's deceiving everyone!"

The fifth time, the young woman went out alone to dig. Unknown to her, the others were planning to move away and leave her. Not a single person except herself would be left in the village. But while they were getting ready to leave, Crow was feeling sorry for the princess; they would leave her to starve. She got two little shells from the river, put some coals in them and closed the shells together. Then she dug a hole near the house post and buried the coals there. "When your mistress comes home," she said, "call her."

When the young woman got home, she found everything torn down; only the rafters were standing. She wept. Then she heard someone talking. "Where is that coming from?" she thought. It was coming from the post. She dug the shells out and found some coals inside from which she could start a fire. She took them and made a fire. She knew that Crow had done this for her. She stayed there all alone. She took sick and gave birth to five little pups, one of whom was a female.

The woman would go each day to the bay to dig clams. The little pups would then gather together, as little pups always do, and play. When their mother was home, they would sleep. But as soon as she would leave the house, they would take off their blankets and become little children; they would have a good time around the fireplace. The eldest boy would sing,

"Sister, see if mother is still there."

If the girl found that their mother was still on the beach, they would play again. Their mother always found them wearing their dog-clothes. When she had returned from her first trip, she had noticed little boys' tracks around the house. "Where do these come from?" she had thought. After her fourth trip, she considered the matter more seriously. "Where do these children come from who play about the fire?" she asked herself. For the fifth time she went out to dig clams. She did no digging but left her torch-light there. She sneaked back to the house where she could hear the children making a noise. Someone was singing,

"Sister, see if mother is still there."

"Oh, those children are my little pups!" she said and ran into the house. The children quickly jumped toward their clothes. But she took the clothes away from them, made a fire and burned them. "You can go without your dog-clothes from now on and be real people!" she said.

The children grew up very quickly. The boys became good hunters and the girl learned how to dig clams and do things of that kind. They had plenty of food — seal, elk and everything of that sort. They filled all the vacant houses with meat.

In the meantime, Crow was thinking to herself, "I must go to see if the princess is still there. She may have been killed by x̣emoi′x̣αmɔi‵[1], the dangerous being (pα′sa); he may have eaten her." She went to the place and saw all kinds of meat there. She began to eat some stuff, for, like the others who had moved away, she was

[1] No description of this being was given.

starving. "Don't eat that stuff! Come up here," the princess said. They fed her and gave her some meat to take home. "Give the meat to your children when everyone else is in bed, so they won't learn that you have been here," they said. Late in the evening, Crow fed her children some seal blubber. The youngest one choked and made a noise. Raven heard and slapped the boy on the back. The blubber came out and Raven ate it. "People," he cried, "this little boy choked on a piece of seal blubber!" Then everyone got busy with the canoes; they would take all their things and move back to their former village. Bluejay made a canoe out of a rotten log, but when he got in the water, the log broke and he could not go any farther in it.

Finally everyone got across. Then in their haste to get to the well stocked houses, they began to push one another about. "This is my house! This is my house!" first one and then another would say. Bluejay claimed a house filled with blubber. But someone shoved him away, saying, "This is not your house! Your house is filled with elk-guts!"[1]

K'walale·'··i.

DOG HUSBAND.

(Fourth Version).[2]

Mouse (sk'wata'ᵊn) made a home and her two grandchildren, a boy and a girl, lived with her; they were growing children. One day Mouse said, "Oh, my grandchildren, you had better get ready and go over that way to the river to catch some salmon to dry." "All right, we'll go," they said. "I want you to travel together but I don't want you to camp close together," she said. "I don't want you to have intercourse with your sister," she added to the boy. "All right, we'll do as you say," the young people said.

They set out. Evening came and they camped far apart. Next morning they went on. That evening they camped a little closer together. Next morning they went on. Night came. They camped a little closer together than before. Next morning they went on. They stopped for the night. They camped not very far apart now. They went on. For the fifth time, they made camp. This time they camped together. They made only one bed and slept together. Next day they arrived at the river and built a house there for drying fish.

---

[1] The narrator added, "The girl, although unmarried, had a baby. It is a disgrace for an unmarried girl — and especially a princess like this one — to have a child. But in the stories, that kind of girl always has good luck." I asked what became of the little dog — the girl's dog-husband — and was told that Bluejay killed the dog before the people left the island.

[2] Told by Mary Heck, 1927; interpreted by Peter Heck.

In the meantime, Mouse felt uneasy — something might have happened. She followed her grandchildren. She came to their camping ground. They had camped far apart. She came to their next camping ground. They had camped a little closer together. She felt uneasy indeed. She came to their next camping ground. They had camped still closer together. "The bad ones!" she said. She came to their next camping ground. They had camped still closer together. It made her angry. At their last camp, there was just one bed. "So they have done it!" she cried. She came to the river. There stood the house that the young people had built. Not far from the house, she heard a baby crying. "Oh, those bad ones, they've done it!" she cried. The baby was in its cradle, which stood by the bed-side.[1] She sat down where the smoke was blowing toward the house. The house was full of smoke; the young people were drying fish as she had ordered. Her granddaughter said to her, "Oh, grandmother, you had better move this way. There's too much smoke there." Mouse did not budge. The smoke was blowing right in her face but she was too angry to move. At last she got up and walked around until she found a small piece of cedar wood. "I'll fix that fellow!" she said. When she went into the house, she was nice and kind. She was happy thinking of how she would punish her grandson. He had not yet returned when she arrived.

Next morning Mouse set to work on the piece of cedar to shape it like a salmon. When she had finished, she threw it into the river but it merely floated, like a lifeless thing. She went to get it as she was not yet satisfied with it. Next morning she went out again and worked all day at the piece of cedar. She threw it into the river. It merely floated down; it would not move about. She could not discover what made it so unsatisfactory. She worked at it six days. The seventh day, it suited her. Although it was somewhat larger than a silver-side, she painted it red to look like a silver-side. Then she threw it into the river. It began to move. It now had life in it. She ordered the salmon to go upstream. He went upstream and then came back. "Now go where the salmon stay, and dig there. If the other salmon run away, don't be afraid. When my grandson spears you, pull him down the river," she said.

That day her grandson went to the riffle. "Oh, there's a big salmon. I'll spear him!" he said to himself. He speared it. But the salmon turned and began to pull him down. He tried to get a good foot-hold but failed. The spear stuck to his hand and he could not let go.

In the meantime, Mouse was as nice as she could be to her granddaughter. Night came but the young man did not return. The young woman could not imagine what had happened. Next

[1] When the baby awakens, the band is removed from its head so that it can look around.

morning she was uneasy about her husband and went out to see what had happened to him. She found the place where he customarily speared salmon. There she saw that he had tried to get a foot-hold and failed. Her husband must have been drowned.

Mouse was still very good to her. But the young woman had followed the river down and had found the place where her husband had drowned. The salmon floated there like a piece of wood. A spear was sticking in it. Realizing what had happened, she came back to the house, determined to have her revenge. "Is there any water?" Mouse said, "I'm getting thirsty." "Oh, yes," the girl replied. She went out to the well and talked to it. "When grandmother comes and stoops down to drink," she said, "fall lower and lower." Mouse went to the well to drink. It was not very full. She could not quite touch the water with her lips. The water dropped lower and lower. She had to lean over farther and farther. At last she had to lean over so far that she fell in and drowned. Her granddaughter came there and saw her at the very bottom of the well, but made no move to take her out.

The woman removed all the wrappings from her little son and tied beads around his head, his neck, his wrists, his elbows, his ankles and his knees. Then she took him out into the woods and set him up in a hollow tree. "If you hear any one pounding, cry at every blow," she said. Then she went to the riverside and dug a place where she could stay. There she covered herself. Every spring time she comes out. She is X̂wala'q'o.[1]

Woodpecker (qaqα'm) came. He was making a canoe. Every time he struck his tools together, he heard something making a noise. He was afraid that it might be a dangerous being (pα'sa). When he got home, he did not mention what he had heard. Next morning he went back to the woods. The noise that he had heard the day before was on his mind. He heard it again. For four consecutive days he heard the same thing. The fifth day he went to work again. The noise continued. At last he discovered that it was a baby's cry. He told his tools to strike against one another. He could hear the baby's cry plainly now and could thus locate the direction from which it came. While his tools were pounding together, he walked away. He walked and walked. He looked into the hollow tree. There was the baby in a cradle, its head covered with beads. He stepped back and looked around, not knowing what to do. He could hear his tools pounding away. He went home. "Where's our daughter?" he asked his wife. "Oh, she's over there asleep," his wife answered. "Well, I don't quite know what to do. I've found a baby. We'll deceive our daughter — we'll pretend you're having a baby," he said. They put up some mats outside and made a little shack. The woman pretended that she had given birth to a child. When the little girl awoke, her father said, "My dear daughter,

[1] A plant; English equivalent unknown.

you have a little brother now. Your mother has just given birth to a son." The little girl was anxious to see her brother.

In five days the boy was quite grown up. He made some straw arrows and shot them about. His sister was always near. "Won't you shoot my hand, brother?" she asked. "No, you might say something about me if I did," he answered. "No, I won't. Since I don't know anything about you, what could I say?" she replied. She coaxed and coaxed. At last he shot her hand and hit it. She squealed and squealed. "Oh, the boy that my father found in a hollow tree has hit my hand!" she cried. "I knew you'd say that!" the boy said.

The boy went to bed and slept five days and nights. Then he arose. He was a grown man now. "I don't know where to go," he said to himself. He took one of his blankets, wrapped it about him and pinned it in the front. Then he set out. He had gone but a short distance when he heard a bird flying over his head. He came to a prairie. There were many women there, digging lacamas. They were camping. One young woman never gave him a glance. All the others discussed the stranger who was passing by. Just as he was about to leave the prairie, the young woman said, "Oh, he's the young man that my father found in a hollow tree!" He turned back and killed her. Her hat fell off, but he paid no attention to it; he left it lying just where it was. He burned the woman up and went on. Just then, he heard a bird fly by again.

He came to another prairie. There were many women camping there, digging lacamas. He saw a young woman who looked very much like the one that he had just killed. She paid no attention to him although the others were busy discussing the stranger. As he was about to pass by, she said, "Oh, that's the young man my father found in a hollow tree!" He turned back. The woman's hat fell off. He killed her and burned her up. Then he went on. On his way he heard a bird fly by.

He came to another prairie. Many women were digging there. "Why, there's the same girl I killed a while ago!" he said to himself. He did not loiter but kept on going. The girl paid no attention to him, although the others stopped to talk about him. "Wonder where that young man is from?" they said. Then the young woman said, "Oh, that's the young man my father found in a hollow tree!" "That is the very same girl I killed!" the young man said to himself. "I wonder how she came back to life!" He turned back. He killed her and threw her into the fire. He threw her hat in, too. He smashed her bones. Some ashes blew up. He said to them, "You shall be the little lark (sqʊtsx̣a′), a mean bird that always tries to quarrel with people."[1]

He went on. This time, he did not hear a bird fly past. He passed many women, as before, but the girl was not there.

[1] Whenever a woman is mean and quarrelsome, she is called "lark."

He came out on the last prairie. He looked about. The girl was not there. But he saw a different girl, a beautiful, shining one. He sat down and began to plan how he could get near her. "Shall I turn myself into a snake? No, that would only frighten them. If I turn myself into a pheasant, they might kill me." Nothing that he could think of was satisfactory. At last he hit upon an idea. "Oh, I shall turn into a tiny dog. I'll use my beads for spots. I'll be a tiny, spotted dog. And if anyone should call me, I won't go to any one but the princess. If she should call me, I'll go, but I won't go to any of the others." He went toward the women. Before long they took notice of him. "Oh, how pretty! Wonder where he came from?" But he ran away from them. The princess was digging off by herself, paying no attention to the others. The little dog lay down on the trail. Finally, the women went to camp but he would not go to any of them when they called him. "Here comes the shining girl," he said to himself. She called him. Happy, he jumped up and followed right at her heels. After he had gone into the house, the other women called him, but he would not go to them. He was afraid, so he pretended. At bed time, he jumped up into his mistress' bed and went to sleep there. Bluejay was there. "What's the matter with that dog? He's afraid of everyone but the princess," he remarked. His sister, Yu'i, said, "Just be quiet. You always talk about everything you see."

Next morning, the women went out to dig roots. When they got home that evening, they fed the dog. He ate the meat that they gave him, but left the bones; he refused to touch them. "That's a strange dog!" Bluejay said. "He won't eat bones! Dogs always like bones." Finally he noticed that the princess had marks on her cheek bones; there were dark streaks across them. "Notice the princess," he said. "She has marks on her face. She's going to have a baby!" He went to the women's quarters. "Oh, little dog, give me some of your food," he said. The dog pushed the bones toward Bluejay's nose. "See, Yu'i," Bluejay cried, "he's feeding me! He gave me something to eat when I asked him for it!"

Bluejay's accusations proved to be well founded, for, when the young woman went to dig, the people saw the marks on her face. Bluejay was right; she was going to have a baby. They decided to move away and leave her, but before they left, they hanged the little dog. They took all their possessions and moved across the bay.[1] They took everything they could lay their hands on; not even a shred of blanket was left. They wanted the young woman to die in child-birth. But Crow did not forget her grandchild. "Oh, I don't know what she'll do for a fire," she moaned to herself. She put some coals in a clam shell and closed it. Then she dug a little hole near the house post and buried it. "When your mistress comes,"

[1] The Upper Chehalis are an inland-water tribe. They have to go some distance to reach a bay. Nevertheless, a bay figures fairly often in their stories.

she said, "even if she is weeping, whinny a little so that she will hear you."

The young woman, weeping, heard a noise and listened. Then she began to weep again. She heard the noise again. It came from the direction of the house post. She found the shell and opened it. "Oh, my grandmother must have done this. She's the only one who has remembered me." She made a fire. Night came and she had nothing with which to cover herself; everything had been taken away. Next day, she took sick. She was all alone when her babies were born. She gave birth to five male pups and one daughter. One of the pups was somewhat spotted. Except for a little fur and a few spots, the pups were otherwise human. "Oh, I can't do anything with these dogs!" she cried. "Now I know why my people left me. But I'll raise my children, regardless of what they grow up to be."

When the tide was out, she would go to the bay to dig clams. Before long, the little pups learned how to eat; they ate the clams that she dug for them. One day, when she returned from digging, she noticed that her room seemed different. Her house was just big enough for one person. Things seemed to have been moved about. But all the little pups were fast asleep. Five times she noticed a change. She thought she saw little boys' tracks in the ashes. "I'll go out again tonight to dig clams," she said to herself, "although there's something amiss here!" When she came back to the house, she found fresh tracks in the ashes. She was puzzled. She went out again the next night. But all the time she was busy digging winter-clams, she was pondering about the little tracks that she had seen. She stuck her torch into the beach and stole back to the house to see what was going on there during her absence. She could hear some children playing near her shack. One of them said, "See if mother is still there." Then her little daughter ran out and looked toward the beach. "Yes, mother is still there," she reported. She crept closer. She could see some little boys and her daughter playing inside the shack. The boys' dog-blankets were heaped on one little spot. She quickly sprang inside, grabbed the blankets and threw all six of them into the fire. The little boys were stark naked. As soon as she had burned their blankets, her children had become real humans. She now had five little sons and one little daughter.

She had the children swim every day. They grew very fast. Before long her sons were growing boys and she sent them out to find tamanoas. They soon succeeded. Each one found either hunters' or fishermen's tamanoas. Those who had the latter, could kill whale and seal; those who had the former, could kill elk, deer, and game of all kinds. They killed any amount of game and dressed it. They now had all they wanted to eat. They hung the dressed game in every vacant house. In Bluejay's and Raven's house, they hung the entrails and anything that was not fit to eat, as these two had demanded more persistently than the others that the young woman be left to die.

Finally Crow thought, "I had better find out if my granddaughter is still alive." She took her little canoe and crossed the bay. "I wonder if my granddaughter has been eaten by X̣emoi'-x̣αmɔi`." The young woman heard someone coming. She listened. "Oh, my poor grandmother is coming, either weeping or singing. Yes! It is she." Crow landed and jumped out. She had not walked very far, when she was seen to look down again and again; she seemed to be eating something. "Don't eat your grandchildren's excrements!" the young woman cried. All the while Crow thought that she was eating marrow. It was hard for her to leave it and go to the house. They gave her all kinds of meat to eat, at which she was very surprised.

After Crow had eaten her fill and was ready to go back home, the princess gave her lots of meat and some seal blubber to take with her. Her canoe was just about loaded down. She began her song, and sang in such a way that the people at home would think that her granddaughter had been killed. The young woman had said, "Don't tell them how I'm living now and don't feed your children until late at night." "Have you been there?" the others asked when Crow got back. "Yes, and there's nothing there. She must have been eaten up after we left," she answered. It was a dark night; since they could not see the things that she had brought with her, they believed her. She packed all her gifts into the house and put the fire out so that the house would be in total darkness. Then she began to feed her children. They ate and ate and ate. Before long, however, the youngest choked on a piece of blubber. The people heard him choking. Raven was on the spot immediately. He slapped the child on the back and the piece of blubber came out. Raven took the piece of blubber and swallowed it whole. "Oh, people, people, people," he shouted, "Crow's little son choked on a piece of blubber!" Then everyone came and questioned Crow. It was obvious that she had found someone still alive across the bay — otherwise her son would have had no seal blubber on which to choke. At last Crow had to confess. "Oh, it's a great place now! Every house is just full of meat and fat!" she said.

When morning came, everyone was preparing to cross back to their former home. All this time they had been starving. They began to squabble over the canoes. "This is my canoe, this is my canoe, this is my canoe," first one, and then another would say. For his canoe, Bluejay hollowed out a rotten log. When they got across, they made a dash for the houses. Then they began to fight over the houses. "This is my house!" one would say. "No, it isn't, it's mine!" another would say. As for Bluejay and Raven, they claimed the house filled with blubber and grease. "This is mine!" each of them said. But the people shoved them away and showed them the house filled with entrails.

K'walale·'··i

SPRING SALMON AND THE YOUNG WOMAN.[1]

A young princess sent word to the people to come to a wrestling match. She sent messengers everywhere to invite the young men to come. The one who could throw her, would be her husband. Many young men had wanted to marry her, but she had refused them.

The invited guests came into her house. She told her servants to prepare a place in the middle of the room. They placed some large mats on the floor where the match would take place. She called Wolf to wrestle with her first. He did not last long; she soon threw him. Cougar, also, was soon thrown. She called Bear. He was no match for her. Then she called Wildcat. She called the Birds. Hawk was thrown. She called Owl. He did not last long. Eagle was thrown. She called Dark Eagle. He was thrown. Not one of them could do a thing; the woman was too strong for them. Spring Salmon came in. "I'd like to wrestle with you," the young woman said. "Oh, no, I don't know how to wrestle; I've never wrestled before in my life," he said. Finally, she induced him to try. Each time she threw him. Everyone clapped his hands and made fun of him. At last he did throw her. Then he walked right out, without bothering to sit down for a while.

Now everyone was jealous of Spring Salmon and wanted to kill him so that they could get the young woman instead. He walked down to his canoe. Wolf jumped on him and threw him down. He tore Spring Salmon's body to pieces. An egg rolled down the hill. Wolf tried to catch it but could not do it.

The young woman packed her clothes, ready to follow Spring Salmon. A man was waiting for her. It was Wolf. "We're waiting for you," he said. "No, you did not throw me," she answered. "Come on," he said, "come with us to our house. We're the ones who threw you. We are five brothers." She did not believe him, but was afraid, as there were five of them. They took her home with them.

The egg began to grow and in five days time was a grown Salmon again. Then Spring Salmon set out to try his luck. He would go to the present home of the young woman. He came to a house. Someone was dancing inside. Two men were dancing around the fire. They were singing:

> Five days have passed since I killed
> Spring Salmon,
> Five days have passed since I killed
> Spring Salmon.

He went in. The two men were Skunks. He clubbed them with a stick for making fun of him.

He finally arrived at the Wolves' house. "Into what should I change myself in order to be safe?" he asked himself. After

[1] Told by Peter Heck, 1926. See p. 409.

thinking it over he decided to become an old man. He would pretend to be the young woman's uncle (L'ax̌we'not).[1] The woman was alone; the others had gone hunting. She was happy for she knew that Spring Salmon was her true husband. As soon as Wolf returned, Spring Salmon changed himself into an old man. "My uncle has come," the woman said. Wolf had smelled Spring Salmon. "It smells like Spring Salmon," he said. He threw the old man about. "Don't hurt my uncle," the woman said. "Oh, I didn't know he was your uncle," Wolf said. He lifted the old man up and took him back to where he had been sitting. Another Wolf came and did the same thing; he and the old man scuffled. "Let him alone," the woman said, "he's your 'in-law'." The three remaining Wolves came in one by one and treated the old man in the same fashion, until the woman explained his relation to her. The four younger Wolves now called him "in-law" and treated him respectfully. "Do you know how to make arrows?" the eldest Wolf asked. "Oh, yes, I used to make arrows in my young days. I'll try," the old man said.

The next morning, the Wolves went hunting. As soon as they had gone, Spring Salmon changed himself into a young man again and stayed with the young woman. He made five arrow heads of agate. One of these he hid. When Wolf came home that evening, he gave him the four arrow heads. "I broke one of them," he explained. "I heated it too much, and it got soft and broke." "Oh, that's all right," Wolf answered. The second Wolf hired him to make him some arrow heads also, as those he had made for his brother were so good. "I'm too old," Spring Salmon protested, "I break them." The following morning, Spring Salmon got more material, made five points and hid one. The woman was very happy that Spring Salmon was with her. When the second Wolf came home in the evening, Spring Salmon gave him four points, explaining that he had broken one. The third Wolf was so pleased with the points, that he, too, hired the old man to make some for him. The old man protested but finally agreed to make them. He made five more points and hid one. Then the fourth Wolf hired him to make some for him. This Spring Salmon did. He made five points and hid one. When he explained again that he had broken one, the Wolves became suspicious. Too many points had been broken. "He smells like Spring Salmon," they said among themselves. The fifth Wolf hired the old man to make him some points. Spring Salmon made five and hid one. The remaining four he gave to young Wolf with the same explanation.

"Now we must go to the well and lay for them when they come to drink," Spring Salmon said to the woman. "I'll help you," she answered. They went to the well. The eldest came and drank. As he raised his head, he looked in Spring Salmon's direction. Spring

[1] After the death of one's father, one calls father's or mother's brother L'ax̌we'not instead of qa'si.

Salmon shot him in the neck. Then he and his wife dragged the body to the other side of the tree, where they had been hiding. The second Wolf came. He stopped at the well to drink. As he raised his head, Spring Salmon shot him in the neck and killed him. They dragged the body to the other side of the tree and hid it. The third Wolf came; he carried a heavy load. He was somewhat wild from thirst and stopped to drink. As soon as he finished and raised his head, Spring Salmon shot him. Then they dragged the body to the other side of the tree and hid it. The fourth Wolf came. He had eyes both in the front and the back of his head. When he stooped to drink, he could see in two directions at once. When he chanced to turn his head aside a little, Spring Salmon shot him. They hid the body. The youngest Wolf came and noticed that something was amiss at the well. He drank only a little at a time, glancing around at every swallow. Spring Salmon shot at him and missed. Wolf, now frightened, ran off. Spring Salmon had wasted one point; it was the last one he had. Wolf had many arrows with him, but was too frightened to stay any longer. Spring Salmon had killed four wolves but had allowed one to escape. That's why we have wolf today. If he had killed them all, there would be no wolves.

Spring Salmon had got his wife back. The couple set out for home. They got to Spring Salmon's canoe and started down river. On the way down, Spring Salmon said to his wife, "I'm getting sleepy. I didn't have a chance to sleep over there. See that the canoe doesn't turn over." He went over to one end of the canoe, covered himself, and went to sleep. They went down and down. The woman began to grow uneasy. "What's the matter with this man? He never wakes up!" she thought. She went over to the bow of the canoe to have a look at him. She pulled the blanket off. Insects flew out. The body was covered with maggots. She wept and wept over her husband who had left her so quickly.

K'walale·′··i — and that's the way it is with spring salmon; they don't last long. They soon become full of maggots. They must be watched very carefully while drying. Unless properly taken care of, they do not last long. Other salmon last longer.

X̱WA′IPS AND THE YOUNG WOMAN.[1]

A certain family had a home place. They had a growing daughter who did not wish to marry. Many men had asked to marry her. Finally, the young woman said to her folks,[2] "It seems I'll have to be a wrestler; the man who throws me shall be my husband." "Do as

---

[1] Told by Peter Heck, 1926. See p. 415.

[2] I use here the English term that the narrator used, for, from later developments in the story, it would seem that the girl is an orphan, which would mean that her present male parent is really her L'ax̱we′not. See footnote 1, p. 111.

you like — don't consider us in the matter," her folks answered. Word of the wrestling match was sent all over the country. Everyone heard about it and was anxious to go, as the girl was very good-looking. All the unmarried men — Cougar, Wolf, Bear and the like — came to the match. The young woman ordered her servants to place a mat in the middle of the floor.

Now X̯wa'ips,[1] a chief, wanted to wrestle with the girl. He found a cedar bough, one slanting down, in the woods. He broke off a nice limb and made a wish on it. His wish was granted; the little limb became a man. X̯wa'ips then took the little man and went to the young woman's house. It was filled with people. The young woman stood in the middle of the room, ready to wrestle. Wolf tried first. She threw him and he sat down, ashamed. Cougar tried next. He did not last long; she soon threw him and he went back to his seat. She called Bear. He tried his best to throw her, but she got the best of him. She called Hawk and threw him. She called Owl and threw him. She wrestled with one after another and threw them all. Then she called to X̯wa'ips, "Come wrestle with me, X̯wa'ips." She pulled him by the arm and said, "A chief should be strong like me." "I can't wrestle," X̯wa'ips said, "wrestle with this little man instead." The young woman and the little man then took hold of one another. The little man was very nearly thrown a number of times. But the fifth time he threw the woman. Then he went out. X̯wa'ips took him home. Everyone was angry that the little man had won.

The young woman arose from the floor, and, without saying a word, took her clothes and went out to find the little man. In the meantime, X̯wa'ips fixed his bed very nicely. He put the little man near the fireplace and blew ashes all over him.[2] "When the woman comes, point to me," X̯wa'ips said to him. The woman came to the house. She looked around and saw a good bed. Then she noticed the little man and pulled the blanket from his face. "Are you the one who threw me?" she asked. "No, he's the one," the little man said pointing to X̯wa'ips. "No, it was you," she said. "No, I did not wrestle," the little man said. The woman was still not convinced, but she went to bed and lay down with X̯wa'ips. X̯wa'ips had got himself a wife. The woman still continued to believe that the little man was the one who had thrown her.

Early next morning, the woman went out to look for roots. When she returned in the evening, she had a pheasant. She said that Hawk had given it to her. X̯wa'ips plucked the feathers. Next morning, the woman went out again. In the evening, she came home with a grouse. X̯wa'ips was pleased. "Next time, tell Hawk to pluck it," he said. Next day, the woman went out again and came home in the evening with some ducks. "How's this?" X̯wa'ips

[1] I was never given an English equivalent for this term. The Cowlitz translate it Mountain Eagle; see p. 182.

[2] To make it appear that he has been sitting before the fire all the while.

asked. "Hawk caught them for me," the woman said. The fourth time, she returned with some geese. This time, X̯wa'ips was not satisfied with her answer. He suspected that not Hawk, but someone else, was killing the fowls for her. He did not pluck the fowls, for he was rather angry. The woman had indeed chanced upon a good-looking man and was planning to leave X̯wa'ips. The fifth morning, she went out again. "I must find out what she's up to," X̯wa'ips said as soon as she had gone. He made some wings and tried to fly. He tried over and over again. At last he could fly a little but soon dropped down. He thought it over — there must be something he had overlooked. Suddenly he realized what it was: on the ends of large wings, there were always some little ones. He added these, made a tail, and flew far up into the air. He could now fly quite well. He flew far up and circled over the place where his wife dug roots. There she was lying with a man. "Look at that nice bird! You'd better shoot it!" the woman said to her lover, Syuyu'wən[1]. X̯wa'ips was now sitting far up on a tree. "All right, I'll shoot it," Syuyu'wən said and shot at X̯wa'ips. The arrow went straight up in the air, but X̯wa'ips blew it back before it struck him. "I've missed that bird!" Syuyu'wən said. "That means that I am going to die! My tamanoas said that I would never miss anything." He shot again, but X̯wa'ips blew the arrow back before it had a chance to hit him. Syuyu'wən shot at him five times but never hit him once. Then X̯wa'ips went away. After a while, he came down to earth and lay in wait for his wife's lover. He had a club made of snow[?], so fashioned that it would kill a person. He killed Syuyu'wən. Then he cut his head off and took it home.

He reached home before his wife. He hung the head right over her bed. He had inserted a stick in the mouth, to make it appear that it was smiling. When his wife came home, she seemed sad. "Did Hawk kill a bird for you to-day?" X̯wa'ips asked. The woman said nothing. He tried to embrace her, but she would not have it. It was growing dark. Something began to drip on the woman's head. "It can't be raining, can it?" she thought. After the fifth time, she felt something like water dripping on her. She could not imagine what it was. "Burn some pitch and see what it is," X̯wa'ips suggested. She burned some pitch. There was a man smiling at her; it was the man she had been with. She was sad indeed.

Next morning, X̯wa'ips said, "Wife, since you are feeling so badly, perhaps you would like to go home." He treated her very kindly. They set out. As soon as they got to the prairie, X̯wa'ips seized her and struck her in the middle of the groin[?]. Her nose[2] began to bleed and bled profusely. They went on. At another

[1] A great hunter, not identified with any bird or animal; see p. 41.

[2] I do not quite understand why, if he struck her in the groin, her nose should bleed. Perhaps nose was substituted for some other part.

prairie, he did the same. And so he killed her. He was unhappy about the other man and was jealous of him. He took his wife far up to the top of a tall cedar and tied her there. "When your folks come, you can call to them from here, for your blood will become strawberries and they will come here to eat them."

The woman's folks came and ate the strawberries. Then the woman called, "That's my blood!" They were eating the blood of an orphan, their niece. "That's my blood!" they could hear her calling plainly now. Then they saw her far up on the top of the tree. X̂wa'ips had killed his wife. He had made the tree as slick as ice. The woman's folks asked the people, "Who of you can take her down?" They asked the Birds and Squirrel, none of whom could make it, although they had been well paid for their trouble. Each one would go a little way and then slide back down. Bluejay was there. "That fellow can't climb!" he would say, "only I can do it!" "Keep quiet," his sister would say, "if those people can't do it, you can't!" Then someone chanced to hear him say that he could do it, and thanked him very much for his offer. He took a basket on his back and flew up. "Kä'tchə kä'tchə," he said, at the same time trying to hold on to a little limb. He tried and fell. The other fellows punched him on the nose. "You talk big!" they said. Then one little fellow, Pape'təna'mɩts (a bird), said that he could do it. He tightened his belt as he climbed, and sang,

Ha'ipvtpʋ'tə,
Haye'.

He had a way of sticking to the tree as he climbed round and round. "There is no reason why I can't stick to this tree — the others can't climb," he meant to imply by his song. He climbed up the tree and then back down, just to show Bluejay what he could do and to arouse his anger still further. He brought the woman down in the basket and received his pay.

The dead woman had five brothers. They dressed up the eldest to make him look like his sister. But he did not resemble her in the least. They dressed up the second and the third brothers. These, then, resembled her just a little. They dressed up the fourth, and he then resembled her much more. Then they dressed up the fifth, the youngest and smallest. They padded him and dressed him as his dead sister had always dressed. He looked exactly like her. "Now, we'll take this young lady to X̂wa'ips," they said. "We'll take a lot of food along." They took the young fellow to X̂wa'ips. "We're bringing your wife back; she got home all right," they had said in a message to him. X̂wa'ips wondered what was up. "Why, I killed her!" he said to himself. "She must have come to life and gone home!" He went into his house to see his wife. The young fellow imitated exactly every action of X̂wa'ips' former wife. "It's she all right!" X̂wa'ips said to himself; he was completely taken in.

Night came and the couple went to bed. X̯wa'ips did not sleep a wink all night. Something seemed to be amiss. The next night, as before, his wife did not remove her clothes. Again, he did not sleep a wink. The following night he tried to embrace her. She pushed him away. The fourth night he tried to embrace her again. She pushed him away, would have nothing to do with him. The fifth night, X̯wa'ips finally slept. Then the young man cut X̯wa'ips' throat with a knife and completely severed his head. He stuck the head back on the shoulders and covered the body with a blanket as if X̯wa'ips were still sleeping.

Bluejay was there. X̯wa'ips slept all day and Bluejay began to grow uneasy. "What's the matter with my master?" he thought. X̯wa'ips slept five days and five nights. Then Bluejay learned that he was dead. When X̯wa'ips' wife had come back to her husband, Bluejay had remarked to his sister, "This woman acts like a man!" Bluejay wept.

*

* *

This story means: the woman was not satisfied with her husband and lay down with another man. Her husband killed her lover in revenge. And the same thing happens to-day; when a man is jealous, he kills his wife's lover.

K'walale·'··i

ORIGIN TALE OF THE TENINO.

(First Version).[1]

There was once a princess at łαmi'x·ilos[2] (Tenino) who did not wish to marry. She refused so many times, that one day her father said, "Well, whom would you like to marry — a wolf?" The Wolves heard this; they were able to understand the old man. And so a Wolf came to the girl and slept with her. But when he lay by her side, he changed himself into a young man. The girl then went away with young Wolf.

One day, the girl's father said, "Say, I wonder what the Wolves are going to pay me for my daughter?" The Wolves were also able to hear this. The girl's father suddenly saw a Wolf driving a great

[1] Told by Peter Heck, 1926. See p. 419.

[2] To be exact, a little south-east of the present town of Tenino, in the direction of Centralia. The people there were called łαmi'x·ilos and their village was known by the same name. Geographically, and linguistically — so it is said, they occupied a position intermediate between the Upper Chehalis and the Squally. They were next door neighbors, so to speak, of the Upper Chehalis, and the two groups used to intermarry. The Skookumchuck River cuts across the łαmi'x·ilos prairie.

many elk and deer right up to his door. The Wolf killed the game right on the spot, so that it would be ready to eat.

From this marriage, the people of łαmi'x·ilos trace their descent. They call themselves the Wolves. They became hunters and were always very successful at killing game, because they were descended from the Wolves.[1]

ORIGIN TALE OF THE TENINO.

(Second Version).[2]

The people of Tenino (łαmi'x·ilos) say that their ancestor was Wolf. There was a pretty girl there. Whenever she learned that someone from another tribe planned to buy her in marriage, she would object. "No, I won't do it," she had said many, many times.

There were many Wolves there in the old days. They seemed to like human beings and could talk the Tenino language. Word came once more that a young man from a certain tribe wished to marry the girl, but she objected. "Well, then, whom do you wish to marry, a Wolf?" her old grandmother asked. The Wolves were outside listening. Of course, the old lady had said this in anger and did not mean it. The Wolves said to one another, "Now they are giving us the girl." They told a certain young man of theirs to go get the girl, as her people were giving her to him. Young Wolf then turned into a human being, I suppose. He spoke to the girl and she agreed to go with him. He took her to his village somewhere.

The girl's parents missed her and looked everywhere for her. Finally, they discovered that young Wolf had her. Old Wolf came over to their village and brought them many elk, deer and other kinds of game. The girl's parents were well satisfied.[3]

SASA'ILAX̣ƏN.[4]

The grandfather of the Sasa'ilax̣ən peoples was living in a house. Not far from his home lived a young princess. Many people had wanted to buy her but she had refused them. People from everywhere had asked to marry her, but she did not like any of those who had asked her. Then young Sasa'ilax̣ən thought, "It would be all

[1] When their parents tell them this story, the younger generation always get very angry, because they do not believe it.

[2] Told by Marion Davis, 1927.

[3] The narrator added at the end of the story, "I believe this story is true. The wolves were always close to the houses. The people of łαmi'x·ilos were great people. They were just like soldiers. What they said, they meant. They were all hunters. Not a one of them could go for long without killing a deer, bear or the like. They were hunters because their ancestors were part wolf."

[4] Told by Peter Heck, 1927; recorded in text. See p. 419.

right if I should go now to see if she is willing to have me. But I shall go secretly. Otherwise, she might refuse me and I would be ashamed. I shall sneak over and find out if she is willing that we make love." He got ready immediately and put some beads around his neck. Then he said to his grandfather, "Get ready; we shall sneak over to see if the princess is willing to marry me." "Oh, all right, grandson," the old man said. They got into the canoe and paddled some distance up the river. They finally got to the place and landed. "Stay here, grandfather. I'll come back here if the woman says 'yes'," the young fellow said. "All right, I'll be waiting for you, grandson," the old man said.

Then young Sasa'ilax̣ən got out of the canoe and started for the house. When he got there, he climbed up and came down through the roof, into the princess' bed, which was next to the wall. After a while, the princess woke up and found herself in someone's embrace. "Who could have come to me?" she thought. She felt around close to her face; there was a man with beads on his breast. "Who can it be?" she thought; "it might be a common person wanting to make fun of me." She got up and reached for some dried salmon backbone that was close by, to strike him on the head. The man arose immediately and climbed back up through the roof.

Sasa'ilax̣ən went down to the river. When he got there, he took his place again in the canoe. "What happened, grandson?" the old man asked. "Nothing," Sasa'ilax̣ən answered. They started back down the river.

Then the young woman began to think, "I wonder who the man was that came to my bed? I felt what was evidently beads on his chest. There were a lot of them. Oh, it must have been Sasa'ilax̣ən who was here! If it were, I'd follow him."

Next morning early, she got ready. She took her travelling-satchel and went out. She went down to the river, and there she saw the canoe going down. "Oh, I shall run after them," she said. She went up the bank and started down the river on foot. She could see them still going down. "Oh, wait for me, Sasa'ilax̣ən," she called (sang). "Oh, grandson, I hear someone calling," the old man said. "Hush, just paddle swiftly!" the young man said. When the girl got down to the bank, they were gone. "Oh, wait for me, Sasa'ilax̣ən," she called again. Then again, the old man said, "Grandson, someone is saying something to you!" "Hush, just paddle swiftly, don't wait!" the young man said. Again, the girl took a short cut and went down to the water. They were gone. "Oh, wait for me, Sasa'ilax̣ən," she called. "Someone is saying something to you, grandson," the old man said again. "Hush, just paddle on," the young man answered. Again the young woman took a short cut and went down to the water. They were gone. "Oh, wait for me, Sasa'ilax̣ən," she called. "Say, grandson, it sounds like a woman shouting," the old man said. "Hush, just paddle swiftly, it's not for me," the young man said. Again the girl took a short cut and went down to the water; they were gone. "Oh, wait for me, Sasa'ilaxən," she called. "Say, grandson, she's asking us to wait for her. It might be the one that you went to see. We'd better wait; it might be the one!" the old man said. "Grandfather, if you say so, then we'll wait," the young man answered. The young woman came down to the river. "She's the one, the princess!" the old man said. The girl was carrying her satchel. "Sit down right in the middle of the canoe," they said to her. The girl got in. "Start to paddle, grandfather," the young man said. They started down the river and finally arrived at their house. They landed and got out of the canoe. The woman took her satchel from Sasa'ilaxən. They went toward the house, and when they got there, went in. Sasa'ilaxən took the woman to his quarters. He put the satchel under the bed. The woman was going to stay as his wife.

In the meantime the girl's parents did not know where she had gone. "She had her satchel with her when she left. Was she leaving to get married? Is it possible that she went to Sasa'ilaxən? Who else could it be? Many people have wanted to marry her, but she was never willing. She must have gone to Sasa'ilaxən. We shall go to see and will take some lunch along. She might be there to eat it." And so they went to their canoe and started down the river. They finally got there and landed. Then they got out of the canoe and started toward the house. When they got to the house, they went in. Indeed, there was the girl in Sasa'ilaxən's house. They sat down. "Oh, daughter, it is all right," they said. "We brought you some lunch. Take it out." The girl got the lunch that they had brought. Now their hearts were cheered; they were satisfied that their daughter was going to have Sasa'ilaxən for a husband. After a while, they went home.

Sasa'ilaxən now had his wife. She said to him, "Oh, let us go to swim." They went down to the river bank. Then they swam. As soon as they had finished swimming, they came out and sat down on the gravel-bar. They combed their hair and when they had finished, the young woman said to her husband, "I am going to look for your louse." She looked for a louse but could not find one. But there was a little sore place on top of his head. "Oh, how does it happen that you have this sore place?" she asked. Then her husband jerked his head away. "What's the matter, didn't you know it was there?" she asked. Then Sasa'ilaxən took hold of his wife and killed her. He left her there dead. "She had no idea what she was doing when she mentioned that!" he said. He had gone mad for a moment, and killed her.

The body of the woman who had been killed by her husband just lay there on the ground. Then a doctor of the lowest class[1] thought,

[1] There are five classes of doctors. A doctor of the fifth class, that is, one who has five guardian spirits of the proper kind, can bring the dead back to life.

"Oh, I shall go down to the river and take a walk." When he got there, he said, "What is that lying over there?" He went closer to see what it was. "Oh, I guess it is the dead woman," he said, "the dead princess. I had better doctor her, so she will come to." He doctored her,

Hard feces,
Hard feces.

But still the woman did not come to. Then he left. Then another one came and doctored,

Diarrhoea,
Diarrhoea.

He stopped, for the woman had not come to, and went away. Then another one came, and started his tamanoas song,

Droppings,
Droppings.

The woman had begun to quiver a little, but still did not come to, and so he got up and left. Another one came and immediately started to doctor. He began his song,

Round feces,
Round feces,
Round feces.

The woman did not move, and so he got up and left. Then Grey-back Louse thought, "I had better go down to the water." She went there, and saw a woman lying there. She went up to her; the woman was dead. The excrements that the others had left were sitting around the dead woman, and were giving off a disagreeable smell. "Oh, those bad people, to make a smell around the princess!" Grey-back said. She sat down and started her tamanoas song,

Move, move,
Try — Try —
Your little finger.

She sang the same thing five times. Already, the dead woman's little finger had begun to move.[1] Then her next-to-little-finger began to move; then her middle finger began to move; then her pointing finger began to move; then her thumb began to move. Then the woman opened her eyes; she had come to. She got up and sat down. She had been brought to life by Grey-back Louse.[2]

K'walale·'··i

[1] See p. 20.

[2] This story is unfinished, so the narrator said. He explained, "That's as far as I ever got with it. My uncle was telling me this story. The folks were talking about eating, and so I asked for something to eat. My uncle said, 'Well, go eat now.' He never told me the rest of it. It was against the law to ask for something to eat while hearing a story."

THE ONE-LEGGED MAN.[1]

A family was living in a certain place. They had five sons and one daughter. The girl had just had her first menses. They had told her that she could bathe in certain places, but there was one place she should stay away from.

The girl went out to bathe. In one direction, she saw a large open place — which her parents had said was "forbidden" (x̣a'x̣a'). She thought, "I had better go to see what is there. My people don't want me to go there." She walked and walked and walked, and at last came out to the large open place. There was a large lake. She sang,

> I thought there was something forbidden here,
> It is only a lake.

She took off her clothes, waded out a little way, sat down, and washed herself. She soon became frightened; someone must be looking at her. She turned around. A man was sitting there. "Oh," she said, "is this why my parents told me I shouldn't come here?" The man repeated what she had said. She stayed in the water. The man knew all her thoughts and repeated them. "I guess he has me now," he said aloud. She came out and tried to get her clothes but he would not let her have them. "This is the first time I have ever seen a One-legged Man (t'ɛ·'tk·'eyʊq)[2]," she said. "This is the first time I have ever seen a One-legged Man," the man repeated. Then he embraced her and pointed to her mouth, saying, "What is this, wife?" (ata'm titati't, k·u'wx·[3]) "My mouth," she said. "Un huh, my mouth, wife," he said. Then he pointed to her nose, saying, "What is this, wife?" "My nose," she said. "Un huh, my nose, wife," he said. He pointed to her ear, saying, "What is this, wife?" "My ear," she said. "Un huh, my ear, wife," he said. He pointed to her head, saying, "What is this, wife?" "My head," she said. "Un huh, my head, wife," he said. He pointed to her hair, saying, "What is this, wife?" "My hair," she said. "Un huh, my hair, wife," he said. He pointed to her neck, saying, "What is this, wife?" "My neck," she said. "Un huh, my neck, wife," he said. He pointed to her shoulder, saying, "What is this, wife?" "My shoulder," she said. "Un huh, my shoulder, wife," he said. He pointed to her arm, saying, "What is this, wife?" "My arm," she said. "Un huh, my arm, wife," he said. He pointed to her chest, saying, "What is this, wife?" "My chest," she said. "Un huh, my chest, wife," he said. He pointed to her breast, saying, "What is this, wife?" "My breast," she said. "Un huh, my breast, wife," he said. He pointed to her belly, saying, "What is this, wife?" "My belly," she said. "Un huh, my belly,

---

[1] Told by Peter Heck, 1927; see p. 414.
[2] This term is always translated The One-Legged Man. Actually, it refers to the man's physical disability which is revealed later. See also p. 240.
[3] See footnote 3, p. 30.

wife," he said. He pointed to her navel, saying, "What is this, wife?" "My navel," she said. "Un huh, my navel, wife," he said. He pointed to her hip, saying, "What is this, wife?" "My hip," she said. "Un huh, my hip, wife," he said. He pointed to her back side, saying, "What is this, wife?" "My back side," she said. "Un huh, my back side, wife," he said. He pointed to her knee, saying, "What is this, wife?" "My knee," she said. "Un huh, my knee, wife," he said. He pointed to her fore-leg, saying, "What is this, wife?" "My fore-leg," she said. "Un huh, my fore-leg, wife," he said. He pointed to her foot, saying, "What is this, wife?" "My foot," she said. "Un huh, my foot, wife," he said. He had asked her to name her body-parts from head to foot. Now he pulled her backward and pointed to her privates, saying, "What is this, wife?" She did not want to say it. "My pri-i-i-i-v—," she said. "Un huh, my pri-i-i-i-v—, wife," he said. He grabbed her by both feet, and slung her, head down, over his shoulder. He left her clothes where they were, and carried her away. He had kept asking her to name her body-parts until she finally came to the part he wanted.

That night they went to bed to sleep. He told her that they should sleep with their legs together — she lying with her head at one end of the bed, he with his head at the other. Then he used his big toe for copulating. Early next morning, he went hunting.

The girl's parents discovered that she was missing, and learned where she had gone. They found her clothes at the lake. "The One-legged Man has taken her," they said. Then one of her brothers said, "I must go to find her." He found the man's place. His sister was there, but the man was not at home. "You must leave now, for he will soon return," the girl said after a little while. When her husband returned, he said, "Has your brother been here?" "Yes," the girl said. "Why not give him this hide?" he said, and went out. He began to shake the hide, and before long the young fellow, who was on his way home, became tired. Then the man overtook his young brother-in-law, killed him and ate him. He went back home, laughing. "Oh, I found your brother. He was glad to get the hide and took it home," he said to the girl. Next morning early, he went hunting.

The next brother thought, "What is the matter with my brother? He has not returned." He went to the place where his sister was staying. "You must go back now, my husband will soon return," his sister said after a little while. When her husband returned, he said, "Has your brother been here?" "Yes," she said. "Why not give him this hide?" he said, and went out. He began to shake the hide and the young fellow became tired. Then he overtook his young brother-in-law, killed him and ate him. He started back home, laughing. When he got there he said, "I overtook your brother and gave him the hide; he was glad to get it and took it home." Next morning early, he went out hunting.

The third brother thought, "What has happened to my brothers? None of them have returned. I must go to visit my sister." "My brothers have not returned home," he said, as soon as he saw his sister. He stayed with her until she said, "You must go now, my husband will soon be back." When her husband came, he asked, "Has your brother been here?" "Yes," she said. "Why not give him this hide?" he asked. Shaking the hide, he ran after his brother-in-law. The young fellow soon became tired. Then he overtook the young fellow, killed him and ate him. Next morning early, the One-legged Man went hunting.

The fourth brother thought, "What has happened to my brothers? Another one has failed to return. I must go to see my sister." As soon as he saw his sister he said, "My brothers have not returned. However, I didn't see anything suspicious looking along the trail." "Well, I can't say what has happened. I do know that my husband always runs after them and gives them a hide," his sister said. After a while, he left. When the girl's husband returned, he asked, "Has your brother been here?" "Yes," she said. "Why not give him this hide?" he asked and shaking the hide, he ran after his brother-in-law. The young fellow soon became tired. Then he overtook him, killed him and ate him. When he got back to his wife, he was very good to her; he laughed and played with her. Before long, he opened his mouth wide; there was a lot of hair sticking to his teeth. "Oh, he's eating my brothers!" the young woman said. She did not sleep a wink all night. She already had two children, a boy and a girl. The man went hunting early next morning.

Then the young woman set to work to gather pitch wood. She gathered all she could find and put it all around the house, covering the door and everything. When her husband came back, he asked, "Your brother didn't come today, eh?" When he learned that the fifth brother had not come, he felt uneasy. The little boy always slept with him. When both were sound asleep, the young woman took the little girl and went out. She fastened the door and set fire to the pitch around the house. Before long the man awoke and shouted to her to open the door. But the house burned to the ground, and he and the boy burned with it. When nothing remained but ashes and charred bones, the woman said, "Nothing like this shall ever happen in the next generation. If a pubescent girl (ma'isx̣ɑm) wants to swim, there will not be a man like this to molest her." Packing her baby girl, she started home.

The woman now had only one brother left. If the youngest one had gone to visit her, the man would have killed him, too. If the man had not laughed and showed his teeth, the fifth brother would have come, also.

The little girl began to grow up and was soon playing with the other children. One day, they heard a child crying, "Oh that girl has pulled my eye out."[1] The girl's mother and uncle then put her in a nice little bucket and threw her into the river.

The child floated down the river to another place. The people there found her in the nice little bucket and kept her. The girl soon became acquainted with the children there and played with them. Then one day a child cried, "That girl pulled my eye out." "Oh, she was troublesome, that's why they threw her away," the people said. They put her back into a nice bucket and threw her into the river.

The girl floated down to another place and someone found her. She played with the other children. Then a child cried, "That girl pulled my eye out." They found out that the girl was a bad child, put her into a nice bucket and threw her into the river.

The girl floated down to another place and someone found her. She became acquainted with the other children and played with them. Before long she pulled out a child's eye. They found out that she was bad, and so they put her in a bucket and threw her into the river.

The girl floated down to another place and someone found her. She soon got into the same kind of trouble, so they put her back in a bucket and threw her into the river.

The girl floated far down until she came to the place where the giant, L'αmx̣αma·'ɪp[2], lived. A man there saw the little bucket and went to get it. When he saw the girl he said, "Oh, she shall be my wife when she grows up." And when the girl was a little older, he married her. The girl's name was Mʊsk·ɪ'ləq'αno't. Her mother's name was (probably) K·ɪ'ləqαno't.

THE DANGEROUS LAKE BEING.[3]

Five brothers had a home at na'k·alł[4]. The eldest brother thought, "I had better go out to hunt something." The following morning, he went out. A pheasant flew up and he shot it. He hung it in a little tree of some sort and went on. Before long he came to an open lake. He looked into the water. There seemed to be an elk-doe far at the other end of the lake. "I wonder how this elk happens to be dead," he said. The elk seemed to be floating about at the other end. He took off his clothes and swam out, intending to bring it to his side of the lake. Half-way out, something pulled him under and he drowned.

"What could have happened to my brother? He's been gone all day," the next brother said. "I'll go out to look for him tomorrow morning." Next morning, he went out. He had not gone far, when

---

[1] See pp. 198, 373.
[2] Ne'pius' enemy; see p. 80.
[3] Told by Mary Heck, 1927; interpreted by Peter Heck. See p. 392.
[4] A little prairie near Lincoln Creek; this prairie was a lake at the time of the happenings in the story.

a pheasant flew up. He shot it and put it in a little tree of some sort — the same place where his elder brother had put his. Then he went on. In a little while, he came to a large open place. There was a lake there. He looked across to the other end of the lake and saw an elk there. "I've found an elk-doe," he thought, "I'll swim over and bring it to this end." He took off his clothes and started across. Just half-way across, something grabbed him and pulled him under.

That evening, the third brother said, "What has happened to my brothers? I'd better go to look for them tomorrow morning." He found the pheasant and killed it and hung it in the place where his brothers had hung theirs. He came to the lake and at the other end he saw an elk. "I guess I'll swim over and bring it over here," he said. He took his clothes off and started over. Just half-way across, something grabbed him and pulled him under. Now the third one was gone.

The fourth brother said, "I guess I'd better go to see what has happened to my brothers; none of them have come home. They must have found something." He saw the pheasant, shot it and hung it in the place where his brothers had hung theirs. In a little while he came to a lake. He looked across and saw an elk at the other end. "I've found an elk-doe. I'll swim over and bring it over here," he thought. It never occurred to him that anything was amiss, and so he did not look about, but thought only of getting the elk. He took off his clothes and started across. Half-way over, something grabbed him and pulled him under the water.

The youngest said, "What has happened to my brothers?" He thought it over and then went to bed. He dreamed: "All of your brothers have been drowned in that lake. There is a dangerous being (pα'sa) there, who puts an elk in the lake to entice them to swim out after it, so that he can eat them. If you should go over there, you will see the lake and the elk. When you see them, you will understand what I am telling you. Stay on this side of the lake. You will find a lot of rocks there. Make a fire and then gather up the rocks. Heat them in the fire. When you have enough, start to roll them into the lake. Soon, the lake will get hot and boil and gradually dry up. That's how you will kill the dangerous being." The young man awoke and thought of his dream. "I must go and see about it," he said. Early next morning he went out. A pheasant flew up but he did not shoot it. He saw the others in the tree; one was fresh, but the first one was decayed. He came to the lake. "This is my dream," he said. There was the lake and there was the elk. He went to the spot to which his dream had directed him. He started a fire and put the rocks on top of it. As soon as the rocks were hot he started to roll them into the water. Before long the water was boiling; one end of the lake was already drying up. He rolled more rocks in and soon the lake was completely dry. Right in the middle of it he saw a dangerous being. The being was pointed at both ends and had a big belly. The young man's dream had said, "When you see the dangerous being, cut him open. You'll find your brothers inside." He went up to the being. Inside of him he found his first, second, third and fourth brother. They had already begun to decay.[1] He started another fire right on the spot. He burned the dangerous being and smashed him up. "In future generations there will be just a lake[2] here," he said.

THE DANGEROUS TREE BEING.[3]

Five brothers made a camp in the woods. The eldest went hunting. He had not gone far when a pheasant flew up and alighted. He got his bow and shot at it. The pheasant dropped. He went after it, got it, and stuck it in the forks of a tree. Then he went on. He had not gone far when it began to rain. It became dark and he could not see. He was getting wet and there was no dry place to go to. He heard someone shouting and listened. The person said again, "Here, here, there is a dry place under a tree." "Ah, he says there is a dry place under a tree." He went in that direction. He got there and found the dry place. It was so dry, it was mouldy. He made a fire, and without removing his clothes, dried them. Then he lay down to sleep. After a while, he slept. Then something came down from the tree.

That evening, the next brother thought, "What has happened to my brother? He isn't home yet. Evidently I shall have to go to look for him." Early in the morning he set out to look for his brother. "What has happened to him?" he thought. A pheasant flew up. He shot it. The pheasant dropped. He got it and stuck it in the forks of a tree. Then he went on. He had not gone far, when it began to rain. Now there was no dry place to go to. He heard someone shouting and listened. The person said again, "Here, under a tree, is a dry place." He went in that direction. He got there, and indeed, there was a very dry place. Dry alder wood for making a fire was stacked against the tree. Then he dried himself. Then he made his bed, and lay down to sleep.

The third brother was worried. "What is the matter with my brothers? They aren't home yet. I must go to see if I can find them," he thought. Early in the morning he set out to look for his brothers. He had not gone far when a pheasant flew up. He shot it. It dropped. He got it and stuck it in the forks of a tree. Then he went on. He had not gone far when it began to rain. There was now no dry place to go to. Then he heard someone shouting. "Over here,

---

[1] Notice that he does not revive his brothers.

[2] I believe that prairie should have been used here instead of lake. It is my impression, from what the interpreter said at the beginning of the story, that the lake was burned dry, forming Na′k·ał prairie.

[3] Told by Peter Heck, 1927; recorded in text. See p. 392.

there is a dry place." He went in that direction. Indeed, he found a dry place. There was alder-wood for making a fire, stacked against the tree. He took some of the alder-wood, broke it in pieces and made a fire. Without stripping off, he dried himself. When he was dry, he lay down to sleep.

The fourth brother was worried. "What has happened to my brothers? They have not come home. I must go to look for them." Next morning early he set out. A pheasant flew up and he shot it. It fell. He got it and stuck it in the forks of a tree. Then he went on. He had not gone far when it began to rain. There was now no dry place to go to. He heard someone shouting and listened. "Over here, there is a dry place." He went in that direction. He found a dry spot under a tree. There was some alder-wood for making a fire stacked against the tree. He took some of it and made a fire to dry himself. When his clothes were dry, he lay down to sleep.

The youngest brother was worried because his brothers had not come home. He felt bad about it. He lay down to sleep. He dreamed: "Your brothers were killed. When each went out, a pheasant flew up. He shot it and hung it in the forks of a tree. Then he went on. He had not gone far, when it began to rain. Then he heard someone shouting. He went in the direction of the noise. When he got there, he found a very dry spot beneath a tree. There was some fire-wood there. When he fell asleep, a dangerous being (pα'sa) came down from the tree. He took out your brother's heart and threw the body behind a tree. There you will find each one's body." Early next morning he got ready to leave. He set out. A pheasant flew up. "There's the pheasant I dreamed about," he said. The pheasant alighted. He did not shoot it; he passed it up. He had not gone far when it began to rain. "This is my dream," he said. He heard someone shouting. "That's the one who has killed all my brothers," he thought. He went in that direction. When he got there, he found a very dry place beneath a tree. There was some dry alder-wood for making a fire. He went around to the other side of the tree. "Here are my brothers!" he said. He went back to the other side of the tree. Then he made a fire. He fixed his bed; he put down some sticks and covered them with a blanket. Then he went back to the other side of the tree to hide. Before very long, it sounded as though someone was coming down from the tree. The dangerous being went right to the bed that he had fixed and grabbed it. Then, suddenly, he shot at the dangerous being. The being jumped. He shot at him again. The being went up into his tree. He shot him again and again, without stopping. Then the being fell to the ground. He shot him again for the last time; the being was dead. He went over to him, took out his knife and slit his belly. His brothers' hearts came out. He laid them aside, together. He made a fire — a very big fire. Then he got the dangerous being and threw him into the fire. He burnt him up. The ashes blew up and he said to them, "Nothing like this shall ever happen again. A dry spot beneath a tree shall be merely a dry spot. In future generations, a dry spot shall never belong to a dangerous being." When he had finished with the dangerous being, he got his brothers and brought them up to the fire. He laid them side by side. Then he got their hearts. He replaced his eldest brother's heart first. His brother came back to life. Then he replaced his next brother's heart. His brother came back to life. He replaced his next brother's heart. His brother came back to life. He replaced his next brother's heart. His brother came back to life. All four of them came back to life. Then the five of them went home.

K'walale·'··i

THE DANGEROUS BEAVER BEING.[1]

Five young men made a home. The eldest said, "Well, brothers, I think I'll take a walk; I might find something." Pretty soon a pheasant flew up. He shot it and it fell down. He hung it up and went on. He came to a little shack. An old man was lying down, warming his back to the fire. "Oh, grandson, you are taking a walk?" the old man said. "Oh, yes, I'm taking a walk; I was tired of staying home," the young man answered. "Oh, grandson, there is a big gathering here above us; people have come from everywhere for the big time. I would like you to help me before you go. When I go to the river to swim or bathe, there is a beaver that always stays near me. I wish you'd kill him for me. I am all alone here," the old man said. "All right," the young man answered. "Here's my spear," the old man said, adding, "now we'll go down to the river." They went to the river. "You stand here, for beaver always comes right through here, and I'll go up above," the old man said. Pretty soon, the young man heard a beaver coming down, splashing his tail. He caught sight of him. "I'll fix you!" he cried to the beaver, who came right close to him. He speared. The spear had no sooner struck beaver's hide, than the point broke off. Beaver then came out on shore, grabbed the young fellow and threw him down. He bit him on the neck and killed him. Then he removed the young fellow's heart and ate it. Then he took off his own beaver clothes. It was the old man himself. He went back to his shack and stayed there.

That evening, the second brother said, "What has happened to my brother? He must be staying overnight somewhere." Next morning he went out. A pheasant flew up and he shot it. He hung it in the place where his elder brother had hung his. Pretty soon he came to a little shack. There was an old man inside, warming his back to the fire. "Grandson, are you taking a walk?" the old man asked. "Yes, I'm tired of staying home. My elder brother did not

[1] Told by Mary Heck, 1927; interpreted by Peter Heck. See p. 391.

come home last night and I am looking for him," the young man answered. "Well, there's a large gathering just above here; the people have come from everywhere for a big time. Your brother must have gone up there," the old man said. Then he added, "There are some beavers here in the river that bother me all the time when I go to bathe; they bother me continually. Something will have to be done about it. Could you help me before you go on?" He gave his spear pole to the young man. When they got to the river, the old man said, "I am going up a little farther; one always stays up there and one comes down here. You kill the one that comes down your way." Before long, the young man heard a beaver coming down, splashing his tail and thrashing about. He stood with his spear raised. When the beaver came close, he speared him. The spear buckled as soon as it touched beaver's hide. Beaver then came ashore, grabbed the young man and killed him.

The third brother said, "I must try to find my brothers." Next morning he went out. A pheasant flew up. He shot it and hung it in the place where his elder brothers had hung theirs. Before long he came to a little shack. There was an old man inside, warming his back to the fire. He went in. "Oh, grandson, are you taking a walk?" the old man asked. "Oh yes, but I'm rather on the look-out for my brothers; they have not come home yet. Did they come here, by any chance?" the young man said. "Why, yes. There's a big gathering near here; they must have gone there after leaving here. You'll surely find them," the old man said. Then he added, "There are some beavers here that always bother me when I bathe. Will you help me kill them? It takes two people to do it." He gave the young man his spear. They went to the river. "You stay here and I'll go up above to watch the others," the old man said. Pretty soon the young man heard a beaver noisily coming down stream and then going back up. Finally, the beaver came a little nearer and he speared him. But the spear buckled — it could not penetrate the hide. Beaver then came ashore, grabbed the young man and killed him.

The fourth brother was growing uneasy. "This is terrible; my brothers have not come home yet. I must go out to look for them." Next morning he went out. A pheasant flew up and he shot it. He hung it where the others had been hung. He came to a little shack. An old man was there, warming his back to the fire. "Oh, grandson, so you have come?" the old man said. "Yes, I'm looking for my brothers; they have not come home," the young man answered. "Oh, grandson, you will certainly find them; there is no reason why you shouldn't, for there is a big gathering near by and they must have gone there. But I wish you'd help me kill some beavers before you go. I made a spear blade just before you came and I will give it to you," the old man said. They went to the river. "You stay here and I'll go up above to watch for one that always comes there," the old man said. The young fellow fastened the blade to the pole. Soon he heard something splashing; a beaver was coming down stream. When the beaver came close, he speared him. The spear broke. Beaver then came ashore, grabbed the young man and killed him. He removed the heart and threw the body to the side of the trail. Beaver ate only his victims' hearts.

The youngest brother was worried. "What has happened to my brothers? They have not returned." He wept and wept. Then he went to sleep. He dreamed and in his dream someone said, "All of your brothers have been killed. After each one left, he saw a pheasant fly up. He killed it and hung it up. Then he found an old man in a shack who asked him to help kill a beaver. He was willing to help. The old man gave him a spear blade that was not meant to kill anything. The old man then left him and went a little farther up the river. He put on his beaver-clothes there and then came down the river looking like a beaver. You will find your brothers' bodies piled up on one side of the trail. If you want to kill the old man, don't use his spear blade. Take his spear pole when he offers it, but put on your own blade."

The young man went out. He heard a pheasant fly up but let it go. He saw where his elder brothers had hung their pheasants. The first one was rotten by this time. "This is just as I dreamed," he said. He came to the shack. "There it is!" There was an old man inside. "This is my dream," he said. He went in. "Oh, grandson, are you taking a walk?" the old man asked. "Oh yes, I've lost my brothers; I don't know where they went," the young man answered. "Oh, they passed by here. There's a big gathering near here; they must have gone there. But grandson, you must help me before you go to your brothers. There are some beavers here that I can't manage to kill. Here's a spear blade; I made it just before you came," the old man said. He added, "I'll go up stream to watch for one and you stay down to watch for the other." They went to the river. "Stand right here and watch; one always comes here," the old man said. As soon as Beaver had gone up stream, the young fellow threw Beaver's spear blade away and tied his own to the pole. Before long he heard a beaver making a noise. "This is my dream," he said. The beaver came close and then went away. He did the same again. Then he came quite close. The spear sunk into his body. The young man had two spears and stuck him again. The beaver grunted like a man; he could not get up. The young fellow beat him over the head with a stick and killed him. He made a fire and then cut the beaver's hide open. The old man was inside; he had put on the hide in order to make himself a beaver. "I've got you now!" the young man said. He burned the old man up. "Beaver will be only an animal from now on and will not deceive travellers in order to kill them," he said. Some ashes blew up. He said, "These ashes shall become harmless beavers. The people may use them for food if they like, but a beaver will never again be a dangerous being." He then smashed up all the bones. "Nothing like this shall ever happen again," he said. He went to the spot where his dream had told him he would find his brothers' bodies. He saw them piled up there.[1]

THE SCATTER CREEK TALE.[2]

A certain young man was living with his grandmother close to Scatter Creek. His grandmother said, "You'd better make a spear. Get ready for the salmon. There will be a lot of them here in a short while. Get ready!" "Oh, the creek is dry; there's nothing but grass. How could they get here?" he answered. "Oh, you'd better get ready, nevertheless," his grandmother said.

In just a few days, the creek was flowing right out on the open prairie; its banks had completely disappeared. The water came roaring down from the head of the creek, and the salmon went up. The young fellow was all excited now. He started to whittle a spear. He held the knife toward him, whittling away, as he gawked at the salmon. As he pulled the knife toward him, it slipped and cut his stomach open. And so he lost out.

Ever since that young fellow cut himself, the people say that one must be prepared and waiting for the salmon on Scatter Creek. There must be no rush about it.

BOIL AND EXCREMENT.[3]

Two old people lived in the same house. They always stayed there and never went to bathe or did any work. They were getting pretty dirty. They had no wood and needed some pretty badly. At last one of them said, "Now we've got to do something. We're pretty dirty and we haven't any wood. We'll have to get some. Either I shall bathe, and you shall get the wood or I shall get the wood and you shall bathe." Then Excrement (mα'ntc) said, "I'll go down and bathe." "I'll go to a good dead tree where there's some nice bark and try to peel it off. I'll get some good thick bark and bring it home," Boil (spo'ᵒs) said. And so Boil went to a standing dead tree and tried to pull the bark off. Some dry, adhering stuff from the

---

[1] The interpreter pointed out that the young man does not revive his brothers.

[2] Told by Peter Heck, 1927. Some details are required to understand this tale. The Upper Chehalis of Grand Mound prairie did not catch fish in the Chehalis River. They would go there and look on while others fished. Occasionally they would catch a few fish if they needed them. But when silver-side came up on Scatter Creek, the Grand Mound people went wild with excitement. After the first snows, the creek flooded and water came roaring down from the source; silver-side then literally poured into the mouth of the creek. This was just what the people were waiting for. See p. 420.

[3] Told by Marion Davis, 1927. See p. 421.

inner part of the tree, fell and burst his eye. That was the end of Boil. As for Excrement, he went down to the river to bathe and thereupon melted and floated; he turned into excrement. In the beginning, the two had been people.

ORIGIN OF THE FRESH-WATER CLAMS.[1]

Some people were living on one side of the (Chehalis) river and some on the other. For some reason or another, someone from one side suggested that they move over to the other side. They then discussed with one another the feasibility of this suggestion. Every last one was willing to go. They boarded their canoe and set out. When right in the middle of the river, they tipped over; evidently one of them had not known how to board a canoe properly. They are there now at the bottom of the river and cannot get away. They had to remain there for good after tipping over. They were once people, but now they are the fresh-water clams.[2]

BEAR AND ANT OR THE CONTEST FOR DAY AND NIGHT.

(First Version).[3]

Bear said that there should be day for a long time and then night for a long time. Ant said that there should be night and day, night and day, one right after the other. And so the two had a race to see who would win. Ant won by making her waist smaller and smaller. That's why Ant has a small waist. If Bear had won, we would have night for a long time and then day for a long time. But because Ant won, we have night for a short time and then day for a short time.

(Second Version).[4]

At the beginning of the world the animals were people. There were Bear, Yellowjacket and Ant. Bear said, "There shall be night for six months. At the end of that time, there shall be day for six months." Ant and Yellowjacket wanted to have night and day right along; they did not want either night or day to last six months at a time. Yellowjacket said, "Day, day, day." Bear said, "Six months night, six months day." Bear now lies down three months at a time and never gets up during that time, he just sleeps. Yellowjacket won. Today, bear tears up yellowjackets' and ants' nests whenever he can find them.

---

[1] Told by Marion Davis, 1927. See p. 411.
[2] About six inches long; similar to the beach clam. Swedes eat them but Indians do not.
[3] Told by Maggie Pete, 1926. See p. 413.
[4] Told by Dan Secena (father of Jonas), 1926. Songs, Appendix, pp. 425, 426.

(Third Version).[1]

Bear was once a person. He said that there should be six months of night and six months of daylight. But Moon (łokwa'ł) said, "That won't do at all; six months of each is too long." If Bear had remained a person, we would have six months of night and six months of daylight, but Moon changed him into an animal. Many of the animals, when they were people, had faults.

MINK KILLS WHALE.

(First Version).[2]

Mink (Stəlä'pcᵘ) was once a person. He saw a large Whale, who stayed in a little bay, digging clams." I'm going to kill that fellow!" he said. "But you have no spear or rope!" someone said. Mink got into his little canoe; he had a knife with him. He dived down alongside Whale and cut a hole in him. Whale did not even feel the cut. Mink went inside the hole, dragged his canoe in after him, and closed the hole. Whale merely jumped a little, thinking the fleas had bitten him. "You'd better go in my direction!" Mink said to the old fellow. They passed a number of places and at each place, Mink would call, "I'm inside the Whale." "Mink is lying!" the people would say. But Mink finally arrived at his own village, where Whale had stopped. He cut Whale's heart. "I'm inside, boys!" he shouted. Whale died and the people towed him down the bay. Then someone noticed Mink inside, already eating. "Oh nonsense," they said to Mink, "you didn't kill Whale; he just got sick and died."

Next morning, everyone came out and looked. Mink was still there. "I'll come out pretty soon; I'll open my door," he said. They saw that he had his little canoe and knife. They went inside and looked. Mink had cut Whale's heart, all right! Mink then invited all the important people down to the beach to eat whale meat.

(Second Version).[3]

One morning, Whale came to the bay. Young Mink said, "I guess I'll take a look at Whale in the salt water." Just as he came out, Whale passed by the camp and jumped. "Next time Whale passes by, I'll kill him!" Mink said. "How would you kill him, you small man?" all the older people asked. "You'll see! You'll eat him yet!" Mink said.

Later, someone said, "Well, Mink, Whale is coming. We want to see you kill him." There were many people camping on the beach. "You have no tools — you can't kill Whale," they said to Mink. "You bet I have!" Mink answered. Young Mink owned a little

[1] Told by Joe Pete, 1926.
[2] Told by Pike Ben, 1926. See p. 405.
[3] Told by Pike, Ben, 1927.

canoe, a one-man canoe. He got a large butcher knife, as sharp as a razor, and put it in the canoe. He had no spear or hatchet. "I have my canoe and my butcher knife," he said. Whale thrashed his tail and spouted. It seemed impossible that Mink, with such a little canoe, could kill Whale. An old lady, when she heard what he was planning to do, said, "Oh Mink, you liar!" (Mink was about twenty-one years old.) His grandmother also said to him, "I want to see how you kill him." Whale stayed there in the bay all day, digging clams. "Watch me now!" Mink said. He got into his canoe and went up to Whale. The latter humped up his back, and Mink, still in his canoe, rode right up on his back. Then he took his knife and cut a hole about a yard square, just big enough for his canoe, in Whale's back. He took his canoe and went inside Whale's belly. Then he slapped the piece of flesh back down. Old Whale felt it; he gave a jump and ran like a turtle. He went down the bay for two days, three days, four days, before he stopped. Then he came back to the place on the beach from which he had started. He had been down to the ocean but had come back to Mink's home. Mink was still inside, talking at a great rate, like a talking-machine. The people could hear him there, talking.

Mink cut Whale's heart. Whale staggered and staggered, then rolled over dead right on the beach, close to camp. He cut off a little piece of flesh and cried, "I told you I'd kill him! Now help me sell him." Everybody then went down to the beach where Whale was lying.

Well, after that old Mink went to call on a certain rich man. Everyone knew old Mink and did not like him.[1] He lied all the time. He had some Spanish-fly[2] — which makes a person go crazy when you put it on his heart. He talked to the rich man's daughter. She did not like Mink, as her family did not approve of him. But before long, she was saying familiarly to him, "Good-bye." He had used the Spanish-fly on her.

The sun set. The girl began to weep, "Poor Mink, poor Mink! I wish he'd come back." "Poor Mink, poor Mink!" she kept repeating. At last her mother noticed what she was saying and exclaimed, "What! That liar!" Before long, the girl was sending a young man to Mink with a message. "Tell him I want to see him," she said to the young man. "Mink," the latter said, "the girl wants to see you." "The girl is no good!" Mink answered. The young man stayed there one day, two days, trying to make some arrangement with Mink. In parting, he said, "Mink, return to the girl in a month."

At last, Mink showed up, dressed in a white shirt[3] and painted like

[1] Compares Mink with a certain man of many affairs.

[2] The narrator may have in mind a native aphrodisiac used by the Upper Chehalis.

[3] At this point, Mr. Ben's wife, who was listening all the while, exclaimed, "No white shirt!" Mr. Ben thought this a great joke. His wife always objected when he brought his stories a bit too much up to date.

a Yakima Indian. "Ah, here's Mink!" the girl cried. She hugged him and kissed him. "Don't kiss me too much," Mink said, giving her one cheek. He had another girl in another village.

And so old Mink won the girl that night and intended to take her home with him. "I'm married to Mink," she said to her parents. "We have no use for Mink. Don't come back home. Mink is a liar. He'll probably give you lots of children," they said.

Before long, the young woman bore Mink a son. At that time, Mink was a man. The woman sent word to her family, "I have a little son." "Don't bring that boy here! I don't want a Mink for a grandson," her father sent word back. When the little boy was about two years old, Mink, his wife, his brother-in-law, and little son, went out in a canoe. The brother-in-law was going to spear little fish and sea-eggs.[1] The woman washed the eggs first and then ate the insides raw. "Help me eat these," she said to Mink. "Throw me a little piece; I'd like to taste them," Mink answered. "Here, taste a little bit of your daddy's," he said to the boy. The woman ate the sea-eggs as though she were sucking eggs. "Are they good?" Mink asked her. "You bet they are! Rich people always eat them," she answered. Mink tried a little piece; he had no more than touched it with his teeth, than he spit it out. "What's the matter with them?" his wife asked. "They're no good! Shame on you for eating them! Let's go on down the bay," he said. The young man kept on spearing sea-eggs and throwing them to his sister. "Here, try a little piece," she said to Mink coaxingly. "Oh, how good they are, how nice!" Mink said this time, eating a whole one. Then he said to the young man, "I'm going to help you get them, brother-in-law." He ate more. "How nice! Eat them, sonny," he urged his little boy. The boy ate them like a little pig. "What's wrong? You're slow!" Mink said to his brother-in-law, adding, "I'll dive in myself. It's not deep. I can catch some in my hand." He took his shoes and pants off, stripped off completely, and dived in. His brother-in-law was sitting on the shore. Mink came out with lots of eggs, put them in the canoe, and dived back in again. This time, he stayed down a little longer; he was eating the eggs. When he came out, he had a half dozen in his hand. "Look," he said to his wife, "how nice!" "But why did you stay down so long?" she asked. "I was looking for other kinds of fish," he answered. He dived in again and stayed there; he went down into deep water, close to some roots. He was gone about a half hour. When he came out, he had only one egg in his hand. "Why did you stay down so long?" his wife asked. "I was playing with the fish," he answered. Well, old Mink dived in again and stayed there. The woman said to her brother, "Look under the water and see what he's doing." "He's eating, eating, eating," her brother reported. "Dirty Mink!" she said. They paddled away. Mink then came out of the water. "Wife, wife," he called, "where are you

[1] See pp. 137, 366.

going? I want to go with you!" "Stay there in the roots. You'll be a mink from now on," she called back. "Throw the little one in, too," she ordered her brother. Then they paddled away from Mink and his son. "You shall be a mink and stay there forever. They'll sell your hide for a lot of money," the woman called back. Before this Mink had been a man.

MINK AND THE GIRL.[1]

Mink went across the bay to see the Leech-peoples' daughter. He talked to the girl for a while and then she said, "You like the girls too well to suit me!"

The girl died. Mink liked her but she did not want to marry him, and so she killed herself. They buried her in a little canoe. The girl's father was living. He was a chief and so his daughter had many friends who came to the funeral. Mink also came to the funeral. He was an old man. He wept and fell down; he was weeping for his "grandchild", as he called the girl. He wore old clothes and carried a cane. "Don't put too many holes in her canoe and don't put it up too high — just high enough that Wolf and Coyote won't eat her," he said.

The same evening, he went out to the canoe and took the girl down. He corked up the holes in the canoe and went away with her in it. One day, someone chanced to pass by the girl's burial place. The dead girl and the canoe were gone. "Old man, you've lost your daughter," they said to her father. Her father ran down and found both his daughter and the canoe gone.

Mink had taken the girl five miles up the bay to a doctor, a cousin of his. "My wife just died a couple of hours ago. Can you help her?" he said. "No, I can't cure her," the doctor said, "she's been dead several days already. Take her eight miles farther up; there's an old fellow there who will help you." Mink paddled and paddled. At last he came to his cousin-in-law. "My wife died about an hour ago. Can you help me out?" he said. The fellow doctored her but was only able to make one of her hands move a little. He was a good, strong doctor! He said, "You must go four miles farther up to the last doctor; he's your cousin." Mink paddled and wept. He came to his cousin. "Your cousin died about an hour ago. Can you help me out?" he said. The fellow began to doctor the girl and by next morning, Mink had a nice wife. About four o'clock in the morning, the girl had got up and combed her hair. Old Mink had a nice looking wife, all right, and a chief's daughter at that!

Before long, the young woman began to show signs of pregnancy. (You could bet on Mink to see to that!) "I'm going to take you home," Mink said to her. He shouted good-bye to his cousin, the doctor, and left. He paddled across the bay to his father-in-law's

[1] Told by P[i]ke Ben, 1926. See p. 405.

place. "Come down to the bay to see me," Mink said, motioning to his wife's little sister. Then Mink's wife said to her sister, "I'm married to a rich man now, a good eater. Tell mother to clean the house and get everything ready."

The little girl went back to the house. "My sister is home; she's come back. Clean the house," she said to her mother. "Don't talk that way! Your sister is dead!" her mother said. "No, she's married," the little girl insisted. After the latter had returned a second time from the beach with the same message, her mother consented to go and see for herself. She came back and got the house ready. Her elder daughter then came to the house; her husband was a fine looking man, a big chief. Two or three days later, the young woman gave birth to a son. The child was not a Mink but a real boy.

Old Mink and his wife went down to the bay to get some fish. He had two or three slaves. The slaves paddled his canoe; Mink did not have to paddle at all. The slaves gathered sea-eggs. Mink's wife told the slaves to wash the eggs in salt water. "Shame on you, my wife, for eating those old eggs," Mink said. "Don't say that!" his wife answered. She ate a half dozen eggs. Mink wanted a little taste of them — just enough for a swallow. He had no sooner tasted one than he spit it out in disgust. His wife started to eat another; there were two in one shell. "Give me half, wife," he said. "Mum, isn't that good!" he said. "You bet it is! I told you so!" his wife said. Then he asked for another and ate it quickly, without first washing it in salt water. "That's no way to do!" his wife said. Then Mink took his clothes off, laid them in the canoe and dived in. "Don't dive," his wife had said. He brought up just a few eggs and laid them in the boat; he had eaten the rest himself, while in the water. The next time, he stayed down longer. When he came up, he had only an empty shell. "Someone has already eaten it," he said. "I'll go down again and get some for my child," he said. He went down again. After a while, the woman said, "Where's that man? Let's leave him there!" Mink came up. "Wife, wife, wife, I've got lots this time," he called. But she paid no attention to him. Then he began to shout curses at her. The woman picked up her little son and threw him overboard. He went in as a real little boy but came out as a mink. "Cedar root is your mother and father!" his mother called back. Mink swore at her. "Good-bye, old Mink," she called back to her husband, as they paddled away. "If you follow us, I'll hit you on the head," she cried.

HO'TSANI.[1]

Ho'tsani[2] wanted to go down to the West Wind as far as he could go. But he could find no way to get there. Before long Cloud came by. Ho'tsani said to him, "I want to go down to the West Wind.

[1] Told by Peter Heck, 1926. See p. 389.
[2] None of the informants, except Mr. Heck, had ever heard of this character.

Can't you take me?" "Oh, you couldn't keep up with me. Sometimes I go slowly but very often I go fast," Cloud answered. "Oh, I'll keep up with you," Ho'tsani promised. Cloud took him as far as he wanted to go. Then Ho'tsani asked to go with Cloud again sometime. But Cloud said, "No, you can't come with me again."

Ho'tsani saw a house. It belonged to two women. They took him in. Each day they went out to dig roots and left him alone in the house. One day he became restless. "I wonder what there is here," he thought to himself. He looked over everything in the house. At last he went over to the place where the two women sat and where they cooked their fish. "They never fish, but still they have fish to cook. Where do they get them?" he remarked to himself. He examined the mats on which they sat and slept. He found that they covered a pool of water. The pool was full of salmon, spring-salmon. "We need this salmon in our own country, but here they are," he said. Then he spoke to the salmon and told them to go to all the different rivers that he knew. Long after the salmon were gone, he suddenly exclaimed, "Oh! I forgot the Chehalis River!" He managed to find a few more somewhere and thus salmon were obtained for the Chehalis River. (But there are not many salmon here.) It was for the very purpose of obtaining salmon, that Ho'tsani had wanted so badly to go to the West Wind. Through Ho'tsani, all the rivers have salmon.

Just as Ho'tsani had about finished his work, Cloud came by, travelling fast. Ho'tsani went along with him. "I'll try to keep up with you," he said. They were headed for home. But Ho'tsani could not keep up with Cloud and was left behind. He landed, I don't know where.

K'walae·'·· i Ho'tsani. That's why we live on salmon.

ORIGIN OF THE FISH.[1]

Once upon a time Jesus was travelling over this world. He was carrying some little salmon bones in his hand. He dropped one[2] into the (Chehalis) river. "You shall become Chinook salmon and there shall be many of you," he said. He went farther down the river and dropped another salmon bone into the water. "You shall become the sucker. The people will eat you, but you will have many bones," he said. He went farther down where there was clear water and dropped another bone into the water. "There shall be trout here, nothing else but trout," he said.[3]

[1] Told by Pike Ben, 1926. See p. 388.
[2] Illustrating.
[3] Mr. Ben remarked here, that the little blue salmon, the best kind of all, live at Tehola but never come up the Chehalis.

ORIGIN OF BEAVER AND DEER.[1]

Beaver used to be a man. Jesus[2] was once travelling and came to him. Beaver was making a nice butcher knife with which to kill Jesus. Jesus was going all over the world hurting[3] people. He said to Beaver, "Give me that knife!" Then he stuck the knife on Beaver's rump and said, "Now, go jump into the river." Jesus then went to the river and said, "You shall be called 'beaver'. The people will eat you; you will make very fine food. Stay in the ash tree forever and get your food from the roots." At present, beaver has a tail like a butcher knife.

Jesus went on and before long, heard a lot of noise. He went down a hill covered with ferns and there found a man in a little shack. "What are you doing?" he asked the man. The old man was Deer. He hit the old man on the tail. At present, deer has a short tail. "Go down into the woods and live there forever; you will make fine food," Jesus said to him.

THE TRAVELLER.[4]

Jesus was travelling. He heard someone splitting rails. He went in the direction of the noise and listened. A man, alone, was splitting a cedar log. "My God!" Jesus exclaimed, when he saw how the man was working. "Well, well, what's going on here?" he said to himself. He went down to where the man was working. "Hello," he said to the man, "have you had dinner yet? I'm rather hungry myself." The fellow stopped and just looked at Jesus. (Jesus was only joking.) He had been using his head for a maul to strike the wedge; he thought his head was an axe! "Hold on there," Jesus said, "come here! Do you see that yew tree there? That's what you should use for making a maul. I'm travelling around straightening up everything. Don't use your head for a maul again; if you do, everybody will do it. Now go down there to that tree and cut it." And so the man obeyed and cut down some little trees about three feet tall. He cut them in two. Then under Jesus' direction, he made a large maul with a small handle. He burned the maul a little to make it hard. Then he made a large wedge. Heretofore, this old fellow had not known how to use his hands as they should be used.[5] "Never use your head again for a maul. I'll watch you now and see how you pound," Jesus said. The fellow pounded and pounded until he had split the log. "Now, how do you like it?" Jesus asked. "Fine, fine,"

[1] Told by Pike Ben, 1926. See p. 388.
[2] Although I brought the question up, I was never able to learn from Mr. Ben whether he substituted Jesus for X̣wɑne' or for Moon. His wife, a Puyallup, once said to me, "X̣wɑ'de is Jesus."
[3] That is, transforming.
[4] Told by Pike Ben, 1926. See p. 389.
[5] Implying that the man was also using his hand as a wedge?

the fellow answered. This happened two or three thousand years ago. At present, no one uses his head for splitting logs.

Jesus went on and came to a river; it was wide and swift. He could hear some commotion there on the gravel bar. A number of men were making a salmon trap, but did not know how to make it properly. They had kept people standing there in the water for two months. They had a bad custom in this place; some women had been kept there in the water to hold the sticks for the trap. An important man owned the trap. They were catching lots of Chinook salmon. "Hello," Jesus, the traveller, said to the owner. The man roared at him. "What's going on here?" Jesus asked. "Fishing,"[1] the man answered. "What are those men and women doing here?" Jesus then asked. "They're posts," the man answered. "Oh my! Who told you to do this?" Jesus said. "I did,"[1] the man answered. "Well, now, aren't you ashamed of yourself?" Jesus asked. "No!" the man said. "Well, sir, you're going to tear out those posts and let the women go! I'll show you what kind of wood to use," Jesus said. The women and men then came out of the water. "Have you an axe?" Jesus asked the owner. "Yes,"[1] the man said. Jesus then cut down three willow trees and cut some cedar limbs for ropes. He tied two of the poles together at the top and then tied the third at the back of these two. "Never use women again for this purpose; use these poles instead, clear across the river," he said. When he had finished Jesus went on.

X̣WɑN AND COON.[2]

X̣wɑn and his brother Coon were living together. They tried to make a living but did not succeed very well; they were half-starved most of the time. At last they became weak from hunger; they could not find anything to eat anywhere. One evening, X̣wɑn said to his brother, "What do you say to wishing for something to eat tomorrow morning?" "All right," Coon said. They found some dried bark and made a wish that the bark would turn into dried salmon. They took the bark home and put it under their pillows: next morning they would look at it to see if it had turned into dried salmon. Coon watched his partner closely. X̣wɑn was snoring. He slipped out and went to someone's house. He crawled through the roof and got some dried salmon. Then he went home. He threw out the bark peelings under his pillow, and put the dried salmon in their place. Later, X̣wɑn said, "Oh, brother, wake up! Remember our wish!" "Look for your's first," Coon said. "All right," X̣wɑn said. He found just the same old bark. Coon lifted his pillow and found two pieces of dried salmon. "Oh, brother, your wish came true and mine didn't!" X̣wɑn said. They shared the salmon.

[1] Said in a big, deep voice.
[2] Told by Peter Heck, 1926. See p. 384.

"Brother, we've got to wish again," X̣wαn said. They went out and got some more bark. That night, Coon went out again and stole some more dried salmon. In the morning, X̣wαn called to Coon that they should look to see if their wish had come true. "Oh, you look for yours first, I'm sleepy," Coon said. X̣wαn looked. There was the same old thing. Coon looked for his wish and found two pieces of dried salmon. "Oh, my wish never comes true, but yours does!" X̣wαn said. But after a while, he began to think, "I don't understand why my wish never comes true but Coon's does. There must be something wrong; mine should be salmon too!"

The fourth time, X̣wαn pretended to be asleep. He was listening closely and heard Coon go out. After a long time, Coon returned. He took the stuff from under his pillow, threw it away, and put the salmon there. "So that's what he's doing! That's why his wish always comes true, and mine doesn't!" X̣wαn said to himself. In the morning, he said, "Get up, Coon, and find your wish. Mine never comes true." Coon ate his salmon. Then X̣wαn said, "You'll have to take me to the place where you get your salmon." "I didn't get any salmon," Coon said. "Oh, yes you did! You'll have to take me!" X̣wαn said.

Night came; they did not have to wish this time. They went to the house. "How do you get up there?" X̣wαn asked. "Oh, I crawl through the roof," Coon said. Coon got some salmon and came back. Then X̣wαn crawled up. It was so dark, he could not see. He found a whole basket of salmon. "Well, I'll take this whole basket full, that's better than just a few," he said to himself. He started to climb back up, missed the pole and fell through. The people waked up and lighted some pitch. There was X̣wαn with a whole basket of salmon! X̣wαn got up. They found a stick to club him with. Finally he managed to get away. "I very nearly got killed," he said to Coon, "I tried to wish a whole basket full of salmon and fell through. I lost my salmon."

They stayed on at the same place, not knowing what to do. Coon took to going to the river to catch little fish. He would wrap the little fish in leaves and bury them in the ashes. He did this day after day. X̣wαn had scarcely anything to eat. One day he said to Coon, "Brother, you'd better be careful. Something dangerous will come around and kill you, if you don't stop that fishing!" Coon paid no attention. "Watch out! Something will kill you!" X̣wαn said again. Coon paid no attention and went back to the river. A little later, he came back. "Something will happen soon!" X̣wαn said again. Coon went back to the river. Then X̣wαn painted his face all over — white and black and red. "The wala'spam[1] and the pi'tspam[1] are always coming around and they will kill you," he had said to Coon. He got himself up to look like a wala'spam. He

[1] Sahaptin terms, although the narrator was not aware of it. He said that as far as he knew, these were just imaginary people.

took his spear and went to the river. Coon was catching little fish with his hands. "Wala'spam!" X̣wαn yelled, and speared Coon right in the side. Then he ran off.

Coon came out on shore, pretty sick. "X̣wαn did this to me!" he said. He went to the house. X̣wαn was asleep. "Oh, brother," he said to Coon, "didn't I tell you that the wala'spam and the pi'tspam come around here all the time?" But Coon was thinking, "X̣wαn did this to me." He lay there, grunting from pain. "I'm a doctor, I'm a tamanoas man," X̣wαn said, "I can help you with my doctor's tamanoas (nawi'kwʋlx·)." Then he told how he would doctor Coon's wound. "I'll suck the blood from it, so that you will feel better," he said to Coon. He took the fat in his mouth, bit and chewed it and pulled it out. "You're killing me!" Coon yelled. "Keep quiet! I'll fix you," X̣wαn said. He was eating Coon's side. "There's no need to worry about food when I can eat you; you are food!" X̣wαn said.

K'walale·'··i, X̣wαn eats his partner.

X̣WαNÄ'X̣WαNE AND SKUNK.[1]

X̣wαnä'x̣wαne went to another country. He found a new companion, a husky, but short fellow with stripes on his body, Skunk (sma·'yɩn). They went everywhere together. Finally there came hard times. X̣wαnä'x̣wαne had to busy himself with finding something to eat. At last the Short-one invented something that had power like poison-gas. X̣wαnä'x̣wαne at first told Skunk to get rid of it, but eventually he, too, saw its possibilities and began to think about it. "I'm going to make a house as large as a winter-house to try your powers," he said to Skunk.

He built a potlatch-house. He would give a feast and distribute gifts. He called people from everywhere. He invited only the most desirable people, — Deer, Elk, Bear, Pheasant, Grouse, Eel and Salmon. He had closed up one whole side of the house. As soon as everyone was inside, Skunk would shoot his poison at them. X̣wαnä'x̣wαne had roasting sticks ready. The guests and assistants had no weapons with them. Skunk shot out his poison-gas. It was too strong for the guests and they were overcome. Then X̣wαnä'x̣wαne clubbed all of them to death. He told Skunk to air the house.

All winter long, Skunk and X̣wαnä'x̣wαne lived in the house in great style. They were killing others right along with Skunk's gas. They kept this up for a long time. No one was a match for Skunk. Eventually a person greater than anyone else would come, for it was the time when Moon was travelling all over the world. Moon finally arrived at the place where Skunk was killing people. He killed Skunk and made a rule for him. "There shall never be

[1] Told by Jonas Secena, 1926. See p. 384.

another person in this world like Skunk. It is cruel and unthinkable. Skunk shall be nothing but a harmless animal in the next generation." Thus Skunk was condemned. (Although X̣wαnä'x̣wαne was a companion of Skunk's, Moon made no mention of him in his law.) Skunk still lives, but he is harmless and no longer kills people with his poison.

X̣WαNÄ'X̣WαNE AND CRANE.

(First Version).[1]

One warm, bright day, X̣wαnä'x̣wαne and his friend Crane (sq'wa's) went swimming in Satsop River. They swam for an hour or so, and then went out on the sand-bar to take a nap. Both fell fast asleep, but their sleep was not natural; it was caused by K'wαtsx̣wɛ', a huge woman. She was not an ordinary person. She devoured people alive. (She was often seen by the people before the Whites came.) She carried a basket of fresh pitch that had just oozed from a tree. She covered X̣wαnä'x̣wαne's eyes and mouth with pitch, leaving only his nose uncovered. She did the same to Crane. Then she put them in her basket, which she carried on her shoulder. She could easily carry two men.

Crane woke up and said, "What are you doing?" X̣wαnä'x̣wαne knew what was up and told him to keep quiet. The woman took them far up to the mountains in Satsop Valley, where she had her camp. She fixed up her winter-house and then turned the two of them loose. She washed their eyes, so that they could see, and their mouths. She told them that she wanted them to be her brothers. She fed them very well and kept them in fine trim. It was her intention to fatten them up, for she would later butcher them for soup. She kept them five days. After the fifth day she said, "You boys go out and get some ironwood sticks, I'm going to roast you alive today."

Both boys went into the bushes, the woman keeping her eye on them. It happened that both of the boys had tamanoas. "What kind of tamanoas have you?" X̣wαnä'x̣wαne asked, and added, "I have tamanoas myself, but I'm afraid I can't do anything to this woman." Crane said that he had power to fix the sticks. "Let's fix them!" X̣wαnä'x̣wαne said. Crane had a long neck; he twisted the sticks into many shapes and gave them to X̣wαnä'x̣wαne. Then he fixed some in the same manner for himself. They went back to camp. Everytime the monster woman sent them for sticks, they brought back crooked ones. She could not get the crooked sticks through them. After the fifth time, she got tired of this. "I'm going to begin talking her out of this," X̣wαnä'x̣wαne said. He began to talk smoothly to her. "Let's have some fun, let's have some taman-

[1] Told by Jonas Secena, 1926. See p. 386.

oas songs. If you do, we'll bring you some straight sticks," he said. The K'wɑtsx̣wɛ' finally decided to give him a trial; she allowed them to have a tamanoas dance, and became interested, herself, in what they were doing. X̣wɑnä'x̣wɑne had the power of the snakes: he held the sticks and on his head, neck, hands and belt, used some small-sized snakes. He told Crane to do the same. X̣wɑnä'x̣wɑne asked the snakes to help them. The monster woman had dry pitch-wood, used for making a fire, piled all over her camp. X̣wɑnä'x̣wɑne had noticed this and was depending upon it. He sang,

Stick your tongues out,
Stick your tongues out,
Stick your tongues out,
My bouquet;[1]
Wonderful bouquet,
Stick your tongues out.

After the fourth night of this, the monster woman could not stand it any longer and gave up; she could not go so long without sleep. "We'll do this just one more night," X̣wɑnä'x̣wɑne said to her, "and then we'll bring you straight sticks." He sang,

My wonderful bouquet,
Your habit of sticking your tongues out,
  of sticking your tongues out,
My bouquet.

Every half hour or so, he would sing this. The fifth night, before the break of day, he got his power. He, the snake and Crane put the monster woman to sleep in her own room; that is what they had meant to do all along.

The three of them began to cover the floor and the door with pitch. They placed a rock near the woman's bed; when the house began to burn, the rock would get red hot. The monster woman, from exhaustion, was dead to the world. They set fire to the pitch. The whole place caught on fire. They stood ready with poles. The monster woman tried, unsuccessfully, to fight her way out. Suddenly, she shot off like a powder-plant. They went in and heaped everything they could find on her. Then they stirred the burning mass with their poles, until nothing was left of her but ashes. Then they left, but not before Xwɑnä'x̣wɑne had made a rule, right on the spot. This was his speech, which he gave like a law-maker: "This shall never happen again, — shall never happen to the people of future generations. At present, people are not real, but hereafter, boys will be able to swim unmolested. This monster woman shall be condemned, so that nothing like this shall ever happen again." Since that time, there have been no monster women.

---

[1] That is, the snakes.

X̣WαN AND CRANE.

(Second Version).[1]

X̣wαn, Crane and three others stayed together at the mouth of Scatter Creek (k·o′ma'nt). One day they went out and ate blackberries directly from the bushes.[2] When they had finished, they came out on the gravel-bar and went to sleep. X̣wαn woke up — all the others were still sleeping — and shouted, "Ah, wake up, wake up, the Qwa′qʷ is coming!" Then the others got up and looked about. They could not see anyone. Then X̣wαn had a good laugh; he was just making fun of them. He did the same thing four times. He did not do it a fifth time, for he was now asleep himself, along with the others.

Then Sqwaqʷsma′ik· came there and found them all asleep. This dangerous being picked X̣wαn up first and put him in her basket. Then she went to Crane and put him in her basket too. The other three, she piled in on top of Crane. Crane and X̣wαn were on the bottom. Then she started home. The three who were on top woke up. The dangerous being crawled under a tree. Then the one who was farthest on top, caught hold of a branch and swung himself out of the basket. The dangerous being went on and he was left there. He dropped to the ground then and went home. The dangerous being crawled under another tree, and the second one also caught hold of a branch, and swung himself out of the basket. He hung there until the woman was out of sight, then dropped down and went home. The dangerous being crawled under another tree. The third one then caught hold of a branch, swung himself out of the basket, and hung there until she was out of sight. Then he dropped down and went home.

Finally X̣wαn woke up and punched Crane. "Now we are in a basket. The very thing I have always warned you about has come true," he said, "we won't be able to run away." The woman got to her house and set her basket down. She treated X̣wαn and Crane very well. They had to stay there; if they tried to run away, she would eat them. She was going to keep them a while and then eat them.

The woman would go out to pick berries and usually stayed all day. X̣wαn said to Crane, "We must think up some way to get the best of this dangerous being, otherwise she will eat us. Tell me what you think is best and I'll tell you what I think is best. Then we'll choose the better scheme." As soon as the woman would leave, they would talk the matter over. "My plan is to have a tamanoas dance (słaiki′kwʊlx·). I think it would be best for us to get this house ready. We will have a chance to work on it for four or five days. We'll get some moss and pitch and cover the whole outside. When we have

[1] Told by Mary Heck, 1927; interpreted by Peter Heck.
[2] That is, without first putting the berries in a basket.

all that done, you will pretend that you are sick, and I will tell her that you want to sing your tamanoas. I'll tell her to invite her sisters to help us," X̣wɑn finally said. This plan was agreed to, and each day, the two of them worked hard gathering pitch and moss. When this was done, Crane began to take sick. He grunted and grunted. "Oh, my good mistress, my brother is taking sick," X̣wɑn said to the woman, "we would like you and your sisters to help us. As a matter of fact, I feel as though I were going to take sick myself. You had better go right away to your four sisters and ask them to help. Our tamanoas will talk and sing for five days and nights."

The other four women came. Crane grew worse. Then he and X̣wɑn started their tamanoasing. Crane tied a snake around his head. The snake kept sticking his tongue out, and Crane's song told what the snake was doing,

lɑ'məlɑm ts'o'wən
tənta'[a]·· mɑlɑ's.

The women helped him sing. Soon X̣wɑn took sick too and wanted to sing his tamanoas. Now he began to dance. He was chewing an old piece of rotten wood. He kept spitting it out on his chest, and it ran red like blood. The women thought he had tamanoas. They thought he was spitting blood. They danced for four whole nights. Then all five women were so sleepy they had to lie down to sleep. There was to be one more night of dancing, but the women were so sleepy, they could not wake up.

Then X̣wɑn said to Crane, "Let's fasten the door, now." They went out and set fire to everything around the place. The flame was hotter on the side where the door was than any other place. After a while, one of the women woke up. She jumped toward the door and tried to open it, but soon exploded. One after another tried to do the same, and exploded. When everything had burned to the ground, X̣wɑn and Crane came back. They gathered up the charred bones and smashed them up. When the ashes blew up, the two of them said to the ashes, "You shall not be a dangerous being to the people of the next generation. If young people wish to pick berries, they may do so without fear. If they want to take a nap, they may do this also without fear. No one shall eat them." These were the words of X̣wɑn and Crane.

X̣WɑN LOSES HIS EYES.

(First Version).[1]

X̣wɑn was taking a walk along the river. Before long, he met a woman with a little pack on her back. "Hello, sister, you're travelling, are you?" he asked. "Yes, I'm travelling; I've been

[1] Told by Peter Heck, 1926. See p. 384.

down here visiting and now I'm on my way home," the woman said, adding, "I have some dried steelhead salmon eggs to take back." "You have something good, all right!" X̣wɑn said. "Well, I'll give you a little," the woman said. X̣wɑn started off, eating salmon eggs as he went. The eggs were very good. As soon as he had eaten them, he ran as fast as he could, and came out on the trail ahead of the woman. "Hello, travelling?" he asked. "Yes, I'm on my way home," the woman answered. She was surprised; this looked like the same man to her. They talked. "What do you have there in your basket?" X̣wɑn asked. "Oh, I have some dried steelhead salmon eggs to take back home," the woman answered. "Well, you have something very nice!" X̣wɑn said. "I could give you a little," the woman said. She opened her basket, gave him some of the eggs, and went on. X̣wɑn ate the eggs. "I'll run ahead and meet her again," he thought. He came out on the trail ahead of her. "There are two of these men, but still they look just alike," the woman thought to herself. "Hello, sister, where have you been?" X̣wɑn said. "Oh, I've been down here visiting, and now I'm on my way home," the woman answered. "Well, I'm going visiting, myself," X̣wɑn said. Then he asked her what she had in her basket. "I have some dried steelhead salmon eggs and I'm going to give you some of them; you look hungry," the woman answered. "Yes, I am hungry for dried steelhead salmon eggs, and I'd thank you very much for some," X̣wɑn said. As soon as he had eaten the eggs, he ran ahead and met the woman again. "Hello, sister, you're travelling, are you?" he said. "You're the very man I met before!" the woman said. "No, sister," X̣wɑn said, "there are five of us, five brothers, and we look just alike." She gave him some of the eggs. As soon as he had gone, she thought to herself, "That's X̣wɑn! I'll fix him, all right!" She found a hornets' nest and tied it tightly to her basket. She met X̣wɑn and he said, "Hello, sister, travelling, are you?" "Yes, and I'm very glad to meet you! Your brother told me that I would meet all five of you," she answered. Then she said, "I have some nice salmon eggs, brother, and I'm going to give them all to you! But go into a hollow stump before you open the basket. Don't dare open it before you get inside!"

X̣wɑn took the basket, went inside a stump, and told the stump to close tightly. The stump closed its mouth. Just as X̣wɑn was opening his basket, something went "tɑm···". "Hey, flies, get out of here! Don't bother me while I'm eating," he said. But the hornets stung him nearly to death.

X̣wɑn was just about dead when the big Woodpecker came and opened the stump. He found X̣wɑn inside, removed his eyes and anus and went away with them. He took them to a gambling game where the people were playing with little round wheels. "I have two eyes and an anus for you," he said. They used the eyes for wheels and the anus for a roller. One side playing with the eyes, sang,

X̣wɑ'ni's eyes,
X̣wɑ'ni's anus.
"ɛ······, missed him!" (they cried).

When X̣wɑn came to, he had no eyes. He found some wild roses and used the centers for eyes. Then he came to a house. A woman was there. "Have you ever seen a star in the daytime?" he asked. "No, not in the daytime," the woman answered. "Well, I have good eyes. I can see one," he said. "Well, I can't see it," the woman said. "Well, if you can't see it, we'd better trade eyes," he said. Then he persuaded her to make the trade. "Now you'll see stars!" he said, as soon as they had traded. The woman was Snail. That's why we can't see Snail's eyes; she has only some stuff for her eyes.

X̣wɑn went to the gambling game. "X̣wɑ'ni's eyes," he could hear the people singing. He sat down on the crosspiece and clapped his hands. They rolled the eyes in his direction. He made a slight move. "What's the matter with him?" Bluejay said. "Keep still!" his sister said. "But he's getting ready to take his eyes!" Bluejay answered. "Just keep quiet, don't bother!" his sister said again. "But he's getting ready to take his eyes!" Bluejay said. They rolled the eyes toward X̣wɑn five times. Then he grabbed his eyes and anus and ran away. "See what I told you!" Bluejay said to his sister, "I told you something would happen!"

X̣wɑn threw the woman's eyes away.

X̣WɑN LOSES HIS EYES.

(Second Version).[1]

X̣wɑn was staying at a certain place. He was getting lonesome. He thought, "Guess I'd better take a walk." He went out on the trail. Before long he met a woman. Her name was Ts'alɛ'sts'als. She had a pack on her back. "Oh, sister, where are you going?" X̣wɑn asked. "Oh, I'm just travelling, I'm just travelling this way," the woman said. "What have you got in your pack?" X̣wɑn asked. "Oh, steelhead salmon eggs," the woman said. "Oh, you ought to give me some," X̣wɑn said. "All right," she answered. She set her basket down, opened it and gave him some eggs. X̣wɑn ate them right away. Then he ran ahead of the woman, turned, and came down the trail. Before long, he met the woman again. "Oh, sister, where are you going?" he asked. "Oh, I'm just travelling," she said. "What have you got in your basket?" he asked. "Oh, I've got some steelhead salmon eggs, some dried ones," she said. "Oh, you ought to give me some," he said. "All right," she answered. She gave him some of the eggs and then went on. X̣wɑn went on a little way and ate his eggs. Then he ran ahead of the woman, turned back, and

[1] Told by Mary Heck, 1927; interpreted by Peter Heck.

started down the trail. "Oh, here's that woman again!" he said. "Oh, sister, did you meet my brothers coming down the trail?" he asked. "Oh, yes, I met them coming, but they look just like you," she said. "Oh, no, sister," he said, "there are five of us and we look just alike. What have you got in your pack?" "Oh, salmon eggs," she said. "Better give me some," he said. "All right," she said. She gave him some and then went on. Old X̣wαn ran ahead of the woman, sat down, and ate the eggs. Then he turned back, and started down the trail. "Oh, here's that woman," he said. "Hello, sister, did you see my brothers?" he asked. "Oh, no, I saw X̣wαn each time." "Oh, no, sister, there are five of us. I am going down the trail after the others right now," he said. She gave him some eggs and said, "These are the last I have. You'd better not ask me for any again." "Oh, no, you are mistaken; we are five brothers," he said. "Don't bother me again!" she said and went on. "All right," X̣wαn said.

The woman went on. "I'll fix old X̣wαn!" she said. She saw a hornets' nest and put it in her basket; it just fitted. She told the hornets to keep quiet. "Just keep quiet until X̣wαn takes you to a hollow tree. He will go into the tree. When the tree closes, sting him as hard as you can," she said. She picked up her basket and went on. "There's X̣wαn coming!" she said. He was close now. "Oh, sister, did you see my brothers coming down the trail?" he asked. "Oh, yes, but it was you each time," she said. "No, I am the youngest of five brothers," he said. Then he asked, "What have you got in your basket, sister?" "Oh, I have some salmon eggs but I'm too fond of them to give you any," she said. "Oh, sister," he said, "that's not the way to do! If you should ask me for some, I'd give them to you. I'm very hungry for salmon eggs." He began to talk to her nicely. The woman finally said, "All right, I'll give you the whole basket, so that you will get enough." X̣wαn went off a little way and then shouted in gladness, "There's no reason why a woman should have food when I, myself, am hungry!"

The woman had told X̣wαn to go to a hollow tree and to close the mouth of the tree while he ate. He looked for the tree and found it. He went in and closed the top of the stump. When he opened the lid of the basket, something went "tαm·, tαm·". "Oh, keep away, you flies! Don't bother me; I'm going to eat lots of eggs," he said. The hornets stung him and stung him. He yelled but no one heard him. His eyes came off, and his anus came off too.

Long afterward, X̣wαn came to. There was not a single hornet in the place. Before long, he heard someone pounding on the outside. "Who are you?" he asked. "Oh, it is I," someone answered. "Oh, my kind cousin, you'd better make a hole in the stump for me, because it closed its mouth and I can't get out," X̣wαn said. Woodpecker (qaqα′m) then began to make a hole in the stump. X̣wαn laid his eyes out first, then his anus; he would put them on as soon as he got outside. But when he got out, he could not find his eyes or his anus. He went on, blind.

He came to a little house. A woman was sitting down there. Then he took some big round berries from a wild-rose bush and put them in his eyes, so that the woman would not notice that he was blind. When he sat down, he said, "Your blanket is full of lice — just full!" The woman looked her blanket over, but could not see any lice. "You are blinder than I. Let us trade eyes," X̣wɑn said. "Oh, no," the woman said. "But can't you see those lice on your blanket?" he asked. The woman looked her blanket over again, but still could not see any lice. "You had better trade eyes with me, if you can't see them!" he said. "All right," the woman said. Then he jumped and took her eyes and put them in his own sockets. Now he could see. He jumped and shouted, "Why in the world should a woman have eyes when I can't see!" The woman with whom he traded eyes was Snail.

X̣wɑn went on, following the same trail. He heard a noise. It was daytime. He came to a house. They were having a gambling game there. He started in, already singing the song that the others were singing,

ta ma'sis t'x̣wɑni'ls
The eyes of X̣wɑni'.

He went right in, and sat down in the center of the room. He helped with the song, so that they would not notice him. He helped both sides. When they rolled the lal[1], he would follow it with his hands. Bluejay said, "What's the matter with X̣wɑn? He's very proud! He very nearly caught the lal that time." His sister said, "Don't say anything about a chief!" X̣wɑn had changed his appearance, so that the others would take no notice of him. He was helping the people right along. They were using his anus to stop the lal. They rolled his eyes — which they were using for a lal — against the stop. X̣wɑn had sat down right alongside his anus. He grabbed his eyes and anus and ran out; they could not catch him.[2]

K'walale·'··i

X̣WɑNE' HAS HIS SALMON STOLEN.[3]

Once upon a time, X̣wɑne' made a trap from sticks to catch a salmon; he had no net. He caught one salmon, butchered it and began to roast it for his dinner. Then he lay down at his camp to take a nap, as he was very sleepy. Wolf came by and found the old fellow lying there. The salmon was now well done. He ate the

[1] The disk.
[2] The game was held on Na'waqʋm prairie, a Cowlitz prairie.
[3] Told by Pike Ben, 1927. See p. 385.

salmon then and there. X̣wαne′ was still sleeping soundly. When he had finished, Wolf put a little piece of salmon on X̣wαne′'s mouth and nose and went away. X̣wαne′ got up after a while, ready to eat his salmon. The salmon was gone. Pretty soon he smelled the salmon on his nose. "I guess I ate it," he said.

The same day, X̣wαne′ left his trap and went down the trail. He met two girls there and said, "Hello, girls, would you like some salmon eggs?" "Yes, indeed! Have you got some? Let us have them. How much do you want for them?" the girls answered. "Oh, I'll give them to you for nothing," he said. "Now open your hands!" he said, holding out his closed fist. He put something in their hands, saying, "Close your hands quickly, now!" It was yellowjackets! The girls ran this way and that. X̣wαne′ had a good laugh at their expense. "You're no good, old man!" the girls called after him.

X̣wαne′ went three or four miles farther down the trail. There he found an old man. X̣wαne′ was a little weak-eyed; someone had taken his eyes and he now had eyes made from roses. The sun had wilted the flowers and left him weak-eyed. He talked to the old man. "Well, my friend, we'll have to do a little trading," he said. "What have you got to trade?" the man asked. "Well," X̣wαne′ said, "my eyes are a little too sharp; I'd like some weaker ones." "All right, I'll trade eyes with you," the old man said. And so they traded. X̣wαne′ had a good pair of eyes once more. Next morning, the old man said to himself, "These are good eyes I have." But by afternoon, when the sun was hot, his eyes had begun to weaken. Then the old man wept because the sun had wilted his eyes. Old X̣wαne′ was smart!

X̣WαNE′ AND THE FISH.[1]

Old X̣wαne′ once put some nice trout in Satsop River, to remain there forever. At present, there are still lots of trout there. He put blue-back salmon in Tehola River. Blue-back seldom come to the Chehalis River for X̣wαne′ put different fish in different rivers. In the Chehalis River, he put black-salmon, silver-side and dog-salmon; they come every year. He put a large falls in the Chehalis, on the other side of Centralia.[2] He made the eels stop at the falls; this is as far up as they go. He ordered them to jump about ten feet high. "When people come here to catch eels, they shall bring a basket with a long handle," he said. On a hot day there are sometimes as many as five hundred eels sticking to these falls; when one eel jumps, the others follow. A man stands under the falls, and the eels fall right into his long-handled basket. X̣wαne′ ordained that eels should be caught in this manner at this particular place.

---

[1] Told by Pike Ben, 1927. See p. 387.
[2] On the road that goes to South Bend.

X̣WαN AND THE GIRL[1].

A small girl was living with her family. Every once in a while X̣wαn would visit that part of the country where the girl and her family lived. He came to this family and noticed that their daughter, who was about thirteen or fourteen years old, was very small for her age. He went away. He came back the second year and noticed that the girl was still just about the same size; she had not grown at all. The next year he came again. The girl was still about the same size; she had not grown at all. The fourth year he came again. The girl was just about the same size. The fifth year he came again. The girl was just about the same size; she did not seem to grow at all. But she was a pretty girl and he desired her. Then he began to tell her about some good medicine that would make her grow. "Now, my little niece," he said, "you don't seem to grow at all. I will tell you about a good medicine — a medicine that is not hard to take: tomorrow go to the sand-bar across the river and take a walk there. When you see a little stick, two or three inches long, sticking up out of the sand, sit down on it." "All right," the girl said, "I want to grow quickly."

Next day, X̣wαn buried himself in the ground, leaving his organ sticking up out of the sand. The girl came to the sand-bar and found the medicine. She sat right down on it and enjoyed it. X̣wαn from under the ground thus had intercourse with her. The girl began to grow immediately; she grew so quickly, they could almost see her grow. It is the same to-day: if a girl has intercourse, she will grow more quickly.

X̣WαN AND WREN.[2]

X̣wαn had a house. He thought, "I had better take a walk; I am getting lonesome." Then he went up the river. He had gone only a little way, when he heard someone hammering. "What is that person doing?" he thought. "I had better go there to see what it is. I wonder if anyone is making a canoe? What can he be doing?" Then he got to the place, unobserved. "It must be Wren (ts'ats'ɛ''αp)." Wren was making a canoe; he was hewing it with a chisel. X̣wαn sat down and looked on while Wren was working. He noticed that there were no chips lying about. He wondered about it. "Where are the chips?" he thought. He got up, to go around to the other side. He went there and looked. Still, he could not see where the worker had left any chips. He went to a bough and sat down. Then he saw what was happening to the chips. Something between Wren's legs was eating the chips right along; it was Wren's "partner".[3] "Ah, so

[1] Told by Marion Davis, 1927. See p. 388.
[2] Told by Peter Heck, 1927; recorded in text. See p. 386.
[3] A polite way of saying organ.

that's it! That's the one who is eating the chips!" X̣wαn said to himself. "I like that; I had better trade with him so that it will be mine." "Ah, old man, I should indeed like to have your 'partner' that eats the chips. Let us trade," he said to Wren. "It would not be safe for you if we traded," Wren said. "Ah, old man, I want it very badly. Let us trade," X̣wαn said. "Ah, it wouldn't be safe," Wren said. "Ah, I want it very badly," X̣wαn said, "you had better give it to me; it won't bother me." "Ah, if you can stand it, we will trade," Wren said. "All right, old man," X̣wαn said. Wren untied his "partner" at the waist, and took it off. He gave it to X̣wαn. X̣wαn took it. He put it on where his own was. He gave his own to Wren. The thing was his now. "If it bothers you, bring it back," Wren said. "I guess it won't bother me," X̣wαn said. "Be sure to bring it back if it does," Wren said. "All right," X̣wαn said. He stood up. Now about his waist was his "partner". "Now, old man, I am going to leave you," he said to Wren, "now I have something good." Then he went away.

He started home; he was happy that he had cheated Wren. He got to his own home. "I had better go to visit someone," he said. He started off. He got to the place and went in. He sat down. "Evidently, you are taking a walk, old man?" they asked. "Yes, I am taking a walk," he said. In a little while, the woman there began to cook.[1] Then X̣wαn told the news — all the news. He was hungry now. In a little while the food was done. They put it on a plate and took it to him. X̣wαn put the plate down where he was sitting. Then he "burnt his fingers from the cook".[2] He took the plate, drew it toward him and put it between his legs.[3] Without paying any attention to his food for the moment, he kept on telling the news. "Ah, I can eat now," he finally said. He looked down at the food on his plate. There was nothing there. He was surprised when he discovered what had eaten it. He became ashamed. Then he went out.

He started off. He got to another house. He went in and sat down. "Ah, old man, evidently you are taking a walk?" the woman there said. "Yes, I am taking a little walk," X̣wαn said. In just a little while, the woman went out. She came in again. She had something in her hand — the back-bone of a dried salmon. She boiled it right away. In just a little while, the salmon was done. She dished it out and gave X̣wαn a plate full. "Thank you for burning your fingers," he said. He drew the plate toward him and set it between his legs. He kept on telling the news without paying any

[1] She was cooking between meals. No matter what time of day a guest shows up, a fresh meal must be cooked for him.

[2] An idiomatic expression. When a guest is served food, he says to the cook, by way of thanking her, "Thank you for burning your fingers for me." At a gathering, some one of the guests gets up and says this to his hosts, or, "Thank you for bothering about us."

[3] He is sitting down on the floor.

attention, for the moment, to his food. When he looked at the plate, he found that all the food was gone; there was nothing there. He was surprised when he found what had eaten it. Then he became ashamed and went out.

He started off. He went back to his own house. He was thinking all the time now, about what had happened to him. Next morning, he got hungry, but still lingered. Then something bit him on one side of the leg; then it bit him again on the other side. "Ah, it is the thing that always eats my food, the thing that was given to me," he said. "I had better go some place again to make sure that this is the thing that is doing it."

He started off. He got there and went into the house. He sat down. "Evidently you are taking a walk, old man?" they asked him. "Yes, I am taking a walk," he said. "You had better wait and get something to eat; then you can go on," they said. They gave him something to eat. He was busy telling the news. When he looked at his plate, there was nothing there; everything had been eaten. Now he knew for sure what was eating his food. He stood up and went out.

He started home. He got to his own house. "What will happen to me if I get hungry?" Then he became hungry. "It is just as Wren said; I guess we will have to trade back. In the morning, I will take it back to him." Night came and he went to bed. In the morning, he found that he was bitten again; a piece of flesh had been taken out of his leg. He got out of bed and went out. He started for the place where he would find Wren. He went up to Wren and said, "Ah, old man, I have brought your 'partner' back. I never have a chance to eat anything now. He eats everything that is given to me to eat." "I told you that it would not be safe. It's all right with me — you can give it back to me," Wren said. Then X̣wαn took the thing off and gave it to Wren. He got his own "partner" back. Then he said to Wren, "I say this to you: nothing like this shall ever happen again. In future generations, this one shall not be the one who does the eating. A man shall use it only for urinating and for intercourse. That is how it shall be in the next generation."

K'walale·'··i

X̣WαNÄ'X̣WαNE AND TAPEWORM.[1]

Tapeworm had a home by himself far off from the people. He was too dangerous a person to live with anyone. He had some strings so fixed, that if anyone should touch them, an alarm would be given all over the house.

A stranger once came to his house and asked, "Where's the trail that leads to the next town?" "Where's the trail that leads to

[1] Told by Jonas Secena, 1926. See p. 386.

the next town?" Tapeworm repeated after him.[1] "I mean what direction should I take to reach the next town," the stranger said. "I mean what direction should I take to reach the next town," Tapeworm repeated. "This is strange," the stranger said. "This is strange," Tapeworm repeated. "Tell me how to ford the trail," the stranger then said. "Tell me how to ford the trail," Tapeworm repeated. "Well, you're certainly acting silly, almost like a crazy person," the stranger said. "Well, you're certainly acting silly, almost like a crazy person," Tapeworm repeated. "My boy, I'll break your bones if you don't stop acting crazy," the stranger then said. "My boy, I'll break your bones if you don't stop acting crazy," Tapeworm repeated.

Tapeworm was short, the stranger, tall. "Come, my children, I'm attacked by a stranger," Tapeworm said. Snakes and tapeworms then came and wrapped themselves around the stranger. Tapeworm threw the dead body into the canyon where it could not be seen, his customary manner of disposing of his victims. Many women and men were lying dead at the bottom of the canyon.

The stranger had six brothers. When their elder brother failed to return, five of the brothers, in turn, went out to look for him and also failed to return. The seventh and youngest then dreamed that someone had murdered his brothers. The murderer was described to him in his dream. X̣wɑnä'x̣wɑne heard of the boy's dream and begged him to give a description of the murderer. Through the boy's description, the people learned that the murderer was Tapeworm, whom everyone feared. A certain person had once run away from Tapeworm and recognized him as the murderer who appeared in the boy's dream.

X̣wɑnä'x̣wɑne studied for two or three years how to get rid of Tapeworm. The latter enjoyed the reputation he had acquired as a dangerous being. At last X̣wɑnä'x̣wɑne hit upon the idea of fastening agate knives to either side of his legs. He went to Tapeworm and said, "Hello, my boy. What are you doing?" "Hello, my boy. What are you doing?" Tapeworm repeated.[1] "Do you know the way to the river?" X̣wɑnä'x̣wɑne then asked. "Do you know the way to the river?" Tapeworm repeated. X̣wɑnä'x̣wɑne then began to tease him. "My boy," he asked, "what makes your stomach stick out so?" "My boy, what makes your stomach stick out so?" Tapeworm repeated. "Whose boy are you?" he asked. "Whose boy are you?" Tapeworm repeated. "How do you manage to live alone in this wild country?" he asked. "How do you manage to live alone in this wild country?" Tapeworm repeated. "How do you murder the people who come here?" he asked. "How do you murder the people who come here?" Tapeworm repeated. "You're acting queer. You've never been beaten by anyone, have you?" he then said.

[1] Tapeworm speaks each time in a big, deep voice.

"You're acting queer. You've never been beaten by anyone, have you?" Tapeworm repeated. "I give you fair warning; we'll fight man to man; the best man wins," X̣wαnä'x̣wαne said at last. "I give you fair warning; we'll fight man to man; the best man wins," Tapeworm repeated. "We'll fight now!" X̣wαnä'x̣wαne said. He had given Tapeworm fair warning. But Tapeworm would not fight. X̣wαnä'x̣wαne then slapped him, spit on him, knocked him down and choked him. Then he let him go. Tapeworm began to shout, "Where are you, my people? I need help!" He shouted five times. At last his people, the tapeworms, came; some of them were like snakes. They wrapped themselves around X̣wαnä'x̣wαne. He tried to strike them with his club. They kept on coming and twined themselves around his arms and legs. It was then that he was able to cut them to pieces. He took his hatchet and hammers and killed Tapeworm. He then looked about the camp and pondered what to do with it. The best thing was to burn it up, he decided. After he had finished he declared, "After this world changes there will be a new generation. In this new generation there shall be no murderous Tapeworm; there shall only be small tapeworms. These tapeworms will live in people but will not kill them."

MOON, X̣WαNÄ'X̣WαNE AND THE DANGEROUS BEING BAT.[1]

A dangerous being lived in the mountains near the peoples' hunting grounds. He was a cannibal and his body was very large.

A man once went to this place where the dangerous being lived. It was in the winter during the rainy season. He found a tree eight or twelve feet in diameter and two or three hundred feet tall; it had fine limbs. There was a little dry spot beneath the tree, so he went there to get out of the rain. This tree was the dangerous being's decoy. Whenever anyone came there for shelter, he would kill him. The dangerous being came down out of the tree and killed the man. He never ate anything but human hearts. He removed the man's heart and blood and threw the body in the canyon. This man was one of seven brothers. When he failed to return, one of his brothers went out to look for him. This one also failed to return. In this way, six of the brothers, one after another, disappeared. Then the seventh and youngest had a dream and learned how his brothers had been killed. (It is mainly through dreams that orphans are eventually able to whip their enemies.) He warned the people about the tree and told them not to go there out of the rain.

Some time afterward, someone was heard to call, "The chief is coming!" Then everybody went out to see the chief. It was Moon, who was conquering all the dangerous beings. All those people who were harmless and loyal, he left as they were. The people told him about the dangerous being in the mountains. Moon then asked

[1] Told by Jonas Secena, 1926. See p. 392.

someone to take him there and X̣wαnä'x̣wαne volunteered. Moon wondered how to get the best of the dangerous being, as the latter was stronger than he. Nevertheless, he made up his mind to fight the dangerous being. He fixed some moss, intending to smoke him out of his tree. When he got near the place, he sent X̣wαnä'x̣wαne in one direction and took just the opposite direction himself. He spied the dangerous being far out on the end of his tree, looking for hunters. He knew exactly what the cannibal meant to do; the latter had seen X̣wαnä'x̣wαne coming out on the camp-ground and was laying for him. This was just as Moon had planned. Moon had some smoke and pitch fixed to smoke him out and burn him up. It was raining as usual. He had told X̣wαnä'x̣wαne to appear on the trail late in the evening and to take shelter beneath the tree; he was not to fall asleep there. He had everything ready. X̣wαnä'x̣wαne appeared at the proper time. Just before he got to the tree, he began to talk to himself, "Oh, I wonder how far I should go before camping. Oh, I'm tired!" He said this just to fool the dangerous being. Then he went up to the tree. "I'm so tired, I must go to sleep here," he said. He had already planned to keep himself awake by singing his tamanoas. He began to sing,

Stick out your tongue, my bouquet.

He always wore a snake on the top of his hat, and he was now ordering the snake to stick his tongue out. The dangerous being had already seen the trap that Moon had set for him, but he thought it was meant for X̣wαnä'x̣wαne. He sent his power out to X̣wαnä'x̣wαne to hypnotize him but failed. X̣wαnä'x̣wαne then began to tease him. "What's that up there? Who's making all that noise? Come down and I'll give you a little fight!" he called up. Toward morning, X̣wαnä'x̣wαne was almost asleep. Then Moon, who was concealed, said, "X̣wαnä'x̣wαne looks sleepy. It's about time to get to work." He started the smoke. Before long the dangerous being, from the top of his tree, called down to X̣wαnä'x̣wαne, "If you don't stop that smoke, I'll come down and get you!" Moon and X̣wαnä'x̣wαne then smoked the dangerous being so much, that he was just about ready to come down. Then Moon said, "I'm the Moon! I'm here to destroy all cannibals and all those who are unfit. I will conquer you. Come down and fight for your life!" They set fire to the tree. "Get sharp pointed poles, one for me and one for you. You jab him with it," Moon said to X̣wαnä'x̣wαne. The fire was now blazing high. The dangerous being came down and began to throw his power but it was too late. They kept punching him into the fire. Finally he burst. The report could be heard for several miles. But the ashes of the dangerous being still remained; they could not destroy them. The ashes turned into small bats. Moon said, "These shall be harmless; they will only fly around camps and smoke-houses."

He and X̣wɑnä'x̣wɑne then went down to the canyon and there they found thousands of bodies from which only the hearts had been removed.

MOON.

(First Version).[1]

X̣wɑn made a home at Lequito (łak'wa'to).[2] He made a fish-trap (ts'i'tpən) on a hard riffle, the only one there. He finished the trap and began to make a canoe. Since he was all alone, he had no one to watch the trap while he worked on the canoe. He did not know what to do. How could he make a person to watch his trap while he worked? What part of himself could he remove to make a person? At last he decided to take off his backside. He talked to his backside and told him how to recognize a spring salmon: it would have a tail, fins and so on. "Whenever you see a salmon, shout for me," he said. Then he left his backside and went back to his canoe. He listened constantly. Soon the fellow shouted, "X̣wɑn, I've got a fish!" Some foam had floated down and lodged in the trap. X̣wɑn ran down to see. In his haste he struck his knee against a stick and tumbled over. When he saw what was in the trap, he became angry at the fellow. "That's not a salmon! A salmon is different. You must pay attention to what I tell you. A salmon will be alive and jumping." "All right, I know," the fellow answered. X̣wɑn left.

Long afterward he heard him shout again, "X̣wɑn, I've caught the fish!" He ran down again. Some little leaves had caught in the trap; he was angry. "That's not a salmon, that's leaves," he said. Then once more he explained how a salmon looked.

Before long his backside shouted, "Come, X̣wɑn!" X̣wɑn ran down to the trap. A bit of trash-wood had caught there. He seized his partner and pushed him about. "This isn't salmon, this is a piece of wood. You're only annoying me," he said. Again he described a salmon and left him.

Soon X̣wɑn heard the fellow shouting again. This time, he did not want to go. The fellow shouted and shouted. At last he went down to the trap. A large piece of wood had caught there. He was angry and now felt discouraged. Again he described a salmon to the fellow, and left him.

Before long the fellow shouted again. X̣wɑn would not go. He could not believe that there was really a salmon in the trap, but the fellow kept on shouting. At last he gave in. "Perhaps he has got a salmon this time," he thought. There was a salmon in the trap. X̣wɑn was very happy. He thanked his partner. "That's right! That's what I've been telling you about!" he said. He took the salmon from the trap and started back home. His partner went with him.

[1] Told by Peter Heck, 1926. See p. 379.

[2] Near the present town of Chehalis.

He dressed the salmon and cut it up. Then he began to cook it. It was a male salmon. He removed the milt, which he thought was very nice, and put it above his pillow. When the salmon was done, he began to eat it. His partner was sitting on the other side of the fire. X̣wαn never offered him a bite. Before long nothing was left of the salmon but the milt. His partner felt very bad about it. He was so hungry his mouth began to pucker up.

After his meal X̣wαn rested. He thought of the milt. He made a wish about it. It was too nice to eat. He wished it would become two girls. When he was ready to go to work, he put his backside on. At present, the backside has a puckered mouth. X̣wαn worked at his canoe. When he looked at the milt again, it was just as he had left it. Next day, he went out again and worked until evening. The milt looked a little different; it seemed to have changed position a bit. X̣wαn felt a little proud. Next morning, he went to work again. When he came home, he looked to see if the milt was in the same position as he had laid it. It was lying differently now. "Perhaps some one changed its position," he thought. When he came back from work the fourth time, it was pointed in an entirely different direction. There was also a foot-print in the ashes. All night long, he thought about it. In the morning he went out to work again on his canoe. His canoe was just about finished. This was the fifth time, now. He went home. When he opened the door, he found two young women sitting down. They were fine looking girls, with white skins. Nothing remained of the milt. He was very happy. "Oh, my daughters, I'm glad you're here. Tomorrow we'll move up the river," he said. "All right," the girls answered.

In the morning they got ready. The girls sat in the stern, X̣wαn in the bow. They started out. But the girls could not paddle well, the boat went zig-zag; there was no one to captain the stern. "Guide the boat right, my wives," X̣wαn said. Then he hastily corrected himself, "Oh, I made a mistake. I didn't mean to call you 'wives'." The girls did not like it. They paddled zig-zag again. "Paddle straight, my wives," X̣wαn said. Then he hastily corrected himself, "Oh, I made a mistake. I didn't mean to say 'wives'." This happened four times. The fifth time X̣wαn chanced to close his eyes as he paddled. The boat went in to shore. "Let's get out," the girls said to one another, "he's talking funny." They put two rocks in their place to keep the canoe steady. X̣wαn went on.

There was a large hill near the river. The girls climbed up the slope. Then they heard someone singing. Finally they saw a swing, in which there was a baby, coming in their direction. It had been swung clear out until it touched the side of the hill where they were. They sat down and watched: an old lady was taking care of the baby. She was singing,

Sleep, baby, my grandchild,
Sleep, baby, my grandchild.

When the swing went back each time, it was a long time before it reached the old lady. Finally the two girls held it for a while and looked the baby over. "Isn't it nice! I'd like to see it!" one said. But the other said, "Perhaps the mother would get after us and kill us. Let it go." They held the swing again. "Oh, the old lady will never know," the one girl said, "we'll fix it so she'll never know it's gone." They let the baby go again. Then they took a piece of rotten log and began to shape it like a baby. When the cradle came back for the fifth time, they took the baby out and put the rotten log in.

The old lady changed her song; she knew something was wrong. She was blind. She sang,

> My baby seems like a rotten log,
> My baby seems like a rotten log.

She stopped the swing and felt for the baby. It did not feel the same. The baby was gone! The child's mother was unmarried; she had never been with a man. One day when she was digging lacamas, she had found a stone, the finest little stone imaginable, somewhat blue. She took the stone home. From this stone she conceived her child. She had no idea how it happened. Her child was Moon (łokwa'ł). As soon as she heard her mother change her song and sing of rotten wood, she knew something had happened. She went back and found the piece of rotten wood. The old lady told her what had happened. She wept. She did not know where to find the two girls. "Let's chase them, they went west," the old lady said. The young woman picked her mother up and carried her on her back. She sang,

> Cause the girls to become small,
> The distance between us shorter.

And then the girls came quite close to them. As soon as the young woman dropped the old lady in order to get at them unhampered, the girls were once more far off from them. They were laughing. She packed her mother again and used her song. She was just about to catch them when she let her mother go. Now the girls were far off, and laughing. The old lady told her daughter to pick her up again. The young woman had just about caught them when she let her mother down; the latter was too heavy to carry, if she were to catch the girls. Now the girls were far off once more, and laughing. She picked her mother up for the fourth and last time and ran after them. The girls were quite close once more. She could just touch them on the back, when she let her mother down in order to catch them more readily. Now the girls were far off once more, and laughing. She gave up. As soon as she let her mother go, the old lady turned into a swamp.

The younger woman turned back. She was Earthquake (yakwa'łtαmx·). When she reached home she wept and wept for her child.

She did not know how to get him back. She took her little son's wet diapers, rinsed them and wrung them out. She put the urine in a wooden dish, covered it and wished that it would become a baby. After five days she looked at it and found that it had become a baby boy.

The two girls had taken Moon westwards somewhere. His mother tried to hire someone to go after him, but no one could find him. Bluejay told someone that he could go. At last the woman heard that Bluejay was willing to go. "If you think you can get there, I wish you would go. I'll pay you anything you ask," she said to him. "I can get there, all right," he answered.

Bluejay got ready and at last set out. He travelled and travelled and travelled. Finally he came to a place where a lever[1] was going up and down, up to the sky and back down again. It was going slowly. He waited a while and then jumped through before it came back down. Just then, the lever came down and clipped one of his tails[2] off. He was safe on the other side. He travelled a long way before he came to another. This one was going up and down a bit faster than the first. He went close and stood there, studying how to make it. It was not going so very fast, but still faster than the first. He ran across while it was still up, but again he lost another tail. He went on. Finally he came to another, going a little faster than the second. He ran under it and reached the other side, but lost a tail again. He came to another one that was going pretty fast. And now he was somewhat frightened. He stood there a long time. "I said I'd find Moon even if I were killed in the attempt!" he thought. He went across, but the lever very nearly came down on him. As usual, he lost another tail. He went on. Finally he came to the last one. It was going so fast it seemed to be in one piece only. He did not know if he could make it. He cried and called upon his tamanoas. He was afraid to go through; he could not slow it down. At last it seemed to be slowing down a bit. "I've got to go; this is the kind of thing I'm used to. Perhaps I'll make it," he said. Several times he made a motion as if to go through and then stopped. The fifth time he made it. He reached the other side but lost another tail. "I'm all right! I'll get there now," he cried.

He went on. At last he arrived at a big winter-house, where Moon was living. Through the open door he saw a man making arrow-points. He flew back and forth in front of the door, saying, "Kä'tcə, kä'tcə, kä'tcə, kä'tcə, kä'tcə, kä'tcə." On the last "kä'tcə", Moon took some little chips from his flakings and threw them in Bluejay's face, saying, "What are you doing here?" Bluejay cried, "Kac, kac, kac. Your mother is spending everything she has to get you back home." "Then why didn't you come in instead of flying back and forth in front of my door? I wouldn't have harmed you had

[1] I use the same word here that the narrator used.
[2] Perhaps tail-feathers is implied.

I known," Moon said. "Come in, Bluejay." He blew on Bluejay's eyes to remove the chips. But a bit remained for Bluejay's eyes still look glassy. Bluejay told Moon everything that had happened. "I'll come home when I have made my preparations," Moon said. Bluejay reached home without any trouble.

Moon was the husband of the two young women who had stolen him. He had grown up in no time at all. They had borne him many children. As soon as Moon was ready, he talked to his children. From the elder of the two women had come all the trees and shrubs. To his favorite son, cedar, prince of them all, he said, "When the people split you, you must do exactly as they wish. They will use your big boards for making canoes and houses. Your bark, they will peel for weaving baskets and for food mats. Your little limbs, they will use for split baskets." The cedar is more useful than any other tree. That's why he was a prince. To red fir he said, "Your bark will be used for making a fire." To white fir, he said, "My son, you won't be good for anything. When they try to use you, you won't burn; you'll be too wet." He called maple. "My son," he said, "when they burn you, you'll crackle and throw out sparks." Maple is very mean that way. He called ash and said to him, "When the people burn you, foamy water will seep out of you." And that is just what happens when people use him for firewood. He called alder. "You, my son," he said, "will be used as firewood for drying salmon." He called dogwood. "You won't be good for firewood. If they should burn you, you'll bubble all the time and make a queer noise." He called willow and said to him, "People will make good use of your bark, and use it for practically everything they wish to tie." That's the way we use willow, for tying. To ironwood, he said, "You'll be used as a straight roasting-stick for salmon, also as a split roasting-stick for fresh salmon." To soapwood, he said, "The future generations will make gambling sets from you. You'll be cut into little wheels (about an eighth of an inch thick). When you're finished, you'll be round and smooth (the lal). The inner bark of the cedar will be peeled off, and when dry, will be smashed on either side, and then rubbed together until soft. The wheels made from you will be concealed in this. From your sprouts, children will make arrows." He said to brush (the reddish-brown bark of which can be peeled off), "Little gambling wheels will be made from you." To bear-brush (that grows on the river-side and bears little clusters of white berries), he said, "People will find Bear eating you; this is the purpose you will serve." To oak, he said, "You will bear oak-berries (acorns); at certain times your berries will ripen and drop down so that the people can gather them for food." And thus acorns always drop when the time comes. All the trees on this earth were Moon's children from the elder of his two wives. They were put here for the use of all Indians, but now it is the whites who derive the benefit.

The younger of Moon's wives had borne all the fish on this earth. Moon then called all his fish-children to him. He told chub that he was going to leave him. Chub cried and tore his mouth. That's why chub has a large mouth. He gave him some little bones and said, "The people of the next generation will use you for food. They will catch you on a hook." He threw him into the river. "This is where you will stay for all time," he said. He called young redhorse and gave him some little bones. "I'm going to leave you," he said. Redhorse cried and blood streamed from his mouth. That's why redhorse has a red mouth. He told him the same thing and threw him into the river. He called whitefish and gave him some little bones. He told him the same thing. "The people will use you for food," he said and threw him into the river. He called another of his children. The boy cried and tore his mouth. Moon was rather fond of him so he did not give him any bones. This was trout. He threw him into the river. "They will catch you with a net," he said, "you'll be a good fish and not bony." He called sucker. When he told sucker that he was going to leave, sucker cried and cried until his mouth drew together and became quite small. He cried and cried and would not stop. He was something of a little prince. Moon gave him many little toys (bones) to pacify him, but still he would not stop. At last, somewhat annoyed, he threw his dip net over him and tossed him into the river. "This is how the people will catch you," he said. He called salmon trout. "I'm going to leave you," he said. Salmon trout cried and tore his mouth. "You'll come in the fall," Moon said, "sometimes you'll be caught in a trap." He threw him into the river. Spring salmon was chief of them all. Moon told him that people would use him for food. "You'll be caught in a trap or in a net basket; you must come up the river early in spring." He called black salmon. "You'll be caught in a trap or speared as you dig on the riffle. You're a big salmon. You'll come in the fall and will be dried for winter use." He threw him into the river and said, "Thus you will be used hereafter." He told silverside that he would be caught the same way as black salmon, in a trap or speared. (There are silverside on every riffle.) He threw him into the river. "You will come in the fall, in September or October," he said, "when the people will catch you for winter use." He called dog salmon (whose sides are spotted; he is very good eating). He told him that he would be caught in the same way as black salmon and silverside, in a trap or speared, and that he would come the same time of the year. "You'll be found in slow water, on little creeks," he said. While Moon was telling certain of his children that they would be speared, he was making a spear and gig whereby it could be done. A bone was used for the sharp point, and was held on either side with elk horn, around which had been wound cherry bark. On top of this was poured hot pitch, which gave a nice smooth finish. Moon told steelhead that he would be speared, also. "When the people see you digging in deep water, they'll strike the bottom of the river with their spears. When you hear this noise, you must come; you'll think it is another salmon and come close. Then they'll spear you. You will come up the river in winter." (Steelhead isn't much used.) "I'm going to leave you," Moon said to sturgeon. Sturgeon cried. That's why he has a small mouth. "I'm going to put you in a bay," Moon said. "The people will catch you on a hook and use your body for drying. They'll make a hook, which they'll attach to a long pole with a long string, for use in the deep waters of the bay." As soon as he had finished speaking, Moon threw him out into the bay. "You will remain there all year round," he added. At last Moon was ready to leave his home and wives. He started out. Some time after he left, his wives returned. The house was empty; not a soul was there. They wondered what had happened. They wept. That is the last of them; I don't know what happened to them.

Moon was on his way back. He saw something close to the trail, watching him. It frightened him somewhat. It opened its big mouth to bite him. He went closer to see what it was. It was a windfall, roots and all. He threw a rock at it, whereupon its mouth closed up tightly. "You will never frighten people like this again," he declared. "Never again will you do this, never again act like a dangerous being. When you fall to the ground, you will always bring rocks up with you." And so it is.

He came to something else going back and forth on the trail. He stopped. "What's it trying to do?" he thought. It tried to strike him. He seized it and held it; it was a needle about a yard long. He took a cat-tail and stuck it through the eye. "People will use you like this for making mats," he said. "They'll use you with a long string for sewing cat-tails together."

Before long he came to another thing going across the trail. It tried to run over him. He grabbed it. It was a mat-smoother. "The people will use you for smoothing mats," he said.

He went on. He heard a noise but did not know what was causing it. As he came closer he heard some people shouting. The people were getting ready to fight; they had heard of a man who was changing everything. "Hwɛᵋ, hwɛᵋ," they were saying, like soldiers on the march. Before long, a stranger came up to them. It was Moon. "Have you been making that noise? What are you doing?" he asked. "We have heard of a man who is changing all our ways. We're going to kill him," they said. "Go close to the prairie," he ordered. "That's where you'll stay forever, here and there and there. If the people like, they may eat you in the springtime." These people became the wild rhubarb. They did not have a chance to learn that here was the man they were looking for; they just did exactly as he said.

He went on. He came to a house. Someone was singing,

We're getting ready for the man,
I'll put the thing that I'm making right over him.

A man was making a kind of net. Moon went right up to him and asked, "What are you making, grandfather?" "I'm going to kill Moon; we want to stay the way we are," the man answered. "Let me see what you're making," Moon said. The man handed it over quickly. "Turn the other way!" Moon ordered. The old man did as he was told. Then Moon threw the netting completely over him. The old man did not know that this was Moon. "Go to the edge of the prairie and stay there forever. The people may eat you if they like," Moon said. The old man became the yalp.[1]

He went on. He heard someone singing again,

We're getting ready for him.

Some people were marching, getting ready to fight. They discovered a man standing close to them. "What are you doing?" the man asked. "Oh, we're getting ready to kill Moon; we don't want to be changed," they said. "So that's what you're going to do!" Moon said. "Stretch out clear around the prairie," he said, "the people will use you in the spring." These people became the wild parsnips.[2]

He came to another place. He heard someone singing, as before,

We're getting ready for him.

Suddenly the people saw him and all stopped. "What are you young men doing?" he asked. "We're getting ready to fight," they answered, "we hear there is a man coming to change everything and we don't want to be changed." "Go out on the prairie," Moon said. They became the spearflowers.[3] These people had been making spears with which to kill Moon.

He went on. He came to a house. Someone inside was singing. He went close and listened. An old man was singing,

I'm getting ready for the man,
I'll kill him with the thing I'm making.

He went in. "Oh, grandfather, what are you making?" he asked. "Oh, I'm making this to kill the man who is changing everything; I don't want to be changed." "Oh, so that's what you're doing!" Moon said. "Let me see it." The old man gave the thing to him and Moon looked it over: it was a scooped out affair, somewhat like a hand in shape, narrow at the bottom and with a long point at the

---

[1] A plant that grows on the edge of the prairie, about two and a half feet tall, with a single wide leaf at the top and white blossoms. The stalk was sometimes eaten. If the stem is spliced, strings are found in the inside.

[2] A plant with round stalk and yellow flowers. The stalk was eaten but not the roots.

[3] About a foot high; bears blossoms red on top with a short spear. The plant is not eaten. The blossom is called ts'its'iya'laqʋm.

top.[1] "Come close," Moon said. The old man came close; he had finished two such objects. "Now look at me," Moon said. The old man looked him in the face, whereupon Moon clapped the two objects on his ears. The old man became deer. Deer has two big ears, now. Moon went outside. "Jump, jump two or three times," he ordered. The old fellow jumped three times and looked back. "That's what you'll do in fright when the people hunt you; you will jump, and look back. They will use you for food. They will dry your meat or use it any way they like," Moon said. Right then and there he changed the old fellow, without the latter realizing what was happening. The objects that he was making, he now uses for ears.

Moon went on. He heard someone making a noise. He went up to the person. A man was sitting on the sand-bar working at some object. It was a wide, wooden thing, curved and rounded on each end. "What are you making, grandfather?" Moon asked. "Oh, son, I'm getting ready to kill the man who is changing everything. I'd rather stay the way I am." "Let me see what you have there," Moon said. The old fellow gave the thing to him. "Come here," Moon ordered. The old man came close. "Now turn around!" The old man turned around. Moon stuck the thing on the old man's backside. "Go to the river!" The old man went. "Now swim! dive!" The old man dived, came up again and looked about as if expecting someone. The object he had been making was now his tail. He raised his tail, splashed the water about with it and made a great racket. "This is what you'll do when someone comes," Moon said. The old man had become the beaver. "You'll make your home in alder roots near the water, where the people will find you and kill you to eat." Beaver always lives underground or among the roots. His home was formerly on the sand-bar, and if it had not been for Moon, he would be there yet. He makes a dam, as Moon told him he should do.[2]

Moon went on. Eventually he came to some people. The giant woman, K'wαtsx̣wɛ', was coaxing them to play swing. Moon did not know what was going on. "What are you doing, aunty?" he asked the woman. "Oh, I'm playing swing with these little rascals. I let them ride on my swing. I push them out and they never come back," she explained. Woodpecker would hold the swing while someone got on. Then the woman would tell the others to sing, "Go and never come back." A man got on. They pushed him out and

[1] "Perhaps a kind of spear."

[2] The people of the older generation say that Moon made one mistake: he should have left beaver on the sand-bar, instead of sending him to make his home in a less accessible place. Had beaver been left on the bar, he would now be much easier to catch. But on the other hand, they say, "Well, you see it's like this: gold is hard to get and it is precious; and that's the way with beaver. Moon must have had something like this in mind, when he did it."

the swing came back empty. "This is a good thing you're doing," Moon said. He looked around. Many people were sitting there laughing. But those nearest the swing were not happy; those who went out would never return. "Aunty, I'd like to swing," Moon said. "Oh no," she answered, "something would happen." "Well, I'd like to try anyway," Moon insisted. Eventually she consented. Now Moon told the people to call, "Come back with the swing." K'wαtsx̣wɛ' wanted them to say, "Go forever." Moon got on the swing. Woodpecker was holding it. When the swing went as far as it would go, Woodpecker pecked at Moon's hand to make him let go. Moon told him to stop. Then he, himself, stopped the swing. Far beneath them he saw two rocks, on which Woodpecker was accustomed to drop the people. Old and young lay dead there. "What a nice swing you have, aunty!" Moon said as soon as they got back. "See, I'm back safely. I don't understand how the others managed to fall off. Why don't you try it, aunty?" he said. "No, I was only playing with those rascals," the woman said. Finally she consented to try. Moon told Woodpecker to peck at her hands, and told the people to sing, "Go forever." K'wαtsx̣wɛ' told them to sing, "Come back." But the people sang instead, "Go to the second-death."[1] They sang gladly. The woman's own pet, Woodpecker, pecked at her hand until she let go and dropped on the rocks. As soon as she was dead, Moon said, "This will never happen in the next generation. If people wish to swing, they may do so without suffering death." That's the reason we have a safe swing.

As soon as he had finished, Moon went on. He came to another place where there was also a gathering. Another K'wαtsx̣wɛ' was there. "What are you doing here, aunty?" he asked. "I'm playing doll with these little rascals," the woman answered. "I'd like to see how you play it," he said. "Very well; I'll play it right now," she answered. She set everyone in a line. If anyone did not move right, she would hit him on the head and he would drop dead. Then she would call another to take his place. "Oh, that's fine! I'd like to try it," Moon said. "No, my nephew, it isn't safe," she said. "But I'd like to try it anyway," Moon insisted. At last she consented. She called him to an empty place. He took the place but did not do exactly as she said, whereupon she hit him on the head. He did not feel it at all, but just laughed and stood up. "You'd better try it, aunty," he said, "it feels very good. I don't see why it kills the others." "No, I'm just playing doll with these rascals," she said. "Better try it, it feels nice," Moon insisted. At last she consented to try. He told her to sit down in his place. She was frightened by this time and did not want to sit down. After she had taken her place, she moved her head a little. He hit her and killed her. He told the people to gather wood, which they did. They built a fire. Now they were ready to burn her. When nothing but her ashes remained, Moon

[1] See p. 24.

said, "This will never happen again. If little children wish to play doll, they may, but not older people."

He came to another place where many people had gathered. Another K'wαtsx̣wε' was there. "Aunty, what are you doing?" he asked. "Oh, I'm playing with these rascals here," the woman said. She was steaming the people, as one would steam potatoes. "Oh, I'd like to see how it is done," he said. "All right," she said. She put a man in the pot, in which there were some hot rocks, sprinkled the rocks to make them steam and put the lid on. She then held the lid down as tightly as she could, to keep the steam in. Before long the man blew up. She had cooked him to death. "Well, aunty," Moon said, "I should like very much to try this." "Oh, it wouldn't be safe for you!" the woman answered. "Better let me try it," he said. "I don't mind doing it with these rascals but I don't want to do it with you," she answered. Before long she consented. She put him in the pot, but he was prepared; he had a piece of ice. She told the others to hold the lid down as tightly as they could. They held the lid down for a long time but Moon did not burst. They grew tired of this after a while and took the cover off. A bit of sweat had come out on Moon's forehead. "This is fine, aunty, you'd better try it," Moon said. "No, I only do it with these rascals," the woman answered. "I don't understand why these people burst, I didn't," Moon remarked again. Reluctantly the woman consented to try. She got in the pot. Then Moon sprinkled the hot rocks with water to make them steam. She lay down. "U·, it's too hot!" she cried, sitting up. "Oh, you'll get used to it," Moon said. She lay down again. He put the cover on and told the people to hold it down as tightly as they could. She struggled to get out but before long they heard her burst. "We've got her now!" Moon said. They took the cover off. She was cooked to death. Then he ordered the people to gather wood and burn her. They threw her in the fire. As her ashes blew up with the wind, they became the lark (sqʋtsx̣a'). As soon as the woman was burnt to ashes, Moon said, "Hereafter, the people may steam food, but not human beings." And so it is now; that is what Moon taught the people. As soon as he had finished, he went on.

He came to five women, all of whom were named K'wαtsx̣wε'. They were standing in a row. They were singers and Moon knew it. "My aunties, I wish you'd sing your song for me," he said. "It wouldn't be safe for you, it's dangerous," they answered. "I don't understand why a mere song should be dangerous," he said. "All right, we'll sing for you," they answered. The first woman said that she would begin, and then the others could join in. She sang,

εnε'
We are the Fire-ladies,
We are the Fire-ladies.

As soon as she opened her mouth, fire streamed out and started a fire in the distance. Then all five women together sang and set fire to everything. They left Moon all alone. He did not know where to go to escape the fire. The water would boil, the river would boil, everything would burn. What should he do? Right there, he had a hard time. Then Trail called, "Oh, grandson, come here and lie down on top of me." The fire burned only on either side of Trail, so Moon was safe. After the fire had run itself out, Moon said to the K'wαtsx̣wε', "There shall never again be a dangerous thing like this. Fire shall never again be sent out from a person's mouth. When a man or woman sings a song, it will be for amusement only." Moon would have burned to death if Trail had not called him. Thus a road or trail never burns; the fire burns only on either side of it.

When he had finished, Moon went on. He came to an open prairie. He heard someone singing. He went closer and listened. He could hear it plainly now. Someone was in the middle of the prairie and on the very trail on which he was travelling. The song was:

He who wants to do this should come.

When he went closer, he saw a K'wαtsx̣wε' lying on the trail, her legs spread apart. "I'm the one who would like to do it," Moon said to her. "No, it wouldn't be safe for you," the woman answered. "Oh, aunty, I want it," he said. "No, nephew, it is dangerous." "But, aunty, I like it very much." Finally she consented. "Close your eyes tightly when I lie on you," Moon said. She closed her eyes tightly. "Now don't look," he said. He got a sledge hammer and an elk-horn wedge. He happened to strike them together. "Hwi·, what's that noise?" the woman asked. "Oh, aunty, that's nothing; it's just my testicles knocking together, I want you so badly," Moon said. He drove the wedge into her vagina and split her open. He saw many dead men lying about on the ground. When anyone had intercourse with this woman, she would cut his organ in two. Moon readily understood what she was up to. He burned her. "Hereafter," he declared, "a woman will never kill a man when he has intercourse with her, will never cut his organ in two." There was sharp agate on either side of her vagina. "A woman shall never again have a vagina like this; a vagina will be entirely of flesh," he said. A woman who has become a widow, one, two, three times is dangerous; for this reason old people advise their young men never to marry a widow. They will have a short life if they do. So today, bad women do not kill men. This was the last of the K'wαtsx̣wε' women.

Moon went on. He travelled and travelled and travelled. At last he came to a place near a river. He heard a noise. "What can that be?" he thought. He went closer to the noise. He could hear someone working. He crept closer to see who was there. A man was singing,

Ouch, my head,
Ouch, my hand.

It was Wren (ts'atsɛ'ʔx̣p). He had put some bark on his backside for a basket. He was using his head as a maul and his hand as a wedge for splitting wood. "The chief, my boss, told me to get some wood," Wren said to Moon. Moon gave him a maul and wedge for splitting the wood and a basket to hold it. "That's not a real basket you are using. Use this basket instead, and use this wedge and hammer for splitting the wood," Moon said. Before long, Wren had a large pile of wood. "Take it down to the bar and build a big fire there," Moon said. Then Moon left and went down to the river.

Someone was making a noise there. He saw a fish-trap (ts'i'tpən) made of human beings. The tallest were used for derricks; they were clutching one another by the hair. Others were tied together at the waist to form stakes. The smallest people formed a kind of dam. They were stretched out clear across the river, standing knee deep in water. Their boss, Raven (sq̣waq̣ʷ), would walk clear across the river, right on top of this human trap. As soon as Wren had built a large fire on the bar, Moon ordered the people to come out of the water and warm themselves. They dropped from exhaustion and cold. Before long Raven appeared. He had gone up the river to get more men. He came with several canoes, each loaded down with men. He landed and got out. He went up to the fire. Moon took hold of him. "Never do this again," he said. "These people here are human beings." He struck Raven twice on the backside. Each time Raven jumped and said, "Q̣waq̣ʷ." After the fifth time, Moon said, "In the next generation, you'll be nothing but a raven. You will stay around camps and live on any refuse you may be able to pick up. Hereafter a fish-trap will be made from stakes and not from human beings." And thus stakes are used now for a fish-trap.

Moon went on. He came to a lake. He did not know how to get across. On the other side, a boy was fishing. He shouted across to the boy, but the boy merely repeated everything he said. "Come after me, boy," Moon shouted. "Come after me, boy," the boy shouted back. Moon shouted the same thing again and again, but still the boy merely shouted back his own words. The boy was catching little fish and eating them. "I'll wade across and slit your stomach open," Moon shouted. "I'll wade across and slit your stomach open," the boy shouted back. Then Moon waded across to him. The boy was Tapeworm, and was accustomed to eat all kinds of snakes and the like. Moon slit the boy's stomach open. As soon as he had done so, everything the boy had eaten poured out. The reptiles entangled themselves about Moon's feet. He slashed them to pieces with his knife, "Hereafter," he declared, "if anyone shouts to a person on the other side of the river to take him across, that person will do so without mocking him."

He went on. At last he saw a river across which a trap of wood was built. He started across on the trap. Half way across he met a man catching fish. "What are you doing?" Moon asked. "I'm catching fish," the man answered. The man wore a small hat on the top of his head. "That's a nice hat you have," Moon remarked, "would you let me try it on?" The man hesitated. "I should like very much to have it," Moon said. "Very well, if you insist," the man answered. He took his hat off and gave it to Moon. Moon put it on. The hat was made of leaves. Before long. Moon wanted to take the hat off, but it stuck tight to his head. The owner of the hat was X̭α'ʼo[1]. Moon did not like the hat, but he could not get it off. He left X̭α'ʼo and went on across the trap. When he got to the other side, he found many people there. No one knew how to remove the cap. "It will never come off. We never ask to try his cap on, for we know it would stick to our heads; it seems to be lined with pitch," they said. Moon was about ready to give up. He offered finally to marry any woman who could take it off. All the unmarried women tried, for Moon was a handsome fellow. None of them could do it. He was weary of the whole thing, and his predicament was rather disgraceful. Sometime afterward, he saw a woman coming. She was the ugliest woman imaginable. She was carrying a little bucket in her hand. She was so ugly, Moon did not like having anything to do with her. "What's the matter?" she asked. "Oh, I borrowed a cap from X̭α'ʼo and now I can't get it off," Moon said, "I have offered to marry any woman who could do it." The woman came close. "Just remain quiet and I'll try to take it off," she said. She took some dog-fish oil from her bucket and with some "dope" worked to remove the cap. She thus worked a charm against the cap and it came off. This charm is called k·ʼɩts'sta'ni.[2] Moon did not care for the woman but had to keep his word. Thus Toad won him. He went back to X̭α'ʼo and returned the cap. "Hereafter," he said, "if anyone wishes to try on another's hat, he may do so without having the hat stick to his head." Moon now had a wife. He said, "Now I have an ugly wife. In future generations, it shall always be like this: an ugly woman will marry a good looking man." (This was his excuse; he had to do something about it.)

Moon left. He travelled some distance and at last arrived at Lequito prairie, his old home. He went to the well and waited there with his wife. Before long a blind boy came crawling along. Moon went to meet him. "Oh, my poor brother, I have returned," Moon said. "Don't say that. Don't make fun of me, Bluejay," the boy answered. "No, I'm not Bluejay, I'm the one who was stolen," Moon said. Then he took hold of his young brother, blew on his eyes and restored his sight, slapped him on the head and restored his hair. "Tell mother to prepare dinner; I have returned," he said.

The boy went home. "My brother wants you to come to the well," he said to his mother. His mother threatened him with a stick. "Bluejay is probably making fun of you," she said. "Oh no, my

[1] A kind of root, stuck all over with bark.

[2] See footnote 1, p. 92.

sight and my hair have been restored," he said. She went up to him and felt his head. There was no doubt of it; his hair had been restored. Moon came to meet his mother. "Poor mother, I have returned," he said. He blew on her eyes and restored her sight; he slapped her on the head and restored her hair. He told her to go back and clean the house and to put up a partition. Later, he and his wife went to the house. He sat down and told his mother everything that had happened. Before long someone called. It was Bluejay calling for the former blind boy. "Clean my backside," he called. "Here, take this piece of burning wood and stick it on him," Moon said to his brother. The boy did this. "There's something wrong," Bluejay said to his sister Yu'i, "he never did this before." He shouted the same thing again, and again the boy burned him. Five times he called, and five times the boy burned him. "He used to clean my backside well; he never burned me before," Bluejay said. Then he peeped through a crack in the partition and saw Moon. He cried and cried.

Moon and his brother went out. "I want you to be the night moon," Moon said. "All right," the boy answered. "I'll be the day moon," Moon said. "You will travel at night," he said to his brother.

The boy went up. As he looked back, he saw shadows on the earth. This frightened him and he came back down. He thought that the shadows were ghosts who would eat him. "They are just mere shadows," Moon said to him. Moon now thought that it was time for him to try out as the day moon (sun). When the day moon had just got to the top of the trees, the people could no longer stand his heat. He rose a little higher and the river began to boil. He saw that this would not do, and came down. "You shall be the day moon," he said to his young brother, "my people cannot stand my heat." He sent his brother up. The boy started and travelled right along. At last he came down. He was just right. "Very well," Moon then said, "I shall be the night moon myself." He went up. Thus they worked, he at night, and his brother, during the day. They were just right. They then took final leave of their mother and the people. "We are going up to be the day moon and the night moon," Moon said.

Moon's mother still travels around the world. When she completes her circuit at the end of a year — when she comes back to the place from which she started — she shakes the whole world, for she is earthquake. This is the work of Moon's mother, — to shake the world.

Whenever Moon's wife puts her hands over his eyes, we have the dark moon. When she takes her hands off, we have the full moon. Whenever a dangerous being devours either sun or moon, we have an eclipse. When he takes them in his jaws, it becomes dark. As soon as he releases them, it becomes light.

K'walale·'··i

MOON.

(Second Version).[1]

In the beginning, this world was only an imitation one. Some people, for instance, were without fire. The present-day animals were people then. This story tells how everything was changed — how the wonderful child, like Christ, was born.

X̣wαnä′x̣wαne was a "crooked" person. He once travelled with the Geese, just for the fun of it. Many people were able to fly at that time. The Geese told X̣wαnä′x̣wαne that he must not pay any attention to the people he saw beneath him on the earth. He travelled a long way with the Geese. Then he began to shout abuses at a man he saw down below. The Geese became tired of this — it was against their rules. They took X̣wαnä′x̣wαne to the highest mountain, removed his wings and left him there. X̣wαnä′x̣wαne lay down to sleep. He was awakened by Night Owl calling, "Hu, hu, hu." Then X̣wαnä′x̣wαne shouted abuses at him. "If you don't stop that yelling, I'll come over there and thrash you!" he said. He said the same thing five times, then went over to Owl. "We're going to have a fight!" he said. He killed Owl and took his wings. He put them on and flew away to a more desirable place. Owl's wings were not made like those of the Geese, so X̣wαnä′x̣wαne was unable to fly very well.

He came to a river. Before long, he saw K'wαtsx̣wɛ′, the monster woman, coming. This woman was more powerful than an ordinary person; no one had ever got the best of her. "What are you doing, sister?" he asked. He gave her a bead for five lacamas. But the bead was not a real bead, it was merely a little stick. He met her a number of times and did the same thing, each time pretending that he was a different person. "There are five of us, all brothers," he would say. The fourth time, the woman said, "You're the same fellow I've met before. Next time I meet you, I'm going to kill you." The women then mixed some bees with her lacamas and left the basket in a hollow stump, ordering the stump to close tightly when X̣wαnä′-x̣wαne came. X̣wαnä′x̣wαne came again and the stump closed up on him. The bees stung his eyes out and he went blind.

He was in the stump for a long time and did not know what to do. He shouted and shouted for help. At last Woodpecker came and helped him out. He had no eyes for the bees had stung them out. He started off, wandering around here and there. At last he stumbled against a winter-house and someone yelled at him. He had made some imitation eyes out of dandelion blossoms and imagined that he could see with these; he had a good imagination. "I'm just examining your house," he said to Snail (or Slug), against whose house he had stumbled. He went in, and told Snail about a great

[1] Told by Jonas Secena, 1926.

many things that Snail had never heard of before. He told him about all the wonderful sights he could see throughout the whole world. "My friend," he said, "have you ever seen clear across the ocean?" Snail went out to see. "You must have wonderful eyes," Snail said. "I'll trade with you," X̣wαnä'x̣wαne said. Finally, Snail agreed to trade, for he believed all X̣wαnä'x̣wαne's lies. X̣wαnä'x̣wαne gave Snail his imitation eyes. At first, Snail could see a little with the eyes, but as soon as they wilted, he was left blind. Since that time, Snail has been totally blind.

X̣wαnä'x̣wαne said, "Well I'm going to make my living in the river." He tried to catch a Chinook salmon but did not succeed. The water was shallow and the salmon ran away. Then he made a maul. "Hammer away while I try to catch a salmon," he said. At first, the maul would not work, but the fifth time, it worked and he caught the salmon.

He ate part of the salmon, which was the finest thing he had ever seen. He admired the insides very much. "Let me create a human-being from this," he said. He took some ashes from the fireplace and buried the milt, mixed with something else, under the ashes. From time to time, he said to himself, "I'm creating a human being." (He knew that the world was going to change.) In five days' time, he could hear some children shouting. The second time, he managed to slip up on them, and discovered that they were two girls. He brought the children up. Later, he tried to make the girls his wives, but they got the best of him and ran away.

The two girls, who were created from salmon organs and ashes, travelled a very long way after they left. They passed through many places and eventually came to a blind old woman at Lequito prairie. In some way or other, the girls had already hit upon the idea that there was a wonderful child at this place. The old lady was swinging a cradle and singing,

> Baby, baby, noble baby,
> Noble-hearted baby.

The old lady was the child's grandmother. The child's mother was a virgin. The two girls stole the baby from the blind woman and left a chunk of old rotten wood in its place. The old woman knew that something had happened. She sang,

> My dear grandchild is gone,
> My dear, my dear —
> A piece of decayed log,
> My dear.

The child's mother was away, picking berries. She heard her mother singing and ran home. This noble-hearted boy, who had been stolen, was the Moon (łokwa'ł). The girls had already taken him a long way off. The child's mother and the old lady got ready to go after them.

The old lady had power to change the earth's surface; she could make it fold. They set out and travelled a long way. The old woman, who had tamanoas, then used her power to fold the earth in order to bring the girls closer to them. When the girls were close, the young woman let her mother down, in order to catch the girls more quickly. Thereupon the earth flattened out and left the girls far ahead. She took her mother up again and started off. The fourth time they got pretty close to the girls, but the same thing happened again, and they failed to catch them. They finally had to turn back, for the girls had now reached the other side of the world where the salmon live. (The two girls were part salmon themselves.) There was a small opening there, where the earth and sky joined, and the girls had slipped through this opening. The earth moved back and forth so quickly, that it was almost impossible to go through.

Rewards were offered for Moon's rescue. Bluejay had no blue uniform in those days. "We will give you a blue blanket if you can get to him," Moon's mother said. "I can go through," Bluejay said. The earth, where it joined the sky, kept moving back and forth very quickly. Bluejay finally managed to stick a stick in, and hold the earth and sky apart long enough to go through.

After he had reached the other side, Bluejay travelled for a number of years. Finally, he heard someone hammering; it was a wonderful, ringing sound. He said, "Kac, kac," and went around the man who was working. "What is Bluejay doing here?" the man asked and threw a little piece of iron at Bluejay. The iron struck Bluejay in the eye. "What do you mean, my boy? I've been hired by your mother to take you home," Bluejay said. He found out that this man was Moon. Moon slapped him on the head and the iron-dust came out of his eyes. Today there is still a cataract on Bluejay's eyes. Moon questioned Bluejay to learn how he had got to the salmon world; he had married the two girls. "We'll get ready to leave," he said to Bluejay after he had learned what had happened. Moon already had some children in the salmon world, a world that we do not know. His favorite child was speckled trout. Before he left, he made his children all kinds of toys [bones] and told them to play with the toys while he was gone. Then he deserted the two daughters of X̣wɑnä'x̣wɑne and started back for this world. Bluejay, in the meantime, returned, and received his blue blanket as pay. That's why he has a blue uniform.

The noble-hearted Moon was going to change the world, because it was only an imitation one. At the first place he came to, he found people fishing in the river. The boss had hundreds of people working for him, lined up clear across the riffle. "What's going on here?" Moon asked. "I've got a fish-trap standing here in line," the boss answered. Some of the people standing there in the water had caught cold, but the boss did not care if they died. Moon said, "My people, I am going to make a real trap here." He put a row of sticks across the riffle, and left an opening that led into a fish-basket. Before this, these imitation people had not known how to make a real fish-trap. "No one shall ever make a human trap again," Moon said. To Raven, the boss, he said, "You shall be punished. No person will ever do as you have done. You shall go back and forth, living on human flesh, and shall say, 'qwa'qʷ'." He turned Raven into a bird.

Moon came to another place and heard some one hammering and hammering. "What is going on here?" he thought. The man was using his head as a maul, trying to split a piece of cedar. "This is not the way a person should do; you are hurting yourself," Moon said. He made a wedge from a piece of elk-horn, and a maul from a piece of rock. He gave these to the man and told him never to use his head again as a maul. "No one shall ever do this again," he said.

Finally, he came to a place where people by the thousands were dancing. These people were the Prairie Chickens[1] who live east of the [Cascade] mountains. "What are you doing?" Moon asked. He learned that the people were dancing on their meat, to cook it. He made a fire drill from willow sticks and told them how to use it. "Turn the drill quickly and a small spark will come," he said. "People will always do this after I am gone," he said.

He came to a certain place and shouted to the people. Everyone got excited. They could not see. Flounder and Salmon were blind. He gave them sight, but flounder is still cross-eyed. [?][2]

On the way, he killed many monsters or told the people how to get rid of them.

One day, Moon met someone who got the best of him. It was old X̣wɑnä'x̣wɑne himself. Moon saw a cap that X̣wɑnä'x̣wɑne was wearing, and said, "Old man, where did you get your cap?" He traded caps with X̣wɑnä'x̣wɑne. The cap got tight on Moon and changed the appearance of his eyes. Now the Moon and his younger brother Sun have cross-eyes. It was X̣wɑnä'x̣wɑne who had done this to Moon.

Moon travelled all over the world showing people what they should do.

At last he arrived home and met his younger brother Sun. "I'm tired of this world," he said to Sun, "we shall go away now. It is a hard life here. Some people have been changed, but those who are civilized enough shall remain the way they are. We shall go away." Before this time, the world was without a sun or moon. "We shall be the sun and moon. I shall go up first," Moon said. He went up and travelled during the day, but he nearly set the world on fire with his heat. Then his brother Sun went up at night, but did not give enough light. Then they changed places. The third time they tried this new scheme, the temperature was mild. The fourth time,

---

[1] See p. 177.

[2] This vague incident is strange to me. The narrator does not repeat it in the version of this story he gave Dr. Boas in text.

it was still more pleasant and the fifth time it was just right. "We shall remain in the sky. We shall furnish light to the people underneath. The world, for this generation, shall now end. You shall always travel during the day, and I shall always travel at night," Moon said. Moon and Sun were born in this world and they were chiefs. Therefore, the people shall always follow their ways and do what is right. We have always believed in the Moon and Sun.

MOON AND THE PRAIRIE CHICKENS.[1]

The Moon was chief of this world. He was travelling through what is now Kittitas County. He came to thousands of people. This country through which he was travelling was cold. The people never stopped dancing for a moment. They were the Prairie Chickens. He noticed some salmon and venison lying about. The people were dancing on the meat. "What are you doing?" he asked. "We are getting the salmon and venison ready to eat. The heat from our dancing will warm it up, and make it tender," they explained. "This is the last time you shall ever do that," he said, "I shall invent another way."

The world was new, it had just become new and the people did not know what to do. He made a vessel for them in which to boil water. He stood it by the side of the fire. He built a fire on top of some rocks and left it there until the rocks were hot. Then he put some meat and some water into the vessel. When the rocks were red hot, he put them into the vessel also. The water began to bubble. He made some stakes and stood them close to the fire. He told the people that they could also cook their meat on the stakes. Indians have cooked their food this way for generations and generations. Moon cut the cooking vessel from cedar. He made a knife, sharp enough to cut wood. He then cut some boards from a cedar and put them together with pitch. The box was square and waterproof. Since that time, Indians have used such a bucket.

---

[1] Told by Jonas Secena, 1926. The story is said to be from the Kittitas, that is, Pcwa'nwa·pam, a Sahaptin group. See also p. 176.

II. COWLITZ TALES.

THE FLOOD.[1]

Spi'tsx̣ᵘ had five brothers-in-law. They often said to him, "Wash your face." He never paid any attention to them; his face was always dirty. This went on for a long time. Finally his brothers-in-law whipped him. Then Spi'tsx̣ᵘ sang,

> Brothers-in-law, brothers-in-law,
> I'm going to wash my face, I'm going to wash my face,
> Brothers-in-law, brothers-in-law,
> I'm going to wash my face, I'm going to wash my face.

He danced and dipped himself in the water. The water began to shake. As he jumped up and down, it rose and rose. He sang as he danced,

> Brothers-in-law, brothers-in-law,
> I'm going to wash my face,
> I'm dancing now.

The water was rising higher all the time. Spi'tsx̣ᵘ's wife said to her brothers, "You whipped him and made him bathe; now we'll float." Spi'tsx̣ᵘ was still singing,

> Brothers-in-law, brothers-in-law,
> I'm bathing now, I'm bathing now.

"You can stop now," his brothers-in law said to him. "But you told me to bathe," he said. The water rose and rose. At last Spi'tsx̣ᵘ turned into a (little brown) bird and flew away. Other people also turned into birds and flew away. Some turned into animals and went far off into the woods. Everyone, like Spi'tsx̣ᵘ, turned into a bird and flew away. Everything was under water because they made Spi'tsx̣ᵘ wash his face.

THE CONTESTS.

(First Version).[2]

Bluejay and his brother Eagle lived on the Cowlitz River. Eagle was a chief. Bluejay used the end of a tree that stuck out over the river, as a latrine. One morning early he went there to relieve him-

[1] Told by Mary Iley, 1927; see p. 413.
[2] Told by Sophie Smith, 1926; see p. 394.

self. Before he had time to fasten his clothes, he saw something strange in the water. He ran back to the house to get his arrows; there were five of them in one bag. He got the arrows, ran back to the latrine and began shooting into the water. He used up the five arrows and then ran back to the house to get another bag full. When these were gone, he ran back to the house to get some more. As soon as the arrows were gone, he would throw his bow, the bag, and then some sticks into the water. Finally he used up five bags of arrows, all that he owned. Then he ran back to the house and said to Eagle, "Brother, I saw a strange looking salmon in the river. I couldn't kill it. Come quickly!" Eagle arose and put on all his fine clothes; he always dressed well. He took five slaves and five salmon-spears and went to the river. Then all got into a big canoe. The five slaves speared and Eagle and Bluejay steadied the canoe. Bluejay was at the bow, Eagle at the stern. Suddenly, a big, long fish appeared and the slaves speared. At the same time, their hands stuck to the spears, and Bluejay's and Eagle's hands stuck to the paddles. It was early in the morning, before breakfast. They were carried downstream very fast. "What's the matter, brother? My hands are stuck to the paddle," Bluejay said. "Hush, hush," Eagle answered. By noon, they had almost reached a place that was inhabited. Then they heard someone calling. "Brother, I hear them saying something, I hear them saying, 'ɛ···, Bluejay's brother-in-law is taking him down,'" Bluejay said. "Hush, the dangerous people have got us," Eagle said. They were taken far down into open water, where the Cowlitz empties into the Columbia. They passed that and eventually got into open water, like the ocean. Early next morning, they landed. They had travelled steadily all day and all night.

The salmon jumped out of the water, took off his fish-blanket and shook it. Then he picked up all the bows and arrows that Bluejay had tried to strike him with. He had saved them all. "Isn't this nice, my brother-in-law?" he said to Bluejay. When he shook his blanket, the water from it turned into ice and covered the ground. He went into the house without inviting his guests to follow. "Oh, oh, oh, I'm freezing! What shall we do now?" Bluejay said. "Follow right behind me," his brother said. Eagle shouted for his power. Then he walked on the ice, and every place he stepped, a hole appeared. Bluejay came right behind him, jumping along and saying, "Kac." The five slaves followed behind Bluejay. They went into the house. The house was nice and clean but there was no fire. They sat down. "Oh — — —, oh — — — —, I'm cold," Bluejay said again and again. "Hush, hush," his brother said. The chief was lying down, high up on a bed. Suddenly he raised his head and said, "Where are you, O'x̣tɪqs?" This was the name of one of his slaves. "Come here and make a fire for my brother-in-law; he's cold." The slave was a little fellow with a long nose. He got a stick about a yard long.

The fireplace was absolutely clean; there was no sign of ashes. "Oh, you make a fire with a very small stick," Bluejay said. "Hush," his brother said. The little fellow split the stick in two with his nose. He laid one piece aside and split up the other piece until he had enough wood for a large fire. Then he built a fire. "Oh — — — —, there's too much smoke, brother," Bluejay said to Eagle. Their host said to the slave, "O'x̂tɪqs, you didn't make a good fire. Come and tend to it." The slave sucked in all the smoke. "Oh, look, look! Look, look! It's the funniest thing I've ever seen," Bluejay said. The fire was now burning very well and the room was free from smoke. In a little while Bluejay said, "Oh, I'm so hungry that I'm sick. I haven't had anything to eat since we left." Then the man raised his head and said to the little fellow, "Get something to eat for my brother-in-law." The slave got a piece of meat that was hanging up and laid it down. He cut it in two pieces and laid one piece aside. He cut up the other piece until there was a large pile of meat. Then he cooked a lot of meat for them. "I want to go out, brother," Bluejay said. They went out. Then Eagle concealed a sack under Bluejay's clothes, close to his mouth. "You must put all the food that you can't eat into this sack. Pretend to eat it all," Eagle said. They went back in and Bluejay kept shoving the food into the sack. After a while, he said, "Oh, I'm still hungry. The food is too fat."

There was going to be a diving contest in the afternoon. "I'll dive," Bluejay said. "I'm afraid you can't do it," his brother said. "Oh, I can do anything," Bluejay answered. He and his brother then went to the river to fix their canoe. They tied it up and piled brush alongside it, close to shore. "You can come here and breathe when you are out of breath," Eagle said. Bluejay and a little sea-bird, a girl, went into the water. The girl was representing their host's side. The two were to remain under water for a number of hours. After a while, Bluejay began to talk to the girl. "Just sit where you are," he said, "I'll wander around under water and explore the country." Every once in a while, he would come out of water, under the brush. "I might smother to death," he thought to himself. He had a little club, a small stone ball with a handle. Finally, he passed the girl and struck her on the side of the head. The girl doubled up and sank. Then Bluejay went to the brush to get some air. He stayed there for a long time, listening. At last he heard the people cry, "Da, da, da." "I guess she is dead now," he said. Then he left the brush and went back into the water. Eagle went out in his canoe to see which one of them was dead. The others followed. Eagle saw that it was not Bluejay. The others brought the dead girl in to shore. After a while Bluejay, far out in the water, was seen swimming toward shore. "I win, I win!" he kept shouting. He won a blue blanket. Then their host announced, "To-morrow, we shall have another game, a climbing-contest."

The contestants were to climb a slick little ladder that was standing straight up. "I'm afraid you can't climb," Eagle said to Bluejay. "Indeed I can, climbing is my trick," Bluejay answered. A little girl and Bluejay started up the ladder, one here, one there. "Kac, kac," Bluejay said, as he jumped along. They climbed far up, so high that no one could see them, and sat there and talked. From time to time Bluejay would come down and then go back up. He and the girl talked for some time. At last he got tired of her and knocked her down with his stone club. Those standing below saw that someone was falling. "Poor boy," Eagle said, thinking it was Bluejay. But it was the girl, coming down bump-ty bump. She was badly smashed. After a while, Bluejay came down. "The girl is missing," he said. He won a blue blanket again and shouted for joy.

Every afternoon they had a game. The following afternoon, they had a shooting-contest. "I'll represent our side," Bluejay said. Then his brother took him into the brush where they would not be seen, and put some little whetstones on either side of his breast. They made Bluejay and a boy slave stand up. Then the chief shot at them. Suddenly, Bluejay fell over backwards. "Poor fellow, he's been killed," his brother said. Then the chief shot at the little boy and knocked him over; he had been shot through. Just then Bluejay jumped up and said, "He didn't kill me. I just got dizzy and fell over." He won another blanket.

The next afternoon they had a sweating-contest. Bluejay and a boy took part in it. They had a little house of rocks, air-tight. Eagle bored a little hole in it so that Bluejay could get some air, for it was very hot inside. Then he sat down on one side of the house, his brother-in-law and a slave on the other side. They sat there for hours. Finally, the boy blew up. "I····, they heard someone burst and thought it was I!" Bluejay said. He won another blanket.

The last game was a "bone-gamble". Bluejay and his brother played together and won. They planned to go home the following morning. From time to time, a little fish, like a trout, would come wriggling up to the place where Bluejay was sitting, and each time Bluejay would try to hit him with his stone club. "Oh, mother," the little fish would say, "uncle wants to kill me!" There were a number of these little fishes and they were Bluejay's nephews. Bluejay's sister, the little fishes' mother, was making a long rope and had completed it at last. It was so long it filled five baskets. The baskets graduated in size and one fitted into another. Bluejay and his brother were now preparing to go home. They were taking back the five blue blankets that Bluejay had won and many other things. Some time before this Bluejay's sister had been stolen and he had been unable to find her. The man who had married her finally let Bluejay know where she was by carrying him off to his village.

When they had finished loading their canoe, the woman said to them, "On the way back, you will pass five thunder and lightning storms. When you pass the fifth one, tear a little piece off your blue blanket, Bluejay, and tie it to the end of this rope. Then let the rope loose." In some way, Bluejay tied the end of the rope to himself. It would unwind as they travelled along. It was early in the morning when they set out. They passed through the first storm safely and then the second, third, and fourth. When they came to the fifth, Bluejay was struck right on the forehead and a little tuft of hair was left sticking out. He fastened a bit of blue blanket to the end of the rope and let the rope drop into the water. The rope stopped pulling [and his sister wound it back up]. When she came to the bit of blue on the end, she knew that Bluejay and his brother had arrived home.

Bluejay got back home safe. He had learned where his sister was living.

THE CONTESTS.

(Second Version).[1]

Once upon a time all the animals and birds were people. Mountain Eagle (x̯wa'ips) was chief. He decided to pay a visit to a village in distant territory and invited his people to accompany him. They set out in canoes. Eagle invited Bluejay and his elder sister Nau to sit in his canoe.

When he saw the party coming, the chief of the village went down to the river's edge and wrung water out of his hair. The water turned into ice. Eagle noticed the ice on the ground and said to his people, "Wait, let me get out first." Bluejay paid no attention, he jumped out first, and slipped and fell on the ice. Someone grabbed him by the hair and threw him back into the canoe. Eagle then got out cautiously. He put one foot forward and the ice melted immediately underfoot. Then he put the other foot forward and the same thing happened. His people followed behind him, walking in his tracks. Thus they finally made their way up the hill to the village.

The villagers welcomed their guests and had a number of people address them. "We'll have a big time tomorrow," a speaker said, "stay over until then." The visitors accepted their invitation. Next morning, there were more speeches. A diving contest for boys was announced. The one who could stay under water longest would win. The villagers wished to bet against their visitors. "I'll enter the contest," Bluejay said. His opponent was little White Duck[2] (kwɛ'lkwʋc). Bluejay's people prepared for the contest: it was the custom to keep some brush in the bottom of a canoe so that the occupants would have a dry place to sit. They took the brush out of one of the canoes and threw it between the canoe and the shore. Then they built a fire on the shore close to the brush. Bluejay could

[1] Told by James Cheholts, 1927.
[2] With black spots on back.

come out of the water and hide under the brush. All the on-lookers were sitting on the shore. Bluejay and White Duck both dived at the same time into a falls. Bluejay got to the very bottom of the falls and so did Duck. Duck then sat down right in the falls. Bluejay said to him, "I'll swing out around you and then come back." He took a wide swing around Duck and came out under the brush, which was some distance away. He sat there for a while and then swam back. Presently he went again to the brush and sat there. By this time he was chilled and began to shake. The brush shook all over. "I'm so tired and cold I'm going to hit that fellow on the head," he said to himself. The third time he came back to Duck, he slipped up behind him and clubbed him on the head. Duck rose to the surface, his head split open. Bluejay just stayed there in the water. He stayed quite a while before he came out. They had taken the other fellow ashore; he was dead now. Bluejay had won the contest.

The next event was a pole-climbing contest. They had taken a tree, cut the limbs off, and hewn it down until very smooth. Then grease was rubbed on it to make it very slick. The pole was then set up straight. It was slick clear to the very bottom. The villagers chose big Hummingbird to represent them in the contest. Bluejay was asked if he would represent his side. "All right," he said, "I'll climb against Hummingbird." Hummingbird started first. He gave one jump, landed on the pole and climbed clear to the top. Then Bluejay jumped onto the pole, examining it closely as he climbed. He spied a little lump and climbed up to it. He stayed there a while, and then let himself slip clear to the ground. "I used to do that a long time ago," he said, "I'm used to climbing trees." He jumped onto the pole again, climbed to the little lump and stayed there. After a while, he slipped to the ground again. The third time he went clear to the top of the pole. And so he won the contest.[1]

The visitors started home in their canoes. Bluejay rode with Eagle. After they had gone a long way, they came to a machine on the water, — a wooden affair that moved up and down very quickly. It moved up and down so quickly it would come down on them before they could pass under. They pulled up close to it, and after watching it for some time, saw that at its present rate of speed they could never pass under it. "Sit down," the chief said to Bluejay. "Get slow," he said to the machine. Thus he made it slow down. "Get ready to pull hard!" he said to Bluejay, "pull so hard that the canoe jumps right under it. When I'm ready, I'll pull. You pull with me." He waited a bit and then said, "Go!" They went right under it. They went quite a way and then came to another machine like the first. This one was going faster. They went close to it and the chief said, "Wait." "Get slow," he said. In just a little while, the machine

---

[1] I judge the clubbing incident has been omitted here.

slowed down. They waited, ready to make the canoe jump under it. When it seemed slow enough, they pulled hard and cleared it. Bluejay, acting as captain, was sitting in the rear. The machine touched him on the back as it came down but did not injure him. They got home safely.

BLUEJAY AND HIS YOUNGER BROTHERS.[1]

Bluejay took his two younger brothers with him to visit some girls. Bluejay already had a wife. One of the girls took a liking to his second brother,[2] but after they had both courted her for a while, Bluejay won the girl's affection. Then the younger gave Bluejay a whipping. He struck him with a sharp-cornered stick and hurt him badly. Bluejay jumped up and said, "I'm still alive." He took a little stick and threw it at the girl to get her attention.

Later on, Bluejay's mother-in-law took his wife away from him, and Bluejay asked his brothers to go with him to try to get her back. The three of them got ready and set out. On the way, Bluejay killed a deer. "What are you going to do with the meat?" the second brother asked. Bluejay told him that he was going to take it to his wife. "Help me pack it," he said. "No, I won't help you. You took my girl away from me," his brother said. Then the youngest brother offered to pack some of the meat to give to Bluejay's wife. "No, you give the meat you pack to my mother-in-law. I'll give the meat I pack to my wife," Bluejay said. "No, I won't pack any meat to give to your mother-in-law," the youngest said. In the meantime, the second brother had taken his share of the meat and was roasting it on a stick. He had no intention of giving any of his meat to his sister-in-law; his elder brother had taken his girl away from him. As soon as the meat was done, he said, "Use this for a cane."[3][?] "No, we'll eat this meat right here," Bluejay said. "No," the second said, "I don't want to eat with you." Then the youngest said, "Go on, go get your wife alone." Bluejay then went off alone, and the two younger brothers stayed where they were, cooking meat.

In a little while, Bluejay returned. "I'm not going for my wife after all. I've decided to get one of those girls for my youngest brother," he said. "All right, I'll go with you," the youngest said. "No, I don't want you to follow me," Bluejay said. Then the second said, "Never mind, just shut up and eat your meat." "I won't eat," Bluejay said, "I'll go alone to get the girl." "Go and get your own wife," the youngest said. "I'll make a canoe and go," Bluejay said. "Stick up a [canoe] pole for me and I'll go with you," the youngest said. "Make me a pole to push the canoe up the river," Bluejay said. "We won't make you a pole. Go get your own wife and forget

[1] Told by Mrs. Northover, 1926; interpreted by Mr. Northover; see p. 398.
[2] That is, next to him in age. All three brothers are Bluejays.
[3] Not very clear, perhaps a pun.

about the girl," the youngest said. "Make me a bow and arrow and I'll get the girl for you," Bluejay said. "I'll make the bow but you make the arrow," the youngest said. "Fix up a lunch for me, I want to go over there and camp," Bluejay said. "I'll put up a lunch and go with you," the youngest said. "No, I'll go alone," Bluejay said. Then the second asked, "What do you think, that I'll get your wife while you are gone?" "No," Bluejay answered, "I'll go get her myself whenever I want her." The youngest then said, "If you don't want to go to get your wife, I'll pack you over myself!" "No, I can go without your packing me," Bluejay said. "I'll go and get the girl myself," the youngest said. "No, I'll get her for you," Bluejay said. "I can go and fetch her here as well as you!" the youngest said. Then the second said, "You'd better kill another deer; we're running out of meat. Don't bother yourself about the girl; you're getting too old." "I'm old, but I think the girl would come with me," Bluejay answered. Then he said to his youngest brother, "Tie ten knots in a string; then you can get the girl." "Tie ten knots in a string and I'll hang you!" the youngest said, and added, "I'll make a pole to push the canoe with. Then I'll get the girl!" The second brother said to Bluejay, "Go kill a deer. We're running out of meat." "When I have the girl here, then I'll kill a deer," Bluejay answered. "Let's go! I'll go with you to get the girl; we're getting hungry," the youngest said. "You two can starve to death. I'll kill another deer for myself, and go alone for the girl," Bluejay said. "Go get your wife," the youngest said. "No, I want to get the girl," Bluejay answered. Then the two younger brothers whispered to one another, "Let's tie him up." Bluejay overheard them. "No, don't tie me up," he said. Then the youngest went up to him and said, "If you go get your wife, we won't tie you up." "All right, if you won't tie me up, I'll go get her," Bluejay said, and left them.

The second brother had whispered to the youngest, "As soon as he goes, we'll go get the girl ourselves." As soon as Bluejay had gone, they left. But Bluejay himself had gone to the girl. They found him there already. When the girl saw the youngest brother, she took hold of him and took him along with her. The youngest took her to the second. Old Bluejay stayed there and cried. "I'll take you to your wife," the youngest offered. "No, I'll stay right here," Bluejay said. That's why bluejays are about everywhere.

WREN KILLS ELK.[1]

Wren (ts'ats'ɛ''αp) was living with his grandmother. He had no father or mother; his grandmother was his only living relative. The old woman told him that they had nothing to eat and that he should go out to get something. Wren went out but he could not

[1] Told by Lucy Youckton, 1926; see p. 406.

find anything. The old woman sent him out five different times. Finally, she made him some kind of a little white knife. "I guess I'll go hunting," he said. His grandmother remained at home. She waited and waited for him. It was a long time before he came back. "I killed Elk," he said. "Don't lie, I'll whip you," his grandmother said.

As soon as Wren had left the house, he had seen Elk and shot at him. Elk could not see who he was. Suddenly, Wren had remembered the little rock knife in his belt. He had called Elk to come down where he was. "Come down, I shall kill you," he had said. Elk had come right down; he had not been at all frightened and said, "You're too little." He had opened his mouth wide and swallowed Wren. Wren had cut his entrails and heart. Elk had suddenly felt like evacuating and Wren passed right out through his anus. Elk had kept groaning; he could hardly breathe for his entrails were cut. Then Wren had run home to his grandmother and told her that he had killed Elk and she had threatened to whip him for lying.

He coaxed his grandmother, "Come, see for yourself." His arrows were all gone. He went back to the elk and spent all day butchering it. When he had finished, he ran home and said to his grandmother, "Grandmother, come and help me pack the meat." He was carrying just a small pack of it with him. "I can't carry much," the old woman said. "Come on," he coaxed. She took a packrope with her. The meat lay scattered on the ground, here, there, everywhere. "Give some of this away. We can't eat it all," she said. Then Wren went to the little Blackheads[1] and invited them to help themselves to his meat. The Blackheads carried and carried it away. "Pack a piece of the meat, just a little piece," Wren begged his grandmother. He cut a piece from the belly and offered it to her. "No," she said, "they'll call me 'belly'." Then he cut a piece from the hind leg and offered it to her. "No," she said, "they'll call me 'hind leg'." He offered her a piece of backbone, the soup bone. "No," she said, "they'll call me 'backbone'." He offered her the little feet, saying, "This is light." She refused it. He offered her the throat. "No," she said. "What can I make her pack? The genitals?" he thought. He had thrown them away. He looked for them and said, "Here, carry this!" He was just having some fun. "Ah, that's what I want to pack!" his grandmother cried.

Then Wren made a cedar-bark rope and tied and tied the meat to his forehead. He started off. His pack fell down and he tied it on again. He went a short way and it fell down again. It fell down five times. Then he went back to the place where he had butchered the elk. There was his grandmother having intercourse with the genitals! She was lying down and singing. "Ah, grandmother is very bad!" he said. He was angry. He started off again. After a while he

---

[1] Birds.

thought, "Where is grandmother now?" Someone was singing. There was his grandmother dancing! She was singing,

> My little grandson killed the elk,
> My little grandson killed the elk.

He took the genitals away from her. "This is something to eat, not something to marry," he said, "you bad one!" He hid the piece of meat so that she could not do it again. Then she got very angry and cried, "If you won't sleep with me, I'll kill you! I had to do it because you won't sleep with me!"

Wren said, "Grandmother, I'm hungry." "Why don't you eat some of the meat? It's cooked," she said. Then she got some dried salmon heads, some cooked roots and salmon berries. "I don't want to cook any more of the elk meat right now," she said. Five times she offered him some cooked lacamas but he refused them. Finally, she offered him some dried berries. "Ah, I don't want to eat that," he said. "Well, what do you want to eat? My backside?" she said. "Yes, that's just what I want!" he said. He dug a hole. His grandmother lay down in it and he had intercourse with her. Suddenly he heard a noise and got up to listen. "Someone will hear of this!" he thought. "Grandmother," he said, "you don't want to have intercourse with me. Get up, get up!" Then he heard someone say, "What is Wren doing with his grandmother?" "Let's get up!" he said to her. Ts'a'maẋwʋl[1] was going down the river in a canoe. "What news do you hear as you travel?" Wren called to him. "I have no news," Ts'a'maẋwʋl called back. Then Wren called again, "What news do you hear as you travel?" "Oh, there is just somebody there lying down with his grandmother," Ts'a'maẋwʋl called back. "Grandmother," Wren said, "he said that I am lying down with you." Then he called Ts'a'maẋwʋl to come and fight. They fought near the camp-fire and both fell. The old woman grabbed a stick and pushed Wren into the fire, thinking it was Ts'a'maẋwʋl. Not long afterward, she heard Ts'a'maẋwʋl down at the river. Then realizing her mistake, she searched in the fire for her grandson. Nothing was left of him but a few bones. Ts'a'maẋwʋl had escaped.

The old woman wept; she did not know what to do. She got some pitch from a tree. Then she took her grandson's little bones, his little head, his little ears and stuck them together with pitch. Wren came to life and began to talk. "You mustn't walk around," she cautioned him. She took him home and put him in the shed. Then she went out to the prairie to dig lacamas so that they would have something to eat. She had left Wren in the shade so that he would not melt. She heard a noise and went to see what it was. Wren had gone out into the sun and melted. She got him and put pitch again on his little head and arms and legs. "Don't go out into the sun again," she cautioned him. Then she went back to the prairie to

[1] See footnote 3, p. 31.

dig lacamas. Wren was hungry and went out to get something to eat. He melted again as soon as he got into the sun. The old woman heard him moving around and thought, "What's he doing?" She found him melted again. She put him back into the shed where it was cool and he got all right again. She was tired and angry now. "I guess I'll have to lock you in," she said. "Grandmother, I'll be all right," he promised. She went back to the prairie. A little later she heard a noise. Wren had melted again. She had stuck him together four times. She put him back again. "I'll stay right here," he said, "but I'm hungry." "I'll go to the prairie and get you some lacamas," she said. She had not yet had a chance to stay long enough on the prairie to get anything to eat. After she left, Wren said, "I'm going away." And so he went west and climbed a tree. Soon he heard his grandmother coming. She hauled him down and said, "I'll feed you soon." Wren was angry because he was hungry and refused to go back.[1] Then the old woman went away because he was angry and turned into the little bluebird. She was a human-being before she turned into a bird. When it rains, one can hear her talking.

CRANE.[2]

Crane (sq'was) built a fish trap (tse'tpən); he got some young people to help him build it. Time and again he invited the people to visit him and share the fish that he had caught. But he never caught any fish in his trap. He never fished but slept all the time. The people would go to see what he was doing. They always found him sleeping instead of fishing. That's why X̣wα'ni let him go. Crane can still be seen in all the streams, trying to catch fish but never succeeding; he just stands there in the water.

BEAR, ANT, GROUSE, FROG AND THE YELLOWJACKETS.[3]

Bear was always going around eating berries. He ate lots of them. "I wish I could sleep a whole year," he said, "I'm so tired." Ant heard him and said, "You shouldn't wish to sleep so long after the berries are gone, it isn't right." "I wish not only I, but everyone could sleep that long," Bear said. "No, that wouldn't do at all," Ant said. "But I might as well sleep, I can't eat in the winter," Bear said. "One night, one night," Ant said. Then big Yellowjacket, black Yellowjacket, Frog and Grouse joined in, five of them against Bear. "One night dark, one night dark," they chorused. "One year, one year," Bear said. "One night dark, one night dark," they chorused. "Tie yourself around the waist," Bear said to Ant. They

[1] Evidently he is the wren now.
[2] Told by Mrs. Northover, 1926; interpreted by Mr. Northover; see p. 410.
[3] Told by Lucy Youckton, 1926; see p. 413.

danced and danced and danced. "One night, one night," they said. "One year, one year," Bear said.

"You've beaten me and now I'm going to eat you," Bear said at last. He looked everywhere for Grouse but could not find him. He sat down again. "One night, one night," someone said. It was Ant and the Yellowjackets. He ate them. That's why bear always eats ants and yellowjackets. The others escaped him. He can never catch grouse and frog. The grouse always flies to a tree and the frog always goes under the water.

"As for myself," Bear said, "I'll sleep a whole winter. You fellows can sleep one night." He went to a cedar tree and made a door in it, just large enough to crawl through. He stayed there all winter, sleeping until springtime. After a while he opened the door and said, "Is it warm yet?" It was perhaps January and still cold. He closed the door and slept and slept. A little later he got up. "Perhaps it's light now, perhaps it's warmer," he said and opened the door. "Oh, it is warm! It must be about March now. Perhaps things are growing already." He swam and swam. Then he found some skunk-cabbage. It was the first thing he ate after his long sleep. He ate and ate. He went close to a house and built a house of his own. "Before long the berries will be ripe; then I'll have a lot to eat," he said. After a while he thought, "Oh, I'm hungry." He found a hollow log in which there were some ants and a yellowjackets' nest. The ants bit him and the yellowjackets stung him but he ate them anyway. "I'm going to eat you fellows, you got the best of me," he said.

FROG AND BEAR.[1]

Frog and Bear, for some reason or other, happened to meet. "Let us sleep four or five years," Bear said. Frog answered, "Ah, ah, ah. One night, one night, one night." Bear got angry and jumped at Frog, but she buried herself in the mud and he could not find her. "Five years, five years, five years," he said. "One night, one night, one night," she answered. Bear got angry and scratched for her in the mud. "Four years, four years, four years," he said. "One night, one night, one night," she said. Then he scratched around in the dirt for her. "One night, one night, one night," she said. "Two years, two years, two years," he answered. "One night, one night, one night," she said. "One year, one year, one year," he answered. Then all the Frogs came out and sat down in a row (on something like a little fence). All bobbed up at once[2] and said, "Only you one year, only you one year." Then all sat down at once.[3] They bobbed up and down five times, saying the same thing each time. "All right, I one

[1] Told by Mary Iley, 1926; see p. 413.
[2] Illustrated by straightening up the fingers.
[3] Illustrated by bending the fingers down.

year and you one year," Bear said. Then all the Frogs said simultaneously, "All right, I one year, and you one year, but people, one night."

Now we sleep one night. Frog sleeps during the winter and Bear sleeps during the winter. When February comes, Bear puts his hand out: it is still cold. When April comes, it is warm. Bear then gets up and goes out. The little Frogs freeze in the ice, but when warm weather comes, the mud softens and they wake up. As soon as they thaw out, they are all right again.

STEELHEAD AND CHINOOK SALMON.[1]

Steelhead came up first on the Cowlitz river. He had five kinds of little fish with him, all very pretty. He spawned up the Cowlitz and started back down. At Mossy Rock, he met Chinook Salmon, who had four kinds of fish with him, all very bony. "How's the country up there where you have been?" Chinook asked. "I'm going to fix him!" Steelhead thought. "Oh," he said, "it's very nice. There are nice shallow places and riffles where the king's-people[2] can float belly up." Chinook got very angry, for it was true, that after spawning, he would not return alive, but would die and float back down the river. "Let's kill him," he said to the boys, his friends. He jumped on Steelhead and grabbed his fat, which he put on himself. He tore Steelhead's head off and put it on. He put his own head, which was full of bones, like white agates, on Steelhead. The Trout, Chinook's friends, tore all the fat off the Suckers, and put it on themselves. Ever since that time, Steelhead has had very poor meat and a skinny back.

Steelhead went home and came back again the following year. Chinook went on up the river and spawned. After spawning, he gets old and dies. He floats down the river, belly up. Steelhead never dies; after spawning, he always goes back to the ocean but returns again the following year.

SMELT AND EEL.[3]

When Smelt and Eel were human beings, they chanced to meet. The first said that he would be the smelt, and the other said that he would be the eel. Eel said that when the people ate him, they should remove his excrements (p'a, a yellow substance) and his head. Smelt said, "The people shall eat every bit of me except my tail." "What would you do if they should remove your bones before eating you?" Eel asked. "I would kill them," Smelt said. "What

---

[1] Told by Mary Iley, 1926; see p. 408.

[2] The term Mrs. Iley always gives to those who are born royal, that is, the chiefs.

[3] Told by Mary Iley, 1927; see p. 411.

would you do if the Taitnepam should clean you before eating you?" Eel asked. "That would be all right; the Taitnepam are strangers and do not know my ways. But should the Cowlitz, who do know my ways, clean me before they eat me, I will kill them," Smelt said.

The people used to die when they removed anything from the smelt except the tail; blood ran from their noses and mouths. It was forbidden to eat the tail. Eel said, "After I am cooked, they must remove my head and throw it away, still on the roasting stick; if the stick falls far off, they will have a long life; if it falls close by, they will have a short life." Smelt said, "If the people eat me as they should, — if they do not mash me, they will not die. If the Taitnepam throw me up, it can't be helped."

DEER AND COUGAR.[1]

Deer and Cougar went to a large gathering. There was lots of fun there. Cougar wanted to play "lal" against Deer. "All right," Deer said. "If I win," Cougar said, "I'm going to kill you and eat you." "You can never catch me. When I run, I run fast," Deer said. Well, they sat down. Many people were gambling now. Cougar started to sing. He sang,

> I wish to gamble quickly,
> So that I can bite and pull hard at Deer's belly.

Then Deer sang,

> No one can catch me,
> No one can do anything to me.
> I am strong enough to run fast.[2]

They gambled and gambled. At last Cougar beat Deer. Then Deer ran away so fast that Cougar could not catch him.

WOLF, COYOTE AND DOG.[3]

Wolf, Coyote and Dog were brothers. They were hunters. They kept their camp-fire burning all the time. One day they were so busy eating the meat they had caught that they forgot to watch their fire. "Why don't you fix the fire?" Wolf asked. "Oh, I have no time," one of the others said. By the time they had finished, their fire was out. Then one said, "Which one of us is going to go to the people and ask them for some fire?" "Well, I can go. I'll ask them to give us some fire," Dog said. "All right," his brothers said, glad to let him go.

---

[1] Told by James Cheholts, 1927; see p. 413.
[2] His guardian-spirit enables him to do this.
[3] Told by James Cheholts, 1927; see p. 409.

Dog went to the people to ask them for the fire. They had some food. "We'll give you something to eat. Stay with us," they said and placed some food in his palm. He never went home. Today, one can see a "cushion" at the base of his palm, where they placed the food. He stayed there for good.

His brothers are still angry with him because he never returned. When Wolf and Coyote meet Dog, they always fight him.

BEAVER, MUSKRAT AND MOUNTAIN BEAVER.[1]

Beaver, Muskrat and Mountain Beaver were brothers. They lived together. One day they talked to one another and said, "Is there any way we can live so that the people can't kill us?" Finally Beaver said, "Well, as for me, I am going to the lake and make a dam there so that I shall never be out of the water. The water is never low there. I shall build a dam in the middle of the lake where people can never come to kill me." Then Muskrat said, "Well, I am going to the river and live there. I shall look for a little hill at the water's edge and dig a hole clear through it. I shall make my home there. In the daytime I shall swim in the river and at night time, in my tunnel." Mountain Beaver said, "Oh, I am going to a mountain or high hill. I shall dig far under the ground and stay there so that no one can catch me."

And so the brothers parted and each went his separate way. Now Beaver lives in the lake, Muskrat in the river, — where he swims about, and Mountain Beaver far underground. In spite of this, the people are able to catch them.

RABBIT.[2]

Everyone was singing and dancing. Each person had a song of his own. Bear sang,

> I dance on the swamps,
> On every swamp.

Elk sang,

> I dance on all the mountains,
> On five mountains, I have a dancing place.

Deer sang,

> I run if they try to kill me,
> To my five mountains
> I run away and leave the people.

All the different kinds of Birds had a song. Pheasant came and sang,

> My children
> Their father was a log.

---

[1] Told by James Cheholts, 1927; see p. 411.

[2] Told by Mary Iley, 1926. This is a story that children like. See p. 410.

While they were dancing and singing, Rabbit (sx̣wa'iks) came in with his bow drawn. He had his arrow aimed at the pole in the middle of the house. He danced and sang,

Move pole, I'll shoot you.

He danced and sang the same thing over and over. The pole began to move. It kept moving, moving, moving, until it was almost at the end of the house. Then everyone saw that the house was going to fall and got ready to run out. Some became feathered and flew out. Rabbit ran out, singing his song, as the old house fell. All those things that are under a house to-day, like mice, lizards, snakes and rats, first went there when the house fell. The rest of the people in the house turned into birds and flew out. Rabbit still dances outside and the people throw sticks at him. He was angry because the others were having a good time.

WILDCAT.[1]

Wildcat was living with his grandmother, Crow. At that time, Skunk, Rabbit, and all the animals were people. Eagle was a chief and he had one daughter. Wildcat was a very ugly fellow; he had sores and scabs all over his body and head.

The chief's daughter had a tamanoas gathering and invited people to attend. "Ha, ha," she sang, holding her head back. She sang like this for five nights. They refused to let Wildcat into the house for he was too lousy; his entire body was covered with sores and scabs made by the vermin. Since they refused to let him in, he climbed each night to the roof of the house and looked down through the smoke-hole. The people beat a stick upon the floor, making a nice noise. When the girl sang, "Ha, ha," her head thrown back, he spit into her mouth. Unknowingly, the girl swallowed his spittle. He did the same thing each night of the meeting.

After the girl had sung her tamanoas, she became pregnant, they say. When she had her baby, Crow was called in to help. "The baby cries all the time. It's a boy," Crow said to her grandson. "To-morrow they will invite everyone to come; the baby will stop crying when its father holds it."

The following day, Crow went again to see how things were going with the baby. The tamanoas-house was packed with people; all the rich people were there. The grandfather gave the child to every man to hold, for it was dying from crying. When he walked past the place where Wildcat's grandmother was sitting, the baby ceased crying for just a moment. Then Bluejay said, "It stopped crying when it came to Wildcat's grandmother." After a while, every man in the place had held the baby. The following day, everyone was invited to come, old and young alike, regardless of who they were.

[1] Told by Mary Iley, 1926; see p. 408.

Coyote came and put his hand over the child's mouth and it stopped crying. "Take it away from him! He'll kill it!" someone said. "Oh, the baby always wants to stop where Wildcat's grandmother is sitting," Bluejay said. No one could make the baby stop crying. Then someone said, "Bring Wildcat in!" "Oh, he's too dirty to come in," someone else said. "We'll let him hold the baby," others said. Wildcat was standing in the doorway and someone passed the baby to him. The rich people present had not been able to make it stop crying. Wildcat took the baby and it stopped crying immediately. Then all the people shouted, "Oh, what kind of a man is the chief's daughter courting!" The girl began to weep; Wildcat was such a dirty fellow. "I've never spoken to him or even so much as looked at him! How could he be the father of my child?" she said. "You must be running after a dirty man!" the people said. The girl's father then became very angry and said to her, "You can live with him! You love him, you had a baby by him!" "We shall move down the Cowlitz river and leave her with her lover," he said to the people.

Everyone got ready to leave. "We mustn't leave any fire," they said. They poured water on all the fires, took all the food, left the houses completely empty. The girl was left only her dress and blanket. But Crow hid a large bundle of dried salmon in the ground, some distance from her house. A string led from the bundle to another hole in which some lacamas were buried and then to a hole with some fire. "Did you put your fire out?" the others asked. "Yes," she said, "my house is empty. I left nothing at all for my grandson."

Everyone left and the girl wept. She prodded Wildcat with the poker. "Make me a fire," she said. Wildcat was still holding the baby. "It's not yours!" she said and took it away from him. He went to his grandmother's house. "I'm sure grandmother left me something," he said to himself. He followed the string and found the lacamas, the dried salmon and the fire. He put the fire on a piece of bark and soon had a large fire going. Then he put the lacamas in a basket and took them and the salmon to the girl. He carried in a lot of wood and built a fire. As soon as he had finished, he lay down in a corner, and scratched as usual. The girl struck him with the poker. "You make too much noise. You'll wake the baby," she said.

Early next morning Wildcat arose and made a sweat-house. He sweated and then rubbed himself. The next morning he sweated again and bathed, to get rid of his sores. His face and hands were already smooth. The young woman noticed the difference. The next day, he did the same thing again and became still more handsome. He went out and killed some rabbits with his bow and arrow. "Can this be the same man?" the woman thought. He sweated for four days and then looked entirely different. The woman always slept soundly at night, and so whenever the baby cried, Wildcat would take it up and shake it. Whenever the woman discovered him doing this, she would strike him with the poker. The fourth night, she thought, "This is a different man, a handsome man. His hair is always nicely combed, his face is smooth, and his body free from sores. Wildcat had sores and vermin, so it can't be he. Now I am going to have a handsome man." In the afternoon, after sweating, the man had gone out and returned with a deer. That night, he slept closer to the woman. He no longer had to touch her with a stick when he wished to wake her up. The fifth night, he lay down alongside the baby. The woman was very proud of her new husband. The sweat-baths that Wildcat had taken had killed his vermin. "I guess that dirty fellow went away," the woman thought. The two slept together, the woman never suspecting that her new man was Wildcat. The man killed many deer and packed them home. He dried the meat and filled every house with it.

The old grandmother thought, "I'm going to look for my grandson." She went secretly to her little canoe and started up the river. When far up, she landed. A little boy was walking around. "Oh, mother," he said, "an old lady is eating what I throw away." The woman knew immediately that the old lady was Crow. "Come in," she said to Crow, "don't eat that. We'll give you something nice to eat. Only you left something for us." They gave her a piece of nice dried fat to eat.

Crow started back home in her little canoe, laughing and weeping at the same time. She wailed,

Oh, my dear, they ate him up.

And then no longer able to restrain herself, she cried, happily,

Ha, ha, that's I.

"Oh, Crow is coming proudly," the people said. Crow had planned to pack up her things, and leave secretly. "Have you visited your grandson?" they asked. "Yes," Crow said, although she was not supposed to tell. "Oh, he's well-off, now. He has lots to eat and a baby old enough to run around. He and his wife are living together and are very happy." Then she showed them the nice fat meat that the couple had given her. (Wildcat had told his wife how he had cured himself and she was in love with him now.) "Oh, we'll all move back," the people said. Everyone got into their canoes and went back up the river. They found every house filled with meat. The chief was proud to have a son-in-law who was able to dress his wife in a nice buckskin dress. He was proud to have such a handsome man for a son-in-law.

FISHER AND SƏMT'I'C.[1]

Fisher and his elder brother Səmt'i'c[2] were living together in the mountains. Səmt'i'c always went hunting and Fisher always stayed home.

A girl lived close by. One day while Səmt'i'c was away, the boy left their home and wandered some distance. "Oh, here's a little house!" he said. He looked into the little house and saw a girl there. "Come in," she said. He went in and sat down and she gave him something to eat. Before he ate, he said, "You haven't burnt me yet."[3] The girl then put him in the fire and burnt him a little. "You're burning me!" he cried. "But you said, 'You haven't burnt me yet,'" the girl said. He started home crying and when he got there, put something on his burn to soothe it. "She burnt me; she's going to be my wife," he muttered to himself. His brother heard him and asked, "What's the matter with you?" "I jumped over the fire and fell down and burnt myself," the boy answered. "No, tell the truth. You said, 'The girl burnt me.'" Fisher then told him what had happened. "Show me her house. Take me to her," Səmt'i'c said. He went to the girl's house and asked, "Why did you burn my brother?" "Well, I gave him something to eat and then he said, 'You haven't burnt me yet,'" the girl explained. "Come with me and be his nurse," Səmt'i'c said. "All right," the girl answered. She got ready and started back with him. "You're going to marry me, not the boy," he said.

The girl made some medicine for Fisher's burn as soon as she got to the house. She stayed on as Səmt'i'c's wife and bore him a son. They told her that she must never go to the middle of the prairie. She obeyed for some time but finally went to see what was there. She found some large lacamas, dug them up and packed them home. She visited the place four times. The fifth time, it was quite warm, so she lay down. A black cloud came by and she made the wish that the cloud would stay there and give her some shade. The cloud came down low and carried her up with it. The baby was left playing on the ground.

When Səmt'i'c came home, he said, "Fisher, where's your sister-in-law?" "In the middle of the prairie, I suppose, digging large lacamas," Fisher said. Fisher went to the prairie to look for her. He found her basket, in which there were a few lacamas. The baby was playing nearby. "The dangerous being must have got her," her husband said, when Fisher returned with the news.

A long time afterward, Səmt'i'c said, "I'm going to look for her." Then lʊslʊ'spiap, the dangerous being, found him and cut his head

---

[1] Told by Mary Iley, 1926; see p. 415.

[2] English equivalent unknown, a gray animal very similar to the fox.

[3] This statement is not to be taken literally so the narrator said. It evidently refers to love-making.

off. lʊslʊ′spiap had two sisters. They took the head and nailed it to the prow of their canoe.

When Səmtʼi′c did not return, Fisher said to his nephew, who was now a big boy, "I believe that your father has been killed. We must look for him." On the way, they stepped on Meadow Lark's leg and broke it. "Poor me, I have been wronged by the one who is searching for his father," she said. "Oh, aunty, we will fix your leg!" they said. They tied beads on each side of her broken leg and she said, "lʊslʊ′spiap killed him. Go to the middle of the prairie. There is some green grass there. Some of it is short and some of it is tall and thus it makes steps that will lead you to the place you want to go." They went to the prairie and the grass turned into steps. They climbed up, passing different places on the way. At last they came to a house, near which was a pond. Meadow Lark had told them what to do when they got there. They hid, as she had said, in a storage-house[1] on the pond. About supper time, two girls appeared. They were making a trip to get something from the storage-house. They were pounding their canoe, making a nice noise. "Bɑm, bɑm," it sounded. They were singing,

We have a brother,
No one is better than he;
A man was looking for his wife,
Our brother killed him;
Now we have his head on our canoe.

They were boasting that their brother had taken a woman derived from chiefs as his wife. Meadow Lark had said, "You must listen closely to their song to get the tune." "I smell Fisher," the youngest girl said. "Let's go home; brother must be hungry." They knew that Fisher was the brother of the dead man whose head adorned their canoe. They landed and went into the cellar. Then Fisher and the youth killed them. They put on the girls' clothes and put the supplies — whatever they were — that the girls had come to fetch, into the canoe.

The woman, hearing the girls returning in their canoe, thought, "It doesn't sound the same." When they came into the house, she observed them closely. "They don't look the same," she thought. She said nothing but kept watching them as they prepared supper. After a while, they said, "Brother, supper is ready." While the man was eating, the youth whispered to his mother, "Mother, we came to get you. We'll burn the man up." After helping to clear away and wash the supper things, the woman, who was pregnant, said to her husband, "I don't feel well. I'd like to sleep with the girls to-night." "All right," the man said, "don't take sick. But if you

[1] Sometimes referred to as smoke-house or cellar-house; a place, evidently, where food supplies were stored. As far as I know, both the Cowlitz and Upper Chehalis stored their food in the main winter house.

do, wake me up." She went to the girls' bed and after the man was asleep, the three of them carried outside all the pretty things that the girls owned. Then they set fire to the house, to the door and everything around the house outside. The man did not wake up until the house was about to fall in. He beat upon the door and cried, "Wake up, wake up! We're burning!" They had locked the door and so he could not get out. The house fell down and he was burned to death. His stomach went "du· · · · ·, du · · · · ·," as it burst.

Fisher then removed his brother's head from the canoe and took it to the place where the remainder of the body lay. He laid the head in its proper place, prayed and walked back and forth over his brother until he came to life. Then they went home, packing along all the property that they had stolen.[1]

Soon after arriving, the woman gave birth to a girl. When the baby nursed, she bit her mother's breasts until the blood came and so her mother had to wean her very soon. As she grew older, she played with other children, but would always claw their flesh. Her mother would slap her but she would do the same again. Once when she was about eight, she tore a girl's eye out and ate it. Her mother gave her a good whipping. The girl then began to cry and would not stop. Finally, she began to roll up from the ground, and then to jump like a fly. Another time, the girl tore a child's eye out and ate it. Her mother gave her a thrashing and she acted in the same way as before. She did the same a third and a fourth time and her mother whipped her. Then for the fifth time, she tore out a child's eye and ate it; each time, she tore out only one eye. Her mother whipped her and she cried and cried. Then she began to rise up from the ground as she had done each time before. Her mother grabbed a stick to strike her but she went up and up and finally appeared in the sky as a small black cloud. "There shall never again be a child like this one. Hereafter no child shall have his eye torn out and eaten by another child. Go home to your father," the woman said.

At present, Cloud merely showers, for nothing is left of him but his daughter.

COUGAR AND SKUNK.[2]

Cougar and his brother Skunk were living together and an old maid and her grandmother were living together. No man had ever found the girl so she had to live with her grandmother. The old lady knew that Cougar was a good man. She told her granddaughter to go to his house and live there. "When Cougar comes home, tell him that you are going to be his wife, that I said so." "No," the girl

[1] The narrator remarked that the story does not tell how they got home.
[2] Told by Mary Iley, 1926; see p. 404.

said, "I'm afraid." "But we have nothing but lacamas to eat," the old lady said. "You must go. Cougar's bed is nice and clean but Skunk's bed is dirty. Go to the clean bed."

The girl went to Cougar's house and saw Skunk's bed. She did not go to it but sat down on Cougar's. Skunk came in and right away fell in love with the girl. He knew that her grandmother had sent her there. "Don't sit on Skunk's bed; sit on mine," he said. He took her to his own bed and hid her there. Cougar soon arrived with a large pack and set it down outside. "Come here, Skunk, and carry in my pack," he called. Skunk always carried his pack in for him. "One would think I was a slave!" Skunk said. But he went out and carried in the pack. Cougar came in and said, "Someone has been here. It smells like a girl." "Don't you know that I smell just like a girl?" Skunk said. Before Cougar came, Skunk had had something to eat; the girl had pounded some food in a bowl for him. He took what remained to Cougar. The girl had put a long hair in the bowl, for she was afraid of Skunk and wanted Cougar to know that she was there. "This is a girl's hair," Cougar said. "No it isn't, it's mine," Skunk said. "It fell in while I was pounding." He took the bowl and said, "I'll put it away for tomorrow." He took it to his bed and hid it there for the girl. During the night, he burst out laughing. "What's the matter?" Cougar asked. "The mice are running up my legs," Skunk said. He was laughing with the girl.

Cougar suspected that something was wrong, for Skunk could not keep away from the bed, but he did not know what to do about it. One evening he left his pack on a mountain, some distance from the house. "I'm very tired," he said when he came in, "I had to leave a big deer over there on the mountain. I was too tired to carry it in. We'll have to bring it in tomorrow morning." Next morning, he sent Skunk for the deer. Skunk came running back five times, on the pretext that he had forgotten something, his bow and arrow, his knife, and so on. He wanted to hide the girl so that Cougar could not find her. After he was out of sight, Cougar found the girl and asked, "What are you doing here?" "My grandmother sent me here to marry you," she said. They went to a very tall rock near a spring and hid there.

Skunk came home, threw the pack down and called, "Where are you, dirty face? Come here and carry my pack in!" He looked everywhere for the girl, in the house, in the brush, but could not find her. Then he sent his musk over everything around the place to kill the girl and Cougar. After a while he became thirsty and ran to the spring to get a drink. As he stooped down to drink, he saw their reflection in the water. He sent his musk into the water to kill them. Five times Cougar called him to come up where they were. Then Skunk looked up and saw them. "What do you mean by dirtying the water?" Cougar asked. "Tuləluləlu', it's funny when I send my musk into the water," Skunk said. "How did you get up there?" he asked. "I tied a rope around my waist and climbed up, upside down," Cougar said. "When I get there I'll shoot my musk at them and kill them," Skunk thought. He started up, backside up. After he had climbed some distance, he asked, "How far away am I?" "You're still way down," Cougar said in a tiny voice, to deceive him. Then Cougar dropped five rocks, one after the other into Skunk's anus. His anus rolled out like a hoop, fell into the spring and rolled away. Skunk fainted as soon as he lost his poison. They took him home, and scalded the house and burned leaves to take away the smell that he had left there.

Skunk was harmless without his anus and so he went away to find it; he could trace it by its smell. "Did you see my property?" he asked at a certain place. "Yes, we saw a shiny thing rolling down the middle of the river, pretty boy," they said to him. He went to another village and asked, "Did you see my property?" "Yes, we saw your anus rolling down, dirty thing," they said to him. At five towns, they told him that they had seen something shining rolling down, and at five towns, they told him they had seen his anus rolling down. At the last of these towns they told him that his property had lodged in a fish trap and that the people there were playing with it. Skunk was happy to hear this and before long arrived at the trap. He crossed over on it, as he had been told to do, and soon heard the people shouting as they played. The hoop was shiny and pearly. The people would play with it during the daytime and take it home at night. They were rolling it down a road two feet wide. Skunk made a hole in the road and buried himself there, backside up. Next morning, the people came back again to play with the hoop. At first, the hoop did not go to the place where it belonged. They rolled it past Skunk four times. The fifth time, he stuck his backside up a little higher than before and the hoop rolled right in. They tried to catch him but he shot his musk at them and killed them. Then he stole all their beads and packed them along. He crossed the river and stopped at a chief's house. "Where is your property?" the people asked. "All good chiefs and people, come in and I will tell you how I saved my property," he said. "We must go in or he will kill us," the people said. They gave him something to eat and then he said, "I stole some pretty things and I am going to give you some of them for helping me." He gave them presents and went on. At another place he stopped at a chief's house. The people knew that he had lost his anus and came to make fun of him. As soon as they were inside, he shot his musk at them and killed them. He also shot his musk over everything outside so that all the people would die. He went to all the different places where he had stopped to inquire about his lost property, and settled with the people according to whether they had told him something complimentary or something insulting. At last he came to the spring and saw his brother coming. "Here comes Cougar. I'll fix Mr. Cougar all right!" he said to himself. Cougar came smiling, thinking that Skunk was still harmless. Skunk turned around and shot him with his musk. Cougar died and Skunk split his hide down through the middle of the back, from nose to tail. He put the hide on, the tail dragging far behind him. "I have beads now with which to buy me a woman," he sang. (As a matter of fact, what he would really do, was to pay some woman to sleep with him.)

Fox was fishing and heard Skunk coming. "What shall I do to escape him ?" he thought. He fell to the ground, turning himself into a piece of wormy meat. "This is a good piece of meat even if it is full of worms," Skunk said. "I'll take it along and roast it in camp to-night. That will kill the worms." He put the piece of meat in his pack and went on. Soon Fox began to cry. Then Skunk sang,

> I can kill all the dangerous things that live,
> I fear nothing but Hwɪ'sələs[1] (the Wolves);
> From the mouth of the Cowlitz to its source,
> I fear nothing but them; I have a chief's tail.

Fox, in the pack on Skunk's back, began to whistle a little. "It sounds like Hwɪ'sələs," Skunk said. Fox whistled five times. Then Skunk said, "It is Hwɪ'sələs! Oh, this pack bothers me too much." He began to run. Fox kept saying, "Hw · · · ·, hw · · · ·."[2] Finally Skunk threw the pack down and ran faster. "Oh, dirty Skunk, he carried me too far," Fox said. He untied the pack and found it full of beads. He stole the beads and went away.

Five Wolves were coming. "Here comes Skunk," they said. Skunk was coming proudly, shaking his tail. "Oh, he's coming proudly; he has a chief's tail," they said. "Oh, the dirty thing; he must have killed Cougar!" Then Skunk stopped in a sunny place to shake his tail. He pranced about, turning to admire his lovely tail as he dragged it along on the ground.[3] In the meantime, the Wolves ambushed him; two crept up behind him and three in front of him. Skunk was now very frightened. "Where did you get your tail ?" the Wolves asked. "Don't you know that it's my tail ?" he said. He was too frightened to shoot his musk. "Where did you get it ?" the Wolves asked. Then the youngest Wolf said, "Don't make the dirty thing talk!" At this, one grabbed him by one leg, one grabbed him by another, and one grabbed him by the nose. They tore the chief's skin off him and beat him up, whereupon he turned into a small skunk. "You will never kill anyone again. When you shoot your musk, there will be a bad smell, but it will not kill people. You will stay in the woods and never go near people except in the winter

---

[1] This is not the ordinary Cowlitz term for Wolf; it is probably onomatopoeic.

[2] Actual whistle.

[3] The narrator stood up and imitated Skunk's actions.

time; when the snow comes, you will steal something to eat from them," they said.

They then went to chief Cougar's house and saw something lying near the spring. "It looks like the chief himself," they said. "Yes," the woman in the house said, "it is Cougar!" They took the hide and put it back on him. Then they walked over him and prayed and he got up. But he fell back immediately. They poured water on his head and revived him again. "What were you doing here?" they asked. "I was asleep," he said. "Where's Skunk?" they asked. "Oh, he skinned me and then went away," he answered. "What did you do to him?" they asked. "I burnt his anus," he answered. Then the Wolves said, "Nothing like this will ever happen again."

The woman had remained in the house and did not know until the Wolves came that her husband had been killed. She cooked dinner for them and Cougar shared his arrows with them. The Wolves were proud to own such fine arrows; they would kill deer with them. They said, "From now on Skunk shall be merely an animal; his musk will smell a little but will not kill anyone." Cougar now had nothing to fear from Skunk; Skunk was dead.

COUGAR AND HIS YOUNGER BROTHERS.[1]

Cougar was a chief. He had a number of wives, each of whom lived in a different place. One day he started out to see one of them. He went up the Cowlitz and then turned east into the wooded hills that follow the river. One of his younger brothers had asked to accompany him but he had refused. The boy, on his own accord, set out ahead of him. After travelling a whole day, Cougar met his little brother on the trail. They camped together that night far up in the hills. Cougar saw a large elk and killed it. He told his brother to run to the cedar brush and get some bark for a cooking basket. The boy found some bark but did not think it good enough and so ran on a little farther to get some more. Again he did not like the bark that he found and ran on farther. Suddenly he ran right into a large man who had a fire burning. "Oh, grandson, what are you doing here?" the man asked. "My brother killed a big elk. Won't you come and have supper with us?" the boy said. "Yes, indeed," the man answered. The boy ran on, found the bark for his basket, and then went back to camp. "I found grandpa and he is going to eat supper with us," he said to his elder brother. "Oh, you bad boy, you've found a dangerous being. He'll eat us tonight," Cougar said. Then Cougar ran out, got some bark and made five cooking baskets. He heated some rocks and cooked five baskets full of meat. Before he had started to cook the sliced meat, he had said to his brother, "Eat quickly before the old man comes." In a little while they heard him coming. The old man grabbed one of the baskets of meat and

[1] Told by Sophie Smith, 1926; see p. 401.

swallowed it, rocks and all. He swallowed all five baskets. After eating all the cooked meat, he ate all the raw meat and anything on which the blood had fallen, like bushes and leaves. Then he spied the head and horns, and folding them into a bundle, swallowed them whole. The little boy looked on, his eyes wide with amazement. The horns of the elk had merely scratched the dangerous being's throat as they went down. Cougar made a fire to keep them warm during the night. Then he laid some large rocks down for pillows and said to the old man, "You must be tired, grandpa, lie down." Aside to his little brother, he said, "Run on ahead. There are five steep hills here. Climb one after the other without stopping. He's going to chase us." All the time, Cougar was busy gathering food and piling up rocks. The old man lay down and muttered over and over again, "ϒm, ʋm, ʋm, you're my breakfast, grandchildren." When the little boy heard this, he was so frightened that he took to his heels. As soon as the old man closed his eyes, Cougar felt him all over with his hands to mesmerize him. During the night, when the old man was fast asleep with his head resting against the rock pillow, Cougar took one of the sharp rocks that he had heated and struck him across the neck with it. Then he ran after his little brother. The old man's body remained where it was, but the head ran after Cougar. "Br · · · ·," it went, like a wind storm, breaking the trees along the way. It went this way, that way, following Cougar until it at last lost him; it went downhill and Cougar went uphill.

Cougar was tired out when he caught up with his little brother, whose name was Wildcat.[1] They travelled all day without eating and when night came, they went to bed without eating. Early next morning, they made a large fire. "Gather some wood to keep the fire going. Don't let it go out. I'll go out and hunt deer," Cougar said. While his brother was gone, the boy played, forgetting to keep the fire up. It was some time before he thought of it. "Oh, the fire is out! Brother will be angry because he told me not to let it go out. What shall I do?" he said. He noticed some smoke across the river. "Oh, that's where I'll find some fire," he said. He jumped into the water and swam across. On the other side he found an old woman who was lying down. She had five logs braided like hair. In the center of the braid, a fire was burning. "I'll try to steal a piece," he said. He waited and when one piece had burned down nearly to the end, he grabbed it and ran. When he started to swim across the river, he put the piece of burning wood on his nose. As he swam, he kept moving it back. By the time he landed, he had it on his tail. He has a short tail now, because the fire burnt a good deal of it off. He started a fire and gathered wood to keep it going. By this time, Cougar had returned. "Hʋm, hʋm," he said, sniffing. "What have you done, bad boy? You've stolen some fire from a dangerous being." "Elder brother, I forgot to watch the fire and it

[1] The boy's name is not revealed until this point.

went out. I swam across the river and took some from an old lady," the boy said. Cougar threw the fire logs into the water and started a fresh fire. "Gather a lot of wood," he said to the boy. The boy gathered the wood and then Cougar sharpened a little axe. "When the dangerous being comes, hit him on the back of the ankle with this sharp axe," he said. Before long, they saw the old woman running into the water, crying, "Who steals my fire, who steals my fire?" The water soon came up to her knees and her skirt got wet. "Oh my skirt is getting wet, oh my skirt is getting wet," she kept saying. Then a man appeared, carrying a whole deer. He dropped the deer and undressed on the run. "Who steals my mother's fire?" he said. He jumped into the water and started to swim across. Cougar was ready for him. The two men fought and the boy finally managed to strike the dangerous being on the ankle with his axe. Then Cougar killed the man and threw him into the fire. He gathered more firewood and piled it on top of the dead man. Then he sharpened his axe. "Don't get excited," he said to the boy, "another dangerous being will come and we'll have to kill him too." Before long, they saw another man on the opposite side of the river carrying a whole bear. When he saw what had happened, the man threw the bear down and cried, "Who steals my mother's fire?" He undressed on the run, jumped into the water and swam across. He and Cougar fought. This man was stronger than the first, but with his brother's help, Cougar finally managed to kill him and burn him. Before gathering more wood, Cougar sharpened his axe again. In a little while they saw another man on the opposite side of the river, carrying a heavy pack.[1] He threw his pack down, undressed on the run and jumped into the water, crying, "Who steals my mother's fire?" He swam across and he and Cougar fought. Cougar killed him finally and burned him. Then he sharpened his axe and gathered more wood. Soon they saw another man who was carrying a heavy pack.[2] He threw his pack down and cried, "Who steals my mother's fire?" He undressed on the run, jumped into the water and swam across. He and Cougar fought. This man was stronger than the others and so Cougar was tired out by the time he got him killed. The boy, too, was tired from swinging his axe. In just a little while they saw another man carrying a live, naked person on his back. He threw his pack down and cried, "Who steals my mother's fire? You can't kill me!" This man was more dangerous than any of the others. He and Cougar fought and fought. He was as hard as iron and Cougar could not kill him. Before the man had reached their side of the river, Cougar had said to the boy, "This fellow may kill me. If we should fight in the air, burn any black meat that falls. Save the white meat, for that will be mine. If you save my bones, perhaps you can put me together again." The two men fought above the

[1] The narrator did not know what animal this man was carrying.
[2] See footnote above.

ground and so the boy could not strike his brother's enemy with his hatchet. He began to weep and kept crying, "Where shall I hit him, brother?" Still weeping, he made a fire and ran back and forth gathering wood. A piece of black meat fell and he threw it into the fire. After a while a piece of white meat fell and he saved it. Pieces of meat kept falling and he saved all the white and burned all the black. Then the internal organs began to fall, first a black piece and then a white piece. They fell so fast he could scarcely tell which was black and which was white. Finally, a mass of tangled bones fell. The two men had been biting one another so hard that the bones were all knotted together. It took him some time to separate the black from the white. He threw the black ones into the fire. Then he put the white flesh back on the white bones and put in the internal organs. After he had everything fixed up properly, he stepped over the body five times and prayed. Cougar then came to life but he could not get up; he was terribly sick. His brother would get him up a little way and then he would fall back. Finally, he spoke. "You've changed my liver. You put a black liver in me. That's the trouble. If people ever kill me to eat, they won't be able to eat my liver, for I have a dangerous being's liver," he said. After a while, he recovered and they went on.

Cougar killed a deer and they ate. Then Cougar said to his brother, "You'll have to go back for if you stay with me, you'll get me killed." The boy did not want to go but Cougar said, "If I kill anything, I'll cover it up and leave it for you. When you find my tracks, you will know that I have left some deer meat or something of the sort for you." "All right," the boy finally said. Cougar gave him a bow and arrow. This made the boy happy and so he turned back at last. Cougar went off by himself, killed a deer and hid it for his brother. Then from a distance, he saw his little brother making a fire. The boy, his hair tied very high, was roasting a rabbit; he thought that he had killed a deer. He had tied his hair like his brother's and was singing as his brother used to sing. When he saw Cougar coming, he cried out, threw his hair over his face and wept for shame. "Never mind, just go ahead. I came to tell you that I have killed a deer for you," Cougar said. The boy was glad to hear this.

Cougar met another of his younger brothers, Mink. "Where are you going? I want to go with you," the boy said. "I'm going to the buffalo country to see my new wife. You can't go with me for you'll get me into trouble," Cougar answered. "Oh, I'll be the best brother you ever had. I'll obey everything you say," the boy said. And so Cougar agreed to take him along. When it came time to make camp, Cougar killed some pheasants and they took them along to cook for supper. "Where are we going to camp, brother?" the boy asked. "I can't tell you; if I should name the place, it would cause a bad storm," Cougar answered. "But you could say it so that I could guess the real name," the boy said. Finally Cougar gave in and said, "De creek is de Tif." "Oh, the little creek is the Ta'ɪx·," the boy said. In just a little while, he repeated it. "That's enough," Cougar said. Then the boy fell down and said again, "We're going to camp on the Ta'ɪx·." He kept repeating it and every time Cougar warned him that he might bring on a storm. This creek was the only one in the mountains, the only place where they could get water. They stopped after a while and cooked the pheasants. "This is the Ta'ɪx·," the boy said. When they had finished eating, Cougar built a shelter in case there was snow or wind during the night. He gathered some cedar bark and sticks and tied them up to make a little shack just large enough for the two of them to lie down in. Then he built a little fire; he would lie on one side of it, his brother on the other. "This is the Ta'ɪx·," the boy said three times. "Come here and lie down with me. This is a good place," Cougar said. He had tied a buckskin hide around the boy to protect him. Cougar soon fell fast asleep. During the night, a strong wind came and it began to hail. The noise woke the boy up. "Oh, it's hailing," he said. The wind blew the little shelter away and the fire went out. Snow began to fall and the ground became soaked with water. Cougar slept through it all, but the boy shivered and cried. "Brother, I'm dying," he said at last. Cougar got up and put another buckskin cover over him. The storm had ceased by morning but there was hail and snow on the ground. Cougar made a fire and they had breakfast.

They left the hills and travelled toward dry country. "Where are we going to stay to-night?" the boy asked. "With my two wives," Cougar said. "Oh, have I a sister-in-law?" the boy asked. "Yes," Cougar answered. They reached Warm Springs before sunset and stopped there. "What am I going to eat? I'm hungry," the boy said. "Go to the springs and sit down there. Cover your eyes tightly with your hands and say, 'Sisters-in-law, I'm Cougar's brother, I'm hungry,'" Cougar said. The boy went to the springs and sat down. He covered his eyes with his hands, but not so tightly that he could not see a bit; he wanted to see what was going on. He said what Cougar had told him to say, but the springs merely gurgled, "Bələlu, bələlu." "Why, the springs are merely boiling. They aren't my sisters-in-law. I'm starving," he said. He ran back to Cougar and told him that the springs merely boiled instead of giving him something to eat. "Close your eyes tightly just for a minute; then they'll give you something," Cougar said. He went back, but deceived them once more before closing his eyes tightly. When he opened his eyes, he found a large dish of food that Yakima peoples eat, — dried roots and fish. "Iiiii, good sisters-in-law," he said. He grabbed the dish and started to eat. He ran back to Cougar and said, "Here, brother. You take one dish and I'll take one dish." "Oh, you eat it. I'll eat after a while," Cougar said. Later on Cougar ate and then they both went to sleep. In the morning, the boy got his breakfast in the same way, but first deceived the women. He did not get anything to eat until he had shut his eyes tightly. When he had finished eating he took the dish back. "Here's your dish," he said. But the springs would not take it. "Oh, funny sisters-in-law, you're just a well," he said. He closed his eyes and when he opened them, the dish was gone.

After breakfast, they travelled east to the buffalo country. They were many days on the way. The night they arrived at their destination, the boy was put to bed at one end of the house, in the corner. Cougar and his wife slept on one side of the house, the woman's father on the opposite side. The boy could not sleep. He had been given a blanket made of small beaver hides and it had been pulled up over his face. Two holes, where the eyes had been, were left in the blanket. He fitted the holes over his eyes and through these could plainly see what was going on, for the fire was still burning. During the night, he saw the old man get up and pull out a long, sharp knife. "What's he going to do?" he thought. He did not know that his brother's father-in-law was a dangerous being. The old man did not know that the boy could see what was going on. He was angry with Cougar and was going to kill him. When the boy saw what the old man meant to do, he cried out, "Hey, what's the matter? Are you going to kill your son-in-law?" The old man quickly jumped back into bed. "Hey, hey, you have nightmare, boy. You'll wake your brother," he said. The boy did not answer, but still continued to peep through the holes in his blanket. The old man pretended that he had fallen fast asleep but five times during the night he got up and did the same thing. Each time the little fellow cried out. He was very much frightened and did not sleep the whole night.

After an early breakfast, the women went out to dig roots. "Your brother-in-law is going to hunt buffalo to-day and you are to accompany him," the old man said to Cougar. "All right," Cougar answered. The old man then loaned him a cap, jacket and a bow and arrow. "Don't take your own things," he said. Nevertheless, Cougar wore his own cap and jacket under those that the old man had given him and took his own bow and arrow. The old man had five sons and all of them went out together to hunt.

After the young men had gone, the old man said to the boy, "You and I are going out to get wood." They got into a canoe and went across the river. They were going to get some bark from a dead tree. (They always cut the bark around the tree to make it fall.) The old man made the boy sit down on the spot where the bark would fall. Then he poked and poked at the bark. The entire piece finally fell with a flop, right on the boy. The old man then jumped on it and cried, "The little fool! If it weren't for him, I would have killed the man last night." He was busy splitting one end of the bark, when the boy suddenly appeared from the water and said,

"I've already put most of the bark in the canoe." "Oh, the nasty thing. How does it happen that he's still alive?" the man said to himself. They filled the canoe completely with bark. "There's no place for you to sit, but I guess you can squeeze into my tool-basket; it's big enough to hold you," the man said. The boy got into the tool-kit and the old man tied it tightly. He set it down in the bow of the canoe, and took a seat just back of it. He started to paddle and after a while, began to rock the canoe. "Oh, oh, sonny, it's blowing now," he said. "Oh, oh, the waves are coming," he said a little later. The little boy thought, "He's going to throw me into the water." While the old man was occupied in shaking the canoe, he began quietly to untie the basket. He already had the basket untied when the old man threw him in. He crawled out of it in the water, and then holding it in his hand, swam under water and reached shore before the old man landed. A number of old women were on the shore. "Oh, grandpa and I nearly drowned, but I saved his tool-basket for him," he said to them. The old man landed, smiling to himself. "Oh, grandpa, I saved your basket," the boy cried. "The nasty little thing! How did he get out?" the man said to himself.

They carried the wood in and the man said, "I want you to do something for me, sonny. Will you do it?" "Yes, I'll do whatever you ask," the boy answered. "I have two pets on a beach. The beach goes out to a sharp point in the center. You will find two nice pups there playing. I want you to get them for me," the man said. The boy ran out to get the pups.

In the meantime, Cougar was going along with the hunters. Shortly after he left the house, he stepped on old lady Meadow Lark's leg and broke it. "A nən, nən, nə," she cried, "you broke my leg. Not that I should want to shorten your life!" "Oh, aunty, I'll fix your leg if you tell me all the stories you know about me," he said. He fixed her leg with long shell beads and she said, "You see, you bought the girls some time ago but you did not come for them right away. This made the old man angry. He is a widower and could have got other husbands for the girls. 'When he comes, I'm going to kill him,' he said. Don't wear the cap and shirt that he gave you and don't use his bow and arrow. Use your own things. When it is time to shoot the buffalo, hang his shirt and cap on a bush, to make them think that it is you. You stand aside. Your wife wants to kill you. The old man's bow and arrow are no good; they're made of weeds. Use your own." Cougar did just as she said. When he heard the men shouting as they drove the buffalo toward him, he hung the cap and jacket on a bush and stuck the bow and arrow on a stick. Then he stepped aside, ready with his own bow and arrow. The buffalo came straight up to the dummy and Cougar killed her. Then he started to butcher her. "ʏh, ʋh, sister has been killed," the men shouted to one another. Cougar was ready to skin the cow. He told the men to hurry up. "Come quickly, hold her for me," he said. He made a pack of the meat and they started home. He had saved the udder to give to his father-in-law. The old man cut the udder up and roasted it on a stick. He started to eat it and cried, "Sk'e, sk'e." To hide his confusion, he pretended that the smoke had brought tears to his eyes; he had realized that he was eating his daughter's flesh.

In the meantime, the little boy had reached the point and had caught the pups, who were two, large dangerous beings, Lightnings. As it happened, his tamanoas was lightning and fire. He called upon his tamanoas, and each of the Lightnings became as small as his fist. He concealed them in his clothing and ran home. While the old man was eating, he threw them into the house and said, "Here they are!" As soon as he threw them in, the Lightnings assumed normal size. Cougar and he jumped out quickly and started for home. The Lightnings tore the house to pieces and killed everyone there,—the old man and all his children.

COUGAR AND MINK.[1]

Mink (mα′stc'əm) and Cougar (swa′wa) were brothers. Cougar set out for his father-in-law's place and took Mink with him. They arrived at the house. Cougar's wife was not there. Cougar had not visited her for nearly three years as he had several other wives living in different places. Because of this, his wife's family was angry and jealous, and to keep him from returning to his other wives, planned to kill him. His father-in-law, old man Thunder, said to him, "Oh, my dear son, go and get me some nice fresh meat tomorrow morning." The woman returned late in the evening; she had been out digging roots to eat. "Oh, my dear daughter," her father said, "your husband has come to visit you. I told him to go hunting tomorrow morning and bring me some nice fresh meat." "All right, father, make him hunt tomorrow morning," the woman said.

They made a little bed for Mink and gave him a mountain-beaver skin for a blanket. There were two tiny holes in the skin where the beaver's eyes had been. Mink covered himself with the skin, fitting the holes right over his eyes, and lay awake. His brother went to sleep and snored loudly. During the night, while Cougar was sleeping soundly, old man Thunder got a big knife and crept toward Cougar, intending to knife him. "Brother, brother," Mink screamed, "your father-in-law is going to kill you with a knife!" Thunder jumped and said, "What are you waking your brother for? Let him sleep!"

Early next morning, the woman went out to dig roots. Cougar got up and ate his breakfast. After breakfast, his father-in-law gave him a bow and arrow and a quiver. Then he started out to hunt.

[1] Told by Mary Iley, 1927; see p. 401.

Before he had gone far, his father-in-law called after him, "Leave your own bow and arrow here." He did not turn back. "No," he said, "I'm taking my own bow and arrow too." On his way he stepped on Lark's (qʋtsx̣a') leg and broke it. "M · · · ·[1]," she said, "your father-in-law is hungry for you." "Oh, aunty, let me fix your leg," he said. He fixed her leg with beads. Then she told him what he should do. He went on.

His father-in-law had told him to go to some trees where Grizzlybear stayed. He went to the place, found a rotten stick and made a dummy out of it. He dressed it in his own clothes and had it holding the bow and arrow and quiver that his father-in-law had given him. Then naked, he hid in the bushes with his own bow and arrow. Soon Grizzlybear, his own wife, came. "It isn't he," she said, looking at the dummy from a distance. "It looks like father's bow though," she said, on second glance. "No, it isn't he," she decided. She changed her mind five times. Finally, she decided that from a distance at least, the figure did look something like her husband, and so she jumped at it. Just as she jumped, Cougar shot her right in the side. Lark had told him that his wife was Grizzly and that she meant to kill him. He shot at her until all his arrows were gone. Finally she fell over. Then he pulled all his arrows out of her and put them back in his quiver. He asked the many little slaves, whom Thunder had sent along with him, to help pack the meat. The slaves were called Ipɛ''sa. Thunder had said, "Take your little brothers-in-law along with you; they will help you chase the Grizzly." The little slaves cried when Cougar cut the body up and cried when he gave each of them a little pack to carry, — but they packed it nevertheless. He carried the udder himself. Thunder had said, "If you kill any game, I'll eat the udder the first thing." He had not known then that he would eat his own daughter's udder. When Cougar got to the house, he cut the udder up — it always cooks quickly — and roasted it on a stick. He gave a piece of it to his father-in-law. Then Thunder began to cry, and said [to cover his confusion], "Shut the door; the smoke is blowing in my eyes."

Thunder said to Mink, "Go get my plaything over there on a big rock." Mink went to the rock. White Agate and Blue Rock were fighting one another. Agate was jumping about like dust but Blue Rock was hard. "Stop that, keep still," Mink said. He grabbed them and put them in his blouse. "Thunder will feel better if I bring him these playthings," he said. He took them to the house and threw them both inside. When he had picked the rocks up, they had become small, but now they became very large. They fought one another and tore the house to pieces. The Ipɛ''sa then turned into little birds and flew away. Thunder turned into a bird and flew up into a cloud. From there he shot his arrows into the rocks and trees.

---

[1] Said with closed lips.

Cougar and Mink went away. At last they came to a nice creek leading from a lake. "I guess we had better part here," Cougar said. "You will always stay here on the creek and on the lake." "All right," Mink said, "I shall always stay here on the creek." Then he turned into a mink and his brother into a cougar.

X̣wα'ni said, "Hereafter a mink will always mate with a mink, and a cougar with a cougar. They shall always mate with their own kind." He also said, "Thunder, you shall always live in a cloud." (I guess Thunder was a very mean person when he was a human being.)

BEAR AND GRIZZLY.[1]

A young man had two wives, Grizzly and Bear. Bear had five young daughters and Grizzly had five young sons. Bear would pick berries and bring back a large basket and a little basket full. She always gave the little basket of berries to her husband to eat. Grizzly would do the same, but the man seldom found any berries in the basket that she gave him, — just a berry here and there among sticks and leaves. Grizzly was a rough picker; she grabbed vines and all. She became jealous of Bear because she was always good to their husband; she gave him nice roots to eat. When Grizzly dug roots, she brought up the whole plant, tops and all. Bear always brought home nice, clean roots. "I'd better kill Bear," Grizzly said to herself one day. Bear usually stayed close to camp when she worked, but Grizzly stayed off in the mountains. One day when they were out together, Grizzly said, "Oh, sister, come look for lice on my head; they're biting me." She laid her head in Bear's lap. Bear looked but could not find any lice. Then Grizzly said, "Let me look for yours." She snapped one finger nail against another[2] to make Bear think that she was crushing the lice, and pulled her hair and twisted her head. "She'll be easy to kill," she thought.

The little Bears sometimes killed small deer, elk, and beavers to roast for their aunty Grizzly.

Bear looked for Grizzly's head lice four days in succession but each time found nothing. In turn, Grizzly looked for Bear's head lice and pretended that she had found some. The fifth day Bear said to her husband, "I think she's going to kill me to-day. She always twists my head so hard. You'll soon learn the kind of berries she'll bring you!" Once more, Grizzly asked Bear to look for her head lice. Bear looked and said, "You haven't any, sister." Then Grizzly said that she would look for Bear's. She grabbed her by the hair and twisted her head around until she killed her. She emptied Bear's berries into her own basket and took them home to her husband.

[1] Told by Mary Iley, 1926; see p. 407.
[2] Illustrating.

"Evidently these are Bear's berries; she must have killed her," the man thought. "Wonder where sister is? She's been gone a long time. It's getting late," Grizzly kept saying. "Where's your mother? It's quite dark," she said to the children.

Bear had not returned by morning and so the man decided to leave. "You'd better leave or something will happen. Grizzly will kill you. I'm leaving because she killed your mother," he said to the Bear children. Grizzly had gone out early. The little Bears said, "Let's wrestle with the Grizzlybears. We can kill them." They had rocks heating in five different places, planning to cook something as usual for Grizzly. They jumped on the Grizzlies and killed them. The youngest Bear jumped on the youngest Grizzly, the second Bear on the second Grizzly, and so on. They roasted a dead boy in each one of the five pits. The youngest Grizzly had two fingers of his right hand bent under. The Bear girls owned a big dog. "If Grizzly asks you where we went," they said to the dog, "you mustn't tell her. Point in the opposite direction." They took all their mother's beads and dried lacamas and left.

Grizzly came home late in the evening, tired and hungry. She stopped at the first fire-place and ate, then at the second. She was quite pleased with what she found. "The girls killed something very nice to eat to-day," she said. When she got to the fifth, she thought, "What could they have killed that tastes so good?" Then she recognized her youngest son by his two bent fingers. "Oh, those girls! They've killed their brothers!" she cried. She dropped the piece of meat that she had started to eat and looked around to see where the girls had gone. She beat the dog and cried, "Where are your owners?" The dog pointed in a certain direction and she ran there. She ran and ran but could not find any tracks. Then she came back and beat the dog again. The dog pointed in another direction. She ran there, but still could not find any tracks. She beat the dog four different times and then he showed her the right direction. On the way, the girls had left some lacamas so that Grizzly would stop to eat. At a second place, they left some greens, at a third, some early berries, at a fourth, some later berries, and at a fifth, still later berries. Grizzly stopped at each one of these places. She dug up the plant stuff and ate it, and picked and ate the berries. At last, she remembered that she was looking for the girls. She shouted to her father who lived in the mountains, "Oh, father, the Bear girls have killed all your grandchildren. Kill them when they come." She knew that she was too far behind to catch up with the girls.

The eldest of the girls saw a house and said, "Let's stop here and cook some lacamas." Then Hot Rock, Grizzly's father, killed four of the girls and roasted them on hot rocks. The fifth one escaped. She went far away, packing her heavy bundle. Hot Rock finally found her and took her home with him. The girl stayed with him as his wife.

A man finally came and took the girl away. Before he got to Hot Rock's home, the man stumbled on Lark's leg and broke it. He fixed her leg and she said, "Stay here and dig a well. When the five Hot Rock brothers come to the well to drink, shove them in with a stick and drown them." The man dug a well and made it very deep except in one spot. The girl's husband came along and leaned over to take a drink, as he was very thirsty. Then the man shoved him over into the deep part with his long stick and drowned him. Another brother came along and the man did the same to him. He did the same to the third. The fourth one came along and also stopped when he saw the well, as he was terribly thirsty. Then the man pushed him in also and drowned him. The fifth one came but was a little afraid to drink; the well looked rather strange and was almost dry by this time. As he leaned over, hesitating to drink, the man pushed him and drowned him. The man then went to the house and found the woman. The house was filled with dried salmon. He took the woman away with him.

MOSQUITO.[1]

Mosquito started down the Columbia at the mouth of the Cowlitz in his big canoe. When still some distance from Portland, he passed some people along the way. "Oh, Mosquito," they called to him, "come and eat with us." "What kind of stew have you, what kind of stew have you?" he asked. "Duck stew," they answered. There was only one kind of stew he wanted, so he refused to eat with them. "It burns me, it burns me," he cried.

He paddled on down the river. When still this side of Portland, he passed some other people. "Oh, Mosquito," they called, "come and eat with us." "What kind of stew have you?" he asked. "Wild goose stew," they answered. "No, no! It burns me, burns me, burns me," he cried. He got burnt although he had not so much as seen the stew. He paddled away fast, as he always did when anyone called to him.

At another place they called to him, "Come and eat with us, Mosquito." "What kind of stew have you?" he asked. "Rabbit stew," they said. "No, no!" he cried, "it burns me, burns me, burns me." He had started to paddle fast as soon as they had called to him.

He was tired now. Someone else called to him, "Come and eat with us, Mosquito." "What kind of stew have you?" "Deer-broth stew," they said. He did not stop.

The people at the next place knew who Mosquito was. They were strong men; there were five of them. Each stuck a knife into his arm and leg and let the blood run out into a pot large enough to hold Mosquito. Mosquito ate people and they were going to kill him. They called to him, "Come and eat with us." "What kind of stew

[1] Told by Mary Iley, 1926; see p. 411.

have you?" he asked. "The blood of people," they answered. "That's just what I want," he said. He sucked the blood from the pot again and again. After he had drunk nearly half of it he was just about to burst. He was a dangerous being and they were going to kill him. They gathered around him, stuck him in the stomach and killed him. Then they declared, "You shall no longer be a dangerous being. You will never again kill anyone. If you so desire, you may suck people just a little." Mosquito used to stick his sticker into a person's neck and kill him.[1] He was a dangerous being a long time ago.

THE DANGEROUS BEAVER.

(First Version).[2]

There were five brothers. Beaver was living near the river. Whenever anyone came to his house, he would kill and eat them. The eldest of the five men went out walking. A pheasant flew up and he killed it and tied it to something along the trail. He would get it on the way back, so he thought. He went down to the river and saw a lot of sticks stripped of their bark and bearing the imprint of teeth. "There must be a lot of beaver here," he thought. He went on down the river, following a little trail, and after some time, came to a little house. An old man was singing,

> I just ate up all the king's-people;
> All the pretty boys and the pretty, pretty, pretty girls,
> I eat them up.

"What are you saying, grandpa?" the young man asked in an angry voice. "Oh, son," the old man said, speaking weakly, "there are a lot of beaver here. You must kill one for me. I can't do it. Stay here in a shallow place and I'll go up and chase them down." The old man was Beaver. He gave his visitor a slice of beaver meat; it was so good that the young man agreed to help him. The old man had cut the meat from his own leg. He gave him a spear and said, "You stay here." He went up the river a little way and threw a beaver blanket into the water. "T'ʊp, t'ʊp," it sounded as it struck the water. "Here comes a beaver," the young man said and got ready to spear it. When the spear struck the hide, it buckled as if made of stiffened paper. Then old Beaver jumped on his neck and killed and ate him.

The second brother visited Beaver and the same thing happened. Then the third and the fourth visited him and the same thing happened. Each time, Beaver would say, "If you kill a beaver for me, there are lots of pretty girls over there that I will show you. They

[1] As a weasel kills a chicken.
[2] Told by Mary Iley, 1926; see p. 391.

throw at me, throw at me."[1] Then he would give his visitor a piece of his own meat, after which the visitor would say, "Show me the girls, grandpa."

The fifth brother thought, "Where have my brothers gone?" He went out to look for them and on the way stepped on Meadow Lark's leg. "Oh, poor me, you have broken my leg," she said. "Oh, aunty, I'll fix your leg with beads," he said. He fixed her leg and she said, "A little farther on, you will see a pheasant fly up. Don't kill it for it is your spirit. Then you will come to a beaver dam where you will hear an old man singing,

> All the king's-people, I'm dressing them to eat,
> The pretty, pretty boys and the pretty, pretty girls.

Then you will ask him what he is doing and he will tell you that he wants you to help him kill some beaver. He will say, 'You stay here and I'll go up above to drive them down.' Then he will offer you a piece of beaver meat. You must say, 'No, no, no! You eat first.' Then you will say, 'Tell me, where is your spear point and pole?' He will give you his spear. Take it, but do not use it. Hide your own spear point under your foot and cut a stick for a pole. When you hear him coming, grab your own spear and kill him."

Beaver asked the young man to help him kill some beaver. "You stay here and I'll go up a little way to drive them down so that you can kill them," he said. He was frightened now for his visitor would not accept the meat that he offered. He gave him a spear made of cat-tails. Then he went up stream a little way and hid there. He put on his blanket and jumped, striking the water with a "L'əp, L'əp". Four times he came a little way out of the water. The fifth time, he came clear out. Then the young man struck him with his spear and tore him to pieces. The pieces became small beaver. "There shall never again be a beaver that eats people. Only you will have done that," the young man said. He looked for his brothers' bones and when he found them, walked back and forth over them until they came to life. The five men then went home.

THE DANGEROUS BEAVER.

(Second Version).[2]

Beaver was living close to the creek; he had a house there. A man came along and Beaver said to him, "Swa'q'ex̣tcιn[3] always go up this creek. You can watch for one and spear it; they are good to eat. I can show you where to find one." He cut off a cat-tail stalk and put a spear on it. He gave the spear to the man and said, "One will

---

[1] The old man is evidently claiming that the girls throw at him to attract his attention.

[2] Told by James Cheholts, 1927.

[3] An unidentified game-animal.

come along pretty soon. You can kill it and I will eat it." The man went up the creek. Then Beaver dived into the creek and came up alongside him. The man struck at him with the spear, thinking he was a swa'q'ex̣tcɪn. The spear crumpled. Beaver then jumped on the man and killed and ate him.

Another man came by. Beaver said to him, "A swa'q'ex̣tcɪn always goes up this creek. Help me catch him. I will give you a spear." He cut a cat-tail stalk and put a spear on it. He gave the spear to the man and the man went up the creek. Beaver then dived into the water and came up alongside him. The man tried to spear him but the spear crumpled. Beaver quickly jumped on him, caught him and ate him.

Another man came by. "A swa'q'ex̣tcɪn always goes up the creek. Help me spear him," Beaver said. He cut a cat-tail stalk and put a spear on it. He gave the spear to the man and the man went up the creek. Then Beaver dived into the water and came up alongside him. The man tried to spear him but the spear crumpled. Beaver jumped on him and killed him. He took him into the house and ate him.

Beaver always stayed there. Another man came by. "Help me catch a swa'q'ex̣tcɪn. One always stays here on the creek," he said. He gave the man the same kind of spear that he had given the others. The man went up the creek. Then Beaver jumped into the water and came up alongside him. The man tried to spear him but the spear crumpled. Beaver jumped on him and killed him. He took him home and cooked him.

A fifth man came by. "Can you help me? A swa'q'ex̣tcɪn always goes up this creek. I would like you to help me spear him," Beaver said. He gave the man the same kind of spear. Then he took him up the creek and showed him where the swa'q'ex̣tcɪn always stayed. "I'll go home and stay there. When you kill it, bring it to me," he said. Now the fifth man knew who Beaver was. He quickly made a real spear. When Beaver came up in the water alongside him, he speared him and killed him.

That was Beaver.

THE BOY AND THE DANGEROUS WOMAN.[1]

The people of Astoria used to send their boys and girls, when about fourteen years of age, over to this side [of the Columbia] to the Rocks to get tamanoas. There was a boy there about eighteen years old who went to the Rocks to get tamanoas, — to become a doctor, a good man, or something of the sort. This boy had been after girls already.[2] He went to a lake and bathed there and played

[1] Told by Mary Iley, 1927; see p. 393.

[2] A youth must be free from sex experience if he wishes to obtain a guardian spirit.

about. Finally, he lay down under a tree. "I wish I had one of my girls here; I would have some company," he thought. He fell asleep and the dangerous woman (pα'sako'wł) came. He awoke to find the woman on top of him. Her body was cold. "Oh, the dangerous woman has found me!" he thought. "No, I'm not the dangerous woman; I'm the one you wished for," the woman said. "What shall I do?" he thought. "Nothing, you wished for me. We'll go home; I live near here," the woman said. "The dangerous woman has got me," he thought. "I'm not the dangerous woman," the woman said. She took the boy home and kept him there.

The boy was very much frightened. For the first two months that he was with the woman, he was frightened all the time. Gradually he became more accustomed to her and finally made her his wife. He spent his time then hunting and fishing. His family learned that he was missing and said, "He must have been eaten up; the dangerous beings got him." Eventually, the boy almost became a dangerous being himself. Whenever he thought, the woman would know what his thoughts were. Then one day, he did not think, but evidently just looked what he felt. (If he had thought, she would have known what he was thinking.) It was early morning, and the woman had just gone away. He jumped up, put his shoes on and went out. He went to the river and shouted across to his own people to come and get him. When he got to the other side, he told the people that they must dig a hole and get in it. His parents did as he said, but no one else would take his advice. "He stayed so long with that woman, he's crazy himself," they said.

The woman came to the opposite side of the river and shouted, "Come, get me. Give me my husband." She stayed there a half day and wept. All the people died when she wept; the very ground shook. She took their breath away from them, caused the air to become different. The boy and his parents were the only ones saved; they had gone into the hole and covered themselves.

After the woman had gone away, the boy said, "You alone have had a real person for a husband. You shall go away forever and never again molest the people." Since that time it has been bad luck to hear a dangerous woman weep. At that time, the dangerous woman killed people when she wept.

THE BAD BOY AND THE DANGEROUS WOMAN.[1]

Many people were living in a certain village. There was a bad boy in this village. He was cranky whenever he ate; he always wanted this and wanted that. "Let's leave this boy. Let's leave him to the dangerous woman (pα'sako'wł)," the people said.

After they had gone, the boy cried and was bad from morning till night. Then he thought, "Perhaps the dangerous woman will come

[1] Told by Mary Iley, 1926; a story that children like to hear; see p. 392.

now." He fixed his house so she could not get in, so he thought, but she came nevertheless. She heated a rock from her basket and roasted a salmon head.[1] She pretended to offer the boy the head, but actually offered him the hot rock. "No, I don't want it. You're not my grandmother; you're the dangerous woman!" the boy said. "No, don't say that, dear. The dangerous woman may hear you," the woman said. "Yes, you just say that because you're the dangerous woman yourself!" the boy answered. He had made up his mind to grab her. He grabbed hold of her arm and pulled until he had torn it off. The woman then went away.

Next morning, the boy followed his people and finally found them. "I managed to pull the dangerous woman's arm off," he said. "Don't lie!" they said, "you cry all the time. If you ever do it again, we'll leave you for good, and the dangerous woman will certainly get you then!" "But I pulled her arm off!" he said. They then sent another boy back to see if this were true. "Yes, it's true," the boy reported.

The older men then went back home. They covered everything with pitch and invited the dangerous women to come so that the boy could put the old woman's arm back on.

All the women came. Coyote said to one of the younger ones, "Let me see how far you can stick your tongue out, sister." She stuck her tongue out. "Farther, farther," he said. Then he jumped at her and bit her tongue off.

Everyone sang,

> Put it on for your sister-in-law,[2]
> Put it on for your sister-in-law.

Everyone was dancing inside the house. The dangerous women were dancing with their eyes closed. The injured woman took her clothes off; her arm was badly torn. While the women were dancing with their eyes closed, the others slipped out, closed the door tightly and started a fire. The girl whose tongue Coyote had torn out had remained on the outside. When she saw what was happening, she tried to cry out, but all she could say, was, "Tət, tət." Finally the women noticed that they were burning up and began to scream. They burnt up.

CHIPMUNK AND THE DANGEROUS WOMAN.[3]

Chipmunk had no father or mother. His grandmother, Roe (tsa'wx̱), reared him. He used to go to a kind of service tree and eat berries there.[4] He was in a tree eating berries when the dangerous

[1] Young children are very fond of salmon heads; they like to suck the nose.
[2] In the levirate sense, so the narrator said. The term is used evidently to flatter the woman.
[3] Told by Mary Iley, 1927; see p. 392.
[4] This tree has little bunches of stickers.

woman came packing her basket. "Come on, grandson," she said, "I have some lacamas from lala·'x̣ʊm for you." "No, no, no!" Chipmunk said, "you're a dangerous being; you're not my grandmother!" "Don't say that! The dangerous woman might hear you," the woman said. "You're the dangerous woman yourself!" Chipmunk said. He threw down some small branches on which there were no berries, — a branch here, a branch there. Then he jumped off the other side of the tree. The woman made a grab for him and left the stripes on his back that are there today. She licked the blood off her fingers. "Oh, how sweet!" she said.

Chipmunk ran home to his grandmother. "Oh, grandmother," he cried, "the dangerous woman almost got me!" His grandmother hid him under a cooking basket.

The dangerous woman came. "Did you see my little food that ran in here?" she asked. "No, be quiet, you might frighten my grandchild," the old lady said. "I'm looking for a little fellow, my food," the woman said. Chipmunk's grandmother was very pretty and white. "Oh, you're so pretty!" the woman said. "Would you like to be pretty like me?" the old lady asked. "Yes," the woman said. "Well then, I shall put pitch on you and you shall jump on this white rock here. Then I shall pull your skin off and you will be white like me," the old lady said. "No, no, no!" the woman cried. The old grandmother persuaded her to try it with her little finger first. She pulled the skin off and the finger came out nice and white. The woman was pleased. "Oh, I do want to be pretty like you!" she said. The old lady then took a sharp-pointed rock and jabbed her in the neck with it. She buried her under the rocks.

Next day the dangerous woman's younger sister came. The old lady had a very nice piece of meat and offered her half of it. The woman was pleased. "Oh, it is very nice! Where did you get it?" she asked. "Oh, I always have a piece of this meat," the old lady said. "If you like, you may have it all." The woman took the meat and ate it. She ate and ate. Then she died. There were five sisters and all of them died from eating the meat.

The dangerous woman had left her children at home. Coyote came to the old grandmother's house and asked, "Where is the dangerous children's mother?" "Oh, I killed her," the old lady said. "How did you do it?" he asked. "I baked her," she answered. "Her children are still living, I must kill them too," he said.

Coyote went to the dangerous woman's house. The children bit him on the legs. He killed them with a stick and threw them away but they came to life again. "Sisters," he asked, "what shall I do?" "If we tell you, you will say, 'I knew that,'" his sisters said. He spit. "Come on, sisters! Come on, rain, kill my sisters," he said. "Oh, brother, we will tell you," his sisters said. "There is something hanging there, — their souls. If you cut them down, you can kill the dangerous beings." He did as they said and all the children died.

Every last one of them died. Then he said, "The people who are coming now will cover the whole world. There shall be no dangerous beings here."

Coyote killed all the young dangerous beings and Chipmunk's grandmother the old ones.

COON AND HIS GRANDMOTHER.[1]

Coon and his grandmother were living together. The old lady had some acorns to eat buried in the ground, a pile here, a pile there. She went to a cache to get some and took out just one. She opened the acorn, took one half for herself and gave the other half to Coon. Coon became very ill-tempered, because she did not give him enough to eat. His grandmother, who was Snowbird (spi'tsx̣ᵘ), was very tiny, but Coon was a good-sized boy. Another time she went to a cache and brought two acorns, one for herself and one for him. She could not eat all of hers but Coon swallowed his in one gulp. A half was plenty for her. Coon became very angry. At last he said, "Grandmother, I'm going myself to a cache and bring back enough to eat for once." She gave him a tiny little basket. He was glad; he would get enough to eat. He filled the basket and started back but on the way, fell down and spilled his acorns. He picked them up. Some were cracked and so he ate them. Finally, he ate them all. Then he ran back and got another basket full. On the way back, he fell down again in the same spot and spilled them all. He picked them up. Some were cracked and so he ate them. Then he went from one cache of acorns to another. He ate one pile belonging to his grandmother, and two belonging to his uncle. "Where's Coon?" his grandmother thought. She went out to see where he was and saw his tail sticking up out of the fifth and last cache. She grabbed him by the tail and whipped him. When she let him go, he ran away.

She went into the house and built a fire, laying one long log across the other. Coon was hiding in the corner. When she saw him, she picked up one of the burning logs and struck him with it. It left a spot on his nose and streaks clear across his back. He ran away and never came back. She was sorry that she had hurt him and wanted him to come back.

Coon ran away to the river and ate crawfish and bullfish. Five times Grizzlybear asked him, "Where did you come across?" The fifth time, Coon said, "Right where your backside opens, that's where I came across." Grizzlybear became very angry. "What do you mean by talking about my backside? I'll swallow you whole. I won't even chew you," he said. Coon had five white, sharp agates around his back. When Grizzly swallowed him, Coon cut him in five places with his agates. "How he scratches!" Grizzly thought. Grizzly died; he had been killing people. Coon ran home, crying, "Grandmother,

[1] Told by Mary Iley, 1926; see p. 407.

I've killed the dangerous being. Grandmother, I've killed the dangerous being." "Don't make fun of the dangerous being! He killed your father and mother," the old woman said. "But I killed the dangerous being," he said over and over. At last she went with him and saw that it was true. Coon butchered Grizzly and started to pack the meat home. The old lady was coming behind, carrying the genitals. When the boy came back for more meat, he could not find his grandmother and stopped to look for her. He looked everywhere for her and at last heard her laughing, "Hi, hi." "What's she doing?" he thought. His grandmother was in the sweat house, astride Grizzly's parts. "The nasty thing!" he said. He shut her in and burned her up. "Tαm, tαm," each part of her went as it burst to pieces.

Coon ate all the bear meat, and then all the crawfishes that he could find. When he had eaten everything he could lay his hands on, he found a piece of soft meat. "What a nice piece of fat!" he thought as he ate it. Before long he became very thirsty and had to go to the creek to drink. Then all his teeth fell out.[1] He realized right away what had happened; he had eaten his grandmother's private parts.

THE HORSE RACE.[2]

An old woman and her grandson, a little boy, were living together. The boy always went hunting and killed chipmunks, rabbits, mink, and small game with his bow and arrow. He always brought the game home to his grandmother. She would say to him, "Don't go too far. The dangerous woman might find you and put you in her basket and eat you."

One day the boy found a little horse, a tiny little horse. He thought it was something to eat and was going to kill it. He drew his bow and shot at it. He nearly hit it. "It's such a cute little thing, I don't like to kill it," he thought. He drew his bow and shot again. He nearly hit it again. At last the little horse said, "Take me home. You will have good luck if you do." So the boy decided not to kill him. "Ride me," the horse said. The boy got on; his feet nearly touched the ground.

When his grandmother saw him she screamed, "What did you bring home, a dangerous being?" She had never seen a horse before; she had heard of a man who owned five race horses but had never seen them. Now she had an opportunity to learn about horses. She went far off and packed green grass to feed to the horse. "Now try

---

[1] The narrator said that Coon probably got himself some gold teeth later on.

[2] Told by Mary Iley, 1927. Mrs. Iley said that her father used to tell this story but she did not know where he learned it. It is supposed to be an Indian story. Mrs. Iley knows many French stories and remarked that it seemed very much like them in places. See p. 421.

me," the horse said to the boy one day. "If I run well, you will be able to win a race." The boy got on and rode him around the prairie. "Now whip me," the horse said. The boy rode the horse around the prairie five times. The tiny horse was now sleek and pretty; at first, he was unkempt and woolly. "I am ready to race now," he said. "Grandmother," the boy said, "go to the man who has the race horses and tell him we will race him." "Oh, my grandson found a little horse. We are ready to race you," the old woman said to the man. "All right, tell him to come tomorrow morning," the man said; he was sure they did not have a horse.

The boy and the old woman came with the horse next morning. The boy had nothing to bet but the horse. "You must have something besides," the man said. "I'll bet my grandmother," the boy said. "Oh no, she's too old," the man said. "She's good enough," the boy answered, "she can dig roots, cook, pack things as well as anyone." Then Coyote said to the man, "Go ahead, let him bet her. If you win, I'll have her for my old woman. She's too old to be a slave; I'll have her for my little woman." "All right," the man said. He bet the horse that he was running and a slave. He ran his worst horse. The boy won; his grandmother would not have to be a slave. He and his grandmother went home. Oh, the old woman was happy that her grandson did not have to leave her behind! The boy now owned two horses and a slave.

That evening, a man came from the owner of the horses and said, "He wants you to come tomorrow morning to race again." "All right," the boy answered. This time, the boy bet his little horse and the horse that he had won the time before. The man bet the horse that he was running and a slave. Now they ran, the boy riding his own little horse. The little horse came out ahead, so the boy won the horse and slave. He went home, riding his little horse. The man who owned the race horses was a chief.

Late that evening the man came from the chief again and said, "He wants you to race again tomorrow." "All right, I'll come," the boy said. He again bet his own little horse and one that he had won against a horse and a slave. They ran and he won. He had won three horses and three slaves. Now the chief had only two horses left.

Late that evening the man came and said, "The chief wants you to come again tomorrow." Next morning the boy went. He won again. Now the chief had only one race horse left; the boy had won four horses and four slaves from him.

Late that evening, a man came from the chief and said, "He's going to run his last horse. Come tomorrow morning." Next morning the boy started out, a slave leading his horse. The chief had a very good horse but the boy's little horse beat him. Now all the chief's horses were gone. He said, "I have an only daughter. If you return all my horses, you may have her. You shall be a bigger chief than I. Bring your grandmother and stay with me."

The boy came with all the horses and stayed with the chief.

PHEASANT AND HER GRANDSON.[1]

Old lady Pheasant and her grandson were living together. The boy always went out to pick q'a'α'n berries. (The berries are similar to the service berries, but grow in little bunches like crab-apples. The bush is very thorny.) One day he mashed some of the berries and made a little ball of them with thorns sticking all around it. "Open your mouth," he said to his grandmother, "I'll throw some berries in." His grandmother opened her mouth and swallowed. The thorny ball stuck in her throat. "Give me water, give me water, grandson!" she cried. The boy paid no attention to her. He just stayed there on the tree; he would not come down to her. Then his grandmother turned into a pheasant and flew away. The boy was left alone.

THE BOY AND THE FIRE.[2]

There was a little boy who became afraid of Fire because it kept following him. He ran away from it as fast as he could. "Oh, what can I do to keep from burning? Can you save me?" he asked old man Tree. "No, if Fire comes, I burn," Tree said. "Can you save me from Fire?" he asked Big Rock. "No, if Fire comes, I get very hot; you'd roast to death," Big Rock said. "Can't you save me? A dangerous being is after me," he said to Little Creek. "What dangerous being?" Little Creek asked. "Fire," the boy answered. "No, I can't save you. I boil; you'd become cooked," Little Creek said. "See if someone else can't save you." Then the boy found Prairie. "Here's someone who can save me," he thought. "Can't you save me? The dangerous being is after me," he said. "What dangerous being?" Prairie asked. "Fire." "No," Prairie said, "all this grass will burn." "Oh, save me," he said to Rotten Log, "Fire is after me." "No, I can't save you. All the rotten part of me will burn," Rotten Log said. He ran and ran and ran. "Can't you save me?" he asked Trail. "Yes," Trail said, "sometimes I burn, but only along the sides. Lie down on me." Then he lay down on Trail and the fire passed over him.

SHARK GIRL.[3]

There were five Crow girls and one girl who was small in size. The small girl had no father or mother. She was a dangerous being; whenever she played with children, she fought terribly. She would tear the flesh from their faces. The Crow girls, accompanied by the small girl, went in a canoe to an island to dig small lacamas. The small girl alone could dig as many lacamas as four or five girls

[1] Told by James Cheholts, 1927; see p. 411.
[2] Told by Mary Iley, 1926; see p. 420.
[3] Told by Mary Iley, 1926; see p. 415.

together. She got more than all the others. Since they got only a few, she divided with them. They visited the island four times. The fourth time, the Crow girls sang,

I'm going to have a best-love,
A rich man.

They did not know that the small girl was a dangerous being. She sang a song of her own, to let the pretty girls know that they could not underrate her,

I'll have the best man of all,
A richer man than yours.

As usual, she dug a great many lacamas. Although small in size, she was rather oldish. By this time, a quite desirable man had taken a fancy to her. On their fifth visit to the island, the other girls said, "We'll throw her away, so that she can never get back home." "Put your basket into the canoe first and then go back after your digging-stick," they said. They had already taken her stick. When she started to go back for it, they pushed off and left her there.

A rich man, who had a number of wives and many slaves, lived near the island. One of his slaves was Coon. She was on the island trying to dig lacamas but could do nothing but scratch around. She had her basket full but there was more rubbish than lacamas. After a while, something caught her attention. "Who can that be over there?" she thought and crooked her finger[1] at the person. The person came over to her; it was a girl. "What are you doing?" the girl asked. "I'm trying to dig lacamas but I can't manage to get anything but the tops," Coon said. "Well, I'll give you mine," the girl said and filled Coon's basket.

The women were surprised when little Coon came home with her basket full. The fourth time, her master asked, "Did you do this yourself?" "No, a girl over there did it for me," Coon said. "How big is she?" he asked. "She's as big as I," Coon said. The man went over to see the girl. "Where did you come from?" he asked. "The Crow girls left me here. I dug with them here for several days and then one day they went off and left me." "I'll take you home with me. You can be my wife." "Do you have any wives?" the girl asked. "Lots of them," the man answered. "And do you have any property?" she asked then. "Thirty-seven slaves," the man said. Coon was his youngest slave. "All right," the girl said. "You'll be well-to-do when you become my wife," the man said, "I'll forbid my other wives to whip you."

The man treated all of his wives well. There was plenty of work to do, berries to pick and lacamas to dig. The small girl always managed to get more than any of the others because she was a fast worker. The other women loved her at first because she was such a good

[1] Illustrating.

worker. But gradually they began to fear her, for when she became angry, she fought them terribly and nearly killed them. At times, she also fought fiercely with her husband and nearly killed him too. Finally, she became pregnant. When her baby was born, she killed it and ate it. By this time, everybody was afraid of her. At last she killed her husband and all the small children that had not already run away to escape her. "I'm going to leave you," she said one day. She went to the ocean and became a dangerous being. When a person, she was much like a shark, and it was a shark that she became. She was the best possible worker; she would work and work and dig fast. When she did any basketry work, her fingers moved with great speed.[1]

MEADOWLARK GIRL.[2]

Meadowlark had one brother. She growled at him continually and tried to hit him and bite him. "I'll leave her; she's bad," the youth thought. He started to go away but she got in his way and growled at him as usual. She would not let him pass, so he killed her with a stick and threw her body to the side of the road. He went on his way but in a little while, there she was again: she had come to life. She called him every mean thing she could think of. He killed her again with a stick and threw her body to the side of the road. He kept on going but in a short while he found her again on the road. She growled at him as usual and said, "Come on — — — — —." "I'm going to kill her. No one has a sister like mine," the youth said to himself. He killed her with a stick and threw her body to the side of the road. Then he went on his way. In just a little while, there she was on the road. "Come on — — — — — —," she said and growled at him. He killed her again and threw her body to the side of the road. Before long he stepped on old lady Meadowlark.[3] She had stuck her leg out for him to break, so that she could then sympathize with him and tell him how to get out of his difficulty. He broke her leg and she cried, "Poor me, you stepped on my leg!" "Oh, aunty," he said, "I'll make you a leg of beads." He fixed her leg and she said, "I'm going to tell you what to do: she has a hat; to kill her, you must take it off her and tear it to pieces." He went on his way and before long, heard his sister again. There she was, growling. "Come on — — — — — —," she said. She was asking him to do bad things; she was asking him to be her lover.[4] She was asking her own brother to do this! That's why he had been ashamed of her all along. He

---

[1] Illustrating. The narrator is one of the best basket makers in this part of the country, so she naturally appreciated the girl's ability in this line.

[2] Told by Mary Iley, 1926; see p. 416.

[3] The narrator pointed out that this was another Meadowlark.

[4] The narrator was a bit modest and so did not reveal the true significance of the girl's demands until she had to.

grabbed her hat off her head and tore it to pieces, whereupon she fell to the ground. His sister was truly dead. It was impossible for him to carry out his sister's demands. No girl could ask her brother to do a thing like that. "No sister dare ask for her own brother's love," he said to her. "Only you will have done that. Now you are dead. Hereafter, a girl shall be glad to have a sister-in-law, and a boy, a brother-in-law."

URINE BOY.[1]

Urine Boy (masα'ntən) had five sisters. He wore his hair in one braid. Every day he danced on a rock. One day as he danced he saw a man running away from a dangerous being. He killed the dangerous being before it caught up with the man. Then he put the man under his braid and took him home to his sister. The same thing happened five times. Each time he took the man home. Each sister now had a man. The eldest girl bore her husband many children. Two of the children fell in love with each other and ran away. Their mother followed them and found where they had camped the first night. They had made a little fire; one had slept on one side of the fire, one on the other. They had gone on the next day. She followed them for five days, but could not catch up with them, for they could travel faster than she. At the fifth camp, she found their beds together. "So that's why you ran off!" she said. She took the two mats and rubbed them together. Then she laid them down side by side.

The youth and his sister ran away to strangers and lived as man and wife. They had one child, a boy. The boy danced every day, and sang,

> My mother is also my aunty,
> My father is also my uncle,
> My mother is also my aunty.

He sang this five times every day. His father could not make him stop and became ashamed. "Someone will find out I married my sister," he said. And so he killed the boy.

Some time later, X̣wα'ni came. "No one shall marry his sister," he said to the man. "Do you see that pretty girl there?" he asked. "Go make love to her and have her for your sweetheart." Then he said to the man's wife, "Perhaps someone will fall in love with you, too, some stranger whom you can marry." "This is the way it shall be done: as soon as they are old enough to know better, sisters and brothers or cousins will not make love to each other," he said.

And so it is today: if a brother and sister act like lovers, it is not nice.

---

[1] Told by Mary Iley, 1927; see p. 416.

SPEAR BOY.[1]

Spear Boy (sα′x̣kən) was living with his sister. His sister had brought him up, for their mother and father were dead. She made their living. She gathered roots to eat, made baskets and traded them for anything she could get, — food and clothes to wear. The boy was now old enough to go fishing. He went out one day to fish for trout but did not bring any home. He went out again but did not return with any fish. Their home was close to the Cowlitz River. One day his sister heard someone calling from across the river, "E···, Spear Boy caught a big fish. He · ·, he · ·, he swallowed it." The young woman paid no attention. "They're making fun of the poor boy," she said. Later on, during the winter, the boy developed a sore arm. He carried his wrist tied up, as if it were broken. During the winter months they used to eat a certain kind of root mixed with salmon eggs. Whenever the boy ate this root, he would say, "Oh, oh!" "What's the matter?" his sister would ask. "My arm hurts," he would say and then he would blow upon it. Sometimes his sister would say, "Oh, let me look at it. I'll wash it and put some medicine on it." But the boy would always refuse to let her touch it.

Spring came and Spear Boy fished all the time, but never caught any fish. One day, his sister again heard someone calling, "Spear Boy caught a big fish." "Let me see," she said, jumping up quickly, "I'm glad. My brother has caught a fish!" Right away she got things ready for cutting the salmon. Then she heard someone shout, "He swallowed it!" "Can it be true?" she asked herself. Then she heard the person shouting, "He's caught another fish." She jumped up to look. It was true that the boy had caught a fish. She stood watching. The same person called out, "He's going to swallow it." She kept watching. The boy held the fish up and swallowed it whole. She sat down and began to wonder, "Has he been doing this all the time?" The thought of it nearly killed her. She had seen with her own eyes what the boy had done. The neighbors had not been making fun of him but had been telling the truth.

She went into the house and began to pack her things. "I'm going to leave," she said. "He's able to catch fish and take care of himself. I reared him and this is how he treats me." She made a large bundle of things, included in which was a little bunch of talu′talo[2] [spear flowers?] that she could not bear to part with. Just as she was ready to leave, she heard the same person shouting about Spear Boy again. While Spear Boy was swallowing his salmon, she slung her pack over her back and started down the river. Then the person shouted from across the river, "Spear Boy's sister is leaving him. She saw him eating salmon and left because she was ashamed." Spear Boy had just caught another salmon. "Come back," he

[1] Told by Sophie Smith, 1926; see p. 417.
[2] A Taitnepam term.

cried to his sister, "I've got a big salmon." But his sister was already out of sight.

The young woman had left home without eating. After five days and nights of travelling, she came to a house. There was no one home, but the house was very clean and there was an abundance of dried salmon about. It was late in the day. "I'll stay over night here," she thought, "there's plenty of dried salmon and I'll cook some for my supper. My, it looks good!" Just then a piece of dried salmon fell down on her. "It thinks I mean to steal it," she said and threw it back where it belonged. She took some dried lacamas from her pack and buried them in the hot ashes, as there was a good fire. After a while she started to uncover the roots. "They're probably done now," she said. The roots were gone; they had burned to ashes. "The nasty thing!" she said, giving the fire a jab with the poker. She sat down and then a man came in bringing a lot of salmon. He arranged the salmon neatly in the middle of the house and said, "Oh, my wife, I'm very glad you came." "My, I never knew I had a husband," the young woman thought to herself. "Oh, oh," the fire went just then. The man explained, "My mother said that she tried to give you some salmon but you wouldn't take it. She said that you fed her some lacamas and that she ate them. You then became angry and prodded her with a stick." The young woman did not say anything but thought to herself, "His mother must be Fire." The man sat down alongside her but still she did not say anything. "Let's eat our supper. Mother has prepared it for us." The food, just enough for two, was nicely cooked. She ate well and was pleased with everything except the fact that the man's mother was Fire. This seemed very strange to her. She started to clear away the dishes but the man said, "Don't bother. Mother will do it. Sit down and I'll tell you about her. My mother is Fire and can do all kinds of work. If you want to feed her, just put something in the fire for her and she will eat it. Just mention anything that you want done and she will do it."

The young woman remained with this man as his wife. Never once was she able to catch her mother-in-law in the act of working. Before she had time to even think of it, the fish would appear nicely dressed and hanging up. Breakfast and supper would appear already prepared. After she had been married about a year, she had a child. Whenever she and her husband went any place, he would tell her to leave the baby behind. She was afraid for the baby was crawling and might get burnt. She wished that her mother-in-law would remain a person all the time, but did not know how to accomplish this, as she had never once seen her in human form. One day while she was out picking berries, she suddenly thought, "Why did I never think of it before! I'll run back and catch her." She ran back to the house and found the door open. A middle-aged woman was holding the baby on her lap. "What shall I do?" she thought. She left her berry basket outside and ran in quickly. She embraced the woman tightly and cried, "Mother, mother, mother. You must never again be Fire. You must always be a person." From that time on the woman remained a person and never again assumed the form of fire. She could now talk to her son and daughter-in-law who were very happy about it.

All this time, Spear Boy was living alone and found that he missed his sister's care very much. After two years had passed, he thought, "I'll look for her." He started out. Wherever he camped, he asked if a woman had passed there. "Yes, a woman stopped here," he was told. "How long ago?" he would ask. And so eventually he found his sister. She had already told her husband that she had an only brother. "Here comes Spear Boy," she said one day. Her husband had a trough full of salmon. When Spear Boy came, he said to him, "You may eat all you want of these raw fish." Spear Boy would stand there by the trough and spear the fish and eat them raw. After he had been there two or three months, he thought, "I'd better go home now." "I've just been visiting you. I know where you live now, so I can go home," he said to his sister. His brother-in-law fixed him up a small pack, one weighing about five pounds, that was not too heavy for him to run with. "Don't untie this pack on the road. Wait until you get home," he said. "After you have gone some distance, you will come to three forks in the road. Take the middle one, which is a short-cut. Don't follow either one of the others. Be sure to do as I say." Then he tied some whetstones to Spear Boy's chest and back, and tied the pack to him tightly. "Don't take the pack off until you get home," he said once more.

Early next morning Spear Boy started home. When he came to the three forks of the road, he thought, "Which one shall I take?" He became confused and took the road to the right. He found it so thick with frogs, snails, bugs of all kinds, and caterpillars that he could not walk. He slipped from side to side and soon became so frightened that he turned back. He then took the trail to the left. Before long he found wildcats that growled at him, and bears, deer, animals of all kinds and birds that looked as though they wanted to bite him. He jumped in alarm and ran ahead. At last he found a girl standing in the middle of the road, who was combing her hair. He tried to evade her, but she ran the comb through her hair, the sharp ends of which pricked him on the chest. She did the same thing again. He tried to get around her but could not get out of the way. If it were not for the whetstones under his clothing he would have been killed; the whetstones dulled the sharp ends of her hair. He suddenly became so frightened that he fell over on his face. Still combing her hair, the girl pecked him on the back. At last he managed to get away from her and ran back. Then he took the middle trail. He was now on the right road. Finally his pack began to tire him very much and he began to wonder what was in it. Perhaps there was something to eat. He stopped and started to untie it; he only intended to see what was in it. No sooner had he untied it, than all the large fish that live in the ocean came out, whales, sharks and the like. They ran right back home. He closed it but too late. Nothing remained but the little fish that live in small rivers. He did not untie the pack again until he got home. Inside, were all the salmon that now live in the Cowlitz River. Big fish never go up the Cowlitz because Spear Boy untied his pack too soon.

NəX̂α'NTCI BOY.

(First Version).[1]

Old man NəX̂α'ntci[2] and his grandson lived on Cowlitz Prairie near ləpa'ləm Creek. X̣wα'ni and his five sons lived at the same place. X̣wα'ni's sons looked for tamanoas and got it very strong. NəX̂α'ntci's grandson was lame.

Some people who lived near the Columbia owned a large hoop. The hoop was shiny, like gold, and changeable in color; it was very pretty. X̣wα'ni's sons decided to steal it; they were very strong boys. "I'll go along with you," X̂α'ntci[3] Boy said to them. "No," X̣wα'ni said, "the people will step on you and kill you. If they can kill strong boys like mine, they would certainly kill you." But the little lame boy decided to go along, nevertheless.

There were five mountains between the prairie and the place on the Columbia River. X̂α'ntci Boy stationed himself on the mountain nearest home. The youngest X̣wα'ni stationed himself at the second mountain, the second, at the third, the third, at the fourth, and the fourth, at the fifth. The eldest of the X̣wα'ni brothers set out alone to steal the hoop. The people were rolling it between two sides. They were shouting and having a good time. Young X̣wα'ni walked to the middle of the playing-field and caught the hoop. He ran with it and the people chased him. When they were about to catch up with him, he threw the hoop to his brother stationed on the first mountain. They killed the eldest boy and started after the second. The second, when he saw that they were going to overtake him, threw the hoop to the third, stationed on the second mountain. They killed the second and started after the third. The third threw the hoop to the fourth. They killed the third and started after the fourth. The fourth threw the hoop to his youngest brother. They killed the fourth and started after the fifth. The fifth then threw

[1] Told by Mary Iley, 1926; see p. 390.

[2] English equivalent unknown. An animal said to resemble mice [sic] but red in color. Old women sometimes chase these animals and kill five or six at a time to eat.

[3] Short for NəX̂α'ntci.

the hoop to old Nəx̣α'ntci's boy, who caught it and ran. They killed the fifth boy and started after X̣α'ntci Boy. When they were about to catch him, he suddenly became very strong and ran as if he had wings. The same thing happened when they came close a second time. Finally all gave up and turned back; they could not catch him.

X̣α'ntci Boy reached the mountain and shouted, "X̣wα'ni's boys were killed—every last one of them." X̣wα'ni was listening for the boys' return. "Oh," he said, "my eldest son is on his way home." "No," Nəx̣α'ntci said, "my grandson says, 'X̣wα'ni's boys were killed.'" "No," X̣wα'ni said, "it was my eldest son and he said, 'Nəx̣α'ntci's boy was killed.'" They argued back and forth. Finally Nəx̣α'ntci said, "Let's settle it now. We'll urinate on one another: the one who turns yellow loses, the one who turns shiny wins." X̣wα'ni agreed. They urinated on one another: X̣wα'ni turned yellow and Nəx̣α'ntci turned shiny. Then Nəx̣α'ntci fixed a big rock so that X̣wα'ni would fall back on it and kill himself when he learned for certain of his sons' death. X̣wα'ni listened closely. The boy shouted again. "Oh," X̣wα'ni said, "that's X̣α'ntci Boy! Oh, my children were killed!" He fainted and hit his head on the rock when he fell back. Finally he wept himself to death.

Nəx̣α'ntci packed the hoop in a bag and went up into the sky where the sun comes out. He took the hoop — the sun — up there. That's why it is shiny there now.

NƏX̣Α'NTCI BOY.

(Second Version).[1]

There was an old man and his lame little grandson living on Cowlitz Prairie. Another man and his five sons were living in a neighboring house. The old man sent his grandson out early every morning to swim. The five boys never went swimming but stayed right in the house. In the evenings, their father would send them out on the prairie to look for tamanoas, — to sing and walk there. The eldest would go fairly far, the second a bit nearer home, the third still nearer, the fourth still nearer, and the fifth and youngest close home. Instead of looking for tamanoas, the boys would build fires and catch grasshoppers.

The old man concealed the fact that his young grandson arose very early each morning to swim: he would blow the ashes from the fireplace over the boy's blanket to make it appear that he slept long after the fire was started.

The second man continued to send his sons out as usual. Each time he sent them a little farther away. Finally he sent them far off on the prairie, — to sing for their tamanoas. The eldest went quite far, the second a little nearer, the third a little nearer still, the fourth

[1] Told by James Cheholts, 1927.

still nearer, and the fifth and youngest still nearer. The boys did not do as they were told, but built fires and caught grasshoppers.

The old man's grandson would always take the same trail as the five boys. He would pass the fifth and youngest one and find him cooking grasshoppers. He would pass the fourth, the third, the second, and find them doing the same. Then he would pass the eldest, go some distance farther, and holler for tamanoas. Next morning early he would go out to swim.

One day the second man came to the old man and said, "You should wake your grandson up early occasionally. He always sleeps so long."

The five boys eventually grew up. They made a hoop and shot at it with arrows — to catch it as it rolled. "You'd better go and play with them," the old man said to his grandson. The five boys could run very fast and so learned to play very skillfully with the hoop. The little boy was not so good at it because he was lame. One day the five boys said, "We're going far down the Columbia River to attend a hoop game." Many people had gathered at a certain place on the Columbia to play the game. The players were divided into two sides and the hoop was rolled back and forth between them. "We're going to leave tomorrow," the five boys said. "I don't want your grandson to go with them," their father said to the old man, "he's too slow; he'll just be in their way." "He's going nevertheless," the old man answered.

Now the six boys got ready and left. They crossed ever so many mountains before they got to the place. At last they came in sight of the game. "We'll steal the hoop and take it to Cowlitz Prairie," the five brothers said. "We'll catch it as they roll it; then we'll run as hard as we can," the eldest boy said. The six boys lined up, standing close to the side that was to receive it. As the hoop came rolling along, the eldest made a motion as if to catch it, and then purposely let it go by. The second, the third, the fourth, did the same. Then the youngest made a motion as if to catch it and then let it go by. When the hoop came by a second time, the lame boy made a motion as if to catch it and then let it go by. "When it comes by again, I'll catch it. Be ready to run," the eldest boy said. The hoop came by and the eldest caught it. Then they ran as fast as they could.

The people chased them. The eldest crossed five mountains. Then the people caught up with him. "He·' · · · ·," he cried, "take this hoop! We are all going to die!" The second brother caught the hoop and ran. The eldest boy was dead now. The second brother crossed four mountains and then the people caught up with him. "He·' · · · ·," he cried, "take this and run. We are all going to die!" The third caught the hoop and ran. He crossed three mountains and then they caught up with him. "He·' · · · ·," he called to his younger brother, "take this and run as fast as you can. We are all going to die!" He threw the hoop to his brother. The fourth caught it and ran. The little lame boy was in the lead all the time. The fourth crossed two mountains and then they caught up with him. "Take it," he cried to the fifth and youngest. The youngest caught it and ran. He crossed one mountain and then they caught up with him. He threw it to the lame boy and cried, "Oh, my friend, run as fast as you can!" The lame boy caught it and ran. He held it with one hand, and slapped his hip with the other to cure it of its lameness. He had been deceiving the people all along; he was not as lame as he had seemed. He had a little sack of fine feathers and untied it. He shook the feathers out and it became foggy immediately. The fog was very thick and those pursuing him could not see him. He slackened his pace. Then he shook the feathers out once more and it became foggy again. His pursuers lost their way and turned back.

In the meantime, the two men were awaiting the boys on Cowlitz Prairie. Finally Nəx̯α'ntci — as the boy was called — came crying, "All of Coyote's boys are dead. Only I am coming." Nəx̯α'ntci the elder said to Coyote (snəkα'l'), "Your five sons are dead." "No," Coyote said, "your boy is dead." They argued about it. Finally Nəx̯α'ntci suggested, "Let us urinate on one another. You urinate on my leg; if it turns yellow, you are right." Coyote urinated on Nəx̯α'ntci's leg but the color remained the same. Then Nəx̯α'ntci urinated on Coyote and he turned yellow. Nəx̯α'ntci was right. "Well," Coyote said, "I'm going to move away from here. I'm going east-of-the-mountains." "I'm going to the snow capped mountains and live there," Nəx̯α'ntci said. Young Nəx̯α'ntci accompanied his grandfather to the mountains, packing the hoop on his back. That's why the young nəx̯α'ntci has a white ring around his back now.

GRIZZLYBEAR AND HIS SONS.[1]

A man had five children. An old man had one grandchild. The first always coaxed his children to go out and look for guardian spirits. The five boys grew up. The old man always sent his grandchild to the creek to bathe. The first said to him, "You always send your boy just a short distance; he will never become educated."[2] "I'm not sending him to school," the old man said.

The first sent his children far off. The eldest kept going and going. Finally he stole another man's wife and started home with her. Before he reached home, the woman's husband caught up with them and killed him. The old man's grandson had followed the young man. He came home and said, "The young man got killed. He stole a man's wife and the man caught up with him and cut his

[1] Told by Mary Iley, 1927; see p. 411.

[2] The guardian spirit training is often compared to our schools. The training is oftentimes kept secret. This accounts for the old man's denial that follows.

head off." Then the old man said to the first, "You never coaxed your children to stay away from another man's wife. There are plenty of unmarried girls they could get."

The first man's second son went off. The little boy followed him. The second son stole some nice things, — some blankets perhaps. Before he had gone far, the owner caught up with him and killed him.

The third son went off. He found some boys playing with some nice horses. "I'm going to steal one," he thought. When the boys went to sleep, he stole a horse. He travelled all day. Finally the boys discovered that one of their horses was missing. They set out to trace it and caught up with the youth. They killed him and took their horse back. The little boy had followed and had seen what had happened. He went back home and reported the youth's death. "Oh, he stole a horse and the owners caught up with him and killed him," he said. Now three of the man's sons were dead. The old man said to him, "Couldn't you have coaxed your children to be good? There is just one way to be good. Couldn't they have taken an unmarried girl as a wife? Couldn't you have bought them a horse? You sent them every day to get guardian spirits; before long you won't have one son left. You have bad boys." The first man had always thought that he had good children.

The fourth son went far off hunting. He slipped on the snow and slid into the water and drowned. The litte boy had followed him. He came back and said to his grandfather, "The youth slipped on the snow and fell into the water and drowned."

When the youth's father heard of his death, he wept and wept. Now he had only one son left. He wanted to do the best thing for the boy, so he went off and bought him a wife. She was Grizzlybear, a very, very pretty girl. Her husband was short and plump and nice-looking. "I'll eat him," she thought. One day it happened that she and her husband went out somewhere together. Then she killed him. The people discovered that the youth was missing and looked and looked for him. Grizzly had gone to her aunt's house and when she got there, she had killed and eaten her husband. The old man's grandson had followed them. He came home and they could hear him calling the youth's name. "His wife has eaten him up. They played and then she jumped on his neck and ate him up," he said.

The youth's father wept when he heard of his death. He did not know what to do; all of his children were gone. He wept and wept and wept. Then he went away. He kept going and going. He was angry and so revealed that he was Grizzlybear. He married his own daughter-in-law and they both went into the woods and turned into grizzlies. No one had suspected previously that he was Grizzly-bear; he must have eaten his own wife. He had reared his children himself and had sent them out to get guardian spirits. But the children must have been bad for they never found any spirits. He had coaxed his children to be good but it had never done any good.[1]

THE CHIEF'S STORY.

(First Version).[2]

There was a young chief who was an orphan; he had no brothers. He was rich and had ten or more wives. The women lived at different places. For instance, it was something like this: two lived in Cowlitz country, two far down the Columbia, two in Upper Cowlitz country, one in Squally, one in Puyallup, one in [Upper] Chehalis country. Occasionally, two or three of the women might live in the same house, but never more than that. When the chief wanted to visit his wives, he had to go from place to place. At each place, he had slaves to help his wives. This chief had a rule of his own: if a wife of his gave birth to a son, the child had to be killed immediately. If she gave birth to a daughter, the child should be allowed to live. Some of the women had no children, some had two or three. Whenever one of his wives gave birth, there had to be witnesses present to testify as to the child's sex.

One of the women lived near the mouth of the Cowlitz River, — not far from Portland. She had a son, but concealed the fact from her husband. The chief's name was Sɩləma'tks; he lived across the river, at Ranier. The boy grew up, but the father never once suspected that he had a son. The son was a very handsome young man. He was very tall, unusually so, was heavily built, had nice brown hair and very fair skin. He was just a little larger than his father. One day he asked his mother, "Where does father live?" "On the opposite side of the river," his mother said. "I'm going over to see him," he said. "No, he would kill all of us if he ever found out about you," his mother said.

The boy had been kept hidden for years. He was about nineteen years old now. He had been taught to sew and could make either men's or women's clothes very nicely. He could also make baskets.[3] One day, he thought, "I'm going to visit my father." He got up early next morning and crossed the river in his canoe. He landed on the beach in front of his father's house. He noticed his father's footprints on the beach and stepped into them to see how his own compared with them in size. "I'm as large as he," he said. The footprints were about a yard long. He went up to the house and walked in. He did not sit down but squatted near the door. "I was walking around on the beach. I wonder who the man is with such long feet? My feet are larger than his," he said. "He must be a very big man,"

[1] Parents tell their children this story as a lesson to them.
[2] Told by Sophie Smith, 1926; see p. 420.
[3] Evidently he was brought up as a girl.

he added. He continued to talk and laugh about the very big footprints he had seen.

After the young man had gone away, the chief raised his head and said, "Watch where he goes." He was told that the young man had gone across the river. "To which house?" he asked. When they told him, he said, "I thought so! They never would let me see that baby." "If he thinks he is a man, very well! Call a slave and send him across the river with a message. Tell him to tell the young man to come to see me; if he's my son, I'm ready to fight him. If he's not a man, I'll kill him!" he said. The slave jumped into a canoe and went across the river. He went into the house and said, "Where's the man who came to see the chief this morning? The chief said to tell him that if he's a man, he can kill him. If not, the chief will kill him." The boy was lying on the bed with his head covered. He raised his head and said, "Tell him that I'll be there immediately." The slave went back. "He'll come," he said to his master.

The boy put on a breech-clout, beaded moccasins and a little beaded cap. His hair was in long braids. His mother wept and wept. "His father will kill him and all of us," she said. The boy started across the river, running on top of the water.[1] Some of his people started to follow him in canoes, but he tipped the canoes over. "Don't follow me; he's going to kill me," he said. All of the people on both sides of the river came out to see the fight. When the boy landed, the old man came out. He was wearing only a buckskin breech-clout. "Are you my son?" he asked. "I think I am," the boy said. "If you are a man, you can kill me. If not, I will kill you; I will not rear a son," the old man said. "All right, I will not say that I am a man," the boy said. They grabbed one another and fought with their fists; they struck and pulled at one another, using only their hands. The old man was hard to throw. The boy was not doing his best; he thought that his father was only joking, and so he laughed all the time they were fighting. It made the old man angry that the boy took it laughingly. He did his best and threw the boy. The boy was hurt a little and the old man tried to choke him while he was down. The boy then got to his feet and threw his father. The old man wanted to try again. The boy then threw him two or three times and nearly killed him. "Do you really mean to kill me?" he asked. "Yes," his father said. Then he grabbed hold of his father by the neck and twisted his head around until he killed him. It took him only a little while to do it. Everybody looked on but no one tried to stop him. After his father was dead, he told the people that he could not believe at first that his father would really object so much to rearing a son; it had taken him some time to realize that his father was in earnest. "As for myself," he said, "I believe in rearing boys as well as girls. Now that my father is dead, this shall be done."

[1] His guardian-spirit enables him to do this; see second version.

Everybody got together and prepared the old man for burial. They washed him and buried him. Then they sent word to all those places where the old chief had a wife living, that the old chief was dead. They wanted all of his wives to know immediately of his death, so that in case one of them was pregnant and gave birth to a male child, she need not kill it.

After his father's death, the young man became chief. The people believed him to be a better man and liked him much better. (The old chief had never had any children but his own put to death.)

In former times, there were many Cowlitz who were very large. That's why they always believe the story about this man.

THE CHIEF'Ṣ STORY.

(Second Version).[1]

There was a chief who bought his wives from various tribes. He lived on this side[2] of the Columbia at lɩ·'niya (Ranier), — near a little mountain. He would always bring his wives home with him, but as soon as they became pregnant, he would send them back to their own homes. "If the child is a boy, kill it," he would say to them. Whenever a daughter was ten or fifteen years old, she would come to see him. One of his wives came from the other side of the Columbia. She had a daughter, but the girl had never come to see her father. Ten years, fifteen years, eighteen years passed but still the girl did not come to see him.

The child was a boy, and for that reason had never visited his father. The boy's maternal grandfather had sent him out to look for tamanoas (sα'x̣tʽkwʋlc) and he had obtained L'ɛ''qʽku, a kind of spider that runs on top of the water.

After twenty-two years had passed, the chief said, "Why does my daughter never come to see me? Why does my daughter never come to see me?"

Shortly afterward, the young man said, "I'm going to visit my father now." The chief was lying on the bed when the young man arrived. The young man kept laughing and talking about the big footprints he had seen. His father was a very large man and had very large feet. He showed his father a stick and said, "I found a dangerous being's footprints this long!" He kept laughing and talking but no one paid any attention to him. After he had gone, the chief said, "Watch him. See where he takes his canoe." "He went up stream and then crossed the river," one of the women in the house said. "That's just what I thought! I know now why my child never came to see me. It's a boy," the chief said. He sent someone to measure the young man's tracks. They were eight inches wide and

[1] Told by Mary Iley, 1927.
[2] The Washington side.

much longer. "I am going to kill him. I will come with all my people," the chief said. He sent word to this effect to the young man. In reply, the young man said, "Let him kill me, but he has no right to kill my people. I don't want them killed. He can kill me if he likes, but he must not harm them." The messenger went back and reported to his chief, "The boy says that you must fight him alone; he does not want his people killed." "No, I will bring my people," the chief said. His name was Sɪləma'tks.

The chief and all his people started across the river. There were many canoes in the party. The chief rode in a very large canoe. "Stay here," the young man said to his people. Running on top of the water, he went out to meet his father. Arrows came flying at him, but none of them harmed him. All the while, he was shooting at his father. He shot him right in two. Then he said to his father's people, "I don't want to harm any of you. My father was determined to kill me. Go back."

After that, it was said, "There shall never be another person like this one. If a man has a son, he shall be happy about it; if a woman has a daughter, she shall be happy about it. Everyone shall be glad to have a son. Only he felt differently. There shall never be another person like him."

The young man married later on, but he never had any children unusually large, like himself. Of course, there were large people, but no one who could compare with him. Evidently his father had been a very tall man.

* * *

Sɪləma'tks was the only one who was a chief and he did not want anyone else to be a chief.[1]

THE WOODEN FISH.[2]

The people used to live near the river, always in small towns. At that time they believed that when a man's wife died, the man, if he were a good hunter or fisher, should cease hunting or fishing for a while and use the sweat-house every day. He was not allowed to eat fresh meat or salmon during the period of sweating.

There was a certain man whose wife died and he was left with a small child and an old mother. His neighbor was catching a lot of salmon, so he asked him to give him some, not for himself, but for the child. "No," the neighbor said, "you might eat a piece and spoil my luck." If the widower should eat any of the meat, he would "spoil" the hunter's shot or fish-hook. His wife had been dead

[1] It is interesting to note how the two versions of this story differ in detail, although told by sisters. Mrs. Iley heard Mrs. Smith tell me her version a year previous.

[2] Told by Sophie Smith, 1926; see p. 416.

five months already, but he was still sweating every day. "How can I get even with the fisherman? My child cannot have any fresh meat," he said to himself.

He made a wooden fish and took it to the river. "Turn into a real fish," he said to it. Then making his wish, he put it into the water. A little later he went back to the river. The wooden fish now looked like a real fish. He told the fish where it should go when the fisherman came next morning. "Take him down stream as far as you can," he said.

Next morning, the fisherman went out in his canoe with his young brother to fish. He saw the fish and told the boy to steady the canoe while he speared it. As soon as he speared, his hands stuck to the spear, and the boy's hands to the oars. Then down the (Cowlitz) river the fish went, pulling them along. They went day and night until they got to the Columbia. Then the fish landed and the fisherman learned that it was only a wooden one. He suspected that the widower had made it to trick him because he had refused him fresh meat for his daughter.

There were a lot of large birds, the size of bears, that tried to bite them. "Stay here on the beach, brother," he said. He pulled the canoe out of the water and turned it over the boy. Then he ran off to look the country over. Before long he chanced upon a one-sided shack. A large, old man was lying inside. "Oh, grandson, where did you come from?" the old man asked. "From the river; I left my brother there," the fisherman answered. "Run quickly! The mosquitoes might bite him!" the old man said. He ran back to the river, but the mosquitoes (the large birds) had already split the canoe to pieces and eaten up his brother. He came back and said, "The mosquitoes must have eaten up my brother; the canoe was split to pieces and nothing remained but blood." "Oh, grandson, the mosquitoes are very bad here; they eat little men like you," the old man said. "I'll cook you some salmon." He made a fire and covered a number of salmon with hot ashes. The salmon came out nice and clean. "P'ə, p'ə, p'ə," he blew upon them and brushed them off with his hands. He gave them to his visitor as if giving only small trout. The visitor took one of them and split it up. He could not eat all of it. "I've finished, grandpa," he said. "What, finished already!" the old man said. Then he, himself, picked up a handful of salmon and ate them in one swallow.

The old man had a large trough to hold live salmon. "Help yourself at any time," he said to his visitor. The fisherman got a stick and clubbed one of the salmon. He cut it up and roasted it but could not eat all of it. "How do you happen to be here?" the old man asked. The man then told him his story. "You should have given him dried salmon for himself, and some salmon only partly dried for the child and the old woman. He evidently meant to be honest. You have lost your brother as the result," the old man said.

X̯wʋ'lpios[1] (the old man) had an enemy, the One-Legged-Man[2] (st'ɛ'dkeɩq), who lived across the river. The old giant was glad to have his visitor with him for the latter made him some stout bows and arrows with which to fight his enemy. Along in the night they heard something going, "Bαm, bαm, bαm." "There's the One-Legged-Man filing my fishtrap," X̯wʋ'lpios said. He grabbed his visitor, who was just a tiny fellow to him, put him in a little hole at the back of his neck where the One-Legged-Man could not see him, and hurried to the trap. From his hiding place the little man shot at the One-Legged-Man, who was trying to break the trap, and struck him in the eye. Every night the One-Legged-Man tried to break the trap down. The old giant, with the little man's help, was able to kill his enemy. Heretofore, neither of the giants was able to harm the other.

After the death of the One-Legged-Man, X̯wʋ'lpios said, "I'm going to send you back home because I am grateful to you for helping me out." The man had been away from home all summer. During his stay, he had dried a lot of salmon that he had got from the trough. X̯wʋ'lpios got a whale and hollowed it out like a canoe. Then he piled it full of dried salmon, clean fresh salmon, clams and all kinds of things. He made a nice bed inside the whale and told the man to lie down there. He covered him up and said, "Don't get up until the whale lands. He will land in front of your house, where you get your water."

The man started home about bed-time. The whale went up the river with a "c — — — — —", just like a salmon. Early next morning, the man landed at his own home. "Kac, kac, kac, your husband is coming," Bluejay had said to the man's wife early that morning. The woman had her hair cut short, in widow's fashion, for it was believed that her husband had drowned. "He's coming back to-day," Bluejay said. And sure enough, her husband appeared. She was very much surprised for she did not think that he would ever return. The man reported that his young brother had been eaten up by the birds.

After that it was decreed that dried salmon should be given to people who were tabu; any kind of dried salmon would serve the purpose. The people were happy to have the fisherman back again and gave a big feast to celebrate his return. Everyone had a good time. By this time, the widower was able to fish again.

THE TWO OLD WOMEN.[3]

There were two old maids who lived back in the woods at Cowlitz. Because they lived alone, they had to do all their own work. They

[1] The Up. Ch. call the old man Ne'pius; see pp. 79, 92.
[2] Up. Ch., p. 121.
[3] Told by Sophie Smith, 1926; see p. 420.

went together to hunt, to pick berries, to gather roots for baskets. When there was any house work to do, they did it together. They also made baskets together. But there was one thing that each could do separately; one could bring water, one could gather wood. In the fall, one would bring home a lot of wood and the other would pack all the water that they needed. After they had spent most of their lives doing this and were quite old, the elder said, "Let's trade work, just for once." The other said, "All right." It was already late in the fall. The elder, taking the younger's place, started out to bring in the water. She was carrying one large basket and a small one that held about a gallon. When she got to the river, she dipped the small basket full and set it out of reach. Then she dipped the large basket into the water and brought it up full. But when she tried to lift it, it was so heavy that it slipped out of her hands. Losing her balance, she fell into the water and smashed to pieces. She turned into rocks there. Sometimes the rocks appear to be wrinkled. They were believed to be good medicine. They were heated and applied as poultices. They are far down the river, close to shore.

In the meantime, the other woman started out to get a lot of bark for winter fire-wood. Having some idea how it should be done, she first cut around the tree and started to ply the bark loose with a long pole. She worked at it for some time. Finally she managed to split a large piece off, but when it fell, it smashed her to pieces. At first, nothing was left of her but blood. After a little while, the blood turned into red huckleberries. The berries can still be seen there on the trees and bushes. That was the end of the two old women.[1]

THE SCATTER CREEK TALE.[2]

There was an old lady who lived at Scatter Creek (waɬa'lən). She had a grandson, a little boy. The little boy played close to the creek. "Scatter Creek is nothing but moss," he said. One day his grandmother said to him, "Cut a spear pole. Before long this creek will be full of silverside. You must have your pole ready; then you will spear many salmon and we shall dry them." "The silverside will never come up here. This creek is nothing but moss," the boy said.

It started to rain and the creek began to rise. Then the salmon started to come up the creek. There were lots of silverside. The boy ran to cut some poles for his spears. He started to whittle, but worked left-handed. He was holding his whittling toward him. Then his knife slipped and cut his stomach open. His entrails came right out. The boy died.

[1] I first heard this story, in abbreviated form, from Mrs. Smith's young grandson, who was about eight years old. When Mrs. Smith learned that I had heard it from him, she was quite amused and offered to tell it to me. She had told the boy the story a short time before.

[2] Told by James Cheholts, 1927; see p. 420.

COYOTE AND THE RIVER BEING.[1]

Coyote was living near the Cowlitz River. He had two young men as neighbors. Every time anyone started to cross the river, they would drown, for a dangerous being would swallow them. "I can kill that dangerous being," Coyote said. "You'd better not try it," his two neighbors said. "I'll choke him to death," Coyote said. He started to make a raft. He got some big, long logs and tied them together. It took him a long time to complete the raft. Finally, he said to the two young men, "I'll start to-morrow morning." The young men were afraid that he would drown. Coyote got on his raft and away he went, shouting and yelling. "Good-bye, Coyote," the young men said. He went up and up and finally disappeared. "Coyote is gone. Evidently he's been swallowed," the young men said. "What shall we do now?" they asked one another. "Let's make a canoe and go after him." They made a canoe and fastened arrow points along the sides. It took five days to complete it. They worked very fast in order to rescue Coyote before he died. "We'll cut the dangerous being open," they said.

The dangerous being had a dog and a little bird to keep watch for him. Whenever the little bird saw anyone coming, it would say, "Yɪt, yɪt, yɪt." This would awaken the dog, and he would bark, "Ha ha, ha ha." The dangerous being would hear the dog and open its mouth. The two young men crept softly up to the bird so that the dog would not notice them. They had some Indian paint and showed it to the bird. The bird began to sing, and thereupon the dog started to bark. "Oh, I was just singing in my sleep," the bird said to the dog. The young men painted the bird very prettily with spots. "Be free. Don't sit here with this dog and the dangerous being," they said. The bird flew away, much pleased with its nice appearance. The dog was now sound asleep. The young men took out a big knife and cut his throat. Then they beat him to pieces. Since that time, people have had only common dogs, not dangerous ones. It was five days since Coyote had been swallowed. The young men got into their canoe and paddled toward the dangerous being. One sat in the bow and one in the stern. The dangerous being opened his mouth and they paddled right into it. They cut him right in two with their sharp-edged canoe. Out came Coyote, still riding on his raft. "Hi · · · ·, didn't I say I'd choke that dangerous being to death!" he said.

Drift logs had formed a jam in the river and this was where the people drowned. "Hereafter, drift logs will pile up for a little while and then burst. They shall never again be a dangerous being," the young men said.

---

[1] Told by Sophie Smith, 1926; see p. 390.

COYOTE AND HIS SON.[1]

Coyote was living up the Cowlitz River, in the hills, with his son. The young man had four wives, who lived together. Each day, he went out to hunt deer. Coyote stayed home and helped the women with the wood. They lived in a long house with a fireplace at either end. Two of the women stayed together at one end of the house, and the other two, at the opposite end. Sometimes their husband slept at one end of the house, and sometimes at the other. Coyote slept along one side of the house, near the middle.

One day Coyote brought in some cedar wood (which pops very readily when burned). The wood popped, and the women, in their hurry to get out of the way, jumped. Coyote could see their legs. "Oh, what white legs you have, sisters," he said to one pair of women. At the end of five days, he desired the pair with white legs. "What shall I do, steal my son's wives?" he thought. One of the women of the first pair had a baby. The other two, whom Coyote desired, had been married more recently, and neither had a baby.

One morning, just at day-break, the old man went out to a little hill and relieved himself there. His excrements were left in a little sharp-pointed heap, resembling a bird. "Hw · · · ·," he whistled to them, whereupon they turned into a pretty bird. Then he said, making a wish about the little hill, "Turn into a mountain." He ran back to the house and found that his son had just got up. The young man was wearing his beaded clothing. "Son, quick, get your bow and arrow. There's a nice bird outside," he said. Both ran out quickly. The young man hit the bird right in the center and knocked it over. Then he began to climb up the hill after it. "Son, take off your clothes before you climb; you might get them dirty," Coyote said. The young man then pulled off his fine beaded cap and clothes and left them at the foot of the hill. The hill grew taller all the time, for Coyote kept saying, "Hw · · · ·, hw · · · ·." When he got to the very top, the young man saw that the bird was nothing but Coyote's excrements; his arrow was sticking to them. "Oh, the dirty thing!" he said. He looked over the side of the bluff but could see nothing but rocks; it was so high he could not get off. If he should fall, he would kill himself.

Coyote put on all his son's clothes and grabbed the sack holding the bow and arrow. Breakfast was waiting. The two women at the far end of the house said, "It looks like Coyote coming." The two women who had white legs did not notice the difference. After breakfast, Coyote lay down on their side of the house and covered up. After a while, he said, "Wonder what became of the old man? He must have gone off somewhere." "Did you see the bird?" the two women asked. "No, I didn't see it," he said. He lived with the women five days and then he thought, "One can never tell; he

[1] Told by Sophie Smith, 1926; see p. 389.

may come back." "Let's move, let's get some fresh air," he said to the women. They packed up, getting ready to move. The two who lived at the far end of the house asked one another, "Shall we go?" "Yes," they finally said, "the others will be angry with us if we don't. Coyote must have killed his son." Before they left, they hid some dried salmon high up in the house, so that their husband, in case he should return, would find something to eat.

They camped four nights. Coyote and the two women camped together; the other two women camped some distance behind them.

The fifth day of the young man's stay on the bluff, old woman Spider came there. "What's the matter?" she asked. The young man then told her the trick that his father had played on him. "Can you help me?" he asked. "Yes, I have some twine," the old woman said. She always walked on twine and had a large basket full with her. She tied him up and lowered him over the side of the bluff. The string ran clear to the bottom. When he reached the ground, the young man ran for home. Everyone was gone. He looked around for something to eat, for he was starving. He found some dried salmon and berries, already cooked, hidden far up in the house. He put on his old clothes and hunted around until he found Coyote's and the women's tracks. He followed them and arrived late in the evening at the place where they were camping. He came upon the two women with the baby. "Coyote and the other two women are a little farther on," the women said. The mother of the baby, just for the sake of starting a quarrel, decided to ask Coyote to give his son's clothing to her for the baby. Coyote pretended that he did not know what she was talking about. The old man refused flatly to give them up. The young man stayed that night with his two [faithful] wives. In the morning, after breakfast, Coyote noticed a man with the two women. Before long, he saw him coming. Coyote had dressed in all his pretty clothes for breakfast. "Give me my clothes," the young man said. "Here are your clothes, son, and your wives. I didn't do anything to your women-folks, I'm too old," Coyote said. "Never mind, you may have the women now," the young man said, and walked off with his clothes. He started back home with his two wives, without inviting Coyote and the other two women to return with them.

The young man and his two wives lived alone at one end of the house. Then Coyote came with the two women and asked to be taken back. The young man killed a deer but gave Coyote only enough meat for one meal. "Come with me early in the morning. I'll kill a big deer and you may have some of the meat," he said.

Coyote and the two women got ready. On the way, they crossed the Cowlitz River on a tree that had fallen across. Then Coyote's son said, "Hw····, hw····," wishing for rain. The rain poured down. He had thought of a trick to play on Coyote and the women. He gave a certain amount of meat to each of them to pack. He had wished for high-water to wash out the foot-log on their way back. When they returned to the river, the foot-log was gone. It was still raining and the river was high. "What shall we do?" Coyote asked. "We'll wade across," the young man said. He made a long stout pole for the others to hold on to, and started ahead. The water kept getting deeper and deeper, and they were soon soaked through. When almost to the other side, the young man let go of the pole. Coyote stumbled and the pole floated down stream. The packs became tangled, and the two women drowned. They turned into mice.

Coyote turned over on his back and went floating down stream. On the way, he grabbed at all kinds of sticks and bushes. "Help me, my brother," he would say. He grabbed at some cotton-wood and it broke immediately. "You're not good for anything. You'll be used only for firewood," he said. He grabbed at all kinds of sticks and gave them names. Oak helped him, he swung him ashore. "You'll be one of the best trees of all," he said, "your bark will be used for skin medicine, your berries [acorns] will be eaten, your roots and everything belonging to you will be put to some use." Fir broke when he grabbed him, so he said, "You'll be good for nothing but firewood." Cedar threw him ashore, so he said to him, "You'll be the best tree of all. Your bark and roots will be used for making baskets, your wood for making canoes, dishes and all kinds of things. Medicine will also be made from you." Each time after being swung ashore, he would jump back into the water and float on.

After floating for a long time, he became very hungry. At last he came to Cowlitz prairie. "Oh, I know what to do," he said, and turned into a large long-handled wooden spoon, lying near the spring. Early in the morning a woman came to the spring to get some water. "What a nice spoon!" she said. She had never seen one before. She grabbed it and took it back to the house. "I found a spoon," she said. She was making a stew and used the spoon to stir it with. Suddenly there was no stew left. "Has it burnt up?" she said. She had some berries in a dish, ready to eat. She wiped the spoon clean and dipped it into the berries. The berries also disappeared. She made some more stew and then something said, "It's Coyote." "Wonder if it is?" she thought, and threw the spoon outside. "E · · ·, I had a good breakfast!" Coyote cried. He went back to the river and floated away. At supper time, another woman found a large wooden dish and put some food in it. The dish ate all the food. At last she thought, "It's Coyote," and threw the dish out. Coyote jumped back into the water and shouted, "E · · ·, I had a good supper!" At Kelso he turned into a horn spoon, and at a fourth place, a cooking vessel. Each time the same thing happened.

At last he came to the mouth of the Cowlitz. Five girls there owned a dam, which kept the fish from ascending the river.[1] "What

[1] See Ho'tsani, Up. Ch., p. 137.

can I do here?" he wondered. Finally he decided to turn into a cute little baby on a cradle-board, prettily beaded. "The girls will find me and take care of me," he thought. He turned himself into a baby and lay on the ground as if drowned. In the morning the eldest girl came to the river to get some water and noticed the baby. It had landed on the beach only a short time before, so it seemed. She looked it over and found it half dead; it was shivering from the cold. She ran with it to the house. "Oh, look, I've found a little baby!" she said. The others ran to see. "It might be Coyote," the youngest said. "Oh, how could it be, such a cute little baby!" the others said. They untied the baby and found that it was a boy. They gave him soup and he swallowed it. "He's dressed so well, he must belong to some rich people; his clothing is elaborately beaded and furred. Perhaps his mother drowned," they said. They tore up their own clothes to make some for the baby. They watched over him carefully and fed him. After a while, in response to their attention, he smiled. He was the cutest thing imaginable! The youngest girl strongly disapproved of her sisters' behavior; she would have nothing to do with the baby. "It must be Coyote," she thought.

Coyote grew to be a big boy; he could now walk around and was always laughing. The girls were delighted with him and kept him dressed very prettily. He learned to whittle and made little things. They put jingles around his waist and tied him to a post, so he would not run off. He had a knife and a stick for whittling and made a nice root-digger for each of the girls. "Don't use it," the youngest said, "he might be Coyote, he grew so quickly." "Oh, you never saw Coyote!" the others said.

The four elder girls used the digging-stick for digging lacamas. One day, one of the girls broke her stick.[1] It smelled like a dead person; the stick had been made from a dead person's rib. Whenever the girls were out digging, Coyote would work at the dam. He would work at it every day, all day long. He would also eat everything he could find in the house. Just before the girls returned in the evening, he would turn into a baby again. As soon as the digging-stick broke, the girls ran home. "Something must have happened," they said. The boy was gone! "It's Coyote," the youngest said. They ran to the river. There was Coyote, working at the dam. He had just a little more to do before the dam would burst. He was wearing a wooden hat to protect himself from their blows. They beat him on the head, but he kept on working. "Hit away at your own head," he said. They broke his hat but he put on another; he had five hats. They broke one hat after another, but he kept on working. Each time they broke a hat, he said, "Hit away at your own head." At last, he burst open the dam. "Hurrah, my people, down!" he cried. He had made a mistake; all the large fish went down the [Columbia] river. "Up, up, my people!" he cried. But

[1] An ill-omen.

it was too late; only small fish went up the [Cowlitz] river. He jumped to the opposite side of the river and shouted across to the girls, "Stay where you are forever and live on dead fish. There shall never again be a dam in the river to keep the fish from going up." (The girls became white birds that live near the ocean.)

Coyote went on up the river. On the way, he became very hungry. "Come, my people, come, my people," he said to the salmon. "C · · ·," he heard, and a fish came to shore. He grabbed it but it was too slippery to hold. He could not catch any fish. "Come, my people," he kept saying. After a while, he thought, "How shall I kill them so I can have something to eat?" "E · · ·, my sisters, what shall I do to kill the salmon?" he asked. "Oh, you will say, 'That's just what I was forgetting,'" [his sisters said]. "If you don't tell me, I'll bring the hail," he said. "When the salmon come in droves, hit them on the head. Then split and roast them on sticks," his sisters said. He put his sisters back where they belonged and said, "Oh, I knew that all along." His so-called sisters were his excrements of huckleberries. They always feared the hail, for it would smash them. He said again to the salmon, "Come, my people." He clubbed and killed five salmon. Then he roasted them on sticks standing around the fire.

The salmon, very nice and reddish looking, were just about done, when five little boys (birds) noticed them. "Oh, Coyote is cooking salmon," they said. "Hw · · · ·, go to sleep, Coyote." Coyote soon became very sleepy. "I'll take a little sleep and then eat the salmon," he said. While he was sleeping, the boys ate all the salmon. Then they greased Coyote's hands and mouth and piled sticks around him. "Hw · · ·, wake up, Coyote," they said, and went away. "Oh, I forgot all about my salmon," Coyote said as soon as he had awakened. "My, it tastes good. I must have eaten some of it. It certainly tastes like salmon." He had tasted the grease on his mouth. Then he noticed the grease on his hands. "It seems I have eaten it already, although I am still hungry." The boys did the same thing to him five times. Then he began to wonder, "Why, if I have eaten, am I still hungry?" He took his sisters out and asked them, "Why is it that I cannot satisfy my hunger?" "When you cook your salmon, some boys come and eat it up. As soon as your salmon begins to cook, eat it," his sisters said. "Oh, I knew that but I forgot," he said. He killed some more salmon and ate them just as soon as they were cooked enough. Finally he became satiated and went on.

He had not gone far, when he noticed something. "Oh, there are the boys cooking eggs," he said. The five boys were cooking pheasant eggs. "Oh, I'm going to pay them back," he said. "Hw · · · ·, go to sleep, boys." The boys became sleepy and lay down. Then he had a good time eating eggs. He smeared the boys' mouths and hands with eggs and put an empty shell alongside each of them. When he had finished, he went a long distance away and said, "Hw · · · ·, wake up, boys." Then he went on, as fast as he could go. After a while, the boys woke up. "You've been eating my eggs," one said to another. "No, you've been eating mine," the other said. They accused one another, but each denied the theft. Then they began to think about it and finally said, "It must have been Coyote; he paid us back. Let's go away from the river, so we won't meet him again."

Coyote kept on going up the river. Finally, he made a camp not far from Cowlitz Prairie, but on the opposite side of the river. He started work on a canoe and caught some salmon. A few of the salmon, he intended to dry. While dressing a male salmon, he noticed two white round things inside. "How pretty these two things are! What can I make from them?" he said. Away from camp, the leaves were beginning to fall. He went there and found two leaves lying side by side. He lay each of the round things on a leaf, and covered each leaf with another. "Whatever you turn into, I shall be very pleased," he said. "I wish for the very best thing I can think of, the best thing I have ever seen." He then went back to the river and spent the whole afternoon working on his canoe. One morning while he was trying his canoe out on the river, he heard someone laughing, "E, ε, ε.." It sounded like girls. If this were his wish come true, it was more than he had expected. He looked far out and then close by. Then he saw two girls, wearing very pretty blankets. They were small, very fair and had hair that was almost red. He was so proud of them that he nearly died. "My daughters, my daughters," he said happily, "come here! This is our camp." The girls covered their heads with their blankets. "Come here, I'll cook you some salmon," he said. The girls then arose and shook their blankets. He cooked some salmon hurriedly. "Your mothers are dead. I had two wives, who died long ago; each of them bore me a daughter," he explained. The two girls stayed with him and he taught them how to make baskets and to dress salmon. When the canoe was finished, he said, "We are going to move now to the place where your mothers died." The girls had been with him several months already. On the way to the new place, his eyes became very sore; he was now almost blind. They had to make camp, for he was too sick to go on. Then he became very foolish; one night he went to the girls and said, "My wives," trying to embrace them. The girls were angry and gave him a pounding. "I'm just an old man, your father," he said. The next day, he said, trying to mislead them, "Oh, daughters, last night I dreamed of your mothers. I dreamed they were with me; maybe I'm going to die soon." The girls pounded him again. Another night he came to them and said, "Be good to me, wives." The next day, the younger girl said, "Don't you think it possible that this old man is Coyote? He might very well be here, right at Cowlitz Prairie." "Well, he's blind; we can soon find out if he is," the elder girl said. Each packed all her belongings in one large basket. Then they put the old man in the canoe and pushed him far out into the river. Coyote knew immediately what had happened: the girls were running away. He looked back and saw them walking up the hill on Cowlitz Prairie. "Oh, daughters," he called, "I'm better now. Come back and get me." "No," they called back.

Coyote went on, wandering, as he had always done. That was the last of him. The girls married very nice men and lived thereafter in Cowlitz country. The girls were very fair. That's why Cowlitz people are fair now.

BUNGLING HOST.[1]

There was Coyote and his wife and Grizzlybear and his wife. Coyote had a son and Grizzly had a daughter. The two young people got married. The young man also married Fish Duck's daughter. Coyote now had two friends — two in-laws — Grizzlybear and Fish Duck.

Coyote and his wife lived on little fish and small game like chipmunks, things that were easy to kill. One day Coyote went to visit Fish Duck. "Ah, in-law," he said to Fish Duck, who was sitting on a tree looking for salmon under the ice. Soon Fish Duck saw a salmon. He dived down, broke the ice and caught the salmon. "Eat it," he said, offering the fish to Coyote. "No, I'll save it for my old woman," Coyote said. "No, eat it, I'll give you another one for your wife," Fish Duck said. He dived down onto the ice again, broke it and caught a big salmon. Coyote packed the salmon home. "I live the same as you do. Come over to see me," he said when leaving.

"I must go to see Coyote, I must see how he lives," Fish Duck said one day. As soon as Fish Duck arrived, Coyote went to a tree and sat there. Then he dived down on the ice to break it and get a salmon, as Fish Duck had done. Instead, he bumped his head and lay there dead. After a while Fish Duck thought, "I'll bet Coyote tried to do as I did." He went out, broke the ice and got a salmon. He brought the salmon back to Coyote's wife. "Your husband will recover after a while. He's lying senseless on the ice," he said. After a while Coyote recovered. He saw the hole in the ice and said, "That's what I thought; I caught a fish."

Not long afterward, Coyote said, "I must see what my in-law Grizzlybear is doing." Soon after Coyote arrived, Grizzlybear sharpened his knife. Then he cut some fat off his wife's breast. It was a good piece of meat. He held it over the fire to cook. Then he held his hands over the fire to melt the grease from them. He caught the grease in a large bowl. He gave the meat and grease to Coyote. "I'll save a piece of the meat to take home to my old woman,"

[1] Told by Mary Iley, 1926; see p. 393.

Coyote said. "Oh no, I'll give you another piece for her," Grizzly said. Then he cut another piece of fat from his wife's breast. "Come to see me," Coyote said when he left.

One day Grizzly said to his wife, "I must go to see Coyote, to see how he makes his living; he never hunts or fishes." "Oh, he'll probably do as you did, and kill his wife or himself," his wife said.

Soon after his arrival, Grizzly heard Coyote sharpening his knife. Then Coyote tried to cut a piece of meat from his wife's breast. She began to cry out. She was too old and skinny. "You can't get anything from me!" she cried. Coyote held his hands over the fire to melt the fat from them. The muscles began to draw up and he wept from the pain. Grizzlybear said, "Oh, you think you can do as I do!" He cut a piece of flesh from each side of his body and gave it to Coyote. Then he held his hands over the fire and caught four or five bowls full of grease. Then he left for home. When he got there, he said to his wife, "Coyote almost killed himself and his wife. He tried to cut some meat from his wife's breast and hurt her. Then he held his hands over the fire and the muscles drew up. I left him some meat and grease."

X̣wα'NI AND COON.[1]

X̣wα'ni and Coon were brothers. They were living at a certain place. X̣wα'ni killed a tiny animal of some sort and cooked and ate it. Coon went out to the road where the Yellowjackets were going by with dried salmon. A Yellowjacket gave him one dried salmon and he took it home. "Where did you get it?" X̣wα'ni asked. "I went over to the swamp and picked some skunk-cabbage. Then I put it under my pillow and it turned into dried salmon," Coon said. "Oh, you'll see, brother! I'll do that and make a lot of dried salmon," X̣wα'ni said. He got a lot of skunk-cabbage and put it under his pillow. The next morning, it was still skunk-cabbage. Then he said, "I'm going to the road and sit there." Both he and Coon went to the road and sat there. X̣wα'ni was smoking and the Yellowjackets, who were passing by, gave him a lot of dried salmon. They gave only one salmon to Coon. They gave more to X̣wα'ni because they were afraid of him; he was smoking, therefore he must be a doctor. X̣wα'ni finally had a lot of salmon, more than ten. Then he stole a pack and then another. "They'll sting us now," Coon thought. Finally the Yellowjackets became angry and stung him. They took all the dried salmon away from him and left him there. His body began to swell all over. He lay there all night. The next morning his face was so swollen that he had to pull his eyes open to see. "You stole their salmon; that's why they stung me," he said to Coon. He was very sick.

---

[1] Told by Mary Iley, 1926; see p. 384.

Coon went to the river and ate craw-fish; he always liked to eat them. "Take your clothes off, close your eyes and sit on a bush; then you'll catch craw-fish too," he said to X̣wα'ni one day. He tricked X̣wα'ni. X̣wα'ni did as Coon said. He took his pants off and closed his eyes.[1] "Let the craw-fish come and I'll catch them," he said. Then after a little while, "Oh, they're going to eat me up now." He opened his eyes but there was nothing but ants between his legs. He got a stick and scraped them off. Next morning, he was badly swollen where the ants had bitten him. Someone was always fooling X̣wα'ni; he would always believe what they said.

One day Coon told him that if he split some cedar-bark [with his organ], the bark would turn into dried salmon. He did as Coon said but did not get any dried salmon.

"The lui'pam and the pi'tspam will kill you if you don't stop eating bull-fish and craw-fish at the river," X̣wα'ni said to Coon one day. Coon paid no attention; he went each day to the river. Then X̣wα'ni painted himself with black stripes, to look like a lui'pam and a pi'tspam. He took his bow and arrow and went to the river. He shot Coon and then ran back to the house. He washed his face immediately and put his bow and arrow back where it belonged. Then he lay down by the fire and blew into the ashes in order to get himself covered with dust [Coon would think that he had been lying there a long time]. Coon came staggering into the house; he was so sick, he could scarcely see. "I can doctor you," X̣wα'ni said. He took hold of Coon's fat and pulled it out. The blood began to run out. He ate the fat and Coon died. Then he skinned him and roasted him. At last he had something to eat. He ate every bit of Coon's meat. Then he became hungry again. "I must go some place and get something to eat, I'm so hungry," he said.

He met old lady Mole. She was cooking lacamas; she had one large and one small pack of lacamas. "Oh, I'm going to eat all her lacamas," he said. "Oh, I'm hungry; give me some lacamas. I'm so hungry. There are five of us and we are very weak now," he said to her. Mole spilled out a lot of lacamas for him and he ate them very quickly. Then he ran off and came out ahead of her. "Did you meet my brother Coon? We are very weak now from hunger," he said. The woman gave him some more lacamas and he ate them very quickly. Then he ran through the woods and came out ahead of her. "Did you meet my two brothers on the way? We're very weak now from hunger," he said. The woman took a good look at his eyes. "This is the same man I met before," she thought. He ran ahead and met her once more. After the fourth time, the woman thought, "I'll bet this is X̣wα'ni. He is known always to want more and more of everything." She found a nest of white-tailed hornets and put it in her basket. Then she covered the nest with a layer of

[1] This passage has been toned down. He is supposed to catch the craw-fish with his organ.

lacamas, about three inches deep. "Oh, here he is again," she said. "Oh, did you meet my brothers?" X̣wα'ni asked. "Yes, four of them," she said. She gave him the basket and told him to eat the lacamas in a hollow stump. He went to a hollow stump some distance away and crouched there inside. "Close," he said to the stump. "Close," he said again, and the stump closed completely. "Open," he said, and the stump opened. "Close, close," he said. Then he ate the lacamas. "Hαm·, hαm·," the hornets said. "I'm eating the last of the lacamas. Go away!" X̣wα'ni said. At last all the hornets came out of the basket and stung him all over his face and body. He fell down and died. (The hornets also died for they die after they sting anyone twice.)[1]

After a while, X̣wα'ni woke up. "Open," he said. But the stump did not open. He was so hungry that he began to tear off his own flesh and eat it. Finally, nothing was left of him but bones. He had even eaten his eyes. Then Woodpecker came and pecked at the stump. It was the big Red-headed Woodpecker (kʋ'təkʋtə). Then all the birds came to help Woodpecker. Together they made a very large hole and carried X̣wα'ni out. He was dead. They walked over him and prayed until he came to life. He could no longer see for his eyes were gone. He picked some dog-wood blossoms and used them for eyes. As long as the blossoms were fresh, he could see well. As soon as they wilted, he got fresh ones. Then he painted the birds for helping him. He painted big Woodpecker red and white, little Woodpecker with black and white dots. The birds were very pleased to have this done to them.

X̣wα'ni met a boy who was hunting with a bow and arrow. "What are you doing?" he asked the boy. "Hunting for deer," the boy answered. "Have you killed any yet?" "No," the boy answered. "Can you see that, — way over there?" X̣wα'ni asked. "No," the boy answered. "Then take my eyes and you can see it," X̣wα'ni said. The boy took X̣wα'ni's eyes. "Do you see it now?" X̣wα'ni asked. "Yes, I see a lot of deer," the boy said. "Pi · · · · · ·," X̣wα'ni had said, to make the deer appear. They traded eyes and first the boy could see everything. X̣wα'ni was glad to have some real eyes. The poor boy's eyes wilted and he was left blind. (His name is weł.)[2]

X̣wα'ni went on and met another boy, who was jumping around. Every time the boy jumped, he flatulated. "Let's trade. It's not nice for you to have such an anus, but it's all right for me, I'm old," X̣wα'ni said. And so they traded anuses. X̣wα'ni flatulated every step he took. "What a funny man I'm going to be now!" he said. After a while he became weak from flatulating so much; all his wind was gone. He had two sisters, to whom he always lied after they gave him advice. "What shall I do?" he asked them. "Trade back," they said. "Oh, I knew that but I just forgot," he said.

[1] A belief which the Whites also have.
[2] A bird?

"Here's your anus; I'm giving it back to you. Give me mine," he said to the boy. The boy took his anus and ran away happily.

X̣wα′ni took his eyes out and threw them into the air, catching them as they came down. He was playing ball with his eyes. Finally, a big black bird, Raven (qwaqʷ), came by. He caught one of the eyes while it was still in the air and ran away with it. X̣wα′ni had no way to get it back. He had to go on with only one eye.

An old woman was mashing lacamas. Her grandchildren were away, attending a game; the people were playing with X̣wα′ni's eye. "What are you doing, grandmother?" X̣wα′ni asked. "I'm mashing lacamas for my grandchildren. They are away, watching a game. Raven found X̣wα′ni's eye; the people play with it each day," the old lady said. "I'll get her granddaughters to take me to the game; then I can get my eye back," X̣wα′ni thought. He killed the old woman and put on her clothes and hair. Then he finished mashing the lacamas. Before long, he heard someone laughing: the girls were returning. He put the lacamas on a large pan and gave them the pan. The lacamas were not mashed well. "Oh, grandmother, these aren't good," the girls said. "Oh, girls, I'm getting old; I can't mash well every day," X̣wα′ni said. "The game has been going on two or three days now. Poor grandmother, we promised to take her to-morrow," the girls said to one another. It was very easy for X̣wα′ni to deceive the girls, for their old grandmother also had only one eye. The next day, they combed and braided their grandmother's hair nicely. They put a hat and moccasins on her. The eldest girl packed her first. "You're hurting me. Don't hold me so tightly; hold me a little more loosely," the old lady said to her. The girl held her more loosely. Then the old lady slid down low and tried to do something bad to her. The girl reproached her. "You'll do the same yourself when you're old like me," the old lady said. When the eldest girl was tired of packing her grandmother, the second eldest sister took her. The four elder girls packed her in turn and each time, the old lady tried to do the same thing. The youngest girl held the old lady high up on her shoulders. "A, a, a, that hurts me! Carry me lower down," the old lady said. The girl held her a little lower and then the old lady tried some funny-business. The girl then held her high up on her neck and ran fast with her. When she arrived at the game, she threw her down hard on the ground. "Why are you trying to hurt your grandmother? You should pack her nicely," the people said. The old lady took a place close to the door. The people were lined up around the room, dancing. They were passing the eye from one person to another. When the old woman took the eye, she sang, "It's my eye." The second time, she also sang, "It's my eye." Now Bluejay used to know everything. He said, "She said, 'It's my eye'". "No she didn't; she said, 'I wish it were my eye,'" one of the old lady's granddaughters said. The third time the old lady took the eye, Bluejay said again, "She said, 'It's my eye.'" "No, she said, 'I wish it were my eye,'" the girl said. The fourth time, Bluejay said again, "She said, 'It's my eye.'" "No, she said, 'I wish it were my eye,'" the girl said. The fifth time around, the old lady jumped and danced. She threw the eye into the air and it fell into her eye-socket. Then she ran outside, crying, "*ɩɯɩ*." "If you have a girl," she called back to the girls, "name it wəpa'ls (handle of a root-digger). If it is a boy, name it tawa'shweyə [roasting stick?]." Then the people shouted, "Oh, you've seen grandmother!" The girls looked for their old grandmother and found her dead. She was naked. X̣wα'ni had killed her and got himself up to look like her. They walked over her and prayed, walked over her and prayed, until she came to life. "What happened?" they asked. "A man came here and asked about you. Then he killed me," the old lady said.

X̣wα'ni went far off. At last he found many young children. They were the children of a dangerous being, the giant woman, who always carried a basket. The children bit pieces out of his legs and ate the pieces. There were ten or fifteen children living in the one house. He took a stick and killed them, but one after another, they came to life. Then he ran off and asked his sisters what to do. "There are some circles hanging from the ceiling. These are the children's hearts or souls.[1] If you cut them, the children will die," they said. "Oh, that's just what I was forgetting," X̣wα'ni said. He went back and cut all the circles. Each child then lay down and died. He cut both little and big circles. That was the end of all the basket beings.

X̣Wα'NI PAINTS THE BIRDS.[2]

Once upon a time X̣wα'ni was travelling far up in Klickitat country. He wanted to make something but did not know what to make. He sang,

What nice thing can I make,
What nice thing can I eat?

Someone was coming, so he hid in a hollow cedar. The stranger looked around. "I wonder who was singing?" he said. Then X̣wα'ni wished that the cedar had no opening. In just a little while, the cedar closed completely. He intended to order the cedar to open as soon as the stranger passed by. He stayed there for a long time. At last he could no longer hear anyone. In the meantime, he had become very hungry. He chewed at a stick but it did not taste good. Then he took a bite of his own flesh. He ate of it until he became very, very thin. "I'm going to eat my testicles," he said. He tossed one into his mouth and bit into it. "Oh, it's fine," he said and sucked

[1] The terms for heart and soul differ. I believe soul is meant.
[2] Told by Lucy Youckton, 1926; see p. 385.

at it. "I'd better eat the other one," he said. It also tasted very good. Then he shouted to the cedar, "Open up! I wish you'd open up." He shouted five times. Finally some little birds heard him. They pecked and pecked and pecked at the stump. "Make a hole for me," X̣wα'ni cried. "Come on," they said, "let's make a hole for X̣wα'ni." Woodpecker and several others, — five in all, pecked day and night at the stump. "Work hard, I'm just about dead," X̣wα'ni said. They kept pecking until they had made a hole large enough for him to crawl out. "I'm going to give you something nice for this," X̣wα'ni said. "I can paint you any color you wish. I can paint you nicely. What color would you like on your head?" Tc'qwɛ'[1] wanted to have his head painted red, some red across his breast, white on his stomach, and black on the rest of his body. As soon as he had been painted, he flew a little. "You look nice, you look fine!" X̣wα'ni said. Tci'ə[2] wanted to have spots all over his body, — red, white, yellow and black spots. It took X̣wα'ni a long time to paint him. He painted his tail orange and red and his wings the same. When he had finished with him, he had him spotted all over. "Go on now, I want to see you fly," he said. "Oh, you look fine!" "What color would you like?" he asked Woodpecker (qaqα'm). Woodpecker wanted only his head painted, as red as could be, and a tiny spot on his wings. As soon as he had finished, X̣wα'ni said, "Go on now, I want to see you fly." "Fine! You look fine!" he said. "Kɛt, kɛt, kɛt," Woodpecker sings on the alders and cedars. "Sit down and I'll paint you," X̣wα'ni said to Robin. "I want just my belly painted yellow," Robin said.[3]

X̣WΑ'NI ON THE CHEHALIS RIVER.[4]

X̣wα'ni was travelling around fixing the world. He was close to the river. He was hungry. "Oh, I'm going to make a trap to catch Chinook salmon," he said. He got some sticks and tied them together with cedar to make a little box. This was on the Chehalis River, not far from Wakina. "Who can tell me when there's a salmon in the trap? I wonder if my excrements can tell me," he said. He sat down and relieved himself. Then he kicked his excrements. "Tell me when a salmon comes in my trap," he said. He had not gone far, when his watchman called, "A salmon is coming!" There was something white in the trap; the water, flowing swiftly, had left a bit of foam there. "That's not a salmon!" he said. "If you lie to me again, I'll call someone to eat you. Make sure it's a salmon before you call me." Before long, he heard his watchman calling. "A salmon has a little bone here and a little bone there," he ex-

---

[1] English equivalent unknown.
[2] See footnote above.
[3] There was a fifth but the narrator had forgotten it.
[4] Told by Lucy Youckton, 1926; see p. 387.

plained. "If you lie to me again, I'll call someone to eat you." His watchman called again. "Oh, he's just lying," he said. When he got to his trap, he found a few dried leaves there. "Come, rain, smash him!" he said. Then his watchman said, "I won't make a mistake again." He walked a short distance away. Then his watchman called him. This was the fourth time. He ran to his trap but when he got there, found only a few little sticks. "I'll throw you away!" he said to his watchman. He walked away. He had just about reached camp, when his watchman called for the fifth time. He let him call for a long time. When he got to his trap, he found a salmon. He was very much pleased. "You're so good to me," he said to his watchman and put him back inside him.

He went to camp. The salmon was very nice. He cut off the head, the tail, took out the insides, cut the body into four or five pieces. Then he made a roasting stick and roasted the salmon over the fire. It looked very nice. By this time, he was tired from running around so much. "I'm so tired," he said, "I'll lie down and take a little rest." Then Mink (ts'mα'lq̣en) came. "I smell salmon. It smells good," he said. Then he saw the fire. "Someone is cooking salmon," he said. "Oh, X̣wα'ni is cooking salmon." He saw that X̣wα'ni was asleep. He ate all of the salmon, — the head, the insides, the tail. After he had finished, he mashed a bit of the meat and smeared the grease on X̣wα'ni's mouth.

After a while, X̣wα'ni woke up. "Oh my, I'm hungry!" he said. "Oh my, I was cooking salmon, wasn't I?" "It's all gone! I must have eaten it all!" Then he noticed the grease on his mouth. "Oh, it smells nice! Did I really eat it?" he said. "Maybe someone came here and ate it." There was a bit of salmon left on the roasting-stick and he ate it. After a while he said, "I'll bet Mink ate my salmon. He's a mean fellow; he always does something like that." He saw someone coming; Mink was thirsty and had come back for a drink of water. Then X̣wα'ni headed him off and urinated in the water. "Here's some water," Mink said and lay down flat to drink. "So I've caught you! You ate my salmon; that's why you're so thirsty," X̣wα'ni said to himself. "Mink is a bad fellow; he left me hungry." And so he ran back and urinated in another creek. He urinated in five creeks. Each time Mink came to a creek, he said, "What a nice little creek!" and lay down to drink. Each time X̣wα'ni hid and watched him. "Maybe he'll get sick from this," he thought. Mink did get sick; he vomited and vomited something yellow. "I'll go up the river now where Mink can't catch me," X̣wα'ni said.

He went up the river to catch some salmon. He turned aside into a creek and started to build a falls. He took some rocks and mud and piled and piled and piled it up. Then he went far off and looked at it. "Over there it is good, but over here it isn't good," he said. He built it over five times. At last he had it built up quite high. Suddenly it began to tumble down. The rocks rolled down, rolled down. Before long some people appeared; they were crossing the river. A little girl carrying a dog in her arms was ahead of the others. They had seen X̣wα'ni building the falls and that was why it had tumbled down. He kicked it to pieces and changed the people into rocks right where they were. The little girl's dog also turned into a rock. (I have seen it; it is a stratified rock.)

X̣wα'ni was angry and went four or five miles farther up the river. "I'll make another falls here where the people can catch salmon on a hook," he said. He piled up a great many rocks to keep the salmon from going up any farther. The people catch salmon there when the salmon fall back as they try to jump the falls. "I wish I could see some eels here. Then I would know whether or not the people can get much to eat here," he said. Before long he saw many eels. There are three holes there in the rocks where one can put eels so they won't run away. X̣wα'ni put some eels in the holes. "If anyone comes here, he can catch eels," he said. There is another little falls in a little creek nearby. X̣wα'ni put it there.

He went farther up the river. He went up and up, perhaps four or five miles. He was going to make another place for eels so that if anyone was hungry and did not know how to catch deer or large game, he could always find something to eat. He took a large stick and pried up a rock. There were many eels under it. "That's good," he said.

He went on again. He made a large falls at Pe Ell to keep the salmon from going any farther. The salmon never go any farther than this falls. It is very high and is far up the river near the mountains. He heard someone coming so he found a good place to hide in a rock. (My father has seen this place where X̣wα'ni is hiding.) "Is there anything else I can make?" he wondered.

X̣Wα'NI TRAVELS.[1]

X̣wα'ni was travelling far up in the country; he had started from Puget Sound. He was making hills as he travelled. He thought to himself, "I'm going to make a snow mountain here. I won't make the top very round; I'll make it in three different parts." He made the mountain and said, "This shall be called 'təx̣o'ma' (Mount Ranier)[2]." From there, he went south, making large hills and small ones and giving shape to the land as he travelled. After he had gone a long way, he looked back: təx̣o'ma was no longer visible. "I'll make another," he said, "I'll make this one round at the top. This

---

[1] Told by Minnie Case, 1926; see p. 387.
[2] See p. 268.

shall be called 'lawe'latə' (Mount St. Helens[1])." After he had finished it, he stood off and looked at it. It was too far away from the first, so he made another about half-way between. "This one shall be called 'tc'ili'ɩł' (Mount Adams)," he said, "this shall be the husband of the two others." They say that lawe'latə got jealous of təx̣o'ma and threw some fire at her. She burnt təx̣o'ma's head off and also burnt her backbone and shoulders.

After he had made the snow mountains, X̣wα'ni thought, "Well, why am I not making streams?" He made large streams leading from both lawe'latə and tc'ili'ɩł; he made the Cowlitz River, the North Fork and the South Fork branching off from it, and still smaller streams. He kept on, making little streams here and there on large hills until he got back to təx̣o'ma. Then he made the Puyallup River and the Nisqually River leading from təx̣o'ma.

From there he went back to the head of the Cowlitz River and travelled down it. Along the way he made little falls. He made one falls rather high, and one very high. The very high one is at Mossy Rock. He also made little hills and gave each one a name. He named Nesika and Silver Creek. "The people on this part of the river will speak a different language; they will speak the Taitnepam language," he said. Some distance below Silver Creek, he said, "The people from here down will speak Cowlitz. They will speak this language clear down to Castle Rock, to Kelso." Then he began to form the land, — to make prairies and so on, places where food-plants could grow. He put in all the plants that people would eat, — the Indian carrot, lacama, tiger lily, button lacama, and a plant resembling the Indian carrot.[2] He made little hills nearby and put in many different kinds of berry bushes — blackberries, black caps, red huckleberries, gooseberries, salmon berries, strawberries, June berries, and wild crab apples. All these things grow on Cowlitz Prairie. After he had finished with the plant-foods, he stocked the country with grouse, wild pheasant, geese and mallard duck; then with bear, elk, deer and all the game animals that we eat. When he had finished, he said, "All these things I leave for the people to eat." Then he put all the fish in the river, the eel, trout, red salmon, calico salmon, steelhead, black salmon, chub, red-mouthed trout, big-mouthed trout, small-mouthed trout, bullhead, crawfish. All these fish are in the Cowlitz River. "This is what people will eat after I am gone," he said. Then he went on down the river. "The sturgeon will come up the river almost as far as Castle Rock and all the people will eat it," he said. "Other fish will come up the river as far as they

[1] According to Mrs. Iley, p. 268. The narrator translated the above Mount Ranier and təx̣o'ma Mount Tacoma. When I pointed out that this was impossible, that the two English terms apply to the same mountain, she still insisted on her nomenclature. Mr. Cheholt's version, p. 268, and the above version agree as far as content is concerned.

[2] With four or five roots to one stem.

can." "Now I have finished with the Cowlitz," he said. He left the Cowlitz and started down the Columbia. "This will be Chinook country," he said. He passed Chinook country and came out on the Pacific coast. He left several different kinds of berry bushes along the edge of the beach, — salal berries, salmon berries, black berries, and a variety similar to the huckleberry. He left some razor-back clams and some crabs on the beach. Then he went inside the bay and left some clams and oysters on the beach near Bay Center. "All these things the people will eat after I am gone," he said. He stocked the hills there with deer, elk, bear and other game animals that are killed with bows and arrows. At the same time, he planned the arrow point of agate. While he was planning this, Bluejay was with him. "How shall I make it?" he asked Bluejay. "Let's fix it this way," Bluejay said. So they made it the way Bluejay suggested. When it was finished, X̣wα'ni found that Bluejay's plan was much better than his own.

When he had finished at Bay Center, X̣wα'ni came on up the Willipa River and left the same fish there as in the Cowlitz, with the exception of the sturgeon. He came on up the Willipa to the source, and from there to the source of the Chehalis. He left the same kind of fish in the Chehalis as in the Cowlitz, with the exception of the sturgeon. Above Ceres and Dryad,[1] he left a little falls. There is a deep eddy at the foot of the falls into which salmon go and stay. Anyone who knows how can get the salmon out. A little farther along, he made a bluff on either side of the river. The water runs very swift there, so swift that the eels can only get up here and there. By making little jumps they can get up as far as Dryad or a little farther, about as far as Boisfort. There is a little bluff between Ceres and Dryad where one can have some fun with the eels if one wants to: one can spit in the water ahead of the eels, and they will turn around and go back along the bluff faster than they came up. Near Boisfort Prairie, about ten miles from the town of Chehalis, he made some holes far up in the bluff, on each side of the river, so that eels could go there. One can take a long pole and stick it in these holes to scare the eels out. The eels are weak and do not run away very fast. One can grab them and put them in a sack. If one sees an eel coming out of a hole, one must not point it out with one's finger, but with one's mouth, otherwise the eel will run so fast one cannot see it. On the hills of this bluff he planted the same kinds of fruit as on the Cowlitz hills. Then he went up to the head of tapa'ł Creek[2] and made an imitation snow mountain. After he had finished with the imitation snow mountain, he came down off it and went almost to the mouth of the creek. Then he looked back at the little mountain and said, "If a stranger appears directly opposite you and looks upon your little creek and prairie, it will

[1] The narrator is now in her own territory.
[2] English equivalent unknown, adjoins Dip Creek.

rain." It will certainly rain and turn bad, if a stranger crosses this creek, it will rain, hail or snow. The second time the stranger crosses the creek it is not so bad, the third the rain stops. When he had finished with his work there, he came over the hill to Lequito and planned things there as in other places, planting fruits and berries all over the hills. Then he went to what is now Chehalis and named it. Then he went to what is now Centralia and named it mαqɛ' (an Upper Chehalis term, — a language between Cowlitz and real Chehalis). Then he went on down and named a prairie ta'łınk'ən (Fords Prairie). He named another L'aqa'yαqł (Grand Mound). He named a creek on the edge of the prairie wała'lən (Scatter Creek). He named another little prairie ıłta'ls (Little Rochester Prairie). He named another place manı'k'oł[1] — across [the river] from Gate City. He named a river sa'ts'αł (Black River) and a prairie t'əa'wən (Oakville Reservation Prairie). From there, he went to Gray's Harbor and came back by the way of Skokomish. From there, he went to Mount tc'ili'ıł and looked back on all his work. "Goodbye to all my peoples," he said, "I am leaving you. Now I shall go to dry country, to Yakima and Klickitat country."

X̣WΑ'NI AND HIS DOG.[2]

X̣wα'ni was travelling. "Now I am going up the river," he said. He set out. Then he noticed that he was back at the place from which he had started. He set out again. Then he noticed again that he had come back to the same place. This happened five times. Then he asked his sisters, "Why do I always come back to the same place?" "You will say again, 'That's what I was forgetting,'" they said. "Oh, come on, come on, rain," he said. He spit, "Tx̂ᵘ, tx̂ᵘ, tx̂ᵘ." He frightened his sisters. "Come on, come on." "Ah brother, ah our brother, we will tell you. It's because we're afraid of the dangerous being over there. He will eat us up, that dangerous being over there. That's what we are afraid of," they said. "Oh, that's what I was forgetting. Come in, sisters," X̣wα'ni said. Then he set out. He relieved himself and said to his excrements, "Turn into a dog, a big dog. Stand up, stand up!" A big dog stood up. "What shall I name him? I shall name him 'Tci·'ləkᵘ'." Oh, X̣wα'ni's dog was big!

Then X̣wα'ni set out. He came to a little prairie and relieved himself there. He said to his excrements, "Turn into people this evening, turn into people. You shall be running around this evening." Then he went away.

X̣wα'ni started toward the trail. When he got there, he climbed a little hill. He saw a big man coming who had a big dog. He said to his dog, "When you see him, show your teeth. If I tell you to stop,

[1] The site of a former Upper Chehalis village.

[2] Told by Mary Iley, in text, 1927; see p. 386.

you must obey." The man reached the spot where they stood. X̣wα'ni's dog showed his teeth. X̣wα'ni stopped Tci·'ləkᵘ: "Keep still. Let your partner alone." Then he said to the dangerous being, "My dog jumps on people; he bites them in two." "Now we shall eat," he said, "how is your dog? He's a little too small. Let us trade." The dangerous being thought, "Oh, all right, I shall trade him my dog." "Oh, all right, we shall trade now," he said. He tied X̣wα'ni's dog up. "My dog is good; if you see any people turn him loose and he will cut them in two with one bite. My dog cuts people in two," he said. Then he said that he would give X̣wα'ni his dog. X̣wα'ni tied the dangerous being's dog up.

"Oh, look," X̣wα'ni said, "there are some people who are staying all night. I'll close in on them from this side, you from the other. We will kill them and eat them." "Oh, all right," the dangerous being said, and went running off. Then X̣wα'ni said to the trail, "There should be a large bank there." The dangerous being ran toward the people. Then the people turned into excrements and he slipped on them and fell. He smashed to pieces. He was still holding on to X̣wα'ni's dog; it was nothing but excrements now. The dangerous being was dead.

The dangerous being's dog was lying tied up. X̣wα'ni started off with him. "How's that man?" he thought. He stayed all night at a place. Next morning he thought, "I shall go to see the dangerous being now." He went to the place: the dangerous being was lying there all smashed up; he was still holding on to the excrements. X̣wα'ni laughed. Then the dangerous being's dog showed his teeth.

X̣wα'ni started off again with no particular purpose in mind. He laughed a little, thinking of what had happened. Then the dog tried to bite him. Oh, X̣wα'ni was frightened. He killed the dog. "Now this is how it shall be: if they do not want a dog — if it is a bad dog — they shall hang it," he said.

X̣Wα'NI AND HIS DAUGHTER.[1]

X̣wα'ni came to the mouth of the Cowlitz River. His daughter had her first menses there. He put her outside in a little house and covered her head with something so that she could not look at people or at the sky. He roasted some salmon until it was very, very dry and gave it to her to eat. She was allowed to eat lacamas or berries, fresh things of that sort, but any meat or fish she ate had to be cooked until very dry.

From the mouth of the Cowlitz, X̣wα'ni moved to Cowlitz prairie,[2] where he made a salmon trap. He wanted to sleep with a woman there and made the trap because they let him have her.

[1] Told by Mary Iley, 1926; Mrs. Iley told the same story in text in '27. It differs a little in detail from the one here. See p. 387.
[2] In the text version, to the mouth of Toutle Creek.

He went to Mayfield next. He wanted a woman and they let him have her. The woman took care of his daughter. He made a little whirlpool there where salmon could be speared. The whirling water shot the salmon out to the surface. He also made a falls of smooth rocks and a pool of still water beneath it. The salmon could be plainly seen when they tried to jump from the still water of the pool to the rocks. He made these places for fish because he had been given a woman. In return, he treated the woman's people well. He told the people that they must not shout when they speared two fish at once. But there was a man[1] who did this. He speared two fish at once and his spear buckled. In his excitement, he forgot the order and shouted. Then all the fish became frightened and ran back to the water. Even the dried salmon went back. The man's wife was carrying a large bundle of dried salmon tied around her neck and her belly. In their haste to get back to the river, the salmon nearly cut her neck off. The people made the man leave. Then they dried more salmon.

X̣wα'ni moved to Tilden Creek next. There he peeled roots and bark and told his daughter to make baskets. She no longer had to eat such dry meat, but he still kept her outside. She was never allowed to look up at old people, boys or the sky. "You are a dangerous being (pα'sa)," X̣wα'ni said. "If you look at men or little boys, you will shorten their lives." It was not forbidden to look at women.

X̣wα'ni moved to Mossy Rock next and made two or three whirlpools where salmon could be caught. He made these places after he had slept with a woman there.

He went to Nesika next. Here he took his daughter into the house and let her eat fresh meat. "People who live here will be dirty," he said.

He then moved to the present site of The Falls,[2] near Nesika. (He was now in thickly wooded country, Klickitat country.) He slept with a woman there, so he made a whirlpool and the falls. Salmon are easily caught there for they fall back into a little well when they try to jump the falls. He made four or five places where salmon could easily be speared. He lost his daughter at this place for she ran away with a man. And so it happens at this place: if a girl wants a man, she runs away with him; her parents do not choose for her. But among the Cowlitz a man must buy his wife. X̣wα'ni did a lot of nasty things there. There was a woman who had killed a lot of men and he killed her.[3]

He then went to Hill and shouted across to his brother at Mossy Rock, "If you want to fish, you will find my pole here." He left a rock and his fishing pole.

[1] In the text version, it is X̣wα'ni himself who breaks the tabu.
[2] Quite large falls in the Cowlitz river.
[3] The toothed-vagina incident, evidently.

He was now without his daughter, she had run away from him. And so in this section of the country, parents never choose their children's mates.

X̣Wα'NI AND THE GIRLS.[1]

X̣wα'ni was travelling. Five girls were digging in the middle of Cowlitz Prairie. Whenever anyone passed by carrying a pack, the girls would ask what was in the pack. X̣wα'ni passed by and they called, "Hey, X̣wα'ni, what have you got in your pack?" X̣wα'ni did not look at them. "What have you got in your pack?" they called again. Still X̣wα'ni did not look at them. They asked the same thing five times. Then he looked at them and said, "Were you speaking to me? I have some roasted eels,[2] one for each of you." "Oh, give us one," the girls said. "Well, come over here then," he said. The five girls went up to him and he laid out a roasted eel for each one of them. Four of the girls ate one apiece. The youngest girl would not eat hers. "Oh, that's X̣wα'ni; I wouldn't eat that," she said. She knew that he was giving them something bad to eat. The eels were nicely cooked. There was one left, so X̣wα'ni put it back in his pack and started off. A little later he turned around and called, "If it is a boy, call it tawa'shweyə (roasting stick?). If it is a girl, call it wəpa'ls (handle of a root-digger)." The girls knew immediately that X̣wα'ni had tricked them and tried to throw up what they had eaten. After that it was said, "Hereafter, young girls shall not run to ask travellers what they have in their packs; old people may do it, but not young people."

X̣Wα'NI DOCTORS A GIRL.[3]

Many people were living in a certain village. A young woman was sick. X̣wα'ni passed by and they told him about the sick girl. "I will doctor her. Then she will get well," he said. "All right, you may doctor her," they said. The young woman's family was living in a large open room. "Make a small enclosure around the sick girl. I will doctor her inside, where no one can see me. You people help beat time on the outside," X̣wα'ni said.

The people gathered outside the enclosure. X̣wα'ni began to doctor. They beat the boards loudly and sang his song. All the while he was singing loudly, X̣wα'ni was having intercourse with the girl. When he had satisfied himself, he came out and said, "I've done all I can do, so I'll leave now. She will recover." Then he went away.

---

[1] Told by Mary Iley, 1926; see p. 388.

[2] His organ.

[3] Told by James Cheholts, 1927; see p. 388.

X̣wα'NI AND THE GIRL.[1]

The people were living in a small village. A young girl there grew very slowly. X̣wα'ni passed by and noticed the girl. Every time he saw her, she seemed as small as ever. "Oh," he said, "I can show my niece a medicine that will make her grow quickly. The medicine will be sticking up on the sand-bar. Let her go there and rub herself." Then he went to the girl and told her how she should put the medicine into her.

He went to the sand-bar and buried himself in the sand, leaving only his organ sticking up out of the ground. The girl found the spot. "X̣wα'ni told me I should come here," she said. She used the medicine for some time and then left.

The next time X̣wα'ni passed by the village, he found that the girl had grown. "You see," he said to her, "I told you what would make you grow."

Today people always say that if a girl is small in size, she will grow quickly after she has had intercourse.

COYOTE AS DOCTOR.[2]

Coyote lived far down the Cowlitz River. He was a doctor. He had one grown daughter, X̣wαna'ye, of whom he was very proud. (He must have stolen her.) Whenever a woman was in child-birth, Coyote was sent for. He always doctored the women at this time and always cured them. There was one woman who had been in labor nearly two whole days. The swelling was in her arm. Coyote sucked at the spot where the baby's head lay and the baby was born. He was given as pay a pretty buckskin dress and beads for his daughter. The girl was always dressed very prettily indeed.

Another time someone sent for him to doctor a woman. This time, the swelling was in the woman's hip. He tore at the spot where the baby lay with his mouth. "Tʊt, tʊt, tʊt," he sucked, drawing the blood out. The baby was born and the torn spot healed nicely.

Every day someone sent for him. He doctored only women. One day a man came and said, "Oh, come quickly, my wife is dying." The woman's leg, below the knee, was swollen very badly. Coyote sucked the blood from the spot where the baby's head lay. The woman then felt all right and had her baby.

Another time he was called in to attend a woman whose breast was badly swollen. He sucked at the spot where the baby's head lay and the woman had the baby. He was given a pretty buckskin dress as pay.

Finally, a man who lived far off came for him to doctor his wife. He found the woman nearly dead. "You're not going to have a baby; you have merely a disease," he kept saying to the woman.

[1] Told by James Cheholts, 1927; see p. 388.

[2] Told by Mary Iley, 1926; see p. 390.

He wanted to mislead her so that he could steal the baby. He always became very fond of every baby that he delivered. He sucked the baby out and hid it in his knee-cap, which he had cut open for the purpose. Then he showed the couple how to have sexual relations properly. Since that time, everyone has known how to do it. Later on, Coyote's patient had another baby.

Coyote left his patient and started home, packing the things that had been given him as pay. After travelling several days and nights, he began to have such severe pains that he could scarcely walk. He was having labor pains as women have. He was almost dead and still some distance from his own house. At last his daughter caught sight of him and cried, "Oh, father is coming! Oh, father is dying." She ran to him and found that his knee was badly swollen. "Let me cut it open," she said. A tiny hair came out of the swelling. "Oh, father," she said, "this looks like a baby's hair." Then a baby boy came out. The girl was very proud of her little brother; Coyote, also, was very proud of his son.

The girl made the boy a spear with which to fish. "You must never make him a bow and arrow," Coyote said. He no longer got many patients, but whenever he did, he always asked for clothes for the boy. "Why can't my brother have a bow and arrow and kill deer as other boys do?" the girl thought. And so one day Coyote made the boy a bow and arrow. "Never go over the hill to the west; always go north, south or east," he said to him. But one day the boy looked over the hill to the west and saw some large deer tracks. He followed the tracks and brought home a deer. On his fifth visit to the hill, he brought home five deer. On his sixth visit, he went farther than usual. A bird had taken his fancy and he was trying to shoot it. Finally he hit the bird and it fell to the ground. He ran to catch it, but it rolled and rolled until it rolled right into a little house. There was a woman inside, standing by the fire-place. She grabbed the arrow sticking in the bird and held it behind her. "Please, sister, give me my arrow," the boy said. The woman made no move to return it. "Please, aunty, give me my arrow," he said. He called her all the appropriate relationship terms he could think of, but still she did not return his arrow.

He went home but returned the following day to the hill to hunt. He saw a still prettier bird and finally shot it. He tried to catch it and was about to succeed, when the bird began to roll upon the ground. It rolled right into the same little house and he followed it. The same woman was there. She took the arrow out of the bird and held it behind her. Again he called her by all the appropriate terms that he could think of, asking for his arrow, but the woman would not return it.

The same thing happened to the boy five times and then he was lost forever. The last time he shot a still larger bird, using the only arrow that remained to him. The bird rolled into the house and he followed it. The woman who lived there was an old maid and she had made the birds from her hair-combings in order to lure a man to her house. "Tell me what I am to you," she said to the boy. "Aunt," he said, then, "mother"; "sister"; he called her everything he could think of except wife, but the woman made no response. Since he wanted his arrow very badly, he finally asked, "If I call you the right thing, will you give me my arrow?" "Yes," she said. "Oh, my dear wife, will you give me my arrow?" he said. The woman then pulled him farther inside the house, closed the door, and took him for her husband. She was older than the boy. Her father and mother were dead.

"You think that Coyote is your father, don't you? Well, he isn't. Your parents live far away," the woman said to her husband one day. She named the place where his parents lived and told him all the things that Coyote had done. Before Coyote showed the people how to have intercourse, so she explained, man and wife had merely embraced one another and conception had taken place as a result.

Coyote knew that the youth was now living with this woman. He also knew that she had informed him of the fact that he was not his real father. He had feared all along that this would happen. One day he said to his daughter, "Daughter, go to look for your brother." "No, you go. You made him the bow and arrow," she said. She refused to go and turned into a river, the X̬wɑna'ye, flowing in the direction that her brother had taken. Then Coyote himself went to the house and found the youth.

After some time, the woman said to her husband, "I'm going to dig some lacamas and dry them. Then we will visit your mother." When the lacamas were dried, she made them into two large packs. The couple now had a baby and Coyote carried his grandchild around. The woman refused to tell Coyote where they intended to go. One night while he was sleeping, the couple got up and set out on their journey. They left him plenty of meat and lacamas to eat. The next day he tracked them. Their tracks were quite deep so he knew that they were carrying a heavy load. After an all night trip, the couple arrived at the home of the youth's parents. The parents knew that Coyote had stolen their baby. "Coyote is following us," their daughter-in-law said. "Oh, he'll get lost," they said. "Now this is the way it shall be: when a baby is taken away from his parents, his parents will eventually get him back; he will always be able to find them," the youth's parents said.

Coyote found them and married a woman who lived there. He went hunting and brought in a lot of squirrels. He stayed there for some time and always brought in the same kind of game. One day his wife said, "I'm going to find out how he catches them; he has no bow and arrow." She watched him and found that he just grabbed the squirrels. "Is that the way he hunts! No bow and arrow!" she said aloud. Coyote was so frightened when he heard her speak that he ran away forever.

XWα'NI AS TEACHER.[1]

There was a man and his wife. The woman had a sore finger. The swelling was about to burst. The man thought that his wife was going to have a child. Xwα'ni arrived at their house and the man told him that his wife was going to have a child. "It doesn't seem that way. Show me her swelling," Xwα'ni said. The man showed him his wife's badly swollen finger. "Why, this isn't pregnancy!" Xwα'ni said. He cut the swelling open and let the matter out. "This isn't pregnancy. I will show you how to have a child," he said. He told the woman to lie down and then told the man what to do so that they could have children. Then Xwα'ni left.

XWα'NI TIES UP HIS WRINKLES.[2]

Xwα'ni was travelling and it began to rain. He had to make camp early in the day. He was making rivers, streams, timber and mountains as he travelled. Wherever he camped, there are no mosquitoes today; the creeks and springs there never go dry; there is always running water. He came to Cascade and made the falls there. Two girls were bathing across the river, directly opposite him. He waded across toward them. Wherever he stepped, large rocks formed. The girls saw that he was an old man with a wrinkled face. He smoothed his face with his hands to make the wrinkles disappear.[3]

Xwα'ni made all the Indian roots, — the Indian macaroni, little carrots, camas, wild carrots, and button camas; also the strawberries, wild raspberries, blackberries, little blue huckleberries, wild service berries, redcap berries and the mountain huckleberries.

GOD AND XWα'NI.[4]

God sent Xwα'ni, the chief, here to teach people how to live. He was to teach them how to work stone and to do all the necessary work. But Xwα'ni did not do as he was told; he just fooled around with the girls and never showed the people the right things to do. God once came to him and discovered him neglecting his work. God looked around and saw that the new people had trains, steamboats, steam-donkies, — all of which Xwα'ni was supposed to have shown the people how to make. Then he threw Xwα'ni on an island where he turned into a rock. In the next world, — when the world

---

[1] Told by James Cheholts, 1927; see p. 388.
[2] Told by Mrs. Northover, 1926; interpreted by Mr. Northover. See p. 387.
[3] This passage is obviously incomplete. I judge that the long distance intercourse incident belongs here.
[4] Told by James Cheholts, 1927; see p. 388.

turns over, X̣wα′ni will be a [real] man. I guess he is still there on the island. I hear people say that he looks like a rock in the shape of a person. He gets up at night and walks when everyone is asleep. A man once caught him in the act: X̣wα′ni was walking around all over the house and seemed to be half-asleep.

COYOTE AND THE RAILROAD.[1]

After he had done too many bad things, they penned Coyote up far off at the end of the world.

Once they were making a railroad through his place. "I don't want it. Take it away; take your tools and go away," he said. "Don't pay any attention to him," the people said, "just go ahead and lay the tracks." The workers paid no attention to Coyote and laid the tracks. Later on, the train went through. When Coyote saw it, he said, "Oh, there's a train going through my place now." "Stay right where you are," he said to the train. Then the train and all the people inside it turned into a rock right on the spot. "You will stay there forever; you will never move again," Coyote said.

THE MOUNTAINS.

(First Version).[2]

Mount St. Helens (lawe′latła[a])[3] had two wives, Mount Ranier (tax̣o′ma) and Mount Adams (patu′ʾ). His two wives quarreled. They had lots of children. They fought and fought. Finally Mount Ranier got the best of Mount Adams; she stepped on all of Mount Adams' children and killed them. She was the stronger. The children were in the way when they were fighting and so they kept stepping on them. The two women and their husband turned into mountains.

THE MOUNTAINS.

(Second Version).[4]

White Mountain[5] was a man. He had two wives and stood midway between them. The two women became angry with one another and started to fight. The one at the south[6] threw fire at Mount Ranier (taqo′mən). The fire hit Ranier but she threw it back at her rival. They kept this up. Finally, Ranier got struck very badly and her head broke off. The other woman got the best of her.

---

[1] Told by Mary Iley, 1927; see p. 390.
[2] Told by Mary Iley, 1927; see p. 387.
[3] Said to be a Taitnepam term meaning "smoking mountain".
[4] Told by James Cheholts, 1927.
[5] Mount Adams? The narrator could not identify any of the mountains except Ranier. See Mrs. Case's version, p. 257.
[6] Mount Helens?

MOON AND SUN.

(First Version).[1]

An old lady had two daughters. The girls went out one day to a certain prairie to dig lacamas. One girl was thirteen or fourteen years old; the other was already a grown-up person. During the night, the younger became angry and cried. To put her in a good humor, the elder said, pointing to the stars shining clearly and brightly, "That big star will be mine, the little one, yours." The girl then stopped crying. After both had fallen asleep, the stars came down and took them up to the sky. The little star was an old man, the large star, a young man. The younger girl got the old man, the elder girl, the young man. The elder girl bore her husband a son.

Every day the two sisters went out to dig roots. "If you find any roots that go straight down, don't dig them," the people said. But one day the girls disobeyed and dug the roots that went straight down. The air came up through the hole and they covered the hole with their skirts. Some men who were nearby asked, "What do you see there?" "Nothing," the girls said, still covering the hole with their skirts. As soon as the men went away, the elder girl said, "Down there is the place we came from." They set to work to twist hazel roots into a long rope. When they got home, their husbands asked, "Why did you get so few roots to-day?" "The baby cries all the time and we have to take care of him," they answered. When the rope was long enough to reach the earth, they tied the baby on. Then the younger girl got on. "When you reach the ground, shake the rope so that I will know you are there," the elder said. They had concealed the rope inside the hole, so that no one would discover what they were planning. As soon as her sister and the baby reached the ground, the second crawled into the hole and went down the rope, like a spider crawling down its web.

They found only their blind old grandmother at home; their mother had gone away. "Grandmother, we've come back. The stars took us up to the sky. We have a baby now," they said. "Oh, give me the baby," the old lady said. From that time on, the grandmother took care of the baby. The two girls went out to dig lacamas. The old lady made a swing for the baby and sang as she swung it back and forth, "Nənə, nənə, nänä." Two girls came by and stole the baby from the swing, leaving a piece of rotten wood in its place. The old lady then sang, "My grandson feels like rotten wood." The younger of the two girls heard her singing and said, "Grandmother says, 'My grandson feels like rotten wood.'" They ran after the two thieves to get the baby back, but could not catch up with them and had to turn back.

The baby had a lot of diapers. "Bring them to me," the grandmother said. She made the diapers into a doll and tied it in a cradle

[1] Told by Mary Iley, 1926; see p. 379.

board. "Nänə, nänə, nänä," she sang, shaking it up and down. The doll made from the soiled diapers turned into a baby. This baby was brighter than the first; he shone nicely and brightly.

The boy grew up and tried to find people who would search for his brother. Finally Bluejay said that he was willing to go. He found the lost boy and said, "Your mother and grandmother want you to return." "If they will buy me five girls from five different countries, I'll come back," the young man said. Bluejay went back and said to the young man's people, "He said that he would come back if you would buy him five girls, one from each of the king-countries, from the Taitnepam, the [Upper] Chehalis, from Kelso,[1] from the Wishram and from the Yakima.

The young man left the place where he was living without saying where he was going. He came to a lake and saw a boy in a little canoe on the opposite side. "Take me over, boy," he called. "Take me over, boy,"[2] the boy repeated. He repeated everything that the young man said. He did not really have a canoe; he used his legs as a bridge. When anyone crossed over on his legs, he would spread them and throw him into the water. He had drowned many people in this way. He finally stretched his legs out for the young man and then dumped him off into the water. The young man, who was tall, then stood up in the water and beat the boy to death with a stick. "Hereafter, no one shall act as a canoe and drown people. Someone will come for them in a canoe and take them across. Only now and then will a person drown when he crosses the water," he said.

He went on and found some boys standing in the river, forming a fish-trap. He ordered the boys out of the water and showed them how to make a real trap. "Who is the chief here ?" he asked. "Raven (qwaq^{w})," they said. The chief was biting himself. Whenever anyone spoke his name, he became very angry. He was so angry now that he was biting himself. The young man beat him to death with a stick. All that Raven could say, was, "Qwaq^{w}, qwaq^{w}, qwaq^{w}." The pieces turned into little ravens and flew away.

The young man came to another place and heard someone saying, "ϒ', ʋ,' ʋ'." "Who's making that noise ?" he thought. Along came a good-sized youth, trying to hold on to the trees and anything else he could find. His head lice were dragging him to the river to drown him. He grabbed the boy and took him to the river. He found some blue mud and washed the boy's hair thoroughly with it. When he rinsed his hair, the lice floated on top of the water. Then he made a comb for him. "Comb and braid your hair every morning," he said, "it will keep you free of lice. People must always do this when they have lice."

He reached home carrying a large pack of beads. He set it down in front of the house and said, "The girl who can carry it in shall be

[1] In Cowlitz territory.
[2] Said very fast and in a squeaky voice.

my wife." The Yakima girl tried but could not lift it. Then the Wishram girl, the Chehalis girl, the Cowlitz girl [the one from Kelso] tried but could not lift it. Then the Taitnepam girl lifted it and carried it into the house; she was the strongest. He took her as his favorite wife. She cooked for him but he would not eat. He refused food for five days. Then he went hunting. Not long after someone noticed a number of dead elk. The young man had evidently killed them but there were no signs of wounds. This person decided to follow the young man to learn how he killed them. He climbed a tree and watched. The hunter took out a feather painted red and shooed the elk with it. All the elk immediately fell dead. Then he made a huge fire from some very large trees; he broke the trees off as if they were mere bushes. From his big cougar-skin sheath, he removed a long, sharp roasting stick and stuck it through the five elk. Then he roasted the elk as one roasts wieners. When they were done, he ate them as if they were a mere bite. The man who was watching from the tree climbed down and ran home to tell what he had seen. "He can't eat at home because he eats too much when he is out hunting," he said.

The hunter came home and learned that he had been watched. He became ashamed and ran away during the night. He is now the Moon. When his wife learned that he was going to run away, she wept and wept, for she wanted to go with him. She jumped on his face and hugged him. He popped his eye open and she jumped in. The mark that she made on his face can still be seen.

The younger boy, the diaper-boy, wept the whole night because his brother had left. Early next morning, he set out, following in his brother's track. The younger travelled during the day, the elder at night. No one could go after them. The elder was the son of a star. One is now the Sun and one the Moon. When the people discovered that he ate too much, the elder ran away to become the Moon.

MOON AND SUN.

(Second Version).[1]

A woman had a baby. She lived with her grandmother who was blind. She went out alone to pick berries and left the baby in its cradle for the old lady to take care of. The old lady pushed her little grandson in a swing. She pushed the swing far out and it was a long time before it came back and struck against the palm of her hand. After a while the swing grew lighter. She found there was nothing but moss in the cradle. Then she sang,

My little grandson is turning into moss.

The child's mother heard her song and returned in haste to the swing. There was nothing but moss in the cradle. The woman had

[1] Told by James Cheholts, 1927.

conceived although she had never had any sexual relations. She took the moss bedding from the cradle and squeezed the urine out. She squeezed at the bedding until the urine turned into another child. The second was just like the first except that he was cross-eyed and so could not see very well.

Later on, they recovered the lost child and the two brothers met. The elder said, "Well, we shall become the moon and sun. I shall travel in the daytime, you at night. We shall arise over the whole world." The younger arose first. As he travelled over the world, he saw many stumps and became frightened. "Perhaps they are harmful, perhaps they will kill me," he thought. "As I travelled I saw some stumps that frightened me. I feared they might harm me and so I turned back," he said to his brother. Then his brother said, "Well, you shall travel in the daytime then and I at night." Moon, the elder, has stronger eyes than his cross-eyed brother Sun. Sun comes in the morning and because his eyes are crossed, he is not as hot as his brother was when he travelled as the sun. Had Moon decided to travel in the daytime, it would be much hotter than it is now, for he has stronger eyes than Sun.

THE STOLEN BOY.[1]

There was a young chief who was living with his mother. The young chief died and left a wife and baby son. The widow continued to live with her mother-in-law. The old lady was blind. She took care of the baby, and the young woman did all the work. One day the young woman went out to dig camas, a large variety that grew about three feet underground. While she was away at work, the old lady was pushing the baby back and forth in a swing. She was singing,

Go to sleep, sonny,
Go to sleep, sonny.

Suddenly she changed her song to,

What's the matter, sonny?
You feel like rotten wood.

The young woman heard her and thought, "What's the matter with the old lady?" She climbed out of the deep hole where she was digging and went directly to the swing. There was indeed a piece of rotten wood, about the size of a baby, in the swing. "What did you do with sonny?" she asked. "Look! Someone must have taken the baby!" the old lady said. The young woman looked, and saw

[1] Told by Sophie Smith, 1926. This story was given as a version of the Moon and Sun myth. I do not believe that it is a true variant, but merely a story to take the place of the original one, which was remembered only in part. See p. 379.

two women running away, in the direction of Chehalis. The two women had the baby. "Quick! Pack me and we'll run after them," the old lady said. The mother took the old lady on her back and started to run. The old lady sang,

> Get short, road,
> Get short, road.

She was the Measuring-Worm and was able to shorten the road. They had caught up with the two women and were about to catch them, when the young woman dropped the old lady. She thought that by doing so, she could catch the two women more quickly, but instead, they left her far behind. This kept up until they reached the beach near Olympia. Just as they reached the beach, the young woman dropped the old lady again. The two women with the baby then got into a canoe and paddled away. The child's mother and grandmother now had to give up and go back.

After she got back home, the mother cried all the time. "Don't cry," the old lady said. "Give me all the baby's clothes — his diapers, cradle board and everything." The old lady made a doll from all these things. The young woman said, "Oh, the crazy old woman, what's she doing now!" The old lady was singing,

> Go to sleep, sonny,
> Go to sleep, sonny.

After a while, the young woman heard something and said, "What's the matter with the old woman? I hear a baby crying." The doll had awakened and had begun to cry. She ran to the child and took it up. It was a girl. They raised the girl and she lived with them until she was about eighteen years old. The mother never ceased weeping for her son. Then Bluejay said, "You should stop crying and send me to look for the boy. I can find out whether he is dead or alive."

Early in the morning, Bluejay started out. He travelled all day and all night. The following morning, he arrived at a house. A man was outside making arrowheads. "Kac, kac, kac," Bluejay said. The man picked up some of the stone chips and threw them at him. They struck Bluejay in the eyes. He cried, "Oh, I bring you good news and in return, you injure my eyes." Immediately the man said, "I'll clean your eyes. Tell me your story." He cleaned Bluejay's eyes and told his wife to prepare breakfast while Bluejay was telling his story. "Your mother has been weeping for you every day since you were a year old. I came to find you and to report whether you were dead or alive," Bluejay said. When he had finished, Bluejay started to eat his breakfast. The man ran to the next house to see the two women who lived there. He had always called each of them "mother". He asked them if it were true that he had a real mother, and if so, how did it happen that they had reared him. The two women looked at one another and then asked, "Why do you ask this?" "I heard this morning that I have a mother who lives in a far-away place. Tell me if this is true," the man said. The women then told him that they had stolen him when he was a year old. "Why did you steal me?" he asked. They told him that they had heard of a young chief who had died and left a son, and since they never had any children of their own, they decided to steal the child. "If you find your mother, we'll go to see her in ten days," they said. "Send this message back." The man was happy and ran back to his house. Bluejay had finished breakfast by this time. "I'll go to see my mother ten days from now. Tell her that I have a wife and baby son," he said to Bluejay.

Bluejay started back right away. He travelled all night and all day and got home the next morning. The woman was glad to see him. "Come in, tell the news!" she said. Bluejay was given a blue blanket as pay for bringing the news.

Everyone set to work to prepare for a large feast. In ten days, the young man, his wife and baby son, and the two women arrived. Everyone was glad to see them. The visitors brought all kinds of food from their own home. They stayed some time and then went back home. The man had found his real mother. From time to time, the two families visited one another.

COUGAR.[1]

An old lady made a little cradle board and trimmed it lavishly with beads. Then she took some smashed cedar bark and fashioned it into a doll, a little baby. She wrapped the doll in a fawn skin and then in a wildcat skin. She put it on the cradle board and laid it down. Cougar came along and stole the doll. That's why a cougar, when hungry, will kill a person. The people tracked Cougar and caught up with him. Cougar knocked them down with his tail; he killed fifteen people in all. They were never able to catch him.[2]

WHITE BEAR TAKES REVENGE.[3]

Two girls lived on Toutle River. One day one of the girls said, "Let us go to pick berries." This particular day, the elder girl was very cheerful and active, although she had never been so before. "Don't make too much noise," the younger one said.

Some time before this, White Bear's little cub had met with an accident. The cub had been playing near the water and had fallen in. The cub did not know how to swim and had drowned. The body had

---

[1] Told by Mrs. Northover, 1926; interpreted by Mr. Northover; see p. 412.

[2] This is a strange little tale. I told Mrs. Northover the Moon and Sun story, hoping that she would recall it. Instead, she gave me the above, saying that it reminded her somewhat of the story I had just told.

[3] Told by James Cheholts, 1927; a true story. See p. 412.

floated clear down to Toutle River and had finally rotted. One day two men who were walking far up the river chanced upon the skull. One of them picked it up and said, "Oh, here's little Bear's skull." He stuck it on a stick and left it facing the river.

In the meantime, White Bear (ca'tqłəm) had learned what had happened and had started down the river. "I'll get even with that man," he had said.

The two sisters started up the river, taking their baskets. "Don't make too much noise," the younger said. "Oh, I'm so happy!" the elder answered. "Oh, I'm unhappy. Perhaps we shall have bad luck," the younger said. At last they came to a sand-bar far up the river. The younger was afraid to go further; she thought she saw something white close to the woods. The elder was not afraid and kept on singing happily. "Let's be careful. I think I see White Bear over there. Perhaps he will kill us," the younger said. "No, no, you are mistaken," the elder said. Then the younger looked towards the woods. There was White Bear, with his head down, looking through his legs as he always does when he is angry. "Look! He's angry, he's angry!" she cried. They started to run. The elder was behind. "Throw your basket to him! He'll tear it up," the younger said. The elder girl threw her basket back and White Bear stopped to tear it up. Then the younger threw her basket back and White Bear stopped again to tear it up. Then they threw a third basket back and White Bear tore it up also. "Let's jump into the water! White Bear doesn't know how to swim," the younger said, and jumped into the water. "I don't know how to swim!" the elder said. She ran to a little tree near by and climbed it. White Bear came to the tree and dug all around it. The younger girl was waiting for her sister out in the water. "Don't wait for me! He's digging the tree; it will fall down and he'll kill me!" the elder cried to her. Still the younger waited. The tree started to fall and Bear ran to the side and caught the girl as she struck the ground. He wanted to pay back the insult to his cub. He tore one of her breasts off and the braid from one side of her head. Then he dug a pit and placed the body in it up to the waist. He had his revenge. He left the dead girl sitting there.

The younger ran home and told her parents what had happened. They tried to send their little dogs to the scene of their daughter's death, but the dogs were afraid to go. I guess they took the dead girl home later and buried her.

III. HUMPTULIP TALES.

MOON AND SUN.[1]

The story of Moon and Sun begins on Humptulip River. X̣wαne'-x̣wαne[2] was living in a house. He had a fishtrap made of rock. He never caught anything in his trap; he thought someone was taking the fish out of it. He went there to defecate and told his feces to holler whenever a fish came. He went back to the house and lay down to rest. Soon his watchman hollered so he went down to the river. Instead of a fish, an old piece of bark had floated into the trap. He took it out and threw it away. Then he told his watchman to let him know only when a fish entered the trap. In a little while his watchman called him. Instead of a fish, there was a piece of water-soaked wood in the trap. He told his watchman to let him know only when a fish was caught. As soon as he got to the house, his watchman called him again. He went down to see what he had caught. Instead of a fish, there was a piece of wood, sharp at both ends. He became angry and kicked his watchman, thus making a disagreeable odor. "You must not call me unless you have a fish; I want to take a nap," he said. He went back to the house and lay down for a nap. He was hungry because he had had no fish. After he had napped two or three times, he heard his watchman call. Instead of a fish there was a large piece of rotten bark. This was the fourth time he had gone out to look at his trap; his watchman had lied again. He punished him again and went back to the house. This time he fell sound asleep. While he was sleeping, something said to him in a dream, "When you catch the fish, you will find two girls inside of it." Soon his watchman called him and he woke up. When he got down to the trap, he found a large steelhead salmon; this was the fifth time. He took the salmon out of the trap. He felt happy. He took the salmon home and set to work to dress it. He found that it had eggs. Then he said to himself, "I'm going to try to find out if my dream is true. I'll wrap the eggs up and keep them warm." As soon as he had covered the eggs, he began to cook the salmon. He ate it and lay down for a nap. While sound asleep, he imagined that he heard someone laughing. He got right up to see what had happened to the eggs. There was no change in them. On the fifth day, near daybreak, he heard someone laughing and talking. (He had turned the eggs over

[1] See p. 379.

[2] The Trickster — culture-hero.

to make them hatch, for he had been told in a dream that the girls were lying on their breath and could not breathe.) He waited until broad daylight before uncovering them. Two girls were lying side by side; they were very good-looking. "Get up and bathe," he said. "I'll go out into the woods to get some cedar bark so that you can make yourselves some dresses." He had some salmon left and gave them some. As soon as they had awakened, he had named them. He had called the elder Säsä'djɪstʊm, the younger, Məlä'-djɪstʊm. He went into the woods to get some bark. As soon as he returned with the bark, he began to work it. He pounded it fine like cotton. Then he wove it and measured it on the girls to see how it should be made. When the dresses were finished, the girls put them on.

That night, when the girls went to bed, he said to them, "I'm going out to look at my fishtrap. Be very careful while I'm gone." The second night, he said again, "Be very careful while I'm gone." The third night a man came to the elder girl to visit her. She would have nothing to do with him. Her father returned very early the next morning and she told him of her visitor. The next night when X̣wɑne'x̣wɑne went out, he said, "Close the door like this," showing them how to close it in a particular way. That night the younger girl had a visitor. "How was the door opened?" the girls wondered. "How could anyone get in when only father knows how we keep the door closed?" This was the fourth night. The fifth night a man came to the elder one and violated her. When the man went away, they noticed that he looked very much like their father. The next night, after midnight, a man came to the younger one and violated her. This time, he did not leave until nearly daylight. Then they learned for certain that the man was their father. "What shall we do?" they asked one another. "Our father has done an outrageous thing." They were ashamed. The younger one said, "Perhaps it would be best to leave him and wander around the world." They got up early, before their father's return. They washed their faces, cleaned themselves up and went out of the house. "What direction shall we take?" they asked one another. Finally the younger said, "Let us travel in the direction from which the sun comes." They started out.

They had not gone far when they heard someone singing a lullaby. They went a little farther and came out on a small prairie. An old lady was swinging a baby in a swinging cradle from one side of the prairie to the other. The prairie was called Hidden Prairie. The old lady was singing,

> Sleep, sleep, little grandchild,
> Your mother is out working for us.

The two girls stood there on one side of the prairie. "Let's steal the baby, it's so cute," they said. When the swing reached their side of the prairie, they hung on to it for a little while and then let it go. The child's grandmother was blind. They took a piece of rotten wood and fixed it to look like a baby; it was the same weight. They could hear the child's mother going, "Tʋp, tʋp, tʋp,"[1] farther back in the woods. The fifth time the swing came back, they caught it and put the piece of wood in the baby's place. The elder girl put the baby on her back and they went away as fast as they could. As soon as the swing went back, the old lady began to sing,

> The two daughters of X̣wɑne'x̣wɑne,
> Whom he disgraced,
> Have run off with the baby.

Then she sang loudly, so that her daughter could hear her,

> My baby smells like rotten wood.

Suddenly the daughter heard her mother singing something that sounded strange. She listened closely. At last she made it out and went straight to her mother. When she got there she found a piece of rotten wood in place of her baby. "The two daughters of X̣wɑne'-x̣wɑne, whom he disgraced, have run off with the baby. Carry me on your back; we have five packropes. We shall follow them," the old lady said. They set out to trail the girls. Sure enough they found their tracks: they were travelling in the direction of the sunrise. "There they are! I can see them carrying my son on their back!" the woman said to her mother. "Now let me down," the old lady said. As soon as she struck the ground, a large lake formed ahead of them. When they reached the girls they found them running on top of the water. The old lady and her daughter gathered up the lake and kept on after them. As soon as they got close to the girls again, the younger woman let her mother down and another lake formed. When they caught sight of the girls again they found them more than half way across the lake, running on top of the water. They gathered up the lake and kept after them. They went on some distance before catching sight of them. When they were quite close the younger woman said, "Here we are!" and let her mother down. Another lake formed. They found the girls running on top of the water again. They were so close to them they could even see the baby.[2] For the third time, the woman picked her mother up. The fourth time they had to go some distance before catching sight of the girls. As soon as they were close, the woman let her mother down. They got as close to them as they possibly could. This time, only a small lake formed; they were losing their power. The fifth time, there was no lake at all, only a damp spot. From that time on, they gave up the chase. They could hear the girls singing far off in the distance. Weeping, they started back home.

[1] The mother is evidently digging roots.

[2] The narrator said that as a child she had wept at this part of the story.

When they got back, they found that the girls had merely slipped the baby out of his clothes. They began to wring out the diapers of moss and shredded cedar-bark. They wrung the urine out of them. They worked at the clothes until the urine turned into another child. The new child was not perfect; his eyes were crossed and his body deformed. He soon grew to manhood. His mother said to him, "You will make your living by fishing. You will go up and down the banks of streams. Always remember that you have a brother who was kidnapped. He would have been the royal chief of this country." Then she made plans for herself. "I'll be a pheasant hereafter and live in bushes because I have been made very sad. I shall be humble all my days. When a person takes sick, they will give him my flesh to eat. A sick person will be able to keep pheasant meat in his stomach. Should a very sick person eat pheasant meat and throw it up, it is a sign he will die." She set to work and cut her hair short except in the middle. Pheasant now looks as if she were wearing a hat, — her sign of sorrow. Then she said to her mother, "You shall live hereafter in lakes. You shall be the hell diver." The old lady cut her hair in the same way. Feathers can be seen sticking up out of her head. The two women no longer lived as people; they became birds.

Shortly after that the news of a chief who had two wives spread through the country. From that time on the people began to hold council. They knew that there was only one chief, the one who had been stolen. They held council after council and finally came to the conclusion that this chief was the right one. As soon as they came to this conclusion, Bluejay said, "Everybody get ready and we shall go to him." Everybody went. When they got to the place where the chief lived they saw a very large house. Between them and the house was a great opening in the earth that closed for an instant and then opened again.[1] All the birds, ducks, and all things that could fly, were afraid to fly across this great space. Bluejay could not even begin to do it. He would go only for a short way and then fall down. When even he failed, they decided to give up temporarily and return home. After their return, they gathered more people for a second attempt. They went to the place again, in sight of the house. They had a very hard time. No bird could fly across. Bluejay would go a little way and fall down. They had to give up and go back home. They called more people together. In the meantime Bluejay was preparing himself. He bathed and cleaned his feathers. Then one night he had a dream. "You had better go to a place where you can get one more feather to put on your wing," he was told in his dream. But he could not find the place, and had no extra feather before the third attempt. They got to the place again, in sight of the house. They did everything possible, made a feast, used "medicine", made a great noise, but still the owner never once

[1] A variation of the "snapping-door" motif.

came out of the house. They stayed there five days as they had done each time before. Then they gave up and went back home. From that time on, Bluejay bathed more frequently. Another council was held. Bluejay began his search before the next expedition set out. At last he found a very small feather in a certain place. As soon as he found it, he put it on and flew. He seemed to be able to fly much farther than ever before. Everyone got ready and set out on the fourth expedition. Bluejay now had more confidence in himself and believed that he might succeed. However, he did not get a chance to fly across; the expedition had to go back. They held another council and gathered more people. This would be their last attempt. Bluejay continually turned over in his mind what he would do: he would look for a place where he could find more feathers. At last, while searching in the place to which his dream had directed him, he found two long feathers and put them on his wings. Then he tried them out and succeeded in flying across the river, which was very wide. This time, he was determined to fly across the opening. He took off his clothes (he was wearing five thicknesses of bearskin) preparatory to making the trip. When the expedition arrived at its destination, a dance was held. Then Bluejay announced, "I'm going to try to fly across." He got ready and all the people stood watching him. When the earth came together, he said, "Ka'tca, ka'tca, ka'tca," and was across in an instant. (He was angry now; when he is good-natured he always says, "Kəla', kəla'.") As soon as he reached the other side, he went up to the house. He looked through an opening and saw a chief dressing some skins. Two women were sitting on either side of the house. There were lots of children there. As Bluejay watched, the implement with which the chief was working broke in two. Bluejay kept looking on and another broke in two. (The implement was made of elk-rib.) The chief started to work again and another one broke. He took another and it broke. He threw it away, barely missing Bluejay this time. He took another, the fifth one, and it broke also. By this time he was out of patience and exclaimed, "What is the matter anyway! They always break; Bluejay must be watching." He threw it out through the door. "Oh, oh, oh, oh, oh," he heard someone groan. He got up and went to the door. Sure enough, there was Bluejay lying on his back. "Poor fellow," he said, "why were you looking in? Why didn't you come right in?" He raised him to his feet and took him into the house. It was some time before he could bring him to. As soon as Bluejay was himself once more, he said to the chief, "Your people have been here five times. They came to the opening; that was as far as they could get. Finally, I was able to fly across. They were coming to get you. They are having a hard time now on your account. They want you to come back for you do not belong here. You were stolen when just a baby." The chief bowed his head when he heard that he did not belong there. He began to whittle. "I'm going back with you; I'll leave my children here," he said. The children began to cry when they heard that their father was leaving them. Sucker doubled up and cried; he has been that way ever since. Red Horse began to cry and tore his mouth far back and made it bleed; it is still that way. Trout tore his mouth clear back to his ears. Sturgeon cried until his mouth protruded far out from his face, and doubled himself up. Salmon cried and tore his mouth. By this time, their father had finished whittling and had begun to distribute the toys[1] that he had made. He gave more toys to Sucker than to any of the others, for Sucker was his favorite. He also gave many toys to Herring, another of his favorites. He did not give many to Porgy (a salt-water fish) or to Trout, as he did not care much for them. Salmon also received very few. Sturgeon received very few, and those only for his head. Their father was now ready to leave them. Then his wives also began to weep. "I am going to leave you, my wives, and our children; you have disgraced me. I am ashamed," he said. He went off with Bluejay.

When they reached the opening, the chief merely wiped his feet there and it closed for all time. They learned that the two women had made it, so that no one could get across. They wanted to rear the child and keep him as their husband.

The chief went back to his people. They were very happy over his return and sang songs of joy. They took him to the prairie where the two women had stolen him from the swing. "This is the place where you were stolen," they said. "Your mother no longer lives as a person; she turned into a bird because of her sorrow. But you have a brother whom you no doubt will run across. He stays on the river, fishing. He is a very lanky fellow called Tapeworm."

Then they held a council. Bluejay said, "Let us go down the (Humptulip) River with him; lots of people live there." They sent a messenger ahead. "We're going to look for a girl for the chief to marry. Get your daughters ready," the messenger announced. "The girl must be of royal blood," Bluejay had said. They boarded their canoes. The chief was assigned a place in the middle of a canoe, all alone. "The girl who can manage to get into the canoe and sit alongside him, shall be his wife," it was decided. They started down the river, with many canoes in the party. They reached a village, the chief of which had a daughter. They stopped in front of his house. Bluejay ran and jumped on top of the house. They led the girl out and started with her toward the canoe. "If you can manage to board it, you shall be his wife," they said. They took her toward the water. "Kʊs, kʊs, kʊs," Bluejay said. The chief's daughter had not even reached the water when she had to urinate. (It was necessary to reach the canoe without fault.) They went on down the river to another village. The chief lived in the middle of the village. Bluejay ran and jumped on top of the house. They got the chief's daughter

[1] I. e., bones.

ready for the occasion. They led her out of the house. Then Bluejay began, "Kʊs, kʊs, kʊs." The girl had not reached half-way to the canoe when she had to urinate. They went to another village. The chief lived in the middle of it. They got his daughter ready. While the girl was on her way, Bluejay began, "Kʊs, kʊs, kʊs." This girl was pretty close to the chief when she had to urinate. They had to go on. They reached another village, the fourth. They stopped in front of the chief's house. Bluejay jumped on top of it. As soon as they led the girl out, Bluejay began, "Kʊs, kʊs, kʊs." The girl was about to step aboard the canoe when she had to urinate. Everyone was very sorry that she did not succeed. The chief was sorry too for he had fallen in love with her. But she was not without fault. They went on to the last village. Frog was living there. She had a grandchild. She bathed her grandchild and cleaned her, combed and braided her hair and painted her face. Bluejay was getting angrier all the time. "A girl of Frog's appearance and position cannot become the wife of a chief," he said. "She has warts on her back; she is ugly." But no one paid any attention to him. The girl's grandmother gave her a little basket with a handle. Before she started out her grandmother put some "medicine" on her that would make a man fall in love with her. She put "dope" on her, — on her breasts; she put some more "dope" in the basket. "Under no circumstances urinate," she said. "While on your way, concentrate on that man's mind and he will learn to love you." The girl started out, her grandmother looking through the door. All the people came out of their houses to look at Frog's daughter. Bluejay was so angry that he did not sing his song fast enough. "Kʊs, kʊs, kʊs," he sang slowly. Frog's daughter did not once slacken her pace. When she got near the canoe, Bluejay began to sing fast, "Kʊs, kʊs, kʊs." The girl stepped right in and sat down alongside the chief. Thus she married him. The people hurrahed. Then Bluejay said, "Well, I always thought she'd be the one to marry him!" They went back up the river to the place from which they had started.

The chief started out to look for his brother. He did not have to go very far; the boy was fishing in a pool left by an uprooted tree. He watched him. He caught a snake, a lizard and a water-dog, and swallowed them right down. After he had watched the boy for some time, he went up to him. "Poor boy," he said to him, "is this the way our mother told you to make your living?" Instead of answering him, the boy only mocked him. "Poor boy, is this the way our mother told you to make your living?" he repeated. Tapeworm was angry and cranky. His belly was bloated. His brother picked him up, held him by the feet, set him on his head and shook him. All the things that he had eaten, — the snakes, lizards, water-dogs, came out of his mouth. Some of them were still alive. After he had shaken everything out of Tapeworm, he took him to the river where the water was clear and bathed him. "I'm your elder brother," he said to him. When he got back to the place where he was living, he said to his wife, "Now you must work on my brother and make a real person out of him." Frog set to work to use her "dope" on the young fellow. She straightened his deformed body, his eyes, shaped his head nicely, and worked at him until she had at last made a real person of him. His cross-eyes were scarcely noticeable. When she had finished, the people came together again. "What are we to do?" the brothers asked one another. "We can't stay on this earth any longer," they decided. "It wouldn't be right for we were disgraced here. We shall be chiefs of the whole world, you and I," the elder said. Then he asked his brother, "What would you like to be, the sun or the moon?" "I'll be the moon; then I can see what the people do at night," the younger said. So they decided that was how it should be. When they were ready, the chief's wife said, "Your younger brother shall also have a Frog with a basket; he shall have my sister." At this time Frog decided that it made no difference what one looked like, as long as one was intelligent. Such a person could marry anyone, even one of royal blood. She decided that if people were intelligent enough, they could marry freely, instead of into fixed classes. The two brothers were ready to start on their journey. The younger went up as the moon. His wife was right there with him; if he should take sick, she was there to give him her "medicine". The elder became the sun. He had no sooner peeped over the horizon, than the water began to boil, the rocks to burst, the trees to split apart and the people to die of heat. The people went to the river to cool off but cooked there instead. At last the two brothers came together again. The younger said, "I'm afraid of the dark. I see everything, the shadows, the young people making love outside. I don't like to see them making love." Then the elder said, "It would be best if you were the sun; my power is too great for the people. Thus on your journey you will see people celebrating weddings, holding potlatches; you will be able to see all kinds of transactions, the bartering of slaves, everything that goes on during the day. On my journey, I shall only be able to see people having a good time at night. I shall only see night happenings." So they changed places. When the younger one showed himself, his heat was not too great, but just right. When the elder started, he threw out just enough light. The younger had shown no light as the moon. When the moon takes sick, he becomes dark on one side. When he gets that way, Frog, who is with him all the time, is able to drive the dark shadow away through the power of her tamanoas[1]; then he appears again. It is the same way with the sun; sometimes he goes out, takes sick. Frog, who is with him all the time, is able to cure him through the power of her tamanoas. When the moon is full, one can see Frog there, carrying a small basket in which she keeps her medicine.

[1] Guardian spirit.

Thus the Frog power is considered the greatest power for doctoring the sick. With respect to the sun, the people are given to understand that they must not look at him. If they do, they will become cross-eyed. (This applies especially to children.)

THE CONTEST IN THE NORTH.[1]

There was a village on Chinoose Creek[2] (Notsa'pac). A chief in this village had two children, a boy and a girl. The chief's name was Sea Otter; he had married Crow's daughter. There were many houses in the village. As soon as the chief's daughter reached maturity, she learned how to shoot arrows while aboard a canoe. She and her brother would always go out in a canoe together to hunt sea-fowl, and following the custom, she would always take the stern and steer. She wore a piece of abalone shell, like a pearl button, hanging from her nose. One day, she and her brother came home, their canoe loaded with ducks, geese and the like. Next day they went out again and came back, as before, their canoe loaded with fowl. As soon as they got home, they began to prepare the fowls for cooking. Instead of plucking the feathers, they skinned the fowls whole, saving the feathered skins for blankets to use at night. The third day they went out it was misting heavily. The girl's face got wet and the moisture dropped off her nose onto her abalone nose-ring. She licked the moisture off with her tongue. They came home with lots of fowl and everyone had a good time feasting. Bluejay was there with the others. The fourth time they went out, the mist and fog were pretty heavy. The moisture collected on the girl's nose-ring and dropped into her mouth. When she got home that night, she felt pains in her belly, moving pains. She spoke to her grandmother about it and the latter told her to be careful — one could not always tell what was happening. Next day, she went out again although she was not feeling well. "Can't you see what's the matter? Her belly is big now," Bluejay said. The girl and her brother returned the fourth time with as many fowl as before. When they started out for the fifth time, the people remarked, "That girl is going to have a baby before long." "Her brother must be the guilty party," Bluejay said. "Let us abandon them," the people said. So they gathered up everything they had, tore down everything and moved away so that the brother and sister would die. Crow said that she preferred to continue to love her grandchildren, but the people forced her to move. Before she left, she braided some cedar-bark, lighted it — it will remain lighted for many days — coiled it, and buried it in the corner of the house, first covering it with a clam shell. She also left some dried salmon, covering it with

[1] See p. 394.

[2] On the map this creek is written Chenois; it empties into North Bay, just east of the mouth of the Humptulip.

another clam shell. "When my grandchildren come home, start to sputter so that they can find you and dig you up. Then they won't starve or die of cold," she said.

The two young people returned home, their canoe loaded with ducks and other seafowl. "The village is gone," they said, "they have abandoned us! This must have been Bluejay's plan." After they had gone from one abandoned house to another, they heard a crackling noise in the corner near their own house. They looked, and found the fire that had been left there. "It must have been our poor grandmother," they said. They started a fire from the braid. The boy got some boughs from a tree and made a shelter, while his sister dressed the birds and cooked them. When everything was ready, they built a large fire. They decided that one should sleep on one side of the fire, one on the other. In this way, they would be able to keep the fire going. They had no covers, but they had gathered some planks and ferns and had made a bed. The fire gave so much warmth that the boy fell sound asleep. After night had fallen, a man came and lay with the girl. "Get up and try to find some covers," he said to her. While she was looking about, he began to spread blankets of duck feathers and sea-otter hides upon her bed. He did the same to her brother's bed. When the girl looked at the other side of the fire, she saw that her brother had the same kind of covers. After the man had been there a little while, he said, "Have your brother get up early and go toward the creek." (The creek was not far from their home.) After he had given her instructions and was ready to leave, he said, "It was my wish and desire for you that caused the heavy mist. In that way I made you pregnant. My name is Hwasq'a'l." As soon as it was daylight, the girl woke her brother up. "Go to the creek; perhaps something has washed ashore," she said. "How can I get up? I'm weighted down with covers. Where did they come from?" he said. He went to the creek close by and there he found a sea-lion on the shore. Alongside it was a piece of whale meat and blubber. He went farther upstream. There was something very red lying there. It proved to be a board large enough to make a good-sized house. He brought it ashore. His sister began to cook. "As soon as I have breakfast, I'll carry in the lumber and make a house," he said. "Where did you get the blankets?" he asked. "From a man, the father of my child," she said. Then she described the man to him, told how he had made himself into mist, and explained that he was chief of the Spətci'yəlαmιc.[1] The man had told her before he left that she must not help her brother lest she have a miscarriage. The lumber was light and so before long the youth had carried all the boards ashore.

Crow had clipped her hair very short and was weeping every day for her grandchildren. Bluejay became very angry when anyone grieved for them. "The children should die for they are no-account,"

[1] These people are later referred to as those from the north.

he said. The people had moved to a high rock, — James' Rock. Crow and her grandchildren usually stayed on top of this rock, from which they could see the site of their former home. They imagined that they could see smoke but never said anything to the others about it. "They must be still alive; they must have found the fire I hid," Crow would say to herself.

When the man came back the following night to the girl, he said, "I brought lots of men with me to put up the house." Her brother was sleeping soundly, he was so well covered and warm. "As soon as your brother wakes up, move upstream. You must move into the house soon; otherwise your child may be born outside," he said. As soon as her brother woke up, she told him to go out on shore. There he found a bundle of blankets made of duck feathers, also some quail meat, blubber, seal and sea-lion meat. The house was already finished. "We shall go into the house and eat there," the boy said. They went in. Everything in the way of utensils that they might need was there. (The man had brought them when he came to see the girl.) They began to smoke the meat. Before long the house was full of smoke. The same day the girl gave birth to her child, a boy. By the next day, the boy had already grown considerably. Every night the man brought something for the baby; he never came in the daytime. When her child was five days old, the woman gave birth to another boy. One morning, they noticed that a whole whale had washed ashore in front of the house.

Crow had a great many small grandchildren. She would say to the little ones, "Your eyes are sharp — what dark object is that in front of the house across the water?" The children would answer, "There is indeed something in front of the house and smoke is coming out." At last they decided to cross over to see what was there. When Crow started, she began to wail, "Ka, ka, ka." When the two young people saw the Crows coming, they said, "Oh, there are the old people!" The young woman then said to her children, "Go down to the beach and breathe in such a way that the wind will bring the old people more quickly." The children obeyed. Soon the noise of Crows could be heard. The Crows quieted down immediately they saw the house. They had noticed the amount of refuse from game and how the place smelled. When the two children saw that the Crows had begun to eat the refuse on the beach, they went out to meet them and said, "Don't eat this. It isn't any good. Come into the house." The Crows went in. So much meat was being smoked that they could scarcely see anything. There were duck blankets and otter-skin blankets. They went wild with joy. The young people told how they had found the fire. The young woman said to her grandmother, "You folks go back, get your belongings and come right back again. Say nothing to the others; we don't want Bluejay to know." That evening the Crows went back. On her way, old woman Crow began to wail in order to deceive those who had abandoned the young people. When she reached the other side, she went ashore. She had some food hidden under her clothes. The people found the Crows sitting in the house, their heads bowed, apparently in sorrow. "Did you find anything?" they asked. "Nothing. They must have died long ago," the Crows answered. That night, the Crows let their fire die down low and then the little ones began to eat. But one of the little ones choked. Bluejay jumped out of bed and thumped her on the back. She vomited a piece of whale meat. "Here it is!" he cried, "the Crows have been keeping something hidden from us." The Crows immediately got ready and started across. When they reached the other side they told what had happened. "That's why we have come back," they said, "by daylight, the whole tribe will be on its way." Sure enough, they soon saw the canoes coming. When the canoes were very nearly there, the young woman said to her children, "Go down to shore and blow in the opposite direction." The wind changed and the canoes were turned back. The fourth time that the children changed the wind, Bluejay upset and nearly drowned. "Better let them alone now. Let them come ashore," the two young people said to the children. They merely meant to annoy their people for having been so unkind. The people finally reached shore. As soon as they had landed, Bluejay began to eat refuse. "Let him help himself; it is his own concern," the others said. They began to rebuild their homes and settle down. When Bluejay came into the two young people's house, he said, "I wonder what chief came to the girl and made love to her? What I thought has come true." He had noticed that many sea-otter hides were hanging from the house and also that the woman was the mother of two grown children.

As soon as the people settled down, they learned that a whale washed ashore every morning. They began to talk about it among themselves. "What kind of man can her husband be? We never see him." Whenever the man came to visit his wife, he would say, "I would like to take you back with me. The children are grown now and I should like my family to see them." She began to consider the matter. At last her brother said, "We had better take her over to her husband's home and leave her there." He gathered all the people together in anticipation of the trip. They got everything ready and prepared a lot of food to take along. Bluejay's sister said to him, "You must go along and stay under the saddle[1]." All boarded the canoes and began to paddle. Before long they heard someone grunting, "ϒnt, ʋnt," under the seat. When they looked to see who was there, they found Bluejay. "What's the idea? Why are you there?" they asked. "My sister said I should stay under the saddle,"[2]

---

[1] A mat or brush, placed in the bottom of the canoe as a seat.

[2] A play on words, a feature that is not uncommon in Coast Salish mythology, and one that always gives rise to a humorous situation. It is impossible to render a passage of this sort adequately in English. From other versions

he answered. They went out into the ocean (toward Alaska). When they arrived at the place, they had to stop far out from shore. They could not go any farther because of the ice. When they managed at last to get in to shore, their chief said to them, "You must stay aboard until I tell you to get out." But Bluejay soon lost patience and jumped ashore. As soon as he struck the ice, he slipped and landed under the canoe, giving his head a good hard bump. They had to pull him on board again. Then they laughed and sang, "When did Bluejay jump on the ice?" But Bluejay was not one whom they could get the best of. "I did that on purpose," he said. "I got so hot I jumped into the water to cool off." At last their leader was told by his hosts that they could come ashore. "Tell your children to kick the ice; then it will disappear and we can go ashore," the leader said to the young woman. The children did as they were told and the party went ashore. When they got close to the house, they stopped. As soon as Bluejay went ashore, he began to eat something red on the ground, which he thought was kinikinik berries; it was the excrements of the people. "When did Bluejay eat the excrements of the Spətci'yəlαmιc?" the others said. "I'm not eating the excrements of the Spətci'yəlαmιc," he said, "I'm only eating kinikinik berries." They stood in front of the house. Bluejay lost patience and tried to jump in, but two large sea-lions guarding the door nearly ate him up. The woman's children kicked at the sea-lions and the latter ran under the bed or under anything they could find to get away from the children. The people went inside. As soon as they were in, their hosts began to cook meat for them — whale and sea-lion meat — also kinikinik berries. They sat down and ate. As soon as they sat down, they were given red-elderberry stalks, the pith of which had been removed.[1] They were to put the stalks through their mouths and out their anuses so that what they ate would go right through. Thus they would not become satiated and ill. Bluejay soon lost patience again. "How shall I ever become satiated? Everything I swallow goes right through me," he said. His people told him not to make such breaks, but he would not stop talking. At last they took the elderberry stalk from him and closed him up. He took a few bites and immediately became satiated. He lay down, sick and pale. As soon as the others had finished eating, they removed the elderberry stalks.

It was dark by this time. One of the northerners challenged Bluejay to a stay-awake contest. The challenger was Shadow. All the others went to bed. Just before the contest, Bluejay's chief put

---

of this incident, I offer the following interpretation: Bluejay's sister tells him to break off some brush and put it in the bottom of the canoe. He understands her to say that he should go underneath the brush in the canoe. See p. 10.

[1] By their own leader or by their hosts? In other versions of this tale, it is the visitors' own leader who gives them the stalks.

phosphorus wood on his eyes so that they would appear to be open all the time. "Bluejay," he said, "you must stay near me." If Bluejay fell asleep, he would jab him with a stick. "Shadow," Bluejay called, "are you still awake?" "Yes, I'm still awake," Shadow called back. Again Bluejay called, "Shadow, are you still awake?" "Yes, I'm still awake," Shadow answered. Bluejay was now on the point of falling asleep. His chief jabbed him with the stick. "Shadow, are you still awake?" he called. "Yes, I'm still awake," Shadow answered. Bluejay was again on the point of falling asleep, and his chief jabbed him with the stick. Bluejay then called for the fourth time. Shadow was slow in answering. The fifth time, Bluejay himself was beginning to snore. His chief jabbed him with the stick. Then Bluejay called, "Shadow, are you still awake?" There was no answer. He called again. Suddenly he heard a loud snore from Shadow. Then Bluejay cried out, "When ever before, through all the ages, has Shadow been beaten?" Bluejay had won this contest. Next day at daybreak, their hosts were going to give them presents. "When they ask you what you want," Bluejay's chief said to him, "tell them that you want a sea-otter blanket." But when they called Bluejay's name, he told them that he wanted a shag-blanket. This was altogether different from what his chief had told him to ask for; it was the cheapest grade of blanket. They asked the chief what kind of blanket he wanted and he said, "Sea-otter." When they had finished, they began to put up food for their guests' return journey. They asked Bluejay what kind of food he wanted, and he said, "Excrements." He put them in his pack-basket. "Why did you ask for such a thing when you could have had seal-meat, whale-meat or anything of the sort?" his people asked him. When they got on board, they put everything together in baskets. The chief did not know what Bluejay was carrying. When they put their weight on the paddles, they smelt a disagreeable odor. This kept up until they got home. Bluejay went ashore, carrying his basket, from which a strong odor came. "What in the world have you got?" they asked. "My sister told me to bring her some excrements," he said. When he got to his sister, she told him to throw the stuff away immediately. "But you told me to get some of this,"[1] he said.

After they had been back some time, they put up food for another visit to the north, where the young woman and her two children were now living permanently. They finally arrived at the place. The young woman came out and before Bluejay had a chance to jump out and hurt himself, scattered the ice with her foot. They went ashore. When they got to the house, the young woman kicked the sea-lions guarding the door and the latter went away. They were given lunch by their hosts and were treated the same as before. Bluejay's people warned him that he should do less talking. He

[1] Bluejay has again misunderstood what his sister said. She probably told him to bring back some food. See p. 20.

made no remarks until the elderberry stalk was removed from him and he had become satiated. Then Seal, one of the northerners, challenged him to a diving contest. All went down to the water's edge and boarded the canoes. The visitors' chief then took the brush from one of the canoes and threw it in the water alongside the canoe. Bluejay and Seal dived overboard. The chief had told Bluejay to come out of the water where the brush was; he would be able to breathe there. Everyone waited and waited. "Has Seal come out yet?" Bluejay asked at last. "No! Keep quiet! They'll see you," the chief said. Bluejay finally began to shiver from the cold. "Keep quiet! Don't shiver!" the chief said. The day was well gone — the sun was pretty low — when Seal came out. The blood was streaming from his nose; he was all in. As soon as he got his wind, he asked, "Has Bluejay come ashore yet?" "No," he was told. Seal came on shore immediately. He had lost the contest. "Now, Bluejay," the chief said, "go under our canoe and go out in the water as far as you can; then come up." When Bluejay stuck his head out of the water, he asked, "Has Seal come out yet?" "Yes." When he heard that he had won the contest, he shouted, "When did anyone ever win from Fable[1]?" They went out after Bluejay but had a hard time getting him aboard, he was so cold. They wrapped him in blankets and had to carry him ashore. As soon as he was somewhat warmed up, they started to give him presents again. When they asked him what kind of blanket he wanted, he told them that he wanted a crane-blanket. As soon as they had finished, they began to put up food for the visitors on their journey home. They asked Bluejay what he would like to eat. He said, "Ma'təmatł." "But how can you eat that?" they asked. It was a kind of file (made from bulrushes). So they put up a pack of food for him. He came to a woman who was relieving herself. "I'm going to buy what you are sitting on," he said to her. "Who would buy excrements!" she said. She would not let him have what he wanted. The visitors finally set out for home. During his stay Bluejay was being continually corrected by the young woman who had married there.

After they had been home for some time, they prepared food and started back. They finally got there and landed at the usual place. The ice prevented them from going ashore. The young woman came down and scattered it with her foot so that Bluejay would not jump ashore and hurt himself. She then made the dogs[2] go away from the door. Their hosts fed them and treated them the same as before. They again made use of the elderberry stalks. When they had finished eating, they removed the stalks. Then Squirrel challenged Bluejay to a climbing contest. A tall, standing tree, with no limbs, had been hewn smooth. It was on this tree, where Squirrel was accustomed to play, that the contest was to take place. As

[1] What he calls himself.
[2] That is, the sea-lions.

soon as he had received the challenge, Bluejay arose and said, "My fellow tribesmen, do not be afraid; I shall win. It is my habit to climb such things." Squirrel began to climb. From the very start, Bluejay seemed to have the best of him. He soon reached the top of the pole. "Ka'tca, ka'tca," he said, for he was angry and excited. It was some time before Squirrel reached the top. As soon as Squirrel caught up with him, Bluejay speared him on the head; Squirrel fell down, dead. The people cheered Bluejay. When he was ready to come down, he jumped from the pole to the top of the house, to the eaves and down to the ground, just to show what he could do. His people knew that if he lost one contest, they would be killed. When they had finished, their hosts gave them presents and food. Then they went home. This was the third time.

They stayed home quite a while and then decided to go again, first gathering together a lot of food. Quite a crowd planned to go. When everything was ready, they started out. They finally got there. Some time after they had landed on the ice floe, the woman came out and scattered the ice with her foot. Then they went ashore. The woman drove the dogs away from the door. Finally, their hosts gave them meat and treated them as before. When they had finished eating, they challenged Bluejay to another climbing contest. The contestants were to climb from limb to limb. This time, Bluejay's opponent was Flying Squirrel. Bluejay said, "All right; I am an expert at climbing trees." The woman put some pitch on the tree where they were to climb, so that when Flying Squirrel hit the tree, it would hold him back. Bluejay was first. He jumped and jumped, and reached the first limb. Then he began to sing,

> Jump, jump, from one limb to another,
> Jump, jump, from one limb to another.

When the race was in full swing, Flying Squirrel began to stick to the tree and had first to pull himself loose before going on. Bluejay was already on top of the tree. "Ka'tca, ka'tca," he said, as he jumped upon Flying-Squirrel's head and dug his claws into him. Flying Squirrel fell down, dead. After their hosts had given them presents and put up a lunch for them, they went home.

They stayed home quite a while. Then they said, "Let us go again to our daughter. It may be the last time we shall ever see her. We may be killed; Bluejay may be beaten." They felt uneasy, knew that something would happen. The leader of the party was the woman's brother. They got ready to go. They finally got there. When they arrived, Bluejay said, "I feel less confident. I feel we are going to lose this time." They landed on the ice. The young man's sister was now carrying a baby on her back. As soon as she saw her brother, she began to weep. "I don't know what will happen. The minute I saw you, I began to feel bad. Take good care of yourselves. This is your last trial. Make yourselves ready and don't forget a thing," she said to him. Heretofore, Bluejay had always had something to say that was out of place, but now, for once, he said only pleasing things. The young woman had given her people advice. They went ashore. She had warned them, "This time, they will take you where a dangerous being — a kind of whale — lives, but they won't take you today." They entered the house as usual. Their hosts began to cook for them and later gave them something to eat. They made use of the elderberry stalks as before. When they had finished eating and it was time to go to sleep, they went to bed without any further ado. One of the leader's nephews slept with him. When it was daylight, they were given something to eat. The woman said to her husband, "Don't take my brother to that place. Your people are going to kill him. Surely you have been planning all along to kill him; that's why you married me." And so her husband did not take them to the place that day. They stayed there five days. The fifth day, the man took them toward the ocean. The woman said to her brother, "If they tell you to spear the first whale, don't do it. Four of the whales are fierce. Spear the fifth one; you can kill it." She wrapped her baby tightly to her body so that she would be free to help her brother. They gave him a harpoon. It took his whole tribe to lift it, they were so frightened. The leader of the opposition cried out, "Good food! good food!" The woman was holding on to the harpoon as her brother raised it. "No," she said. "Don't say a word," she said to Bluejay. When the first whale appeared, the people of the north cried out, "Kako'iloc."[1] When the second whale came to the surface, they again cried out, "Kako'iloc," but still the young man did not spear. When the third whale appeared, they again cried out, "Kako'iloc." Just as her brother was ready to spear, the woman held him back. When the fourth whale appeared, they again cried, "Kako'iloc." "You must not repeat what they say; that would be unfortunate," the woman warned her people. "Let this one go and spear the next," she said. The whale disappeared. When the fifth one appeared, her brother let go of the harpoon; he had speared too late. The woman caught hold of the harpoon, but she was too late also. Bluejay had said, "Ka — —,"[2] as the harpoon struck. The harpoon finally slipped from the woman's grasp. Her brother and all the people holding onto the line — the entire tribe — were carried away. All the young woman was able to grasp were Bluejay's tail feathers. She turned back from shore; she had saved nothing but Bluejay's feathers. She blew the feathers back to her tribal home. The whale had dived into the ocean with all the others; not one was saved.

She went back, took her baby from her back and said to her husband, "Here is your son. I don't care where I go to die. You have done me a great wrong. I loved my brother, my family and my

[1] Good food?

[2] He starts to repeat what the Northerners have said.

people." Then she left. Her husband followed her. He could not overtake her and gave up.

The woman travelled aimlessly day and night — through the woods and everywhere. A stick struck her eye and put it out. Finally she chanced to meet her husband at the lake — or body of water — where the dangerous whales lived. She went straight into the water. Her husband ventured to speak to her. "My dear wife, come back. Your children are weeping for you." "Let them weep," she said, "you have done me a great wrong." Thereupon she dived into the lake. Her husband sat down facing her. "You must not dive," he said. She paid no attention to him. When she came to the surface, she asked, "Do I still look like a person?" "Yes. Come ashore to me. Your children are weeping," he said. "Let them cry. I love them but I also loved my brother," she answered. She dived again. "Do I still look like a person?" she asked for the second time. "Yes. Come ashore, otherwise you will become a dangerous being," he said. "No matter; I loved my brother," she answered. She dived again. When she came to the surface for the third time, she asked, "Do I still look like a person?" "You don't look like a person now. You look different, but come ashore nevertheless," he answered. She dived for the fourth time. When she came to the surface, her entire body was covered with hair. "Do I still look like a person?" she asked. "No, you look like a dangerous being, but come ashore nevertheless," he said. She dived for the fifth time. When she came to the surface, she had horns on her head. "Do I still look like a person?" she asked. "You are a dangerous being now; you look different, but come back to our children," he said. Then she advised him about the children and dived for good. He never saw her again. He gave up and went back home. The children were weeping. "There is no reason why we should remain people any longer," he said, "we have done wrong. I loved my wife but today she is gone. We shall turn into birds and remain homeless forever. We shall eat our food raw." Then they left their homes and began to float on the oceans. The entire tribe broke up in this manner. They became the Hwasq'a'l.[1] It is a great sight to see them when they come far south.

When Bluejay's tail feathers got back home, they turned into a Bluejay again. That's how the people know this story; Bluejay told them.

BLUEJAY AND HIS SISTER YO'I.[2]

Bluejay and his sister Yo'i lived on Chinoose Creek. Every day Yo'i went out to dig lacamas and other roots. Bluejay shot arrows for a pastime and managed to shoot a few birds to eat. "You should

[1] English equivalent unknown; a large bird with white breast and black spotted wings and back.
[2] See p. 396.

shoot the geese. They annoy me more than any other birds, by peeping under my skirts," Yo'i said to him. She had a digging stick, sharp on one end, with a cross-piece for a handle. When she stuck the stick in the ground, she would bear far over to pry the roots out. Once when she was breaking the ground and stooping over more than usual, an arrow struck her in the backside. Bluejay had done it; the ducks were all around her. She cried, "Oh you old thing! Why did you shoot me?" At the same time, she called him a name; she could see the tuft of feathers on top of his head. "But you told me that the geese hang around under your skirts," he answered. Next day, Yo'i went out to dig again, but Bluejay did not come around; he was afraid of her.

The evening of the following day, Bluejay said to her, "Yo'i, you should marry with the dead." Next morning Yo'i went out to dig. She had a strange feeling and began to sing,

There is fog over the Land of the Dead.

Next day she went out to dig again. Fog began to settle down over the place where she was digging. She sang the same song. The third day, the fog began to settle very close to her. The fourth day, a man came up to her. He was not a real man, but fog in human shape. The fifth day, the fog spoke to her. "I am here now, the one you have been wishing for; I am from the dead," he said. He asked her to marry him and Yo'i accepted; Bluejay had told her to marry a ghost. She agreed to go away with him. "There is no reason why I should remain here any longer; I'm married to you," she said. She got ready to go with him. "I'm going away with a man from the dead," she said to Bluejay. "Where is your husband? I can only see fog," he said. "What do you mean by talking like that about a chief!" she scolded. "Whenever you want to visit me in the Land of the Dead, make five square buckets and fill them with water. There are five prairies there, always burning," she said. Then she left with her husband, having given her brother instructions how to visit her.

Her husband told her to close her eyes and to keep them closed. She closed her eyes, but feeling afraid, soon opened them. As soon as she had done so, she no longer seemed to move. Her husband made her close her eyes again. They went down to the depths of the earth. When they passed through this danger, he said, "Open your eyes now." When she opened her eyes, she found they were in a very lovely country. They came out on a prairie so full of beautiful flowers that it seemed to be on fire. After they had crossed five prairies like this, they came to one that was truly on fire. "Don't be afraid," her husband said, "I travel here; this is my trail — the trail of the dead." They started across and soon reached the other side. Yo'i did not even feel the heat for the fire seemed to draw apart and leave a path. They went on and reached another prairie, also ablaze. In a short time, they reached the other side. They came to another burning prairie which they soon crossed. They came to the fourth and crossed it in the same manner. The fifth was blazing more than any of the others; the flames nearly reached the sky. This time her husband said, "You must close your eyes and keep them closed; you are living, not dead. Under no circumstances open your eyes." As soon as they were across, he told her she could open her eyes. Shortly after they were through the most dangerous part of their journey—dangerous for Yo'i but not at all for her husband—they came to a river. Her husband called someone to come after them. "Ko, ko, ko, ko,"[1] he called; this is the language of the dead. As soon as he called, a skull began to roll down the opposite bank and got into a canoe. The canoe landed on their side of the river, although Yo'i could see no one paddling. After they had started across, she noticed that there was a hole in the bottom of the canoe.[2] She was afraid it would sink. "Don't be afraid," her husband said and put his foot over the hole. For the first time, Yo'i was actually able to see her husband. He was nothing but a skull, with holes where his eyes and nose had been, and entirely without flesh. They started toward the house, following the other skull as it rolled along. When they reached the house, her husband said, "Go in. This is my house." Yo'i could see nothing but skulls, some of which were lying on the bed. When she had been there only a short time, she could hear, "Ko, ko, ko." Then the skulls began to move toward the fire. She saw them get some bark and stand it against the flame; the bark was full of pitch. There was also a lot of bark hanging over the fire. Before long a skull, carrying a piece of board with some bark on it, came toward her and set it down in front of her. "How can I eat bark?" she thought to herself. "This is not bark, it is steelhead salmon that was roasted on sticks before the fire," her husband explained. "You must close your eyes when you eat it." She took hold of it and twisted it; it broke easily. She closed her eyes for a moment, but as soon as she got it up to her mouth, she saw that it was nothing but a piece of bark. On her fifth attempt, she managed to keep her eyes closed long enough to eat it and found that it tasted like good fish. She broke off another piece, keeping her eyes closed, and raised it to her mouth. But then she opened them again and saw that it was only a piece of bark. She closed her eyes and swallowed it. Then she made up her mind to keep her eyes closed, as she was hungry. It was really quite good, so she kept her eyes closed and so managed to get a real meal.

As soon as night fell, she heard, "Ko, ko, ko," again and got frightened. That night she went to bed with her skull-husband. They had very good covers. Very early in the morning, the skulls began to talk again. Her skull-husband rolled out of bed and began to talk

[1] Spoken very fast.

[2] Many of the Coast Salish bore holes in their burial canoes to let the water run out.

with the others. As a matter of fact, he had gone to see his trap. He soon came back, carrying two large pieces of bark. "Dress and roast this steelhead salmon," he said to her. He showed her how to cut it; it cut easily. She dressed it as she would have done a real salmon. She set it up to roast. Pitch began to run from the bark. "That's fat from the fish," her husband explained. She took the piece of bark out and they ate it for breakfast. She found she no longer had any trouble keeping her eyes closed. As soon as they had finished eating, her husband rolled outside, saying, "Ko, ko, ko." In five days' time, Yo'i gave birth to a child; it was nothing but a skull. After five more days she had another baby, also a skull.[1]

Bluejay soon became lonesome living alone and decided to visit his sister. One day he met Wedge. "How would you like to go along with me to the Land of the Dead? I am going to visit my family over there," Wedge said. "We'll make five buckets and then go," he added. Bluejay was pleased to accompany him. They made the five buckets and set out. "You must close your eyes if we are to get there," Wedge said. They had not gone far, when Bluejay opened his eyes. After five trials, he kept them closed. "You mustn't try any funny business when you travel with me — we might die," Wedge said. They came at last to the prairie full of flowers, that seemed to be on fire. "Phosphorus wood prairie,"[2] Wedge said and they passed through. Thus they crossed the five prairies. "We will soon reach a prairie that is really on fire," Wedge said. Before long they came to this blazing prairie. "I'll carry four buckets and you carry one," Wedge said to Bluejay. "Whatever you do, don't drop it; we might die." Bluejay began to shiver, he was so frightened. "Why did I come?" he said. Wedge began to sing, "Słαts, słαts," as he sprinkled water from a bucket, thus making a path through the fire. "This is what they call 'Fire prairie'," he said to Bluejay. Bluejay was so frightened he could not speak. They came to the second prairie on fire. "Słαts, słαts," Wedge said, sprinkling water with his hand. He gave Bluejay the empty bucket to carry. Bluejay was so frightened, he could not even sing with Wedge. They got across safely, having emptied another bucket. They went on. "Słαts, słαts, Fire prairie, słαts, słαts, Fire prairie," Wedge sang. He emptied the third bucket. "We have two more prairies like this to cross and then we'll be through the danger," Wedge said. Bluejay never opened his mouth. They came to the fourth. "Słαts, słαts, Fire prairie," Wedge sang. They had one more bucket left. Then Bluejay made a break. He ventured to ask, "What shall we do if there is not enough water in this bucket?" "Well, this is all I ever have carried; I've never run short before," Wedge

[1] The interpreter explains, "Now the story comes back to Bluejay."
[2] This is the term the interpreter used. I should prefer to substitute Glowing or Luminous prairie. What is implied here is, that the flowers on the prairie produce an effect like the glow from phosphorus wood.

answered. At this, Bluejay began to pick up a little courage. They came to another that was blazing pretty high. Bluejay was so frightened, he shivered all over. "Don't let your mind wander; wish only that the water will hold out," Wedge said. "Słαts, słαts, Fire prairie," Wedge sang, as both of them sprinkled water on the fire. When they got to the other side, they found there was a little water left in the bucket. Bluejay was happy to have crossed alive. They continued their journey. They reached the river. "I'll leave you here; I'm going up a little farther; my family lives there," Wedge said. "How long will you stay?" Bluejay asked. "Oh, some time; I plan to have some fun with the girls," Wedge said. "Well," he added in parting, "enjoy yourself and don't be bashful."

While Bluejay was waiting on the river bank, his sister came out. "Oh my little brother, my little brother," she cried. He noticed three skulls rolling down the bank behind her. She boarded the canoe and the little skulls rolled into the bow. They reached the other side. Then he heard the children saying, "Ko, ko, ko, ko," and became frightened. "Why did you put dead people in the canoe?" he asked. "Don't talk that way about your little nephews!" Yo'i said. "But how can I have dead people for my nephews? They are only skulls," he said. "I won't get into that canoe. There's a hole in it; it might sink. Go back and bring another." So Yo'i went back to get another canoe. "And don't put skulls in it again!" he called out. "Don't talk that way about your nephews!" she answered. "But how can I have skulls for nephews!" he called back. When she boarded the canoe, three little skulls rolled in again; she could not keep them out. When she got across to Bluejay once more, he said, "Those skulls are here again! I'm afraid of them. I won't get in! There's a hole in this canoe. Go back and get another one without a hole. And leave the skulls out! I'm afraid of them." "But all the canoes have holes in them," Yo'i explained. She crossed back over. She had to go five times before Bluejay was convinced that all the canoes had holes. As soon as they were on their way, the little skulls began to roll back and forth. "Oh, these skulls! I'm afraid of them," Bluejay said. "They're your nephews; don't talk that way about them. They are glad to see you and call you 'uncle'," Yo'i said. "How can they be glad to see me when they only make 'talk'!" Bluejay said, pushing one out of the canoe with his foot. Yo'i had a hard time catching the little fellow; he was just about ready to sink, all the time keeping up a rapid fire of, "Ko, ko, ko." "Don't treat my children like this; their father is of royal blood. Why do you come here anyway if you mean to act like this! My child is cold; he has swallowed a lot of water," Yo'i said angrily. "How can a skull get cold!" Bluejay said. When they were near the shore, Bluejay threw another skull overboard with a paddle. Yo'i began to cry. The little skulls began to roll ahead of them. "The children are afraid of you now and will tell the people how mean you treated them," Yo'i said. "Since you're here, behave yourself and let the people alone. Don't bother them. You're the one who told me I should marry here. You shouldn't treat my children so roughly," she added. She was angry with her brother.

They went into the house. Bluejay looked around. There was nothing but skulls. Some were walking about, others were lying on the beds; all were wrapped in good blankets. The little skulls lay by the fire. "Little skulls, sitting by the fire," Bluejay began to cry. "You mustn't talk that way to your nephews; they're cold. You kicked them into the water," Yo′i said. "I don't understand how skulls can get cold," Bluejay answered. "I'm afraid to sit down, there are so many skulls around." Yo′i spread a mat before him. "Here's a place," she said. He sat down, first kicking a little skull out of the way. "Be careful, you may hurt him or kill him!" Yo′i said. "I only did it because I didn't know where to stretch my legs; I had to kick it out of the way," he said. While he was sitting there, Yo′i took down a piece of bark and put it near the fire to roast. The pitch ran off. "What are you cooking that for?" he asked. "That's for your dinner," Yo′i answered. "I won't eat that — a piece of bark full of pitch!" he said. "Don't talk like that here! These people are very high-class; you insult them," Yo′i said. She took the piece of bark away from the fire, put it on a board, and set it before him. "Close your eyes and eat now," she said. "How can I eat a piece of bark with pitch running from it?" he asked, and threw it into the fire. "That's how bark should be used — for firewood!" he said. Yo′i had a hard time trying to get it out of the fire, burning her hands in the attempt. "If you don't eat it, you'll starve," she said. "I'll never eat bark! How could I chew it?" he said. "If you'll only close your eyes, you'll find you can eat bark; it's really steelhead salmon," she explained. "It's strange that you yourself don't starve if you only eat bark," he said. "But I told you it was steelhead salmon," she said. Then she placed some before her children and they ate it with zest as they were hungry. Bluejay was surprised. "How can skulls eat!" By this time his sister was tired out and began to cry.

Bluejay went out to look the place over. Toward evening, Yo′i took down some more bark and set it in front of the fire to cook. The place was noisy with, "Ko, ko, ko," for it was meal time. The skulls began to stir about. "Get some water for your father to wash his face," Yo′i said to her children. Bluejay was so frightened by the "talk", he could not even stir. "I can't go anywhere but what I find skulls talking," he said. The little skulls soon came back with the water. "How can skulls carry water?" he asked. Before long the skulls began their "talk" again. "Oh, my brother," Yo′i said, "these people say that you clubbed them when you were out walking." "I couldn't help it. I had to do it. I was afraid of them, they talked so much," he said. "But they were only glad to see you," Yo′i explained. When it was time to go to bed, Yo′i said,

"One of your nephews would like to sleep with you." "Why should I sleep with a skull, I'm afraid of them," he answered. "You'd better eat something before you go to bed," she said. "As long as I have only bark to eat, I won't eat it," he answered. They finally went to bed. "I don't understand how you can sleep with a skull; he has no eyes, only eye sockets, and his teeth show," Bluejay said to Yo'i. "Why do you speak of these people like that? They feel insulted," she answered. After he had got into bed, Bluejay could hear the house full of "talk". He finally fell asleep.

Early in the morning, his skull brother-in-law rolled off the bed saying, "Sko, sko, sko." Bluejay cried out, "I'm so frightened! The skull sleeping with my sister talks." As soon as her husband went out, Yo'i said, "Don't talk like that. Your brother-in-law went out to look at his trap." "But he'll bring back bark, not steelhead salmon," Bluejay answered. "Keep quiet; you make me tired," his sister said. Finally Yo'i got up, washed her face and built a fire. The children started to talk as soon as they got up. "Your father went to his trap. Go meet him; he may catch more than he can carry," Yo'i said to them. Bluejay began to laugh. "How can these skulls do anything, anyway?" The little skulls went down to the river. Sure enough, a skull soon came back with two large steelhead salmon. The people began to talk when they saw them. Soon the little skulls rolled in, all talking. "Did you cover the fish?" Yo'i asked them. They told her that their father had caught a lot of fish. Bluejay noticed that the skulls began to roll out. "The skulls are beginning to roll out," he said. "Don't talk to the people like that," Yo'i said. "They're going down to the river; there's a canoe load of salmon there," she explained. The smallest skull began to say, "Ko, ko, ko —," to his mother, meaning, "We have picked out the best fish for uncle, who must get up and wash his face." "Oh, even the little ones talk," Bluejay said, "but it isn't real talk, it's something dangerous." Yo'i finished cooking breakfast and set the best fish before her brother. She took another board, placed some fish on it and set it before her husband. One of the little ones began to roll toward his father. "My youngest child says he wants to eat with you," Yo'i explained to Bluejay. "I don't want a skull to eat with me; he has no eyes," Bluejay answered. He watched his sister while she ate, for he was hungry by this time. "I'll try to do what she does," he thought to himself. He closed his eyes tightly and raised the food to his mouth. He opened his eyes. It was nothing but a piece of bark. He managed to hold his eyes shut tightly and began to chew. It was very good fish. He finished breakfast with his eyes shut. It tasted good as long as he kept them shut. "It's good enough food!" he said. Soon one of the little skulls rolled out. When he rolled back in again, he had some water. He set it down in front of Bluejay. "Your nephew brought you some water to wash your hands," Yo'i explained. "Why should I have a skull for a nephew?" Bluejay asked, adding, "I'm so afraid of skulls. I'll become one myself if I don't watch out!"

Before long he heard the noise of talking. Suddenly his sister's husband rolled out as fast as he could go, with a pack-rope. "The people say there is a whale on the beach and to help yourself," Yo'i explained. Bluejay went out. When he got to the beach, there was nothing but skulls. His sister went along with him to keep watch over him; she noticed that he had a stick and was striking people with it as they went by. He got to the place where the whale was supposed to be. There was nothing there but a large log, white on top with skulls. He got on top of the log and began to roll the skulls off. He peeled off a fairly large piece of bark and carried it home. "I'm going to use this for all-night firewood, so the skulls won't talk," he said. "This isn't bark, it's whale blubber," his sister said. "No, it's bark from a tree. I didn't see any whale. There's only a tree on the beach," he said, But Yo'i dressed the bark and hung it up to dry. Before long, Bluejay heard a lot of "talk". "They say that when you got to the whale, you threw the people on the ground, struck them and hurt them badly," Yo'i said. "Don't do it again."

Bluejay began to make some buckets. He wanted to go back home. As soon as he had finished one, he said, "Now I'll go back. I'm afraid to stay here any longer." "On your way back," Yo'i explained, "you will find five prairies called 'Phosphorus wood' that you can cross without water." "But why don't you go back with the person you came with?" she added. "That man is having a good time with the girls. I can't wait for him. As for me, I don't care about having a good time with skulls," he said. The skulls soon began to talk among themselves. "Your brother-in-law has to go to his trap first; then he'll go along with you to see that you get there safely," Yo'i explained to Bluejay. But he refused to have it. "He would make 'talk' and I'm afraid of it. I can't understand him anyway," he said.

He started home alone. He had five buckets of water; he had managed to make the necessary number of buckets. He came out on the first prairie and began to sing, "This must be the prairie my sister told me was 'Phosphorus wood prairie'." "Słαts, słαts," he sang and began to sprinkle the water. He did not have to use all the water in the first bucket to get across. As soon as he reached the other side, he began to boast, "When did they ever beat Fable?"[1] He came to the second one and began to sing, "This must be the prairie my sister called 'Phosphorus wood prairie'. Słαts, słαts." He got across without using up all the water from the first bucket. Then he began to boast louder than ever, "When did they ever beat Fable?" He came to another. He began to sing, "This must be the prairie my sister called 'Phosphorus wood prairie'. Słαts, słαts." He got across and began to boast again. "I've crossed three prairies

[1] See footnote 1, p. 290.

with only one bucket of water. Wonderful! I'll get through without using all my water!" He went on. He came to the fourth prairie and began to sing, "This must be the prairie my sister called 'Phosphorus wood prairie'. Słαts, słαts." He got across, having used just a little water from the second bucket. He came to another — the last of the Phosphorus wood prairies. He got across, without having to use all the water in the second bucket. He had crossed five prairies with one and a half buckets of water.

He came to another prairie. This one was actually on fire. When he got there, he began to think, "Surely we used five buckets full of water for these five prairies." The other prairies were only ablaze with flowers; these prairies were truly on fire.[1] He began to sing, in a humble voice now. "This must be the prairie my sister told me was on fire. Słαts, słαts." He managed to get across with the water that remained in the second bucket. He now had only three buckets of water left with which to cross four burning prairies. He felt sad. He tried to turn around and go back, but had forgotten how to turn around. He came to another; there was a large fire. He began to sing, half crying, for he knew he was short of water, "This must be the prairie my sister said was on fire. Słαts, słαts." He got across, with a little bit of water left; he had made it go as far as possible. He had three burning prairies to cross and only two buckets of water. He came to another. It was blazing still higher. He began to sing his song. He thought to himself, "I'll run through as fast as I can; then I won't have to put the fire clear out." Sure enough, he got across with some water left in his bucket. "It's obvious that I'm going to get a little burnt, but I'll go through any way I can. I'll strike the fire with my buckets. I've got five bear-skins and I'll use them, too." He had two more prairies to cross and had only one full bucket and a little water left in another. When he came to the next one, he tried to go through as fast as he could. Although he was running fast, his hair and body caught on fire. He kept right on, throwing a little water as he ran. He got across. He now had only a little more than half a bucket of water. "I shall surely die," he thought. He kept going and came to the last, bigger than any of the others. He began to sing, at the same time crying for his sister. He went as fast as he could go. Not far from the end, the water gave out. He began to spit on the fire, striking it with his bearskin blanket. "Stʻo, stʻo," he spit. The last bucket of water was gone. He used the

---

[1] Notice that the order of the prairies on the return trip is reversed, a fact which the interpreter, if he noticed it, did not call my attention to. Heretofore in the story, those coming from the world of the living found first the five flower prairies, then the five fire prairies. The latter were not far from the village of the dead. Here, on his trip home, Bluejay finds first the five flower prairies and then the five fire prairies. I suppose this reversal of order is necessary to work up the proper suspense: Bluejay's journey must become more and more dangerous. The other way round, his journey would become ess and less dangerous.

rest of his bear-skins. Near the very end, his fifth bear-skin burnt up. When his saliva was gone, he began to strike the fire with his head. He had only a few steps more to go, when he began to shrivel up and roast. Suddenly he died, his claws drawn up together.

He was back at the river once more, now calling, "Ko, ko, ko." He was saying, "Sister, come after me in the canoe." The children ran out and cried, "Our uncle wants the canoe." Yo'i began to cry, "My brother — he's dead, now." She went down to the water; she could see Bluejay on the other side. He was saying, "Ko, ko, ko," meaning, "Take me across." He was dead. "Oh, my brother, I knew he would die," she said, and wept. Bluejay could see the children getting into the canoe. "How beautiful they are! Is there a hole in that canoe? How beautiful! It's a different one, isn't it?" he said. "It's the same one. You are dead now and you see things differently," Yo'i explained. "How beautiful your children are. Where did you get them, anyway?" he asked. "They're the same ones that you kicked overboard and this is the very canoe you were afraid to ride in before," Yo'i said. "No, it's not the same canoe; there's no hole in it," he said, "and these are not the same children I threw overboard; the others were skulls. These are my nephews whom I love dearly." As soon as they reached shore, he took his youngest nephew in his arms. Yo'i went to the house, weeping. Bluejay met a lot of people, who formerly only appeared to him as skulls. She could hear him talking, "Ko, ko, ko." She told her husband that her brother was now one of the dead. "If I had taken him back," her husband said, "this never would have happened." When they went into the house, Bluejay found that all the people were very kind and good. "Is that your husband — the royal person there in a blanket?" he asked Yo'i. "Yes, he's the very one you used to throw around," she said. "No, I never threw him around, I only threw skulls around," he said. "You are dead now. If you had let my husband take you through, you would not have died," she explained. "I'm not dead! I wouldn't feel or look like this if I were dead!" he said. He went out and soon came back with a steelhead salmon. "What a beautiful salmon this is. Let us dress it right away. Salmon is salmon, not bark," he said. "This is what you used to throw away," Yo'i said. She cooked it for him and set it before him. "I want my three nephews to eat with me," he said. He took hold of the fish and put it into the children's hands, he loved them so much.

Soon he went out. One of his nephews went with him. Some people came into the house, saying, "Ko, ko, ko." Yo'i got up and went out. Sure enough Bluejay had gone in the direction she had forbidden him to go. Not far away the people were dancing, holding cooking utensils, some of which were made of bone, in their hands. "I told you not to come here. This is where people go when they die the second time," she said to Bluejay. "I saw these things and I wanted to bring one back to you," he explained. She made him go back home. She got him home and then forgot about him. The children came in. "Uncle is going to that place again," they said. Yo′i ran out. She found him dancing with the people. She got him home and then forgot about him. The children came in. "Uncle is going to that place again." Yo′i ran out as fast as she could. This time, Bluejay was already making motions with his hands like the other dancers. She took him home and then forgot about him. The children came in. "Uncle is going to that place again." Yo′i ran out quickly. She saw Bluejay dancing, bending over, about to fall on his head. The people whom he was with danced upside down. He was singing, "Tce′yeyʊk." Yo′i wept and the children wept also. "Why are you weeping ? I came over here to get you a dish of bone," he said. She took him back home for the fourth time. She forgot about him. The children came running in. "Uncle is over at that place again." She found Bluejay dancing on his head. She went home alone, weeping for her brother. He had stayed with her just one night and then had gone to the Second-death. She would never be able to see him again or communicate with him in any way.

Wedge got shut in among the dead because Bluejay had spoiled the road home to this world. If Bluejay had not made a mistake, we would be able to go to the Land of the Dead to visit and the dead would be able to come here and visit us. But Bluejay made a mistake on the way back. The dead, at the present time, come to visit us but trip and fall down when they are just about here. When they fall down, they forget our language. Sometimes they can be heard near the house, saying, "Ko, ko, ko," night or day. They are afraid of us and we are afraid of them. All we can hear is, "Ko, ko, ko." It is Bluejay's fault. We would have been able to visit them, and they us. They would be able to speak our language and we would have no fear of them, or they of us.

BLUEJAY BECOMES A TATTLE-TALE.[1]

Bluejay went to Bear and told him that Bullhead had said that he had a dirty face, an ugly nose, and a big appetite. Bullhead lived in a puddle left by the out-going tide. When Bear heard what Bullhead had said about him, he became angry and went to him to see about it. He began to chase Bullhead to catch him. But when Bear tried to catch him, Bullhead jumped into the water and stuck his horns into him. He pulled his head under water and crawled under a rock. Just then the tide started to come in. Bear tried hard to get away, but could not do it. By the time the tide was clear in, he was full of water; he turned over and died. When the tide went out, Bluejay was first on the spot to offer to help skin Bear. He had a fine feast.

[1] See p. 398.

Next day, Bluejay went back to the woods and said to Deer, "Bullhead called you a dirty name. He called you 'big-head' and 'ugly-big-nostrils'." Deer was angry and went to Bullhead to learn why he should say such things about him. He went to his puddle and said, "What do you mean by calling me names? I'll kill you!" Bullhead then jumped out of the water, stuck his horns in Deer's head, drew his head under the water, and hid under a rock. Soon the tide came in, and before long Deer was out of breath; he died there. Bullhead's friends came and helped drag the body ashore. Then they skinned him. Bluejay and everyone else had a fine time at the big feast.

Next day, Bluejay went back to the woods and called Calf Elk. "Bullhead called you dirty names," he said. Elk was angry and went after Bullhead. "What do you mean by calling me such dirty names?" he demanded. Then Bullhead jumped out of the water on to Elk's head, drew him under the water, and hid under a rock. The tide turned and started to come in. Elk was drowned and they dragged him ashore. Bluejay had a fine time eating. All those who took part lived there on the shore; this was at Georgetown on Shoalwater Bay.[1]

Next day, Bluejay went back to the woods and told the same story to Cow Elk. She was angry and said, "I'll go down there where Bullhead is and choke him to death." She went to Bullhead and demanded, "Why do you call me names?" "I never called you names," he answered, jumping at her. He stuck his horns between her ears and dived into the water, pulling her head under. The tide turned and she drowned. When the tide went out, all went down to the beach and dragged her in. Everyone had a good time and Bluejay ate all he wanted.

Next day, Bluejay went to Male Elk and told him that Bullhead had said something about him. "He said that you have big nostrils and big eyes, and funny eyelashes." Elk got angry. "I'm going to kill you, Bullhead!" he cried. So he went to Bullhead and asked, "Why do you call me dirty names?" Bullhead then ran down the beach to his puddle, Elk right after him. When Elk caught up with him, he said, "I never called you dirty names." With this he jumped at Elk and caught him right between the horns, and pulled his head under water. Just then the tide began to turn. Elk did not last long. They dragged him ashore and had a fine time eating his meat. Then Bullhead said to Bluejay, "This is the last time you will ever repeat what I have said, for my horns are short now." Both of them had been in on the scheme.

---

[1] The narrator said that Grays Harbor stories were not told any farther south than Shoalwater Bay; from there, Willipa stories were told.

RAVEN AND EAGLE.[1]

Raven and White-tailed Eagle were brothers. Eagle was the younger. He had a son and Raven had a son. After a while, Eagle's son died of cold; he was always in the water catching herring and caught cold. Eagle went to his brother and consulted him. "Now what is going to happen to a person when he dies? Let me resolve before you this day: when a person dies, he shall come back to this world and live again." Raven answered, "When has an Eagle ever come back from the dead? When his eyes are gone from his skull, has he ever come back? When a person dies, let him die for good."

Eagle went back home and began to mourn for his son and made preparations for his burial. He wept so much that his eyes became sore. (Eagle, it seems, had always been luckier than Raven; tamanoas was always coming his way and he had "caught" much of it.) Raven went to visit his younger brother and found him at home. He was sitting with his back to the wall, facing the fire, silently mourning his son. "Eagle," he asked, "how do you manage to catch so many herring?" It was some time before Eagle answered. At last he said, "I have a son; he is my eldest child and my favorite. I put some rocks in a basket, tie the basket to my son and sink him in the water. When he stops pulling on the rope, I pull him up. That's how I catch so many herring."

When Raven got home, he took a basket, put a rock in it, tied the rock to his son and put him in the basket. "Now I am going to let you down into the water," he said to the boy. "When the basket is filled with herring, stop pulling and I will pull you up to the surface." Then he took him out and lowered him into the water. Soon the boy began to pull on the rope; he pulled very hard. Then he suddenly stopped pulling. "Oh, my son, the basket is full of herring," Raven said. He began to pull the basket up to the surface. Then he noticed his son's face; the boy's eyes were almost bulging out of his head. He hauled him out. There were no herring in the basket. His son was stiff and cold; he had drowned. He took him ashore, dead. He then went immediately to his brother Eagle. "Let us resolve," he said, "that when a person dies, he will come back to life." But Eagle answered, "When has a person whose eyes are gone from his head, ever come back to life? When he dies, he will die for good, from this day on." Raven, then, did not weep for his son, but buried him. No sooner had he buried him, than he heard some one singing and whistling close-by. He ran ahead of the noise and began to dig down under the ground. He could not find his son in the ground and came out. No sooner had he done so, than he heard his son again. He began again to tunnel under the earth, ahead of the sound. Before long, he came out again. When he reached the surface, he heard his son making a noise, this time quite some distance away.

[1] See p. 400.

He ran ahead and dug down into the ground. When he came out this time, he heard his son whistling far in the distance. He dug again, but when he came to the surface, he heard his son still whistling far in the distance. He dug again, but without hope. This time he worked very hard and dug quite a way, but could find nothing. He gave up; he could not find his son. So he went back home.

"Hereafter," Raven said, "I shall not need a home." From that time on, he became a wanderer without a home. As he wept, mucus flowed from his nose, and he flung it here and there; it became the white moss on the trees.

Since that time, brothers and sisters do not always agree. If Raven had agreed with Eagle when the latter asked that the dead should return to life, people would still come back to life after death. The members of a family still disagree; there is always something wrong.

CROW SINGS TAMANOAS FOR RAVEN.[1]

Crow was taking a walk along the beach. She had many children and was looking for salmon with which to feed them. This was at Demon's Point. There were two families living there, Crow and a neighbor. There was illness in the latter's house. Crow went along the beach, looking for salmon that had been washed ashore; she wanted only Chinook salmon. Before long, she found just what she was looking for and took it home. As soon as she got there, she began to bake the salmon. She heated some rocks, dressed the fish, put some wood on top of the rocks and placed the fish on the wood. Then she covered the fish, poured some water on and left it to steam. But in a short while someone came along and said, "The people in the next house want you to come; Raven (qwaq^w) is sick and they want you to help sing tamanoas." So Crow went over to her neighbor's house. Raven was lying on the bed. He was singing his song,

My beak, how it shines.

He had diarrhoea and while the people were singing his song, he had to go out. He came in but soon had to go out again. Evidently, he was pretty sick. Many people had come — Crane, Crow, Kingfisher — and they were making a terrible racket. No sooner would Raven come in than he would have to go out again. It was a bad case of diarrhoea. The fifth time, he did not come back. Soon they heard a noise outside, "Qwaq^w, qwaq^w, qwaq^w." "Oh there's the sick man!" they cried. "He's outside!" So they stopped tamanoasing and went out. They saw him jumping from one place to another, saying, "Qwaq^w." When they got to the baking fish, there was not

[1] See p. 400.

a piece left. Crow turned the wood over and found some scraps here and there. With these, she fed her children. Raven had eaten her fish while she was singing tamanoas for him.

THE WOLVES AND THEIR BROTHER DOG.[1]

Five brothers — four Wolves and their younger brother Dog — were living on Humptulip River. The four elder brothers were hunters. All five went out together to hunt. Each of the elder ones killed some small game, — a deer or an elk. Dog killed a rabbit. Each one took home what he had killed. They did not stay out long as they had left a fire burning at home.

Next day, they went out again. When they got home, they found that their fire was still all right. They ate through the whole night. By morning, everything that they had killed the day before was gone.

They went out again. When they returned, they found their fire a little low. They ate all night. By morning, everything that they had killed the day before was gone.

The fourth morning, they went out again. "Don't stay out long," they said to their younger brother. "When we come home, you may have all you want to eat." Dog stayed out only a little while and then came home. He did not get anything. The fire was very low. He had a hard time getting it started. When his brothers came, he said to them, "I had a hard time getting the fire started." His brothers began to eat. They threw him his share of food. Then he said, "If the people over there use fire, I'll go there and live with them. I don't like the way you give me my food. You throw it to me instead of handing it to me."

The Wolves went out for the fifth time. When they got back, they were very hungry. Dog had stayed home to keep the fire up. They cooked their food and began to eat it with their eyes closed. They were very hungry and ate as only wolves can eat. Dog looked on. The fire was going out. "Let it go," he said, "I have no respect for them." They only threw him the parts they did not like. "Why not blow the fire?" they asked one another. "No, I can't, I'm chewing my food," first one and then another said. Then they told Dog to do it. "No, I'm chewing, too," he said. One of the Wolves looked at the fire; it was just about out. He started to blow it with his mouth full of food. He blew his food right into the fire and put it out entirely. They did not know what to do. "We'll send our little brother over there to the people to get some fire," they said. "Go over there and get some fire from those people. Tell them we'll pay them a deer," they said to Dog.

Dog went to the place. The people gave him a feast of lacamas. "Did you let your fire go out?" they asked. "Yes," Dog answered.

[1] See p. 409.

Then he explained what had happened. "My brothers have such big appetites, they have no time to look after it. They tried to blow it with their mouths full of food and put it out." "Take some lacamas back with you," the people said. They offered him five and some fire. "No," Dog said, "I won't go back. I'll stay with you forever; my brothers have too big an appetite."

When the four brothers learned that Dog was not coming back, they said, "If we ever find our little brother, we'll eat up every bit of him except his head and tail."

There is only one way that a dog can escape a wolf: if he can urinate in wolf's eyes when the latter tries to bite him, wolf will let him go.

THE WOLVES KILL THE DEER.[1]

The four Deer and their younger brother Rabbit had a house at Copalis. One day, the Deer said, "Let us catch some crabs." They went out, hunted for crabs and found a great many. They brought them ashore and began to bake them. They got some rocks and heated them. They piled boards on top. Then they swept the fire off and piled the crabs on as high as they liked. They covered them with boughs and poured on some water to steam them. As soon as the crabs were done, they said to Rabbit, "Go up to the Rocks where the five Wolves live and invite them to eat with us."

When Rabbit got there, he peeped into the house. The Wolves were lined up around the house, lying crosswise on the beds. "My grandfathers, I'm inviting you to eat with us," he said. As soon as he had finished inviting them, he started back on the run. The Wolves, in full speed, came right behind him. When the Wolves got to the place, they began to eat, "Tca, tca, bαk, bαk," like hogs. They ate up a lot of crabs in no time at all. As soon as they had finished, they went back home.

Next day, the Deer went out to the beach again for more crabs. As soon as they had cooked them, they told Rabbit to go to his "grandfathers", the Wolves, and invite them to feast on crabs. Rabbit peeped into the house and saw the Wolves sprawled out every which way. As soon as he had invited them and had just turned to go back, he muttered, "You-with-your-eyes-hanging-down." The Wolves did not hear him. When they got to the place, they found two piles of crabs. "Tca, tca," they ate as only wolves can. They ate one pile in just a short time and started on the other, "Tca, tca." They ate it up in no time and then went back home.

Next day, the Deer found more crabs. This time they had enough for three piles. As soon as the crabs were done, they told Rabbit to go to his "grandfathers", the Wolves. "Just invite them and don't say anything more," they warned him. "I am inviting you, my

[1] See p. 410.

grandfathers," Rabbit said to the Wolves, adding in a little louder voice than before, "You-with-your-eyes-hanging-down." The Wolves stopped and listened; they did not quite catch what he said. Rabbit started home, running as fast as he could go. When the Wolves came, they seemed a little rougher in action than before. The eldest of the Deer brothers said, "Our little brother must have said something. The Wolves are a little rough today." When the Wolves got to the place, they began to eat as fast as they could. They went from one pile to another, until they had eaten all three. As soon as they had finished, they went home. "Now tell us," Rabbit's eldest brother said to him, "did you say anything insulting to them?" "Not a thing," Rabbit answered.

Next day, the Deer went out to the beach for more crabs. This time, they had enough for four piles. They baked the crabs and as soon as they were done, sent Rabbit to invite the Wolves. "Don't say anything insulting; they'll get angry and eat us," they said to him. Rabbit got to the Wolves' house, where he saw them lying every which way. "My grandfathers," he said, "I'm inviting you to eat with us," and then still a little louder than before, "You-with-bogey-eyes-and-lips." This time, they heard him very plainly. Rabbit ran back as fast as he could go. Sure enough, the Deer brothers saw the Wolves coming right after Rabbit. Just as the Wolves were about to get him, he jumped aside and they missed him. "Our brother must have said something insulting. The Wolves are angry. They are coming fast," the Deer said. When the Wolves got to the place where the crabs were, they began to eat, "Tcαk, tcαk, tcαk." They finished with one pile and went to the next. They finished all four piles.

Next day, the Deer brothers gathered even more crabs. "This is our last day if you persist in calling the Wolves names," they said to Rabbit. They sent him to invite his "grandfathers". "Don't say anything bad. They'll surely eat us up today if you do," they said. When Rabbit got to the Wolves, he found them stretched out in all directions. "I'm inviting you to eat with us, my grandfathers," he said. As he ran, he yelled back, "You-with-bogey-eyes-and-mouth." The Wolves heard plainly. They started after him. When they were about to catch him, he landed on top of one of the Wolves' heads. Then he jumped off in another direction. The Deer ran to the house and jumped under the bed covers or anything they could find, to hide. There was a basket hanging high in one corner of the house. Rabbit ran into the house as fast as he could and jumped into the basket. While he was there hiding, he could hear the Wolves outside, eating the crabs, as only wolves can eat. They were eating so fast they were breaking wind in all directions. When they had eaten everything they could find, they came into the house. They found the eldest brother under the house and pulled him out. He squealed as they began to eat him alive. They ate him up in no time. They pulled the second out and ate him up. They looked around for the third and ate him up. They found the fourth in the corner of the house, pulled him out and ate him up. They had eaten up all the Deer brothers. Then they began to search for Rabbit. They looked high and low. They looked under the bed, upset everything, but still they could not find him. Finally they gave up and went away. Then they played among themselves and had a good time.

After they had gone, Rabbit came down from his hiding place. The Deer were nothing but bones. He thought to himself, "It's too late, now. My fault. Now I shall become a traveller. I shall be easy game for everyone. Even a dog will be able to catch me easily. I'll eat anything green, like grass." He went toward the shore. "I'll wander around until I find a lot of moss; then I'll lie down there. Hereafter my name will be 'rabbit'."

THE COUGARS AND THEIR BROTHER WILDCAT.[1]

There were four Cougars and their younger brother Wildcat. The five of them lived at James' Rock. Whenever the four elder brothers went out hunting, they left Wildcat at home to keep the fire burning; another fire would be hard to start. The eldest would always say to Wildcat, "You mustn't go away. Keep the fire up." The eldest would usually come home first. Once he brought home a large elk, its legs tied together. After he had dressed it, he said to Wildcat, "What part would you like?" "I want the diaphragm," Wildcat answered, as usual. He cooked that part of the meat for Wildcat. Then he set to work, cut the meat and hung it up to dry. As soon as he had finished, the next-to-eldest came in with a smaller elk, one that was not full grown. He and his elder brother skinned it. "What part would you like to eat?" the second asked Wildcat. "The kidney tenderloin," Wildcat answered, as usual. He cooked the tenderloin for Wildcat and he feasted upon it. The two brothers together worked on the elk; they skinned it and dressed it. "When you are thirsty, catch the drippings of the meat as we roast it; it will make you strong," they said to Wildcat. It was not long before Wildcat was red from his mouth to his nose. When they had finished with the second elk, the third brother brought in a somewhat smaller one. While they were skinning the elk, the third brother asked Wildcat, "What part of the meat would you like?" Wildcat began to cry. "I'm tired of elk meat; I want deer meat," he said. Then they said to one another, "Perhaps our next-to-youngest-brother will bring in a deer." Before long they heard him dropping his pack outside. Sure enough, he had brought home a large deer. As they began to skin it, the fourth asked his little brother, "What part do you want?" "I'd like the tongue," Wildcat said. He roasted it for Wildcat and the latter ate it. Then the elder brothers

[1] See p. 401.

cooked for themselves and ate before going to bed. Wildcat had gone to bed as soon as he had finished eating, for his brothers always left him very early in the morning.

They woke him up early. He got up and looked after the fire. After a big breakfast, he went out for a walk. While he was out walking, he saw some small snipe. "I'd like to eat them, I'm tired of elk meat," he said. He got a long stick and threw it at them. He killed a few, took them home and buried them in the ashes. As soon as they were done, he ate them. He gathered up the refuse and feathers and hid them. His brothers might see them and scold him. He was not allowed to leave the house; he had been disobedient.

When the eldest brother came in with a large elk, he found Wildcat asleep near the fire. "What's the matter? You seem sick. Is there something wrong?" he asked. "No, I'm not sick. I just fell asleep," Wildcat answered. The eldest began to skin the elk. "Are you hungry for any part?" he asked. "No, I'm tired of eating elk meat," Wildcat answered. "How do you expect to become strong like us and hunt for yourself if you don't eat elk meat?" his brother asked. The second brother came in with an elk. "What part will you have?" the two brothers asked Wildcat. "Nothing; I want deer meat," Wildcat answered. "Perhaps our third brother will bring a deer and you may have some of it," the second brother said. The third brother came in with an elk. "What part would you like?" they asked Wildcat. "Nothing; I want deer meat," Wildcat answered. It was not long before they heard a noise like the dropping of a pack. Sure enough, the next-to-youngest brother had killed a deer. "What part do you want?" they asked Wildcat. "The kneecap," he answered. When it was time for the elder brothers to get their supper, Wildcat went to bed — early, as usual.

Next day, his brothers went out to hunt again. When Wildcat got up, he said to himself, "I don't think I'll eat elk meat today; I'll eat some snipe." Before his brothers had left him they had said, "Don't go away; the fire might go out. The fire you can see on the other side of the Harbor belongs to a dangerous being who will eat you if you go there." Not long after getting up, Wildcat went out to hunt snipe. He did not go far, but still, it was a considerable distance from the house. When he got back, he found the fire pretty low. He had a hard time getting it started. He set to work to cook the birds. When they were done, he took them outside to eat so that the feathers would blow away from the house. Soon the eldest brother came home. He found Wildcat asleep by the fire. This was the third time. "What do you do anyway? Do you ever go away and leave our fire?" he asked Wildcat. There was no answer. "I notice snipe feathers around. Do you ever hunt for snipe?" he asked. Wildcat denied that he ever did. When his remaining brothers came home one at a time, they found that he was not hungry. "He must have eaten something," they said. Wildcat went to sleep, stretched out on his back, his mouth open. They noticed a piece of something, like snipe flesh, between his teeth. They picked it out. It was snipe flesh. Then they gave him to understand that he should never hunt for snipe again. They warned him of the dangerous being across the bay, who would destroy them. He should never leave the house but should stay to take care of the fire.

As soon as they left him, Wildcat went out to look for snipe again. He went farther than he had ever gone before. "The fire might be out," he thought. He went back. The fire was almost out. He had a hard time getting it started. After he had cooked and eaten the snipe his eldest brother returned. "What would you like to eat?" he asked. He had noticed some snipe feathers outside. Wildcat thought to himself, "My brothers are suspicious. I'll fool them. I'll tell them what part of the meat I want." "I'd like some of the rib, roasted on a stick," he said. His brother fixed it for him. He noticed that Wildcat had already eaten so much that his ribs were sticking out. Wildcat began to eat, but soon had enough. The second brother came home. "What part would you like?" he asked Wildcat. "The marrow," Wildcat said. The third brother came home. "What part would you like?" he asked Wildcat. "The nostrils," Wildcat answered. The next-to-youngest brother came home. "What part would you like?" he asked Wildcat. "The kidney," Wildcat answered.

It was soon time for Wildcat to go to bed. The elder brothers talked among themselves. "We must reprimand our little brother," they said. "It is obvious that he leaves the house. If he lets the fire go out, he'll probably cross the bay and borrow fire from the dangerous being."

Next morning, Wildcat went out for more snipe. This time he went a long way from the house. He suddenly remembered the fire and ran back. When he got there he found the fire was out. He tried unsuccessfully to start it. He thought to himself, "I might as well die. I'll go over to the dangerous being." The tide was pretty well out. He started to swim and in a short while reached the other side.

A strange feeling came to the eldest brother's heart. "Our little brother has let the fire go out," he said. By a sign, he and his brothers met.

Wildcat sneaked into the dangerous being's house. He turned into a fly. The old lady was sitting near the fire. She had five firebraids on each side, the ends tied together. The fly had no sooner appeared than she knew who it was. "It must be Wildcat who always throws sticks at the snipe and thus lets his fire go out," she said. Thereupon Wildcat changed himself into a cinder, sailed down from above and landed on the firewood. Failing again, he turned into a flea. Soon the flea jumped upon the firebraids. The old lady began to strike him with a stick. "Why did you throw sticks at the snipe and neglect your fire?" she asked. This was Wildcat's third trial. He changed himself into a mosquito and came sailing into the house. As soon as the old lady saw the mosquito, she knew it was Wildcat. "Why did you throw at the snipe and neglect your fire?" she asked. Wildcat had very nearly given up hope of stealing the fire. "I wish she'd sleep for a moment," he thought. He changed himself into smoke and mingled with the real smoke of the fireplace. The smoke seemed to roll toward the firebraids. The dangerous being started to fall asleep. This gave him a chance to steal the firebraid. He started for home.

The old lady was K'wαtsx̣wɛ'. She woke up and looked around. Her firebraid was gone. Wildcat had tied the fire to his tail, as he had a long tail at that time. She followed him. "I'll swallow you alive," she said. She had five packropes around her waist. As soon as she reached the water, she threw one in. It became a sand-spit. Wildcat reached the spit and ran across it as fast as he could go. When he came to the end, he jumped into the water and started to swim again. The old lady threw another rope into the water and it became another spit. Wildcat reached it, ran across it like the wind, jumped into the water again and swam. By the time the old lady had reached the end of the second spit, Wildcat was far out in the bay. His tail was now nearly burnt off. The old lady threw another rope into the water and formed another spit. Wildcat's elder brothers had now reached home. Sure enough, they saw Wildcat, K'wαtsx̣wɛ' right behind him. When his tail was burnt short, Wildcat moved the fire to his forehead. His eldest brother swam out to meet him. K'wαtsx̣wɛ' threw the fourth rope into the water and formed a fourth spit. His tail burnt short, Wildcat moved the fire to his forehead. The old lady threw her fifth packrope into the water and formed a fifth spit. The eldest brother reached it and met Wildcat. "Now you see what has happened! You should have stayed home and watched the fire!" he said. He took the fire from Wildcat's forehead. The latter's eyes, nose, and forehead were now drawn up together. "Hang on to my tail and we'll swim ashore," his brother said to him. Wildcat held the fire in one hand while he hung on to his brother's tail with the other. By the time they got to shore, K'wαtsx̣wɛ' had reached the end of the last spit.

They took the fire into the house. "What shall we do?" the elder brothers said. "K'wαtsx̣wɛ' will eat us." "I'm not afraid," Wildcat said, "I can kill her. Climb to the top of the tree overhanging our house and I'll attend to her!" He kicked the door. It turned into a rock. He kicked it again and raised the rock a little. He kicked it again and raised it a little higher. The old lady came. "Oh, my grandchild, why did you run away? If you had only asked for the fire, I would have given it to you. If you won't come out here to me, then let me come in to you. Are you all alone?" she said. "Yes, I'm all alone," Wildcat answered, "my brothers are not home. Come in; the door is just high enough for you to get through. I can raise it a little higher if you like." "How shall I come in?" she asked. "On your belly, head first," Wildcat answered. She started to crawl in under the rock, head first. As soon as she was under it, Wildcat kicked the rock. It came down on her head and smashed it. He killed her, just as he had said he would. "My brothers, come down now; everything is all right. Now we can start a fire," he said. They dragged the old lady from under the door and burnt her up. They cooked their dinner and ate it. As soon as they had finished, the elder brothers asked one another, "What shall we do now? There is nothing for us to do but to become wanderers. If this fire goes out, there are lots of dangerous beings who will continually molest us." The next-to-youngest brother asked, "What shall we do with Wildcat?" The eldest said, "Let us take him with us until something happens. Perhaps we will be able to keep him with us."

They left their home. They took no food of any kind with them. "Hereafter," they said, "we shall always eat our food raw." They started toward the sea. On their way, they practiced jumping in all directions. Wildcat tried to do what his elder brothers did. They got to Grass Creek. Then they proposed, "Let us see what we can do. Let us jump across the creek." "Who shall jump first?" "Our next-to-youngest brother." "No, our eldest brother, so that he can make the banks of the river come closer together." The eldest jumped clear across. The second jumped clear across. The third jumped clear across. The next-to-youngest jumped clear across. Only Wildcat was left. Then he, too, jumped clear across. The others were glad that he, as well as they, could do it. Their little brother's tail had been gone and his ears and face drawn together ever since the time he stole the fire. They went on. They reached Chinoose Creek. "This creek is narrow, but we'll jump it just the same." One after another, the brothers cleared the creek. Wildcat was the last, as usual, but he made it. The others were glad. They went from there to Humptulip River. They said, "We'll all jump across here." One after another, the elder ones made it without mishap. Wildcat was last. It was all he could do to make it. His brothers felt badly; he did not have their strength. They went on. They came to Esło'ts. Wildcat was the last to jump it. This time, he knocked some dirt loose from the bank with one foot. They went on. They came to Nota'wəwapc. It was a large river. The eldest jumped across, and then one after another the three younger ones made it without any trouble. Wildcat alone remained on the other side. He went up and down the river looking for the narrowest point from which to jump. At last he jumped. He merely struck the opposite bank and then slid back into the water. They pulled him ashore. Then they sat around him, weeping for his plight. "Now we shall lose our little brother." "You will remain here on this creek where you will work for your own living. It is obvious that you cannot travel with us any longer," they said to Wildcat. "Where shall we go from here?"

they asked one another. "I am going out to sea," the eldest said. "I'll go with you," the second said. The two younger ones said, "We shall go to the woods. We shall hunt for a living and eat our food raw." Then the two latter said to Wildcat, "When you are walking along a hill and smell meat, you must dig around there. When we kill an elk, we will always bury it for you so that you can dig it up and eat it. That's how you shall make your living hereafter. You will find a deer, that we have left for you, buried in the ground. We are sorry for you and would like to take you along, but you have lost your tail." Then the two elder ones said, "When you come to the beach, you will find a sea-lion, seal or blackfish that we have sent ashore for you to eat." After they had held their little brother on their knees, the two latter went to the sea to try themselves out. They jumped far out into the water and came back. They did the same thing five times and on the last time, stayed out forever. "Anyone travelling on the beach will find a white substance like fat, the remains from our excrements left at sea; it will be good luck to anyone who finds it," they had announced before going into the water for good.

The two younger brothers, who were to live in the woods, started out. They went up the creek to a little hill. "We'll find some game and leave it for you soon," they said to Wildcat before going into the woods. "Whenever there is to be a death in a family, the family will hear Wildcat cry," they declared. They left the poor boy by himself.

Wildcat lay down by the water and wept. Finally he fell asleep. When the sun was low, he thought to himself, "My brothers said I should go inland." He went up the creek. Sure enough, he found a cow elk, already dressed. He stayed there and feasted. Then he went to sleep. He ate all night. When morning came, he was still feasting. The next night, someone came. Wildcat could hear him breathing, "P^{u}, p^{u}," through his mouth. It was Bear. Bear rolled him off his food. When he had eaten all he wanted, Bear took the rest of the food along with him and hid it. He steals Wildcat's food whenever he can find it.

THUNDER.[1]

There were five brothers. The youngest was called Sət'α'msət'αm.[2] They made their living by hunting. They lived half-way down Humptulip River. The four elder brothers went out to hunt. The youngest stayed home to watch the fire. Each of the four brothers brought home an elk, its legs tied together. They went out three times and soon had the house filled with elk meat. The youngest

[1] See p. 401.

[2] The youth is not referred to by name throughout the rest of the story.

thought to himself, "I wonder who is going to eat all this food; we have so much on hand." The third day, while his brothers were still out hunting, he decided to take a walk. He began to sing,

I wish someone would come who never gets enough to eat,
I wish someone would come who never gets enough to eat.

In the meantime, his brothers had returned, each with one elk. The eldest felt uneasy. He thought to himself, "My little brother may be saying something." When the youngest returned, he said to him, "You must be careful what you say." They went out for the fourth time. The youngest went for a walk. He began to sing,

I wish someone would come who never gets enough to eat,
I wish someone would come who never gets enough to eat.

While hunting, the four elder brothers met. "There must be something wrong at home. Our little brother must be saying something," they said. Each had a dog to help him in his hunting. When they got back, they said to their little brother, "You always say something. We know it. If you sing, the dangerous being will come and eat us." They went out again for the fifth time. After they had killed their game, they met. They soon felt that all was not well at home with their little brother and started back.

During their absence, the youngest was taking a walk and singing as usual. "A he′," he heard someone laugh. "Here I am grandson. I'm the one who never gets enough to eat." When he heard the dangerous being coming, the boy ran into the house and hid under the bed. The dangerous being then came in and sat down by the fire. Soon the eldest brother came in with his game and found the old man sitting there, laughing to himself. When all the others had returned, the old man said, "My grandchildren, here I am at last. My little grandchild here always calls me." It was Huno′nx̂ᵘ (Roaring Sound of the Ocean). "What would you like, some fresh meat?" they asked. "Yes, I'm ready to eat fresh meat," he said. "My youngest grandchild, who always calls me, must sit alongside me while I eat." "Now you'll have to sit alongside the dangerous being! Serves you right; this is just what you've been looking for," the little fellow's elder brothers said to him. The eldest took a hot rock, put it inside the elk that he had brought home, and threw it to the dangerous being. The latter caught it in his mouth. It went down his throat like nothing. He had swallowed it whole. "He, he′, thank you, my grandchildren," he said. The next-to-eldest then threw his elk filled with red hot stones into the dangerous being's mouth. He swallowed it without any effort. The third brother then threw his elk filled with hot stones into the dangerous being's mouth. The youngest brother all the while was sitting alongside the dangerous being. He was shivering all over. "Serves you right!" they said to him. The fourth brother filled his elk with hot rocks and threw it to the dangerous being, who swallowed it in one gulp. Then they began to feed him dried elk. They made it into a bundle the size of an elk, put a sharp limb in and wrapped it in an elk hide. The dangerous being swallowed it without any effort. After he had eaten ten elk at one sitting, he started to get sleepy. "As soon as he is fast asleep, we'll try to run away somewhere," they said. "I'd like my little grandson to sleep with me," the dangerous being said. The others said to their little brother, "Sleep with him. When he is sound asleep, move away." They had a long limb ready. The dangerous being began to snore soon after lying down. They got up, took their younger brother out of the bed, and left the limb in his place. They set out for Demon's Point.

After they had gone a long way, the eldest said, "I feel that the dangerous being is awake now." They knew that he had said, "A he′, my grandchild!" and had then swallowed the limb. "He's coming now!" they said. They could hear him say, "A he′, my grandchild, why did you run away from me?" Then the eldest said, "My dog, lie down between us and the dangerous being." As soon as the dog lay down, he became a large mountain. After they had gone on some distance, they looked back. They could see the dangerous being on top of the high mountain, all doubled up and carrying a cane. It was all he could do to move but he was still coming. By forming the mountain, they had managed to get some distance away from him. As soon as he got close he gave an "A he′" and asked, "My grandchild, why are you running away from me?" The eldest said to his dog again, "Lie down!" The dog lay down and formed another large mountain. Not long after, they saw that the dangerous being had reached the top of the mountain. He was soon close to them again. The eldest then told his dog to lie down again. This time, the mountain was not as large as formerly. They went quite a way before they saw the dangerous being coming over the mountain. It was some time before he began to catch up with them. This time, the dog turned into only a small hill. The fifth time, the dog turned into a very small hill. The dangerous being had no sooner reached the top of the hill, than he bit the dog and swallowed both him and his master. The next-to-eldest then used his dog in the same way. The dog lay down and formed a large mountain; he did this five times. The fifth time, the dangerous being caught both dog and master and swallowed them. Now two brothers were gone. It was the same with the third brother; the fifth time, the dangerous being caught both dog and master. It was the same with the fourth brother; he made five hills with his dog. But just before the fifth hill was formed, he said to his younger brother, "Run as fast as you can toward the end of the Point! We're done for now, and it's your fault!" Then, on the appearance of the fifth hill, the dangerous being ate both dog and master.

The little one ran away. He came to the end of the Point. When he got there, he saw an old man sitting on the other side of the river, making a net. He called to him, "Have pity on me! Take me across the river. I'll give you my belt. The dangerous being who never gets enough to eat is following me. He ate up all my brothers." The man answered, in an angry voice, "I have lots of belts." "I'll give you my hat." "I have lots of hats." "I'll give you my knife." "I have lots of knives." "Oh, my grandfather, I wish you'd take me across. The dangerous being is close. He'll eat me! I'll give you my arrow sheathe." "I have all the arrow sheathes I want." "I'll give you some sinew." "That's just what I want! Thank you, thank you." Then the old man, who was on the Westport (Ts'x̣e'lɩs) side, made his legs good and strong and stretched them across the mouth of the river. The little fellow ran across them easily. When he got to the other side, the old man drew his legs up again and resumed his work. After the young fellow had told him his story, the old man, Thunder, said to him, "My house is just a little way along. I have a daughter there."

The dangerous being came to the water and laughed. "Did you see that fellow I'm chasing?" he asked. "You're always chasing someone," Thunder answered. "Will you take me over?" the dangerous being then asked, adding, "I'll give you my hat." "I have lots of hats." "I'll give you my arrows." "I have lots of arrows." "I'll give you my belt." "I have lots of belts." "I'll give you my sinew." Thereupon, Thunder stretched his legs clear aross the mouth of Grays Harbor, first making his legs slender. "Don't touch my legs with your cane! If you do, I'll draw them up and you'll fall in!" he said. The dangerous being started across, shivering in fear to cross such a narrow footing without the use of his cane. Sure enough, when he was only half-way across, he became so frightened that he put his cane down on Thunder's legs. Thunder became angry. "I told you not to touch my legs with your cane!" he said. He drew his legs back, and the dangerous being fell in. After some time, the latter's hat came to the surface and finally floated ashore. The dangerous being, himself, had floated on downstream. Then Thunder said, "This is how it will be for all time: when the evening is to be cold and stormy, you, Huno'nx̂ᵘ, will be heard roaring in the ocean. When there is a wind coming from the Quinault, you will be heard rolling instead of roaring, because you have turned your back to the wind. When it is to be good weather, you will be heard making a humming sound, because you are so far out your feet can't touch bottom." To this very day, the Lower Chehalis have this dangerous being for a weather sign; they can always tell when stormy weather or a change of weather is coming; he continually makes a noise in the water.

It was just about evening when the young man reached Thunder's house. He and Thunder's daughter married. The young woman set an entire meal before him. "I haven't much appetite," he said, "I'm so broken up over my brothers' death." "The dangerous being who was chasing you will never eat anyone again. He will live in the ocean forever, where he can never harm anyone. He will have a disagreeable time there forever," she said.

When it was late in the evening, the young man's wife asked him to take a walk with her, on the pretext that she was grieving deeply for his brothers. They went to a place where there was lots of gravel. She looked around until she found a thin, round, good-sized stone. When they got back to the house, she told him to lay the stone over his heart when he went to sleep. "My mother is bad," she explained. Then they went to bed and fell asleep. The young man had placed the stone over his breast as his wife had directed. Five days later, the young woman noticed that her mother's nose was bleeding. Then Thunder said to his wife, whose name was L'opa'lαkwł, "What's the matter with your nose? It's bleeding." "Ha, ha, ha," the woman said. One night they heard her say, "My son-in-law, my son-in-law." She was trying to peck a hole in his heart. Instead, she struck the stone and smashed her nose. After that she became good; she changed her mind and began to like her son-in-law.

By this time, the young man's wife had two grown children; she had been married only five days, but had borne a child every other day. Whenever Thunder went to the ocean to hunt whale, he would say, "Don't let the children go out. They might laugh at me." Suddenly they heard, "X̣o, x̣o." It was the peal of Thunder, and all went out to see what had happened. There was Thunder in the ocean, clutching a whale with his feet. He flew out of the water. Whenever the whale struggled, it carried him under. The children's mother forbade them to laugh at their grandfather. The children were too frightened to laugh anyway. They all went back into the house as it was contrary to Thunder's rule to be seen by anyone while whaling. Late in the evening, Thunder came into the house. He was carrying a wooden canoe-bailer shaped like a spoon. In the bailer was a fish about the size of a mud-fish. He set it down in the middle of the house. When morning came, the small fish had become so large that its back was sticking out through the roof. They began to cut the whale up right in the house. As soon as they had it dressed, they began to smoke and dry it.

Thunder finally went out hunting again. This time the children went outside; their mother had forgotten about them. When they saw their grandfather having a hard time in the ocean, they began to laugh, causing him to lose hold of the whale. Thunder came back to the house, went to bed and covered up his head. "Tell your children to stay inside!" he said to his daughter.

Next day, he went out again, but this time he took his grandchildren along with him in the canoe. He took them to a place where some porpoises were playing and ordered them to catch one. One was to catch it by the head, the other by the tail. When the children at last managed to get hold of the porpoise, they found it was so heavy they could not fly out of the water with it. It kept pulling them down under the water. Thunder laughed to get even with them. At last he helped them get the porpoise ashore.

He took them out again next day and ordered them to catch a still larger porpoise. After the children had learned how to catch porpoises successfully, they went out alone to catch whale. They no longer needed their grandfather's assistance. Their grandfather came home, and angry for no apparent reason, went to bed and covered up his head.

When the old fellow woke up, he uncovered his head and said, "My son-in-law, you must come with me today and help me fell a tree for making a canoe." The young man's wife had already warned him, "If father should tell you to do anything, go ahead and do it, but think of me, and whatever you do, pray for help; I shall always help you." They went out and felled the tree. Then they started to split it in two. When they had made only a slight opening, Thunder said, "Get into the crack and split the tree in two; that's how I used to do when I was young like you." The young man squeezed into the opening, thinking of what his wife had told him. As soon as he was inside, Thunder pulled the wedges out, letting the sides of the tree close in on him. Then Thunder went home angry. He went to bed and covered up his head. As soon as the young man found he was caught, he began to plead with the cedar, "My grandfather, take pity on me; split open." The cedar did as he was asked and split open. As soon as he was out, the young man said, "I wish you would take pity on me so I could carry you in two pieces, limbs and all." He took the two pieces home on his shoulder. Thunder heard the noise of a load being dropped and went out to see what it was. "Oh, my son-in-law," he said, "I didn't realize you were bringing that tree home." He seemed very pleased. As soon as the young man got into the house, he told his wife what Thunder had done to him.

Soon Thunder went to bed and covered up his head again; he had something on his mind. At last, he suddenly uncovered his head and said, "Oh, my son-in-law, I should like to eat some snow. I want you to bring me some from five different mountains." Then the young man's wife said to him, "You must think of me while you are gathering snow. Bring the snow home in the form of a small ball." The young man went to five different mountains as directed and gathered snow. At the fifth mountain he made the snow into a very small ball. He took it home, and handing it to Thunder, said, "Here's the snow that you wanted." "What a small amount! There's not enough for a mouth full," Thunder said. He began to eat it. He took a large bite but still there was plenty left. He ate and ate but still the snow ball did not decrease in size. At last in anger he threw it into the middle of the room. Next morning, he tried to lift his blanket but could not do it; it was weighted down with snow. Then he called to his son-in-law, "Will you please gather up this snow and take it back where you got it? It's smothering me." The young woman then said to her husband, "Wait until he is very nearly exhausted before you get up and help him." After a while, the young man got up, gathered up the snow and took it back to the mountains.

Before long Thunder had something on his mind again. He went to bed and covered up his head. When he at last uncovered his head, he said, "Oh, my son-in-law, when I was a boy I had a pet bear; I should like to have him again now." The young woman then said to her husband, "When you find the bear, talk to him. Tell him that he was once Thunder's pet." When the young man found the bear, he spoke to him as his wife had told him to do. "All right, I'll go with you," the bear said. He then made himself into a small cub, as he had agreed to do. The young man carried him home. When he reached the house, he said to the bear, "Now I'm going to throw you into the house. Don't kill my father-in-law, but slap him all over the face." "Here's your pet," he said to Thunder, as he threw the bear inside. "Thank you, son-in-law," Thunder replied. When he took hold of the bear to pet him, the bear slapped him and threw him around. He took Thunder by the foot and threw him to one end of the house and then gave him a good spanking. Thunder then began to beg his son-in-law to take him away from the bear. As soon as the bear had entered the house, he had assumed his normal size. "He's killing me!" Thunder cried. The young man then took his father-in-law away from the bear. "Take him back," Thunder said, "he doesn't seem to recognize me any longer."

Before long Thunder had something on his mind again. He went to bed and covered up his head. When he uncovered his head, he said, "Oh, son-in-law, I want you to go after a pet that I had long ago, a cougar." As the young man was starting out, his wife said, "When you find the cougar, tell him what you want him for and he will come." He found the cougar and talked to him as his wife had directed. "All right, I'll come with you," the cougar said. When they got to the house, he explained to the cougar, "When I throw you to my father-in-law, don't kill him, but treat him rough; hurt him a little." In the meantime, Thunder had bathed and combed his hair, in expectation of his pet's arrival. As soon as he took hold of the cougar, the latter assumed his natural size and struck him on the head; he tossed Thunder up in the air and kept him there, tossing him about as if he were playing ball. "Take me away from him!" Thunder cried. The young man then took the cougar back to the place where he belonged.

Before long Thunder went to bed again and covered up his head. When he uncovered his head, he said, "Oh, son-in-law, I want you to go after a grizzly bear, a pet I had long ago. I used to play with him." Now the young man's wife was sad. She told her husband what to do and say when he found the grizzly. The young man talked to the grizzly. "You were once Thunder's pet," he said. Then he explained what he wanted him to do. "All right, I'll go with you," the grizzly said. He made himself small and the young man took him under his arm. As soon as they got to the house, the young man threw the grizzly in. "Here's your pet!" he said. "Don't kill my father-in-law but treat him rough," he had said. The grizzly gave Thunder pretty rough treatment. After a while, when the grizzly had him in the air and was keeping him there, Thunder cried, "Son-in-law, take him away! He's killing me!" So the young man took Thunder away from the grizzly. Then Thunder said, "He doesn't seem to remember me any longer." His son-in-law took the grizzly back to the place where he belonged. Then everyone laughed at Thunder.

Soon Thunder covered up his head again. When he uncovered his head, he said, "Oh, my son-in-law, go over there where the people are gathered and get the thing that they are playing with." The people had gathered at a certain place and were having a good time. The young man now felt low in spirit. "I don't see how I shall be able to do it; there are so many people there," he said to his wife. But she understood the situation and said, "You must take good care of yourself. I and my children will be ready to help you in case of need." The young fellow wept and then set out. Sure enough, when he was still some distance away, he heard the sound of a happy gathering. It was night and he could see that there was a bright light there. "What are they doing with this thing my father-in-law told me to get?" he thought. The place was indeed filled with people. They were rolling something — a hoop — on the ground. Whenever it was rolled, it gave forth light. When he got to the crowd, he went some distance in, and stood there, studying how they rolled the hoop. After he saw how it was done, he decided that his task would not be so difficult after all. These people were the Tamanoas (sα′x̣tʿkwʋlc). He noticed that they rolled the hoop up twice and then down twice. "When they roll it down, I'll take my chances," he thought. Soon Thunder and his wife L'opa′lαkwł felt that something was going to happen; their hearts were pounding hard. The hoop was on its way down and the people were shouting. As it rolled in, the young man jumped for it and started to run. It became dark immediately. Then Bluejay said, "I knew that Thunder was going to send his son-in-law over here." The Tamanoas, lighting their way with torch lights, started after the young man. "Oh, my people at home, why don't they think of something!" he thought. Although he was running with all his might, it did not seem to him that he was moving at all, the people behind him were coming so fast. Suddenly he heard a roar, "Notʋ′ptʋp, hwo′ · · · ·." It was the peal of Thunder. He quickened his speed immediately.

Thunder then began to make a rattling noise. He ran faster than ever. Suddenly a number of torches were extinguished, but some could still be seen. Bluejay and his sister had not gone far, when their torch lights went out and they lost their way. Bluejay's bear-blanket was so wet that he could not go any farther. Thunder pealed five times, and with each peal brought rain. But the rain was not the kind we have now; it was Thunder's urine. By this time only half the torches were extinguished and Thunder's urine was all gone; he could not make any more. He said to his wife, "Take my place. I can't do anything more. You must urinate for me now." He then went to the place where the people were following his son-in-law and pealed and rattled but without effect. He could not extinguish another torch. His wife urinated five times. One light still remained. Soon the young man's two sons, the young Thunders, began to rattle. One managed a slight trickle and put out the torch. This last torch to be extinguished belonged to Shark.[1] From there on, the young fellow managed without any trouble. His father-in-law soon showed that he was very pleased to have him back. But his wife advised, "Don't give the hoop to him right away. Wait until he is out of patience."

Toward evening, Thunder's patience was exhausted so he went to bed and covered up his head.[2] After dark his son-in-law said, "You'd better get up now and play with the hoop. You can roll it and play with it." Thunder got up then. "Oh, I am so happy! Thank you, my son-in-law," he said. "Now go to the other end of the house," the young man said. Thunder obeyed, jumping up and down with excitement. The young man then rolled the hoop toward him. As it rolled, it lighted the house as bright as day. "If you catch this hoop with your arm, it will be yours. But if I catch it with my arm, it will be mine," he said to his father-in-law. Thunder got ready to do his best. As the hoop rolled toward him, he slipped his arm through it with no trouble at all. He shouted for joy. The hoop was his. He said to his son-in-law, "This is the last time I shall ever ask you to do me a favor, for you have been able to do everything that I have asked." His son-in-law answered, "Hereafter, when you are angry and thunder, you will throw a light. Whenever your peal is heard — whenever there is a storm — a light will be seen." Thunder then said, "This hoop will be my property until the end of the world. I shall always keep it with me. This is what my son-in-law gave me as an expression of his good will — as a present in exchange for my daughter."

Thereafter it was known that whenever heavy peals of thunder were heard quite low down, it was a sign that the whole family was

[1] Shark is the highest tamanoas that can be obtained; a person who obtains him as guardian spirit can cure any kind of illness.

[2] The old people used to do this when they were angry. Oftentimes they would not get up to eat for four or five days.

taking part — Thunder, his wife and two grandsons. Sometimes the thunder is not very heavy and the light that accompanies it is like the light of children at play; that is caused by the two children. When it rains, it is a sign that Thunder's wife is out with him; she is urinating as well as he. When Thunder is looking for a whale, he peals very loudly for he has to work hard. The same is believed today. Before he obtained the hoop, Thunder had no light.

LAND OTTER'S SON.[1]

There was a village at Mulla on the southern side of Grays Harbor. Two large houses were there on the river. A young woman who was known as an expert clam-digger lived across the bay at Grays Harbor City. The people of Mulla heard of her fame and decided to cross the bay to her village to see if they could make arrangements for her marriage to one of their young men. They went over to buy the girl. The girl's parents agreed to give her to Land Otter's son, a young man of royal blood. The Mulla people took her home with them. Shortly afterward, they heard of a young woman who was an expert fruit and berry picker. She did not live on the bay, but in the mountains. As was customary, they went over to buy her for a youth of royal blood. Her parents let them have her and she, also, was given to the same young man. He now had two wives.

When the tide went out, the first young woman went to the beach to dig clams. The second joined her and the other women. The first dug clams with her bill, which was very long. The mountain girl could not dig clams for her arms and legs were very short. When the tide came in, they went back to the house, bringing all kinds of clams. Their husband was there. His face was painted and he was lying down. When the two wives had finished their feast of clams, they went up to the hills to pick berries and dig roots. The first wife tried to dig roots with her nose but could not do it; her nose began to bleed and she had to stop. The second wife had no difficulty in gathering roots. In a short time she had gathered a large quantity. It always required both women to carry back what the one had gathered. When they got back to the house, they found five piles of empty clam shells. "I had company while you were gone," their husband said. "I gave them some clams; there are the shells."

Next day, when the tide went out, the two women went to dig clams again. They always dug a great many. When the tide came in, they started home. When they got back, they found their husband asleep. All that remained of the berries and roots, were the leavings, heaped in piles. "I had five guests while you were gone. I gave them something to eat," their husband said.[2]

[1] See p. 409.

[2] A second trip to the mountains may have been omitted here; at any rate, it is implied.

The following morning the first wife found that she was very hungry for lacamas and began to cry over and over again, "I wish I had some shelled lacamas." The second then sang, "Come, then, help yourself." But when the hungry woman went to get the lacamas, she could not find any. The two then went out to dig clams, both very hungry. When the tide came in, they went ashore. When they got home, they found their husband asleep. His face was very pale.[1] The two then decided that they were going to get something to eat before their next trip. They had plenty of clams, so they ate as many as they wanted. When they had finished eating, they went up to the mountains; this was their third trip there. When they had as many roots and fruits as they could carry, they started back home. When they got there, nothing remained of the clams but the shells. Their husband told the same story, "I had five visitors while you were gone and gave them something to eat." Then the two women talked the matter over. "Why is it that his visitors always come when we are gone, and eat so much?"

When they came back from the shore once more they found nothing but the leavings of their roots and berries. Before the morning was over, they planned to go into the mountains again. They ate their lunch before they started. They had dug a canoe-load of clams only the day before. They decided, this time, that they would pick berries for a short while only and then return to learn what their husband was doing with the clams. So they returned sooner than usual. When they got near the house, they saw some smoke coming through the smoke-opening in the roof. They walked lightly so that he would not hear them and peeped through a crack. (They had gathered a few mussels along with the clams.) Their husband had his hair tied on the top of his head; his face was painted and he was cooking clams. He made five piles of the cooked clams. When he had finished eating one pile, he would hop to another. While he was thus occupied, they opened the door. "What are the names of your visitors who always eat our food?" they asked. "We're not going to look for anything to eat again; we're tired out. As for you, you shall be the sea worm." No sooner had they told him what he should become, than he crawled into a mussel shell. "You shall never again be like a person," they said to him. He became a kind of worm, purplish or reddish in color, about eight or ten inches long, found in salt-water mussels and clams.

The two women then sat down facing one another and wept over their plight. They wept for a long time. The first at last asked, "Where do you intend to go?" The second answered, "I shall go to the mountains. It is the only place where I can make my living easily. I shall live there forever." The first then said, "I shall go to the sea-shore. When the tide goes out, I can always find plenty

[1] Evidently he has eaten their berries and roots this time.

of worms and clams. And let it be understood that we shall hereafter eat our food raw. We shall never eat cooked food as people do." Then she added, "Now I am going to try to fly; I'm going to be a bird." But she had a hard time before she could manage to grow wings. She first had to sing a song — calling upon the elements to assist her. She had been very much disappointed in her husband. After she sang, she found she could fly. The second wife said, "Hereafter, I shall be a food animal. The people will find that I am very easy to catch. My flesh will be their food, and my fur, their blankets." Because of what she said, the Indians of the older generations made a very simple trap to catch her with when she came out of her burrow. Her eyes are eaten raw, as is also a ball of grass in her chest. All this is as she ordained. If a sick person craves her meat, it is a sign that he will recover. This is the end of the two wives and their husband. He became the sea worm, the first wife, the large-snipe, and the second, the mountain beaver.

LAND OTTER.[1]

Young Wren and his grandmother Long-legged Spider lived together in one of the two houses at Mulla.[2] There was a large run of herring, so Wren made a kind of trap of cedar boughs where the fish would go to spawn, leaving a door large enough for a canoe. He also made a dip net of hemlock roots; the roots were split and twined and woven into a net. He went to the trap and dipped for herring until he had his canoe full. Then he and his grandmother dried the fish. On his second trip, after his canoe was full, something came out of the water and ate nearly all his fish. He went right home, for he was afraid. "Something comes and eats my fish," he said to his grandmother. On his third trip, someone again boarded his canoe and ate his fish. So the fourth time, he ran his canoe ashore just as soon as it was loaded. The stranger again boarded the canoe and Wren ran home immediately. The following night his grandmother went with him. She tied a packstrap around her waist and took a large knife of yew wood. Since the stranger had not appeared by the time the canoe was full, they ran it ashore. They had just reached the shore when the stranger got in. The old woman jumped out, struck him square on the head with her weapon and killed him. After they had pulled him ashore, they found that he was Land Otter.

The people noticed that Otter was missing. "What's the matter? He hasn't been home all night," they said. So they sent Bluejay to

---

[1] See p. 406.

[2] This story was told immediately after the preceding one. The narrator pointed out that the same people figure in both stories, that is, the villagers of Mulla. The Land Otter of this story is the father of the young man who became a worm.

look for him. Bluejay got into his canoe, and began to wail as he paddled,

> Oh, paddling, paddling my canoe,
> Here I am, paddling my canoe,
> Searching for my friend.

Finally he arrived at Spider's house. "Has Otter been here?" he asked. Since Otter was a royal chief, his loss meant a great deal to the people. The house was full of fish hanging overhead to smoke. Bluejay lay down on his back. As he was lying there, a drop of fat fell down. The smell was familiar. He looked up and there was his friend; he had been skinned, his fur was stretched on a board. He got up immediately and without saying a word, left the house.

Bluejay was heard coming up the river, singing,

> I smell something like my friend.

When he reached his tribesmen, he informed them that their chief had been murdered. They called a council and asked, "What shall we do with Wren and his grandmother?" At last they decided to invite them to a tamanoas gathering and sent someone with the invitation.

Wren and his grandmother arrived at the place where the feast was being held. The old lady had concealed a club, shaped like a knife, on her person. While still outside, she started her tamanoas song. Wren entered first, dancing. Then the old lady entered, singing,

> I'm the one that hit Otter on the head.

They gave her a basket for a present and put it over her head. While she was dancing with this basket over her head, they kicked her grandson into the fire. The old lady became excited as she sang her tamanoas, but when she did not hear her grandson helping her, she took the basket off her head. She saw her grandson in the fire; he was burnt to cinders. She gathered up the cinders and took them home with her.

She held the cinders in her hand and began to blow on them. The cinders then began to assume a tiny form. "You can't be a person any longer," she said to her child, "you're too small and you can't speak. I'll blow you into the air and you shall be the wren." After he had become a bird, she said to him, "You will have no faults; you will be honest and will never steal what people have worked hard to produce. When you bathe, or put your head under water, you will say, 'Sʊp, sʊp, sʊp.' That's the only sound you will ever be able to say, for you were burnt." When wren is seen taking a bath and saying, "Sʊp, sʊp, sʊp," it is a sign of rain. Then the old lady added, "As for myself, I shall be the spider. It will be my job to make thread — on which I will climb. That will be my work, hereafter." Her threads can be seen to this day — threads stretched from one bush to another through the woods. This is the end of the story about Land Otter who was murdered; the tribe punished the murderers by throwing one of them into the fire.

DOG HUSBAND.[1]

The daughter of a chief was living at Westport (Ts'x̣̱e'lɩs). Her family owned a large white dog. During the night, a nice handsome young man would come to the girl's bed. He wore a white blanket. She wondered where he came from. After he had visited her three times, she found that she was pregnant. She slept on a raised platform, the old people on the ground beneath her; the dog slept some distance away. When it was dark, the dog would jump up on her bed. When the people saw that she was pregnant, they were ashamed and left her. The girl still did not know where the man came from. She had to live there all alone with only the large dog for companion. The first night after her desertion, the man came to her again. "Don't be sad because you have been deserted," he said, "I will work for you." She said nothing. When daylight came, he got up to go away. She still said nothing but observed in what direction he went when he left her bed. He climbed down and went a short way. She could hear him lie down; it sounded like an animal. So she watched. "Oh," she said to herself, "it is that dog that has disgraced me! I am ashamed of myself!" She expected her child the next day. She gave birth to five children — all pups. The old dog came in with a large rabbit.

Next day, she left the pups at home and went to the beach to dig clams. When she returned for the fourth time from the beach, she noticed that things seemed strange. The pups were quite large by this time. Whenever the old dog came near her, she would hit him with a club. She went out for the fifth time to her usual place, but left a stick with a basket on it sticking up out of the beach. Over this she threw a mat to make those in the house think that she was still there. When she got back to the house, she could hear people inside having a good time dancing. There was one grown person with them. A pile of dog skins was lying near by. The youngest pup had been told, "Look toward the beach to see if mother is still there." "Oh yes, she's still there," he had answered. After that, they had resumed their fun-making. When the children and the grown man had danced their way back to the end of the house, the woman rushed in and threw their dog skins into the fire. "Oh, you dogs!" she cried, "you have been people all the time, but I have had to suffer disgrace!" The dog skins burned up. The children sat down; they had nothing to say. There were two girls and three boys. Their

[1] See p. 399.

mother was angry with the old dog; she took a piece of burning wood and beat him with it. "Ouch! Ha, ha, ha, don't hurt me," he said. She let him alone then. "You dogs," she said to the children, "shall be people from now on, but a disgrace to your tribe. Other people who live here will be of royal blood, but you will be a disgrace." Then she helped the two little girls make some dresses. "I'm going to leave you," she said to the men, "but I'm taking the two girls with me; you might make them pregnant. You're nothing but dogs!" So she left them.

MƱSPʻ AND KƏMOʹL.[1]

Chief Woodpecker lived on the present site of Humptulip City. The village was composed of twelve large houses. Woodpecker had a son and while the boy was still quite young, he taught him how to make a canoe, for he himself was a carpenter by trade; he had built all the houses in the village. So he taught his son how to make a canoe. They went out into the woods and felled a cedar-tree. Later, he left the boy to his own resources. He had given strict orders to his tribesmen that no one should help his son; the boy should rely on his own judgment as to how a tree should be felled.

The boy went out into the woods and felled a cedar as he thought it should be done. The same day, he put the outside shape to his canoe. Next day, he went out to continue his work and managed to do the inner rough work. The third day, he found a large lacamas in his canoe. It was tied to a single black hair as long as the stretch of both arms. He was very much surprised. He did not take it home with him but hid it. The fourth day, he found two lacamas, each tied, as the first, to a single hair. He hid them in the same place. The fifth day, he found three lacamas, each again tied to a single hair. The sixth day, he found four lacamas and a piece of elk-marrow used for greasing the face. The seventh day, he found nothing. After working but a short time, he became very drowsy and lay down in his unfinished canoe to sleep. After he had fallen asleep, he dreamed that a pretty young girl was sitting by his side. Her hair was exceedingly long and on her back she carried a flat, soft pack-basket. She asked, "Why do you not eat the lacamas that I bring you? I have learned to love you, for I hear you are of royal blood. I want to marry you." When he awoke, he found a young woman sitting by his side. "Why do you fear me? I love you very much," she said. "Who are you, and where do you come from?" he asked. She named a place above Humptulip City. "And what is your name?" "My name is SɨLʼoʹcən," she answered. "That being the case, will you go home with me?" he asked. "If you will wait until late this evening, I will go with you; you see, I am very bashful," she answered.

[1] See p. 383.

They waited until quite late before starting home. When they got to the young man's house, the woman unbraided her hair and let it fall over her face before entering. She took a seat but sat down with her face to the wall. After she had been there some time, Bluejay asked, "Where did this young woman come from?" When she arose next morning, she again sat down with her face to the wall. She ate her breakfast of lacamas, still sitting in the same position. By this time, Bluejay was talking incessantly, demanding to see her face; he wanted her to laugh so that he could laugh with her. After four days of his chatter, she began to lose patience. The fifth day, she said to her husband, "Today, you are to go far beyond the prairie[1] with me." So he went with her. When they got to the place, she began to dig a very deep hole. At that time, they had dug-out boxes large enough to hold one person. She told him to get into the hole which she would cover with a box. "You must not think for a moment that I am going to laugh with you today — I am going to laugh with Bluejay," she said. Before she left him, she stuffed his ears and nose with cedar-bark batting, so that he could not hear her laugh. After she had started back toward the village, her husband said, "I'm going to raise this box just high enough to hear you laugh."

The woman went back to her husband's home and began to dress up. She combed and braided her hair, greased her face with marrow and painted it. She was getting ready to laugh with Bluejay. She went into his house, her face uncovered. "I'm going to laugh now with Bluejay; he's been wanting to laugh with me for a long time." She clapped her hands and cried, "Ha, ha, yo·′·· Bluejay, we're going to laugh now." She had no sooner spoken, than Bluejay fell prostrated. By the time she had finished laughing, everyone in the house, including Bluejay, had fallen dead. Their tongues lolled out and their eyes fairly bulged from their heads. Then she went to another house and cried, "I am going to laugh with Bluejay! Ha, ha, yo·′··" Every last person in the house dropped dead. She went to another. "Now I'm going to laugh with Bluejay! Ha, ha, yo·′··" And again all the people there dropped dead on the spot. She went from one house to another and every occupant died. When every person in the village was dead, she went to the place where she had covered her husband. There she found him, his eyes bulging, his tongue lolling out. When she saw that he was dead, she began to weep. "What shall I do?" she asked, when she had ceased weeping. She took him out of the hole and set to work to remove his breast and genitals. These she put into the basket that she had been carrying when she first met her husband. Then she set out for her own village ten miles farther up the river. (There was a Humptulip village there then, but there is only a prairie now.)

---

[1] About a mile and a half away; they were living close to the river.

When she got home, she hung her basket up in the corner opposite the door. Her bed was near the basket. Along about evening, the basket began to move. She took it down and went to bed with her husband's remains. After she had slept with his remains, her belly began to stir and she knew that she was pregnant. In five days she gave birth to twins. The elder was called Mʊspʻ, the younger Kəmo'l. She loved only the older one and threatened to eat the younger one when he cried. When they were two days old, the children began to walk and she made each a bow and arrow to play with. Whenever she went out to dig lacamas, she told the children that they must never look in her basket; its contents were her secret. She also forbade them ever to go down the river. The children noticed that their mother would get up during the night, take the basket down and put it in her bed. Then she would laugh and enjoy herself for the rest of the night. After five days of this, the children, who were now full grown men, were curious to know what was in the basket. So they climbed up, during their mother's absence, and peeped into it. When they saw what its contents were, the elder said, "This must be our father's remains; this is why mother laughs all night long." The same day, they went down the river. When they arrived at Humptulip City, they found eleven houses. They went from house to house and looked in but could see nothing but skeletons. "This must be the place where father lived and died," they said. Their mother had told them that her real name was not SɩL'o'cən, but K'wαtsx̣wɛ'. "There are five of us," she had said, "myself and four sisters, each one of us living at a different place along this river." They started back and when they got to their house, they said, "We'll burn our house and travel." This particular day, K'wαtsx̣wɛ' felt queer — her heart beat fast and she was excited. This was the day that her sons burned their home.

The two young men had the finest bows that could possibly be obtained; the bows were perfect. As soon as they had burned the house, they started down the river, Mʊspʻ keeping his younger brother in front of him all the time. After they had gone quite a way, Mʊspʻ said, "That dog has discovered that we have burned the house. But we'll keep going and when we find a dead tree with loose bark, we'll climb it, for she'll eat us if she catches us." In the meantime, their mother, while digging, noticed that a cinder had fallen close by. When another came, she held out her hand to catch it. "This cinder is the same shape as the design on my basket!" she said. And, indeed, the cinder was in the shape of a person. Then she realized that her basket was burning. "The boys must be burning the house! I'll eat that Kəmo'l!" She started home. The house was burned to the ground, and with it, had gone her basket and its contents. So she went down the river to the village where she had formerly lived with her husband. She peeped into the houses for some sign of the boys. At last she discovered some tracks and followed them. "They must be travelling in this direction," she said. She scouted around until she found a division of the tracks. She soon discovered Kəmo'l's tracks; right behind his were Mʊspʻ's. She set out on their trail, singing,

Ts'ana'sən,
Ts'ana'sən.

She was singing to weaken them — was singing for something to catch them by their backsides and slow them up. The two young men had not gone much farther, when the elder caught sight of their mother. "Here comes that dog!" he said. It just happened that they were close to a dead tree with loose bark and no limbs. They quickly began to climb it, begging the tree not to let the bark go; the "dog" would eat them if it did. "What kind of song can we sing to help us climb you?" they asked the fir. "Say 'pαt, pαt, pαt,'" the fir answered. Every time they said, "Pαt," their hands and feet stuck to the tree. Far at the top, there were a few limbs, and on one of these, Mʊspʻ put Kəmo'l. When their mother was still a little distance away, she caught sight of them and said, in a voice half weeping, "Nice Mʊspʻ, why do you do that to your brother? He'll fall; be careful!" And when she got close to the tree, she asked, "What did you say when you climbed the tree? What did you say to get up there?" The elder boy answered, "Say 'pαt, pαt' if you want to get up here." Their mother began to climb, saying, "αhe', αhe'," occasionally remembering to say, "Pαt, pαt." This helped a little and after a while she managed to make pretty good time. When she was close, Mʊspʻ pushed the loose bark with his foot and she began to slide down with it. When they saw that their mother was completely smashed to pieces, the two brothers came down. They stood there and asked one another, "Where shall we go from here?" Finally the younger suggested, "Our mother used to say that she had four sisters. Let us look for them and kill them. If these women live, they will always be eating people." "Yes, let us do that," the elder said.

When they neared Humptulip City, they found a prairie that was rather hilly, and whose slope was in the form of steps; there was a rise and then a flat, and so on. In this prairie stood two trees, their tops together; between them was a swing. The steps were filled with children. The children were crying and dirty and seemed afraid of being punished. "Why do you look like this?" the two brothers asked. "Any minute now, the person who lives on this prairie is going to eat us; we are afraid," the children answered. The brothers then walked up to the swing and there they found the owner. "Why are these children so sad?" they asked. "They are my food," the woman answered. The children were called Always-tears, because the tears were continually streaming down their faces. When the two brothers had left the fir tree, the elder had tied a cord around the younger's chest to make it appear that the latter was ill; he was prepared for anything. "My nephews," the old woman said, "I am glad to see you. Where is your mother?" "Our mother is on her way; she is carrying a very large pack," they answered. "Come Kəmo'l get in my swing; I'll give you a ride," the woman said. Just at the spot where the swing swung farthest forward, there was a large rock. (This rock and the two trees are still there.) "My little brother is ill; I'll take a ride in his place," Mʊspʿ said. The children had already told them that the woman would put a child in the swing; he would then fall on the rock and she would eat him. The rock was covered with blood. "Now give me a push," Mʊspʿ said to his aunt. As she pushed him off, she said, "Go and never come back." At the same time, all the children also said, "Go and never come back," as she had always ordered them to do; they feared she would eat them if they did not obey. When he was close to the rock, Mʊspʿ jumped and landed on the other side. "Oh, my nephew," his aunt, the K'wɑtsx̣wɛ', said, "you are very brave!" "Now, my aunt, it's your turn to take a ride," Mʊspʿ answered. At last she agreed to ride. She had a very big belly. "Go and come back," she then ordered the children to say. But Mʊspʿ had already told them to say, "Go and never come back." So when she came to the rock, she fell on it and burst her belly open. All the children that she had eaten then came out. Some were still alive but some had already begun to rot. The two brothers set to work right away to wash these children. Those who were dead were difficult to revive, but those whom the woman had eaten only recently were easily revived. When they had finished, they also cleaned those who had escaped being eaten; they washed them, combed their hair and painted their faces. They then seated them. To these, they said, "When you come into existence again, you will be long-lived people." To those who had been in the woman's belly but who were now alive, they said, "When you come into existence again, you will die when half-grown." To those who were already dead, they said, "You will be the still-born children." The name of this place is The-place-where-the-children-were-seated.[1] As soon as the two brothers had finished with the children, they continued their journey.

They travelled down Humptulip River until they came to another prairie, called Notcu'kł, on the present Highway. There they heard someone saying, "Ha he' yo." They soon saw that they had arrived at a girls' game. A figure shaped like a child, and covered with clam shells, had been built of dirt; it was sitting upright on the ground. Behind this figure, there were children sitting. There were five seats, each full of children. Near by, was a large rock. Just before they had reached the spot, Mʊspʿ had tied a rope around his brother's chest and head.[2] "Where is your mother, my nephews?" their aunt

[1] The narrator's maternal grandmother was a native of this place.

[2] The narrator said that Indians in olden times used to do this when they were ill.

asked when she saw them. "She's coming a little later; she has a very large pack," they explained. The woman then said, "Kəmo'l, sit down there with the children." They were playing doll. "No, I'll play doll instead; my younger brother is very ill," Mʋspʻ answered. When he took his place with the children, he asked them, "What's the trouble? What does she do to you?" The children were crying bitterly. "Do you see that stick sticking up there by the figure? Well, if we can't take that stick without laughing, she beats us to death against the rock and swallows us," they explained. When one child went for the stick, the others, following the old woman's orders, had to say, "Go and never come back." Mʋspʻ's aunt now said to him, "Get that stick and don't laugh." As he started forward, she told the children to say, "Go and never come back." But Mʋspʻ got the stick without laughing. "Now it's your turn to be the-doll-who-is-punished," he said to his aunt. So K'wαtsx̣wɛ' took her turn. All the children then began to say, "Ha he'yo," to make her laugh so that she would not come back. Before she got to the stick, K'wαtsx̣wɛ' fell back laughing, saying, "Ha he' yo." Mʋspʻ then went to his aunt to strike her against the rock. He grabbed her by the feet and she said, "You won't hit me hard, will you? You might hurt me." He promised that he would not hurt her. Then, still holding her by the feet, he picked her up, slung her against the rock with all his might and burst her open. They found numerous children inside her. Each time they killed one of his aunts, Kəmo'l, for a person who was supposed to be ill, showed very quick recovery. The two set to work and bathed the children, combed their hair and painted their faces. (These, like the aforementioned children, were supposed to be in existence before their birth.)[1] Then they said to them, "When you are born, you will have royal parents." At the same time they named this place The-place-to-play-doll. Three of the five sisters were now dead.

From there, the two brothers went to a prairie called Nɩcəg'wa'k'e. Before they had quite reached it, they heard someone laughing, "Ha he' yo." At this place they were playing spear, aiming at a large sized fungus. "What do they do to you?" the two brothers asked the children. The latter explained, "This woman here always makes us sit down on the fungus. Then she spears us and eats us." "Kəmo'l," his aunt said to him, "come over here and sit down. I'll use you as a target." "No," Mʋspʻ said, "your nephew is very ill. I'll sit down in his place. You can use me as a target, instead." When Mʋspʻ sat down, she raised her spear, saying, "Oh, my nephew!" Mʋspʻ answered, "My aunt, you'd better spear me!" She then let the spear fly at him, but he caught it before it struck him. Then he jumped and shouted. "Now, my aunt, you sit down on the fungus, and I'll use you as a target," he said. K'wαtsx̣wɛ' started toward the fungus. "ɛhe', ɛhe'," she grunted as she walked,

[1] The narrator or interpreter may mean to imply rebirth by this statement.

her belly was so heavy. Mʊspʻ picked up the spear and drove it into her heart. Then he took her to a rock and smashed her against it. Many children spilled out of her belly. Mʊspʻ and his brother set to work to bathe the children. When they had them clean, they combed their hair and painted their faces. Then they seated them and said, "When you children are born, you will be spirit people. You will be the hunters' tamanoas." Four of the sisters were now dead.

At last the two brothers came out on the prairie at Carlyle, where the last of the five sisters lived. Someone was laughing, "Ho ho′ yo." There was a game of see-saw here. On either side of the see-saw, there was a large rock. "What do they do to you?" they asked the children. "She sets us on the see-saw. Then we fall off on the rocks and she eats us," the children explained. "Where is your mother?" K'wɑtsx̣wɛ′ asked. "She'll be here a little later; she's carrying a large pack," her nephews answered. "Kəmo′l will have to sit on the see-saw," she said. "No, he's ill," Mʊspʻ said, "I'll sit on it." So he went over and sat down on one end of the see-saw, his aunt on the other. She bore down hard on her end, and Mʊspʻ went up in the air. "Go and come back," the children said, as he went up. Then he bore down hard on his end, and jumped off while his aunt was still up. She fell on the rock and burst open. They found many children, that she had swallowed, inside her. Then they set to work to clean the children. When they had finished, they said, "When you are born, you will be hunters." This was a boys' game. The members of the tribe that used to live in this place were all hunters—even the women. The last of the five sisters was dead. In parting, the two brothers said to the children, "You now have nothing to fear; those who were eating you are all dead."

The two brothers then left for the mouth of the Humptulip. When they got there, they decided, "We shall travel and reform the people. Everything that is wrong, we shall make right." (Considering the way these two lived, one should think of them as Christ-like.) "The mouth of this river shall be a place for fish traps. Hereafter, the people shall always catch fish here," they declared. "We shall now go west — downstream."

So they went to a place called X̣wɛ′tyɪt. There they heard someone shooting arrows inside a house. Bluejay was among those living there. It was raining; the roof was leaking and the people did not know how to stop the leak. They were shooting at it. Bluejay thought he could shoot the raindrops on the head. Mʊspʻ and his brother entered. "What are you doing?" they asked. "Your Honors, the house is leaking," Bluejay answered. The two brothers then started to investigate and found that the shingles were laid just opposite from the way they should have been. "Who in the world ever told you to build a house like this?" they asked. Then they tore it down and built it so that it would not leak. "Hereafter, the roof of a house should always be built like this," they said.

From there, they started toward the ocean beach. They saw a house and when they got close, heard something going, "Tαp, tαp, tαp." It was Bluejay on top of the roof. "What's going on up there?" they asked. "Oh, our chief is making love to his girl," they were told. Then they called up, "It's wrong to do that; come off the roof!" They took Bluejay into the house and there was his sister Yo'i, older-than-he. They closed the house and made it dark. Then they showed them how to conduct themselves properly as man and wife. "Hereafter," they said, "such acts will be carried on privately and in the dark. No one shall cohabit on the roof, where others can see them." From that time on the people there conducted themselves in a respectable manner.

The two brothers then went a little farther along the beach. There they saw many clams stuck on sticks standing upright in the ground. The clams were left to cook by the heat of the sun. When the sun shone brightly, the clams would open. "What are you doing?" they asked the people. "We are cooking clams." "That's not the way to cook!" the brothers said. So they set to work to make a fire with fire-sticks. Then they taught the people how they should cook their clams. They put the clams on top of the sticks and built a fire under them. "Hereafter," they said, "this is how you should build a fire and cook."

Then they went out to the very end of the beach — where the surf strikes. There they found a man walking on his head, with a piece of wood between his legs. Mυsp' and his brother stood the man on his feet and said, "This is the way you should carry wood. If you put it on your left shoulder, it will fall off; but if you put it on your right, it will stick on. And you should walk upright from now on, instead of on your head." Heretofore, all the people in this place had walked on their heads.

They went on a little farther up the coast (to the place where Samson John now lives). They found a house there and heard someone groaning inside, "Ouch my head, ouch my hand." They found a man splitting wood, driving the wedge in with his head. This was why he was groaning. "Split, split," he was saying. "What are you doing?" they asked. "I'm splitting wood," he answered. "That's not the way to split wood!" they said. Then Mυsp' made a mallet for driving in the wedge. "From now on, this is how wood should be split," they said to him. The people in this place were cooking clams by dancing.[1] "You people get your nets ready to catch Chinook salmon," the brothers said. Instead of getting nets, the people got their sticks for digging clams.

They then went to Corner Creek. There they saw a man sharpening a large clam shell. He was singing,

I am making this for the Reformers.

[1] This passage was at first omitted by the interpreter; for this reason, a few details may have been overlooked.

They went up to him and asked, "What are you going to do with that?" "Oh," he said, "there is someone coming who is changing things." "Let me see these things you are sharpening," Mʋspʿ said. There were three shells. "What are you going to do with these?" he then asked. "In case I should meet the one who is changing things, I'll murder him," the man answered. "So the Reformer is coming?" Mʋspʿ asked. "Yes, we heard he was." The man was Deer; at that time, he was like a person. "Turn around this way," Mʋspʿ said. He stuck the shells on the man's backside to make a tail. "Now let me see you jump!" Deer tried to jump but did not do very well. The third time, he did much better. "Now jump toward the ocean and look back now and then," Mʋsp said. "Your name shall be 'deer', hereafter. When people hunt you, you will always run a little way and then look back. When the wolves hunt you, you will run toward the ocean; that's where they'll find you," the two brothers said.

They left him and went to Copalis. There, close to the water, they saw a man. He was saying, "ɛhe', ɛhe'." He seemed to be having a hard time. "What are you doing?" they asked. He said, "I am very lousy; my louse is dragging me to the water; he will drown me." "Have you any urine?" they asked. "Yes, I have some in the house."[1] "Lice never killed anything or anybody. Come on, we'll wash your hair," they said. They washed his hair first in urine and then in fresh water. Since making articles of necessity was part of their work, Mʋspʿ and his brother made the man a comb from wood. They oiled his hair for him and then combed it into a braid which they fixed into a knot. "If you should feel any lice in your hair in the future, wash it and comb it again. Always do that hereafter," they said. "Get your nets for catching Chinook salmon!" they said to the people. But the latter, instead of getting nets, got their sticks for digging clams again. "Always do that hereafter," they said.

They went on and came to the Rocks. There was a Wolf there, eating crabs raw. "Crabs aren't eaten raw; they are cooked first. You are still a person and should act accordingly," they said to him. "We don't want to become real people. It's too much work to cook; we'd rather eat our food raw," Wolf answered. There were four Wolves; their younger brother was Dog. Mʋspʿ said to the Wolves, "You folks can go on eating your food raw; you will be real wolves from now on and will always be hungry." Wolf then said, "We once had a fire but it went out."[2] "Will you let us build you a fire?" Mʋspʿ asked. "No!" Wolf answered. Mʋspʿ then declared, "From now on, no matter how bad your food is, you will have to eat it as you find it."

The two brothers then went to Moclips. There they found people who were totally ignorant of the proper manner of cohabitation.

[1] The people used to use a tightly woven basket for a night vessel.
[2] See The Wolves And Their Brother Dog, p. 307.

They cohabited through their ears, eyes and mouths; they did not know any better. "What are you doing?" they asked. The people told them. Then Mʋsp' laid them in the proper position. "This is the way to have sexual relations," he said. They called this The-place-of-cohabitation.

They went to Rock Creek. There they found a person, his face painted with charcoal, lying among the rocks. All around him in the sun were lying clam shells. The two brothers took the clams and stuck them on his front teeth but he did not wake up. They named him X̣wɑne'x̣wɑne. (He was a great liar.)

From there, they went to Tehola. "Get ready and go to your fish traps! Get your nets and all your implements!" they called to the people. The latter did just exactly as they were told. The brothers then showed them how to make a basket from which the fish could not swim out.

They then went to Large Stream. No one was living there. "What shall we do about it?" they asked one another. They looked around and found many buildings, all empty. They followed the stream down to the mouth. There they saw a very deep, suspicious looking whirlpool. There was something there. They built a fire, heated some rocks and threw them in. Before long the water began to boil. And soon there rose to the surface a huge black creature with an enormous mouth. It was a supernatural creature. They pulled him ashore, belly up. Then they began to cut his belly open. They found even a canoe inside. There were whole families there (houses and all), and skull after skull. Only those who had been in the monster's belly but a short time could be revived. They could do nothing with those who had been dead a long time; their flesh was completely shrivelled up. Bluejay and X̣wɑne'x̣wɑne were both there. Since the latter had still a little life in them, the two brothers were able to revive them. "What shall we do to increase the population here? There are so few people left," the brothers said. Then X̣wɑne'-x̣wɑne spoke up, "I shall be the one to plan for the new population." "Rub up your skin," he said to Mʋsp' and his brother. The latter rubbed and a little dirt came off. They rubbed this dirt into little rolls between their palms. "Give me some of the dirt," X̣wɑne'-x̣wɑne said to Mʋsp'. Then he put it with that which he had rubbed off from his own skin. "Now blow upon it," he said. The two brothers blew, and the little rolls of dirt became people. The latter located at this place; they are called Those-made-from-dirt. X̣wɑne'x̣wɑne then built a fish trap for these people so that they would have plenty to eat. He did his part; this was his way of showing his gratitude to the two brothers for reviving him. Bluejay then explained, "There were once people here, but when they started to move across the river, the whirlpool swallowed them."

From there, they went to Səla'tx̣. "Build fish traps!" they called out. The people here had modern things — fire, houses;

everything was in good shape, but the people themselves were dirty. Mʋspʻ and his brother made them bathe, first showing them how.

They then went to Quillayute. "Put up fish traps!" they cried out. The people, instead of putting up traps, pushed their canoes out into the surf and let out their trolling lines. Then someone threatened to murder the two brothers so they ran away. After they had got a safe distance, they declared, "Let them be a mean people, a bad people!"

They then went to Ozat. "Put up fish traps!" they called out. Instead of putting up traps, the people went out to troll; a few went up to the hills to hunt. So they left these people because they did everything properly.

From there, they went to Nəgwi'lau. "Put up fish traps!" they called out. Instead of putting up traps, the people went out to sea.

They then went to Noẋa'pɑq'. "Put up fish traps!" they cried out. Instead of putting up traps, the people got their arrows and other implements for war. "Hereafter, you shall be warriors," they declared.

From there, they went to Qwəneo'tsot. "Get your dip nets!" they called out. Instead of getting their nets, the people went out with hooks and lines. "Hereafter, you shall always fish in this way," the brothers said. The people then said, "If you are the Reformers, you can help us out by telling us what comes out of the hill back of our village and eats us." The two brothers heated some rocks and threw them in the lake that was pointed out to them. The water began to boil and before long a dangerous being, belly up, came to the surface. Everyone present then called upon the dangerous being to come ashore. They tried to cut him open but their knives would not penetrate. So they heated some more rocks and laid them on his belly to burst him open. They found many people inside, some still alive but others pretty well gone. The people were happy when the dead were brought to life by the two brothers. These revived people were then bathed. The two brothers had to stay some time in this place, straightening things out. The place was full of large rocks through which it was difficult to make one's way. They made the country more open and left an island there as a kind of lighthouse. The people had formerly had great difficulty at this spot. There had been so many rocks on the point that a whirlpool had formed. They were glad that the brothers had saved them from this.

They then went to Chinook country to complete their circuit. When they got to Clatsop, they called out, "Get out your fish nets!" Instead of getting their nets, the people caught crabs. Before they left, the brothers pronounced Clatsop the birthplace of royalty. "Anyone with Clatsop blood, will be a chief," they declared.

They went to Astoria and called for nets. The people did as they were told and came out with their nets to fish for the royal Chinook salmon.

They crossed the river to Miggley. There they found the people drying sturgeon heads on a rock. "What is that hanging on the rocks?" they asked. "We're drying fish heads," the people answered. "That's not the way to dry fish!" the brothers said. Then they taught them how to smoke the heads, and also how to dress and dry fish. "If you don't follow our directions hereafter, the fish will become scarce here," they said.

They then went to Qwɪ'lsɪł. There they found people who did not know how to eat; they put the food in their noses, eyes, and ears, and when they drank water, they spilled it on their heads. "What are you doing?" Mʋsp' and his brother asked. "We're eating our lunch," the people answered. "That's not the way to eat!" they said to them. They then taught them how to hold the food, how to put it in their mouths, and how to chew and swallow it. These same people also did not know how to sleep. When night came, instead of going to sleep, they would put phosphorus wood on their eyes, so that it would always be light. This kept them from sleeping. After the brothers had taught them how to sleep they left them. They also taught these people how to fish with a net.

From there, they went to Qwatsa'mɪts. They found the people ready to move; some were lying crosswise on the bed. They thought that by having everything ready to move, they could get where they wanted to go during their sleep. The two brothers said to them, "That's not the way to move! You just think you move; when you wake up, you're still here. Hereafter, when you want to go some place, pack your things, put them in a canoe and paddle. After a while you will find that you are there." So the people found out how to travel. The two brothers left them after setting things straight.

They then went to Fort Columbia. The people in this place had large serpents for pets. If the serpents were not fed sufficiently, they would eat one of their owner's small children. The owners did not know what to do with them. "If these serpents keep on multiplying, they will eat you up. You must kill them," the brothers said. So they gathered all the snakes together, took them to the top of the high hill at that place, and killed them; it took three whole days to get rid of them all. Mʋsp' was so tired out from the effort that he had to sit down for a rest. This spot is now called The-place-where-Mʋsp'-was-sitting. After all the snakes had been killed, they burned them. The two brothers then said, "If you should find another serpent, by all means kill it; otherwise it will multiply and eat you." The people agreed to do this. At the present time, people are told not to go to this particular hill as there are so many snakes there. There is a rock on this hill in the shape of a duck; this rock is called Mʋsp'.

From there, the two brothers went to Chinook City. They found that the place was infested with wood rats. The rats came from the swamps back of the village and ate the people alive. So they started to kill the rats. They burned the ground over so that no rat could escape. The rats could be heard squeeling as they were caught in the flames. The two brothers then said, "If you should ever see a rat here, take a stick and club him; you can kill him quite easily." "Do you have any fish nets?" they also asked. In reply, the people went out with their nets and caught Chinook salmon.

They then went to Illwako and Mʊspʻ called for nets. In reply, the people came out and went fishing.

They went from there to Ts'eyʊ'k'w and called for nets. In reply, the people came out with their clam "guns".

They then went to Nesɑ'l. "Bring out your nets!" they called out. Instead of bringing their nets, the people went out hunting; a few went out to hook sturgeon. These people had no fire, so they taught them how to make fire with fire-sticks and how to cook clams.

From there, they went to Nemah and called for fish nets. In reply, some of the people went out hunting. Others built small fish traps; for that reason, this place is now full of small salmon.

They then went to Bay Center. "Bring out your nets!" they called out. Instead of bringing nets, the people went to their herring traps; for that reason, the herring are plentiful in this place.

They went to X̣wax̣ʊ'ts. "Bring out your nets!" they called out. Instead of bringing nets, the people brought sturgeon hooks and caught sturgeon.

They went across to Q'wa'pks and called out for nets. Instead of bringing nets, the people brought their spears for spearing salmon.

They then went to Nomol'x̣ɑnł and called for nets. Instead of bringing nets, the people went to catch crabs and dig clams.

They went to Westport (Ts'x̣e'lɪs) and asked for nets. Instead of bringing nets, the people went out to catch crabs and dig clams. When they left, they said, "A whale will always wash ashore here; you are good people."

They went to łəmi'ətʊmc. "Bring out your nets!" they cried. Instead of bringing nets, the people fished for herring.

They went to Yate'kł and called out, "Bring out your nets!" Instead of obeying, the people went out to fish for herring. These people did not know how to wash their heads, so they taught them how.

They then went to Ts'e'tc. "Have you any nets?" they cried. Instead of fishing, the people went out to hunt elk. So they said to them, "You shall always make your living by hunting. You will be good natured people. Everyone here will be equal in rank; no one will be disgraced by slave blood, for all will be born royal." The Harbor people originated from this group.

They went to Mulla and called for nets. Instead of bringing dip-nets for herring, the people brought hooks for catching sturgeon. So they said to them, "You shall continue to make your living in this way."

They went to Hoquiam and called out, "Bring your nets!" Instead of bringing nets, the people either went to their herring traps or brought hooks for catching sturgeon. Anyone with Hoquiam blood is usually small in stature.

They went to James' Rock. "Have you any nets?" they asked. Instead of bringing nets, the people started to build herring traps. These people had a canoe shaped something like a box; a canoe of this shape was always inclined to tip over. So they taught them how to make the proper kind of canoe. This new canoe had a bow and stern exactly alike.

They went to a place called Owl. The people there had the habits of an owl. They asked for nets. But instead of going out with nets, the people went to the prairie and caught gophers. So the brothers said to them, "From now on, you shall be owls and live like them; you shall know no other way of life."

They went to Chinoose Creek. "Have you nets?" they asked. In reply, the people came out with sturgeon hooks and also began to build herring traps. So the two brothers said, "Hereafter, you shall make your living in this manner."

They went to a place called Cold-water. "Have you nets?" they asked. The river here was very small. Instead of bringing nets, the people built salmon traps. The two brothers then said, "This is how you shall make your living hereafter." "There will be no dog-salmon in this stream — no large-sized salmon — only silver-side," they declared.

From there, they went to the mouth of the Humptulip, the first place they had visited as Reformers. "Here we are!" they said to one another. "We have travelled around the whole world without any difficulty. We have killed many dangerous beings and by doing so have saved the people. Now what shall we do?" "We'll settle down in the water," Kəmo'l decided. "We'll be a kind of duck." After this was decided, they said, "We'll make our appearance during the middle of the fishing season. After seeing us, the people may then cut their fish in any manner they desire." Before the appearance of the ducks, the people had to dress the fish with a sharpened clam shell. A rack was then placed over the fire. The heads of the fish were hung down over one side of this rack, the tails over the other. Both the tails and heads had to be broken off the body. The portion that included the back was not held upright by a roasting stick, but was laid on a board before the fire.[1] This method of handling the fish was also laid down by the brothers; if it is not followed, the fish will become scarce. But as soon as the ducks arrive, the people are free to cook the fish as they like.

The two brothers became ducks — about the size of the Mallard duck. This kind of duck always lives in rivers; it never appears in flocks but in pairs. The ducks go north in the spring and return in the fall. It is their fall appearance that means so much to the Indian.

[1] The narrator said that she cooked fish this way when she was young.

IV. WYNOOCHEE TALES.

X̣WƏNE′.[1]

An old lady had a house near the river. She had built a dam in the river to keep the fish from going up any farther. People who were hungry for fish would sometimes come to her and ask for them. Then she would grab a fish and butcher it. X̣wəne′ finally broke the dam, making a channel through it, so that the fish could go up the river. If he had not broken the dam, we would not have fish. Now there are fish everywhere.

X̣wəne′ was a smart man; he could make anything but he would lie and cheat people. Once he was staying on a gravel-bar. "I wish I were on top of a hill, on top of a bluff," he said. He lay down to sleep and when he awoke found himself on top of a bluff. He was very hungry and began to weep. He wished and wished and wished for something to eat. It was a hot day and he began to perspire. He licked the perspiration off with his tongue. He happened to touch his eye and found that it tasted very good. He ate it. Then he ate his other eye. Now his eyes were gone, so he began to wish for eyes. He wished and wished and wished that someone would come and help him. Perhaps Wind would come. Instead Owl came. X̣wəne′ took him by the neck and strangled him to death. He took his eyes out and put them in his own sockets. Then he pulled his wings off and put them on himself. Now he had wings so he flew down to the ground. He kept Owl's eyes but threw his wings away. He was very hungry.

He walked and walked. Finally he met an old woman who was packing lacamas. She was K'ʊwutsx̣wɛ′. "Ah, nephew," she greeted him. "What are you packing?" he asked. "Cooked lacamas," she answered. "My slave is just coming around the point in a canoe. If you give me one of your baskets of lacamas, I'll let you have him," he said. She gave him a basket of lacamas and he ran away. He was very hungry and ate up all the lacamas. After a while, the woman thought she saw the slave coming around the point in a big canoe. She had mistaken a large root riding the waves for a canoe. X̣wəne′ had lied to her. She stayed there on the beach waiting for the slave to come in to shore. "Come on, come on, I bought you," she called. "Come on, come on, I bought you," she called again. The canoe never came to shore.

[1] Told by Jack Williams, 1927; see p. 385.

X̣wəne′ came again; he cheated all the time. K'ʋwutsx̣wɛ′ was hoping he would come again. She was ready for him. She had found some large bees, a very mean kind, and had put them in one of her baskets. She had fastened the basket securely and had told the bees what to do when X̣wəne′ opened the basket. "Oh, my aunt, what are you packing?" X̣wəne′ asked. "Lacamas," K'ʋwutsx̣wɛ′ answered. "I'd like to buy some," he said. K'ʋwutsx̣wɛ′ readily agreed to sell him some. "Take the whole basket along," she said. "Open it inside a hollow tree, but first see that the tree is closed tightly." X̣wəne′ took the basket and ran away. He went to a hollow tree and had it close tightly. Then he opened the basket. Something came out and went, "B · · · · ." The bees stung him all over. X̣wəne′ was in the stump with nothing to eat. He was very hungry and ate his eyes. Now he had no eyes; he had eaten his own eyes for the second time. He stayed there in the stump, begging it to open up for him. "Open for me, I want to get out," he kept saying. The stump did not open. He wept and wept. He stayed there for many days. Finally he heard someone knocking. "Open the stump for me, Yellowhammer," he cried. Woodpecker (qa'qʋ′m) pecked and pecked and pecked at the stump until X̣wəne′ was at last released.

X̣wəne′ had no eyes; he had torn them out and eaten them. He was still hungry. He wept and wept. He had been imprisoned in the stump for days and days. He wandered about blind. Sometimes he would fall into the water and have to drag himself ashore. He wandered here and there, feeling his way along by means of the timber. Finally he came to some timber that was standing on end. It was a house. He groped his way along the house, muttering to himself, as he felt for the door. "What are you doing?" someone asked. "I'm measuring your house. Oh, you have a big house! How many fathoms long is it?" he said. Then he said, "Hwu · · · · , ɛ · · · · · · , do you see that star over there?" Snail, the owner of the house, looked in the direction in which X̣wəne′ pointed. Snail had very good eyes. "No," he said, "I don't see any star." X̣wəne′ had put some blossoms in his sockets and was using them for eyes. "I have good eyes. Let us trade," he said, "then you'll have good eyes." Snail traded eyes with him. The blossoms soon wilted. Now Snail has no eyes; he cannot see. "Hw · · · · · ," X̣wəne′ whistled, happy to have good eyes once more. He was always fooling someone.

BUNGLING HOST.[1]

Bluejay set out to visit Fish Duck. He kept going and going and at last got there. "Wait, old man, I'll go out and get you a salmon," Fish Duck said. He dived into the water and came out with a Chinook salmon. Then he heated some rocks and boiled the salmon in a

[1] Told by Jack Williams, 1927; see p. 393.

trough. Bluejay ate the salmon. Then he left for home. "Come to my house and visit me," he called back.

Fish Duck returned the visit. Bluejay went out, and flying this way, that way, dived down into the water to get a salmon. Instead, he struck his head on some rocks and was knocked senseless. He had missed the river completely. He lay as if dead. Fish Duck picked him up, carried him to the house and put him to bed. Bluejay finally regained his breath and recovered. Then Fish Duck went out, circled over the river, dived in and came out with a salmon. He left the salmon for Bluejay.

After his recovery Bluejay set out to visit Bear. He got to Bear's house and went inside. "Sit down, old man," Bear said. After a while Bear got a knife and cut some meat from his feet. There was a lot of fat on Bear. He cooked the meat on a big rock and gave it to Bluejay. Bluejay ate it; it was very good. Then he started home. "Come to my house, come to my house," he called back.

Bear returned Bluejay's visit. After a while Bluejay heated some rocks. Then he sat down and started to cut some flesh off his feet. His poor little feet began to draw up; he had cut through the muscles. "Uh, uh," he peeped like a chicken. Bear worked at Bluejay's feet to heal them and rubbed him to bring his breath back. Then he cut some flesh off his own feet. He had only to rub them a bit to make them normal again. He left the meat for Bluejay and went home.

THE HOOP.[1]

Now people were travelling, five of them.[2] This was before the world was changed. Coyote (snətcu'l) had four sons; they were fast runners. One old man, Stəhe·'n,[3] had one grandchild, a very strong boy.

Far away some people were playing with a hoop. These people were the tamanoas. They were racing back and forth with the hoop which shone brightly as it rolled. "Let's go and steal the hoop," the Coyote boys said. Stəhe·'n's grandson went with them. They travelled and travelled. At last they got to the place and the eldest Coyote went alone to steal the hoop. Bluejay was there. "Hai · · · · · ·, he has come to see the tamanoas play," he said when he saw young Coyote. Young Coyote stood waiting. When the hoop came his way, he slipped his arm through it and cried, "Bə · · · · · ·." He ran as fast as he could. The people ran after him and finally caught up with him. He then threw the hoop to his next brother. The tamanoas seized the first boy and killed him. The second boy ran as fast as

[1] Told by Jack Williams, 1927; see p. 390.

[2] This may be a formalized opening, or it may refer to the five boys when they set out to steal the hoop.

[3] An animal said to resemble a dog.

he could with the hoop. It was heavy and made him tired. They were gaining on him, so he threw the hoop to his third brother. They killed the second boy and started after the third. The third threw the hoop to his youngest brother. They then caught up with the third and killed him. Now three boys were dead. The fourth boy grew tired and threw the hoop to young Stəhe·'n. "B · · · · · ·," young Stəhe·'n squealed as he caught it. They killed the fourth boy and started after young Stəhe·'n. As the boy ran, it became foggy. He made the fog come; perhaps he had doctor's tamanoas.

Old Coyote heard someone coming. "Now my children are coming," he said, giving old Stəhe·'n a push, "your little grandson was killed." They argued back and forth. "It's my little grandson you hear. He's strong, he wouldn't get killed," old Stəhe·'n said. Stəhe·'n won the argument.

V. SATSOP TALES.

X̣WƏNEʹ AND THE WOMAN.[1]

There was an old lady who stayed in the woods a great deal of the time. She was busy drying lacamas. One day she came out to the beach, carrying a basket on her back. Before long X̣wəneʹ came and asked, "What are you packing in your basket, aunt?" "I have some dried lacamas," she answered. "Well," he said, "I have a string of beads with which I could buy one." "All right," she said and gave him a lacama so long and so wide.[2] She put the beads inside her dress and went on. X̣wəneʹ ate the lacama. Then he went on ahead and met the old lady again. "Oh, where are you going, aunt?" he asked in a nice voice. "I'm packing some lacamas home that I dried in the woods," she answered. "I have a string of beads with which I could buy one," he said. "All right," she said. She took a lacama out of her pack and gave it to him. X̣wəneʹ was a great one! He ate up the lacama — it was quite a large one — and set out to overtake the old lady again. He caught up with her and asked, "Did you see my brother?" "Yes," she said, "he bought a dried lacama from me." Then she noticed that he looked very much like the man she had met before. "Aren't you the man I met before?" she asked. "There are five of us; we are brothers and look just alike. My brothers are travelling this way, too," he explained. Then he said, "I have a string of beads; I could buy one of your lacamas." "Oh, I have lots I could sell," she said. She took the beads and gave him a lacama. X̣wəneʹ ate it quickly and then went on. He caught up with the old lady again. This time she was rather certain that he was the same man. She was tired out now and rather annoyed. "I have a slave coming behind me in a canoe," he said. Then he asked, "What have you got on your back?" "Dried salmon eggs," she said. "Well," he said, "my slave who is coming can pick you up in the canoe and take you the rest of the way home." She accepted his offer and gave him some salmon eggs. He went on and she waited for the canoe. She stood on the beach and called, "Come this way, come this way." She called and called. Finally she went farther out on the beach and saw that what she had taken for a canoe was only a big stump. X̣wəneʹ had said that it was his slave coming in a canoe. The tide was washing the stump ashore.

[1] Told by Mrs. Simon Charlie, 1927; see p. 385.
[2] Illustrating.

"I'll fix you, X̣wəne′!" she thought. She got as many yellowjackets as she could find and put them in her basket. Then she went on. After a while she met X̣wəne′. "I have some dried salmon eggs in my pack," she said. "I'll buy them from you, aunt," he said. He showed her a string of beads. He had strung some little red fruit, like little crab apples, on a long string. The old lady thought they were real beads. She took the string and gave him her basket. "Don't open the basket until you get to a place where you won't catch the wind. Go far inland," she said.

X̣wəne′ did as she said. When he opened the basket something went, "Bəm · ·." The yellowjackets stung his eyes out. This was what the old lady had planned. X̣wəne′ had no eyes now. "Where shall I go?" he thought. He crawled about, trying to find his way. Finally he came to a house and began to feel his way about it. A woman asked, "What are you doing?" "Nothing," he said, "I'm just measuring your house to see how long it is." X̣wəne′ always had an answer ready. The woman was Snail and the house belonged to her. X̣wəne′ sat down. Snail noticed that he had no eyes. She was somewhat blind herself and held her hands over her eyes to shade them. "You've got good eyes," he said and snatched her eyes out. Then he put ground berries in her sockets and left her. The bad old thing! That was X̣wəne′; all stories about him are like this.

A great many people had gathered at a certain place to play slahal and X̣wəne′ went there. They were playing with his eyes.[1] He joined the game and pointed with the others. They were singing,

X̣wəne′'s eye,
X̣wəne′'s eye.

"e · · ·," he said as he pointed. The eyes came toward him and he snatched them up and ran out. Now that he had his eyes back, he decided to look for the old lady who had played the trick on him. "Where shall I go to find her? What shall I do to her?" he thought. The story ends here; he never went to look for the old lady.[2]

BUNGLING HOST.[3]

Bluejay was a great one to fool people. He had a sister named Yu·′i. One day he said to her, "Well, sister, let's get ready and visit Bear." Yu·′i got ready and sat down in the canoe. Bluejay paddled and paddled up the river and finally arrived at Bear's place. Bear was a human being at this time. Bluejay and Yu·′i got out of the

---

[1] Evidently an incident has been omitted.

[2] The narrator remarked: X̣wəne′ lived a long time ago. He was an important person and a very foolish one. He made the rivers and hills. He was full of fun and did everything he could think of. If a person can do everything, or if he is very foolish, they call him "X̣wəne′".

[3] Told by Mrs. Simon Charlie, 1927; see p. 393.

canoe and went to the house. As soon as they arrived, Bear made a fire; he was going to cook for them. He got his knife and cut a piece of meat off his thigh. Then he slapped his thigh and the flesh grew back on again. He cooked the meat and Bluejay and his sister ate it. They stayed a little while after eating and then got ready to leave. When he got to the door, Bluejay said, "Come tomorrow morning to see us." Then they went home.

Next morning Bear got ready to visit Bluejay. He went down the river to Bluejay's place. When he got there, he went into the house and sat down. In a little while, Bluejay said to his five little children, "You children go out and get some trout for Bear." The little Bluejays went out and dived into the water to get the trout. The youngest one dived for good, — he drowned. The children came back and said, "Father, we couldn't get any trout. We lost our youngest brother." "Too bad, old man," Bear said to Bluejay. Bear then got ready to go home. He cut another piece of meat from his thigh and left it for Bluejay.

Old Bluejay did this kind of thing time and again. He would pay a visit to a house and when the visit was returned, would do something foolish. He was foolish and a liar. In this respect, he was second only to X̣wəne'.

BLUEJAY GOES TO THE LAND OF THE DEAD.[1]

Bluejay was staying with his sister Yu·'i. One day he said to her, "I wish you would marry a dead person, I wish you would go far under this earth where the dead live and marry someone there." Before long Yu·'i died and went to the place where old Bluejay had wished she would go. She married and stayed there. There was nothing but bones in this place; there were bones everywhere.

Not long afterward Bluejay thought, "I'm going to look for my sister now. But how can I find her?" He went to someone and asked, "How can I get to the ghosts?" He asked again and again, "How can I get to the ghosts?" Finally old Bluejay learned how to get there. He came to a river and hollered, "Io·'ii." "That looks like Bluejay," Yu·'i said. She started across the river in a canoe to get him. "Don't bring that canoe, it's got holes in it," he said, "it will sink before it gets here." He sent her back a number of times for another canoe. Finally she managed to get him across to her house. Bones of dead people were lying about everywhere and Bluejay began to kick them. "Gosh, they're lots of dead people's skulls here!" he said and kicked a skull. "Don't kick my husband!" Yu·'i tried to stop him. "Just keep still," she kept saying.

Finally Yu·'i got tired of him. "Go home now, we're tired of you," she said. She made him five little buckets in which to carry water

---

[1] Told by Mrs. Simon Charlie, 1927; see p. 396.

for his return trip. He would have to pass through a burning place and would need the water to put the fire out, she explained. Bluejay started back, splashing water along the way. He splashed it on the prairies which were full of brilliant flowers. Then he came to a place that was on fire. He should have saved the water for this place. When the water was all gone, he tried to beat the flame out with his topknot. He burned to death. He was back at the river once more, hollering for his sister. "You're dead now," she called back. She started across in a canoe to get him. "Oh, you have a nice canoe!" he said. "It's the one I came in before," she answered. When he got to the house, he said, "Gosh, your husband is nice-looking!" "He's the man you kicked around before," she said.

VI. SOME PUGET SOUND TALES.

PUYALLUP TALES.

THE CONTESTS.[1]

In olden times, it was the custom for a tribe to choose athletes from their own number to compete with those from another. For instance, one band of people might challenge a band that lived across the bay. In this story, the Seal nation represents one side, the Freshwater animals, such as, Otter, Mink, Beaver and Weasel, the other. All were human beings at the time. They had challenged one another to play certain games. As a rule everyone talks about a contest of this sort and knows when it is to take place. Bluejay (ska′ikai), like everyone else, heard of the contest. "Grandmother," he said, "the people from here are going to play a tribe across the bay on a certain date. I want to go." His grandmother was Mouse (skwatə′n). "Look here, grandson," she said, "you'd better forget about it. You can't compete with those big men; you're just a child." Next day Bluejay said again, "Grandmother, I want to go to the contest." "No, those people who are competing are trained. They have skəlä′letut (the power of bravery)[2] and x̂ᵘnä′m (doctor's power)[2]." All of the young men who were to take part were well prepared, they could face anything — war or games — and so were very brave. The date of the meet had already been set. Every day Bluejay begged his grandmother to let him go. Finally he said, "Grandmother, I'm going to ask you for one favor. If you don't grant it, I'll stay home." By this time his grandmother was out of patience and angry with him. "What do you want? You annoy me all the time. Now what is it?" she said unpleasantly. "Grand-

[1] Told by Jerry Meeker, 1926; see p. 394.

[2] The narrator's translation. Anyone who desires a guardian spirit must go through a rigorous training. He must bathe in a river, a lake, or the Sound. Eventually, if the spirits choose him, he falls into a trance and floats ashore as if dead, or is beaten ashore by the waves. Then in spirit he is taken to another world, the place where the skəlä′letut live. When he finds himself in this world, he is told what power he is to receive, — whether for doctoring, war or whatnot, depending upon the spirit that has chosen him. The spirits themselves are human beings, but invisible to the naked eye. They talk with the person and what they have to tell is "unknown to human beings on earth". Anything they reveal must be kept secret. See also p. 354, footnotes 1–3.

mother, I want you to cut the hairs from your privates and let me use them for a tassel,"[1] he said. His grandmother did not want to let him go for fear the other men would shorten his life,[2] but finally granted his request.

The appointed day arrived and everyone got ready and crossed the bay. Before landing on their opponents' grounds they sang their spirit songs, keeping time with their paddles, either waving the paddles in the air or beating them against the sides of the canoes. All the big sportsmen finished with their songs. Then it was Bluejay's turn. "Now you must sing your song, Bluejay," they said to him, "sing your spirit song. Let us see what you have learned since you became a man. You've got to show it now." Bluejay shook himself. Then he took out his tassel, shook it a bit and stuck it in his hair. It was a pretty tassel. He sang,

äniyäə, äniyäə
tən əx̣weəkwa.

The song referred to the material from which his tassel was made but he had changed the words so that the reference would not be too obvious. Everyone sang his song but did not suspect its implication. At last they said, "Now you're all right. We think you'll be able to manage."

Before they had left home, Bluejay had made a little club with a handle and hid it in his blouse. As soon as they landed on their opponents' ground, they began to plan the games. They decided on a diving contest as the first feature. When he heard this, Bluejay ran down to a canoe, began to pull the brush out and throw it into the water. (Brush is usually kept in the bottom of a canoe to keep the canoe from soiling.) "What's the matter with Bluejay? He's throwing the brush into the water," someone said. The opposition chose Seal to represent them in the contest. Bluejay's people would have to choose either Otter, Mink or Beaver to represent them. Which should it be? As they deliberated, Bluejay got up and volunteered. "Why, you don't even know how to dive!" they said. At last they gave in to his entreaties. Bluejay went into waist-high water and stayed there. The one who was short-winded would have to come out first; this one would be the loser. Bluejay dived under the canoe from which he had thrown the brush and came up in the

---

[1] The narrator explained: The people here never used more than two feathers in their hair for decoration. More than that was considered very bad taste, an implied insult. "Too much of anything is worse than nothing at all." A feather or two worn in the hair indicates the spirit the person met while training. When a person who possesses a spirit goes to a contest, he sings his spirit song which also indicates what power he has, whether for bravery, or for wealth, for acquiring things easily.

[2] If one professes to have a power and does not, or does not have a power strong enough to meet the demands of the occasion, others who do have strong powers will kill one.

brush. He poked his bill out, but kept it concealed. He stayed there breathing the fresh air. At last he said to himself, "I'm getting tired of this!" He still had plenty of breath left. He started to crawl toward the spot where Seal was submerged. He struck Seal on the head with his club and Seal came up as dead as a hammer. At last Bluejay came out at the place where they had dived in. He was out of breath now. He came out of the water and shook himself. "Has Seal come out yet?" he asked. "Why, he's been dead for a long time," they said.

The next event was a tree-climbing contest;[1] they were going to see who could climb the highest. The opposition chose Tiny Woodpecker to represent them. Bluejay again volunteered to represent his side. Tree climbing was one thing in which Bluejay excelled, but his people at first refused his offer. "No," they said, "we must have someone more powerful than you." The fact that he had a club to help him out made Bluejay brave. The others did not know that he had the club; they had real power, not some material object to give them courage. Finally they decided to let him climb. He and Woodpecker then started to climb the tree. Woodpecker kept climbing and climbing. "My, he's high! How can I get up that far? I'm not used to going so high," Bluejay thought. "My good gracious, he never will stop!" He went to a shady spot and stayed there. When Woodpecker came back down, Bluejay struck him on the head. Woodpecker dropped; there was blood on his head. Then Bluejay's people said, "There's something wrong somewhere! Bet Bluejay has a weapon of some sort. There was blood on Seal's head and now there is blood on Woodpecker's head." They kept their suspicions to themselves. The games were over; Bluejay had won them all. They went back home.

THE SPIRIT OF WEALTH.[2]

A number of families in a certain village were giving their children the customary tamanoas training. The children were sent out each morning before daylight to swim, to cleanse themselves and to do any number of required tasks. In this village there was a family that had two sons, both of whom were considered lazy and slothful by other families. They always slept by the camp-fire until sunrise. Consequently their blankets were dirty and covered with soot. The villagers would come to the boys' family and make complaints about them. "Why don't you train your children as we do?

[1] There was also a gambling contest but the narrator had forgotten which side won.

[2] Told by Jerry Meeker, 1926. This story is told to children to educate them, — to make them brave. It is a winter story, and the telling of it is sure to bring on cold weather. See p. 420.

They'll never amount to anything!" they would say. "We can't help it. We can't get them to do anything," the boys' parents would answer. Other trainers[1] would come to the boys' parents and threaten them because they did not train their children properly. But all the while, the two boys had been training secretly; they did not want anyone to know what they were doing. They had been going out every night from two to four during the winter. They did all their work after midnight.

The other children in the village kept up their training. Some were ready to go off by themselves.[2] They were already hunting game. "How well he can do things, what a good shot he is," grown-ups often remarked about certain of the children.

When the two boys were about twelve or fourteen years old, they let the villagers know that they were training. They made them think that they had just begun; they admitted that it was a little late. "It's too late now, you won't get anything," the villagers would say. But the two boys had already obtained Tuo'łbəx̂[3] as a protector, the spirit of wealth. They would now go openly to a spit or lagoon and test their power there. They found they could mesmerise any kind of fowl: ducks would drop dead and float ashore. The people would find the ducks, take them home and eat them. The two boys would also go into the wilderness and test their power on game animals. They would command a certain place to become filled with game of all kinds, such as deer and elk. Upon going to the spot, they would find the game there. Everything came easily to them, involving no labor. At last the two boys were satisfied that their power was all it should be. "Now we're through," they said to

---

[1] A trainer may be a relative, or, as in the case with certain bands, someone appointed by the head chief. It is the trainer's duty to see that a child trains properly. Before the child bathes, he must rub himself with yew wood or some smooth hard wood to make himself tough. If the trainer thinks he has not rubbed himself hard enough, he will turn him across his knee and spank him. If he likes, he may wake him up during the middle of the night and punish him again. This time, he lashes him a half-dozen times with a little bunch of switches tied together. This does not hurt very much. A child who wishes to obtain a spirit must be pure. He is forbidden to have any relations with women; he will taint himself if he does. He must excel in marksmanship, know how to handle hooks and spears for salmon, and play games well.

[2] After a child has shown himself capable in his preliminary training, he is sent out alone to the wilderness to fast — during which time he will obtain his spirit.

[3] The power which this spirit conveys is called ya'bədɨb and is "strictly for riches". It brings untold wealth without any effort on the part of the possessor. The term tuo'łbəx̣ is said to mean something great, wonderful, like the meeting of the sky and earth as far as the eye can see. When a youth is ready to go out by himself, his parents say to him, "Go out and look for ya'bədɨb. Don't accept any other. If another is offered to you, ignore it." It is obvious, however, from other powers the narrator mentioned, such as doctor's and warrior's power, that the youth does not always obtain this particular power.

one another. "We evidently have the spirit our parents told us to obtain. We have completed our training."

Some time later, the two young men began to sleep continuously. While the young men slept, their father and mother could hear something rumbling and singing. Tuo'łbəx̱ had given the young men certain songs to sing. They must eventually sing these songs to please him, otherwise he would get angry and make them ill. Their mother would hear constant rumbling and singing; it was coming from the young men's stomachs. Finally one of the young men became ill and his stomach began to swell up. They could hear a song coming from it; his spirit wanted to come out and sing. The young fellow was holding it back, and so it was making him ill. At last he said to his family, "I'm getting ill. Something must be done about it; invite all the tribes around the Sound to come.[1] I've got to practice and sing my songs. It is the only way I can recover."

The guests came and began to sing his song. As they sang, the swelling began to subside. They had a good time at night singing and pounding sticks against the roof in time to the songs. (The sticks are pounded straight up and down. When the meeting gets lively, the sticks will shake up and down on their own accord. They become alive but one must not let go of them.) Finally the young man said to his parents, "Get certain of the boys in the village and send them after game." There was nothing in the house to eat but, in keeping with custom, the young man's family had to feed the guests to please his spirit. The young man told the boys where to go to find the game. He sent two or three of them to one place, and several to another. "You'll find game there," he said, naming the places. The boys went out, taking their bows and arrows. At one place they found the ground literally covered with ducks. At the young man's command, the ducks had floated ashore dead. The boys took the ducks back to the house and the women boiled them for stew. (As regards tamanoas training, this legend is true. The events took place long before the flood, when Indians were almost animals, — before the Transformer came.) The young man was now improving rapidly. Whenever any meat was needed, he would send the boys out. They would go to the place he named and find whole herds of game animals. The animals were easy to kill and died quickly. By the time the feasting was ended, the young man was well. Thereafter his tamanoas only bothered him once or twice a year. It never bothered him afterward [to the same extent]. (As a rule, one's spirit comes to one and makes demands only in the winter time. It is my personal opinion that the spirit does this in order to bring the people together for a good time.)

---

[1] As a rule, the Puyallup, Skokomish and Upper Chehalis were invited.

STAR HUSBAND.[1]

Five very industrious sisters lived in a certain village. They always gathered the food for the family. One day they talked of gathering fern roots. They would have to go to a place where the roots were nice and fat. They would camp over night there.

When their day's work was done, they made camp and fixed their beds. They had no shelter, evidently. The night was bright and clear. Before long the stars began to appear, thick and brilliant. It was a pretty sight. The girls began to wonder about the stars. The youngest noticed a bright one and wished for it. "I wish that star could be my husband," she said. The second wished for the next brightest star, and so on, until the eldest wished for a dim one. At last they fell asleep. When they awoke the next morning, they found themselves in heaven, living with the stars. The youngest found herself living with a sore-eyed old man, for the bright stars are old people, — bright from sore eyes; the dim stars are young people. They resigned themselves to this ridiculous situation. The stars are people living above us.

They went out to work as usual. They began to dig for fern roots. "How in the world shall we ever get home? How shall we go about it?" they asked one another. They dug and dug, for the fattest roots ran far down. Suddenly, the eldest girl felt a whiff of fresh air. "Oh, my goodness," she exclaimed, "if we keep on digging deeper, we'll get there!" They got home late. They excused themselves to their husbands by saying that the digging was hard. They roasted the roots and gave them to their husbands to eat. The next day, they stayed out longer, making a rope of hazel brush. The fourth day, they were very late. They got very few roots as they had spent most of their time making the rope. They had to make some excuse to their husbands. "The digging was very hard today," they said. "We'll surely reach the earth tomorrow. We'll go and never return," they said to one another. The afternoon of the fifth day, the rope reached the earth. They slid down on it and found their way home. As soon as they got there, they began to tell this story, how they had found themselves in the star-world after wishing the night before to become the wives of the stars. "There are people living up there; we are not alone down here on earth," they explained. From that time on, the people knew that the stars were people like themselves in another world.

MOON AND SUN.[2]

Five sisters and their blind old grandmother, Toad, lived in a certain village.[3] The third sister bore a child whom they called Moon.

[1] Told by Jerry Meeker, 1926; see p. 418.
[2] Told by Jerry Meeker, 1926; see p. 379.
[3] The Puget Sound peoples lived in villages along the shore.

When the child was born, the people invited everyone to a great gathering. A feast was given and all kinds of games were played. The most popular feature in the way of entertainment was a swing: all the young athletes were trying to find out which one of them could swing the highest. A swimming contest, a foot-race, the spear game and the bow and arrow game also furnished entertainment.

The five sisters left the baby with their grandmother and went to attend the games. Whenever the baby ceased to cry, the old lady would feel carefully to see if he were still there. She felt uneasy when he did not cry, for something might be amiss. The baby was in a cradle that was suspended from a sharp-pointed hazelwood stick.[1] His bedding, skirts and napkins were made of nice soft shredded cedar-bark. His mother and her sisters returned every evening about sunset from the games.

The fourth or fifth day all the well trained athletes were invited to try the swing. Tiger, Panther, Mink, Weasel, Beaver, and Otter were considered the swiftest and most courageous of all the athletes. Now Shitepoke, who was something of a clown, was considered untruthful and any story he had to tell was disregarded. During the gathering, he had told many funny but untrue things and had made interferences in the games. The others had merely made fun of him. This particular day, the old lady sang the lullaby she always used to put the baby to sleep,

> Rər, rər, rər;
> Rock-a-bye baby.

Then suddenly she began to sing,

> My grandchild has turned into punk wood.

Almost simultaneously, Shitepoke shouted, "Hawk, Hawk, listen!" No one paid any attention to him. Everyone was shouting and yelling in his enthusiasm over the best athletes. Shitepoke cried again, "Hawk, Hawk, listen! I hear something!" After a while, someone said, "Do you hear? Shitepoke is shouting over there. He says, 'I hear grandmother singing that her baby's face has turned into punk wood.'" The old lady had felt the baby's face and found it dry, not moist. They ran to the place where Toad was; the sisters and their grandmother lived some distance away from the other villagers. The oldest sister got there first. Sure enough, the baby was gone. She shouted and the entire gathering came. They began to discuss the matter and finally came to the conclusion that the child had been kidnapped. They had learned that five sisters who lived in the underworld — a world beneath us and difficult to reach — had taken him to their home. They began immediately to choose those who should follow in pursuit. In the meantime, the oldest sister said, "Where are the baby's napkins? We must wring

[1] This kind of cradle was swung with the toe.

them while they're wet, before they get too dry." They took the bedding, which was still damp, and wrung the urine out. From this, another child, Sun, was formed, but one eye was very badly crossed from the wringing. Finally Tiger, Beaver, Otter, Lion, Mink, Weasel, Eagle and all the strong birds were chosen to follow the kidnappers. Bluejay was there: "I'm going too!" he volunteered. They set out.

It took three or four days to reach their destination. (The women had heard of the baby's fame and had decided to steal him.)[1] When they got to their destination, they found a door, made lengthwise, that automatically opened and closed every few seconds. They chose the swiftest man to go through. Everyone tried, but the door closed too fast. Even Eagle, who was very swift, could not do it. Finally, they came to Bluejay. He braced himself and flew in front of the door. He followed it back and forth two or three times. "Kɛ'tcəkɛtc," he said, and on the fourth time, went right through. But the door clipped him on the head and knocked his tassel down. Instead of standing straight up like Quail's, Bluejay's tassel flops right down.

Bluejay had been instructed what to do on his journey. He came to the first house. There was a woman there and he questioned her about the child. "They took him on ahead," she said. He came to a second house and made inquiries there. (Several years must have passed already.) He came to a third and was told that they had taken the child on ahead. He came to a fourth. "Go on farther," he was told. Finally, he came to a fifth, where the child had been taken. A young man was sitting in the house making hard baskets with an awl. Bluejay went in. He flew around three times, and said, "Kɛ'tcəkɛtcə," each time he passed the door. The young man picked up the basket in which he had been soaking his roots, and threw the water right at Bluejay. The water struck him in the eyes and blinded him. Bluejay then said, "Your uncles and aunts sent me over here to find you." The young man took pity on Bluejay and washed his face and eyes. Bluejay noticed that the young man had his hair tied higher than was customary.[2] "Your mother, uncles and aunts are waiting for you. They sent me to take you home," he said. Moon removed as much of the water as he could from Bluejay's eyes, but even after Bluejay was able to see again, a whitish film, like a cataract, covered his pupils. This whitish film still remains under his lids. Moon said, "I don't think it would be wise for us to return together, for the people with whom I am associated have witchcraft."[3] "Remember the houses you passed on the way?" he asked. "Yes," Bluejay said. "Well, they'll give the alarm, so you go back alone and tell my family I'll try to find some way to get back. When you reach the automatic door, turn to the left; it opens slowly there. There's a secret passage-way."

---

[1] The narrator remarked that the child must have been like Christ.
[2] A sign of maturity?
[3] The narrator's term.

It was not until he had got out of the underworld, that Bluejay remembered he was to tell the young man of all the dangers he would encounter on the way back. "Well, I saw him," he reported to the people as soon as he reached the other side. "I gave him your message. It did not seem wise for him to come with me, so it was agreed that he should come later." "Did you tell him of all the dangers he would find on the way back to our country?" they asked. "No, I forgot all about it," he confessed. There was witchcraft, torments of various kinds, — things on the trail like the "Sʊt-sʊt" chorus of Fire, all of which he had forgotten to mention. The entire gathering went back to the young man's home to await his coming. They played the same games and celebrated as on the occasion of his birth. Everyone was happy. Little Sun was growing fast, but was still cross-eyed.

Finally, the young man started back from the underworld, following the route over which he had been taken. He still remembered it, although he had been a mere baby at the time. He did many good things as he travelled, and passed through some dangerous places. He heard a man singing, "Oh, the side of my head!" The man was in agony. He was striking his head against a glut-wedge. He walked up to the man and found him using his head as a maul to split a cedar. He said, "Man, what a terrible thing! I'll show you how to make a stone maul. Here, use this as a maul. Hereafter, always use this instead of your head." The man was very pleased. How nice it was! As soon as he had finished, he went on. Finally he came to a river that he had to cross. There he found a number of derricks stretched across the river, parts of a fish-trap. Each derrick was formed by three men who clutched one another by the hair. There were four derricks like this, supporting a timber platform. The men had to stand there in the cold water. "This is wrong," he said. "You should make your trap of timber. Get some alder wood and I'll show you how." He crossed the timber stakes at the top and tied them together with rope made from twisted hazel brush. As soon as they saw the first derrick, the men said, "That's fine, that's reasonable." Altogether they made four derricks. Then he showed them how to build the platform on which to walk. The people were very happy that so much good had been done. He came to another river. There was no one living there except an old fellow on the opposite side. He shouted and the old man came out. "I want to go across," he said. The old fellow merely repeated what he had said. He tried in every way to make some approach, but still the old man merely repeated his words. Finally, Shitepoke heard him. "I haven't any canoe," he said, "but I can stretch my legs across for a foot log." When Moon was half-way across, having just reached Shitepoke's joints, the latter exclaimed, "Oh, my! You'll break my legs!" But he braced himself and Moon reached the other side safely. Moon thanked Shitepoke and went on. He heard a beautiful, mellow song. It was sweet to the ears. When he got nearer, he discovered that it sounded like young people singing, some girls perhaps. It was a very beautiful song. Suddenly, it stopped. He turned around to catch the echo. Then he saw five little children, all very small but with enormous stomachs. He went up to them. "Weren't you children singing?" he asked. "Yes, we were singing a while ago," they answered. "Won't you please sing again? It was such a beautiful song." "No, sir, we cannot sing it. It would not be right for us to sing it." Then he questioned the little boys, as a stranger would naturally do when he comes to a new place. "We don't want to kill you," they insisted. "But I want to hear your song." "No, we might kill you." He begged them to sing. At last they consented. "It will not be our fault if you are killed," they said. They sang,

sən sa'de, sən sa',
sən sa'de, sən sa',
sʊt sa'de, sʊt sa'.

They had no sooner finished, than the whole place caught fire. Moon was forced to save himself. He ran to a fir tree. "Do you burn?" he asked. "Yes," the fir answered. He ran to some rocks. "Do you burn?" "Yes." He asked everything he could possibly think of and got the same answer. Then he asked a little trail. "Sometimes the fire passes over me," the trail answered. He lay down flat on the trail. After this, he had no more trouble. He had passed all the dangers.

By this time, the people were quiet, awaiting his return. Little Sun was already a big fellow. The news was sent far and wide, "Moon has returned." All the people were invited to attend a large gathering. They were to hold a council to talk matters over, to make plans for the future. After the appointed time everyone gathered at the water front. They began to make their plans. Naturally, they were delighted to have Moon back. "We must have someone to rule the earth by night and by day," they said. They broached their plans to Moon. "Now, you, Moon, must rule the day," they said. "Very well, I'll try it," Moon said. He arose about seven in the morning. By noon, the people were suffocating. They could no longer bear to remain in the open, they had to take dips in the bay for relief. By the middle of the afternoon, even the water was hot. Moon came back. "How was it?" he asked. "It was entirely too hot; we were nearly suffocated. Your young brother had better try instead," they said. Moon's eyes were too sharp, but "Cross-eyes" could look every way at once, especially when he became angry. Sun now rules the earth by day, Moon by night. Moon took his grandmother with him, where she still remains.

WHITE RIVER TALES.

MINK KILLS A CHIEF'S SON.[1]

The people were living in a certain village. The chief's son was found murdered but nobody knew who did it. They did not know whether he had been killed by someone from his own tribe or from another tribe. He had been found dead, that was all they knew. The chief sent several of his people everywhere to find out who killed him.

Finally Mink (ts'mα'lqen) said, "I had better confess and give a song. I'll gather the Frogs and any animals that say, 'Wa'ä' wa'ä''." Crane always said, "Wä' wä' wä'." He got together all those who sang like that. When he had them all together, he said to them, "I am going to sing now." He sang,

otso'təb		ota'tcalale''i	
They	say	by someone different[2] (was killed)	
kwe	bə'da'	as	x̣wex̣weya'le[3]
The	son	of	,,
gwa'	ota'tc'	α'ts'a	
It	was	I	(who killed)
kwe	bə'da'	as	x̣wex̣weya'le
The	son	of	,,
awax̣i'x̣i		wax̣i'x̣i[4]	
wax̣i'x̣i		wax̣i'x̣i	

"Wä''ä'," chorused the others. They sang the song five times. "Oh, was it he who killed my son?" the chief said to his people as they listened to Mink's song. Then they caught Mink and butchered him up. They took his limbs and shot them off with a bow and arrow. They shot his foot in one direction; his leg, in another direction; his hip, another; his backbone, another; his neck and hand, another; his fore-arm, another. Each time they shot off a limb, it went off on fire, like fire-works. His elbow, his leg, his foot, his hip — all went off like fire-works.

CROW DOCTORS HER DAUGHTER.[5]

Crow had one son, Ts'i'tsix̣wʊn, and a daughter.[6] They lived in a village close to the bay. One morning Crow said to her son, "I'll have to go to the bay and try to get some more clams." She had a few small clams in the house. "If your little sister wakes up and

[1] Told by Marion Davis, 1927; see p. 406. Song, Appendix, p. 426.
[2] Meaning foreigner, evidently.
[3] The chief's name.
[4] No meaning; said to be words of joy.
[5] Told by Marion Davis, 1927; see p. 400. Song, Appendix, p. 427.
[6] The girl has no name.

cries, get some of the clams and cook them. You must roast them and give them to her." "All right, I'll do it," Ts'i'tsix̣wʋn said.

His mother went to the bay to dig clams. When she got to the house, both her little daughter and Ts'i'tsix̣wʋn were gone. In a short while the boy returned. "Where's your sister?" she asked. "She's outside," Ts'i'tsix̣wʋn answered. "Go get her," she said. The boy went out. "She's not there," he said. "Well, where is she?" she asked. "Perhaps she's over there where the children are playing doll," he said. The girl was not there, for Ts'i'tsix̣wʋn had roasted her. His mother had said to him, "t'et'sa'pcɪd tcax̂u ts'a'a tsu'-tsuq'wa aq'sa'x̂o' (Roast some clams for your little sister)." He had understood her to say, "t'ɪt sa'pʋd tcax̂u tsaat tsu'tsuq'wa (Roast your little sister's backside)." And so when his little sister had awakened, he had roasted her before the fire until she died. He had lied to his mother about his sister, he was afraid to tell her the truth. He had thrown her in the gooseberry bushes, where Crow could not find her. When Ts'i'tsix̣wʋn came back for the second time, he said, "She isn't there, I can't find her." "Well, where is she then? You should know where she is!" his mother said. "Maybe she's over there where the children are swinging," he said. "Well then, go after her and bring her home," Crow said. In a little while he came back and said, "No, she's not there. Maybe she's over there where the children are playing the laughing game." "Well, go get her," she said. He ran to the place, he was afraid to tell his mother the truth. The fifth time, he told her what he had done: "Why, mother," he said, "you said, 't'ɪt sa'pʋd tca'x̂u tsu'tsuq'wa.'" "No I didn't," Crow cried, "I said, 't'et'sa'pcʋd tcax̂u ts'a'a tsu'tsuq'wa.'" "What did you do with her?" she demanded. "Well, when she woke up I roasted her before the fire and she died," he explained, "then I threw her in the gooseberry bushes." "Well, go get her," she said.

The boy brought his little dead sister home. Crow tied her pack-strap around her middle, wrapped her hair around her head and tied it on her forehead, preparatory to doctoring. Then she began to sing, holding her right forearm against her forehead,

łała'ᵃ babα'lx̂weis[1]
łała'ᵃ babα'lx̂weis.

She sang the song over and over until the little girl came to life.

Crow went to the bay five times to dig clams. The fifth time, while digging, she noticed that the tide was coming in. There was a seal in the water right in front of her. "Oh, what can I do to catch him? I wish he would come close, then I could club him." She wished and wished that he would come ashore. Finally, she began to sing,

tc'e'tc'i ta'sx̂u de'di sx̂wa'datcʻ
Come near, seal, go down, bay.

[1] The narrator did not know the meaning of the song.

The seal came nearer. The water began to withdraw and left the seal marooned in the sand. Crow got a club and ran after him. She struck him with the club and killed him. Then she carried the body back from the shore and resumed her clam-digging. When she had finished, she packed the seal home. First she rolled it in the fire to singe the hair off. Then she rolled it out and scraped the burnt hairs off. Then she butchered it and roasted the meat in a pit over hot rocks. When the meat was done, she invited all the people to come to her house and eat it. Everyone came and had a good time eating seal fat. Raven (qwa'q^u^) heard that his sister had invited everyone to her house to feast except himself and this made him angry. But she had not forgotten him; right away she had sent Ts'i'tsix̣wʊn with a large piece of fat for his uncle. But the boy had turned off the trail and eaten the fat himself.

Raven went to see Crow. She saw by his eyes that he was angry and asked if he got the piece of fat she sent. "No!" he said. Ts'i'tsix̣wʊn's stomach looked rather distended. "You've got it all in your stomach!" Raven said to himself. "I'll call him to look for my louse," he thought. They say that Raven's knife was pretty sharp. "Come here, my nephew, and look for my louse," he called, "it's right in the front of my head." Crow did not see what was going on. Ts'i'tsix̣wʊn went close and Raven pointed his knife at the boy's stomach where it was bulging out. Then he ripped his stomach open and the piece of fat came out. Ts'i'tsix̣wʊn died right there. Raven ate the piece of fat that had been in the boy's stomach. Then he thought, "What shall I do with him? I guess I'll throw him in the river and let him float down."

So he took hold of Ts'i'tsix̣wʊn and threw him in the river. The boy floated down. (I think it was still the fall of the year, for the leaves that were falling from the trees overhanging the river were floating down.) Ts'i'tsix̣wʊn was still alive in his heart. "Oh," he thought, "I wish the leaves would come right into my stomach and heal me." He floated down and down, thinking this all the while. Finally a leaf fell right into his wound and suddenly it knit together. He swam out to the river bank and stayed there quite a while. "Perhaps I can walk now," he thought. No, he could not do it. He tried five times; then he stood up and walked. Then he thought, "Oh, how shall I get even with that fellow who killed me? I'll surely get even some way." And so he turned toward home.

He walked a long way and finally came to a lake. "Perhaps there is a fish here," he thought. No, there was no fish, so he kept on going toward home. He came to another lake. "Perhaps there is a fish here." No, there was no fish there, so he went on. He came to another lake, the third one. "Perhaps there is a fish here." No, there was no fish, so he kept on going. He came to another. "Perhaps there is a fish here." Yes, there was a little fish in the lake. He went on. When he got nearer home, he found a larger lake. There was a big fish there. "Oh, what could I use for a hook to catch it with?" he thought. He went to a gooseberry bush and pulled out a sharp thorn. Then he got something to use for a string and tied it to the thorn. He caught one fish but threw it back in again. Then he caught a second fish and threw it back in also. The third time, a whole school of fish came. He soon had a large pile. He broke off a forked stick and slipped the fish on by their heads until both prongs of the stick were full. The stick was so weighted down with fish he could hardly carry it. He kept on going toward home and finally arrived in front of the house, where Crow saw him. They now had a lot of fish and started to roast them. While the fish were roasting, Raven came along. He noticed the fish and became very happy. "That's the kind of boy I wanted you to be! That's why I killed you," he said to Ts'i'tsix̣wʋn. "I sent you floating down the river so that you would get such a tamanoas."[1] Raven was happy because he thought he would have some fish to eat before long. When the fish were done, they put almost all of them on a mat and gave them to Raven. He ate and ate and ate. When the fish were about gone, he began to say, "Ä'ʿ, ä'ʿ, ä'ʿ, ä'ʿ." The bones were sticking in his throat. He kept on gagging and finally died right there. Ts'i'tsix̣wʋn got even with Raven. (Ts'i'tsix̣wʋn was a great eater like his uncle Raven.)

SKOKOMISH TALES.

MINK.[2]

A chief had a daughter. Many men wished to marry her, but both she and her parents always refused them; her parents did not wish her to marry. Mink was a funny fellow, always in mischief. At night, when everyone was asleep, the girl had a visitor. During the day, she did not see him. Mink was always loitering around the chief's house. Night came and again the girl had a visitor. He slept with her. She had no idea who he was. "That fellow must be her lover," Mink said, for in some way he had discovered the nightly visits. "I'll fix him," he said, "I'll make a trap to catch him!" He did not reveal his secret to anyone. He watched. The visitor came. While he was with the girl, Mink set his trap. The girl's lover was Whale, who had come ashore from the bay. "When he goes home, I'll catch him!" Mink said. Next morning Mink went out. How pleased he was! There was Whale in the trap. "Folks," he called, "sharpen your knives! Here's a dead whale. We'll have a big feast." They butchered the whale. All got their share. The women got some and cooked it. The girl still did not know who her lover was. She ate some of the meat. Mink sat grinning while she ate her lover's flesh.

[1] That is, one that will enable the boy to get a lot of food.

[2] Told by Mary Adams, 1926; see p. 405.

He kept walking in and out. At last he said, "It's very strange that you should eat your lover." The girl did not hear him. He said it again. Then she heard him more distinctly. She felt ashamed and let the meat drop. She lay down in bed, wrapped herself up, even her head. They say she had a fine pin of deerbone in her blanket. When she lay down, she had driven it into her heart. She had committed suicide in her sorrow and shame. She failed to get up next morning at breakfast time. They called her several times but she did not stir. Her mother said, "What is the matter with my daughter?" She pulled the covers from the girl's face. Still she did not move. It was entirely Mink's fault. Her wealthy father gave her an enormous funeral. No one mourned more deeply than Mink. He mourned for his "niece". They buried her in a Chinook canoe. They merely pulled the canoe ashore and left it there. They say that Mink wept and wailed. "I'm going to stay with my niece, I am going to stand guard over her body; Crow may come and dirty on her," he shouted. He continued to weep and shout in the same vein. Everyone went home but him. He remained there at her burial-place. As soon as everyone had gone, he tried to push the canoe into the water. He had relations with the dead girl and made her pregnant. He paddled off with her in the canoe. "I have five brothers, all doctors. They will cure her, they will bring her back to life," he said. Each of the five doctors whom Mink had spoken of lived on a different point along the river. He went to his eldest brother who lived on the first point. He shouted, "Oh, dear brother, my wife was ill. She died just as we came around the point." His brother came out. They carried her out of the canoe. Then his brother began to doctor. He doctored her for a long time. "No, I can't revive her," he announced finally. They put her back into the canoe. Mink went to his next brother. "Oh, brother," he cried, "your sister-in-law died just before we rounded the point." His brother doctored her a long time. Before he started he said, "I doubt if I can revive her." The woman was becoming larger with child all the time. Mink went to the third doctor. "Oh, brother," he cried, "your sister-in-law died just before we rounded the point." They took her out of the canoe. The doctor began to work on her. Before long her body began to get warm. "Take her to the next doctor; he may be able to help her," the doctor said. When Mink came to the next point, he cried, "Oh, brother, your sister-in-law was sick. She just died." The fourth doctor worked on her. When he had finished, she could raise her head, but could not stand up. "Take her to our youngest brother," he advised. When he came to the next point, Mink cried, "Oh, brother, your sister-in-law died just as we came round the point." They took her out of the canoe. Then the youngest doctor began to work on her. Before long she stood up, well.

The woman gave birth to a daughter. Then they left. A little later, she gave birth to a son. She was Mink's wife now. Mink had married his "niece". After their children were born, Mink started home with his wife to visit her family. How important he felt! When they got to the place, they directed some children to the chief's house. "Tell them to clean the house; the one who was dead has returned," they said to them. "Did they believe you?" they asked the children when they returned. "They began to weep," the children said. "Why should they weep!" Mink said. At last the girl's family sent someone over to find out if the report was true. "It is indeed your daughter," the person reported. "She is married and has children." Then they had a big time. Mink came with a canoe load of food. His father-in-law had slaves. He gave some to his daughter. Mink and his family started home. He no longer had to paddle his own canoe. They were travelling near shore. It was a nice calm day. They could see clear to the bottom of the water. Then the slaves noticed some sea-eggs and called their master's attention to them. The slaves dived for the eggs. "Would you like to eat some?" they asked their mistress. "Yes," she said. "Oh, my children's-mother, don't eat that stuff!" Mink said. "But wouldn't you like to try some?" his wife asked. Mink spit and spit to show his disgust. He would not eat them; he wanted his wife to think he was a high-class person. He tried to persuade her not to eat them. Finally, he consented to try a taste himself. "Oh, my children's-mother, how good they taste!" he cried. "I'll dive for a few myself!" "No," his wife answered, "we have our slaves for that." But Mink stripped off and dived in. He stayed down a long time. He was eating down there. He ate so much that his hind parts stuck out of the water. At last the woman realized who her husband was. She told her slaves to paddle away. The slaves left him behind. She knew now that she had married Mink! "Oh, my children's-mother," Mink cried, "here I am!" The woman paid no attention, only directed her slaves to keep on paddling. She threw her son overboard. As the boy floundered about, Mink cried, "Try to reach those snags! Try to swim ashore to your grandfather's root!"

The woman's slaves paddled her homeward. In the meantime, Mink and his son had reached shore. While they were on the beach, Mink found a dead salmon. He built a fire and cooked it. Then he grew sleepy. The entire fish, including the head, was done now. "Watch the salmon while I take a nap," he said to his son. But before long the boy, too, fell asleep. A man came along and ate the fish. When Mink woke up, he found the fire out and the salmon gone. "Why did you eat it all? Why didn't you leave some for me?" he asked his son. "But I didn't eat it!" the boy said. "Oh yes you did; your teeth are full of salmon." "But so are yours!" the boy said. Mink wanted to put the blame on his son although he knew who had done it. The person he had in mind had filled their teeth with salmon. Mink was sure of this. "After a man has eaten salmon, he gets thirsty," Mink thought. He went off and made some spring water from his urine. The spring was bubbly and lovely. The man drank. Then he drank from a creek. He drank from a lake; it was nice and sparkly. "This is a good lake," he thought. He drank at every place he came to. Then he drank so much he began to swell up. This man was Dukwe'bał, the Creator. He found himself pregnant. When the time came for his delivery, he was very much disturbed, for he was a real man and different from a woman. He worried and worried. Then he ran to all the trees and asked them if they had anything that would enable him to make himself like a woman. At last he came to a wild-cherry tree. He took some of the bark, stretched it and made some female parts; wild-cherry bark stretches readily. This man gave birth to a child, the price he had to pay for his sin. The child was a boy. As soon as it was delivered, he threw it away. But whenever he travelled, the child would follow after him. "Ma ma, ma ma," it would cry. He threw the child down and killed it. "Don't call me 'ma ma'," he said. Still, he could not get rid of his child. It followed him everywhere. "Call me 'pa pa'!" he would say in disgust. Finally, he made a lake, a river and some thick high mountains, so that the boy could not reach him. It was the Creator who had this sin.

Mink was in everything!

CROW DOCTORS RAVEN.[1]

Raven had a sister, Crow. Crow had a little daughter. Whenever the tide went out, Crow would go down to the beach to dig clams. One day she noticed a little seal bobbing up and diving back in. She sang,

> If I were a baby seal,
> Every time I came up
> I would go close to shore.

When the baby seal came close, she killed him. Then she heated some rocks to steam him. While she was busy doing this, her brother took sick. They sent for her for she was a doctor. Raven was in very great pain; he was so sick he was going to die. Crow doctored him. His shadow[2] was running around outside. Finally Raven said he had to go out to move his bowels. "No, we'll bring you a receptacle," they said. Then Crow changed her song,

> The sick man really isn't sick,
> His lower parts are all that bother him.

She knew that he only wanted to eat something. At last Raven insisted that he did not want to have his movement in the house. While he was gone, he was eating everything in his sister's house.

[1] Told by Mary Adams, 1926; see p. 400.
[2] His soul ?

It was just for this purpose that he had pretended he was sick. Crow's little daughter cried, "The sick man is eating!" "Shut up," Raven said, "or I'll burn your backside on the rocks!" He ate everything there was. Then he killed his niece and threw her behind the rocks. At last the little girl's mother came; she had refused to come when her daughter first called. She looked about for her little girl but could not find her. "Where's my daughter?" she asked Raven. "She's playing with the other children," he answered. She could not find her. She asked Raven again where she was. "There's a crowd of children swinging over there. She must be with them," he said. She could not find her there. She asked Raven again where she was. "She's in swimming," he said. Crow hunted for her there but could not find her. "Raven must have killed her!" she said. She found her daughter's dead body. She wept and wept. Raven had killed the girl while her mother was doctoring him.

RAVEN EATS HIS SISTER'S BERRIES.[1]

Some women went out in a canoe to pick berries. They took Raven along. He stayed in the canoe while they picked. They brought some berries to the canoe and went back again. Raven ate all the berries. Then he poured the juice all over himself to make them think he was bleeding. When his sister came he began to groan and groan. "I'm dying," he said, "some people came and beat me and stabbed me." Crow began to weep,

A big crowd has tried to kill my big brother,
A big crowd has tried to kill my big brother.

She did not miss the berries until later. Then she discovered that Raven had eaten all of them and poured the juice over himself.

BUNGLING HOST.[2]

Bluejay was talking to an old fellow in a crowd. The old fellow was Bear. He invited Bluejay to visit him. "I'll give you a good meal," he said. "All right, I'll come," Bluejay said.

Bear cooked some fish and got a clam shell to hold the grease. Then he held his hands over the fire; the fat ran into the dish. When the fish were done, he dipped them in the grease. "This is fine food," Bluejay said. He ate and ate and ate. When he was leaving, he invited Bear to visit him. "All right, I'll come," Bear said. "Come early in the morning," Bluejay added. "All right, I'll be there," Bear said.

Bear went to Bluejay's house. Bluejay began to cook, thinking he would do the same as Bear. He held his hands over the fire but they cracked open. Today one can still see where Bluejay's hands are cracked open.

[1] Told by Mary Adams, 1926; see p. 401.
[2] Told by Mary Adams, 1926; see p. 393.

ROBIN.[1]

Robin's wife was sick. She fainted. Robin called a doctor but she died. He wept and wept. "My dear wife, I'm going to call you every spring," he said. Every spring one can hear him saying,

> tsɩs· tsɩs tsɩtco'wac, my wife tco'wac
> My wife. —

CRANE AND HIS UNFAITHFUL WIFE.[2]

Crane is a great fellow to fish. His wife was little Helldiver. She was always sick and could not eat. She would wish for a little fish and would send Crane out to get one for her. Sawbill was in love with her. As soon as her husband would leave the house, she would comb her hair, paint her face and scent herself for her lover's visits. As soon as Crane appeared, she would rumple her hair and go back to bed. "Oh, I'm so sick, so sick," she would say. Then off Crane would go to get her a little fish. To this day, one can see the male sawbills, — white —, drifting down the river, in love with the helldivers. At last someone said to Crane, "What's the matter? Your wife is going around with Sawbill. Better watch her!" "All right, I'll watch her," Crane said. When his wife said to him again, "I'm so sick," he went out and hid. Before long he saw her coming out. Her hair was combed and face painted very nicely. Then Sawbill came ashore and met her. The two went into the house together.

Crane kept watching; he had no intentions of fishing. He had caught them indeed. He would not punish his wife's lover but he would punish her. He built a fire. Then he rubbed his wife's face in the hot ashes. She went blind; her face became cooked and red. She is still blind. They say that whenever she goes out at night she says, "Oh look at the light in the bay!" But it is only her eyes deceiving her; they have been red ever since her husband punished her.

Crane, when he had to fish so much for his wife, burned his legs black with pitch wood so that he could creep up on the fish without their seeing him.

THE HOOP.[3]

In early times the poor people had very few luxuries. They could not buy toys for their children as the rich could. The rich people owned a hoop to roll and often gathered together to play with it. Only the children of rich parents were invited to play with it. They would roll it downhill and it could be heard far off. Some poor children wished to own it but their parents could not afford it, so they were tempted to steal it.

---

[1] Told by Mary Adams, 1926; see p. 410.
[2] Told by Mary Adams, 1926; see p. 410.
[3] Told by Mary Adams, 1926; see p. 390.

There was one old man who had five sons and another old man who had one grandchild, a boy. The second old man's name was Stuhe′. He kept his grandson so dirty that the boy developed sores on his head. The first man would say to his sons, "Keep away from that boy." He sent his sons out every day to swim and fast, — to get tamanoas. "You must be prepared," he would say. The other old man would send his grandson out every night to swim. The boy would stay out the whole night. "You might get your power; then you could go with the other boys if they should go to get the hoop," he would say. He would smear his grandson with ashes and water to give the impression that the boy was too lazy to stir from the fireplace, and so consequently too dirty to obtain tamanoas. But all the while, he was sending him out secretly at night. Other children would have nothing to do with the boy. The first old man finally put his sons through a rigid examination to see if they had completed their training. "I guess you are all right," he said.

At last the hoop proved too great a temptation to the poor boys and they decided to steal it. The people would shriek with delight whenever they rolled it. The first man's five sons went to the place and sat down as if to watch the fun. The dirty boy went with them, although they had tried to keep him from going. "Keep him home, he's not fit to go along," they had said to his grandfather. The eldest boy grabbed the hoop and started to run with it. The people ran after him; they had recognized him right away — he was Fox's eldest son. The boy ran toward the beach. He became exhausted after a little while and threw the hoop to his second brother. When they were about to catch him, the second threw it to the third. When they were about to catch him, the third threw it to the fourth. One after another they caught and killed the three elder boys. They ran after the fourth but before they caught him, he threw the hoop to his youngest brother. They killed the fourth and then ran after the youngest. By this time, the dirty boy had just about caught up with the youngest. Just as they were about to catch him, the youngest threw the hoop to the dirty boy — the sixth. The dirty boy caught it and ran as fast as he could. He had some down feathers wrapped in a piece of woven cedar bark and let them loose. The feathers floated up and turned into fog. The people could not see beyond their noses and so could not catch him.

The five boys were dead; only the dirty boy was able to keep the hoop. He came to the cove opposite his home and shouted to his grandfather. The two old men were arguing about their boys. "You had no right to send your boy along with mine, to get in their way," the first said. After a while they heard someone calling. "Listen, old man, they're calling you. Your grandson was killed," the first said. "No," the second said, "it's the other way round. 'All your sons were killed.' It couldn't be my boy, for that's he calling." "Clean your ears well! They are calling, 'Your grandson was killed,'" the first answered. "No, that's my boy calling. He was saved, for he was prepared," the second said. "Well, if that is so, he was the cause of my boys' death," the first answered, "he was not fit to go with them." They heard someone calling again. "Come on," the first said, "let's settle it, let's have a urinating contest. If my boys were killed, my urine will reach only half-way across the bay. If yours was killed, your urine will reach only half-way across." The two old men urinated. Stuhe′ urinated first and his urine reached clear across. Then Fox urinated and his urine reached only half-way. Their urine is now the rainbow: one rainbow reaches clear across the bay, one reaches only half-way.

The boy reached home and told what had happened. He gave his grandfather the hoop. "You got the hoop because you were well prepared. I trained you in the right way," his grandfather said. Fox began to weep. "You were the cause of my boys' death," he said. The two old men began to argue again, this time about possession of the hoop. "My boys —," Fox would say. "No, my boy —," Stuhe′ would say. Old man Stuhe′ still has the hoop.

THE SHARPTAILED MAN.[1]

A young woman of high rank was having her first menses. She was told to swim night and morning but was forbidden to go to a certain lake. "It is bad," she was told. They would never tell her what was in the lake. "What's the matter with that lake?" she would ask. "You must obey," was the only answer she could get. At last she made up her mind to go there. "It's a nice lake for swimming and it has a nice beach," she thought to herself. She stripped off and waded out. She sat down in the water, her back to shore. After a while she thought, "I'll go ashore now and dress." A man was sitting on her clothes. Every word she thought, he repeated aloud after her, in a big bass voice.[2] "What shall I do?" she thought. "What shall I do?" he said. "How shall I get my clothes?" she thought. "How shall I get my clothes?" he said. "What shall I call him, 'uncle'?" she thought. "What shall I call him, 'uncle'?" he said. "What shall I call him, 'grandfather'?" she thought. "What shall I call him, 'grandfather'?" he said. "I don't know what to do! This is what I get for disobeying. Now I'm caught," she thought. Finally she thought, "Now I shall call him 'husband'." "Yes, my wife. You should have said that a long time ago," the man said. This was just what he had been waiting to hear. He was the Sharptailed-man. He took her home with him.

The young woman's disappearance was soon discovered. On the way, she had dropped bits of twisted cedar-bark on the ground and had also tied bits of it to the bushes to mark the trail. They hunted

---

[1] Told by Mary Adams, 1926; see p. 414.
[2] Illustrating.

and hunted for her. At last they discovered that she had been to the lake. "The dangerous man has taken her away," they said. The young woman had five brothers. The eldest found her; he followed her tracks. Her husband was not home at the time. He was a great hunter; their house was filled with hides of all kinds, — deer, elk. The woman had already given birth to a daughter. She gave her brother some meat to take home. He started back to give the news to his family. The woman did not know what kind of a person her husband was. When her father came home, the little girl said, "Uncle was here. Mother gave him some hides and meat to take home." "I think I'll run after him and give him some more," the man said to his wife. He had a song that he sang to weaken his brother-in-law. The young man soon found that he was unable to walk. "Wait a minute," the man said when he caught up with him, "I've got something for you." Then he stuck him with his tail and killed him. He took the heart out and threw the body into the brush. Then he swallowed the heart. "I couldn't find your brother," he said to his wife when he got home.

The eldest brother did not return. Next day, the second brother set out to find his sister. He discovered the signs that she had left along the trail and finally found her. "Where's your husband?" he asked. "Oh, he's always out hunting," she said. She gave him some meat and he started home. She now had a second child, a boy. "Don't tell your father what happened today," she said to her daughter, for she had learned that her eldest brother was missing. But as soon as their father appeared, the children said, "Uncle was here today. Mother gave him some meat to take home." "I'll run after him and give him some more," the man said to his wife. He sang his song to weaken his brother-in-law. The young man soon became so weak that he could not walk. "Oh, say, brother-in-law, wait! I have something for you to take home," the Sharptailed-man said when he caught up with him. "I'm unable to walk," the young man said. Then the Sharptailed-man stuck his tail into his heart and killed him. He threw the body into the brush and swallowed the heart.

Next day, the third brother went out. He found the signs that his sister had left on the trail and tracked her to her home. "Oh, brother," she cried, "go away! I have a bad husband. I think he has killed our brothers." "Don't tell your father what has happened," she said to the children. When her husband came home, he said, "Tʊm, tʊm." "Oh, father," the children said, "uncle was here today. Mother gave him some meat and hides to take home." "Perhaps he would like some more," the man said to his wife and set out after his brother-in-law. He had never once mentioned to her that he had killed her brothers.

Now the youngest brother[1] went out alone. He fasted and swam

[1] The narrator evidently forgot to tell about the fourth brother. From later events it is obvious that he met the same fate.

in order to obtain power that would enable him to overcome his sister's husband. He stayed out day and night, fasting. At last he was prepared. He had obtained his power according to the custom. Then he began to test his power. He talked to the trees, to see if he could make a man from wood, but was unsuccessful. Then he came to a pitchy stump. "Do you think you could move and turn like a man?" he asked the stump. "Yes. You can make a man from my pitch," the stump answered. "Then stay right here," he said. He dressed the pitchy stump like a man. "When I yell to you, turn around. A man will come here. You must do as he says," he explained. "I'll do it," the pitch-man agreed.

The young man set out to find his sister. He tracked her to her home. "Oh, brother," she cried, "go home!" "Yes, it is your husband who kills people," he said to her. "I ask the children not to tell but they always do," she said. "Well, I'll go home now," he said. "Don't tell your father what has happened," the woman said to her children. But they had no sooner heard their father's footsteps, than they began to tell. "Uncle was here today. Mother gave him some meat to take home," they said. "Did you give him some meat?" the man asked his wife. "Yes," she answered, "but don't run after him as you did the others!" She knew that her brothers were dead. Her husband set out after his brother-in-law. He began his song. At last he came to the pitch-man. His youngest brother-in-law was hiding. "Wait a minute, brother-in-law," he said to the pitch-man. The pitch-man turned around. "Oh, brother-in-law, I have something for you," the Sharptailed-man said. Then he turned around and stuck his tail into his supposed brother-in-law. His tail caught in the pitch. It stuck there and he could not pull it out. Then the youngest of the five brothers appeared. He had been able to fashion the pitch-man by means of his power. He went up to his sister's husband and killed him. Then he opened him and found four hearts. He took them out and laid them down. Then he searched for his brothers' bodies. He arranged them nicely. The heart that had been consumed first belonged to his eldest brother. He set to work to revive his brothers. He stepped over them repeatedly and used his power. The youngest of the four came to life first. It took considerably more power to revive the eldest. As soon as his brothers came to life, he went back to his sister's house. "Your husband is dead and our brothers are safe. Get ready to return with us," he said. "We'll leave the boy here and burn the house. I'll take the girl with me," the woman said.

As soon as they got home, the men said to their father, "You must invite the people to see your daughter." They called the people and everyone had a good time, as those of high rank always do.

The little girl's nails were so sharp that she scratched other people's eyes right out. They could not stop her. They determined to get rid of her in some way. There was a rich man; the Crows were his slaves. They hired the Crows to take the girl out in their canoe and leave her somewhere. They put her into the canoe. The Crows began to paddle. They could not get started right off; one had her paddle turned the wrong way and the others were holding theirs the same way. They sang,

Become foggy,
We're going out to dig buttercup roots.

They mentioned the roots to mislead the girl. When they got into the fog, close to the shore, the Crows rose up and flew away, leaving the girl all alone in the canoe. Since she was of a chief's family, she did not know how to paddle. She did not know what to do; she was alone in a strange place. There was a woman on shore digging buttercup roots. It was Coon, the slave of the man who lived at that place. She came there every day to dig roots. The girl noticed her. The two became friends. The girl helped Coon dig. Then Coon invited her home; she was lucky that day for the two of them together had dug many roots. She kept the girl hidden. The next day she went out again to dig and took the girl with her. She came back with better roots than she had ever got before; they were very large ones. Then they began to question her about them. That evening they heard Coon-language. Her master said. "Oh, you're laughing with someone." "It is only my niece," Coon answered. He could hear them laughing and whispering. Coon did not want to tell him about the girl. At last he thought, "I'll have to watch and see what is going on." He saw the girl with Coon. They say she was a nice-looking girl. He fell in love with her and made her his wife.

MOON AND SUN.[1]

There were two sisters. One of them had a child. They were busy all the time gathering wood or digging roots. They always left the baby with their blind old grandmother. The baby was kept on a cradle-board which was so fashioned that it worked up and down like a spring-board. "Never refer to the baby as a boy," the young women had warned their grandmother. Whenever the old lady sang to the child, she spoke of it as a girl. When the young women came home in the evening, they always found the baby there. The next day they would go out again to dig roots. One day the old lady made a mistake and referred to the child as her grandson, but quickly corrected herself. Another day she said, "Oh, my grandson, — I mean my grandchild." Two women were watching her secretly. One day she said, "My granddaughter smells like rotten wood." The two

[1] Told by Mary Adams, 1926; see p. 379.

women had stolen the child. They had dressed a piece of rotten wood like a baby and had left it on the cradle-board.

The two young women returned in the evening expecting to find the child there as usual. They were very upset when they found him gone. The women who had gone off with him had fixed many dangerous things on their trail so that no one could follow them. The child's mother hired people from all the different nations, all the birds that could fly, (they were human beings at this time), to search for him. All the different peoples gathered at a place on the trail where the women had left an obstruction. It was something like a cedar-stump and opened and closed so quickly that it would crush anyone trying to go through. Everyone was puzzled by it. They asked all the different birds if they could go through. "No, I can't do it," each would say. Then someone said, "I can do it; only I can do it." It was Bluejay. He was confident he could do it, he was so quick and lively. He started to jump through. His head was caught and flattened but he was soon on the other side. He was the only person who could go through.

As soon as he was on the other side, he inquired for the lost boy. He kept on going although some of the places along the way were dangerous. At last he heard something making a noise. "What is that?" he asked. "Someone is pounding," he was told. He heard a man singing. The man was peeling bark from a tree, using the side of his face for a wedge. It seemed a strange thing to do Bluejay thought but did not tarry. He came to some crooked trees. They looked strange. "What's going on here? I'm anxious to find out," he said. The trees began to unwind themselves. He was frightened to death. Then a man did something or other and he heard a loud "s· · · · ." The trees were alive with snakes. He went on, making inquiries about the baby as he went. He came to another dangerous place. There was a noise throughout the whole place. "What is it?" he asked. "We're just playing," he was told. "I want to see what you do; it must be something strange," he said. "You'd be frightened," he was told. Then a fire broke out and burnt everything within reach. They say that Bluejay ran and ran. He ran to a tree. "Are you going to burn?" he asked. "Yes, I'm going to burn," the tree answered. "Are you going to burn?" he asked a rock. "Yes, I'm going to split," the rock said. "Are you going to burn?" he asked the water. "Yes, I'm going to boil," the water said. "Are you going to burn?" he asked a trail. "Yes, I'll burn but I'll be cut into furrows in which you can crawl for safety," the trail said. Then Bluejay lay down on a little spot on the trail. As soon as the danger was over, he said, "That's bad." "We told you it was dangerous," he was reminded. He was getting close to the place where he thought the boy was. He had been many years on the way. He came to a place where some people were living. "We think we know whom you are looking for," they said. He kept on going. He came to another place and made inquiries. "It won't be long, now," they said and described the house in question. When he got there, he hopped around, looking about. The place was very quiet. He went up to a house. A man was at work there, chipping bullets. The two women who had stolen him were always away working, like his mother and aunt. Bluejay hopped in and out, in and out, chattering all the while. The young man grew tired of him and threw some of the chippings at him. "Kɛ'tcəkɛ'tcə," Bluejay said, for he was angry. He tried to explain why he was there. "— — — — living with other women —, kɛ'tcə — — —, that's why I'm here," he said. "What are you talking about, Bluejay?" the young man asked. "— — no one could pass by except me," Bluejay kept saying. "Come, I'll doctor your eyes," the young man said. He picked the chips out and Bluejay could see again. This young man was the one who had been stolen. Bluejay explained everything to him. "Well, come to think of it, these two women do act strange. They seem jealous of one another; first one claims me and then the other. I've often wondered about it," the young man admitted. "Go back and tell my mother that you have found me."

The young man packed up his things for his trip home. He went back the way that Bluejay had come. He also found the dangerous places that the two women had made. When he came to the place that made the noise, like Bluejay, he was anxious to find out what it was all about. He asked to see what it was. "No, you'd be frightened," he was told. He insisted. They started the fire. He did just as Bluejay had done: he finally lay down on the trail. When the danger was over, he said to the man there, "This will never happen again. It is too dangerous." When he had finished with that, he went on. He came to the place where Bluejay had passed the snakes. He found the same enormous man who owned the snakes. The man burst and the snakes crawled all over the young man.[1] He was as frightened as Bluejay had been. The man was a dangerous being. After a while the snakes crawled back into the dangerous being's stomach. If this happening had not taken place, there would be no snakes today. The young man said, "This will never happen again." He came to the place where the man was getting wood, pounding with his head. He made some tools and showed the man how to use them to get wood. "Hereafter tools will always be used for this purpose," he said. He kept going, doing away with dangerous things as he travelled. He heard someone yelling. It was a woman. He went up to her. "What did you say?" he asked. "Nothing," she answered, "I was just talking for fun." "Everyone likes to have a little pleasure," she added. She needed a man so badly, she was yelling. Whenever a man came, she would grab his organ and cut it off. The young man lay down on her. Just at the moment

---

[1] This incident seems to vary a little when retold.

when he was ready to have relations with her, she opened her eyes and asked, "What's that noise?" She was frightened. "It's just my testicles rattling," he said. As soon as she had closed her eyes, he cut her up. He was doing away with everything bad. He came to łała'baqˀeʊs. She had a basket on her back in which she was packing children. She was heating rocks to steam the children with. She had covered their eyes with pitch. "What are you doing?" he asked. "She is going to cook us and eat us," the children said. The woman was fixing her fire. "Watch her. When she comes in front of us, help me push her into the fire," he said. He and the big boys pushed her in. Then he greased the children's eyes. Their eyes came open. He had saved the children from death. As he walked along, they followed after him. All of them began to talk at once. Then he blew on them. They blew up into the trees, where they became little birds. He was now near home.

His mother, after he had been stolen, had taken what was left of his bedding and clothing and had washed and squeezed it. Then she had heard a cry; another son had come into existence from her child's clothing. She had no intentions of making another child, it had just happened. This boy was now a big fellow. His legs and body were twisted and his eyes crossed.

There was a spring near a hill not far from their house. The young man went there and stayed there. The cross-eyed boy came crawling along for some water. His mother always sent him to get the water. As he dipped down for some, he saw the reflection of a face in the well alongside his own. He looked up several times but could not see anyone. His elder brother hid each time. The boy went back. He told his mother he had seen something strange, the reflection of a man's face in the well. "It was just your imagination," she said. He was so frightened he had forgotten the water. He had to go back. He saw the man's face in the water again and looked around. A man stepped up and spoke to him. "Run home. Tell your mother that her lost son has returned," he said. The young man knew that the boy had come into existence from his clothing. The boy went home. His mother wept and whipped him. "How do you know that you have a brother who was stolen?" she asked. The boy went back to the well. He told the young man how his mother had whipped him and what she had said. The young man went up to him. He fixed his legs, his arms, his stomach, his eyes. "Now go back and tell mother that I'm here. Tell her to clean the house and invite the people," he said. The boy ran home. "Your son who was stolen told me to tell you to clean the house. Just look at me if you don't believe it," he said. The woman looked at her son. He was now nice-looking.

She invited everyone to her house. All the different peoples came. Before long the house was filled. They waited there for the lost youth to appear. The two brothers appeared dressed just alike; it was impossible to tell one from the other. They came into the house. All the unmarried young women were there. They were going to choose a wife for the young man. It would have been impossible to tell the two brothers apart, were it not for a satchel filled with property that the elder held. He had brought it back with him. When he came into the house he just set it down by the door. It was extremely heavy. "Any girl who can lift that satchel and pack it to me shall be my wife," he announced. The daughters of all the high-class people were there, dressed in their finery. Toad's little granddaughter was there also. The girl was an orphan. Toad had greased her with dogfish oil. "Get out of here. The chief will see you. You smell to high heaven!" someone said to the girl. "We have a right to see him as well as you high-class people," she answered. All the young women tried to lift the satchel. None of them could do it, it was so full of gold. The daughters of all the birds and animals tried. Then Toad's little limping granddaughter, Frog, tried. She lifted the satchel as if it were filled with nothing but paper. The young man knew all along that she would be the one to do it. She sat down by his side. Now she was his wife. All the daughters of the high-class people were so upset that they missed the door going out.

After that, the young man said to his brother, "I shall be the sun." But he gave so much heat it was intolerable. Then he said to his diaper-brother, "You shall be the sun and I'll be the moon. You won't be as hot as I was." So they exchanged places. Now the stolen youth is the moon, his younger brother, the sun. Frog and her satchel can still be seen on the moon. Ever since that time a homely woman always marries a good-looking man.

ABSTRACTS.

The abstracts have been rearranged in an order which corresponds to the folkloristic emphases of the tribe.

UC	Upper Chehalis	Sa	Satsop
Co	Cowlitz	P	Puyallup
H	Humptulip	WR	White River
Wy	Wynoochee	Sk	Skokomish

Comparative material has been listed in parentheses for each tale from the following collections:

Sahaptin Myths by Melville Jacobs. Columbia University Contributions to Anthropology, Vol. 19, Pt. 1. Listed CU.

Some Tales of the Southern Puget Sound Salish by Arthur C. Ballard. University of Washington Publications in Anthropology, Vol. 2, No. 3, pp. 57—81. December, 1927. Listed UWP 1.

Northwest Sahaptin Texts, 1 by Melville Jacobs. University of Washington Publications in Anthropology, Vol. 2, No. 6, pp. 175—244. June, 1929. Listed UWP 2.

Mythology of Southern Puget Sound by Arthur C. Ballard. University of Washington Publications in Anthropology, Vol. 3, No. 2, pp. 31—150. December, 1929. Listed UWP 3.

Mythology of Puget Sound by Herman Haeberlin. Journal of American Folk-Lore, Vol. 37, No. 145—146, pp. 371—438. July-December, 1924. Listed JAFL.

Zur Mythologie der Indianer von Washington und Oregon von Franz Boas. Globus. Illustrierte Zeitschrift für Länder- und Völkerkunde. LXIII. Bd., S. 154—157; 172—175; 190—193. Braunschweig, 1893. Listed Globus.

Upper Chehalis Texts, MS. by Franz Boas. Listed Boas MS.

Hanis Coos Myth, dictated in text and translated by Mrs. Annie Petersen, in Miluk Coos, to Melville Jacobs. August, 1933. Listed Jacobs MS.

MOON. UC87,88. MOON AND THE PRAIRIE CHICKENS. UC89. MOON AND SUN. Co62,63; H1; P4; Sk9. THE STOLEN BOY. Co64. (CU 40, 76, 139, 146, 188, 238; UWP 3: 69; JAFL 372, 373, 375, 391; Globus: 155; Boas MS.; Jacobs MS.) 158—73 177 269—71 276 356 374 272

X̣wαn stations his backside [feces H] at his fish-trap; the fifth time it calls, there is a salmon in the trap (cp. p. 387). At present the backside has a puckered mouth because X̣wαn did not feed it any of the salmon. He saves the salmon milt, makes a wish over it, and after five days it turns into two girls. The girls leave X̣wαn after he addresses them as wives four times [violates them H] (cp. p. 390). They steal a baby out of a swing and substitute a rotten log to fool the child's blind grandmother. (The child, Moon, had been conceived from a stone its mother had found.) The mother, Earthquake, carrying the child's grandmother, sings her song to overtake the girls [the mother and grandmother form lakes H], but they escape. The grandmother turns into a swamp. The mother obtains a second boy out of the urine from her first son's diapers. She engages Bluejay to look for her stolen child. [The mother and grandmother cut their hair short except in the middle and become pheasant and hell diver. Pheasant looks as if she were wearing a hat. Bluejay sets out with the people to find the stolen chief H.] He gets past five levers, losing a tail at each one (cp. p. 396) [he finds himself additional feathers and on his fifth attempt succeeds in flying across the opening in the earth H], and reaches Moon's house. When Moon hears Bluejay's errand, he removes the chips he had blown into Bluejay's eyes. A bit remains; that's why Bluejay's eyes still look glassy. Moon gives his children borne by his elder wife, all the trees and shrubs, and those, borne by his younger wife, all the fish, instructions as to their use in future generations. Chub cries and tears his mouth; that's why he has a large mouth. Redhorse cries and blood streams from his mouth; that's why he has a red mouth. Moon was fond of trout [did not care for him H], so did not give him any bones [Trout tore his mouth clear back to his ears H]. Sucker cries until his mouth draws together and becomes small [Sucker doubles up and cries; he has been thus ever since. He was his father's favorite and received most bones H]. Sturgeon cries; that's why he has a small mouth. Moon makes a spear and gig for catching the fish. He starts home (H). He transforms dangerous objects into a windfall, a needle, and a mat-smoother. He transforms people preparing to fight him into wild rhubarb (cp. p. 417), yalp, wild parsnips, spear-flowers, deer, and beaver, respectively. 1. He persuades a first giant woman, K'wαtsx̣wɛ', to follow his example and take a ride on her swing, and thus brings about her death. That's why people have safe swings now. 2. He plays doll with a second, hits her over the head, and kills her. Older people must not play doll. 3. A third steams him in her pot without harm, for he has a piece of ice in his possession. He steams her and she becomes the lark. People may steam food, but not humans. 4. Five K'wαtsx̣wɛ' women sing and cause everything to burn. Trail saves him. Fire shall never again come from a person's mouth. A road or trail never burns (cp. p. 420). 5. He splits open and puts an end to the last K'wαtsx̣wɛ' woman who had been cutting men's organs in two by means of her sharp vagina. He teaches Wren the use of a maul and wedge for splitting wood and of a basket for carrying it. He transforms Raven, who owned a fish-trap made of human beings, into a raven. Fish-traps shall be made of stakes (cp. p. 389). He slits Tapeworm open, for one person shall take another across the river without mocking him. He puts on X̣α'ʾo's hat and offers to marry any woman who can take it off. All fail but Toad. People shall be able to try on each other's hats. Ugly women shall marry good-looking men. He arrives home and restores his brother's and mother's sight and hair and has his brother burn Bluejay's backside five times (cp. p. 418). His brother rises as the night moon, but is frightened. Moon as the day moon burns everything up. Thus he becomes the moon, and his brother, the sun. His wife is with him. His mother is earthquake UC87.

The stolen chief arrives home. The girl who gets into his canoe beside him without fault is to become his wife. The fifth girl, Frog's granddaughter, is successful, when Bluejay does not sing his song fast enough. The chief finds his deformed brother Tapeworm, whom his Frog wife makes into a real person. The younger boy is also given a Frog with a basket. Since he becomes afraid when sent up as the moon and his elder brother is too hot as the sun, they exchange places. When either one takes sick, Frog who is always with him cures him. Thus Frog power is the greatest for doctoring the sick Hl.

The Geese with whom X̣wαnä'x̣wαne is travelling deposit him on a mountain and remove his wings, when he shouts at a man below. He kills Owl and takes his wings; meets a woman with camas; has his eyes stung out by the bees in her basket; is rescued by Woodpecker; and trades eyes with Snail (cp. p. 384ff. for details). He catches a salmon, when his maul hammers, saves the milt, etc., as noted above, UC87, but in brief form and with the following variations: Bluejay is promised a blue blanket, if he gets through the opening between the earth and the sky and finds Moon. That's why he has a blue uniform. There is still a cataract on Bluejay's eyes from the iron-dust Moon got into them. Moon teaches the use of the fire drill to the Prairie Chickens, who had been dancing on their meat to cook it. He gives Flounder and Salmon sight, but flounder is still cross-eyed. When X̣wαnä'x̣wαne's cap gets tight on him, it gives him cross-eyes UC88.

Moon teaches the Prairie Chicken people the use of a cooking vessel and stakes for cooking their meat UC89.

Two girls are taken to the sky as wives of two stars (cp. p. 418). They descend to earth by means of a rope, and the elder brings her baby. Their blind grandmother minds the child in a swing. Two girls steal it. The grandmother creates a new child from the stolen baby's soiled diapers. Bluejay finds the lost boy who sets out for home, when promised five girls from five different countries. On the way he kills the boy who drowns people in transporting them across the lake on his legs; condemns Raven's human fish-trap; and teaches a boy to comb and braid his hair in order to get rid of lice. He takes the Taitnepam girl, who succeeds in carrying his pack of beads, for his favorite wife. When a man sees him roast and devour five dead elk at which he had pointed a feather, he becomes ashamed and runs away. He becomes the Moon. His wife jumps into his eye. The mark she made on his face can still be seen. His younger brother becomes the Sun Co62.

A baby boy is stolen from his swing; his mother makes a new boy from his urine; he is recovered and becomes the moon, since his younger brother is afraid to travel at night; the younger, who is cross-eyed, becomes the sun Co63.

Two women steal a baby boy from his swing. His mother and grandmother, Measuring-Worm, fail to overtake them. A doll made from the boy's clothes turns into a girl. Bluejay finds the young man and is paid a blue blanket. After ten days the man, accompanied by his wife, son, and the two women, pays his mother a visit Co64.

Toad, the blind grandmother of five sisters, minds the third sister's child, Moon, while the girls attend games. Shitepoke hears the grandmother singing that the baby has turned into wood, and the theft is discovered. The younger child, Sun, is created. He is cross-eyed. The people set out to the home of the five sisters who stole Moon. Bluejay flies through the snapping door of the underworld which knocks down his tassel. That's why Bluejay's tassel flops right down. He arrives at the fifth house, where he finds Moon. He still has a whitish film under his eyelids from the water Moon threw at him. On his way home Moon teaches people the use of the stone maul and timber fish-traps. Shitepoke stretches his legs across a river to enable Moon to cross. A trail saves him from a fire caused by the singing of five children. He arrives home, and after the usual trial he becomes the moon, his brother, the sun. His grandmother is still with him P4.

A blind grandmother refers to her granddaughter's baby, whom she is minding, as a boy, and the child is stolen by two women. Bluejay has his head flattened in jumping through a snapping opening in his search for the stolen boy. He is obliged to pass many dangerous places and to lie in a trail to escape being burnt, before he finds him. On his way home the young man, in turn, passes through the same dangers, fire, snakes, and the woman who cuts up men's organ, and he puts an end to each one of them. He teaches a man how to get wood with tools and burns up a woman about to steam children blinded with pitch; he transforms the children into birds. He meets his deformed brother at the spring and makes him nice-looking. Toad's granddaughter, Frog, is the only one able to lift his satchel and becomes his wife. A homely woman always marries a good-looking man. After the usual trial he and his brother become the moon and sun, respectively. Frog and her satchel can still be seen on the moon Sk9.

MUSP' AND KƏMO'L. H14. (cp. above, and JAFL 379; Globus: 173.) 329

Chief Woodpecker sends his son into the woods to make a canoe. Six days a girl leaves camas for the boy. On the seventh he dreams of her, she appears and goes home with him. After five days she conceals her husband in a hole and agrees to laugh with Bluejay. All the people drop dead when she laughs, including her husband who peeps and hears her. She keeps his breast and genitals in a basket and has intercourse with them. In five days she gives birth to twins, the elder, Mʋsp', the younger, Kəmo'l. The children discover their father's remains in the basket and find the skeletons of their father's people. They burn their house and flee with their mother in pursuit. A dead fir tree tells them what to sing in order to climb up safely. Mʋsp' pushes the tree's loose bark down upon his mother and kills her. He sets out with Kəmo'l to kill his mother's four sisters. The first K'wαtsx̣wɛ' kills children for food by giving them a ride on her swing. Mʋsp' swings in place of Kəmo'l, who feigns illness, and is uninjured. The K'wαtsx̣wɛ' rides and is killed. The brothers revive the dead children. Mʋsp' similarly overcomes the second K'wαtsx̣wɛ', who plays doll with children, — sending them to get a stick without laughing; the third, who places children on a fungus and spears them; and the fourth, who kills children by means of her see-saw. The brothers travel on as Reformers. They declare the mouth of the Humptulip shall be a place for fish traps. They teach people how to build a roof which will not leak; how and where to cohabit; how to build a fire, and cook clams; how to walk upright and carry wood; how to split wood with a wedge and mallet; how to make a fish basket; how to bathe; how to dry fish; how to eat, to sleep and to fish with a net; how to travel, to make a canoe. They stick the shells with which a man is planning to kill them on his backside for a tail and transform him into a deer (cp. p. 388). They teach a man to wash and comb his hair in order to get rid of lice. The four Wolves, with whom their younger brother, Dog, is living, are transformed into wolves who will eat their food raw, since they no longer wish a fire (cp. p. 409). The Reformers name X̣wαne'x̣wαne. They cut open a monster in a whirlpool and revive those people, including Bluejay and X̣wαne'x̣wαne, who had been in its belly but a short time. X̣wαne'x̣wαne makes more people from dirt Mʋsp' and his brother rub from their skins and builds the people a fish trap. The Reformers visit many peoples, call to them to bring dip nets or to set up traps, and the manner in which a specific people responds accounts for its present day customs. Salmon are plentiful at Nemah, because the people there built fish traps; herring, at Bay Center, because the people used herring traps. The brothers lay hot rocks on a dangerous being in order to kill him and revive the people inside; kill serpents which people keep for pets; and burn up rats which have been eating people. They return to their starting point and become ducks, upon whose arrival each fall the people may abandon the prescribed method of handling fish and cook them as they like H14.

142 XWαNÄ'XWαNE AND SKUNK. UC76. (CU 98, 177; Boas MS.)

X̣wαnä'x̣wαne and Skunk, companions, have nothing to eat. Skunk invents his poison-gas, and together with X̣wαnä'x̣wαne invites people to feasts. The guests are killed by means of the gas and used for food. Moon arrives and makes Skunk harmless UC76.

140 XWαN AND COON. UC75. XWαN LOSES HIS EYES. UC79,80. XWα'NI
146—48 AND COON. Co46. (CU 54, 76, 100, 107, 188, 207; UWP 1: 75, two
250 versions; JAFL 388, 407; Globus: 174; Boas MS; Jacobs MS.)

X̣wαn and Coon, brothers, live together. They place bark under their pillows and wish that it may turn into salmon. Coon steals salmon and substitutes it for his bark each night. The fourth time X̣wαn spies upon him. In stealing a whole basketful of salmon, X̣wαn falls and is clubbed by the owners. Coon catches little fish. X̣wαn warns Coon four times against dangerous enemies, then disguises himself as a wala'spam and spears him. He pretends to doctor Coon and eats him up UC75.

Coon receives a dried salmon from Yellowjacket. He tricks X̣wα'ni into believing it came from skunk-cabbage he placed under his pillow. The Yellowjackets give X̣wα'ni some salmon. He steals more and is badly stung. Coon catches craw-fish; he tricks X̣wα'ni into undressing and closing his eyes to fish. X̣wα'ni is bitten by ants. He splits cedar-bark thinking it will turn into salmon, as Coon had led him to believe. Disguised as a lui'pam and a pi'tspam, he shoots, doctors, and kills Coon Co46.

At this point the myth continues into the episodes of X̣wαn Loses His Eyes, UC79,80 (cp. p. 381):

X̣wαn contrives to meet a woman [Mole Co] four times and each time receives salmon eggs [camas Co] from her. She finally recognizes him as the same person and the fifth time puts a hornets' nest in her basket. X̣wαn opens the basket in a closed stump and is nearly stung to death (Co). Woodpecker pecks him out of the stump and takes away his eyes and anus [X̣wαn cannot find his eyes and anus UC80]. X̣wαn uses wild-rose centers [berries UC80] for eyes, until Snail woman is tricked into trading him hers. He comes to the people who are playing with his eyes and anus. Bluejay suspects him, but he successfully retrieves his property and runs away UC79.

Upon awakening in the stump X̣wα'ni eats up all his flesh. The Woodpeckers peck him out and revive him. He paints big Woodpecker red and white, dots little Woodpecker black and white. He uses dog-wood blossoms for eyes, until weł is tricked into exchanging eyes with him. Weł becomes blind. X̣wα'ni tries out a boy's anus, but it weakens him and he gives it back. He juggles his eyes and Raven steals one, with which the people play games. X̣wα'ni kills an old woman and takes her disguise. While her granddaughters are carrying him to the games, he tries to have intercourse with them. At the gathering Bluejay suspects him, but the fifth time the eye is passed to him, he puts it triumphantly into his socket and runs away. The girls revive their grandmother. X̣wα'ni is bitten by the basket being children, whom he cannot kill. His sisters instruct him to cut the circles hanging from the ceiling which are the children's hearts (cp. p. 392) Co46.

X̣WαNE' HAS HIS SALMON STOLEN. UC81. (cp. above.) (JAFL 382,391.) 150

Wolf steals X̣wαne''s salmon, while X̣wαne' is sleeping and tricks him by leaving a piece on his mouth and nose. X̣wαne' offers some girls salmon eggs and hands them yellowjackets instead. He tricks an old man into trading eyes with him. The sun wilts the rose eyes which he gave the old man UC81.

X̣WƏNE'. Wy1. X̣WƏNE' AND THE WOMAN. Sa1. (cp. above.) 343
(Boas MS; Jacobs MS.) 347

X̣wəne' breaks an old lady's dam, in order that the fish can ascend the river. He wishes himself on top of a bluff, becomes hungry and eats his eyes. He kills Owl, extracts his eyes and flies down to the ground on his wings (cp. p. 381) Wy1.

The myth continues at this point into the episodes of the Satsop version:

X̣wəne' buys camas [and salmon eggs Sa] from a woman [in exchange for beads Sa] and [the fourth time Sa] promises her his slave [to take her home Sa] in return. She receives nothing and puts bees [yellowjackets Sa] in her basket which she tells him to open inside a stump [far inland Sa]. He eats his eyes while in the stump; Woodpecker pecks him out [the yellowjackets sting his eyes out Sa]. He trades eyes made of blossoms to Snail who becomes blind. [He snatches Snail's eyes and gives her ground berries, comes to some people playing with his eyes and retrieves them Sa.] Wy1.

X̣Wα'NI PAINTS THE BIRDS. Co47. (cp. above.) 254

While a stranger is passing by, X̣wα'ni hides in a cedar and eats his own flesh. Since the cedar will not open up, Woodpecker and four other birds peck X̣wα'ni out. In return he paints Tc'qwɛ' red, white and black, spots Tci'ə red, white, yellow and black, paints Woodpecker's head and a spot on his wings red, and colors Robin's belly yellow Co47.

154 XWαNÄ'XWαNE AND TAPEWORM. UC85. (Boas MS.)

Tapeworm repeats all the questions a stranger asks of him. The stranger and he fight. Tapeworm and his children wrap themselves around the man and kill him. This happens to five of the man's younger brothers. The seventh brother dreams of the murderer. After two or three years X̣wαnä'x̣wαne fastens agate knives to his legs and prepares to kill Tapeworm. Tapeworm repeats X̣wαnä'-x̣wαne's questions and the two fight. Tapeworm shouts five times for his people to help him. They are cut to pieces on X̣wαnä'x̣wαne, who kills Tapeworm. Tapeworms shall live in people but not kill them UC85.

143—5 XWαNÄ'XWαNE AND CRANE. UC77. XWαN AND CRANE. UC78. (JAFL 437; Boas MS.)

The dangerous being, K'wαtsx̣wɛ', puts X̣wαnä'x̣wαne and Crane to sleep after a swim and carries them off in her basket. [The dangerous being, Sqwaqʷsma'ik·, carries off X̣wαn, Crane, and three others after berrying. Each of the latter three catches hold of a branch and swings himself out of her basket UC78.] (Five times when she sends them for roasting sticks, Crane uses his tamanoas and they bring back crooked ones). They prepare for a tamanoas song and dance. [By feigning sickness they get the woman's sisters to come and help them sing UC78.] The fifth night of tamanoasing with the help of their snake power they put the monster woman [and her four sisters UC78] to sleep and burn up the house which they had covered with pitch. The woman [and her sisters UC78] is burned to ashes. X̣wαnä'x̣wαne ordains the end of monster women UC77.

260 XWα'NI AND HIS DOG. Co50. (CU 64, 96.)

Five times X̣wα'ni sets out but always arrives back at the same place. He takes out his sisters who tell him they are afraid of a dangerous being and his dog at the place to which he wishes to go. He changes his excrements into a dog, and into people who shall appear in the evening. He deceives the dangerous being and trades him his dog of excrements. The people, pursued by the being, turn back into excrements upon which he slips and is killed. X̣wα'ni kills the dangerous dog Co50.

152 XWαN AND WREN. UC84. (CU 74, 102, 238; Boas MS.)

X̣wαn sees Wren's "partner" (that is, his penis) eating the chips, as Wren hews a canoe, and insists on trading "partners." He pays a visit, and while he is telling the news, his new "partner" eats up all his food. This happens in three houses. His "partner" begins to bite him in the leg. He returns him to Wren. The organ shall henceforth be used solely for urinating and intercourse UC84.

XWα'NI TRAVELS. Co49. THE MOUNTAINS. Co60,61. (CU 228, 238; Jacobs MS.) 257 268

Xwα'ni makes təxo'ma mountain (Ranier), lawe'latə (St. Helens) and tc'ili'tł (Adams). lawe'latə throws fire at təxo'ma, which burns her head, backbone and shoulders. Xwα'ni travels on. He creates and names the present mountains, hills, rivers, streams, creeks, falls, and prairies. He leaves plants, berry bushes, game birds and animals, seafood and fish in the various places (for specific references see text). He makes the arrow point of agate according to Bluejay's plan Co49.

Mount Ranier (taxo'ma) and Mount Adams (patu'ʾ), the two wives of Mount St. Helens (lawe'latła[a]), fight. Mount Ranier wins. She steps on all Mount Adams' children, who get in her way. The two women and their husband become mountains Co60.

White Mountain's two wives fight. Mount Ranier's (taqo'mən's) head is broken off by the fire White Mountain's wife at the south throws at her Co61.

XWαNE' AND THE FISH. UC82. (CU 74, 79; Globus: 155.) 151

Xwαne' puts trout in Satsop River. There are still many there. He puts blue-back salmon in Tehola River, black-salmon, silver-side and dog-salmon in the Chehalis. He puts a falls in the Chehalis which blocks up the eels. People shall stand below and with long-handled baskets catch them when they jump UC82.

XWα'NI ON THE CHEHALIS RIVER. Co48. (JAFL 378, 400; Globus: 155.) 255

Xwα'ni appoints his excrements watchman at his salmon trap. Four times the watchman makes a mistake, the fifth time he calls, there is a salmon in the trap (cp. p. 379). The salmon is stolen (cp. p. 406) by Mink. Xwα'ni urinates in five creeks, from which Mink drinks and becomes sick. Xwα'ni rebuilds a falls five times, but some people had seen him and it tumbles down. He transforms the people into rocks. He makes more falls where the people can catch salmon and eels, and keeps the fish from going any farther than Pe Ell. Xwα'ni is hiding in a rock Co48.

XWα'NI TIES UP HIS WRINKLES. Co57. (Jacobs MS.) 267

Xwα'ni travels about making rivers, streams, timber, mountains, falls, rocks, roots and berries. Wherever he camped, there is always running water without mosquitoes. He wades across a river to two girls and smoothes his face to make the wrinkles disappear Co57.

XWα'NI AND HIS DAUGHTER. Co51. (CU 228.) 261

Xwα'ni segregates his daughter at her first menses. She eats dry meat and may look only at women. Wherever Xwα'ni is given a woman, he leaves salmon traps for the people. When a man shouts upon spearing two fish at once, all the peoples' fish hurry back into the river; the man is sent away. At Nesika X̣wα'ni takes his daughter into the house; people there will be dirty. In Klickitat country she runs away with a man. Thus parents never choose their children's mates there. X̣wα'ni kills a woman who had killed many men (cp. p. 380). He leaves a rock and his fishing pole at Hill Co51.

263 X̣WΑ'NI AND THE GIRLS. Co52. (CU 102.)

Five girls ask X̣wα'ni five times what he is carrying in his pack. He gives each girl a roasted eel. The youngest refuses to eat hers. X̣wα'ni leaves and calls back a name for their children. Young girls shall not ask travellers what they have in their packs Co52.

152 X̣WΑN AND THE GIRL. UC83. X̣WΑ'NI AND THE GIRL. Co54. (CU 207.)
264

X̣wα'ni notices a girl who never seems to grow. [The fifth year he sees her she is still the same size UC.] He instructs her how to use some medicine out on the sand-bar. It is his organ sticking up out of the ground; it makes her grow. If a girl has intercourse, she will grow quickly Co54.

263 X̣WΑ'NI DOCTORS A GIRL. Co53. (CU 102, 238; Jacobs MS.)

X̣wα'ni doctors a sick girl, while all the people beat time outside the enclosure. He has intercourse with her Co53.

267 X̣WΑ'NI AS TEACHER. Co56.

A man thinks his wife who has a sore finger is with child. X̣wα'ni doctors the finger, then teaches the couple how to reproduce Co56.

267 GOD AND X̣WΑ'NI. Co58.

God sends X̣wα'ni to teach people how to live. X̣wα'ni neglects his work. God throws him on an island, where he turns into a rock. In the next world X̣wα'ni will be a real man Co58.

138 ORIGIN OF THE FISH. UC72.

Jesus deposits Chinook salmon in one river, the Chehalis, sucker in a second, and trout in a third UC72.

139 ORIGIN OF BEAVER AND DEER. UC73. (UWP 3: 81; JAFL 379; Globus: 155, 173; Boas MS.)

Jesus sticks the knife Beaver is making to kill him with on Beaver's rump for a tail and sends Beaver into the river to be food for people. He hits an old man on the tail, making it short, and transforms him into deer (cp. p. 383) UC73.

THE TRAVELLER. UC74. (CU 213, 238; UWP 3: 81; Boas MS.) 139

A man uses his head for a maul to split a cedar log. Jesus teaches him how to make a maul and a wedge of yew wood. An important man keeps men and women standing in the water as posts for his salmon trap. Jesus teaches him how to make a trap of willow poles and cedar rope (cp. p. 381) UC74.

HO'TSANI. UC71. (UWP 1: 69.) 137

Cloud takes Ho'tsani down to the West Wind, where Ho'tsani lives with two women. He discovers a pool of water in their house and sends the spring-salmon in it to all the different rivers (cp. below). That's why the people live on salmon. He almost forgets the Chehalis River; thus there are few salmon there. In returning home he cannot keep up with Cloud and is left behind UC71.

COYOTE AND HIS SON. Co44. (CU 79, 91, 103, 191, 213; UWP 3: 144, two versions; JAFL 400; Jacobs MS.) 243

Coyote's son has four wives, two with white legs, whom Coyote desires. Coyote has his son shoot at a bird, which he has made of excrements, then undress and climb a mountain to get it. He causes the mountain to grow steadily taller and returns home in his son's clothes. The two women with white legs do not suspect him and after five days move on to a new camp with him. The other two camp apart. Old woman Spider lowers Coyote's son from the bluff, after he has been stranded there five days. The young man fetches his clothes and his two faithful wives home again. Coyote and the other two women return. His son gives the three of them meat to pack across the river and wishes for heavy rain. The two women are drowned and become mice. Coyote floats downstream. He names the trees at which he grabs; oak and cedar, which swing him ashore, shall be two of the best. He becomes a wooden spoon which consumes a woman's stew and berries when dipped into them. The woman throws the spoon away. In the form of a dish, a horn spoon, and a cooking vessel, respectively, he steals food from three other women. He becomes a baby and is found by the eldest of five girls who own a dam blocking up the fish. The youngest girl will have nothing to do with him. One day one of the four elder girls' digging-sticks, which Coyote had made for them, breaks. The girls discover him breaking up their dam and attack him. He sends the fish down the Columbia river; only the small fish are left to go up the Cowlitz (cp. p. 418). The girls turn into white birds. When Coyote threatens his excrement sisters with hail, they tell him how to catch salmon by clubbing them. Five times five boys steal the cooking salmon, while Coyote sleeps, and grease his hands and mouth. His sisters tell him what the trouble is. He steals the boys' pheasant eggs and smears grease on them. He makes a wish and the two white things which he has found in a male salmon turn into two fair girls. When he tries to mislead them, they run away. They marry and settle in Cowlitz country. That's why Cowlitz people are fair (cp. pp. 380, 387) Co44.

242 COYOTE AND THE RIVER BEING. Co43. (CU 126.)

Coyote sets out on a raft to kill the dangerous river being formed of drift logs. The dangerous being swallows him. After five days two men go to his rescue. They paint the dangerous being's bird prettily and inveigle it not to sing and awaken the dangerous dog, whose bark would arouse his master. They kill the sleeping dog and paddle into the river being, cutting him in two, and freeing Coyote Co43.

264 COYOTE AS DOCTOR. Co55. (Jacobs MS.)

Coyote doctors women in child-birth. He sucks at the spot where the baby's head lies and the baby is born. He is paid with clothes for his daughter. He steals one woman's baby and hides it in his knee-cap, then shows the people how to have proper sexual relationship. Coyote's daughter cuts the baby boy out of his knee. The boy is forbidden to hunt to the west. Five times he brings home deer from the west and five times shoots a bird there which rolls into a woman's house who keeps the five arrows. The sixth time in order to regain his last arrow he becomes the woman's husband and she reveals to him his true identity. Coyote's daughter refuses to look for the boy and turns into a river. Coyote finds him. The boy, his wife and their baby return to his real parents. A stolen baby shall always find his way back. Coyote follows them and marries a woman there. When she discovers that he catches squirrels by grabbing them, he runs away Co55.

268 COYOTE AND THE RAILROAD. Co59.

Coyote does not want a railroad to go through his place. The workers build it in spite of his orders. He transforms the train and the people in it into a rock Co59.

70 FOX AND STEHE'N. UC35. NəX̯Α'NTCI BOY. Co35,36. THE HOOP.
230—1 Wy3; Sk7. (CU16, 168.)
345
369 Fox [Coyote Co36] has five children, Stehe'n [Nəx̯α'ntci Co36; Stuhe' Sk] has one lame [dirty Sk] grandchild. The six children are sent out to look for tamanoas five times [until Fox finds them all right Sk]; the five Foxes [Coyotes Co36] spend their time

catching grasshoppers. [The children practice playing with a hoop Co36.] Fox sends his five children to steal a shining hoop [the poor boys cannot resist stealing the rich people's hoop Sk]; Stehe'n's grandson goes along. When the hoop has been rolled five [two Co36] times, the eldest Fox runs off with it. When caught, he throws it to the next eldest, etc. The five Foxes are killed; young Stehe'n [Nəx̣α'ntci boy Co36] by means of his tamanoas, Swan, [by shaking out feathers Co36; Sk], brings a fog and escapes with the hoop. (The pursuers become the Tamanoas, see p. 403.) He shouts to his grandfather, and Fox and Stehe'n argue as to whose children were killed. They urinate on one another; Fox turns yellow and loses. He is still yellow. [They urinate; Stuhe''s urine reaches clear across the bay, Fox's only half way. Their urine is the rainbows Sk. Coyote moves away east-of-the-mountains Co36.] Stehe'n and his grandson each keep half of the hoop. [Young Nəx̣α'ntci with his grandfather packs the hoop on his back to the snow capped mountains. That's why the young nəx̣α'ntci has a white ring around his back Co36. Stuhe' still has the hoop Sk.] UC35.

X̣wα'ni sends his five sons to look for tamanoas, and they get it strong. Nəx̣α'ntci has a lame grandson. The five X̣wα'ni boys steal the hoop and are killed, as above. X̣α'ntci Boy, running with the hoop, suddenly becomes strong and outdistances his pursuers. X̣wα'ni turns yellow in the urinating contest with Nəx̣α'ntci and weeps to death for his sons. Nəx̣α'ntci takes the shining hoop up to the sky. That's why the sun is up there now Co35.

Coyote has four sons, fast runners. Stəhe·'n has one very strong grandchild. They decide to steal the tamanoas people's hoop. Young Stəhe·'n succeeds, as above. Old Stəhe·'n wins an argument with old Coyote as to whose children were killed Wy3.

THE DANGEROUS BEAVER BEING. UC61; Co22,23. (CU 17; UWP 2: 200, 234; UWP 3: 114.) 128 214—5

Each of four elder brothers, after killing a pheasant, meets an old man who gives him a worthless spear and stations him at the river to help kill a beaver. [In return for his assistance Beaver gives him a slice of beaver meat and promises to show him pretty girls Co22.] The spear buckles and he is killed by the beaver who is the old man. The fifth brother learns what has happened in a dream in which he is advised to use his own spear blade [he steps on Meadow Lark's leg who instructs him how to do away with Beaver Co22]. He kills the old man in his beaver hide and burns him up. [He steps over and revives his four brothers Co22.] Beavers shall never again be dangerous beings UC61.

Beaver gives each of four men a spear made of a cattail stalk and sends him out to kill a swa'q'extcιn. The spear buckles and Beaver kills each man. The fifth man knows who Beaver is, makes a real spear and kills him Co23.

126 THE DANGEROUS TREE BEING. UC60. MOON, X̣WɑNÄ'X̣WɑNE AND
156 THE DANGEROUS BEING BAT. UC86. (CU 43, 171; UWP 2: 204; UWP 3: 114, two versions; JAFL 427; Boas MS.)

Each of four brothers kills a pheasant, gets caught in the rain, hears a voice calling him, and sleeps under a tree. Each sleeper has his heart removed by a dangerous being. The youngest brother learns of all this in a dream, hides at the tree, shoots the dangerous being when he descends, recovers his brothers' hearts, and burns him up. He revives his four brothers UC60.

The youngest of seven brothers dreams of the dangerous tree being who has killed his six brothers. Moon arrives and sends X̣wɑnä'x̣wɑne to take shelter under the being's tree. X̣wɑnä'x̣wɑne sings his tamanoas song to keep awake. Toward morning Moon begins to smoke the dangerous being out and together with X̣wɑnä'-x̣wɑne burns him up. His ashes turn into bats UC86.

124 THE DANGEROUS LAKE BEING. UC59. (CU 14; Globus: 172.)

The eldest of five brothers goes hunting, shoots a pheasant and hangs it on a tree. He sees a dead elk-doe in a lake and is pulled under in swimming out to it. This happens to three of his brothers. The youngest has a dream and learns a dangerous being is killing his brothers. He is instructed to roll hot rocks into the lake to boil it dry. He sees the four pheasants hanging on the tree but does not shoot any, dries out the lake, and finds his decaying brothers inside the dangerous being UC59.

218 CHIPMUNK AND THE DANGEROUS WOMAN. Co26. (CU 64; UWP 3: 107, 109, three versions; JAFL 388; Boas MS.)

The dangerous woman finds Chipmunk eating berries in a tree. She grabs at him and leaves the stripes that are on his back. His grandmother, Roe, hides him. She kills the dangerous woman under the pretense of pulling off her skin to make her white. The dangerous woman's five sisters die from eating the meat Roe feeds them. Coyote succeeds in killing the dangerous woman's children, when his sisters, threatened with rain, instruct him to cut down the children's souls (cp. p. 385) Co26.

217 THE BAD BOY AND THE DANGEROUS WOMAN. Co25. (CU 121; UWP 3: 106, two versions.)

A cranky boy is deserted by his people. The dangerous woman comes and offers him a hot rock, pretending it is a salmon head. He tears her arm off. He finds his people, tells them, and the older men return home. They invite all the dangerous women to come and have the woman's arm restored. The youngest woman remains outside the house, which the men have covered with pitch; Coyote bites her tongue off. The others are burnt up while dancing inside Co25.

THE BOY AND THE DANGEROUS WOMAN. Co24. 216

A boy out seeking tamanoas wishes for a girl and the dangerous woman, who knows all his thoughts (cp. p. 414), carries him off. She becomes his wife. One day he escapes and returns to his people. He tells them to get into a hole. Only his parents obey. All the other people lose their breath and die, when the woman weeps. The boy sends her away forever Co24.

BUNGLING HOST. UC5, 6, 7; Co45; Wy2; Sa2; Sk4. (UWP 3: 98, 99.) 3—9 249 344 348 368

1. Bluejay and his cousin (brother), Skwikwi'k^{w}, visit Skwit. Skwit's children gather salmon-berries for the guests. Skwit and his children return the visit. Bluejay's children cannot find any berries. The Skwit children gather five basketfuls for Bluejay. 2. Bluejay and his cousin visit Tsia'kwawa and again receive salmon-berries, which Bluejay's children in turn are unable to find. 3. Bluejay and his cousin visit Beaver. Beaver's children collect branches and mud for Bluejay which Bluejay does not eat. Beaver and his children return the visit. Bluejay's children fetch willows and mud; Beaver eats and is satisfied. 4. Bluejay and his cousin visit Bear. Bear frightens Bluejay with his noise five times. He cuts his hand in five places and serves Bluejay the grease which drips out. He returns the visit. Bluejay fails to frighten him, then hurts himself cutting his hand. Bear provides grease for Bluejay. 5. Bluejay and his cousin visit Sea Lion. Sea Lion frightens Bluejay, then cuts flesh off his side for him. Bluejay imitates and injures himself. 6. Bluejay and his cousin visit Fish Duck. Fish Duck's children dive for fish for Bluejay. Fish Duck and his children return the visit. Bluejay's children cannot catch any fish. Fish Duck's children provide Bluejay with some. 7. Bluejay and his cousin visit Shadow. Bluejay tries to take some beads. Invisible people cook for him. Shadow visits Bluejay, but Bluejay cannot see him. Shadow leaves UC5.

As above: 1. Bluejay, his grandmother, and four children visit Bear. (Bear cuts a piece of meat out of his thigh and cooks it.) 2. Bluejay and his family visit Fish Duck. 3. Bluejay and his family visit Seal. Seal kills and cooks his smallest child for his guests. The little Seal comes to life again. Seal and his wife return the visit. Bluejay kills and serves his smallest boy, who does not revive. 4. Bluejay and his family visit Beaver. 5. Bluejay and his family visit Shadow. (It is uncertain, if Shadow ever returned the visit.) UC6.

1. Bluejay visits the Shadows. 2. He visits Bear. 3. He visits the ghosts. Here he makes mistakes as at the land of the shadows. When the ghosts visit him, they will not eat the food he serves. 4. Bluejay misunderstands his sister and is almost killed hanging under the canoe saddle, but the youngest boy passenger finds him in time (cp. below). He neglects to mix food with the oil served him and takes sick. He visits Beaver. (Bluejay eats the wood and mud Beaver serves him.) UC7.

Coyote's son marries Grizzlybear's daughter and Fish Duck's daughter. 1. Coyote [Bluejay Wy] visits Fish Duck, who dives for salmon for him. In imitating Fish Duck, Coyote is knocked senseless on the ice. Fish Duck leaves him a salmon. 2. Coyote [Bluejay Wy] visits Grizzlybear [Bear Wy]. Grizzlybear cuts fat off his wife's breast and cooks it in grease from his hands. [Bear cuts meat from his feet Wy.] Coyote tries without success to cut meat from his wife's breast and to melt fat from his hands. [Bluejay tries to cut meat from his feet Wy.] Grizzlybear cuts flesh from the sides of his body and melts grease from his hands to leave with Coyote Co45; Wy2.

1. Bluejay and his sister, Yu·′i, visit Bear. Bear cuts meat off his thigh. He returns the visit. Bluejay sends his five children to dive for trout. They fail to get any and the youngest drowns. Bear cuts off another piece of meat for Bluejay Sa2.

1. Bear invites Bluejay. He serves fish in grease melted from his hands. Bluejay holds his hands over the fire. One can still see where they are cracked open Sk4.

12—15 THE CONTESTS. UC9, 10; Co2, 3; P1. THE CONTEST IN THE NORTH.
178—82 H2. (CU 153; UWP 2: 216; UWP 3: 64, three versions; Jacobs MS.)
351
284 The introductions preceding the contests vary for the several versions:

X̯wa′ips, Skwikwi′k^{w} and Bluejay chase Sea Otter. Sea Otter comes out on shore as a man and shakes the water off himself. The water freezes. [The people make a trip to get provisions. Bluejay misunderstands his sister, Nau, and almost dies hiding under the brush in the canoe (cp. above) UC10.] Bluejay jumps ashore and slips. X̯wa′ips [the chief UC10] leads the way up the icy bank and into the house guarded by two dogs. One dog [servant UC10] makes a fire from a small piece of wood, the other draws in the smoke. The dogs serve much food from little, which the guests and Bluejay swallow through elderberry tubes [put into sacks underneath their clothes Co2] UC9.

Bluejay shoots five bags of arrows at a salmon and pursues it with his brother, Eagle, who takes along five slaves. The slaves' hands stick to their spears, Bluejay's and Eagle's to their paddles, and they are carried downstream to the village where Bluejay's sister, who had been stolen, is living. The salmon turns into a man, Bluejay's sister's husband, etc., as above Co2.

Chief Mountain Eagle and his people visit a distant village. The people follow up the icy shore in Mountain Eagle's footsteps and are welcomed for the contests Co3.

The Seal nation challenges the Freshwater animals in games. Bluejay begs his grandmother for hairs from her privates to make into a tassel, sings his spirit song, and is taken along. He conceals a club in his blouse P1.

Chief Sea Otter marries Crow's daughter and they have a son and a daughter. While the brother and sister are out hunting together in a fog, the girl is impregnated by moisture falling into her mouth. The fifth day the people desert the two. Their grandmother, Crow, leaves them fire (cp. pp. 399, 408). The girl's lover supplies them with blankets, a house, and food. She gives birth to two children. Crow and her grandchildren visit and are supplied with food. Bluejay discovers them eating the meat they have brought back, and his people set out for their former home. The deserted woman's children blow their canoe back four times, before allowing them to land. The people prepare to take the woman and her children to her husband's home. Bluejay hides under the canoe saddle by mistake, the people get up the icy shore, pass the sea-lions guarding the door of the house, and use elderberry stalks when eating H2.

The contests follow at this point:

In the first Cowlitz version, which is typical, Bluejay represents his side five times: 1. Bluejay and seabird girl dive to see who can stay under the water longer. Bluejay comes up for air in the brush alongside his canoe. He finally strikes the girl on the head and she floats up dead. He wins a blue blanket. 2. Bluejay and a girl climb a ladder. After a time he knocks her down with his club and wins another blanket. 3. The chief shoots at Bluejay and a boy slave. Bluejay protects his breast with concealed whetstones. The boy is shot through. Bluejay wins another blanket. 4. Bluejay and a boy remain in a sweathouse. Eagle bores a hole through which Bluejay may obtain air. The boy blows up. Bluejay wins another blanket. 5. Bluejay and his brother play together at a "bone-gamble" and win. His sister makes a rope for his and Eagle's return. The two pass through five thunderstorms; during the fifth Bluejay is struck on the forehead and a tuft of hair is left sticking out. Bluejay ties a bit of blue blanket to their end of the rope and lets go. His sister winds the rope back up and learns of their safe return Co2.

1. Bluejay beats White Duck [Seal P] at diving. 2. Bluejay beats Big Hummingbird [Tiny Woodpecker P] at pole-climbing. [The visitors go home P1.] Eagle causes two wooden machines operating as levers to slow down so that their canoes may slide through safely, and the party arrives home Co3.

In the first Upper Chehalis version Bluejay wins a foot race, a climbing, a diving, and a sweating contest. 1. Bluejay wins in running by hitting his opponent, Coyote, with his club. X̂wa'ips thus wins a paddle from Sea Otter. 2. Bluejay similarly beats Squirrel in tree-climbing and X̂wa'ips wins another paddle. 3. Bluejay similarly beats Seal at diving. 4. Bluejay keeps cool with ice, hits his opponent, Mud Hen, and wins at sweating. He wins five paddles in all. He and X̂wa'ips are again hindered by levers of ice on their way home. Each of the five levers clips off some of Bluejay's tail (cp. p. 380) and his five paddles are broken. X̂wa'ips borrows Spider's rope to get the rest of the way up the river. The party arrives home. X̂wa'ips jerks the rope and Spider pulls it back UC9.

1. Seal comes up floating; thus Bluejay wins at diving. 2. Bluejay and Beaver are targets for shooting. Bluejay escapes by his quickness. The fifth shot hits Beaver. 3. Bluejay hits Squirrel with his club and wins at climbing. He takes excrements home to his sister, for he had misunderstood her UC10.

The Humptulip version includes a stay-awake, a diving, and two climbing contests during the people's first four visits to the country of the woman's husband. 1. Bluejay and Shadow contest at staying awake. Bluejay's chief puts phosphorescent wood on Bluejay's eyes and jabs him with a stick whenever he is about to fall asleep. The fifth time Bluejay calls, Shadow is asleep. Bluejay asks for a shag blanket and excrements as presents to take home. 2. Bluejay beats Seal at diving, when Seal is finally forced to come out. Bluejay asks for a crane blanket, and a kind of file as food to take home, and tries to buy a woman's excrements. 3. Bluejay beats Squirrel at climbing. 4. Bluejay beats Flying Squirrel at climbing. Pitch on the tree holds Flying Squirrel back, then Bluejay digs his claws into Flying Squirrel's head. The woman's brother and his people pay her a fifth visit in her husband's land. On the fifth day of their stay they are sent to spear a whale. The woman tells her brother to spear the fifth one. Bluejay begins to repeat their opponents' cry and the whale carries his entire tribe away. The woman grasps Bluejay's tail feathers which return home again as a Bluejay. She leaves her husband and children, dives into a lake five times, and becomes a dangerous being. She goes into the water for good. Her husband and his tribe become Hwasq'a'l birds H2.

21—29 BLUEJAY GOES TO THE LAND OF THE DEAD. UC12, 13, 14, 15; Sa3.
349 293 BLUEJAY AND HIS SISTER YO'I. H3. (CU 55, 190; UWP 2: 227; UWP 3: 128, seven versions; Boas MS.)

Bluejay shoots his sister, Yo'i, in the backside, while she is digging camas. He tells her to marry with the dead. The fifth day a man of fog, a skull, takes her for his wife. Yo'i gives Bluejay instructions how to visit her. Her husband takes her with her eyes closed down to the depths of the earth. They pass through five prairies of flowers and five burning prairies. A skull in a canoe with a hole in the bottom takes them across a river. The people are all skulls. Yo'i roasts bark and eats it with her eyes closed; it tastes like steelhead salmon. She gives birth to two skulls. Bluejay and Wedge set out for the Land of the Dead. After five trials Bluejay keeps his eyes closed. They use their five buckets of water to get through the Fire prairies. The fifth time Yo'i comes for him, Bluejay agrees to travel in the canoe with the hole. Twice he pushes a skull child out of the canoe; he kicks and clubs his skull nephews. The second day of his visit he succeeds in eating bark with his eyes closed. He tells Yo'i the skulls' whale on the beach is only a log. He prepares to go home and refuses to have his brother-in-law take him. He uses up one and one-half buckets of water on the prairies of flowers and burns to death on the fifth fire prairie, when his water gives out. He returns to the river as one of the dead and admires the canoe, his nephews and the salmon. Four times he goes to the Second-Death, where the people are dancing, and is brought back by Yo'i. The fifth time he must stay there. If it had not been for Bluejay, the living and the dead would still be able to visit each other H3.

The Upper Chehalis have four versions of Bluejay's visit to the Land of the Dead which have but few variations from the Humptulip account:

Bluejay's sister had married a dead man. [Bluejay pretends to be dying and the fifth time persuades his sister, Nau, to stand over his face a long time to cure him; thus he may examine her. He makes her marry a dead man UC13. A dead man marries Bluejay's sister and takes her to the Land of the Dead. They cross prairies and come to a river. She closes her eyes and gets across safely in a canoe with holes UC14.] Bluejay prepares to visit his sister [his daughter who had died suddenly UC15]. He shouts [five times UC13] to be taken across the river, but to no avail. He yawns, and immediately his sister sends her husband to get him in a canoe with a hole. He gets across safely, as soon as he keeps his eyes closed. He kicks many bones [and tears a child's bead from her nose UC14]. He tells his sister the whale meat the people have is only a tree. [He gambles with the ghosts and wins their berries and fruits. Thus we have lots of berries UC15.] (He goes fishing with his brother-in-law and throws the trash his brother-in-law catches and his brother-in-law's bones out of the canoe. Yo'i gives him a basket and sends him home. He opens it on the way and lets the bees, which would have become fir-cones and berries, and the first-born baby in it fly away. He visits his sister a second time and again mistreats the bones.) He is sent home with five buckets [a small vessel UC14] of water, saves the smallest bucket for the fifth and largest prairie [wastes the water UC13, 14], and burns to death. [The baby his daughter had given him returns to the World of the Dead UC15.] He lives at the end of the village with the dead who have died by fire. [In this Second-Death people sit head down; that's why children are born head down. The bluejay on earth is the sparks that flew up when Bluejay burned UC13.] UC12.

The short Satsop version is identical with the Humptulip version with all details omitted. Yu·′i dies, goes to the home of the dead, and marries there, as Bluejay had wished she would. Bluejay follows, is finally paddled across the river by Yu·′i, kicks many skulls, and is sent home. He uses up most of his water on the prairies full of flowers, is burned to death, and returns to the dead whom he now finds beautiful Sa3.

20 BLUEJAY AND THE YOUNG WOMAN. UC11.

Bluejay steals from a tree the body of a woman who had been dead five days. The fifth doctor to whom he takes the woman revives her, and Bluejay takes her for his wife (cp. p. 405). Her parents recognize her and take her from him. He therefore decrees, the dead shall never be brought back to life again. The woman dies UC11.

11 BLUEJAY AND CRANE. UC8.

Bluejay asks Crane for salmon. He injures Crane for not answering him. Crane decides to fight. Bluejay enlists the aid of Nettle, Bull-Thistle, Slipperiest Mud, Rotten Meat, and Skunk. He puts excrements about the house. Crane tramples all Bluejay's aides but Skunk to death. Skunk shoots his musk in Crane's eyes. Bluejay and Crane make up UC8.

303 BLUEJAY BECOMES A TATTLE-TALE. H4.

Bluejay tells Bear that Bullhead has been calling him names. Bear chases Bullhead. Bullhead sticks his horns into Bear, holds him down in the water while the tide comes in, and drowns him. Bluejay, Bullhead and his friends feast. Bluejay and Bullhead similarly trick Deer, Calf Elk, Cow Elk, and Male Elk. Then Bullhead's horns become short and they stop H4.

184 BLUEJAY AND HIS YOUNGER BROTHERS. Co4.

Bluejay, who is married, accompanies his two younger brothers on a visit to some girls. He wins the elder brother's girl away from him and as a result his mother-in-law deprives him of his wife. The three brothers go to get her back. Bluejay kills a deer which the elder of his two brothers refuses to help him pack. He plans to fetch a girl for his youngest brother instead of going for his wife, but his two brothers send him for her, on threat of tying him up. They go to get their girl and find Bluejay with her. She leaves Bluejay and goes to them. Bluejay stays behind and cries. That's why bluejays are about everywhere Co4.

DOG HUSBAND. UC49, 50, 51, 52; H13. (CU 79; JAFL 418.) 96—103 328

The pet dog of a young woman [who had refused to marry UC49] secretly becomes a man and impregnates her. She is deserted by her people, [who hang the dog UC52], but a member of her family [her grandmother UC49; Crow UC51, 52] leaves her fire (cp. pp. 395, 408). The young woman gives birth to four male pups and one girl child [five male pups and one daughter UC51, 52; two female pups, three male H]. After about ten days [the fifth day UC51, 52], she leaves her torch on the beach, returns early from digging, and discovers the pups are boys [the girl confesses the fact to her mother UC49]. She surprises the boys at play and burns their dog coats. The boys become great hunters. [The five pups become people. She declares they shall be a disgrace to their tribe, beats the old dog, her husband, and leaves with the two girls H13.] UC50.

Bluejay discovers that the young woman's grandmother has been obtaining food from her granddaughter. The people start back in their canoes and all but the grandmother are drowned UC49.

In the Upper Chehalis version 52 the Dog Husband narrative is preceded by the following: Mouse sends her grandson and granddaughter to catch salmon and warns them not to camp close together. They sleep closer each night and the fifth night sleep together (cp. p. 416). Mouse tracks them by their camps and discovers their baby. In seven days she fashions a salmon out of a piece of cedar and instructs it to carry off her grandson, when he spears it (cp. p. 416). His wife takes revenge on Mouse by causing the water in the well to drop. Mouse stoops to drink, falls in, and drowns. The girl puts beads on her baby and places him in a hollow tree with instructions to cry if he hears pounding. She becomes the plant X̱wala'q'o UC52.

Woodpecker at work in the woods hears a baby's cry. The fifth day he leaves his tools at work and seeks the baby. He and his wife pretend to their daughter that it is their own son. The fifth day the daughter persuades the boy to shoot her hand, whereupon she cries out his identity. After five days he leaves and follows a bird to a prairie where five women are digging camas. The girl is there to taunt him on his origin. He shoots her and burns her up, but her hat falls to the side, and another bird, which he follows, flies off to a second prairie. Here the burning is repeated. The third time (fourth UC51) he throws the girl's hat into the fire as well, and transforms her ashes into the lark, (cp. Meadowlark Girl, Co32, p. 416). (An adopted person shall be treated like a brother UC51.) On the fifth prairie he changes himself into a dog in order to get near a beautiful girl. Bluejay suspects the dog, because he comes only to the princess who begins to have streaks on her cheek bones; he does not eat bones; and he seems to understand Bluejay. The princess becomes pregnant and the people desert her UC51, 52.

Here follows the dog husband narrative given for version 50, as noted. The conclusion of 51 and 52 reads as follows:

Crow visits the deserted princess and is fed. She returns home with meat for her children. Raven detects the youngest boy choking on blubber. The people return to the princess and quarrel for possession of the houses which have been filled with meat. Bluejay (and Raven UC52) is chased away to his house filled with entrails UC51, 52.

305 RAVEN AND EAGLE. H5. (Jacobs MS.)

Raven and White-tailed Eagle, brothers, each have a son. Eagle's son dies. Raven decides the dead shall not return. Eagle tells Raven he gets herring by letting his son down into the water in a basket and leaving him there, until he stops pulling at the rope. Raven is thus tricked into drowning his son. Eagle says the dead shall stay dead. Five times Raven digs in the ground to reach his son; the mucus flowing from his nose as he weeps becomes the white moss on trees. Thus people do not come back to life and members of a family disagree H5.

306 CROW SINGS TAMANOAS FOR RAVEN. H6. CROW DOCTORS RAVEN.
367 Sk2. CROW DOCTORS HER DAUGHTER. WR2.
361

Crow finds a salmon to feed to her children and leaves it to steam, while she is away singing tamanoas for her sick neighbor, Raven. Raven has diarrhoea and goes out of the house four times. The fifth time he steals Crow's fish H6.

Raven goes out of the house to have a movement, while Crow, his sister, is singing for him inside. He eats the seal Crow left at her home to steam and kills Crow's daughter. Crow finds her daughter's body Sk2.

Crow's son, Ts'i'tsix̣wʋn, misunderstands his mother and roasts his sister's backside instead of roasting clams for her. Four times he tells Crow he cannot find his sister; the fifth time he confesses that he roasted her. Crow revives the girl. She kills a seal and gives a feast. Ts'i'tsix̣wʋn eats the fat he is supposed to take to Raven. Raven has Ts'i'tsix̣wʋn look for his louse, cuts Ts'i'tsix̣wʋn's stomach open and throws him in the river. Ts'i'tsix̣wʋn makes a wish; a leaf falls into his wound and heals him. He starts home and catches many fish in the fifth lake to which he comes. Crow and he roast the fish and feed many to Raven. The bones stick in Raven's throat and he dies WR2.

RAVEN EATS HIS SISTER'S BERRIES. Sk3. 368

Raven eats some women's berries and pours the juice over himself. His sister Crow believes he is bleeding to death from an attack by many people. Later she misses the berries and learns the truth Sk3.

SYUYU′WəN. UC23. (UWP 3: 92, two versions; JAFL 379.) 41

Syuyu′wən shoots an elk. Raven tracks it and claims it as his kill. He butchers it and carries home some fat and meat. The fat turns into white moss, the meat into rotten wood. He and his children find nothing but rotten wood where the elk had been. Syuyu′wən shoots another elk. Pheasant tracks it, but denies it is his. Syuyu′wən gives it to him. Pheasant feeds his children some of the meat. Raven hears one of the children choking on it. He fetches the rest of the elk with Pheasant and asks for a piece of the hide. He pulls out a hair as a blanket for each of his five boys. They freeze to death UC23.

COUGAR AND WILDCAT. UC31, 32, 33, 34. COUGAR AND HIS YOUNGER BROTHERS. Co18. COUGAR AND MINK. Co19. THE COUGARS AND THEIR BROTHER WILDCAT. H9. THUNDER. H10. (CU 113, 133, 217; UWP 2: 192, 219; UWP 3: 118; JAFL 425; Boas MS; Jacobs MS.) 60—69 202 209 310 315

Type 1: Cougar [the four Cougar brothers H9] leaves his little brother Wildcat at home to watch the fire and cook, while he hunts. [Wildcat becomes tired of elk meat and the second, third, and fourth times goes out and catches snipe. His brothers return, discover snipe flesh between his teeth, and warn him of the dangerous being who owns the fire H9.] The fifth time Wildcat lets the fire go out and steals some from the dangerous man, łała′mak'wʊs. [Wildcat turns into a fly, a cinder, a flea, and a mosquito, but the dangerous woman, K'wɑtsx̣wɛ′, recognizes him each time. He turns into smoke and steals a firebraid from her, while she sleeps. She pursues him and throws five packropes, forming five sand-spits in the water H9.] Wildcat puts the fire on his tail, which is burnt short [as it is now Co18, H9], then on his forehead, so that his scalp becomes drawn together (H9). łała′mak'wʊs arrives and has a tree fight with Cougar. Wildcat saves Cougar's pieces of flesh, but puts aside łała′mak'wʊs's liver by mistake, which Cougar is forced to use in reassembling himself. Cougar shoots an elk. Wildcat invites someone to eat with them. Q'ama′psəm comes and swallows all their food. Cougar cuts Q'ama'psəm's neck in two. Q'ama'psəm kills four Cougars; the fifth and youngest escapes. Wildcat in fleeing makes five mountains behind him. Arrived at the last one, Q'ama'psəm turns into a cyclone. The surviving Cougar and Wildcat make a new camp. Twice Wildcat trades his elk skin blanket with two women for camas, the third time he brings the women home. Their singing frightens away Cougar's game, and he and Wildcat are forced to move again. Cougar gives Wildcat a bow and leaves him. Wildcat shoots a field-mouse, long-tailed mouse, mole, gopher, and rabbit for game. Cougar finds him cooking them and promises always to provide him with big game. Thus cougar always leaves game for wildcat, who follows after him UC31.

The conclusion of the Humptulip version varies from the above as follows:

Wildcat sends his brothers up a tree and awaits K'wαtsx̣wɛ' in the house. He kicks the door and turns it into a rock which falls down on her head, as she crawls in on her belly. The five brothers burn her up. The Cougars become wanderers and take Wildcat along. He jumps across four creeks after them; at the fifth he falls in. They pull him ashore and prepare to leave him at the creek. The two elder go out to sea and will send sea-lion, seal or blackfish in to him. The two younger go into the woods and will leave him game. Wildcat finds a cow elk left for him. Bear steals some of it. Bear steals Wildcat's food, whenever he can H9.

Type 2: Q'ama'psəm comes at Wildcat's invitation, eats all Cougar's and Wildcat's food, and kills all but the fifth Cougar. Wildcat changes himself into a hill five times to escape. [The dangerous man's head pursues Cougar and Wildcat UC34.] Thunder takes Wildcat [and Cougar UC34] across the river and sends him to his house. Q'ama'psəm crosses on Thunder's legs, is toppled off, and drowned. The roaring of his head is an omen of good or bad weather (UC34). Wildcat marries Thunder's daughter. Thunder has him crawl into a log to split it, removes the wedges and leaves him inside. Wildcat splits the log in two and carries one half home. Thunder strips bark off a tree, drops it on Wildcat, and leaves him for dead. Wildcat crawls out from under the ground unharmed and packs home the bark. Thunder has him go inside a basket, takes it out in his canoe, and topples it overboard. Wildcat unties the basket and comes ashore. Thunder sends him to the mountains for snow. Wildcat brings back a small snowball which Thunder cannot eat up. He throws what Thunder leaves of it away and it covers the house. He rolls it up and takes it back to the mountains. He fetches Thunder's two pet lions. They frighten Thunder and he takes them away again. Thunder does not bother him any more UC 32.

The Humptulip tell a detailed version of the second type:

Four elder brothers hunt elk, while the youngest boy, Sət'α'msət'-αm, watches the fire. The third, fourth, and fifth times Sət'α'msət'αm sings for someone to eat with them; the dangerous being, Huno'nx̭^{u}, comes. Huno'nx̭^{u} has the boy sit beside him, while the four brothers feed him ten elk in which they put hot stones and sharp limbs. Huno'nx̭^{u} sleeps with the boy alongside him. The five brothers flee, the boy leaving a limb in his place. Huno'nx̭^{u} pursues. The eldest brother uses his dog five times to form five mountains, before he and the dog are overtaken and swallowed by the monster. This happens to the boy's four elder brothers. The boy gives Thunder sinew and Thunder lets him cross the river on his legs. Huno'nx̭^{u} touches Thunder's legs with his cane while crossing in pursuit and Thunder draws his legs back. Huno'nx̭^{u}'s noise in the water is still a weather sign. The boy marries Thunder's daughter. Thunder's wife tries to peck a hole in her son-in-law's heart, but smashes her nose against a stone his wife had given him for protection. Thunder goes out alone and catches a whale. He loses a second one when his daughter's two children come out and laugh at him. He teaches them to catch porpoises and whales. His son-in-law escapes out of the split cedar, from which Thunder had removed the wedges, and carries the tree home. He brings Thunder a ball of snow and takes it away again, when it almost smothers Thunder. He fetches in turn Thunder's pet bear, his pet cougar, and his pet grizzly and takes each of the pets away again, after it has treated Thunder roughly. Thunder sends him for a hoop with which the Tamanoas people are playing. He seizes it and the people pursue him with lighted torches. Thunder peals five times and brings a rain of urine which extinguishes half the torches; his wife urinates five times and but one light, that belonging to Shark, remains, which one of the young Thunders puts out with a trickle. Thunder catches the hoop on his arm and thus obtains his light from his son-in-law. Whenever he peals, a light is seen. When it rains, Thunder and his wife are urinating. When it peals loudly, Thunder is looking for a whale H10.

Types 1 and 2: Q'ama'psəm comes to eat at Wildcat's invitation. Cougar manages to kill him. Cougar and Wildcat desert the Geese women who frighten away all their game. Wildcat steals the dangerous being's fire. Cougar fights the being and Wildcat saves Cougar's flesh. Cougar has the liver of the dangerous being; that's why people won't eat it. The head of the first dangerous being, Q'ama'psəm, pursues him. He crosses the bay on Thunder; Q'ama'psəm's head follows and is rolled off into the water. By means of his tamanoas Cougar makes huge trees small five times and carries them into Thunder's camp. Thunder frees him. He always buries venison for Wildcat UC33.

Cougar sets out to visit one of his wives. Young Wildcat accompanies him in spite of his older brother's disapproval. Wildcat invites the dangerous being to eat with them. Cougar kills the being, whose head pursues him, until it gets lost. At the brothers' next camp Wildcat lets the fire go out and steals some from the dangerous woman. The woman's five sons arrive in turn and fight with Cougar. Wildcat strikes the first four on the ankle with his axe and Cougar kills each one of them. The fifth fights Cougar above ground. Wildcat saves Cougar's white flesh to put back on his bones. Cougar now has the dangerous being's black liver which people cannot eat. He sends Wildcat away and promises always to leave hidden game for him. Cougar's younger brother Mink goes to buffalo country with him. Mink breaks the taboo and repeats the name of the creek, where he and his brother camp. A hail storm comes up and almost kills him. Cougar sends Mink to the springs for food. When Mink keeps his eyes shut, his sisters-in-law in the springs bring food and remove the empty dish. Mink watches through two holes in his blanket while Cougar and his wife are sleeping in the house of Cougar's father-in-law. Five times he cries out when the old man is about to kill Cougar. The next day Cougar goes out hunting with his brothers-in-law; his father-in-law takes Mink out. The old man tries unsuccessfully to kill Mink by dropping bark upon him and by putting him into his tool-basket and toppling it out of the canoe. Meadow Lark warns Cougar his father-in-law wishes to kill him, because he did not come sooner for his wives, and advises him to set up a dummy to fool his buffalo wife, then shoot her with his own bow and arrows. Cougar thus kills her and feeds her udder to his father-in-law. The old man has sent Mink for his two pets, the Lightnings. Mink with the aid of his tamanoas fetches them, and they kill the old man and his children. He and Cougar go home Co18.

A second brief Cowlitz version includes Mink's visit with Cougar to Cougar's wife, Grizzly Bear, and her father, Thunder; Mink's cry of alarm at night, when Thunder is about to murder Cougar; Cougar's killing with Lark's aid of his wife, Grizzly; and Mink's fetching of Thunder's two playthings, White Agate and Blue Rock. The two rocks tear Thunder's house to pieces, Thunder flies into a cloud in the form of a bird, and his slaves, the Ipɛ'ʔsa, turn into birds. Cougar leaves Mink at a creek. The one becomes a cougar, the other a mink, which henceforth mate each with his own kind Co19.

46 198 SKUNK. UC27. COUGAR AND SKUNK. Co17. (CU 42, 202; UWP 1: 63, two versions; UWP 2: 207; JAFL 421.)

A chief instructs his two daughters to follow the trail sprinkled with red paint. The elder takes the trail sprinkled with bird feathers. [A girl's grandmother sends her to Cougar Co.] Skunk takes her in with him. After five days Skunk's master [Cougar Co] discovers her [the girl puts a hair in Cougar's food to make known her presence Co], and the sixth day he runs away with her beyond the sky [to a tall rock Co], while his slave, Skunk, is carrying in their meat. Skunk pursues and shoots his musk four [five Co] times at the couple's reflection in the water. He discovers the two up above and calls five times, before they direct him to ascend backside up. They mislead him about his progress and when he is very near, roll hot rocks into his backside. His anus shoots out his mouth and floats down the river. He follows and questions people at five [ten Co] houses about it. It is being used as a fiery hoop at a hoop-game. Skunk drops in at the game (disguised as an old man) and sits in such a position that the hoop rolls back into the proper place. He shoots his musk at the people and kills them. On his return up the river he shoots his musk at all those people who had spoken of his anus and speaks kindly [gives presents Co] to those who had referred to his property (Co). Skwikwi'k^{w} turns himself into a blanket covered with maggots to escape Skunk. Skunk packs the blanket along for his wife. He is frightened by Skwikwi'k^{w}'s whistling, shoots out all his musk and dies. A skunk shall never again kill people UC27.

Skunk shoots his musk at Cougar and puts on Cougar's hide with its chief's tail. Fox turns into a piece of wormy meat which Skunk packs. Fox whistles, Skunk discards the pack and Fox steals the beads in it. Skunk meets five Wolves who tear the chief's skin off him and beat him; he becomes a harmless skunk. The Wolves revive Cougar, who gives them arrows Co17.

MINK KILLS WHALE. UC68, 69. MINK AND THE GIRL. UC70. MINK. Sk1. (CU 183; UWP 1: 66; UWP 3: 123; JAFL 382, 391, 393; Boas MS; Jacobs MS.) 133 136 364

Mink takes his canoe and knife and prepares to kill Whale. He cuts a small hole in Whale, enters and is carried along inside him. He cuts Whale's heart. The people see him inside eating. He invites them to eat (UC68). He calls on a rich man and uses Spanish-fly on the man's daughter to make her like him. She becomes his wife against her parents' wishes. They have a son. Mink, his wife, brother-in-law, and son go out in their canoe to spear sea-eggs. His wife teaches him to eat the raw eggs. He dives down for some and stays down eating them. His wife and brother-in-law paddle away and leave him and his son to become minks UC69.

The Leech-peoples' daughter does not wish to marry Mink and kills herself. Mink goes off with the dead girl in her burial canoe. After two cousins have failed, his third cousin doctor revives her for him (cp. p. 398). He takes her back to her former home, where she gives birth to a son. She deserts her son and Mink, when Mink stays under diving for sea-eggs UC70.

Mink traps Whale, the lover of the chief's daughter, and holds a feast. When he tells the girl whom she is eating, she commits suicide. Mink steals the dead girl in her canoe and has her revived by the fifth and youngest doctor to become his wife. He returns to his wife's home with his wife, a son, and a daughter. He is deserted by his wife while diving for sea-eggs, for she recognizes who he is. He and his son reach shore, roast a salmon, and fall asleep. Dukwe'bał, the Creator, eats the salmon and leaves bits of it in their teeth (cp. p. 389). Mink makes water from his urine which the Creator drinks. He becomes pregnant, makes himself female parts, and gives birth to a son. He cannot get rid of the boy, till he separates himself from him by a lake, river, and mountains Sk1.

361 MINK KILLS A CHIEF'S SON. WR1.

The chief's son is found murdered. Mink calls together all the animals that say, "Wa'ä' wa'ä'ʿ." He sings to them five times that he is the killer. The people shoot each of his limbs off in a different direction WR1.

33—36 WREN KILLS ELK. UC18, 19; Co5. (CU 179; UWP 3: 137, two
185 versions.)

Little Wren goes hunting. He calls Elk and sends away in turn Tiny Mouse, Mouse, Deer, and Bear [Bear, Cougar, Wolf, Deer, Wildcat, Skunk, Fisher, Coyote, and all the little animals UC19]. At last Elk comes. Wren jumps into his anus, cuts his heart [liver and entrails UC19], and comes out through his mouth. [Wren is somewhat yellow today from Elk's bowels UC19. Wren shoots Elk, is swallowed by him, cuts his entrails and heart, and comes out through his anus Co.] Elk is butchered. Wren fetches pack straps and his grandmother. [He gives some meat to the Blackheads Co.] His grandmother refuses to pack any of the meat but the genitals (UC19). Wren's pack strap breaks five times, when she copulates with them (Co). Wren finds the Elk marrow which he had saved gone. He hits his grandmother on the throat and the marrow comes out. She weeps. The people dress her up and take her to Wren for a wife. The fifth time she laughs, she opens her toothless mouth, and Wren recognizes her UC18.

Wren cries [refuses to eat Co], until his grandmother has intercourse with him. He digs a place for her humpback and they lie down together under the elk hide. Ts'a'maẋwʊl (and Sɔ·'ts'i) detect them. Wren fights Ts'a'maẋwʊl. Nau burns Wren by mistake; Ts'a'maẋwʊl escapes. Nau sticks Wren's bones together with pitch (and blows upon him). Wren melts [four times Co] in the sun and his grandmother fixes him up again. [The fifth time he climbs a tree and refuses to come back Co.] The real Wren's ashes became the wren. [His grandmother turns into a bluebird Co5.] UC19.

31 WREN KILLS OTTER. UC17. LAND OTTER. H12.

326 Every day Wren goes out to catch fish. One morning all his fish are gone. [A stranger boards his canoe and takes them H.] This

happens four times. The fifth day he keeps watch and clubs and skins Otter, the thief. [His grandmother, Long-legged Spider, is with him and clubs Land Otter H.] Ts'a'max̣wʊl [Bluejay H] is sent to find Otter. Wren feeds him Otter's meat. Ts'a'max̣wʊl sees Otter's hide. Otter's parents invite Wren [and his grandmother H] to a tamanoas gathering (H). They stuff the cracks of the house with moss. Bluejay says he alone can kill Wren. Five times he pounces upon him with a scoop spoon, but catches Snail, the drummer, by mistake. Wren sings his tamanoas song and escapes; he is never caught. Snail becomes covered with slime UC17.

Wren's grandmother is presented with a basket, which is put over her head. While she sings, Wren is kicked into the fire. She blows on his cinders and he becomes a wren. She turns into a spider H12.

COON AND HIS GRANDMOTHER. UC25; Co27. (CU 179, 217; Boas MS.) 43 220

Coon finds some grasshoppers. He eats them all and feeds his blind grandmother twigs. She strikes him on the nose with a piece of charcoal and leaves a black streak UC25.

Coon becomes dissatisfied with the one acorn his grandmother, Snowbird, feeds him. He obtains a basketful from the cache, spills the basket and eats the cracked acorns. In this way he consumes the acorns in four caches. His grandmother whips him at the last cache. Coon hides. She strikes him with a burning log and leaves a spot on his nose and streaks across his back. He runs away and insults Grizzlybear who swallows him. The five agates on his back cut Grizzly in five places and kill him. Coon fetches his grandmother. She carries home Grizzly's genitals and cohabits with them in the sweat house. Coon burns her up (cp. above, Wren Kills Elk). He eats bear meat and crawfish and a piece of flesh which proves to be his grandmother's private parts, for when he drinks at the creek, all his teeth fall out Co27.

LION AND BEAR. UC26. BEAR AND GRIZZLY. Co20. (CU 45, 79, 159; JAFL 422, 436.) 43 211

Woodpecker has two wives, Lion and Bear, and five sons by each. Bear picks ripe berries for Woodpecker; Lion brings him red ones. The two women hunt for lice in each other's heads. The fifth time Lion chews Bear's head off. The youngest Bear sees Lion roasting his mother's breasts. Woodpecker gives each of his children a bow and arrow; the Lion children's arrows are made of weeds. The five Bears kill the five Lions and are sent by Woodpecker to their grandmother's. Woodpecker stands the youngest Lion boy up to fool his mother and makes himself wings to fly away. The Bear boys run around the house five times and ask Black Bug and Snail to delay

Lion. They take the wrong road and arrive at old man Wolf's house. Wolf locks them in for his five sons' breakfast. The eldest Bear digs a tunnel underground and they escape. They reach their grandmother's, After-birth's, house. Lion tracks them here. After-birth tells her to come in backwards and the snapping door cuts her in two. The Bears burn Lion's body. If a man has two or three wives, they shall be good to one another UC26.

The Cowlitz version repeats the above in all but the following details: A man has two wives, Bear and Grizzly, five Bear daughters and five Grizzly sons. Grizzly brings her husband mostly sticks and leaves. The five Bear children wrestle with, kill and roast the Grizzlies, after their mother has been killed. Grizzly beats the Bear's dog four times before he shows her the girls' tracks. She stops five times to eat camas, greens and berries which the Bear girls have left on their trail. Hot Rock, Grizzly's father, kills four Bears, the fifth he takes for his wife. Lark instructs a man, who fixes her leg, to build a well where he can drown the five Hot Rock brothers. The man thus gets the Bear girl Co20.

193 WILDCAT. Co15. (CU 27; JAFL 393, 414; Boas MS.)

Wildcat, an ugly, scabby fellow, is not permitted to attend a tamanoas gathering at the house of the chief. Five nights he spits through the smoke-hole into the mouth of the chief's daughter, while she is singing. She gives birth to a baby. When Wildcat holds it, it stops crying, which proves him to be the child's father and consequently the woman's husband. The people desert the three. Crow, Wildcat's grandmother, leaves them salmon, camas, and fire (cp. pp. 395, 399). Wildcat takes sweatbaths four days and becomes handsome. He kills many deer and fills all the empty houses. Crow visits and is given dried fat. She tells the people and they return to plenty Co15.

72—3 STEELHEAD AND SPRING SALMON. UC36, 37. STEELHEAD AND
190 CHINOOK SALMON. Co9. (UWP 3: 133, three versions.)

The brothers Steelhead and Trout stay in the Chehalis River during the winter. In the summer they travel to the ocean. At one time they meet Spring Salmon and his brother, Silver Eel. Steelhead insults Spring Salmon. While the two fight, Trout cries; ever since his mouth has been of normal size. Steelhead loses. Spring Salmon takes his flesh and fat, Silver Eel, his oil. Ever since they have been nice and fat. Trout gathers and arranges Steelhead's bones and Steelhead recovers with the aid of his tamanoas. He uses vine-maple leaves and blossoms for entrails, vine-maple limbs for bones; vine-maple oil is in his flesh. He is still thus. He and Spring Salmon both live in the Chehalis River now UC36.

In a brief second version Steelhead uses iron-wood for a new backbone; that's why he has a tough backbone. He takes snake skin for his skin. Spring salmon and eel have his fat. That's why he becomes thin when he goes downstream UC37.

Steelhead accompanied by five kinds of Suckers comes up the Cowlitz River to spawn. He meets Chinook Salmon accompanied by four kinds of Trout and insults him. Chinook takes Steelhead's fat and head for himself. He gives Steelhead his own head, full of bones. The bony Trout take all the Suckers' fat. Ever since steelhead has poor meat and a skinny back. He never dies. After spawning Chinook dies and floats belly up Co9.

SPRING SALMON AND THE YOUNG WOMAN. UC53. (CU 47; JAFL 383.) 110

A princess announces she will marry the one who can throw her in a wrestling match. Wolf, Cougar, Bear, Wildcat, Hawk, Owl, Eagle and Dark Eagle fail. She persuades Spring Salmon to try, and he throws her. Wolf kills him, but out of his body rolls an egg which in five days grows into Spring Salmon again. He proceeds to the home of the five Wolf brothers who have taken the woman, killing two Skunks on the way for making fun of him. He pretends to be the woman's uncle, and is hired by each of the five Wolves to make arrow heads. He gives each Wolf four, keeping a fifth for himself in each instance. He hides at the well and shoots the four eldest Wolves, when they come singly to drink. He misses the youngest who escapes. That's why we have wolf today. Spring Salmon starts home with his wife. He lies down in the canoe and his body becomes covered with maggots. Spring salmon do not last long UC53.

LAND OTTER'S SON. H11. 324

Land Otter's son is given an expert clam-digger and an expert fruit and berry picker for wives. The women complete four trips to the beach for clams and four to the mountains for berries. Each time they return, their husband says five guests have eaten the food which they brought on their previous trip. The fourth time they return early from the mountains and discover him eating all the clams. He becomes the sea worm. The first wife becomes the large-snipe, the second, the mountain beaver H11.

WOLF, COYOTE AND DOG. Co12. THE WOLVES AND THEIR BROTHER DOG. H7. (Boas MS.) 191 307

Wolf, Coyote and Dog, brothers, let their fire go out. Dog is sent to the people for fire. There is a "cushion" at the base of his palm where the people placed food for him. He stays with them. Thus Wolf and Coyote always fight Dog Co12.

Four Wolves and their younger brother, Dog, go hunting. The fifth day Dog is left at home to keep the fire up, but neglects it, because his brothers always throw him scraps to eat. One Wolf with his mouth full of food blows it out entirely. Dog is sent to the people for fire and stays with them. Dogs can only escape from wolves by urinating in their eyes H7.

308 THE WOLVES KILL THE DEER. H8.

Five times the four Deer send their younger brother, Rabbit, off to invite the five Wolves to eat with them. The fourth time the Wolves hear Rabbit, as he calls them an insulting name and they come for the food more boisterously. The fifth time they hear him again. They eat the four Deer, but Rabbit escapes. He becomes a rabbit, easy game to catch H8.

192 RABBIT. Co14.

At a gathering Bear, Elk, Deer, Pheasant, etc. each sings his song and dances. Rabbit sings and makes the supporting pole move from under the house. Mice, lizards, snakes and rats go under the house, where they are today. The rest of the people fly away as birds Co14.

41 CRANE. UC22; Co6. CRANE AND HIS UNFAITHFUL WIFE. Sk6.
188
369

Crane's faithless wife [Helldiver Sk] continually sends him out for fish [she pretends she is sick Sk]. In his absence she dresses herself up and summons her lover [Sawbill Sk]. Crane is thus always fishing (Sk). He cuts the flesh from either side of his legs in order to walk lightly. This is why he has such thin legs UC22.

Crane burns his legs black in order to creep up on the fish unnoticed. He is warned and spies upon his wife. He blinds her with hot ashes to punish her. She now always sees an imaginary light in the bay, for her eyes are red. White male sawbills drift down the river in love with helldivers Sk6.

Crane with the help of some young people builds a fish trap. He sleeps all the time and never catches any fish. Crane still stands in the water trying in vain to catch fish Co6.

30 ROBIN. UC16; Sk5.
369

Robin's wife removes all the peels of the camas she digs. She brings nothing home. The fourth day Robin spies on her. He burns her face in order to kill her. She rolls her hot body to which rocks stick down into the water and becomes the periwinkle. The rocks are her house. Robin mourns for his wife. Mornings and evenings he sings for her UC16.

In a Skokomish fragment Robin's wife becomes sick and dies. Robin weeps. Every spring he calls her Sk5.

DOVE. UC20. (see text.) 40

MOSQUITO. Co21. 213

Peoples along the river invite Mosquito, a dangerous being, to eat duck stew, wild goose stew, rabbit stew, and deer-broth stew, but he refuses each in turn. Five men feed him a potful of their blood, then stick him in the stomach. He bursts. He shall just suck people hereafter Co21.

PHEASANT AND HER GRANDSON. Co29. 223

A boy throws a thorny ball of mashed q'a'α'n berries into his grandmother's, Pheasant's, mouth. It sticks in her throat. She becomes a pheasant and flies away Co29.

SMELT AND EEL. Co10. 190

Smelt and Eel stipulate how the people shall eat them. The Cowlitz shall die, if they remove any part of smelt but the tail. Eel's head must be thrown away on the roasting stick; if thrown far, the person will have a long life, if near, a short life Co10.

BEAVER, MUSKRAT AND MOUNTAIN BEAVER. Co13. 192

Beaver and Muskrat decide to live in the water, Mountain Beaver far underground, in the hope that people will not be able to kill them Co13.

ORIGIN OF THE FRESH-WATER CLAMS. UC64. 132

Some people are crossing the Chehalis River. Their canoe capsizes and they become the fresh-water clams UC64.

GRIZZLYBEAR AND HIS SONS. Co37. 233

An old man secretly sends his good grandchild to bathe for power. Grizzlybear's five bad children fail to find guardian spirits. The eldest steals a wife and is killed by her husband. The second steals blankets; their owner kills him. The third is killed by some boys whose horse he has stolen. The fourth slips and is drowned. The father marries the fifth to Grizzlybear who eats him. The father and his daughter-in-law turn into grizzlies Co37.

43 BEAR LOSES HIS TAIL. UC24.

Old Bear, who used to be a man, once sits down on the ice. The ice melts, then freezes again. Bear jumps two or three times and loses his long tail UC24.

274 WHITE BEAR TAKES REVENGE. Co66.

While out picking berries, a younger sister warns her older sister of White Bear. White Bear comes seeking revenge for the insult paid to his dead cub, whom some men had stuck up on a stick. The girls throw Bear three baskets to tear up. The younger jumps into the water, the elder climbs a tree to escape him. Bear uproots the tree, kills the girl and leaves her sitting in a pit Co66.

274 COUGAR. Co65.

An old woman makes a doll of cedar bark and wraps it in a fawn and a wildcat skin. Cougar steals it. That's why a hungry cougar will kill a person. He is tracked, but never caught Co65.

52—3 MOUNTAIN LION AND RABBIT GAMBLE. UC28, 29. (UWP 3: 135, two versions; Boas MS.)

Rabbit and Mountain Lion play slahal. Mountain Lion is losing and tries to catch Rabbit. [Mountain Lion sings his song for rain UC29.] Rabbit sings his tamanoas song [for clear weather UC29]. He melts the ice on the lake just a little. On the fifth night he flees across the ice, which he tests for Lion by letting a ball of dirt [five feces UC29] skim over it. The ice breaks under Lion and Rabbit holds him down with a pole UC28.

55 WOLF AND DEER GAMBLE. UC30. (UWP 1: 69.)

Wolf challenges Deer to a game of lal. The Wolves and Deer alternate singing, each side playing till hit. The first two Deer receive a second turn before they are hit. Three Wolves and Bear play for the Wolves; two Deer, Red Salmon and Rabbit for Deer's side. Then Old Wolf plays and his side jump at the Deer who flee forgetting little Fawn. Wildcat wounds Rabbit. Four times Old Wolf sends Fawn out for a roasting stick and Fawn returns without one. The fifth time Fawn flees UC30.

DEER AND COUGAR. Co11. 191

Cougar challenges Deer to a game of lal. Cougar beats Deer, but cannot catch him Co11.

BEAR AND ANT, OR THE CONTEST FOR DAY AND NIGHT. UC65, 66, 67. 132—3
BEAR, ANT, GROUSE, FROG AND THE YELLOWJACKETS. Co7. 188
FROG AND BEAR. Co8. (CU 3; UWP 3: 54, two versions; Boas MS.) 189

Each of the five versions explains the present division of time into day and night:

Bear wants a long day, followed by a long night. Ant wants night and day immediately succeeding each other. The two race and Ant wins by making her waist smaller. That's why Ant has a small waist and we have short successive nights and days UC65.

Bear wants night for six months [one year Co7], followed by day for six months. Ant and Yellowjacket [Ant, big Yellowjacket, black Yellowjacket, Frog and Grouse Co7] want a successive night and day. [Ant ties her waist, all dance and Co7] Bear is beaten. Bear now sleeps three months [a winter Co7] at a time and tears up yellowjackets' and ants' nests. [Grouse always escapes Bear by flying; Frog, by going under water Co7.] UC66.

Moon changes Bear into an animal because Bear wants six months of night and six months of daylight UC67.

Bear wants to sleep five years, Frog one night. They finally agree they will each sleep one year (winter), but people, only one night Co8.

THE FLOOD. UC1, 2, 3, 4; Co1. (UWP 3: 49, four versions, 51, 63; Boas MS.) 1—3 178

Thrush's mother-in-law asks him five times to wash his face. At last he agrees. [The people finally persuade Thrush to wash her face UC2.] His face becomes streaked. That is why he has scratches on it. It rains for perhaps forty days and nights [fifty or sixty days UC2] and many people are lost. Thrush's parents-in-law and wife land in Upper Chehalis territory. Muskrat dives for dirt five times and makes Tiger Lily (Black) Mountain for the people. The earth becomes just like new UC1. Muskrat, the smallest boy, is paid a fur coat for diving. At Gate, near Mima Prairie, the earth remains like waves. Thrush becomes a bird. A flood shall never again occur when one washes one's face UC2. This is ordained by Moon, after it rains a long time. He turns Thrush (male) into a bird UC3.

The flood drowns all the people but Pheasant. Pheasant flies to the tallest tree on the highest hill. The water leaves a mark on Pheasant's tail UC4.

Spi'tsx̣ᵘ never washes his face. His five brothers-in-law whip him. Thereupon he sings and dances in the water. It rises until everything is flooded. Spi'tsx̣ᵘ flies away as a little brown bird. The other people go away as birds and animals Col.

75 NORTHEAST WIND AND SOUTHWEST WIND. UC39. (UWP 3: 53, 55, seven versions; JAFL 378, 398; Boas MS.)

Northeast Wind, who lives in the sky, always freezes the people. Southwest Wind, who lives in the ocean, declares war upon him. With all his people he makes a trail to the sky which Snowbird pulls down by the aid of his tamanoas. No one from Southwest Wind's side is killed, but Snake and another are missing. Snake's sister, Toad, makes fun of his cross-eyes. When he returns, he murders her. Thus a snake always does to a toad. In a second fight Southwest Wind cannot overcome the seven Northeast Wind brothers with boiling water. His grandmother makes a water-sprinkler to help him, and five of the seven brothers are killed. Snow and frost no longer freeze people to death. Southwest wind melts them. Southwest Wind also overcomes Elk, a star, who was killing earth people UC39.

76 THE BATTLE WITH SNOW. UC40. (CU 145; UWP 3: 53; JAFL 378.)

The people and animals go up to the sky to attack Snow who buries them under every winter. Mouse cuts the strings of four of the five Snow brothers' bows. Only the youngest Snow escapes. Thus there is no longer deep snow, for only the youngest brother brings it. The Earth-people leave Snake and Rattlesnake in the sky to gather up the leavings from the battle. Snake finally returns to earth and gives Water-dog a buck-skin, Lizard some basket straws for mourning for him properly. That's why water-dog has a tough hide and lizard, stripes. The other basket straws are on Snake's back; that's why some snakes have yellow or white stripes. Snake's cousin, Frog, receives nothing because he mocked Snake (cp. above). It is thus that snakes kill frogs UC40.

121 371 THE ONE-LEGGED MAN. UC58. THE SHARPTAILED MAN. Sk8. (CU 11, 174; UWP 2: 236; UWP 3: 105; Globus: 172; Boas MS; Jacobs MS.)

A pubescent girl bathes in a forbidden place. One-legged Man [Sharptailed Man Sk] watches her, knows her thoughts (cp. p. 393), and takes her clothes. He embraces her and has her name her body-parts from head to foot, while he repeats the names after her. He comes to naming her privates, carries her off and copulates with her with his big toe. [She finally calls him husband; he takes her home Sk.] One of her brothers comes to visit her. Her husband learns his brother-in-law has been there, [his children tell him Sk], overtakes him by shaking a hide [by singing a song Sk] to weaken him, kills and eats him. This happens to four of the girl's five brothers (Sk). The fourth time the woman sees her brother's hair sticking to her husband's teeth. She sets fire to the house, in which her husband and son are sleeping, and goes with her daughter to her surviving brother. The daughter pulls a child's eye out (cp. below) and is sent in a bucket down the river. Four times people find her but throw her away again when she pulls out another eye. The fifth time a giant makes her his wife UC58.

The youngest brother trains for power and on the way to his sister's house alters a pitchy stump to resemble a man. The Sharp-tailed Man mistakes the stump for his brother-in-law and sticks his tail into it. The youngest brother kills him and revives his four brothers. His sister, her daughter and he return home. The girl scratches people's eyes out. Thus the Crows paddle her out in their canoe (cp. p. 420) and desert her. She meets slave Coon, whom she helps dig roots. Coon's master marries her Sk8.

SHARK GIRL. Co31. (cp. above.) 223

A small girl, a dangerous being, digs camas on an island with the five Crow girls. Their fifth trip to the island the Crow girls desert her. She meets Coon, the slave of a chief, and four times fills Coon's basket with camas. The chief marries her. She fights with the people and kills children, her baby, and her husband. She becomes a shark Co31.

FISHER AND SƏMT'I'C. Co16. (CU 142.) 196

While Səmt'i'c is out hunting, Fisher, his younger brother, goes to the house of a girl who "burns" him. Səmt'i'c takes the girl for his wife. Five times she goes to a forbidden place. The fifth time she makes a wish and is carried off by a cloud, lʊslʊ'spiap, the dangerous being, who marries her. lʊslʊ'spiap beheads Səmt'i'c looking for his wife. Fisher and Səmt'i'c's son step on Meadow Lark's leg. She directs them to lʊslʊ'spiap's house. They kill lʊslʊ'spiap's two sisters and enter the house in their disguise. When lʊslʊ'spiap is asleep, they take his wife and supplies outside and set fire to the house. lʊslʊ'spiap is burned to death. Fisher revives Səmt'i'c. Səmt'i'c's former wife gives birth to a girl. Five times the girl tears out a child's eye and eats it (cp. above). The fifth time she rises up to the sky as a small cloud. Now Cloud merely showers, for only his daughter is left Co16.

X̂WA'IPS AND THE YOUNG WOMAN. UC54. 112

A man whom X̂wa'ips has made out of a cedar limb succeeds on his fifth try in throwing a girl in a wrestling match (cp. p. 409).

X̮wa'ips takes the girl for his wife despite her protest. Every day she brings home fowl which she claims Hawk caught for her. The fifth morning X̮wa'ips flies above his wife and her secret lover, Syuyu'wən, disguised as a bird. Syuyu'wən shoots at the bird five times and misses. X̮wa'ips clubs him and takes home his head, which he hangs above his wife's bed. Five times something drips upon her and she discovers Syuyu'wən's head. The following morning X̮wa'ips kills her on the way to her parents' home and ties her to the top of a tall, slippery cedar. The Birds, Squirrel, and Bluejay fail to get her down. The small bird, Pape'təna'mɩts, succeeds. The youngest of the woman's five brothers is dressed up to resemble his sister and taken to X̮wa'ips. He sleeps with X̮wa'ips and the fifth night cuts off his head. Five days later Bluejay discovers the murder. Whenever a man is jealous, he kills his wife's lover UC54.

225 MEADOWLARK GIRL. Co32. (cp. p. 399.) (Jacobs MS.)

Meadowlark growls at her brother to become her lover. Four times he kills her, but she comes to life again. He steps on old lady Meadowlark who instructs him to tear up his sister's hat in order to kill her forever. Sisters and brothers shall not make love to one another Co32.

226 URINE BOY. Co33. (cp. above.)

Urine Boy comes home five times with a man under his braid. Each of his five sisters thus obtains a husband. Two of the eldest girl's children fall in love, run away, and live as husband and wife. Their mother finds their beds together at their fifth camp. They kill their boy for singing of their true relationship. X̣wα'ni separates them. Sisters, brothers, or cousins shall not make love to one another Co33.

77 238 THE SEAL HUNTER. UC41. THE WOODEN FISH. Co40. (UWP 1: 77; JAFL 428, 430.)

Five brothers have tamanoas; the third eldest has sea-hunter's tamanoas, the eldest is a canoe maker. Three times the canoe maker's wife keeps the seal meat which the hunter has given her for her husband. The canoe maker carves a wooden seal (cp. p. 399) and after five alterations leaves it in the bay. His three brothers spear it and are towed away for five days. When the seal lands, the two elder brothers hide the youngest under their canoe and go up to the house of the giant Ne'pius. The youngest is eaten up by mosquitoes. Four times the two brothers peep while Ne'pius fishes, and he loses his fish. The fifth time he catches a whale for their food. They help him fight L'αmx̣αma·'ɩp, who has been trying to spoil his fish-trap. The two boys enter a hole cut in Whale, their "grandfather," and he sets out with them. On his fifth stop he comes out at their village. The people come to get whale blubber. The whale rolls over on all the young men's enemies and kills them UC41.

A fisherman refuses to give a widower fresh salmon for his child, (for if the widower should eat any of it, it would spoil the fisherman's luck). The widower makes a wooden fish which tows the fisherman and his young brother to the Columbia River. The boy is eaten up by mosquitoes, the fisherman is fed by X̣wʋ′lpios. He hides in a hole in X̣wʋ′lpios's neck and shoots One-Legged-Man (L'αmx̣αma·′ιp, UC). X̣wʋ′lpios sends the fisherman home in a whale. Henceforth dried salmon shall be given to people who are taboo Co40.

SPEAR. UC45. SPEAR BOY. Co34. (CU 148.) 87 227

Spear's sister, Pαsi′nos, [Spear Boy's sister Co], gives him roots to eat. He keeps all his fish for himself. She suspects him and leaves (Co). She marries chief silver-side. Spear visits her. He is fed. Sqwe′lius, father of the salmon, calls an elk and sends its empty hide off to become a new elk. Spear's brother-in-law's sister, World's End, provides a small dishful of huckleberries which Spear cannot eat up. The five nations of salmon, the black-salmon, silver-side, dog-salmon, spring-salmon, and steelhead-salmon, each holding what property it owns, come in dancing and stay the night. World's End cooks her nephew, silver-side, for Spear. Spear saves the bones and the boy revives. The fifth day Spear leaves a piece of meat on the boy's cheek-bone and he cannot be revived. Spear is sent home. He stops at Thunder's house and receives Thunder's daughter for a wife. He flees when he fails four times to become like Thunder. He is given another wife by the Pitch People who cause a board to stick to his back. An old woman removes it and he goes on. He follows an old man's warning, climbs a fir to escape łała′mak'wʋs and throws the bark down upon him. He burns up łała′mak'wʋs's body. Ne′pius gives Spear his daughter for a wife. Spear kills Ne′pius' enemy (cp. above) and Ne′pius as well, for no one shall have a trap above another. He restores an old lady's, Tax̣wa′'asti's, sight and follows her warning to hide and shoot Cougar, who switches people to death with his tail. He burns Cougar up, and transforms his ashes into cougars. An old woman, To′tαmx·, warns him of people on the prairie preparing to kill him; he transforms them into the wild rhubarb (cp. p. 380). He finds his sister back home and the two transform themselves. Spear becomes spear-flower (sheep's nose) to be used for children's toys UC45.

Spear Boy's sister reaches a man's house whose mother is Fire. Fire does all the housework and eats food put into her to cook. Spear Boy's sister marries the man and has a baby. She takes her mother-in-law by surprise, and the old lady remains a person. Spear Boy spends two or three months with his sister. His brother-in-law ties a pack on him which he is not to open and directs him to take the middle fork of the road. Spear Boy follows first the right fork, then the left, and is beset by slimy bugs, wild animals, and a girl who combs her sharp-pointed hair upon him. He opens his pack too soon and all the large fish in it escape. Thus big fish never go up the Cowlitz (cp. p. 389) Co34.

83 THE YOUNG MAN WHO WAS STOLEN BY LION. UC44. (Globus: 192; Boas MS.)

Lion and Crane steal a woman's baby. Lion gets lizards, Crane finds salmon for the boy. After five days Crane makes him a bow and arrow and tells him what to do. The boy wounds Lion from the front, then escapes up a tree belonging to Crane. Crane shoots Lion five times, kills her, and flies away. The young man climbs to heaven. He meets a grey man, Dawn, who sends him to his five daughters. On the way he meets a black man, Evening, and reaches the home of Evening's five girls. Evening brings home a dead deer and a dead man for food. The grey girls arrive and win the young man, who prefers them, from the black girls. He receives the youngest Dawn girl for a wife, but later discards her for a pretty girl he finds in a basket. The latter bears him twins stuck together. He sees the earth through a hole and with his father-in-law's permission takes his wife and children and descends in a basket which Spider lowers to earth on her rope. He restores his brother's and mother's sight and hair and has his brother burn Bluejay's backside, instead of cleaning it as usual (cp. p. 381). Bluejay separates the twins the fifth time they walk past him and they die. Twins shall never again be born stuck together UC44.

74 MALɛʼʼ. UC38.

Five evenings the grandson of Malɛʼʼ makes arrows with which to kill Lion, and hides them in canyons along the Chehalis River. The canyons are called X̣aʹlsənʾ, because he did not have to use the arrows. Lion always walks with his head between his legs to watch for enemies behind him. The young man surprises Lion from the front (see above) and cuts his throat. Nɩx·qʾwaʹnx̣tən prairie receives its name from the fact that Lion's skin was spread out there to dry. The young man never returns to Malɛʼʼ who with his two dogs turns into a rock UC38.

95 STAR HUSBAND. UC47, 48; P3; see also p. 381. (JAFL 373, 375.)
356 Two girls sleep out. One [the younger UC48] wishes for a large, bright star; the other for a tiny, dim one. [Each of five sisters wishes for a star for her husband, the youngest for the brightest, the eldest

for a dim one P.] They awake [in the sky UC48; P] and the first finds an ugly, old man with sore eyes sleeping with her, the second a nice young man [thus we know the stars are people living above us P] UC47.

Spider puts one girl at a time in a basket and lets it down to earth on a string. Spider comes down also. It is bad luck for girls to wish for anything far off UC48.

In digging roots in the sky the girls make a hole to earth. The fifth day they finish a rope of hazel brush and slide down upon it P3.

SASA'ILAX̣ƏN. UC57. 117

A princess refuses all suitors. Sasa'ilax̣ən and his grandfather arrive secretly, Sasa'ilax̣ən embraces the girl, he and his grandfather paddle away again. The girl follows their canoe. When his grandfather hears her calling for the fifth time, Sasa'ilax̣ən waits for her and takes her home as his wife. Her parents visit. In examining her husband's head for lice one day, she notices a sore place. He goes temporarily mad and kills her. She is successfully revived by Grey-back Louse, doctor of the fifth class, after his four predecessors fail UC57.

ORIGIN TALE OF THE TENINO. UC55, 56. 116—7

When a princess at Tenino refuses all suitors, her grandmother [father UC55] asks her if she wishes to marry Wolf. Hereupon young Wolf comes and gets her. The Wolves pay her parents much game in exchange. The people of Tenino are descended from the Wolves UC56.

THE QWEQWASTA'IMʊX̂. UC42, 43. (JAFL 429.) 81—2

A northwest warrior in a borrowed canoe is carried off by a storm. He lands among the imaginary Qweqwasta'imʊx̂ tribe, with whom he lives about three years. The Geese drop feathers on the Qweqwasta'imʊx̂ and kill them. The Qweqwasta'imʊx̂ revive when the warrior pulls out the feathers. He gives them, as well as a second tribe, the bow and arrow for a weapon and teaches them to eat the Geese. After six or seven years he returns home UC42.

Two men are carried off by a Qweqwasta'imʊx̂ man, from whose fingers they had stolen salmon. The two are freed, when they show the Qweqwasta'imʊx̂ how to fight and cook their enemy, the Ducks and Hell Diver. The men put pitch on their canoe bottoms, to which the dentalia shells which the Qweqwasta'imʊx̂ possess stick. That's how dentalia first got here UC43.

235—7 THE CHIEF'S STORY. Co38, 39. (CU 123.)

A chief has a number of wives in different places. He issues orders that they shall always kill their male babies. One boy is concealed. When he gets to be about nineteen [twenty-two Co39], he finds his footprints are as long as his father's. His father challenges him to a fight. The boy runs over the water [he has L'ɛ''q'ku tamanoas Co39]. He kills his father and becomes chief. Male babies shall live Co38.

95 THE ORIGIN OF MENSTRUATION. UC46. (Jacobs MS.)

An old man menstruates through his eyes. Some girls make fun of him. He throws the blood at them. Thus women menstruate instead of men UC46.

40 CROW AND THE WOMEN. UC21. (UWP 3: 106; Boas MS.)

Crow and five other women set out in a canoe. They push their paddles edgewise through the water and cannot get ahead. The captain discovers the paddles should be held broadside. They make good time UC21. (cp. also Sk, p. 415.)

223 THE BOY AND THE FIRE. Co30. (cp. p. 380.) (JAFL 391.)

Fire follows a boy. Tree, Big Rock, Little Creek, Prairie, and Rotten Log cannot save him. He lies on Trail and is saved Co30.

353 THE SPIRIT OF WEALTH. P2.

Two boys train secretly, until they are about twelve or fourteen years old. They obtain Tuo'ɬbəx̣, the spirit of wealth, and are able to mesmerize all kinds of game. One boy becomes ill. His stomach continues to swell, until all the people arrive and sing his song to appease his spirit. Whenever meat is needed, the spirit tells the boys where to find much game P2.

131, 241 THE SCATTER CREEK TALE. UC62; Co42.

A woman tells her grandson to make a spear and get ready for salmon. He refuses. In a few days the dry creek fills up and salmon come. He starts whittling a spear; in his hurry his knife slips and cuts his stomach open UC62, Co42.

240 THE TWO OLD WOMEN. Co41.

Two old maids do all their work together with the exception of fetching water, which is performed by the younger, and gathering wood, performed by the elder. At one time they trade jobs. The elder falls into the water and is smashed into rocks. A falling piece of bark kills the younger. Her blood turns into red huckleberries Co41.

BOIL AND EXCREMENT. UC63. (CU 107.) 131

Two people neither bathe nor work. Finally Excrement, the one, takes a bath and floats away as excrement. Boil, the other, peels bark from a tree and some pithy substance falls and bursts his eye UC63.

THE HORSE RACE. Co28. 221

A boy tries to shoot a tiny horse, until it tells him to stop. He races the horse against one of a chief's five race horses, betting his grandmother and the horse against the chief's horse and a slave. He wins. In this way he obtains possession of the chief's five horses, as well as five slaves. He returns the horses in exchange for the chief's daughter Co28.

APPENDIX: SONGS

The following songs were transcribed by Dr. George Herzog. Page references to the tales have been listed after the songs.

EXPLANATION OF THE SIGNS USED IN THE TRANSCRIPTIONS.

+ above a note or in the signature: somewhat higher than noted (approximately a quarter tone higher)

− above a note or in the signature: somewhat lower than noted (approximately a quarter tone lower)

(♩), pitch uncertain

cry, parlando, pitch uncertain

weak stress, ornamental tone

strong glide (glissando)

portamento

pulsations subdividing the tone

lengthening (not above half of the value as noted)

shortening (not above half of the value as noted)

brief rest without rhythmic significance ("Atempause")

⋮ tentative division

P.R. Phonograph record, collections Adamson and Boas, in the American Museum of Natural History, New York.

D.R. Dictaphone record, collection Adamson, in the American Museum of Natural History, New York.

NB. All songs are understood to have been sung an octave lower than noted or indicated. The texts of the Nutsaq song (p. 430) and of the chant for rain (p. 429) are uncertain; they have been written down from the phonograph records.

BLUEJAY'S SONG (p. 25, sung by Davis; P.R. 14a, 13a, 13b)

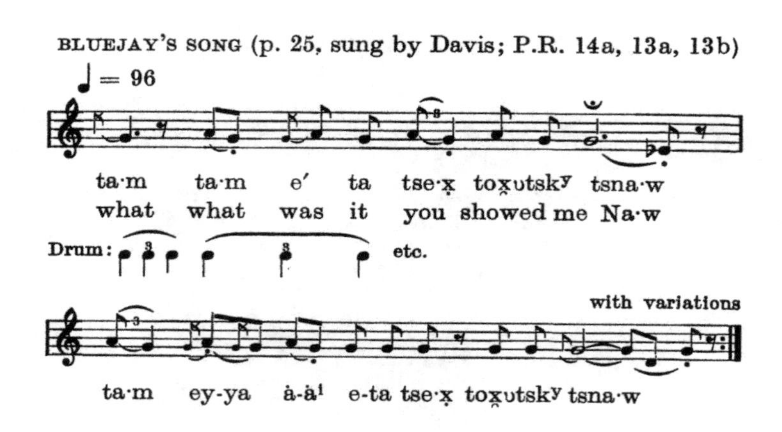

CHANT, WREN CALLS ELK (p. 36, sung by Davis; P.R. 15c)
= cca 56 (molto rubato)
(original sung half tone higher)
tc'e·ʻ sa tc'e·ʻ sa qʷel qʷe le tə·n s.il ɩl ax̣ wol yaq' to·x tcɩł
tc'e·ʻ sa tc'e·ʻ sa qʷel qʷe le tə·n tc'e·ʻ sa
etc.
tc'e·ʻ sa qʷel qʷe le tə·n s.il ɩl ax̣ wol yaq' to·x tcɩł
LION'S GAMBLING SONG (p. 52, sung by Secena; P.R. 24a)
= cca 168, rubato
(original sung major third lower)
Drum: etc.
ho kwo kwo kwa— tcʻo - o
qwa— kwo kwa tcə kwɛ—— hwi - iy ——
kwo—— kwo— kwa tca kwɛ - ɛ - - ɛ
hi - i—— hui - yiy - yi - i - ya——
with variations
hui - yi - i - ya—— hui - yi - i yi - yi - ya - a ho

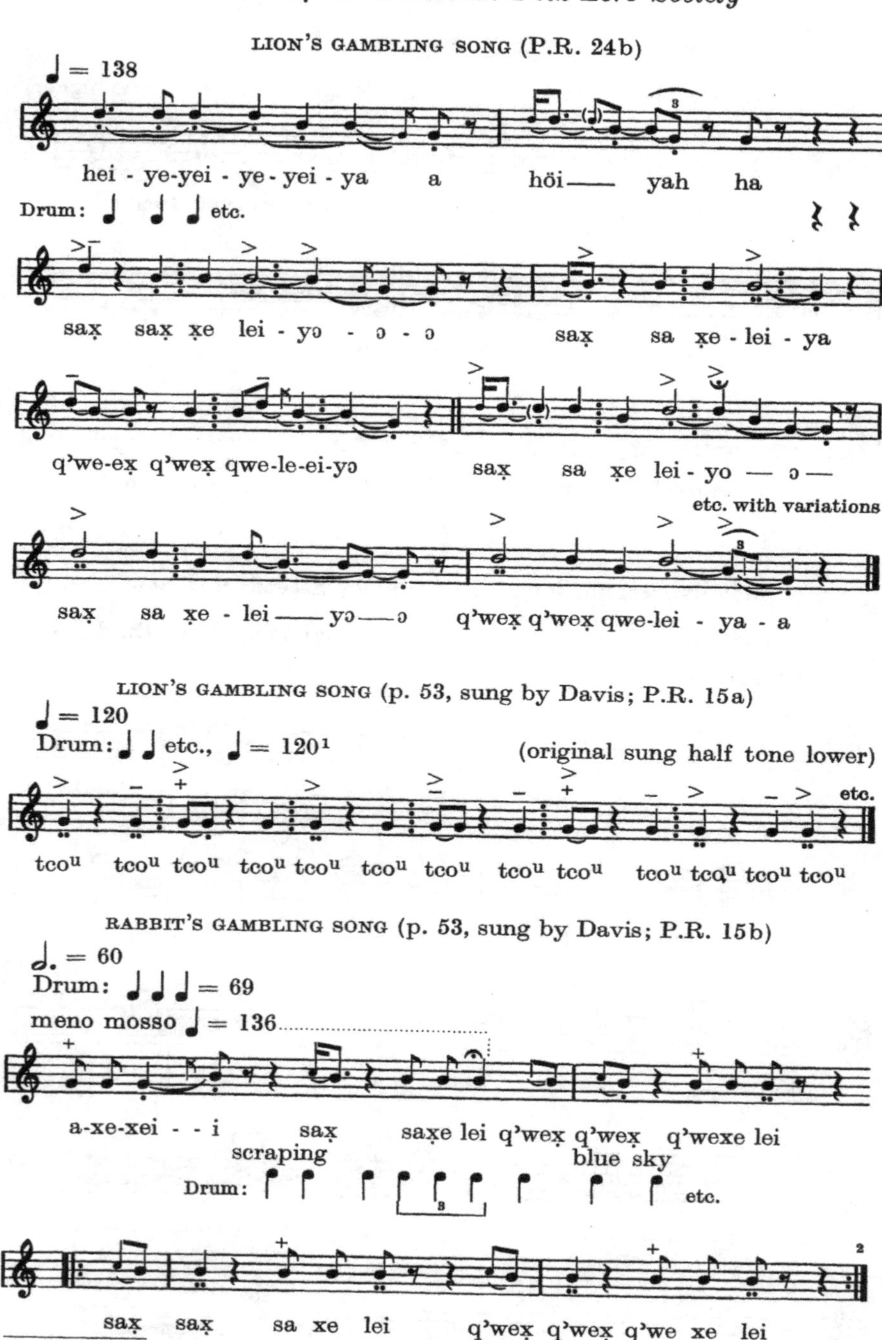

[1] almost syncopating with the beats of the singing
[2] interspersed with cries, calls, yells, etc.

WOLF'S GAMBLING SONG (p. 55; P.R. 5a)
= 114, poco rubato
(original sung diminished fifth lower)
ma·' L'i na' ma·' L'i na' ts'i·ł tsoł tseł quntsmαn tcαn k'wos
stir it! stir it! I will tear up
Drum:
etc.
with variations
End:
na·łetc'ιn man kwos na·łetc'ιn man
intestines intestines
hei - - yà-à
Drum:
etc.
Cries
höi - iy - yà hoi - i - yà - à hoi-i - yà ho ho hi
BEAR'S SONG (p. 132; P.R. 8a)
= 72, molto rubato
Drum = 126—132
natc pa·nxu ?........... natc pa·nxu mo·' SE hEmtcł natc-
Drum:
etc.
L'a skus
one year will be night one year we sleep
pa·nxu L'as mo·'sExEm ?.... ɔ·ts's L'ic L'as
mo·semtcł
one year will we sleep one winter will be
kwa - - ι - sa ɔ·——ts's L'ic L'as
night
kwa sa ɔ·ts's L'ic L'as kwa-s

YELLOWJACKET'S SONG (p. 132; P.R. 8b)

MINK'S SONG (p. 361, sung by Davis; P.R. 17b)

[1] the intonation of the parts with the syllables *le* and *x̣i'x̣iwa* is uncertain; notation approximate.

CROW'S SONG (p. 362; P.R. 30a)

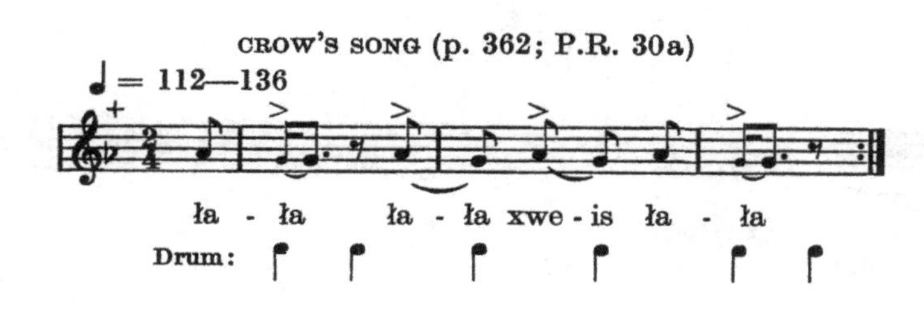

MALƐ' SHRINKS THE EARTH (sung by two men; P.R. 6)

[1] with variations

CRADLE SONG OF MALɛ', MOON STORY (sung by two men; P.R. 7a)

[1] with variations

SPITSXU CHANT TO BRING RAIN (White River song; P.R. 14b)

SNAKE SONG, TRICKY CHIEF STORY (sung by Jonas x̣wan; P.R. 23a)

SONG OF THE CHILDREN WHEN SPαLəWE· GOES BY (P.R. 30b)

NUTSAQ SONG (D.R. 1)

NUTSAQ SONG (D.R. 2b)

CPSIA information can be obtained
at www.ICGtesting.com
Printed in the USA
LVHW011643161022
730831LV00008B/477

9 780803 226685